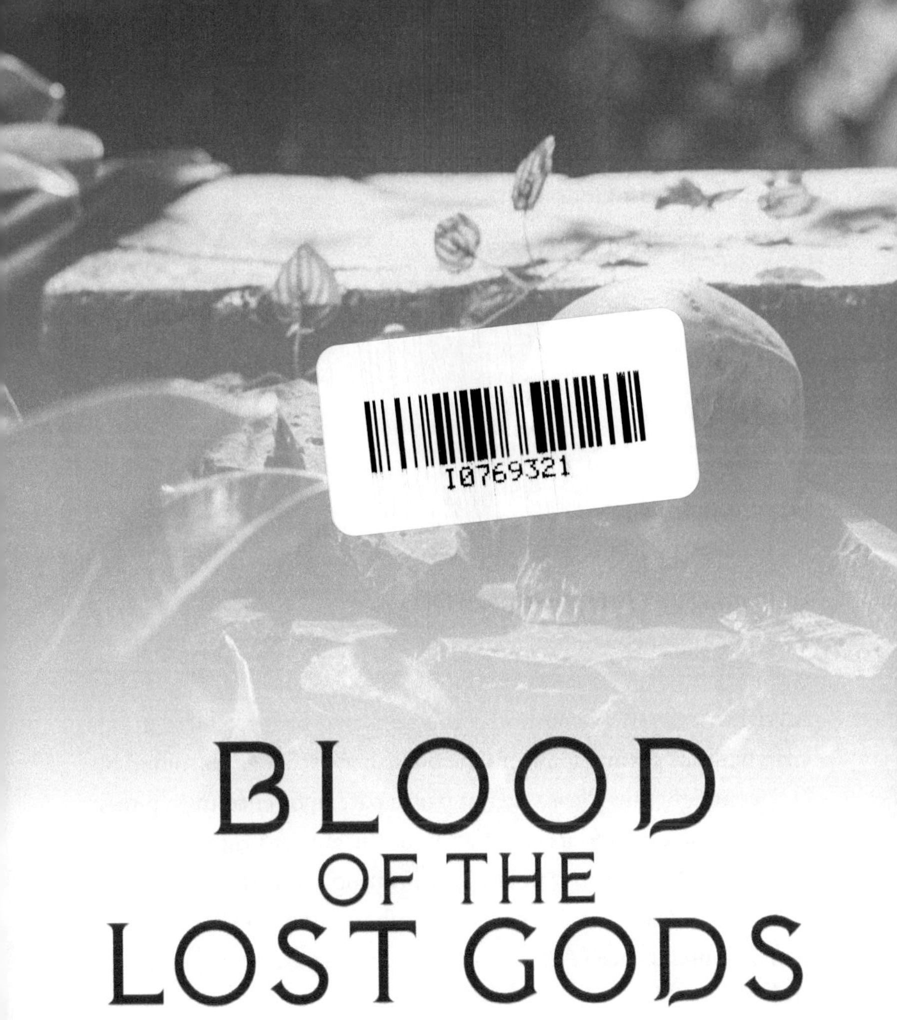

BLOOD
OF THE
LOST GODS

JESSICA J. AYALA

PRAISE FOR
FALL OF THE HORIZON

"*Fall of the Horizon* is what a fantasy reader's dreams are made of! Ayala has built an intricate world that's rich with history and fully immersive down to the last detail, complete with complex characters and a beautifully vulnerable romance."

Nicole Platania, author of *The Curse of Ophelia* series

"Hauntingly beautiful and devastatingly commanding, this heart-pounding romantasy is the first in what will be the next great high fantasy series! For fans of the morally gray love interest, this one will hit."

L.B. Divine, author of *The Prince of Snow* series

"Bursting with action, magic and sizzling romance, *Fall of the Horizon* is an epic tale sure to be adored by fantasy lovers. Ayala's starkly detailed world, rife with war and sinister dealings, is highlighted by a cast of fiercely determined characters and a wonderfully executed mystery. The ending is both satisfying and bound to leave readers longing for more."

Max Francis, author of the upcoming dark academia fantasy novel *Honor & Heresy*

"*Fall of the Horizon* brings the reader to a new world that feels like home from the first page: the incredible worldbuilding, the originality of the lore, the complexity of the characters and their stories . . . Ayala executes every aspect to perfection. An incredible first book for a very promising fantasy series."

Chiara Gala, author of *The Goddess and The Hawk* series

ALSO FROM
JESSICA J. AYALA

The Dusk and Dawn series

Fall of the Horizon

Blood of the Lost Gods

Of Fangs and Shadows

A NOTE TO THE READER

This book contains subject matter that might be difficult for readers such as graphic violence, emotional trauma, grief and loss, slavery, physical abuse, mentions of sexual assault, as well as sexually explicit content.

The fictional world of *The Dusk and Dawn* series is inspired by events, myths, and legends from various parts of the world. None is intended as a faithful representation of any one country or culture at any point in history.

For those who love deeply and fiercely, who are always willing to give their hearts to those they care about. Know you are worthy to receive love too.

This is also for my little sister, Emily.

YOU AND THE CHAOS

you and the chaos you carry.
a hurricane on two legs.
the finality of the thunder.
the bitter cry of the rain.
nothing hits the ground without an echo.
no disaster walks away unscathed.
even if it is a scrape of the knee,
a slightly tattered heart;
i want you to know that i see you.

i want you to know that
i am not afraid of your storms.

Fleeting Things, Rachel H.

THE CONTINENT OF RIBERA

Realm of Elios

The High Realm, residence of the High King and the Council of Deities; new home to the archangels and deities who waged the War against the Primordials as well as to elves, shifters, and humans; member of the Aligned Realms.

Realm of Ikarria

The draconic realm, residence of the ether-wielding elves as well as shifters and humans, once home to the dragons; independent from the Aligned Realms.

Realm of Adrastea

The vampiric realm, original residence of the vampires; member of the Aligned Realms.

Realm of Kairos

The realm of the sands, residence of the shifters, especially the jackals and the wraiths; member of the Aligned Realms.

Realm of Valenzia

The guardian realm, sister kingdom to Damalis, charged to protect the Gates of Celestrea; destroyed during the War of the Skies; surviving citizens were either slaughtered by the High King or are now scattered about the Continent.

Realm of Damalis

The guardian realm, sister kingdom to Valenzia, charged to protect the Gates of Celestrea; destroyed during the War; the guardian realm still lives.

Realm of Celestrea

The ethereal realm, kingdom of the Primordials and original home of the deities and archangels; the Gates of Celestrea had allowed the gods to sustain the mortal world; the Gates were destroyed as a result of the War, removing any contact between the Primordials and the mortal world.

CELESTREA
ASHERAS
DRAGON'S TEETH
IKARRIA
DAE ASARI
THE JADE SEA
THE CONTINENT OF
RIBERA

TEOTLAN
DAMALIS
VALENZIA
NEPHTYR
WRAITH'S DEN
KAIROS
ESTRELLA TERRITORIES
ADRASTEA
ROZA
SOLEIRA
ELIOS

BLOOD
OF THE
LOST GODS

PROLOGUE

Every day that passed was a blade wedged deeper between the young man's ribs. Cold steel bit into the skin of his wrists, chains that silenced the powers inside him. Darkness ate at his mind, pulling him farther and farther into the void.

Icy water splashed his face, and the young man gasped awake. His vision swam before meeting eerie cerulean eyes.

"I'm afraid you cannot leave me yet," the specter said. Its lion-like face was mere breaths away from him. *"We are not finished."*

The young man spat out a wad of red. "Pity."

He shifted slightly, wincing at the ache throughout his body. They had decided to string him up this time, leaving him with his back against the wall, arms tied up above him. Blood had long dried on the stone ground, the young man's skin slowly healing itself.

The specter leaned over a table, its hand drifting above the array of wicked instruments. *"Let's try this again. I will release those shackles, and you will show us what you're capable of."*

"Torturing me so that I'm too weak to truly use my powers against you." The young man chuckled, the sound strained. "It won't change anything; I will not cede to your demands. Do what you want with me."

"Months have passed since you were first brought to this place, and you still fight. I like that about you."

Was that how long it had been? He had given up on keeping count. The mere fact he hadn't lost his mind to the shadows was a miracle.

The young man groaned as the last of his wounds stitched back together. "All this time and none of you have bothered to tell me why you want me."

A third voice echoed from beyond the cell bars. "We wish to understand the ether in your veins."

Deep and melodic. Full of ice and iron. The sound sent chills down his bruised spine. He blinked through the droplets of blood that fell across his eyelashes, dragging his gaze to the archangel with wings white as snow. How long had he been standing there?

It had been some time since the mysterious male had appeared within these cells.

The specter bowed to the archangel. *"Fallen, I will soon discover whether this prisoner holds the ability we are seeking."*

"Do so, and quickly." The archangel's expression was unreadable. "The hunt has begun."

Chains wailed against the stone as the young man struggled against them. He gritted his teeth. "What are you talking about?"

The specter's eyes brightened. *"The elf and the archangel."*

He didn't understand who the creature was referring to.

Something flickered across the archangel's blue eyes, though it quickly faded. "Their time is running out and our Creator wants them in our grasp before then. The Continent is no longer safe for them."

Shadows moved throughout the halls, heavy footsteps echoing. The blood drained from the young man's face at the sight of a figure cloaked in black. Broad shoulders, massive arms and legs clad in leather and darkness. Across its back was a scythe, grinning in the dim light. A hood was draped over its head, a crown of silver fire perched atop. Though it did little to hide its face: it was that of a skeleton, gleaming with bronze.

The young man knew it was the same monster that had taken him from his home, the same one that had killed his family…

The skeletal warrior brushed past the archangel, stepping further into the darkened hall of the prison, stopping in front of the cell.

That was all the young man knew of this place. A dark, cold prison tucked away somewhere on this Continent.

"This mortal world is decaying, it is only a matter of time before it meets its end," the archangel said. "You aren't allowed to die yet."

Sweat rolled down the young man's battered skin. He didn't understand what the male was speaking about, but one thing echoed through his tired bones. He wouldn't let them know the truth about him.

The specter picked up a jagged dagger, stalking toward him. *"Where did we leave off? Will you show me what rests within those veins today?"*

The young man's breathing turned shallow. He clenched his teeth as the specter grabbed his chin. *"Should I use steel or ether this time?"*

The young man jerked against his chains. "Please… *no*."

Those cerulean eyes burned brighter. *"Ether it is."*

His world exploded in silver light just as the chains were released from his wrists. He crashed to the ground, all while screams tore through his throat.

PART I

STARS MADE BY THE SUNS

ONE

Zara Santos contemplated her bleak options. A step back would send her flying off the cliff's edge and into the thick canopies of the jungle below. Any sudden movement forward would surely spook the jaguar, its reddish-yellow eyes heavy on her. The Ikarrian mercenary was also confident the female warrior sitting on top of the animal would skewer Zara with the spear in her hand. If the large cat didn't eat her first.

Every possibility led to certain doom.

Río stomped his hooves on the ground, clearly agitated because of the massive carnivore several yards away. He pulled against the reins firmly grasped in Axar's hands.

The shifter murmured gentle words to the horse. "Easy, easy."

Zara's blood turned hot. "Do you mind? You are scaring my horse."

She glared at the mysterious elven warrior who wore a skeletal mask over the lower half of her face.

The elf narrowed her green eyes but said nothing.

She was unlike anything Zara had ever seen. Her armor was the same midnight blue as the blade of her spear, and seemed to fit her strong body like a second skin. Strong, flexible material, with emerald-green pauldrons and dark leather armguards.

Intricate designs and images covering the armor on her legs and abdomen oddly reminded Zara of the murals she would often see in mercenary temples. Around the warrior's collar was an array of bright gems—red, orange, yellow, green, blue and purple—stitched into the chest leather piece, arranged to resemble sun rays.

Zara braced herself as the warrior raised her spear.

"Soraya, enough."

That liquid dark voice. Zara was met with a confusing onslaught of emotions at the sound, clashing with the undying throb in her heart. A pain that hadn't left her since the events in the abandoned temple in Soleira. When the blood of her mercenary family had pooled around her under a dawn sky, ready to drown her in grief.

Zara closed her eyes to shut out the images.

Her face betrayed nothing as she opened them again to find Ronan Menodora walking toward the warrior. The skin under his gray eyes was bruised purple. Exhaustion lined his strong jaw and scarred mouth, though he still seemed composed. His usual black fighting attire was stained with dirt and some flecks of blood. Her gaze narrowed on that.

The elf swiveled her gaze toward the archangel, a flare of emotion there. She scoffed but hitched the spear behind her back. The jaguar whined and took a few steps back, its spotted tail swishing over the jungle floor.

"You've been gone for years and *that* is the first thing you say to me?" Soraya's voice was smokey, laced with that same accent Ronan held—though hers was thicker, the words rolling over her tongue. Zara couldn't help but think how attractive it sounded.

Ronan's expression cracked, glancing away. "I'm sorry," he said softly. He turned his attention to the jaguar and lifted his hand; the animal pawed the ground excitedly before ramming its snout against his palm. Ronan smiled. "I have missed you, too, Kenzo."

Zara's jaw slackened.

"What is happening?" Axar muttered.

She wasn't quite sure herself but she was glad to know the chances of getting mauled or speared were a lot slimmer now. Zara released a heavy breath, the sweet scent of tropical fruit and damp wood filling her lungs. Her ears rang with the sounds of birds and other creatures she wasn't familiar with. Sunlight kissed her exhausted body, its warmth touching the sweat and bruises that coated her skin.

This land had been long considered dead when it was anything but. The Continent of Ribera had truly been fooled.

Soraya observed Ronan as he continued to pet Kenzo. "Orion informed us you were planning some sort of attack against the High Throne. The other érendira and I have been keeping watch for your return ever since."

The archangel's lips thinned. "It was a grave risk. One I was willing to make."

"It is only when *your* life is at risk that you come home, it seems."

Ronan gave the warrior a sharp look. "That is not—" He stopped himself, staring at her. After a moment, his expression softened. It might've fallen a little, too. "You are angry with me."

Soraya scoffed and tugged on the reins loosely tied to Kenzo, urging the jaguar to take a few more steps back. Away from Ronan. "It is fine. No need to explain yourself to me, *Your Majesty*."

Zara was unsure what to make of the scene unfolding before her. There was some history between them, though it was not something she cared to get involved in.

The archangel must have felt her stare on him; he glanced back and waved a hand. "I'm sorry you had to witness our family spat. This is Soraya Delgado. She, Orion and I grew up together."

Zara blinked in surprise. Though Ronan's family was no longer alive, she knew that the brawny archangel Orion was like a brother to him. Something warm fluttered in her chest knowing there was someone else that Ronan cared for. Someone who had been waiting for him to come home.

Soraya grumbled something under her breath before nodding her head to Zara and Axar in greeting. She moved away and disappeared into the trees before Ronan could stop her.

"She is an érendira," Ronan continued with a sigh. "An elite class of Damalisan warriors, composed only of women. They protect our land. I'm afraid my stubborn, little sister isn't happy with me."

A flurry of questions was on the tip of Zara's tongue. Before she could ask anything, Axar shuddered, his body teetering back and forth.

She caught her mercenary brother as he sank to one knee. *Suns,* the shifter was heavy.

"You used too much ether traveling in your wolf form," Zara said. "Stay on Río for now."

Ronan appeared beside them, pulling Axar to his feet. The shifter groaned. "No, I will be fine. *You* travel on Río."

"Don't be stubborn."

The archangel helped Axar on top of the warhorse's saddle. "It's better you avoid straining yourself. Soraya will escort us to Teotlan, the capital of Damalis." He paused with a wince. "It's a three-week journey from here. Maybe longer depending on our pace."

Axar released a string of curses at that.

Teotlan.

The word buzzed through Zara's head. The capital of one of the two guardian realms. Somehow, hearing the name made everything more real. That all the weight and pain she had carried had not been in fact a dream. A nightmare. There would be no waking up to a life where she hadn't lost the people she loved.

The back of her eyes burned, her hands curling into fists.

Soraya cleared her throat. Zara hadn't even realized she had returned. "There's no sign of the Elios soldiers that were following you. We'd better move, though," the warrior said, before sweeping her eyes over Zara and the now-woozy-looking wolf-shifter. "I don't think the people of the guardian realms will react well when they find out that we are hosting mercenaries—*Horizons,* at that—within our borders. Especially the *Rogue.*" The elf jerked her chin toward Zara who widened her eyes. "I am a protector of my people. I knew who you were as soon as I saw you. You've killed countless of our own."

Zara gritted her teeth, her hand flying instinctively to the dagger sheathed at her thigh. The jaguar caught the movement and jerked its head toward her, snarling. She stilled.

"You and your people are justified in your hatred against the mercenaries. I am not your enemy, but I can be. The Rogue was a role I was forced to play to keep *my* loved ones safe."

Zara was relieved that her voice did not waver, though there was still a tremble within her heart. She didn't know why she was spilling pieces of herself to this stranger. Perhaps it was a way to tolerate the ugly sensation that sat in her stomach.

She had failed to protect her loved ones after all, hadn't she? Hakim and Eshe were *gone*. Ikarria overrun by Adrastea. The fate of her sister and pater still unknown to her. Her hands were stained with blood from trying to keep these people safe, and—it had all been in vain.

Everything had gone to shit.

Soraya growled. "Even if you didn't choose that path, it doesn't bring back those you have slain, Rogue."

Ronan stepped between them. His voice was low, yet still had the power of thunderstorms. "Do *not* call her that, Soraya. She is no longer the Rogue, no longer bound to the High Throne. Many of us have had our choices taken from us, and it was the same for Zara. Besides, we cannot afford to fight amongst ourselves when—"

An arrow whistled through the air. Soraya moved to dodge it, her senses knife-sharp, though she was not the target. Ronan jerked his head to the side with a grunt.

Cold fear froze every limb in Zara's body. Everything in her mind screamed Ronan's name, only for her to realize that she had actually shouted it out loud. She didn't understand what this visceral sensation meant—couldn't bring herself to consider it—but all of that quickly faded when Ronan moved. The arrow in his hand.

"Fucking bastards," he growled, snapping the stem. "I thought I had lost them in the mists."

A line of red trickled down his cheek. The arrow had grazed him, the speed with which the archangel had moved a testament to his skill as a warrior and survivor. It had been too close though, Zara thought with a grimace.

Kenzo let out a roar, causing everyone—even Río—to jump. He

turned toward the trees, hairs bristling. Soraya unsheathed her spear once more.

"The Elios soldiers," she said. "How did they manage to get this far past the borders?"

Ronan cursed under his breath. "They are after me and Zara. They won't stop. We are what the High Throne wants."

Soraya studied him. "Why?"

The ether in Zara's soul growled and red light flickered across her skin. If Hakim were alive he would've scolded her for showing her power so recklessly. She had been hiding this abnormal light for most of her life after all. Though none of that was relevant anymore.

"Oh." Soraya's voice sounded far. "Is *that* why?"

Zara couldn't respond. There was the rustling of leaves, the scampering of critters along tree branches, and in the distance, the flapping of wings and the clangs of armor.

Her gaze drifted to Axar's pale face, his body slumped on Río's saddle. Seeing her mercenary brother like this, the sole survivor of her guild—the pain in her heart sharpened, like she'd taken a dagger to the chest. All of this was happening because of *them*.

Ronan brushed a thumb across the blood on his cheek. His black wings flared, the daggers strapped to his body gleaming. "We will have to kill them here. They cannot go any further."

To protect the surviving citizens of Damalis and Valenzia. All the effort he had gone through over the years to ensure the safety of his people and of the other guardian realm.

Soraya shifted her midnight-blue spear into position, the daylight's reflection on the blade almost blinding. Her other hand tightened around the jaguar's thick reins. "I will attack from above."

Above? Kenzo dove into the jungle. Zara sprinted after them, thinking she'd misheard, Ronan beside her. They followed the sounds of the approaching soldiers. Leaves and branches whipped at her sides and arms—but it was easy to ignore them. Especially when white cloaks emerged in the distance, glowing like shattered gems under the sparse rays of sun.

The jaguar was far ahead, moving over the wild terrain with ease.

Kenzo lunged toward a tree trunk and scaled the wood, practically gliding up and along the massive branches. Soraya moved to stand atop the jaguar's back. What were they doing?

A pair of archangel soldiers soared toward them. Soraya crouched, her spear grinning in her hand. The jaguar sprinted along a thick branch as one of the archangels prepared to swing his blade.

Zara felt the world slow as Soraya leaped off Kenzo. The érendira drove her spear forward and clashed with the soldier's sword, their weapons ringing out. She used the momentum to twist herself up and around the archangel. The male could barely move before the elf jabbed her weapon into his back, wedging it between the steel plates of armor, and yanked it out. A ribbon of red followed.

The soldier screamed as he fell, wings splayed out awkwardly, slamming onto the next branch below. Bones snapped on impact and blood spewed out of the male's mouth.

Soraya gazed at the lifeless soldier from above her skeletal mask, like a reaper of the afterlife.

"Welcome to Damalis," she snarled.

A second soldier hurtled toward her, but the warrior was already moving. Soraya swept her hand out in a crescent-shape motion, flares of ether following her fingertips as water materialized in the air. She directed it toward the archangel; the water sharpened, its tip freezing like a knife and piercing the male straight through his neck.

Ah. A water-wielding elf. Zara could only grin at what she was witnessing. She had seen the elemental elves of her pater's army in battle, but had hardly had the opportunity to admire such power up close. The sight sang to her blood-ridden soul.

Ronan's voice cut through her thoughts. "Move, Santos!"

Zara leaned into her instincts at the urgency in his tone. She slid across the dirt, ducking low enough to avoid an Elios soldier. There was a collision of wings above her, as well as the song of blades.

Deep within her soul, a white-hot anger surged forward. It bore fangs and claws, consumed by a hunger that craved something other than flesh and bone. A force that stirred the ether in her blood.

Zara had to trust that Ronan could handle the soldier, especially as the remaining unit of archangels appeared through the trees. She unsheathed her twin khopesh swords, the obsidian steel so dark it swallowed the light. All she could see were those fucking white cloaks.

Red light danced around Zara's legs as she lunged into the air, crossing her blades across her chest, the sound and ether drawing every soldier's gaze to her. She leaned into the white-hot feeling and sank into the wild waves inside her.

The soldiers watched as a crimson mist enveloped her entire being. How her eyes flickered to a deep red. To them, she would've looked more demon than elf. A nightmare made real.

Zara crashed into the archangels, twisting and turning as she met every blade that rushed toward her, quick on her feet. She slid her sword into the gaps of a soldier's armor. He bowed over and coughed blood. Zara laughed that cold, empty sound that came out whenever she made a kill. She almost expected the fyrebrand, her ether-imbued tattoo to flare. But it didn't. Beneath her bracer, there was now a blank space where the ink used to be. It would never again force her to submit to the will of another.

An archangel began to shout. "We need her alive! Remember: we either take the Rogue or the King of Damalis."

Zara yanked out her blade just as another soldier swung their warhammer toward her. She kicked her leg out to hit the female between her neck and shoulder. The archangel cried out and crumpled to the ground.

"I have been hunting marks for most of my life." Zara straightened, watching the soldiers gather around her in a circle. The mercenary didn't bother to count how many were against her; her senses told her enough: there were too many. Untamed ether was devouring her energy, but she held on. "And now I am the hunted."

The soldiers lunged as one. Zara ducked low, dirt and leaves smearing her skin as she sliced the muscles of someone's leg. Her ether gave her an extra boost of strength to help her cut through armor—though she couldn't do it cleanly and quickly and left them there to bleed out. It would have been a hassle to hack through steel and skin.

Every soldier she went against was a walking weapon. They

managed to nick and pierce her skin, punch and kick her body. Someone bashed the end of their weapon's pommel against her temple and Zara's vision blurred. She gnashed her teeth together and thrust her sword through their gut.

A soldier kicked Zara's ribs, knocking the air from her lungs. Pain shot through her side, her grip on her weapons loosened. The archangel grabbed her hair and yanked her head up.

He hissed in her ear. "Such trash. To think you were the late High King's *personal* assassin. Don't you realize that you will always be chained to someone stronger than you? Stop resisting and serve your role."

Zara thrashed in his grasp. The ether inside her screamed, though she was losing focus. Images of that night in the temple flashed in her mind. The deities' ethereal eyes on her. Axar being taken away from her. Raziel killing Hakim and Eshe. Their bodies before her. *No no no.* Her heart was being peeled apart—she couldn't breathe.

Blue, scalding light erupted around the soldier's arm. The archangel's eyes went wide as he let her go. "What is this? What's happening?"

His questions twisted into a scream as the unnatural power crawled up his shoulder. Blue as the deep sea, even as the sky above began to turn blood-orange. It wreathed the soldier's body, and he rolled on the ground in an attempt to put out the fiery light. Not that it did him any good: the ether still devoured him.

The other soldiers went pale. More blasts of blue shot through the crowd, giving Zara time to catch her breath and get to her feet. Her head rang as she lifted her gaze to see the Elios forces turn to Ronan.

She knew she recognized that ether, had seen it once before when it blew an entire wall of the coliseum into chunks of rock and stone. Ronan had saved her with it. Ethereal light danced around his body, similar to how hers did, but it wasn't as bright as it had been moments ago. Certainly not as strong as it had been back in Elios. Ronan's energy was waning, and soon, hers would too.

His eyes met hers for a moment. They were separated by enemy forces, the air filled with steel and the smell of ash. The archangel winked before swinging his sword toward a soldier. His ether exploded once more, devouring those within close range.

Beyond him, Soraya was still locked in b. Torrents of water plowed through rows of soldiers, drowning them or smashing them against trees. The érendira switched between her ether and the spear as her jaguar maneuvered around their foes.

Blood trickled down Zara's brow, nearly blinding her. She surged forward with her power, appearing in one spot and then another to cut soldiers down. Pain ricocheted throughout her bones as she collided against strong armor.

A numbness was washing over her body, her mind going quiet. Ether spiraled inside her. That pure, unadulterated anger rushed through her veins.

Her power slipped from her reins. Red-purple light poured off her arms and legs, lashing out at nearby soldiers. Their armor turned hot, singeing their skin. They fell back while others pushed through the heat.

Zara landed on top of an archangel's shoulders and slashed the bloodied edge of her khopesh at his throat.

"None of you will be returning home," she growled.

The trees seemed to spin as Zara continued to cut through the horde. A soldier tried to grab her a moment before they caught on fire. The smell of burning flesh and metal was thick in the air. Ether continued to pool around her, eating at the archangels surrounding her.

The world was burning before her eyes; power rushed through her body and mind, a tidal wave that had been unleashed from the unknown. Zara gasped for breath, falling to her knees.

The familiar power she had grown up with had become a stranger to her. A foreign creature that was impatient and hungry. She clutched the leathers over her chest, her breathing rampant. If Hakim could see what had become of her...

A deep voice cut through the crimson haze. "Zara!"

She blinked a few times and found Ronan kneeling before her. His expression was focused; those silver eyes betrayed nothing. He cupped both sides of her face, his rough palms warm against her skin.

"You are doing so well," he said. "Now I need you to take a deep breath and reach out to your ether. Call it back to you."

Zara hated how a part of her recoiled at Ronan's touch, while another wanted to melt into it. It was an aching battle on the rise. She breathed through clenched teeth, shoving those feelings away for now.

She clung onto his words and willed the last thread of her strength to tug her ether back. The red-purple light slowly returned to her; every pull had her body quivering with exhaustion.

Ronan still held onto her, the ether never harming him. Perhaps due to the power he also possessed. A connection of some kind between them.

Once Zara's senses were back to normal once more, she felt her boot sink in something wet. Her arms, legs—even her hair was sticky. Still in the archangel's arms, she dragged her gaze up.

Bodies surrounded them. Wings had been ripped apart, feathers scattered about. Torn limbs tossed to the side, hands stuck reaching to the sky. Every soldier dead. Had she and Ronan done this?

The archangel brushed the hair from her face. His own was riddled with cuts and bruises. "There she is." He smiled at her. "How are you feeling?"

Zara blinked a few times, her eyelids heavy. Before she could speak, he pushed her to the side. Away from him. Her head smacked against something hard, and she was forced to watch as a soldier aimed their sword at Ronan's chest.

No.

How could Zara not have sensed them? She and Ronan had dropped their defenses for a mere breath without checking for any survivors. The soldier had taken advantage of that. Ronan raised his arm as if to block the blade.

Zara reached for him just as a slash of silver light materialized in front of the archangel. Like a tear within the fabric of reality. A black panther ran through the gash. Zara must have hit her head harder than she thought—but no: what she saw was *real*. The panther took the soldier down, tearing their neck apart with its fangs.

Ronan fell to the ground, his jaw agape. Silver lined his eyes. "Nyota?"

The panther licked its snout clean before letting out a mewl. It charged the archangel, and Zara's chest tightened as he toppled back into the dirt. Ronan wrapped his arms around the muscular animal, a ragged laugh escaping him. As tears trickled down his face.

"Suns Above, Nyota, it *is* you. You found me."

Zara pulled herself upright, wincing at the slight pain in her head. Her gaze lingered on Ronan's smile, at the light that brightened his face. One she hadn't seen in a while.

"Who's this?" she asked.

Ronan turned to her just as shouts rose from beyond the trees, as another wave of Elios soldiers charged toward them. Zara pushed herself to her feet and reached for her twin swords. Even as her fingers trembled. Her ether had guttered out.

Ronan rose as well, the panther prowling before them. "This was not how I wanted to introduce you to our homeland."

Zara shrugged. "I'd say it's quite fitting for us."

Her voice was light despite how her heart hammered against her ribs. The soldiers tore through the large plants, dove between the branches. There were too many. She couldn't see Soraya anymore. Where had the warrior gone?

Shadows rushed past her. Sharp bird calls echoed above them, causing chills to run along her arms. Zara was familiar with this tactic: it was something she had done with her guild many times. It was a song of the hunt, a call for blood.

Jaguars scaled the magnificent trees, moving along the vines. Atop them were women clasped in midnight-blue armor and steel, each of them wearing the mask of a skeleton, like Soraya.

Pride touched Ronan's voice. "The érendira have arrived."

Soraya was among them, spreading her arms. The warriors let out a final war cry before they unleashed themselves upon the Elios soldiers.

With their intricate armor glinting under the setting sun, the women looked like shooting stars. Many of them commanded fire and wind, flares of their elemental power cutting through the jungle.

An érendira and a male soldier landed on a nearby root of a tree, which was wide and thick enough to count as part of the battleground. The warrior's spear was a slash of deep blue with how fast she moved the weapon, but the archangel slammed his wing against her chest, throwing her off the root. The elf backflipped midair and summoned a pillar of rock to rise from the ground and break her fall.

Zara stumbled back. "Fucking Suns."

The érendira gave a low shout—a signal—and her jaguar launched itself from a wall of leaves and bit down on the archangel's wing. The male gave a bloodcurdling scream as the jaguar dragged him through the shrubbery. As soon as they were out of sight there was the wet sound of squelching flesh, and red pooled from behind the branches. The animal reemerged, licking its chops.

Ronan shuddered. "That's terrifying… and disgusting." He glanced at Zara. "I can practically see stars shining in your eyes right now."

Zara closed her mouth, unaware that she had been gaping.

A sharp gust of wind plowed through the remaining group of soldiers, sending them to the ground. Another érendira rode atop her jaguar, her hands controlling the air, the force of it growing stronger and faster. Someone whistled from above, and another jaguar sprinted down the length of a branch.

Soraya. She flew off Kenzo's back, spiraling toward the ground where the soldiers were struggling against the ethereal wind, many of them gasping for breath, scratching at their chests and throats. Zara's face paled when she realized that their air was being stolen from them.

Water formed at Soraya's command, a torrent that danced around the warrior as she fell. The érendira sent the water crashing down against the soldiers just as the wind dissipated. From the height it came from, the weight of it must have been brutal. The archangels were crushed to the jungle floor, many of them dying on impact.

Kenzo leaped out to catch Soraya midair, the pair landing on a giant plant's leaves.

"Incredible," Zara breathed, her legs shaking.

Spots fluttered across her vision as the last of her energy was sapped from her body. Before she could crumple to the ground, strong arms wrapped around her.

"I have you, little wolf," Ronan said.

Zara wanted to reach out to him, to help him, too. This sense of helplessness was so aggravating, but the darkness was swallowing her whole.

All she could do was watch as the érendira defeated the last of the Elios soldiers before she fell unconscious.

TWO

Zara woke several times. The first was to a campfire, a warm blaze that wrapped around her exhausted body. Her eyelids were too heavy, everything unfocused and tilting on its axis. Still, Zara was able to make out the érendira gathered around the makeshift camp. They stood proud, their jaguars waiting among the trees, where only their glowing eyes could be seen. All of their gazes were on Ronan who was before Zara, his body angled protectively toward her.

Under the amber light, the tattoos along his neck seemed darker than before, shadows that danced along his skin. "They are under my protection," he said.

Zara wanted to move. To stand at his side. He shouldn't have had to do this alone, but her body betrayed her. She couldn't even speak. The darkness enveloped her.

The second time Zara woke up was to a night sky filled with a sea of stars. Her head was heavy but she felt familiar hands wiping a damp cloth over her face. Ronan was bowed over her, his jaw bracketed with tension as he poured water down her scalp.

"Just cleaning you up, Santos," he whispered. "I can only wash your hair and face. You will be able to have a proper, warm bath soon, I promise."

Zara moved her mouth, though she didn't know if she actually said anything. Ronan seemed to understand, his voice warm like honey. "Axar is fine. He's right here, sleeping near you. Río too."

Good. The relief was so strong that her head lolled to the side and darkness found her once again.

And the third time she opened her eyes... was to a dream. One filled with fiery ether, sending her blood thrumming. Zara was suspended in a nothingness that she couldn't comprehend. Something in the distance called to her, a hum that spoke to the energy that lined her soul.

Until someone grabbed her jaw and yanked her forward. Golden-brown wings unfurled, wine-red hair flowing with unseen energy. Raziel. As glorious as the day she'd killed him. The late High King smiled, the golden hue of his eyes burning like embers. His grip on her tightened to the point of pain.

"The god is looking for you," he said in a sneer.

She yanked herself from his grasp—

Zara jerked awake and scrambled toward a random bush before vomiting. No, not a dream. A nightmare. She swished some water from her waterskin in her mouth and spat it out.

Raziel is dead. Raziel is dead. Raziel is dead. He can't hurt you anymore.

Her eyes adjusted to the dark, noting all the small campfires that were now dim and close to ashes. Jaguars were huddled around their partnered warriors, all seemingly asleep. This area of the jungle looked different from where they'd had the battle against the Elios soldiers. They must have traveled some way before settling for the night.

Río and Axar were near her bedroll. The shifter was fast asleep underneath his blanket, his closed eyes just peeking out over the hem. Her warhorse lifted his head, dark eyes on her.

She walked to him and ran her hand down his snout. "I'm sorry if I startled you."

Río nudged her palm and Zara kissed the space between his eyes before venturing across the camp. Anything to get rid of the nerves that still shuddered through her body after that nightmare.

Roots covered the ground, tall and wide, looking like the spines of a beast. Plants were filled with long, blood-red leaves. Monkeys with iridescent blue-green feathered tails huddled together along the large branches. Zara's mouth fell open in wonder.

Just within the camp's outskirts were Soraya and Kenzo, the jaguar curled around the sleeping warrior. He lifted his head, watching Zara pass by. She quickened her pace.

The mercenary reached a small hill, silver ribbons of starlight waiting beyond its peak. Zara gulped down the cool air as she trudged up to the top. She heard someone murmuring and moved closer to the sound.

"I've missed you."

Zara would recognize that deep timbre anywhere.

"It's been too long."

She cocked her head; Ronan sounded so… affectionate. He was sitting at the base of a tree. His powerful black wings shifted and she could see his profile, the slope of his nose touched by the moonlight. Ronan was—Ronan was *petting* the black panther.

Her jaw slackened. Now that the chaos had died down, she was able to properly admire the animal who had come to their aid. The panther was stunning, with a sleek coat that rippled with muscle. It snuggled its muzzle into Ronan's palm and he smiled, running a hand down the animal's back.

Zara was about to take another step but faltered when she saw flickers of light flowing between the archangel and the panther. Whispers of ether danced in the night air; Zara wasn't sure if she should be concerned at the sight.

"Are you going to keep standing there, Santos?" Ronan glanced over his shoulder, his eyes shining silver in the night. The corner of his lips curled upward. "Or will you come meet my *nahual?*"

The animal's bright green eyes gazed at Zara curiously. Its tongue darted out, revealing thick fangs.

"A nahual?" Zara moved closer.

The archangel went back to petting the panther who nestled its head under the crook of his arm. "They're also known as a familiar.

Nahuals are animal guides, birthed by ether. They are spirits who come from beyond the bounds of Celestrea and bond with a mortal of their choosing." He scratched behind the animal's ear. "Zara, allow me to introduce you to Nyota."

Nyota licked Ronan's cheek before making its way to Zara. The panther's paws were large, with sharp claws that dug into the dirt. There was a faint sheen of an iridescent deep green and blue along the nape of the panther's neck, the same color as the monkeys she'd seen a few moments ago. Zara hadn't noticed that before, though it wasn't as if she'd had the time to admire the animal in the midst of the battle.

She lifted a hand and waited. Nyota slowly pressed its forehead against her palm, starting to purr not long after.

"I apologize if Nyota scared you earlier. When I entered guardian realm territory, she felt my presence through our bond," Ronan said. He jerked his chin to the panther. "She wasn't willing to wait any longer for the reunion, especially when she sensed I was in danger."

Zara scratched the back of Nyota's ear. "You speak as if you know what she's thinking."

He stretched out his long legs. "Because I do. Anyone with a nahual can speak with them."

Zara recalled how ether had flowed between Nyota and Ronan. It had faded once he'd acknowledged her presence. "What does it mean to be bonded to a nahual? I have never seen such companionships within the realms of Elios and Ikarria."

"It doesn't surprise me. They are very rare nowadays. During the Age of the Primordials, nahuals were much more common, but I think the animal spirits have become more selective over the years. You've probably seen some familiars with their mortal partners; you just didn't know it. Though compared to the other kingdoms, the animal spirits are more likely to be found in the guardian realms."

Ronan tipped his head back to look at the sky. "A nahual is a guide, a mirror to your soul, and they can speak only to you. They are your guardians, your support." A small smile formed on his lips. "Really, they are there to love you."

Zara's chest warmed at his words. She couldn't help but stare at the archangel. With his wings splayed out on either side of him, starlight dappling his tattooed neck, it made him look like some otherworldly painting. One that portrayed the darkness embracing the ethereal. Beauty crafted from the places most people would fear.

Ronan glanced her way and she averted her gaze. Nyota decided to lie at Zara's feet and began to lick her paws.

"Nyota says she likes you," he said. "She doesn't like anyone."

The panther made a whining sound; it only made Zara smile. She continued to pet the panther. "How come you didn't reveal Nyota before?"

Ronan sighed. "To protect her, mostly. Nahuals are immortal in theory, but they can die in the mortal world. If they do, they will be sent to the Otherworld, and it may be thousand of years before they can return again. It is never a risk you want to take. If I'd walked around with Nyota in the Stone Orchard, it would have made me stand out even more." His expression turned pained. "She didn't like it of course. It has been years since we last communicated; the ether between us has waned and our connection nearly faded into nothing."

Hearing him speak of this was unreal, as if Zara had stepped into an entire different world than the one she had always known.

"What was it like when the bond between you two weakened?"

His eyes went to Nyota. "It was terrifying. I felt alone in a way I had never imagined," he said, his voice low. "Though, when I was with you, that seemed to change."

Zara sucked in a breath when he met her gaze, and she looked away. Emotions washed over her, mixed with warmth and guilt. All while the pain in her heart throbbed. She couldn't find a response. Zara swallowed back the thick emotion gathering in her throat, battling the bone-deep sorrow she wasn't sure how to handle.

They sat in silence underneath the canopy of stars, the only sounds the subtle rustling of leaves and the occasional cawing of night birds.

"How does it feel knowing you are back in your home realm?" Zara asked, still not meeting his eyes.

The skin between the archangel's brows pinched together. "A part of me is happy, though the other is *terrified*. I have been avoiding my kingdom for so long, using the Sombra Quarter as an excuse to stay away, when the truth is… I was too ashamed to go back after the War."

Zara tried to imagine a younger version of the archangel. The one who had escaped from the Elios prisons and started to take over the shadow markets. She wondered what he had been like back then.

"Now, with the High Throne at our heels, we will have to shift our priorities," Ronan said as Nyota curled up between them, her bulky body big enough to take up the whole space there. "Our ethers have been freed from the binds after so long and will begin to mature."

Ronan ran a tattooed hand through his hair; the act snagged Zara's attention. She stared at the inked designs peeking from where his fighting leathers dipped at his collarbone. He wasn't wearing sleeves and her gaze focused on the empty space around his left bicep. The ether-binding tattoo that used to be there…

"We have the powers of a Primordial," she whispered, remembering the moment she found out. Back in the abandoned temple, when her ether had torn through the dawn sky… after Hakim and Eshe were killed. Ronan had witnessed that power then, told her what it was. It was what had freed him of his ether-binding tattoo.

Zara's eyes narrowed. "What does it mean to have such powers?"

Shadows seemed to crowd over him. "The full answer to that question will require us to be fully rested. But to satiate your curiosity for now, I can say that Primordial power is *not* hereditary, it is given. The natural ether of this world, the force that is above the gods themselves, decided to bestow this strength onto *you*."

Zara's heart raced. Out of fear or bewilderment, she didn't know. Most of her life she'd thought she was some anomaly. Elves were blessed with the ability to control one of the four elements, but she had been born with the ability to summon light. Now, that light seemed to be manifesting into something else. Ethereal flames. *Maturing*, as Ronan had called it.

The archangel gazed out at the wild terrain. "Now that we know the atrocities the High Throne and Council are committing, we must decide our next steps."

Fucking Suns, how could she have stopped thinking about any

of that? The specters possessing mortals, the Spirits of the Midnight Sun appearing even years after the gates were destroyed, as well as the apparent involvement of the Primordial of Fate and Time, Khaos. Not to mention…

Zara's hands balled into fists on her lap. "Adrastea has overtaken Ikarria. I need to find out what happened to my pater and sister."

Ronan nodded. "Which prompts me to ask you this," the archangel gave her a sidelong glance. "What is it you want, Zara Santos?"

She felt the gravity of his question. All that had happened that past hunting season had brought her here, to a land long-forgotten. Her path was and always would be entangled with the male before her.

"Power," Zara said. "I do not care how it sounds. I want the strength to be rid of the Council and their influence. To avenge the people they took from me."

Her voice broke and she swallowed.

"Raziel is dead, but they still want me—and you—in their possession. No longer will I allow others to control me. Now I have an ether with a potential unknown to me, I will not let this opportunity go to waste." Red light wreathed around her fingers, albeit weakly.

Ronan's lips curled. "Violent little wolf. The High Throne and Council have always seen the guardian realms as their enemies, and now they know we still exist. It will only be a matter of time before they come for us." The archangel grabbed Zara's hand, lifted it into the moonlight. "Will you work with me once more, Horizon?"

Zara had no idea where this path would take them. She felt as if she was standing on the edge of a cliff, with nothing but the unknown waiting below. Everything was so different now. The promise of vengeance burned through her, even as tears threatened to burst.

"Yes," she said. "You have a deal, archangel."

Ronan gave her a soft smile; it pulled her gaze to the scar on his lips. He still held her hand, his thumb sweeping over her skin. Zara was staring at him. She remembered how it had felt to kiss him… The hot touch of his body against hers, entangled in bedsheets—

The thought brought a surge of heartache. Zara had been so happy in that moment—all while her mercenary family were fending for their lives. It wasn't fair, nor was it Ronan's fault. Her grief was misplacing her emotions, this she knew. Yet, it still persisted.

Zara pulled her hand away from his. "I think we should talk about… us."

Her heart was thumping wildly against her ribs. Ronan was looking at his now-empty hand, and the skin between his brows pinched together. "I don't intend to put any pressure on you, especially after all you went through."

She considered his words. "It's not as if I am the only one going through hardship. After more than fourteen years, you have returned to your kingdom; I'm sure it will come with many obstacles."

Ronan's expression darkened, a twist of pain there. The strands of his black hair fell over his brow, but Zara was sure she saw a sheen in his gray eyes.

"Yes," he said. "And I have a score to settle with Erebus."

Nyota growled at the name of the newly crowned High King. The panther stood, stretching her powerful limbs before strutting into the trees. Zara was grateful they could now talk privately.

"Do you want to talk about it?" Zara asked. Erebus's expression when he'd seen Ronan at the coliseum burned through her mind. Full of shock, and maybe even… *relief*. She wondered again how far in the past the relationship between the archangels went.

Ronan was silent at first. "I will. But not now. Once we reach Teotlan, we will talk about this, and more."

She nodded. Thinking of Erebus caused her chest to tighten. Besides her family and guild, he was the only other person she'd trusted in Soleira. The archangel had provided her an escape in many ways. They'd spent many nights talking to one another in the comfort of each other's arms.

Suns, she had considered him a *friend*. And he had betrayed her. Turned out, there was little Zara had actually known about the male.

"I do have a question, though, if you're willing to answer," Ronan said. His gaze was distant, voice soft. "What was your relationship with Erebus?"

Zara blinked in surprise. He continued, "I think I have been curious about it for some time. In the coliseum, the way Erebus acted towards you made it seem there had been… *more* between the two of you."

"Erebus and I never had a romantic relationship, if that's what you're asking. Though, yes, we've been together. For a while, I thought we were friends."

Ronan ran a hand across his jaw, still not looking her way.

"Does that bother you?"

"I must admit, the thought of him touching you—of anyone touching you—doesn't please me, but at the same time… I'm glad you both had each other, especially during a time when all must have seemed lost in the darkness."

Zara couldn't blame Ronan for his curiosity.

Her attention dragged to his cheek. The wound the arrow had inflicted had already healed, the archangel's ether quick at work. Zara brushed her fingers across where the cut used to be.

Ronan stilled under her touch, his gaze heavy on her. Zara suddenly couldn't breathe. A memory of their bare bodies, slick with sweat, as they drowned in each other—the abandoned temple filled with *blood*.

She quickly pulled away.

Something ugly gnawed at her bones. Guilt that she had been with Ronan, *happy*, while her guild was in danger. Guilt that she couldn't face being with him now. Guilt that it was affecting Ronan.

"I'm sorry," Zara whispered. "I don't know if I am able to give you what you are seeking. At least, not right now…"

It hurt to see how the light cracked in Ronan's eyes. Zara couldn't blame him if he was disappointed. The archangel had given himself to her, fully, just like she had to him.

Ronan gently held her chin, tilting her face toward his. "I do not expect or demand anything from you, Zara Santos. As we said, we both have our own battles to overcome, and this *bond* between us can take its time to strengthen. Until and if you are ready."

Zara felt like she could choke on the emotion that sat so heavily in her chest. He was being too kind. Too merciful. She didn't know if she deserved it.

Tears burned behind her eyes. "Maybe we should set a boundary between us. We will be working together, and it would be best that we keep it at just that."

He dropped her chin. The absence of his touch made her feel cold and she almost regretted her words—*no*. This was what they needed.

Ronan didn't give her time to doubt and gave her a gentle smile. "Agreed, my Horizon." Something raw touched his voice, and it twisted her heart. "I am your blade, and I will have whatever you give me."

THREE

Daria Calderón watched as flames hissed to life above her palm. The ball of fire pulsed and rotated, red tongues lapping at the air. She turned her hand and swept it out; sweat beaded her brow as the flames followed her movement, the length of the fire growing longer and thinner. Good.

Daria held her breath and stepped into a lunge. She used her other hand to push the rope of flames farther out. This, practicing her control on the ether, was the only thing that offered reprieve nowadays.

It had been a month since the raid on Ikarria, and Daria had become a glorified hostage within her own home. There was access to food and basic necessities. She was even able to walk the castle grounds and venture into the capital, though there were many vampire soldiers about keeping an eye on her. No need for a personal guard.

Daria gritted her teeth as she lifted her foot and twisted it into a kick. The fire didn't obey; it flowed along her hands but did not transfer to her leg and foot. Her ether shuddered before dissipating into embers.

She sighed. "Well, that can't be right."

Daria glanced at the tome she had propped up on a stand. Various fighting stances and techniques poured from those worn pages, satiating her thirst for knowledge. For now. A valuable distraction. Ironic that the book came from the very person that caused her need for it. She shut down any further thoughts of him.

Daylight poured from the glass ceiling, bouncing off the pool of water that surrounded the stone platform where she was training. Thankfully, there was no one around, the statues of the Primordials her only audience.

Her eyes went to the Primordial of Life, Genesis. The goddess was judging her, she was sure of it. Daria rolled her eyes. "Oh, hush."

"Your Majesty?"

Hearing her new title sent a cold rush through Daria's veins. *Queen.* She was queen now.

It was all wrong.

The advisor to the Ikarrian court walked into the chamber. Basira was a strong woman, with dark shoulder-length hair, broad shoulders and an uncanny skill with the blade. Her brown skin was all brawn, even though the elf had long retired from swordsmanship and gone into politics.

By some grace of the Suns, the Ikarrian advisors and castle staff were permitted to keep serving their duties, so as to have *some* internal order in the realm. Any visiting nobles or other officials had been removed from the obsidian castle. Only the necessary leading figures were allowed to live there. Forced, even. Daria supposed the reason was so the vampires could maintain control of the Ikarrian authority.

The advisor observed Daria's training garb, which consisted of loose slacks and a blouse, and the queen's expression. "If I can make an assumption, your ether winked out on you."

Daria tried not to slump her shoulders. "I don't understand how our soldiers can fight *and* control the elements at the same time. It feels impossible."

Basira glanced at the tome. "For one, the stance you are attempting is too advanced for you. What you need to focus on is strengthening your mental control. Simply trying to summon your fire multiple times throughout the week will help with that. It is a practice, like anything else, and eventually the flames will listen. As I've said before, Your Majesty."

Her advisor was right, she had mentioned this to Daria various times during their many training sessions. Learning about fighting techniques and battle tactics was a different world compared to the politics and cultures she'd studied.

She exhaled a sharp breath. "My progress is far too slow, I need to expedite my training. To be of some use with my ether. My kingdom needs me *now*."

"At least the vampires allowed you to use it," Basira replied. She raised a hand, showing the iron bracelet wrapped around her wrist. "Adrastea made certain that no other elf can tap into their power."

Guilt washed over Daria. Every elemental elf, whether a soldier, tradesman, or a regular civilian, had been forced to wear ether-imbued bracelets that locked their ether. All except the children and, for some reason, her.

"Truthfully, I think they simply aren't threatened by my power." Daria wiped her hands on her slacks. "What can I help you with, Basira?"

Her advisor grimaced. "He has requested your presence again."

He. Daria's stomach twisted. A month since the raid. A month since she had even seen Ares. She had refused all his previous attempts to speak with her. At first, Daria was worried there would be consequences to denying the war general of Adrastea, but none came. The thought of seeing him…

Basira's expression was grim. "It's different this time, Your Majesty. I would advise that you go to this meeting."

"Why?"

"It looks like the vampires received new orders from their king." Basira folded her arms. "Adrastea has been sending forces to all major cities within Ikarria."

Suns Above, that was not good. "I must go then."

She went to grab the tome from the stand while her advisor stared at the statues. "You've been coming here a lot, Your Majesty."

"The vampires don't come to the Primordial Sanctuary. It's safe for me to practice."

Besides, if Daria stopped moving even for a second, all she would do would be thinking about her pater and sister. Only the gods knew where Idris had been taken and what he was currently going through. As for Zara—there were too many unknown variables. It hurt to even think of her sister. Zara had been branded a traitor. Word had quickly spread about the High King's death and the revelation that the Damalisan king was alive.

The Damalisan King—*Ronan Menodora*, leader of the Sombra Quarter. Daria had only met the male once but the thought that she had been in the presence of the long-lost ruler of a guardian realm was surreal. Zara must have known this truth too.

Daria needed to talk to her sister.

And Hakim and Eshe… The news of their deaths had been delivered through Ares, ironically enough. He had slipped the information under her door one night after she had rejected yet another meeting with him. It was better that way; Daria had been able to cry and mourn the mercenaries on her own.

"Allow me to change, and then we'll see what Adrastea wants."

As they exited the Sanctuary, Basira eyed the thick book in the queen's arms. "That is a rare edition on elemental training. Where did you get it?"

Daria kept her gaze forward. It was the same book *he* had come across in the forbidden library of the High Throne, and it had somehow found its way into her bag while the Adrastean forces marched toward Ikarria. She could only wonder what the vampire general had been thinking when he put it there.

Daria hugged the tome a bit tighter. "Nowhere special."

Two vampire soldiers guarded the doors to the war chamber. More of Adrastea's forces strolled down the halls, while others lounged in the grand dining hall. Daria hardly ever interacted with any of them; most of the time they would sneer or ignore her. Though, occasionally, she felt that *they* were keeping their distance from *her*.

One of the males raised a hand, stopping her and Basira. "I apologize, Your Majesty, but this meeting is only meant for you."

Basira looked insulted. "I must support my queen," she said, her lips twisting in anger.

"My general commanded that no one else enter the meeting aside from Queen Daria." The vampire bowed his head. He was young and seemed *genuinely* apologetic.

Daria couldn't help but gape at the male.

The other soldier flashed her fangs at him. "Why are you being so polite? We do not serve the Ikarrians—they serve *us*."

That was more like it.

Daria waved a hand to Basira. "Thank you for escorting me. I will come for you afterwards."

Her advisor bowed to her, though she looked worried. "I know you can handle it. Be safe, Your Majesty."

Those parting words were a comfort Daria didn't know she needed.

Entering the war chamber, the first thing that caught her eye was the obsidian table. Its black glass surface reflected the carved structure of a dragon protruding from the ceiling. Daylight beamed through the open wooden shutters where Daria could see the rustling leaves of the ancient Ikarrian trees. Cool mountain air nipped at her skin, a sign that winter had arrived. Though it didn't snow in Dae Asari, the Dragon Teeth's mountain peaks would soon be drenched in white.

Daria's heart thumped against her ribs at the nostalgia that hit her in the war room, but it quickened for a different reason when she saw who sat at the head of the table.

The vampire general had an elbow propped on the armrest, jaw resting on his fist. His long dark hair flowed down past his waist, the sunlight catching the tint of violet there. A thin trail of red smoke curled from a rolled piece of parchment between his lips. His brows were furrowed, as if he were deep in thought. Those violet eyes slid up to her.

The words were clogged in her throat. They stared at one another, as if standing on separate cliffsides, a gorge between them. Daria supposed that was true: Their last conversation had been an argument, one where she'd severed any kind of friendship. All with good reason.

She tried to pry into that cold gaze of his. For some kind of proof that the male she had gotten to know was not completely gone. But Ares was too good at wearing a mask.

Silas stepped to the general's side. The Second stood proud, hands clasped behind his back. He was as handsome as always, with his curly black hair slicked back and the same easy smile that had made Daria mistake him for a kind and friendly ally—while he was actually a snake in disguise.

Silas grinned. "Welcome, Your *Majesty.*"

Daria didn't respond and seated herself at the opposite end of the table. Ares's gaze was heavy on her, but she refused to shrink away from it.

"You're here," the general murmured.

Daria hated how her body stiffened at his deep voice, even more so since he sounded *bored.* She lifted her chin. "After all my refusals to meet, you could sound a little more pleased at my presence."

Silas whistled. "I like the attitude, Your Majesty. Not so timid now, are you?"

Well, it was not like she could admit sweat was beading along the nape of her neck.

Ares's jaw clenched. "Silas," he warned.

His Second raised his hands. "I apologize, General."

Ares plucked the roll from his lips and crushed its end on a little plate on the table. "It has been some time since we've properly spoken. Adrastea has finally placed all its forces where they need to be and I thought it was time we had a discussion about the future of the draconic realm."

He leaned to the side, and that was when Daria noticed bandages wrapped around his left arm and wrist through his long-sleeved coat. He had been burned in the fight against her pater, and the general must have been recovering this entire time.

Her gaze continued down to his hand, honing in on the obsidian circlet around his middle finger. Ares still wore the ring she had given him back in Soleira.

The vampire crossed one leg over the other. "King Matías has made his orders clear. Ikarria will function as it always has, though under the formal rule of Adrastea and the High Throne. Our king will require reports of the trade and business within your kingdom, and anything he wishes to change of the draconic realm will be adhered to."

Hurt cleaved through Daria's chest as a different type of fire flared within. It burned her blood, those unseen wounds in her heart making it hard to breathe. After all this time, *this* was what Ares wanted to speak about.

Beneath the table, her hands balled into fists. She bridled the clash of emotions, unwilling to let any tears rise. "So, I am to be a puppet of a ruler."

"You are to stay *alive*," he said, his expression still unreadable.

Before Daria could interpret what he meant, Ares scoffed under his breath. "Or you could disobey and risk my king's wrath. Do whatever you wish."

Right. Disappointment curled in her stomach. "You told me that Matías wanted Ikarria as a reward for aligning himself with the late High King. There's more to it, isn't there? I don't see what benefits the Lord of the Vampires could achieve from Ikarria. What is his true purpose in all this?"

Ares searched her face, his stone-cold face betraying nothing. But it was Silas who cackled, placing a hand over his chest. "Isn't it obvious, Your Majesty? Do you not remember what I asked you back in Soleira?"

Daria searched her memory; she recalled questions about her home realm, specifically about . . .

She felt the color drain from her face. Ares's brows pulled forward. He didn't know what Silas had spoken to her about.

His Second didn't relent. "Honestly, why would I show such interest in this lonely corner of the Continent?"

"The dragons," Daria whispered. Her vision swayed. "The Lord of the Vampires is interested in the dragons."

Ares blinked, the most reaction he offered. "Yes," he said. "King Matías wishes to bring them back. A common goal, is it not?"

Daria's heart fell. How long had he known of the true intentions of the vampire king?

She gritted her teeth. "I have already said this before, the dragons disappeared a hundred years ago. There has been no sign of them since."

"Matías believes they are able to return." Ares glanced down at the obsidian table, at the reflection of the carved dragon between them. "Much like your own father."

Daria narrowed her eyes. "You still haven't said where you took him."

"I could've told you, but you've been avoiding me."

"A message would have sufficed."

Silas glanced between them with a growing smirk. He was enjoying this.

Ares met her gaze. "The Iron Isles. Have you heard of the place?"

Daria sucked in a breath. "Of course." The Iron Isles were a stretch of islands within travel distance from Soleira's harbor, with a fortress on one of them that was used as a prison. "It is reserved for the High Throne's most wanted."

The general tilted his head back. "It is where prisoners usually go to die."

Fear swept over her like an icy wind. "What does the High Throne plan on doing with him?"

Ares shrugged. "Idris is a valuable asset. They will most likely keep him alive to ensure your cooperation. Should you try to thwart Matías's plans, such as using the dragons against us, your pater would suffer the consequences."

The skin over her knuckles tightened. "And what does your Lord of the Vampires want to do with the dragons?"

"Think about it. Why else would a kingdom want winged beasts with a hide stronger than armor and the power to douse the skies in flames?"

The world came to a screeching halt.

"Weapons," Daria said softly. "Adrastea wants to use the dragons as weapons against the other realms, and the High Throne approved such a plan. The two powerful kingdoms have allied themselves to become the most superior forces in the Continent."

She wondered what else the High Throne and Council were planning. Given the other darker forces amassing within the Continent.

Silas chuckled, but Ares ignored him. "Learn how to rule your people, even under the supervision of the vampires. Soon my king will ask about your progress on the search for the dragons; he wants to find them as soon as possible."

"You mean he wants *me* to find them as soon as possible."

"Princess—"

Ares closed his mouth, the word falling like a needle on hard floor in the silent room.

Daria stared at him and—by the Suns, she hated how tears welled in her eyes. While he'd been her guard in Soleira, the title he'd used to address her had turned into a term of endearment. Daria didn't expect her heart to twist hearing him say the word again. She blinked the tears away.

"*Your Majesty*," Daria said. "I'm your queen now. Be sure to address me properly."

Ares raised an eyebrow, a slight curl to his lips. One wouldn't have thought much of the general's reaction; they might have assumed he was simply amused by what she said. However, Daria saw a flicker of something else in his eyes. Something almost like pride. Like *longing*.

Silas, however, was thoroughly enjoying what was happening. "I feel like this has become a lovers' spat." He pulled out a chair and sighed loudly as he sat. "Just how far did your relationship go exactly?"

Daria wanted to disappear. Silas was under the impression that there had been more between her and the general. Not that she could blame him: He had stumbled upon them when they were secretly investigating the offices in the Soleira castle and, in the spur of the moment, Ares had closed in on her, backing her against a statue. His lips a mere breath from hers. They had been so, *so* close—

Her breath hitched.

It had all been to prevent Silas from figuring out what they were doing. An act. And the general was never really helping her.

She remembered how her blood had burned under Ares's cool touch. How his lips had brushed the bridge of her nose. The heavy presence of his body bowed over her.

Something tugged at her heart. Daria would never experience something like that again. Not with him.

"He was my personal guard," she said to Silas, folding her arms. "Just that and nothing more."

Ares didn't respond. Simply stared at her, emotionless, cold, unfeeling.

Silas whistled again. "From what I saw, it seemed a bit more than that. Though I suppose it's a relief you know where you both stand, Your Majesty. Ares is not one for heartfelt promises and everlasting connection." The vampire looked sidelong at the general. "He is Matías's *favorite* for a reason."

Daria felt her cheeks turn hot; she wanted nothing more than to sprint out of the room.

The general waved a hand, as if it all meant nothing to him. "That is all for today."

For the love of the gods… Daria cleared her throat. "Before I take my leave, I would like to inquire about the state of my soldiers. I understand they have either been imprisoned or are under strict supervision. If I am to rule under the formal leadership of Adrastea, I would like my own forces to be released so they can continue to serve my kingdom… while I serve yours."

Ares lifted his chin, that shine returning to his violet eyes. Daria pressed on, "Allow some sense of normalcy for my people and let our warriors be amongst them. They all wear the ether-imbued bracelets, after all. My soldiers are not a threat to yours."

After several beats of silence, the general said, "So be it."

Silas snarled, but Ares raised a hand to silence him. "The day-to-day livelihood of the capital needs more support. Our own can't monitor all that needs to be done. The Ikarrian forces can help, under our supervision."

His Second flashed his fangs. "Fine," he hissed.

This was a small victory for her people, but it was the best Daria could hope for. Her pater was being used as leverage and while she despised the thought of moving forward with the vampires' plans, risking *him*…

It's meant to be you. It was always meant to be you!

Her pater had left her with this wish, and she had made it into a vow. The only way she could truly save Ikarria was to find the dragons.

Ares met her gaze in a silent challenge, and Daria could've sworn the fires of her ether growled in anticipation.

FOUR

Teotlan was exactly as Ronan Menodora remembered it: a glimmering spectacle of red stone and limestone cliffs, stretching all the way down to the beach. Jungle morphed into palm trees that swayed in the salty, jasmine-kissed air; azure waves rolled over opalescent sands. The city was an expansive grid of pyramid-shaped buildings, domed structures, and residential villas. The ether in the air made Ronan's blood hum, beckoning him closer.

Soraya led them into the city, her back to him. The érendira had long removed her skeletal mask, staying atop Kenzo most of the time. She hadn't spoken to him once during the weeks spent traveling the wild terrain, crossing jungle, grassland, and mountain ranges. Ronan didn't blame her. He had failed many people in his life.

The other érendira marched close, surrounding him and the Horizons. The warriors hadn't welcomed the mercenaries with overwhelming enthusiasm, though neither had they outwardly shown hostility. It was the best case scenario Ronan could have hoped for. The érendira were charged to protect Zara and Axar in the capital, as they were guests of the crown. Of Ronan.

His heart pounded against his ears as they ventured deeper into the city. They began to pass shops and other businesses, banners of colorful parchment fluttering overhead. The citizens in Damalis were of all the races—elves, shifters, humans; vampires, who were not only from Adrastea but from other parts of the world, too; and archangels. There were many of the winged race, some from Celestrea, while others had been born right here, in the guardian realms.

People filled the streets with their vibrant clothing of jade, yellow, and red fabrics. Their hair was fashioned with gleaming gold jewelry, as well as their ears, necks, and arms. Since Damalis had taken Valenzia's surviving citizens under its care and rule, the city had become an even brighter mixture of different cultures.

"It's breathtaking," Zara whispered.

Something inside him ached at the sound of her voice. It felt like ages since he'd heard her speak; Zara and Axar had mainly kept to themselves. The shifter had healed and had been traveling in his wolf form for the last few days.

Ronan pointed at the limestone cliffs. "There's my home."

The Damalisan palace stood atop the peaks, overlooking the sweeping city. Made of crimson stone and marble, the center building was pyramid-shaped with a flat rooftop. Multiple tall structures and domed towers lined the borders of the royal grounds.

Zara raised her eyebrows. "You grew up there?"

He nodded, even as the back of his eyes threatened to burn. Out of happiness or sorrow, it was difficult to determine. Zara nudged his shoulder, offering him a small smile. A gesture of support, that she was there for him. Even though he knew she was breaking apart inside.

Suns. Ronan could see the pain behind that soft gaze.

Without a second thought, he reached for her. To caress her cheek, cradle her face. *Something.*

But Zara averted her gaze and moved away, back to Axar's side.

He shouldn't have tried to touch her, even in an attempt to comfort her. Not with the boundary they had drawn between them.

You are worried for her.

Hearing his nahual's voice in his mind warmed his chest. Ronan still couldn't believe he was back with her. He hadn't dared think of Nyota while in the Sombra Quarter; the separation from his familiar would have killed him if he had. It almost did.

Since their reunion, they had been speaking to each other constantly. Ronan recounted everything that had happened to him, from his confinement in the Elios prisons, to his rule over the Stone Orchard, and his alliance with the Ikarrian guild. Nyota told him of her time in Damalis, how she'd stuck by Soraya's side, and had rarely ventured back in the veil—the thin fabric of reality between Celestrea and the mortal world that existed for the animal spirits.

Ronan patted her large head as she walked beside him. *I am. Zara lost her family, and her home kingdom was raided.*

Nyota nuzzled his hand. *Knowing you, I am sure you already have some plan in the works to help her.*

I might.

The panther looked up at him with bright eyes. *I wish you hadn't forced me away. You're different now, and time hasn't been kind to you. The scars you carry, both on your body and within your spirit… They pain me.*

Ronan's chest cracked. *I'm sorry.*

Nyota nudged his leg with her snout. *I am proud of you, though. You found the strength to come back. And it seems that now you have another reason to keep fighting.*

Ronan followed the panther's gaze, his eyes landing on Zara. Specks floated around the mercenary as she walked through beams of sunlight. A lethal radiance surrounded her, sharp as a blade.

Pain tugged on his heart the longer he stared. It hurt to look at her.

Citizens started to notice the érendira and who they were escorting. Some of the jaguars acted as a barrier between the people and the mercenaries, while others scaled the buildings where their bonded warrior could keep watch from above.

Ronan kept his gaze ahead as every pair of eyes fell on him. Whispers prowled from every corner, growing louder and louder. He could feel an unseen weight land on his shoulders, a pressure against his throat the longer people stared. His heart raced with every step, sweat trickling down his neck.

The central plaza stretched out before them where a crowd had gathered. The wide steps that led up the cliff to the palace were within walking distance. So *close*.

"Your Majesty."

Ronan stilled, silence falling like a gentle wave. Their whole entourage came to a halt. Waiting.

Long ago, they would have been addressing his father with those words. Not anymore. Ronan looked toward the voice, his gaze landing on an older woman. He held his breath, wary and unsure how the people would react to his return.

Then the woman bowed as far as her frail body could allow. "Welcome home."

One by one, the people followed suit, until everyone was on their knees for their king. It was so quiet, the sounds of the distant waves and birds could be heard.

Ronan swept his gaze over the citizens before him, words failing him. He wasn't sure what he had been expecting, but it wasn't this.

He should say *something*. His father would have already spewed out a smart and inspiring speech. That wasn't Ronan though. At least, not at this moment.

The King of Damalis brought two fingers to his heart, before moving it toward the people in a low sweep. It was a common gesture among the guardian realms, one of welcome and farewell. Of respect. The crowd returned the greeting, some people letting out cheers. Even the érendira surrounding him responded in kind.

He was home.

Ronan felt the warmth of Zara's stare. Her face was shadowed by her dirty black hood—apart from her eyes. That green gaze shimmered with emotion at the scene in front of them. Ronan was overwhelmed by a sudden need to sweep her off that horse and take her in his arms. He wanted—he *wanted*—

It was a mistake to look at her. Some of the people followed his gaze and the whispers returned with the heat of boiling water.

Their expressions changed. Their previous awe morphed into a wary curiosity and eventually into a cold realization at who the two strangers amongst them were. An understanding that bled into anger and fear.

"They are Horizons from Ikarria!"

"Isn't that the Rogue?"

"Did our king bring them as prisoners?"

Among the shouts, some clutched their young ones and backed away, and Ronan watched that temporary peace crumble away. How could he have expected his people to react any other way? Many of them had been waiting for their loved ones to return home, but most of them had been hunted down by the mercenaries. Yes, those acts had been done by order of the High Throne, but that didn't remove the pain of these people.

"Execute them, Your Majesty!"

"Let us get back at the High Throne!"

"The Rogue has killed many of us, she is a *monster*! Why not have our revenge?"

Ronan's body tightened as if preparing to launch into battle; even Nyota bristled at his side. Anger burned through him. For Zara, he would defend. He would stand against his own kingdom for her.

Ronan.

He froze. A voice resounded in his head, and it wasn't Nyota. It almost sounded like…

Ronan met Zara's gaze again, and it held him in an ironclad grip. Gone was the previous light that had shone in her eyes, replaced by that familiar emptiness. She shook her head, and Ronan hated that he knew what she was trying to say. Zara didn't want him to take any action.

He did not want to stand by while people demanded her and Axar's life. However, the mercenaries must have understood where the people were coming from. The Horizons simply stared ahead, letting the crowd throw their grievances their way.

Ronan felt the back of his eyes burn once more, and he didn't realize how tightly he'd curled his fingers until blood trickled from between his knuckles.

The ghosts of Ronan's past lingered within the Damalisan palace. He could almost still hear the laughter that used to weave through the lattice windows, the small feet that used to run along the mosaic tiles. Time had had its way with his childhood home. Lush gardens had turned to green beasts. Pools of water now filled with scattered flowers.

Ronan rubbed a hand over his chest. "Are any citizens still living here? I thought the palace had remained open to those who lost their homes during the War?"

Soraya slid down from Kenzo's saddle, patting the jaguar's snout. She was the only érendira who'd led them up the cliff to the palace, the others having stayed in the city.

"Many did for a while, but eventually they were able to move into homes of their own. All thanks to the funds your shadow businesses made."

He let out an exhale; it reassured him that all his efforts had not been for nothing.

Ronan turned to Zara and Axar. "Soraya will take Río to the stables, and I will escort you to your bedchambers. You are both safe here."

Zara's gaze was downcast, as if the weight of the world was crashing down on her. He could've sworn her eyes watered as well. Axar slipped a strong arm around her shoulders as they trudged after Ronan down a long passageway.

Vines crawled from above, twisting around the stucco pillars that made the inner courtyard. Dust gathered across the framed paintings on the walls. Small yellow birds bathed in the stone fountains.

He stopped at a dark wooden door. Neither one of the mercenaries seemed to have noticed their surroundings.

Ronan's lips thinned, keeping the worry out of his tone. "You can stay here, little wolf. Axar can take the room next to yours."

Her brother tightened his hold on her. "Can Zara and I have a moment, archangel?"

"Of course. There are bathing chambers inside and I will have spare clothing dropped off. Get some rest. We will reconvene in the morning."

Ronan left the Horizons to their business, understanding that they needed some time together. To mourn and reconnect.

His body kept walking, as if it knew where he longed to be. Ronan halted at a threshold—fuck, he felt like he couldn't breathe.

This wasn't just any office. Unlike the elaborate walls throughout the rest of the palace, the ones here were plastered white. Dark brown beams stretched overhead, mirroring the deep wood-paneled flooring. The grand desk in the center was a lighter shade, a layer of dust atop its surface. Indoor olive trees had managed to survive all these years, their leaves rustling in the ocean breeze sweeping through the open arched windows.

His father's office. The late King Elijah of Damalis.

Ronan took a breath and stepped into the room. His mind conjured the image of the royal archangel, sitting at his desk. Elijah had his head propped up on a fist, frowning at whatever scrolls had been given to him to review. The lively noise of the palace—of children playing and staff bustling about—filtered through the chamber, unable to break the king's concentration.

Ronan's thoughts conjured the image of another person. The late Queen Miriam was scouring the floor-to-ceiling bookshelves that filled the office walls. She tucked a book under her arm as she approached the king. He sensed his wife's presence and, without tearing his gaze from the papers, reached to pull Miriam closer to him. The queen's soft chuckle warmed the chamber and the tight lines across the king's face smoothed out.

Tears pricked the corner of Ronan's eyes as the scene disappeared before him.

"I have sent word for the castle staff. They will be arriving in the morning to tend to the rooms and courtyards." Soraya's curt voice sliced through the quiet air, causing his wings to stiffen.

Guilt settled in the pit of his stomach. He wasn't the only one in pain.

Ronan turned to face the elf as she walked toward him, a small smile tugging at his lips. "You've grown since the last time I saw you, little sister."

Soraya shoved him; the pure strength behind it sent him stumbling back a few steps. She glared daggers at him, each blade filled with emotion.

Her lips twisted into a snarl. "It was only through Orion that I discovered you were even *alive*. All this time, and you never even responded to my letters. Not once!"

He flinched, but Soraya pressed forward, "I tried to get Orion to bring me along on his trips to the Stone Orchard, but like the loyal bastard that he is, he followed *your* orders to prevent me from seeing you."

Ronan's heart cracked. He had considered reaching out to Soraya, but at the time the guilt and self-hatred had consumed him. It had already been difficult to face Orion, but when it came to the little girl whose innocence was shattered the day the deities brought war to their sands…

"I'm sorry," Ronan whispered. "I understand why you are angry—"

"When I realized you did not plan on coming back, I gave up. Just knowing that you were alive was enough." Soraya shook her head, lips trembling. "I only thought I meant more to you. So much for being like *family*, Ronan."

The skin between his brows pinched together. How wrong she was, for Soraya was *still* and would always be family to him. He would always cherish the childhood memories of teasing her and Orion during training camp, training together under the blazing sun, confiding in one another until the late hours of the night.

Something else was bothering Soraya, though, he could sense it. "What's wrong?" Ronan asked. "What is it you are not saying?"

Soraya faltered back a step. She blinked and he caught the broken emotion in her shimmering eyes, but then the elf glowered and tore her gaze away from him. "Forget it. There are other more pressing matters at hand. Orion warned us about the risk of the High Throne discovering the truth about our survival, and told us about the specters and the Spirits of the Midnight Sun you were fighting against."

She folded her arms. "So what exactly happened in Soleira that had you racing back home?"

Ronan sighed. He knew the woman before him, and she would open up to him when she was ready. For now, he would simply be there for her. Would try to mend the cracks in their relationship.

He took a breath. "It was Erebus all along."

Soraya frowned. "What?"

Ronan told her what happened in the coliseum. The people of Damalis had found out that Erebus was alive and well when he became the Hand of the High King. They also knew of his betrayal against Damalis. What they could never have imagined was the extent of Erebus's deception. How twisted his hatred and desire for revenge had become.

One day, I will be remade into a Primordial, he had said in the coliseum. The idea was insane. Erebus should know that wasn't possible, unless you were selected by the ether.

Soraya's expression fell the longer Ronan spoke. Because Erebus had never merely been the Hand of the High King to them. Nor just a friend.

No, not to Ronan. Not to any of them.

They were all a family once. Ronan, Orion, Soraya… and Erebus.

Soraya seemed to be holding her breath and turned to pace around the office, her spear a terrifying contrast to the bookshelves and leather seats. She ran her fingers along the book spines before curling her hand into a fist.

Ronan looked out the window to the jungle. "Erebus made some sort of pact with Khaos."

He could hear the clatter of a book falling to the ground. Soraya gasped. "The Primordial of Fate and Time?"

"Who else bears that name?"

She cursed. "Erebus is a fool. He signed his life away."

"I think he knew what it meant to strike a deal with a Primordial and did it anyway." He could feel Soraya's heavy gaze on him, and his blood began to race.

"Why would Erebus take such a risk?" she asked. "What happened to him, Ronan?"

His heart pounded louder and louder. The pain inside him welled until it braced the walls of his lungs.

Soraya took a step forward. "Growing up, it was always all of us together. Then you and Erebus left for Celestrea and everything changed."

Gods, Ronan couldn't speak—*breathe*—

"So, why did Erebus betray us? You never told us—"

He doubled over, gasping for breath. Erebus's words echoed throughout his mind. *You had failed me.*

Ronan often heard the screams of his dying family, saw the flames that tore them apart. And the chains that had bound him all those years post-War. Those were the chords that wailed at his soul.

But this—no, this was something else entirely. Another fucking wound that had been flayed open. Being here, within these familiar walls, was digging into parts of himself he had been running away from.

Perhaps Ronan shouldn't have returned.

"Erebus is lost," Soraya whispered. "You know that, right?"

Ronan didn't want to admit it, let alone talk more about the male he had been close to all his life. Even now, despite everything, he couldn't help the affection he felt toward him. Twisted as it was.

"I know," Ronan said, his voice rough.

He wiped a hand over his face, aware of Soraya slowly approaching him. The archangel straightened as he battled for breath. "I've had enough for today, if that is all right with you, érendira."

Ronan didn't mean for his voice to come out so sharp, but it didn't seem to faze the elf. She narrowed her eyes, as if seeking an answer from his tortured expression.

Eventually, Soraya sighed. The tight lines across her mouth and forehead softened.

She started to make her way out of the office before stopping. "Sleep, Your Majesty. I'm sure Orion will come by to see you soon— he's been busy training the imperial soldiers while the general is away on patrol. Tomorrow the Elders will want to speak to you. And your *guests.*"

"Thank you," he said, watching the elf disappear into the hall.

Ronan fought back the groan that crawled up his throat. Another wave of emotion threatened to send him to his knees.

Shit. He didn't want to be in this room any longer than he needed to be. There were simply too many ghosts, too much pain within these walls, floors—every fucking framed portrait.

Ronan fled the office; he had been naive to think he was strong enough to face the shadows waiting to devour him.

FIVE

Zara's vision swam when she opened her eyes. She was in what looked like a… temple? Painted walls of dark stone surrounded her, carved windows revealing a sky of dusk and dawn. This was certainly not her bedchamber within the Damalisan palace. It was a dream—it had to be. But she could see crescent suns nestled in the sky, could feel the cool air drift from the windows, hear the trickle of water.

Her body felt as if it was filled with molten lead. Zara rolled onto her stomach, a cold slab of stone pressed against her skin. Channels of sapphire water gurgled on either side of her, rushing through whatever building she was in.

Zara's vision blurred once more. Her senses screamed for her to get up, but not even her ether responded. There was a deathly quiet where her power usually roared.

And she wasn't alone. The presence that always lingered in the shadows called out to her. Familiar. It was so familiar. She lifted her head to see a black wolf.

The same wolf that always appeared at her lowest moments. It had even guided her through the jungle, led her to Damalis. The wolf stood on a slab of stone across from hers, half-touched by the celestial light from outside.

Zara tried to speak, but her tongue felt heavy. What was happening? Where was she? Why was she seeing the creature *here*?

The wolf pointed its snout to the wall of darkness ahead of them. A gentle wave of warm air blew out from there. As if someone or something had *exhaled*.

Zara's skin prickled. She followed the wolf's gaze to two orbs of silver light emerging from the black.

They rose, and the world trembled. Once, twice. Then, Zara saw the outline of thick shoulders and long legs—

No, those aren't orbs, she realized. They were a pair of *eyes*.

Zara breathed heavily through her nostrils and tried to push herself up. Slowly. Almost painfully.

The creature stepped into the columns of red light. It had a skeletal, humanoid face and wore a headdress of blades that resembled feathers. Dangling around its throat was a necklace made of bones and teeth.

This was no mere creature; Zara had seen many murals and statues depicting him. This was a being carved by the natural ether that made all that existed. A force that was one with the suns and stars.

Mikatán, the Primordial of Death.

"Are you afraid?" A cold breeze came with his voice. A sound that was deep and gentle, the night and the moon. "You should be."

Zara's ether finally tugged at her mind, clawing its way from the depths. It was far too weak here. She tried to scramble away, falling onto her back.

Mikatán leaned down. He smelled like damp, rich earth with notes of rosemary. Terror struck her frozen. Terror twisted with *awe*.

"That frail mortality is becoming a nuisance; it will destroy you the longer you stay here," he said, lifting a finger. "You aren't ready. Try again, Zara Santos."

Her eyes widened at hearing the god of Death speak her name. The Primordial touched her brow and the world dropped from below her. Zara couldn't even scream as she spiraled down into a pit of darkness.

Zara vomited into a basin. She gripped onto the porcelain, cracks exploding from beneath her fingertips. The dream had felt too real, the Primordial of Death's piercing gaze lingering with every blink of her eyes. She didn't know what to make of it.

After rinsing her mouth, Zara stepped out of the bathing chamber to find Axar rolling a tall food cart made of brass into her room.

"Your archangel left us some breakfast." His voice was still rough with sleep.

Zara scoffed, pushing off the threshold. "How do you know it was Ronan?"

"I could smell him on the other side of the door when he left this spectacle behind."

She went to sit at the long settee where Axar started to arrange the food on the table in front of it. Freshly cooked meat and eggs topped with sliced tomatoes, onions, and coriander leaves; small bowls of chopped potatoes alongside plates of sliced fruit, some of which Zara was not familiar with. There was also a basket of round flatbread wrapped in white linen, and delicate ivory cups of tea that smelled of chamomile.

"Suns, bless that male." Axar hummed in delight, rubbing his hands together.

Zara imagined Ronan—the *King* of Damalis—in the royal kitchens preparing this meal for them, and it was nearly comical. And endearing. She ripped off a piece of flatbread and used it to scoop some of the egg and ham. The taste of spicy herbs fell over her tongue, and her body slackened.

They ate in silence for a breath until Axar said, "I couldn't quite ask this of you while we were traveling with those terrifying women with spears and massive jaguars—" He shuddered. "But what exactly happened between you and Ronan?"

The food suddenly tasted dry in her mouth. "Why?"

He flicked her arm playfully. "I see you're ready to close your-self off. Don't."

"You are a bully." Zara hissed, rubbing at the spot. "Nothing happened between us. We are still... allies."

Axar set down his fork. "Santos. If it's because of what hap-pened to Hakim and Eshe, you know it wasn't your fault, right? Hakim wouldn't have wanted you to push your feelings away—"

Zara clenched her eyes shut and let out a shaky breath. "When Raziel and the Council attacked you, I was with Ronan. I was... *happy*, while you were all suffering."

Hot tears filled her eyes. "Maybe I could've saved you if I had gone to Soleira sooner. What if I had left when my wounds healed? What if I hadn't stayed with Ronan?" Zara shook her head. "I wasn't there for you when you needed me."

"Oh, Santos." Axar pulled her into his arms and hugged her tightly. Her tears threatened to burst. "Don't think such thoughts. There is no point in torturing yourself like this. Nothing from the past can be changed. To be honest, I think Raziel always intended to kill them. If it hadn't been then, it would've been later."

Zara flinched, before releasing a deep exhale, the sound ragged. "Remember what we say?"

Her chest tightened. "We are stars made by the Suns."

"The Suns, the gods, however we want to refer to them—we were made by them. That means the will in our hearts is just as strong as theirs, if not more." Axar pressed his brow to hers. "Do not force yourself to do anything you are not ready for. Mourn as much as you need to, as will I. So long as you press forward. So long as you allow yourself to be happy."

Zara knew her brother was right. So damn right. And one day she would. As of now, that bone-deep pain was met by a festering anger. The Council who had caused this still lived. Raziel might have been gone but his poison was still thriving in the world.

She didn't voice that, though. Axar didn't need to hear it; he was suffering just as much as she.

"How are *you* feeling?" Zara asked, before pausing. "Eshe was like a mother to you."

He pulled back, and she noticed the purple underneath his eyes. The sunken skin around his cheeks. The haunted look in his hazel eyes.

"Eshe taught me everything I know," he said, clearing his throat. "I will try to live up to her expectations."

That was her brother: always persevering. Zara squeezed his hand. "What is going to happen to us?"

"I can't speak for the future, but this morning we are to attend a meeting with a group called the Elders. Ronan left a note about this—"

Axar suddenly flinched and swiped a cup off the tray; it smashed against the wall into glittering pieces.

Zara lurched from her seat. "What's wrong?"

Her brother's face paled as he stared at his hands. "I—I thought I saw something."

They were alone in the room; if there had been something amiss, she would've sensed it as well. Axar seemed to realize this. His fingers trembled as he ran a hand over his head.

"I'm sorry, I don't think I slept enough." He pushed himself to his feet and started to head toward the door. "I am going to freshen up."

Something in Zara screamed to reach out to him. She grabbed his hand, the words carefully leaving her lips. "Axar, you were imprisoned by the High Throne for a week." It was a battle to fight off the rage at the thought of her brother in the late High King's clutches. "You still haven't told me…What happened during that time?"

When he didn't answer her, another question crossed her mind. "Did Erebus come to see you?"

Axar growled, his eyes flashing the yellow of his wolf. "*Don't ever say that name to me again.*"

Zara dropped his hand. She was no stranger to arguing with

him—they had clashed multiple times before—but the bite in his words was sharper. Deadlier than she had ever heard.

He blinked, as if remembering who was before him. Not just anyone. But his sister. Axar took her hand again, curling his fingers around hers, giving them a firm squeeze.

"I'm sorry, Santos," he said roughly. "I—I need a moment."

Axar stormed out of the room, leaving Zara with an uneasiness spreading throughout her stomach.

SIX

"Find the dragons? How ludicrous. The vampire king must be more deranged than we thought." The Ikarrian advisor laughed, leaning against the bookshelves. "We should take advantage of this absurd task. Organize a rebellion while the Adrasteans are chasing the past."

Daria tapped her nail against the mahogany desk. It was odd to see the Ikarrian diplomats gathered in her pater's—*her* office rather than in the war room. With all the vampires in the castle, there had hardly been an opportunity for them to meet in secret, except for a few afternoons when the soldiers were too busy to notice the politicians' movements. Hiding in plain sight. Or Daria and the advisors were simply not seen as any type of threat.

She suppressed a sigh. "It would only risk our people's safety. For now, we must track the vampires' rotations and job duties within the castle and city. Learn as much as we can about our enemy to prepare a strong revolt, while I search for the dragons."

Silence fell over the room. Many of the diplomats shared glances. Others kept sipping their tea.

The first advisor who had spoken gave her a pitiful look. "With all due respect, Your *Majesty*, you have only recently stepped into the role of queen, and under dire circumstances at that. We have been in this profession for many years; Idris Calderón has always trusted our judgment. Attempting to find the dragons is not worth our effort… unless you *truly* believe they can return?"

How he said it. As if Daria's belief stemmed from a place of pure naivety. Of delusion. She winced at that. The truth was that she did believe. Some part of her, deep within, had always hoped that the ancient magnificence Ikarria had originated from would rise from the past.

Basira, who was standing beside her, interjected. A sweet mercy. "Our queen has little choice, regardless. The vampires will be monitoring her progress and the king of Adrastea will expect results. We must support her."

The other advisors mumbled under their breaths, their doubt almost tangible. Daria felt the contents in her stomach churn. What would her pater do in this situation?

She sucked in a breath. "I managed to convince them to let our soldiers walk freely about the capital, to help sustain our day to day lives, albeit under the vampires' supervision. Every single one of us must study our enemy. Learn their strengths and weaknesses, so that we can fight back, but only when we are ready. Do not bring unwanted attention to yourselves or the citizens. Any misstep could lead to lives lost."

She lifted her chin as her court's wary gazes grew heavy on her. Her pater wouldn't have cowered under their uncertainty, and neither would she.

Basira bowed to her and after several beats of silence the other advisors followed suit. Daria knew she had the support from at least one of her court members. The others were afraid and angry; it was understandable to doubt the capabilities of a young and inexperienced monarch. The same had happened when she became an ambassador of Ikarria.

Still, it didn't stop her own worry from fluttering through her.

Daria returned to her training in the Primordial Sanctuary. Every droplet of sweat lessened the frustration wedged within the marrow of her bones. The sun began to set, the evening air cooling her body.

She commanded a column of fire, the fiery length a beast that roared as she moved about the stone platform. Her senses sharpened and Daria twisted around, shooting her ether toward the doors.

The newcomer dodged the attack with an irritating amount of ease, moving like the shadows that had began to rise from the darkening sky.

"Your power has become much stronger," Ares said. The corner of his lips lifted. "You knew it was me."

They were alone, for the first time in weeks. Daria kept her hands raised, tendrils of flame licking her palms.

"Of course. How could I miss the broody aura that intruded on my space?"

Ares smirked. "After so much time spent together, I too can sense your presence in any room."

A growl ripped from Daria's clenched teeth. She sent spears of fire toward him, her ether crackling in the dim light.

"Don't talk as if we are close, *General*," she snarled. "It's unbecoming to lie."

Ares didn't respond, not while he twisted and turned between the shots of flame. Shadows illuminated the deep violet of his eyes as he drew closer with his unsettling speed.

Daria stumbled back, her fire dissipating. Darkness now surrounded them, save for the dim candle and torchlights. The vampire assessed her as he would an opponent on the battlefield. Like he was calculating his next steps.

He glanced at the tome sitting on the stand. "I'm glad the book has proven to be useful. I hoped you wouldn't stop practicing your ether."

Her heart hammered against her ribs, words clogged in her throat. When she didn't respond, Ares said, "Make sure no one from Adrastea sees you training."

"Is there a point to you being here?"

"I wanted to speak with you privately; some news arrived after our meeting." He slipped his hands into his pockets. "I've been called to Soleira so I will be leaving tomorrow."

Suns Above, Daria didn't understand the sharp sting at his words. A sense of uncertainty, and maybe even of *loss*—as much as she hated to admit it. She curled her hands into fists as tendrils of fire slipped between her knuckles once more. "The nerve you have, Ares. You took control of my home and now you are going to waltz back to your king, leaving me alone with the mess you created."

Ares's jaw clenched. "I will return as soon as I hear what Matías has to say."

"What a relief." Sarcasm was thick in her voice. She could almost hear Zara's approving chuckle. It was comforting.

"I thought it better that you heard it from me first." He gritted out. "Especially since Silas will lead in my absence."

Daria shuddered at the thought of Silas in charge. Ares wouldn't be here to control his soldiers.

He seemed to sense where her thoughts had headed. "I suggest you be on your best behavior."

The general turned to leave.

"Are you still in communication with Ronan? Does he know what you did?"

Ares glanced at her, his brows furrowing slightly, most likely at the sudden change in topic.

"Are you still playing the double life?" Daria's voice echoed in the chamber, leaving a heavy silence in its wake.

Ares searched her eyes, something flickering in his expression before it smoothed out, the walls drawn up once more. "I don't think that is any of your concern."

Daria remained silent, waiting. She couldn't help asking, trying to reach him, the vampire she had grown close to in Soleira. But it was futile. There was no shred of the male she thought she knew. She caught how his gaze lingered on the dagger strapped to her waist— the weapon he had gifted her. She couldn't bring herself to get rid of it, not when it was something to defend herself with while surrounded by enemies.

Ares's lips parted, as if to say something—

He jerked his head toward the shadows just as Basira strode into the chamber. The advisor eyed him like one would a wild animal. "Is everything all right, Your Majesty? I've come for your training. Have you already started?"

Before Daria could respond, Ares turned around again, his cloak flapping through the air. "I expect some progress on the dragon hunt when I return."

Reality returned with a cold vengeance as she watched him walk away. That gorge only split wider, driving them further apart. *It's better this way,* she told herself. And tried to believe it.

SEVEN

Soraya arrived to escort them to the meeting. Zara was not fond of the idea of getting involved in whatever politics were at play in yet another realm, but since she had been given shelter and food, she would play nice.

"The Assembly of the Elders was formed after the War to maintain order within the surviving guardian realm," Soraya explained. The érendira had forgone her brilliant armor today and wore dark blue form-fitting garb. The absence of the skeletal mask revealed a light splash of freckles along her cheekbones and nose. "There are five members in total: Taraji, Riyad, Ezrah, Orion, and myself."

Ah. Orion. Zara was still reeling over the fact that the male was Damalisan. The brute had often threatened her if she ever hurt Ronan. It had been amusing. Now she was walking about his king's palace.

"It's impressive that you have such influence within Damalis," Axar said.

He walked beside the warrior, sunlight lining his athletic frame. Even Soraya's curly hair seemed to glow as she waved a hand. "As leader of the érendira, I have a place there."

The briefest ripple of surprise flitted across Axar's expression. "How long have you been head of the warriors?"

Zara eyed her brother. After his little incident, he seemed back to normal. The shifter wore a loose, long-sleeved shirt, the fabric rolled up to his elbows, his body tattoos visible. The short braids on his head had grown, tied back with a leather band, whereas the lower half of his head was freshly shorn.

Axar noticed her staring and shot her an easy smile. She narrowed her eyes in return.

"You've been silent, mercenary." Soraya turned to Zara. "I'm sure you have many questions."

The problem was that there were too many racing through her mind. They stepped onto a terrace, where palm trees and gardens basked in the sun. Her gaze was drawn to the jungle and capital below the limestone cliff the palace sat atop.

Her thoughts went to their short encounter with the people of Damalis. How their faces had twisted into anger and disbelief at the sight of her. Fucking Suns. That had not been new; Zara had endured it for so long: the hatred that people would throw at her. Their insults and cries were bricks of stone laid upon her shoulders. And she would carry that weight for the rest of her days. She didn't mind—it was her price to pay.

Zara met Soraya's gaze. "From how you acted when we first met, I'm sure you'd rather push me off this cliff than answer questions."

Axar grumbled something at her, but the érendira seemed unfazed.

"Is that an invitation?" Soraya shrugged. "While it would give me no small amount of satisfaction, my king, on the other hand, would not be pleased."

"Because we are under Ronan's protection."

Soraya's expression shuttered at his name. "As I understand it, you helped him, so you will not experience ill will—not from the érendira at least. You made an alliance with our king. As long as that stands, we will give you the roof over our heads and the food from our table."

That brought a smile to Zara's lips. "Sounds like Ronan talking."

The érendira clamped her mouth shut and averted her gaze. It seemed like the archangel was sensitive territory.

A massive shadow soared overhead. Zara ducked on instinct, her hand going to the dagger sheathed at her thigh, only to see an eagle flying by. To say it was big would have been an understatement; its brown wings seemed to envelope the sky and its talons looked capable of crushing stone. Another eagle rushed up from the cliffside, sending a blast of wind onto the terrace. Axar cursed under his breath, bringing up his arms to protect himself from the stray dirt and leaves.

Soraya looked amused. "The Damalisan eagles don't come by often; usually they keep to themselves in the mountain ranges or stay within the border region. Sometimes they like to hunt along the Jade Sea," she said as a way of explanation. "They sensed we had new guests in our realm."

"Fucking Suns," Zara muttered. She clutched a hand to her chest, leaving her weapon alone. This world was much bigger than she'd ever anticipated.

The saltillo tiles beneath her boots shifted to smaller, squared ones arranged in various shades of brown as they moved through the palace. Slender pillars lined the halls, their bodies carved in intricate designs. Greenery covered archways, crawling up the stone as hummingbirds drank from the red flowers there.

They approached the royal meeting chamber just as a male's voice echoed from within. "I beseech you, Your Majesty. The Horizons may have helped you in your time of need, but they have served their purpose. Renounce whatever truce has been declared—"

"I won't hear anymore of it, Riyad. The Horizons are under my protection; you will relay this to the people." The deep voice belonged to Ronan, and he sounded *irritated.*

A pause. "Yes, Your Majesty."

"I still don't understand why we had to have this meeting first thing in the morning."

This time, a woman answered. "We've been eager for your return. Orion informed us of what's been occurring in the Continent and we hoped you would fill in the gaps."

Their voices fell silent as Zara and the others entered the chamber.

Sea wind and daylight swept through arched windows, illuminating a massive painting that covered the high domed-ceiling. It was a depiction of the Three Sun Gods: Life, Death, and Nature, the main Primordials reigning over the mortal world.

Aside from Ronan and Orion, the other three she did not know: two males and a female. The familiar brawny archangel started to make his way to her.

"Santos," Orion said.

She felt herself tense. Back in the Stone Orchard, Zara hadn't had much opportunity to get to know the male. Did he still see her as an enemy?

Orion's expression softened a fraction. "I'm sorry for your loss."

Zara blinked in surprise, but she couldn't speak. The archangel spared her, giving her a gentle smile before turning to clasp Axar in a quick embrace. Ah. Orion and her brother had had more time to bond and seemed to have become genuine friends. Good, that was good.

Ronan flashed them an easy smile. "Don't you both look well rested. Much better than yesterday, I must say."

His voice was light. Teasing. Yet, his eyes said something else. Ronan was surveying her, scanning her from head to toe.

She folded her arms. "I'm assuming you slept well, too, since your vibrant personality seems restored."

Ronan actually looked striking this morning, but she wasn't going to say that out loud. The archangel wore a fine dark, long-sleeved top with matching trousers, threaded with midnight blue. His collar split low down on his chest, his tattoos fully visible. No crown on his head though; she wondered if the King of Damalis even had a crown.

"Riyad, if you are going to continue glaring daggers, I suggest you speak."

Ronan slid his gaze to one of the males, an older elf, who was standing in a wide-stance, his arms tense at his sides. A warrior ready to break onto the battlefield. Riyad had long black hair and brown skin. His rouge eyes made Zara think of a dawn sky after a rainfall. His dark robes couldn't hide the muscular body underneath.

The elf placed a hand over his chest and bowed. "No, Your Majesty. I will respect your wishes."

Something in her chest pinched at the thought that Ronan had gone out of his way to ensure their safety. Going against his advisors. However, it seemed his people's loyalty was firm.

Ronan's eyes slid back to her. "Riyad is the commander of the Damalisan Imperial Army. They have different duties from the érendira and make up the realm's general defense force."

"I thought Orion was your commander. In the Stone Orchard, he oversaw the soldiers there."

"Orion is my Second. While Riyad led the defense forces here in Damalis, Orion managed the ones in the Stone Orchard."

Riyad looked at her. There was something familiar about him. "As far as my soldiers and I are concerned, we will honor our King's word in giving you sanctuary." His lips twitched into a snarl. "But if you risk the safety of our realms any more than you have, trust that I will cut you down where you stand."

Zara didn't miss the emotion that swam in his eyes, and suddenly she understood. How many of his loved ones had she killed? It was difficult to blame him for his apprehensions, razor-edged as they were.

She raised her chin. "I would expect nothing less."

"Leash that temper, Riyad." A woman's voice boomed with authority. Thick, curly brown hair framed a delicate face and heart-shaped lips. The woman was human.

"My name is Taraji," she said when Zara turned to her, her wide circular earrings glinting in the light. "I was First Advisor to the late King Elijah and Queen Miriam, and now to Ronan. I am the Head of the Elders, which help rule over the guardian realms in His Majesty's absence."

Taraji smiled, but Zara wasn't fooled. Though she didn't feel anything malicious from the woman, there was something behind her grin that said she wouldn't hesitate to smite down anyone who posed a threat to their home. The guardian realm surely lived up to its name.

The other male Elder was an archangel. He bowed before Zara, forest-green wings folding over his back. Iron beads decorated the golden tendrils of his shoulder-length hair that was partly tied back. His ears were also pierced and clasped with silver cuffs.

Zara froze. Surely, this male wasn't bowing *to* her?

He smiled at her. "Pleasure to meet you, Princess of Ikarria. My name is Ezrah and I am the head healer of Damalis."

She stumbled back a step. "No—the title 'princess' belongs to my sister. 'Horizon' is fine."

Ronan stepped in, hands clasped behind his back, as if sensing she needed a moment. "Ezrah has been instrumental in the development of our academies, advancing our healers' training as well as the kingdom's general education. He has the ability to use ether in his medical profession."

Zara had to remind herself that archangels had powers that were more ethereal in nature than others. She had hardly ever been exposed to those abilities, the winged race very private when it came to using their powers. To know that there was an archangel able to manipulate ether as a means of healing was fascinating.

Taraji interjected. "King Ronan, I believe you had some news to share with us."

King Ronan. Zara still couldn't believe the male who had been leading shadow dealers and running illegal businesses when she met him was the actual *ruler* of a realm.

Axar gave her a gentle push. She glanced up to see Ronan extending a hand toward her, his gray eyes bright. "Do you trust me?"

Zara had no idea what the archangel was planning. What she did know was that the male before her had fought alongside her and her guild, had helped her fight through her own self-hatred. Had been there for her.

She smirked. "I suppose I do kind of trust you."

Ronan seemed delighted at her teasing. "Stubborn wolf."

He led her to the center of the meeting chamber and addressed the Elders. "You have already been made aware of the threat that is rising within the Continent—something we can assume all the Aligned Realms are aware of, as the High Throne is at its forefront. Specters have entered our world, possessing mortals' bodies and eradicating entire cities. The Spirits of the Midnight Sun have arrived, bringing the end of the world, and the ether-born are being taken. For reasons still unknown to us. Not to mention the natural ether of our mortal world is *fading, dying*, weakening the earth. Crop failure each year, each harvest less bountiful than the last. And this, we can conclude, is due to the Primordials being cut from us."

The Elders looked at each other, unease written across their faces. Something about what Ronan said had Zara glancing at him. "Ether-born, those who descend from deities, no matter how thin that blood relation is?"

It was what Erebus had told them in the coliseum. Shadows fell over Ronan's expression. "I think it is more complicated than that. Deities may have descendants within the mortal world, but who's to say that Primordials don't as well? I believe the ether-born could have bloodlines from both the lesser and higher gods."

Zara suspected that was another result of the guardian realms' constant exposure to the ethereal. At least, the exposure they'd had before the Gates of Celestrea collapsed.

Ronan continued, "How they determine who is ether-born is also a mystery, though I suspect the Spirits and specters have sharper senses that are able to detect such lineages."

"The specters—they speak the ancient language of the gods. We could understand them." Her lips thinned. "Does that mean *we* are ether-born?"

Ezrah perked up at that. "Any person who has a connection to Celestrea will be able to understand the original language of the gods."

Ronan gave her a soft smile. "I don't believe we are ether-born. At least, I don't think that's the reason we can understand the specters."

More questions came to mind, but before Zara could voice them, Riyad interjected.

"Must we really focus on these details?" The male folded his arms. "How does all this involve the mercenary?"

Ronan's wings unfurled, stretching out behind Zara. She could feel their shadow, the presence of those dark wings. Strong and comforting, like the night.

"The late High King had a keen interest in Zara for most of her life. Rather than tell you why, I'll show you," Ronan said.

Deep blue mist formed along his shoulders, rolling down his

body and legs. Blood-orange light twisted around his arms into fiery ropes of celestial flame. The veins of his throat bulged as he focused on his power.

The members of the Elders gasped, their eyes wide with shock. Not out of fear but more like awe. And maybe relief.

Orion's eyes glistened as he stared at his brother. "It feels stronger."

Meanwhile, Zara's power was growing impatient, shivering so close to Ronan's ether. She gritted her teeth as she tried to grapple her unnatural light. The destruction she'd wrought in the jungle flashed in her mind: it was the last thing she wanted to do. Especially here.

She must have whispered that out loud as Ronan tenderly slid his palms over hers. "With me, you are safe. We are only showing what our individual powers could do, and if you lose control, I will be right here. I promise."

Zara let plumes of red and purple burning light rise from her hands. Ronan did the same with his, their ether too close not to touch. Sparks flared on impact, the twin flames dancing around each other. His power tasted like lightning, the weight of it enough to send everyone in the room to their knees.

Zara had never felt this energy from him before. It was baffling how all this strength had been chained within the tattoo he used to wear.

"Easy," Ronan murmured. "Lean into the ether. Resist it, or it will fight back."

Sweat trickled down her brow as streams of starlit fire continued to flow out of her. The chamber room now bathed in their celestial light.

Ronan closed her hands. "Follow my lead and breathe."

Zara obeyed, holding his gaze. His blue flames slowly folded over hers—as if coaxing her ether to settle down. She felt it snap back, unwilling to return to its restraints.

Ronan ran his thumbs over her skin and she exhaled. Bit by bit, Zara pulled her power back, until both of their ethers had sunk back into their bodies, sparse flames dissipating into colorful embers.

"Not bad." The archangel was gasping for breath. "It's been a while. I will need more practice controlling my ether."

Zara doubled over, hands on her knees, grateful that they were no longer touching. "Liar. You looked more than capable to me."

He smirked. "That was not the full extent of my strength. You will eventually understand as your power grows."

She rolled her eyes, though deep down she shivered at the thought. To think that this was nothing to how her ether could be in full maturity was daunting and exhilarating.

Everyone in the chamber was silent as they slowly got to their feet, gaping at them. Even the birds outside had quieted.

Ezrah's voice was filled with wonder when he spoke. "Ether of a Primordial. A different phenomenon from those of the ether-born and specters. We believed Ronan was the only one—but now there's another. The energies are similar, like they are mirrors of one another."

Zara shared a look with Ronan.

"I believe our *power* is the reason we can understand the specters; it is what connects us to Celestrea," Ronan murmured.

Ezrah was gazing at her. "Horizon, may I inquire about the history of your power?"

Her skin prickled at all the eyes on her. "I've been told my ether is rare—for an elf to wield light, it had never been seen before. But it was always weak and I hardly ever used it, though it did give me heightened speed and strength. It wasn't until recently that it developed into something *more*."

Ronan quickly went over how she'd worn the fyrebrand for years. And the ether-binding tattoo he'd placed on himself to leash his power.

Ezrah looked deep in thought. "The fyrebrand certainly would have hindered your ether's growth, Zara, and now it is almost trying to catch up. And what about your parents? Who are they?"

She stilled. It had been a long time since Zara had thought of them. Her mater was now merely a blurry image in her mind, her pater even less so. "I don't know. They're dead."

Ezrah bowed his head. "I'm sorry, Horizon."

Ronan was staring at her, something swimming in those eyes.

He glanced at the archangel. "Primordial ether doesn't take heritage or bloodline into consideration."

"No, but it may be good to know where Zara came from to try and understand it."

"I was born in Valenzia," she said. "After the War of the Skies, I was raised as an Ikarrian."

A wave of shock rippled through the room. Something like realization dawned on Ezrah's face. "Valenzian. Like you, Riyad."

The archangel glanced over his shoulder to the elf, who stared at Zara with an unreadable expression.

"You are considering training her, aren't you?" Riyad said, turning to Ronan. "We can't seriously allow that to happen. For a potential foe to become stronger."

Zara spoke through gritted teeth. Her patience was wearing thin. "Then I will not be able to help your king eliminate his enemies. The ones who almost destroyed your realm." When the others fell silent, she scoffed. "That is why Ronan wanted us to show off our ether. I can help you. And those enemies are just as mine as they are yours—I have nothing to gain in attacking Damalis."

The air hummed, the ground trembled, and the trees outside shuddered. It took her a moment to realize that the energy was coming from Ronan. The archangel stepped around her, his black wings swept back as he stared down the Elders.

"I think you need to remember that Zara Santos is my guest. Every single one of you knows the significance of this Primordial power. What it means to hold it, the risks that come with it. It won't be long before the specters mature into their true forms and become a bigger problem for all of us." Blue light crackled along Ronan's feathers. "Our realm is not untouchable. The High Throne will come for us. For me *and* Zara."

Riyad clenched his teeth and averted his gaze, though the other Elders seemed to comprehend the gravity of Ronan's words.

Soraya, who had been silent for most of the meeting, spoke up then. "While it's great that we have two people who can wield

Primordial ether, it means nothing, since the Gates of Celestrea are broken."

"Zara and I will need to be able to harness our ethers at their full potential before that becomes an issue, anyway," he said. "For now, we must strengthen our patrols and protect the outlying cities from any ambushes."

Issue? Zara wasn't sure what the archangel meant. Ezrah took a step forward. "Then I will support you. I will mentor both of you on how to strengthen the mind. It will help the growth of your powers."

Zara perked up. "How?"

"Your ether is not like the others. It is connected to the celestial realm. Even with the Gates being broken, it still means something. That power can be used for more than mere combat." There was a twinkle in the male's eyes. "I can teach you how to reach the gods."

She thought of Mikatán appearing in her dream and wondered if it was related to what the archangel was saying.

Taraji gestured to Zara. "Although you are a guardian by birthright, given the dire circumstances I imagine you would like something in return for helping us?"

The statement sent a thrill through Zara's blood. She could sense the discomfort and morbid curiosity in the room; it was nearly tangible. Primarily from Riyad. The male hadn't stopped watching her like a hawk.

Her lips curled into a smirk. "As long as I can kill the Council of Deities, I will do what I must here."

Taraji didn't seem surprised. "I'm afraid we must have our warriors keep an eye on you. We can't take any risks."

Ronan interjected. "Zara is not a prisoner, and she will not be treated as such. Let us end the meeting here and focus on ways to increase our security."

Taraji bowed at the archangel, placed two fingers to her chest and made a gentle swooping gesture toward the king before leaving.

Riyad bowed to Ronan and practically stormed out of the room without so much as a second glance. Ezrah, however, swept in to take Ronan into his arms, nearly lifting the male off the ground.

"You have grown and learned so much, boy." Ezrah mussed his hair.

Ronan rolled his eyes, though a smile stretched his face. "I can't take all the credit. You did teach me most of what I know."

Zara was witnessing a mentor reuniting with his student. The sight tugged on her heart. *Little warrior,* Hakim would often call her, usually before reprimanding her for slacking during training.

Ezrah was now playfully holding Ronan in a headlock, who squirmed against him.

"Come visit us soon," the older archangel said. "Tobias has missed you."

The archangel king finally managed to free himself with a chuckle. "I will."

Ezrah then bowed to Zara. "I look forward to working with you, Horizon," he said with a wink before disappearing from the chamber.

"Tobias is Ezrah's husband," Ronan told Zara. "They've been as much of a family to me as my—" He stopped himself and cleared his throat, looking away with a pained grimace. Zara placed a hand on his arm gently before pulling away.

Orion yawned, oblivious, stretching out his arms. "Fuck, I need a drink."

Once all the Elders—aside from the brawny archangel and the érendira—had left the room, Zara turned to Ronan again. "What did you mean when you said we are to harness our powers to their full potential *before that becomes an issue?* What issue?"

His expression fell. "Remember how I said that Primordial power is not hereditary, it is given?"

Something inside her dropped as Ronan continued, "When the natural ether selects a mortal to wield such a force, the ether is not guaranteed. We could lose our powers completely."

EIGHT

Ronan's words still rang through Zara. Clogging the air in her throat. The light she could always wield—that was just starting to grow—it could leave her?

"Would you like some?" Orion asked, holding up a basket of fluffy flatbread.

Zara stared at him, dumbfounded. After the meeting with the Elders, they had moved to one of the many dining halls of the palace. *To talk*, as Ronan had put it.

Before them, on a mahogany table, were plates of fried beans with melted cheese. Orion and Soraya sat across from Zara while she was wedged between Axar and Ronan.

"The doom and gloom is written all over your face," Orion said. "It's healing to share our worries while eating with friends."

Zara slowly took the flatbread from the archangel. She had never heard him speak like that to her. So… amicably.

"I am a bit unsettled by your kindness."

Ronan chuckled, pointing a fork in Orion's direction. "It's true. You're usually *so* overprotective of me you almost bite people's heads off."

"Not always." The archangel swept his dark, plaited hair over his shoulder. His eyes lifted to Zara's. "But you saved my brother, freed him from his ether-binding tattoo—so I thank you."

She didn't expect the warmth that rushed through her at that. Her actions *helping* someone was not a common occurrence. Quite rare, in fact.

One of the palace staff placed a tea set on the table, its pot hot with the scent of chamomile. The royal halls had come alive overnight: from the time Zara had left her bedchamber, she'd noticed staff members cleaning each room, dusting every surface. Cooks were back in the kitchens and gardeners were tending to the wild shrubbery.

"That sounds like Orion," Soraya muttered. She sank back into her seat, bringing her knees up to her chest, a cup of tea cradled in her hands. "He's always been like that but only with Ronan. It only became more intense after we lost Erebus."

The name wrought a blade of deafening silence through the room, a deep-rooted tension emerging in its wake. *We.* The white-winged archangel was connected to all of them. She saw it every time his name was mentioned and Ronan's expression would crack. The way dark clouds seemed to form above Orion and Soraya. Pain linked these three Damalisans, and it all went back to Erebus.

"You said that Erebus grew up with all of you," Zara looked at Ronan at her side. When Soraya had said Erebus's name, he'd seemed to freeze in place. Zara hesitated. "What is his story? How did he become the Hand of the High King?"

Soraya's gaze jumped between the two silent archangels. "We have to talk about him sooner or later."

Silence dragged for another long painful breath. Zara felt guilt churn in the pit of her stomach.

"Only if you are ready, Ronan," she whispered.

He snapped his head up, focusing on her, as if waking from a dream. Or nightmare. The corner of his lips tipped up, a smile that didn't reach his eyes.

"I'm ready." Ronan took a breath, running a hand through his hair. "Erebus is actually from Celestrea, was born and raised there. His family were servants to a household of deities. The realm had its own social hierarchies: Primordials were at the top, deities came second, and at the bottom were the archangels. Those fortunate enough could work their way up to the middle or upper classes. Stories of old would say that deities only created archangels to serve them, and that belief has survived throughout time."

Fucking Suns, Zara had never known any of this. Erebus had always been secretive about his past when they were together, though he often spoke about the Primordials and deities with distaste and with what she now realized was hatred.

Ronan continued, "When we were young—perhaps around eight years of age—there were initiatives attempting to bridge the social and political gap between the guardian realms and Celestrea. Since Valenzia and Damalis were charged to protect the Gates, there was much desire to partner up with the ethereal realm. The deity Erebus served sent him to Damalis to learn the ways of the mortal world, and to eventually become an advisor on behalf of Celestrea." Ronan's face drew carefully blank. "That is how he came to live with us at the palace."

Orion watched Ronan, his eyes full of sorrow. He gave him a weak smile. "The Crown Prince and his little advisor in the making. You two were inseparable."

Ronan's face softened. An echo of pain there. "My parents accepted him as if he were one of their own. Enrolled him in the same academic studies and training as me—a Crown Prince had to be skilled in sword fighting and ether-wielding. When I came of age, I was enlisted as a soldier. Erebus, too."

"Is that where you two met?"

She turned to Orion who shook his head. "My mother is the retired leader of the érendira. My father was a politician, a trusted advisor of the late King's. My parents had a close friendship with the Crown; Ronan and I have known each other since birth."

That the brawny archangel descended from an érendira seemed… fitting. She'd known there was more to the male, and in the short time Zara had spent with him and the warrior women, she assumed they had trained him. She recalled the elaborate tattoos on his back, inked in a different language. There was a story there.

"As for Soraya—" Ronan jerked his thumb toward the elf.

She waved a hand, cutting him off as she set her cup down. "My mothers were blacksmiths, their work often requested by the Damalisan armies. We lived a humble life in a small town within the jungle. While I loved it, I also craved to expand my world, so I enrolled as a new recruit to the Imperial army. It was grueling."

"We all bonded on the training ground," Orion added. He patted Soraya's head. "Until this one caught my mother's eye; she convinced Soraya to enter the trials for the érendira."

The elf batted his hand away, a small smile touching her lips. "And I will always be grateful to her for it."

"Why didn't you seek to be an érendira in the first place?" Axar asked, his mouth half-full.

The warrior's eyes sharpened. "Becoming an érendira requires us to walk the path of our patron goddess, Junya, Primordial of Hunt and Harvest. It is a trial that can cost you your life."

"Similar to how Horizons swear the ancient oaths of the mercenaries, the érendira experience their own rite of passage. That is where the woman becomes a warrior, and is chosen by a jaguar." Ronan clarified for Zara and Axar. "Not all are lucky enough to be selected."

Zara shuddered at what was implied by that. As if on cue, Kenzo appeared. The dining room was in an open-air courtyard; while an ornate ceiling arched above them, pillars stood guard to the outside. A fountain gurgled crystalline water into a pool filled with blossom petals. The jaguar lumbered by, before disappearing between the short palm trees.

"Enough about me," Soraya snipped. "We were discussing Erebus."

Whatever warmth had returned to Ronan's face vanished as soon as the archangel's name was brought up again. The skin over his knuckles turned white and his throat bobbed.

Zara hesitated. "Erebus grew up alongside you—all of you," she said, gesturing to the three Damalisans. "So why did he… defect?"

There was that tension again, and a simmering anger, one mostly shared by Orion and Soraya. Ronan looked to be more in pain.

Soraya straightened in her seat, her gaze heavy on him. "That is what we want to know as well."

Orion glanced at Zara and Axar. "As I'm sure you know, Erebus led the rebelling deity armies into the guardian realms. Raziel created his so-called Aligned Kingdoms, with the High Throne and Council at the top and—you know the rest. But once Erebus helped raze Damalis and Valenzia to the ground, he vanished. After Ronan was taken by Elios, there was no news of Erebus until he reappeared as Hand of the High King." The archangel lowered his gaze, staring at the food on the table. "I remember the confusion I felt… and the sting of betrayal. It hurt so much knowing that I had lost two of my brothers. I didn't know whether Ronan was alive or not at the time."

Throughout this, Soraya's face became more and more ashen.

Orion continued, "We kept an eye on Erebus from a distance. There was no point in pursuing a traitor, especially as our kingdom was still recovering. Our focus was on finding Ronan and getting him back."

Shadows soared past the courtyard as eagles flew by, sending a gust of warm wind through the pillared dining room. Their massive wings were brown blades against the blue sky. Zara's heart fluttered at how free the animals seemed here, and she felt a twitch in her legs. Like she wanted to run after them.

Ronan was also gazing at them.

"Erebus's defection was my fault." His deep, broken voice caused everyone to still. "And yet, not even I know the full story of what brought him to betray us."

Orion's brows bunched together. "How is it your fault? Was it when you went to Celestrea?"

The world came to a screeching halt. *Celestrea.* Ronan had been to the realm of the Primordials. It had crossed Zara's mind before, but she'd never asked him. So, it was true. The male beside her had actually been to the ethereal kingdom. Had walked among *Primordials.*

Ronan's gaze slid to hers. A small smile appeared on his scarred mouth.

The current circumstances were forcing him to wade through

traumas he hadn't fully overcome yet. Zara wished there was wine, but resorted to simply making herself another cup of tea. Her fingers shook as she did so. Fucking Suns, why was she so nervous?

"How does our Primordial ether connect with you having gone to Celestrea?" she asked. The silver light in Ronan's eyes seemed to dim. "It is rare, but the natural ether of our world—of both the mortal and ethereal realms—at times selects a mortal capable of wielding Primordial powers. The mortal undergoes a series of physical changes and enhancements that include strength, speed, and sight. They may also go through otherworldly changes, like having visions or dream walking. The process is called '*Izcali*' and it is never the same for every user."

At that, Orion and Soraya's expressions turned grim. The former watched Ronan with a pained look. Zara didn't know why, but she felt like she was teetering on the edge of a cliff.

Ronan twisted around to fully face her. He held her gaze in an iron grip, seeming to forget the others in the room; this part of the conversation was meant for her alone.

"The mortal could lose their Primordial power if they do not complete the Crossing."

Zara's eyebrows drew forward. "The light I am able to summon… I could lose it all?"

He nodded slowly. "The mortal selected will eventually have to make a choice. A decision they can never take back." Ronan grabbed her hands, holding them. "To have powers of a Primordial means to *become* one."

A faint ringing started in Zara's ears. "What?"

"The mortal will undergo the *Izcali* and, eventually, when their ether has fully matured, they will receive a sign to make the decision. If they choose to become a Primordial then they must complete the Crossing. They will shed their mortal lifespan and become a god."

His expression was a mix of sadness and exhaustion. "If the mortal chooses not to take the Crossing, then they walk away from the powers the natural ether gave them. Over time, those abilities will become embers of their former selves and the mortal's lifespan will be cut in half. There is no telling when they'd meet their end."

Axar cursed under his breath. "This doesn't seem real."

The archangel ignored him, his eyes on Zara. She wasn't even sure if she was breathing. Her eyes searched Ronan's for a lie or a joke. Surely, the archangel would bust out laughing and slap her on the back for being so gullible.

No. Ronan held her gaze, letting her see the truth laid out within him. On his beautiful, tortured face.

Power. Zara desired power to defeat the Council and High Throne, to avenge her loved ones—and this was what it came down to? A decision that would change the trajectory of her life forever. How was this even possible? She wanted to run, cry, and fall.

Zara forced her voice to remain steady as she pieced everything together. "The Crossing... is that something that happens in Celestrea?"

Ronan nodded. "The gods oversee it. Before the War, those selected few would stay in Celestrea and study with the deities before attempting the Crossing."

Her hands were still in Ronan's. This time, she tightened her grip. Holding *him* now. "You were going to complete the Crossing, weren't you? All that talk of your destiny and that is what you meant. Suns Above, Ronan, you were so young. Why do it then?"

"The tension between the celestial and guardian realms was beginning to seep into the mortal world. Damalis—as well as Valenzia—had the responsibility to ensure the safety of the Gates, so anything that happened in Celestrea was our concern. Since I had been selected by the ether, I thought I could become that bridge." Ronan pulled back from her grasp, shadows gathering in his expression. "Erebus went with me to Celestrea and I began my initiation with the deities. It was during our time there that things changed between us. We were growing distant and had an argument and... Erebus disappeared on me. When he returned, it was with the rebelling deities at his heels."

Ronan looked at Orion, a harsh silver light flashing in his eyes. "That is what I meant when I said it was my fault. I broke a promise to Erebus, and the world was ruined." He gnashed his teeth together.

Orion stared at his brother, the color draining from his face. "I'm sorry, Ronan."

Zara was still reeling from what she'd learnt. To know that Ronan had been about to leave his mortal life behind, so young, it almost terrified her. How different things would have been if he had completed that path.

Ronan dipped his head to meet her eyes. "Right now, what we need to focus on is honing our Primordial powers. My concern is that the Gates of Celestrea are broken and our access to the Crossing is closed."

Zara felt a rush of panic. "If the option to participate in the Crossing is inaccessible to us, would that mean our powers would fade in time? Will we be able to keep our ether long enough to fight our enemies?"

She couldn't bear the thought of being without it. It was so alive, a constant companion within her soul. If it were to suddenly leave, there would only be an emptiness there. This was new territory for Ronan, too, Zara realized. Not even he knew what to expect. Losing the Primordials and access to Celestrea had changed everything.

Ronan opened his hand and a thread of blue light wreathed around his fingers. "There is a place called the Oasis of Dreams. It is described to be the only corner of our mortal world still connected to Celestrea, its aura kindling with ethereal energy. A nexus point, so to speak. I have a theory that, if we can enter it, we will be able to amplify our ether to its full extent. And maybe—*maybe*—we can find a way to keep our power *without* the Crossing, and have the strength and time needed to defeat our enemies."

"So there is no telling how long the *Izcali* will last." It wasn't a question, but Ronan still shook his head. Zara had her sister and pater to think about as well. They needed her help, and she couldn't afford to simply wait for her power to mature on its own.

"Where is the Oasis of Dreams?" Zara asked.

Ronan flashed her a wicked smile. "Near Nephtyr, the capital of Kairos. We'd have to leave soon, though it would only be us going.

Us and maybe Tallon. Orion and Soraya will have duties to tend to here while I'm away."

The brawny archangel protested but Ronan ignored him.

Axar swore again. "That is on the opposite side of the Continent. Need I remind you both that you are wanted criminals by the High Throne?"

The archangel willed his blue flames to disappear and leaned back against his seat. "What a great way to make things more entertaining."

Zara and Ronan shared a look, and she could see the question in his eyes. Zara didn't need to consider it.

"When do we leave?"

NINE

Ares Valdemar tucked a fresh roll of bloodroot between his teeth as he stormed through the halls of the Soleira castle. The earthy scent, touched with that delicious hint of copper he had been painfully waiting for finally erupted within his lungs. Anything to scratch the itch in his throat.

Vampire soldiers stationed in the castle saluted him. Royal advisors murmured their congratulations on the successful raid of Ikarria. Ares barely acknowledged them, his muscles slackening as the drug's effects bled through his body.

The citrus smell of orange trees wafted in the warm air. Castle staff shuffled down the ivory halls, the marble floor bathed in daylight.

Ares pushed through the doors to Matías's office and skidded to a halt. He should've heard the wet kisses, the moans. How could he have forgotten that his king kept a bed in his own office?

Two female courtesans jumped in surprise, the bedsheets slipping off their naked bodies. By the grace of the gods, Matías was covered, though a wide grin spread over the male's face upon seeing him.

"Ares! Welcome back, General. You should have sent word that you'd arrived; I would have been more decent."

Ares pinched the roll of parchment between his fingers and blew out a thin trail of red smoke. "Apologies, Your Majesty. I will come back later."

Matías waved a hand. "Nonsense! You have traveled all this way." He sat up and sank against the bed frame, his dark and gray hair slightly mussed. The two courtesans relaxed on either side of him; one rested a hand on his bare chest while the other pressed her cheek to his shoulder.

"I was eager for your report, General Valdemar," Matías said. "I'm glad all went according to plan, and that the dethroned draconic king has been taken care of."

Ares's lips remained in a smooth line, no creases forming between his brows. "The Ikarrians proved to be worthy adversaries, but their efforts were in vain. We have secured control of the capital and the realm's major cities."

"Your brief report also mentioned you'd received a parting gift from Idris Calderón." Matías's eyes brightened. "Show me."

Ares shrugged off one sleeve and with one hand tugged on the strings of his cloak. The long-sleeved shift fell low over the slopes of his chest, enough for him to slip out his arm.

Ragged lines of reddish skin wrapped around the length of his arm. The healer had managed to tend to the wounds, but the scars had been unavoidable.

Matías clicked his tongue. "A token of your battle won."

The vampire king grabbed one of the courtesan's hands. She turned her palm upward, offering her wrist to him. The king bit her skin and drank, and the courtesan sighed, her head resting on Matías's shoulder.

Ares could hear the gush of blood, and its rich scent rushed through his senses. His body stiffened, his mouth watering—though a sense of nausea hit him too. *Fuck.*

After the king had had his fill, he asked, "The task I assigned to our newly appointed ruler… can she manage it?"

A flash of amber-brown eyes, and the fierce determination behind them, rushed through Ares's mind. He squared his shoulders. "Daria Calderón will find the dragons."

"I hope so, for her sake. And for the sake of Ikarria." Matías licked blood from his thumb. "You have proven yourself loyal, General. I'm sorry I doubted you."

Ares released a growl through his fangs. "My allegiance never swayed."

"That is not how I remember our last conversation." The king's gaze slid to Ares, his expression darkening. "For a moment, I was concerned that I was losing a valuable asset."

Ares took another drag of the bloodroot, thinking back to the evening after he had introduced the princess to his mother. When his king had revealed the plans to raid Ikarria.

His lips curled. "I told you the Ikarrian heir would be more useful alive, did I not? She is more than capable of finding the dragons. Having Idris imprisoned only adds to your advantage. Two Ikarrian royals, one true ruler. You."

"The once-poor boy turned into a valiant soldier. I knew I wouldn't regret picking you from the slums of Adrastea to join my ranks. From *nothing* to something." Matías cocked his head. "You seem a little worn out, Ares. When was the last time you had a drink?"

The general stilled. The lingering sensation in his throat burned hotter. The corners of his vision blackened and his fangs felt sensitive to the touch.

Matías gestured to one of the courtesans lying beside him. "Feed my general."

Ares's heartbeat dulled as the courtesan slipped from the king's bed; she held an ivory sheet to her chest, though it did little to hide her nudity.

He took a step back. "That won't be necessary."

The vampire king raised his eyebrows. "I remember the days you would feast on my personal staff with abandon. There were even times when you became too excited and accidentally killed them." He chuckled.

Ares kept his face neutral, but something sharp struck his soul. He would rather forget those days. A poor boy who had known nothing except starvation and had leaped into the pleasures of knighthood.

He had tasted fresh blood for the first time, and with no proper instruction, his younger self found it difficult to control the bloodlust.

He'd learnt to leash himself, to enjoy feeding. Though the thought of doing so now abhorred him. He'd never believed that could ever happen to him.

"I wouldn't want to use up your sources, Your Majesty. I have my own stock," Ares said.

"Oh I insist, General. Unless there is another reason you don't want to drink? Maybe you prefer something more… *royal*."

Ares stiffened, just slightly. Silas must have been talking. Too much for his own good. Ares needed to remind his Second of his place. He willed the brewing storm inside him to silence.

The general smirked. "The princess served her purpose well, but I tire easily."

Matías laughed and gestured to his courtesan again. "I should've known. You tend to play with your food. Allow me to repay you with this small gift."

The human woman brushed her hair to the side, baring her neck. "How will you have me, General?"

Ares steeled himself against the sickening feeling that curled in his abdomen. It was foreign to him. Normally, he would have been glad to dig his fangs into the flesh of willing sources. But everything was different now.

He was keenly aware of Matías surveying him.

"The neck will do," Ares purred.

The courtesan dropped the bedsheet, her breasts almost brushing his chest. Nudity was hardly something to be ashamed of within vampire culture, but he still found himself refusing to look anywhere except the woman's eyes.

He slid his hand around the back of her neck and tilted her head up. Bloodlust surged through his veins, and his throat itched for what was to come.

Ares plucked the bloodroot from his lips before piercing the courtesan's skin. Blood bathed his fangs, dousing the fires that coursed through his throat. He did not pay heed to the woman's soft moans as she went slack in his arms nor would he think about the twisted sensation that thrashed throughout his body.

He finished drinking, though he was hardly satiated. Ares looked at Matías expectantly. "If you will, Your Majesty, could you tell me why I was summoned? I imagine it was for more than a mere update."

The vampire king was now sitting on the edge of the bed, the other courtesan draping a robe over his body.

"Raiding Ikarria was the first step of my plan. I want to show you what the High Throne and I have been working on," Matías said, his fangs flashing. "And how it will benefit Adrastea."

TEN

Ares didn't expect his king to lead him to the lower levels of the Elios castle. Torchlights illuminated the stone archways, though were unable to remove the chill that lingered in the air. Ares hardly ever visited these lonely halls.

"Your Majesty, will you tell me why we are here?" Dust curled from the heel of his boots. "Or are you trying to keep me in suspense?"

Matías walked toward a large stockroom. "You are ruining the surprise."

As a child, Ares had always been bold with Matías. At first, the other soldiers beat him for showing such disrespect, but the king only laughed. He considered it an endearing trait, so much so he decided to take the young vampire under his wing. The other soldiers liked that even less.

They entered the stockroom, Matías made an approving sound. "This sight never fails to amaze me."

Ares halted. A forge took up the opposite end of the storage space, chimneys rising toward the high ceiling. His nostrils flared at the scent of ash and coal.

Lines of enormous ballistas were stationed along the sides. Something ugly and heavy sank deep in Ares's veins.

Matías waved him over to one of the machines. "This is what I wanted to show you."

Long, thick javelins were stacked upon weaponry racks. Custom made, designed specifically for the great ballistas, Ares realized. The projectiles were barbed, and the blades shimmered with silver.

Ares narrowed his eyes. "The ore that was used to make these…. It is not of our world, is it?"

"Good eye. We used astral ore, a material originating from Celestrea."

His heart pounded against his ribs. "How did you manage to secure such a resource? I thought that the Gates of Celestrea were broken."

The vampire king scoffed and ambled further inside the grand room. "The Gates, the Gates, the Gates. That is all anyone ever has to say when it comes to Celestrea. Yes, you are correct: the main entryway to the ethereal world is closed. Most of the material was brought over by the deity armies when they first made the crossing during the War."

Ares caught something in his king's tone. "This is not all the ore you have managed to obtain, is it? There is more."

A wicked light shone in Matías's eyes. "By grace of our one true ruler, Erebus ensured—through certain… *means*—that we received access to the astral ore."

The vampire general mulled over his next words carefully. "Does all this have anything to do with the battle in the coliseum? I read the reports: three skeletal figures clad in armor wearing crowns of silver fire appeared alongside Erebus. It sparked my curiosity—and I wanted to know more about them." The lie flowed from his lips. Ares couldn't tell Matías he had helped the long-lost King of Damalis research about the specters and Spirits.

He ran a finger along the length of the spear. The iron felt like ice. "It is said they are the embodiment of the world's end. Should I be concerned?"

The vampire king rolled his eyes. "Dramatic, isn't it? Yes, the Spirits will bring the ruin of the Continent, and Erebus will cleanse this world, remaking it without the influence of the lost Primordials." He waved a hand in dismissal.

Suns Above, Matías had known everything all this time. That heavy weight in Ares's chest thickened. *Cleanse this world?*

The general kept his expression smooth as he rubbed a crumb of debris between his two fingers. "There is something I don't understand. Why get involved in these efforts in the first place? Will we not become victims to that destruction as well?"

Matias was silent at first. "We vampires do not control ether in the form of the elements like the elves, nor do we shapeshift or hold a shred of otherworldly capabilities as do the other races. Instead, our ether made us into creatures with fangs with the need for blood to survive." A growl echoed behind his words. "In this world, aside from humans, we are the lesser species. We are *powerless.* That is why Adrastea made an alliance with the High Throne. We will make our own strength, and the other realms will cower to *us.*"

Ares frowned. "It won't guarantee the safety of our people."

"Sacrifices are necessary for a greater purpose."

The general held his tongue, even as something sharp and fiery boiled between his ribs. In desperate need for a distraction, he grabbed one of the enormous javelins, his eyes widening at the weight of it. "What is this for exactly?"

Matías grinned. "Finally, you are asking the right questions. Do you know much about astral ore? It is the one mineral that can scar and disable a god—a Primordial. It can also kill them."

Ares stilled. "And Erebus approved such manufacturing?"

His thoughts went to Ronan and what this would mean for him.

Matías nodded, pointing at the array of chains stored along the walls: iron binds of various sizes. "What you see here was imbued with ether, designed to lock the power of those who are bound by it." He laughed. "A parting gift from our dear Raziel—may he rest in peace."

Ares looked down at the javelin. The tip of his fingers accidentally brushed the sharp edge of the astral spear and a hiss was yanked out from between his teeth. His skin was cut open, blood spilling onto the dirt.

"Careful, General. Astral ore is dangerous for a *god*—imagine the damage it could do to a mortal." The vampire king grunted. "It can even pierce dragon hide."

Ares watched the red trickle down his hand. "This is how you intend to control the dragons once they are found."

"Precisely. Our beloved Ikarrian queen is the key to the beasts, but as there is no guarantee those animals will follow her or be willing to fight alongside us, the astral ore is our way to ensure their loyalty."

"You mean to threaten them."

Matías grasped his shoulder. "Does it matter? The creatures are *meant* to be used. Now that you know what I have planned, I trust you will see to it that my reign is strengthened, and that the Calderón girl finds the dragons."

The vampire king exited the chamber, leaving Ares alone. His eyes went back to the ballistas. Weapons made to make dragons fall.

Ares curled his gloved hands into fists.

He needed to make a visit.

Spike-tailed seabirds soared through the evening sky, disappearing beyond the ivory fortress of the Iron Isles. Guards patrolled the great walls while others rode armored pegasus over the various strips of land. Large hyenas with patches of rough hide could be seen sauntering between the thick groves.

Tension coiled along Ares's shoulders the moment he saw those towers. It had been about fourteen years, more or less, since he'd last seen this place. After graduating from the Academy, his first assignment had been as a prison guard; a shoddy task that the senior officials enjoyed passing off to the rookies. It wasn't long before he was ordered to watch over Ronan, the most valuable war prisoner at the time. And eventually helped him escape.

The boat moaned as it slowed to a stop, and Ares stepped onto the wooden dock. Sprays of salt water sprinkled his sharp cheekbones, his wine-red cloak billowing in the breeze.

A captain waited for him at the start of the pathway to the prison's iron gates. "General, I was surprised to hear your request to visit the Iron Isles. Did you miss the ol' stomping grounds?"

Ares arched an eyebrow. "Hardly. I'm only here to visit the prisoner."

The captain let out a belly-laugh. "Of course, of course. Young ones hardly look back to their roots. Can't say that's always a bad thing. Come with me, General, I will take you to him."

Ares followed the male past the gates and into the halls. The walls of pale stone were bright even under the dying light. They reached the upper levels, from where the central courtyard could be seen below; it must have been after dinner-time as inmates were loitering about the smooth dirt.

He wouldn't be there. No, not a prisoner of that high caliber.

They turned into a secluded wing, and Ares's lungs tightened. There were less prisoners on this floor, reserved for the High Throne's most wanted. He stopped walking when his gaze landed on a familiar prison cell. No one occupied it now—even the cot and chains had been removed.

Ares noticed the faint hues of red along the stone. The blood that still stained these walls. He could almost see Ronan there, chained and lying in his own waste. His body always torn, always broken—

"We are here, General."

Ares blinked, brushing away thoughts of the past. His gaze settled on a larger cell and the corner of his lips lifted. It didn't smell like urine or waste. Strands of hay covered the stone floor. A cot was chained to the wall beneath a small, barred window, nothing but a meager blanket and pillow on it.

"I'm surprised the new High King allowed such accommodations," Ares said, clasping his hands behind his back. "Given who you are to the High Throne."

The former King of Ikarria, Idris Calderón, narrowed his eyes. "Almost two months since your soldiers locked me in here and *that* is what you have to say?"

The draconic ruler sat on the cot, his back against the wall.

Although the cell seemed better than the rest, there was no denying the dull sheen on the male's silver-white hair, his braids now frayed and unkempt. Dark circles had grown under his eyes.

Ares gave the captain a sidelong glance. "Thank you, I will take it from here."

The male hesitated. "Be wary, General. The Ikarrian can bend fire."

"You forget, Captain, that I fought this man with a mere sword and *won*." Ares gestured toward the chains around Idris's wrists. "Besides, every bind within this place has been imbued with ether that neutralizes any powers."

"Of course, I meant no offense. But one can never be too careful."

"On that, you are correct." Ares waved a hand. "Off you go. I prefer to work alone."

Ares's cold expression didn't waver once the captain had left. Not even as an ugly sensation raged forward from the trenches of his heart.

Idris rested his head back against the window sill, watching him with a cool look. "Can you really say you defeated me?"

"We could call it a draw, since you did manage to leave your mark." He gestured to his left arm where the burn scars were hidden beneath his clothes.

Idris's expression darkened. "I had to make it believable, that is what *you* said."

Ares raised a gloved finger, cocking his head to hear if anyone was eavesdropping.

The elven king lowered his voice. "It was a gamble I was willing to make, and now you must meet your end of the bargain."

"That is why I am here. It has already begun."

"Will it work?"

"Yes."

Idris nodded, satisfied. After a moment, his brows bunched together. "My daughters… How are they?" The Queen and the mercenary were always the elf's first priority. Not his realm nor his own fate.

"They're safe," Ares said, softly. "Daria is at the castle and Zara is…"

Ares stopped at the sound of footsteps down the hall and they both glanced down the walkway.

He considered his next words. "You will not die here."

The sound of chains echoed as Idris approached iron bars. He was just as tall as Ares, though much brawnier.

Idris searched his gaze with familiar amber-brown eyes. He saw through Ares, barrelling past those unseen walls and witnessing the blackened roots there. And yet, the vampire's mask did not break.

The corner of Idris's lips lifted. "You are a good liar."

His chest tightened. How the male said it… it was not out of unkindness, but more out of a twisted sense of admiration. With a shade of sympathy. Ares was unsure what to make of it.

"It has helped you survive this far." Idris continued before the general could respond, turning away from him. "I will be waiting to hear of your next move. Go back on your word and I will kill you."

A shadow of a smile touched Ares's lips as he turned and left.

ELEVEN

Zara spent the next several days recovering in the palace from the journey to Damalis. Thoughts of the Crossing still buzzed through her brain. To become a *Primordial*—what an outrageous concept. The vetting process surely needed some improvement if *she* had been presented with such an opportunity.

And the Crossing was not even doable, not with the broken Gates. Later. That would be a concern for later.

Ronan had been busy returning to his role as king, as well as arranging their journey to Kairos through the Sombra Quarter. Apparently, the archangel was coordinating with the shadow dealers to secure a safe route, and that in itself would take some time.

One evening, Zara found herself entering one of the many grand offices within the palace. Sunset poured through arched windows, illuminating rows of bookshelves. On one side of the room was a crescent-shaped desk with various instruments to study the stars; an artisan rug rested beneath it, and large ceramic vases filled the space.

Zara brushed her hand along golden trinkets, lifting her gaze to a portrait that hung in the center wall between the windows. Her eyes widened.

It was the royal family of Damalis. They were posing on a cliff, the Jade Sea glimmering behind them. She immediately recognized

Ronan. He was tall and lanky, with bright eyes and a wide smile. The archangel closely resembled the late King Elijah, who was standing behind him. Gray eyes and black wings.

The boy clinging onto Ronan's hand, however, wore a serious expression. His eyes were dark and his wings were a beautiful midnight blue.

"That's Hael."

Zara jumped at the sound of Ronan's voice. She had been so engrossed in the portrait she hadn't even sensed his presence.

The archangel walked into the room, his gaze heavy on the artwork. "He'd hated having to stand still for the artist."

"I don't think you've ever spoken about him."

Emotion swam in Ronan's eyes. "I'm ashamed to say—I feel like I'd almost forgotten what he looked like. It hurts to think of him, of my parents, so I often avoid doing so…"

The air grew heavy.

"What was Hael like?" Zara asked after a few moments.

Ronan frowned, as if peering into a memory, before his face softened. "He was a rascal. Always following me around, especially when I was with Orion and… and Erebus."

"It sounds like Hael admired you a lot."

"He would have turned twenty-eight this year."

The archangel was still facing the portrait, tension bracketing his jaw. Zara's fingers twitched at her sides, tempted to smooth out the lines on his forehead. He wouldn't have seen how she reached for him. Felt the phantom binds tightening around her insides. How her mind immediately flashed with the image of a dagger, slicing into Hakim's throat. Blood spilling, light fading from his eyes—

She curled her hand into a fist and withdrew it.

"What about your parents?" she asked shakily.

"They were kind, loving. My father was strict with our education and training, while my mother was patient. She often took us to the city to see how our people lived." Ronan brushed his knuckles over the painting. "I've been meaning to ask you this… Do you recall your parents?"

Zara stiffened. Remembering her life before Ikarria was a hot blade dragged over an old wound. The memories always came in blurred fragments, constantly slipping through her fingers.

For a moment, she saw flashes of a red sky, someone hiding her in the temple where Idris had found her. She shook her head.

"I never knew my pater. If he was ever around, I don't remember him. And the few memories I had of my mother have faded over the years. Isn't that terrible? To not be able to honor the person who raised you?" She rubbed her temple. "Though I do remember a jungle and—and mangoes."

Ronan's lips twitched. "Mangoes?"

"Don't laugh at me," she deadpanned.

"I'm not, it's just…" The archangel flashed his brilliant teeth. "I find it adorable."

Zara huffed, turning away from him. Something fluttered in her chest, and a part of her hated that.

Ronan chuckled. "I actually came to invite you out to the capital tonight. You've been cooped up in this place, and I thought you might like to explore the city."

"Palace," she corrected. "I've been cooped up in a *palace*. These are the best accommodations I've had in a long time; I think I will be fine here."

The thought of being alone with him right now made her uneasy, for many reasons. That dull pain… The grief. It echoed through her bones. And the longing. This urge to cry out to him. To be held. To push him away.

Ronan grunted. There was the sound of clinking and Zara swerved around, catching one of the small telescopes from the desk before it could hit her.

She made a sound of disbelief. "Did you just *throw* this at me?"

"Oh, good. Your senses are still sharp." The corner of his lips curled. "Because I could've sworn it sounded like you were just *giving up*."

Zara snarled, launching the small instrument back at him. "Do you not remember what happened when I first stepped into the city? Your people will not be happy to see me out there."

He caught the object with ease. "So, you are going to just imprison yourself here? Because I would never do that to you."

The archangel moved so quickly—a rush of jasmine and ocean— appearing before her and cupping her jaw. His grip was gentle, though firm enough to hold her attention.

"Do not punish yourself any more than you already have. You have worked so hard to get where you are, do not stop now. You are *more*."

Those words… There was a pounding in her ears and an ache in her chest. It pierced through her flesh, digging deep into her. *You are more.*

Zara squirmed in his grasp. "How did you—"

"I heard Hakim say that to you." Ronan's face softened. "Come out with me tonight. Axar and Orion will be joining as well."

Fucking Suns. Zara could feel her determination withering.

She shoved the archangel away. "Why didn't you say that before? You could've made this conversation much easier for yourself."

Ronan grinned. "Where's the fun in that? I'm quite fond of your bite."

The nightlife of Teotlan pulsed with music and dancing. The sound of string and brass instruments filled the air as people ambled up and down the streets. Vendors bargained their goods, families dined at various eateries.

Zara pulled the hood of her cloak over her head, leaning against a high table. "I don't think anyone has recognized us."

Axar snorted. "How could they when they're so enamored with their long-lost king, back from the shadows?"

As if on cue, a wave of whispers slowly grew from the crowd gathered around the food stall next to them, where Ronan and Orion were ordering from. The citizens kept a modest distance from the archangels, but their genuine delight and awe was practically tangible. A male and female, clearly a couple, flirted with the males, trying to invite them out for the evening. The archangels declined.

Zara couldn't blame their admirers, even though her jaw tightened. The two males were too handsome for their own good, in their dark blue leathers, swords sheathed down their backs. Not to mention being morally ambiguous heroes of the realm had its charm.

When the archangels returned, they all feasted on flatbread topped with sauced meat, coriander leaves and onions. Orion disappeared and brought back ceramic mugs filled with chilled alcohol. Zara had groaned throughout their meal, Ronan's jaw tightening with every passing second.

After dinner, they explored streets bathed in colorful blossoms. Baskets and wreaths of flowers filled the sides of the roads, crawling up along buildings, and over the beams that arched overhead. Banners of white parchment fluttered above them, bundles of golden bells jingling in the ocean breeze.

Shops and stalls sold dried fruit and melons, while others had trays of wrapped sweets and candies. Some sellers offered leather shoes, bags, and saddles.

A few times Ronan got a few streets wrong and had them turning back, ignoring Orion's good-natured teasing.

"Do you even remember where everything is?" the archangel chuckled.

The Damalisan king rolled his eyes, averting his gaze. "It's slowly coming back to me."

They came across a stand with tables of ceramic skulls painted with intricate designs, as well as stone knives that resembled feathers.

Axar bent to observe the trinkets. "What are these?"

Orion slung an arm across the shifter's shoulders. "These beauties are a treasure to our people. You will see more of them toward the end of the year when we approach the city's main holiday."

"What holiday?"

The archangel smiled, his dark plaited hair shining under the moon and torchlights. "The Festival of the Three Suns, of course. It is an annual celebration where we honor life, nature, and death."

"In the guardian realms, death is seen as a new beginning, a dawn of another life, after having lived this one to the fullest," Ronan added. He picked one of the feather-shaped blades, spinning it between his fingers. "I'm sure you will recognize the design that represents Mikatán, one of the Three Sun Gods."

Zara's lips parted, but she stopped herself from speaking. She still hadn't mentioned to anyone that she'd seen the Primordial of Death in her dream. The god hadn't made another appearance. It might have been nothing but coincidence. Though, given all that she had learned, it didn't seem likely.

"Ikarria has a similar holiday," she said. "We light paper lanterns and release them into the sky. Many of them are shaped like dragons, flying toward the stars."

Thinking of the draconic kingdom cleaved through her. Ronan had received word that Daria had been crowned *Queen* of Ikarria—under Adrastea's control—and their pater was imprisoned somewhere in Elios.

The power in her veins growled—she needed to get back out there, as soon as possible.

"What a beautiful tradition, I'd love to see it one day." Ronan purchased a small ceramic skull and dropped it into her palm. He winked. "A little souvenir for you."

Zara cupped the trinket with more care than she expected, her worry and sorrow temporarily retreating. Her thumb brushed the blue and red flowery design of the skull. No one except her family or her guild had ever gifted her anything before. Zara didn't feel worthy of it, especially as it was from a guardian realm.

Though she couldn't help but be selfish and pocketed it.

Orion dragged Axar farther down the street. "You might get to enjoy the Festival of the Three Suns with us after your excursion to Kairos."

The shifter smiled as the two males continued down the busy street, getting lost in their own conversation.

Zara cocked her head. "I didn't realize how close those two had become."

Ronan followed her gaze. "You and I were a bit caught up with our own problems at the time. You know, chasing specters and all."

"I remember. It was very thrilling."

He snorted at that and gestured toward the brawny archangel. "Orion has stuck with me all this time, but he has been lonely for a while. He's been losing himself in countless trysts that have left him feeling hollow, so I think he needed a true friend who was not me. Someone he isn't duty-bound to." Ronan ran a hand over his jaw. "Especially since I was probably not very *emotionally* available… Not that Orion ever held that against me."

Zara observed Orion more closely. The archangel and her brother were now buying desserts, laughing about something. "What's his story?"

Ronan sighed through his nostrils. "Years ago, he was engaged to be married. His betrothed was another archangel soldier; he was killed in the War of the Skies."

Betrothed. Zara couldn't fathom the pain of losing the person you hoped to spend the rest of your life with. She tried to imagine what it would've been like for Orion during the War. Ronan had been taken prisoner, so Orion would've lost his love as well as his brother in a very short amount of time. She felt a newfound respect for the male, who had managed to persevere through so much.

The fine hairs on Zara's arms rose. Passersby had begun to notice her, their gazes hardening with a clash of emotions. Silent wails, unheard curses. *Monster. Beast.*

Ronan turned them around, gently urging her to keep walking. "Let's go," he murmured. "Orion and Axar will find us later."

Zara followed the archangel. The torchlights from the heart of the city thinned, and the smell of salt water thickened. Her heart began to race when he led her to the beach. The pearly-white moon swelled, water lapping at the sands. Within the shallow parts of the Jade Sea, canyons of moss and greenery looked like fangs in the dark.

They weren't alone: more dining places were posted along the beach, the air thick with the scent of cooking meat and pineapple;

bands of musicians played their trumpets and guitars; people danced and talked in the firelight.

Ronan tapped Zara's nose with his finger as he brushed past. "Stay here. I'll be right back."

She pressed herself between two near-empty stalls, feeling the sand beneath her boots. It wasn't long before her senses started to buzz.

"I can feel the murder in your stare." Zara sighed before looking up.

Elder Riyad stood a few paces away, his glare strong even in the dim firelight.

"Our king is a kind male; one could argue a little *too* kind," the elven male said. "I know there is a purpose to the arrangement between you and him, but I'd like to make one thing clear."

Zara remained silent. Waiting.

"The fact that you are Valenzian means nothing. You will *never* be one of us."

His words struck something inside her. It was a prick to her heart, and it became a burn that lasted longer than she would've liked.

She lifted her chin. "That is not what you really wish to say to me, is it?"

"No," Riyad snarled. Tears welled in his rouge-colored eyes. "Do you remember your marks, Rogue? I speak of two in particular—an elven male and a human girl; they were trying to flee Soleira."

The blood drained from Zara's face. A memory flashed in her mind, from the past hunting season. There had been darkness and rain. Two marks running in the mud. A girl's neck in her hands. An elf begging her to stop, to show mercy—

A cold stillness overtook her body, her stare heavy on Riyad. Her voice came out lower, *softer* than she wanted. "Yes, I remember them."

Those tears now ran down Riyad's cheeks, glistening like broken gems. "They went to learn more about the High Throne and the Council, but they were caught and detained in the Soleira castle. An elf and his human pupil, hardly dangerous enough to be considered a threat, let alone war criminals. I did everything in my power to help them escape that wretched place; I was *waiting* for them! I was there on the outskirts of Soleira, waiting in the rain… But they never came!" He brought a hand to his brow, sobbing. "And you killed them! He was my cousin, and you *killed* him!"

The world dulled in Zara's ears. She could no longer hold her emotion back, not as her face fell. The truth was a knife piercing through her chest, threatening to puncture her lungs.

Raziel had revealed to her that the marks assigned to her during the hunting season were Valenzian. Many of them distant members of her family. All because Raziel wanted to hurt her.

It was then that the late High King had told Zara that one mark—the elf with the green eyes—had been her uncle.

And if he had been Riyad's cousin, then it meant…

Zara took a step back, her eyes wide. She was standing in front of someone *related* to her. Someone who absolutely despised her.

"*Riyad.*" Ronan's voice was deadly calm. Zara hadn't noticed him returning from the stalls. "I think that is enough."

The Elder didn't wipe the tears from his face. "Your Majesty, I have every right to be angry. Keeping *her* here is an insult and an outrage—"

"I have also lost loved ones," Ronan said, a silver storm flashing across his face. "*Zara* has as well. And it is because of this War and every individual behind it—not her. What kind of ruler do you make of me? Do you think I would have allowed someone who truly meant us harm into our realm?"

Riyad breathed through his nostrils. "I believe you would side with a dangerous force without hesitation if it meant protecting whom you care most about."

Ronan prowled closer, his wings flaring. A beast of night and darkness.

Zara's chest began to burn; it was like a fire that scorched through the plains of her heart, leaving cracked earth in its wake. The sensation was hot, though there was something else lingering beneath the flames. A pain that brought tears to the back of her eyes.

Anger and sorrow. That's what she was feeling. So sudden, as if they had almost been forced *into* her. She clenched her teeth, her gaze drifting to Ronan.

He stopped before the Elder, and his lips curled. "On that, we can agree."

Riyad's jaw tightened. Before he could respond, the archangel said, "I understand you are grieving, but you must trust my judgment. And you must respect Zara."

By now, citizens had begun to take notice of them. Riyad seemed to know it too. He closed his eyes for a breath, and when he opened them again his expression was weary.

Without another word, the Elder bowed to Ronan and went back to the city. As soon as they were alone again, the boiling sensation lessened to mere crackling embers. Zara braced herself against the wall as the rush of emotion left her. She stared after Riyad, unsure what to make of it.

Questions thrashed within her. Questions that threatened to change everything. To yank open a door to another world, one she was not ready for.

Her vision shifted then. It was brief, a flash of fire—of *Teotlan* up in flames. Specters were swarming the streets, people screaming. Zara was slammed back into the present, her eyesight returning to normal.

A cold sweat broke across her skin as she scanned her surroundings. No fire. No destruction. Everything was fine. So, what had she just seen?

"I'm sorry. I wanted to give you a night free of burden, and I failed." Ronan's deep voice tugged on something inside her. He hadn't noticed anything. She went to meet his eyes, her gaze landing on what he was carrying.

"Are those… *mangoes?*"

Under the moonlight, Ronan gave an awkward smile. "You said you used to eat them as a child. Thought I'd give you a reminder of home. Though I hoped you could enjoy them under different circumstances."

Riyad was right. Ronan *was* too kind. Zara's chest warmed. That's what she admired about him. "Thank you."

The archangel gazed at her, longer than necessary. A stretch of silence filled with unsaid promises and unheard pleas. Zara wanted to say more, but couldn't trust herself. She looked away.

Ronan let out a soft exhale and flipped out a knife, slicing into the fruit, juice flowing down his wrist.

Something else rushed over Zara—another emotion. As if it had burst through an invisible door, crashing through her mind. It gnawed at her heart, and she clutched her chest.

When it lessened, Zara looked at Ronan, her head cocked. The archangel seemed oblivious, cutting the mango into slices and offering her some. All while shadows loomed over him.

TWELVE

The following morning, Zara found herself deep in the jungle, trailing behind Ronan. Axar and Río were also with them, her warhorse being led by the archangel.

She squinted in the bright sunlight. "Where are you taking us?"

Ronan didn't look back. "You agreed to train and become stronger while in Damalis, did you not?"

If Ronan had been upset the night before from the altercation with Riyad, there was no sign of it today. The male seemed his usual witty self.

Zara sighed. "Then I assume this attire you forced us to wear fits whatever you have planned?"

The dark blue fighting leathers were snug against her skin, plates of silver covering her shoulders, forearms, and legs. Her khopesh blades were strapped to her back; she had missed their familiar weight.

"Forced? More like *strongly* encouraged." There was a smile in Ronan's voice. "I think you will like where we are going."

Axar rubbed his temple. "You are both far too energetic this morning. I have a splitting headache."

Zara shot her brother a look. "You shouldn't have gone out drinking with Orion last night. I know you came back to the palace late."

"I didn't get drunk."

"Then that explains the perfume coming from your room."

Ronan smirked. "Did you have overnight guests, Axar?"

Her brother groaned. "Please, both of you leave me alone."

"Well, I'm glad not all people of Damalis hate the mercenaries." Zara tried to keep her voice light-hearted but there might've been more bite than she intended.

Axar shot her a look and she shrugged before turning to Ronan, "Did you send my message to Daria like I requested?"

The archangel didn't hesitate. "Of course. The note was given to the shadow dealers, along with my orders. It may take some time before it reaches her." He glanced over his shoulder. "Don't worry, they will get the message to Daria without risking her safety."

Zara knew she shouldn't doubt the capabilities of Ronan's shadow dealers. While he had been making arrangements for their journey to Kairos, she had asked to send communication to Daria. Not knowing how her sister was faring was too much; she couldn't wait any longer.

Eventually, a path made of saltillo tiles emerged under their feet. Short pillars of stone held large braziers made of brass. Within the mossy trees and thick vines above, jaguars lounged on the branches.

Ronan tossed his head back and inhaled the woodsy air. "This place brings back so many memories."

Ether flared beside him just as Nyota appeared. The panther nudged her head against his leg and he reached to scratch her ears.

The archangel and panther approached some steps that led up to a limestone archway. Without another word, they walked up and stepped through. Zara shared a glance with Axar before following.

She had to raise her hand to block the blinding sun as Ronan said, "Welcome to the érendira stronghold."

The light peeled back, revealing another—city? It was the closest comparison Zara could make. In front of them, steps led down to a training ground; surrounding it were many buildings and villas where citizens ambled about, carrying baskets of fruit or tending to their businesses. A river flowed on one side, its waters filled with fishermen.

Ronan gestured to the landscape. "The érendira train and live here. Their families reside on these grounds as well, so this place has grown a lot from the village it once was."

Many warriors were already training, jaguars lingering close by. Some practiced battle formations with swords, dual blades, or spears. One érendira commanded fire in the shape of a serpent, while her opponent parried the attack with a column of water. Steam billowed on impact, obscuring the two fighters from view.

A sense of thrill rushed through Zara. "Impressive."

Ronan chuckled, walking down the steps. "I knew you would like it."

When they reached the training ground, they found Soraya observing the warriors. The elf narrowed her eyes at Ronan. "You're late."

The archangel raised his hands in apology. "I appreciate your willingness to take us in today."

"When you came to me with this request, I thought you were mad." Soraya's eyes slid to Zara. "Though I must say, I am curious."

Zara felt a challenge in the air. She arched an eyebrow. "Curious about what exactly?"

The érendira raised her spear, the blue blade mere inches from Zara's face. "I want to see what makes the Horizons so special. Whether you can keep up with *us.*"

The warriors started to close in around them, grinning and banging their weapons against the ground. It sent a chill across her skin.

"We shall play our favorite game." Soraya hitched the spear across her back. "A round of Junya's Hunt, what say you?"

Axar took a step back. "Why do I have a bad feeling about this?"

"This is just part of the érendiras' training methods. Something I think will come in handy for the battles to come." Ronan clasped a hand around the shifter's shoulder, but his attention was on Zara.

"Are you ready for the challenge, little wolf?"

"The Hunt was created many years ago by our beloved Primordial, Junya. It tests not only your physical agility and strength, but also your *mental* ability. It shows how capable you are in adapting in the midst of battle." Soraya was saddled atop Kenzo, the jaguar pacing back and forth as the elf spoke.

Zara realized why Ronan had insisted on bringing Río along. Her hands tightened around the reins, her warhorse standing in a line of massive jaguars. Six of the érendira had agreed to play this round, the lower half of their faces covered by their skeletal masks. Axar shifted into his wolf form while Ronan hovered in the air.

"White targets have been placed along the game's territory," Soraya said. "Whoever hits the most wins. It is a race from here to the finish line. As usual, fights between participants are encouraged. Act like this is a real battle."

Zara stared ahead at the stretch of dense jungle and touched the throwing daggers sheathed on her body. She and Río may have been at a disadvantage against jaguars, but her competitiveness hummed through her blood. It felt... good. Normal. Like home.

There was the blare of a brass horn and they all ran into the jungle. Río galloped over tree roots, dodging branches and thick plants, the érendira blasts of wind on either side of Zara.

She saw a white target in the branches of a tree, several yards above the ground. A jaguar was already leaping from branch to branch to get to it. The érendira slid to its side, flinging out a throwing dagger and hitting the target dead center.

Axar whined beside Zara. "*Suns Above, my head hurts.*"

"Don't leave me now, Tallon." She grunted, coaxing Río to run faster. "I still have to find a way to reach those heights. Next time, maybe don't drink so much."

"*I didn't get drunk last night!*"

Ronan dove from overhead, striking the same target. He saluted Zara with two fingers at his brow before disappearing into the canopies. She gritted her teeth. The bastard was taunting her.

Axar veered closer to Zara. "*On me!*"

She moved to stand on top of Río's saddle, copying the movements she had seen the érendira do, and willed her ether to push her off and onto Axar's back. The breath was knocked out of her lungs as she struggled to cling to the wolf's thick fur, her body splayed awkwardly on top of him.

Axar began to climb a tree, though he was nowhere near as nimble as the jaguars, his claws sloppily shredding the wood.

She heaved herself further up on the wolf. "They just threw us into this game with little to no preparation."

They were higher up now, the target a bright beacon within the thick greenery. Zara sucked in a deep breath and leaped off Axar just as he shifted into his human form. They threw their daggers, hitting their mark.

Zara landed and rolled along a branch; her boots slipped on the moss and she toppled over the edge. "Shit!"

Axar caught her wrist, yanking her up. "We can't stop now. Keep going."

They maneuvered between the branches, much like how the other warriors had. Zara's mind was racing. As a Horizon, it was not the first time she'd hunted within the trees, but the way the érendira utilized the jungle was something beyond her.

Zara broke away from Axar. Ether spiraled around her body as she whistled for Río, who popped out of the orange shrubbery below her. She sailed through the air, the world seeming to slow. Her heart was pounding, adrenaline pumping through her veins. A bubbly sensation swelled within her chest, a thrill that burst throughout her body.

Like a crack of lightning, Zara's vision shifted. One moment she was airborne, and the next she was watching *herself* fall. Ether caressed her other self's body; crimson light unfurled behind her like wings. It illuminated the unfamiliar light in her eyes.

As quickly as that moment had come, she was slammed back into her own vision. Zara landed on top of Río's saddle, nearly toppling off her horse. It had not been some trick of the eyes—she had truly watched herself from the outside. Some odd out of body experience. How was that possible?

Zara glanced up. Ronan hovered in the air, wings flapping. He cocked his head, a curious look in his eyes.

Could it have been…

A sound tugged her attention toward the trees. It was no animal. She could smell the sweat from their skin, hear their ragged breathing. There was the rustle of feathers and a deep flap of wings as an archangel burst from the bushes. The white armor was too bright to miss—it was an Elios soldier, flying away.

More soldiers emerged from the trees, their backs to her. It was a small unit, not big enough for a large-scale attack. Were they scouts?

Without a second thought, Zara spurred Río into a gallop. If the archangels were to report what they'd seen here in these lands: how the people of Damalis had survived, how they were *thriving*… The thought turned her blood cold.

The soldiers dove between vines, the canopies too thick for them to rise into the sky, flying over a massive root that blocked the path. Zara pushed herself into a crouch on Río's saddle and sailed over it. She moved so quickly, tendrils of red light flared in her wake.

The archangels spilled into a clearing where the trees finally peeled open to sunlight and blue skies. *No*—they were going to escape. Ether whispered along the length of her arms, rolling into spheres at her palms. She couldn't let them go, couldn't—

Someone pulled her behind the thick plants. A hand clamped over Zara's mouth, her eyes clashing with Soraya's glare.

The érendira bared her teeth. "Careful, lest you fall in their path."

Zara furrowed her brows; Soraya brought a finger to her lips before slowly releasing her. Zara was ready to argue when a roar sounded through the jungle. The ground rumbled, shaking the loose stone and wood.

One of the soldiers pointed at something deep in the trees. "Watch out!"

Eagles slammed into the clearing, their massive talons pinning the archangels to the ground. Screams filled the air as the giant animals tore the soldiers apart.

Zara sucked in a sharp breath. It was a blessing that Soraya had pulled her back when she did.

The warrior pointed toward the trees across the clearing. "Watch."

Three-horned rhinoceroses charged out of the jungle, plowing through the Elios soldiers. Bones and guts exploded; wings were trampled on.

Zara stumbled back, watching them kill all the remaining soldiers, a line of sweat trickling down her neck. "What—what was that?"

Soraya pushed herself to her feet. "The animals of the guardian realms protect these lands. How do you think we have remained a secret all this time?"

Of course, that made sense. Her mind was fumbling for coherent thoughts, desperate to catch up with what she'd witnessed.

"Were they commanded to do this?"

Soraya shook her head. "No one controls them, not even Ronan. They act out of their own will. The guardian realm is their home, too." Her brows furrowed as she stared at where the archangels had been heading. "What concerns me, though, is how close the soldiers got."

Zara's limbs trembled as she struggled to her feet. She glanced at the clearing once more, nothing but blood and body parts and flattened ground. A shiver ran down her spine.

"It looked like they were scouting the area."

"We need to tell Ronan."

Zara grunted in agreement. "Speaking of, where is he?"

Suddenly, Kenzo sprinted to Soraya's side. He curled around her body in a protective stance, baring his teeth.

The érendira brushed a hand along his fur. "What's wrong?"

Ronan and Axar appeared over the peak of a small hill. The archangel was grappling with the wolf and they tumbled into the clearing. Ronan threw the shifter across the red-stained grass.

Sweat and blood ran down the archangel's face, a hand pressed against a nasty claw mark on his side. "Get a hold of yourself!"

Axar thrashed his head from side to side, his tongue lolling out of his mouth. *"I need to bring you to him. He demands it."*

A sense of dread engulfed Zara as she rushed toward the shifter. "Talk to me, Tallon. What's going on?"

Her brother snarled at her. *"I need to bring the both of you to him."*

There had been signs that something was wrong. When Axar flinched in her room because he thought he'd seen something. His headaches, even though he hadn't gotten drunk the night before. Shit, she was an idiot.

Zara sank to the ground. A sickening feeling filled her lungs—she had to do something. To help her brother.

But every logical thought flew out of her mind. Zara was unable to move as Axar lunged toward her. His fangs bared for her neck.

THIRTEEN

Daria trailed her fingers across the armrests of the obsidian throne. The black glass reflected the frown on her face. She had tried researching the dragons in the royal office, but there had been nothing noteworthy, except for ancient retellings of the first bond created between the creatures and Genesis, the Primordial of Life. The disappointment had sent her wandering about the castle, and to the throne.

She sighed. "How am I supposed to find something with no physical record? It is as if their existence was purposefully wiped from our textbooks."

The thought tickled something in her head just as the obsidian stone beneath her hands trembled. Whispers rose from the depths, as if answering a call. Reaching ghostly fingers toward her.

Daria froze. This had happened before. Voices, in a language she didn't understand, coming out of the throne. No one else could hear them. Only her.

The torches in the throne room warmed the air, and sweat trickled down her back. She pressed her fingers onto the black stone and leaned back against the seat.

"What are you trying to say?"

There was a deep rumble—and then, an image appeared in her

mind. She could see a flame, dancing in a void of nothingness. Above it, a reptilian eye opened. It was like the voices were speaking to her through these depictions.

Please, Daria begged, *what are you trying to tell me?*

The reptilian eye blinked before retreating back into the dark. She almost cried out after it, wanting to reach a hand into the depths of her head, when the flame snapped brighter, flickering over an elven male's face. Angry claw marks scarred his cheek, just below amber brown eyes…Why did he look familiar?

Daria gasped when the image dissipated like smoke, the voices going silent. The throne had spoken to her—shown her something valuable. A piece of information she needed to understand. Her fingers shook as she tucked a strand of hair behind her ears.

"Comfortable, Your Majesty?"

Daria jumped at Silas's voice. It had been two months since Ares had left for Elios and, unfortunately, his Second had made it a hobby to constantly inquire on her progress. More so to annoy her, she was sure of it.

"What can I help you with, Silas?"

The vampire donned his usual smirk. "I am merely checking in."

Daria's eye nearly twitched. "If I had anything to report, I would've done so already."

"That best be the truth. I don't think you'd like to find out what would happen to your realm or your precious father if you withheld any information on the dragons."

She clenched her teeth. "Like I said, I have found nothing. Honestly, there don't seem to be any actual records on what happened to them. There is no way to know where the dragons might've gone."

"Then you need to look elsewhere. Stories—*life*—exist beyond pages and textbooks, you know." Silas cocked his head, looking at her with disdain.

For a moment, Daria imagined driving her dagger through the male. "I don't need *advice* from you."

"I see, you would rather have Ares lend you a hand, right?" The vampire leaned toward her, his smirk even sharper in the dim firelight.

Daria scoffed, pushing off the throne and brushing past the male. "I'd rather have all of you vampires out of my castle."

Silas's laugh echoed against the obsidian marble floor, following her as she left the throne room. While the male's existence was an annoyance equivalent to that of a bug, something about what he said prodded at her mind.

Stories—life—exist beyond pages and textbooks, you know.

Daria thought of the elven male the throne had shown her. Her eyes widened. *Suns Above,* of all people, Silas had actually given her an idea.

Priestesses bowed when the Ikarrian queen entered one of the chambers of the Primordial Sanctuary. Thorny vines snaked along its ceiling, white flowers nestled in the greenery. Garlands wrapped around thin pillars encircling a raised, central platform. The stone there was etched with various symbols Daria had never understood.

"I know it has been some time since Your Majesty interacted with the *Mirari.* Do you recall how to use it?" A priestess jerked her chin toward the altar at the end of the room.

Daria brushed her braids over her shoulders, running her hands down the length of her deep-blue satin dress. The smell of incense was thick in the air. She eyed the smoke, its pale claws reaching for the columns of daylight.

"I will be fine, thank you."

As soon as she was alone, Daria approached the altar. Waiting for her were a vial of a rose-scented incense blend, a wooden bowl of charcoal tablets, and a small black cauldron. Glass containers filled with pink and white powder lined the shelf above.

Her hands moved as if of their own accord, memory finding its way through her limbs as she plucked the charcoal and powders from the shelves, dropping them into the cauldron. When she was done, she snapped her fingers and fire erupted inside it.

Ether from the powder shimmered within the pale smoke, and

Daria inhaled. Energy shuddered throughout her body, and when she opened her eyes, they'd turned a milky white.

The *Mirari* was a place to *view* stories of old. Tales of Primordials and Ikarrian historical figures could be witnessed here, narrated by acolytes.

It was not a safe practice: some extremists had gone so far they'd permanently changed their vision. To always be connected with the gods, they said, and to never live in the present moment. It was why her pater forbade her and Zara from ever using the *Mirari*—even though Daria attempted it once during her academic education. So much time had passed since then, it was no wonder she hadn't thought of using it before now.

"I seek the story of the late King Arzhel Calderón," Daria whispered.

The room darkened, despite it still being bright outside. Smoke rolled out of the cauldron and onto the central platform.

A voice belonging to one of the acolytes echoed in the chamber. *As has been known throughout Ikarrian history, the bond between the Ikarrian elves and the dragons started with the Primordial of Life, Genesis, the first dragon rider. Through the goddess, that bond was passed onto the royal bloodline of the draconic realm.*

The smoke morphed into the shape of a male. The scar down the side of his face was harsher now.

Daria's lips parted. "I knew it. The throne showed me *you.*"

She had heard many stories of her ancestor. The *Mirari* stored lesser-known anecdotes, a well of information the people of Ikarria could not access. If the throne had chosen to show Daria a member of her family, then perhaps there was something about them she needed to learn.

The narrator continued, *The bond between dragon and elf was a vow forged in fire and blood. A connection with the potential of achieving something grand, filled with purpose—only to be broken by one of the Ikarrian kings.*

Daria's eyes widened. She didn't recall this part of her family's history. It must not have been commonly known.

Those promises were violated by King Arzhel Calderón, the last dragon rider.

What? Someone of her bloodline had broken the dragon bonds?

The smoke-figure of King Arzhel stared at her, and she felt the hairs on her neck rise.

The bond between dragon and elf was a vow forged in fire and blood. A connection with the potential of achieving something grand, filled with purpose—only to be broken by one of the Ikarrian kings.

Daria frowned. "You already said that."

She knew there would be no response, it was a mere recording. But the acolyte's voice repeated the same words.

Those promises were violated by King Arzhel Calderón, the last dragon rider.

Was the *Mirari* broken? No, that couldn't be it. The story must have been recorded incorrectly. Unless—

Chills ran down Daria's arms. Her gaze drifted back to where Arzhel was standing on the platform. He still watched her, slowly cocking his head.

She took a step back. "Something's wrong."

A male's voice resonated in her head, slicing through the narrator. "*Descendant.*"

Daria stumbled back.

The smoke-figure didn't move, but the voice returned. "*If you are listening to this, then it means the Primordial contract has selected you, as a member of my bloodline, to uncover my secrets.*"

"What are you saying?" she whispered.

"*Find me, Descendant, and I will tell you what I've done.*"

Daria's heart was beating wildly against her ribs. "The dragon bonds. What happened to them?"

White light blasted across her vision. The last thing she saw was Arzhel raising a finger to his lips.

Daria was thrown back to the ground. Panic wrapped around her lungs and she blinked several times until her eyesight returned to normal. Her palms slapped the stone as she hurled the contents of her stomach. The use of the *Mirari* had been too much for her body, though what she just witnessed was even more concerning.

A *primordial contract.* There was not much she knew about them, only that when the Gates of Celestrea were still open, mortals could make contracts with gods, in exchange for whatever they desired. For a price. It had been an uncommon practice, and highly discouraged, even dangerous—and Arzhel had made one to break the dragon bonds…

Find me, Descendant, and I will tell you what I've done. It seemed there was a missing piece of Ikarrian history. One she would have to dig out from the void. From the dead.

After several more attempts to glean more information from the *Mirari*, Daria decided to leave the chamber. It was dark within the Primordial Sanctuary, save for the candlelight; only a few priestesses remained, bowing as she passed before returning to their nightly routines of worship and prayer.

Daria stopped in a dim hall near the entrance as one of the priestesses draped her cloak over her shoulders.

"A word, Your Majesty?" Before Daria could respond, the woman slipped a sealed letter into her hands.

Daria sucked in a sharp breath and whirled back toward her. "You're not one of ours, are you?"

While the woman wore the usual gown of the priestesses, she also had a hood that covered most of her face. Her lips curved. "My Lord has business in all parts of the Continent. I was instructed to wait if you'd like to provide a response."

Daria blinked. Her heart hammered against her chest as she ripped the seal open. Tears welled in her eyes when she recognized the handwriting. *Zara.* The woman's 'Lord' must have been Ronan, which meant she was a shadow dealer.

Daria should've known the archangel would conduct illegal transactions in her realm—the male didn't discriminate. But how had someone from the Sombra Quarter managed to sneak their way into Ikarria, let alone the Primordial Sanctuary and castle?

She clutched the letter tighter. Suns Above, Zara was all right. She hungrily devoured all of her sister's words, her heart racing even faster.

They were preparing to depart for Kairos. To sneak into Nephtyr and use the Oasis of Dreams to amplify their ether.

I will come for you, her sister had written.

Daria let out a choked laugh. As fugitives, Zara and Ronan were planning on using the Sombra Quarter to get the realm of sands. It was too dangerous. The Queen of Kairos and its citizens were not people you wanted to risk getting on the bad side of. Though Daria knew they were lacking options.

Her mind went to the Queen of the Sands. She had briefly met the Kairos royal during the Summit, and Kamari had extended an invitation to Daria to visit her kingdom…

A plan started to morph in her head. Her progress on the dragons had reached a dead end here in Ikarria. There was a connection between Arzhel—who was long dead—and the dragons' disappearance. The realm of Kairos specialized in the otherworldly, and the Oasis was a prime example of that. Daria might be able to learn something of value there.

And if Zara and Ronan needed to get to Kairos, then perhaps she could help them. Not just anyone could enter the Oasis; it required permission, granted by the kingdom's ruler. Daria could help them pass through the city gates—maybe even into the royal walls. From there… Well, that would be a problem they could address later.

Daria glanced at the shadow dealer, who still waited in the dark. "I'd like to send a reply."

FOURTEEN

Ronan hissed between gritted teeth. "Santos, your treatment is *unique*."

He glanced down at Zara, who was crouched before him and wrapping a white bandage around his bare torso none-too-gently. She let out a growl.

"Maybe you'd prefer to have someone else tend to you?" The violent wolf might have added more pressure against his wound.

Ronan's growing smile turned to a wince. He still managed a rough chuckle. "Hurt me all you like. It does not matter to me."

Zara narrowed her eyes. "Or maybe I should have let Axar finish the job instead."

Ronan turned serious. "I think he was going to end *both* of us."

He didn't want to think about that moment. How Axar had attacked him, and then Zara—had nearly *hurt* her. Before the shifter could do anything, Ronan had slammed the wolf to the ground, hands squeezing his throat until he lost consciousness.

They were now in the infirmary of the palace, while Axar had been taken to the healers' chambers to be examined. The wounds the shifter had given Ronan would heal on their own, but that hardly mattered.

Zara was still tying the bandage. She was so close to him. The skin between her brows was furrowed. He could see the weight that pressed on her shoulders. Could hear the silent cry of her spirit.

He reached to cup her cheek. Or to brush a strand of hair behind her ear, he wasn't sure. But he stopped himself.

Instead, he said, "Do not blame yourself, Santos. You couldn't have known something like this would happen."

"I am still trying to understand." Zara paused, her breath hitching, as if she'd just noticed how close she was to him, and pulled away. "Axar attacked you first. Can you tell me what exactly happened?"

"When you went after the Elios soldiers, he kept complaining about his headaches. He was in severe distress, with dilated pupils and severe salivation. I thought he was dehydrated or just exhausted, but before I knew it, he was attacking me." Ronan ran a hand across his jaw. The words carefully rolled from his tongue. "He said Erebus ordered him to bring us in."

Something broke in Zara's eyes. "It's just as I thought."

Before she could say anything else, Ezrah opened the door to the healing chambers, blond locks plastered to his temple. "Axar is awake. He'd like to talk to you. Please come in."

Ronan shared a look with Zara before they followed the archangel.

A small fountain sat in the heart of the chambers, pouring water into a shallow pool made with emerald green tiles. Thin trails of mist lingered in the air, smelling of mint and jasmine.

In the corner of the room, shielded by a wooden divider, was Axar. He was in bed, sipping on tea. When his eyes lifted to Zara, he abandoned what he was doing. "Thank the Suns you're unharmed."

Zara flung her arms around him. "I'm so happy you're all right."

While Ronan was also relieved to find the male back to normal, he couldn't help the tension that bracketed his body. Prepared to dive to Zara's defense in case the shifter went ballistic once more.

Axar's gaze landed on Ronan's bandages, the archangel was still shirtless. The shifter winced. "I'm sorry about that."

"It will take a lot more than a few gashes to take me down." Ronan folded his arms with a smirk. "You'll have to try harder next time."

The shifter gave him a dry look, relief flooding his features, until

Ezrah cleared his throat. "Axar, would you please share with the others what you told me?"

Darkness fell over the mercenary's face; his eyes went distant and there was a tremble to his fingers. Zara grabbed his hands.

"Before you saved me at the coliseum, I was Raziel's prisoner for an entire week." Axar swallowed. "Or rather, I should say I was *Erebus's* prisoner. He—he showed me things. Painful realities."

Ronan was struck speechless. Suddenly, he began to understand what was happening here. The look Ezrah shot him only confirmed his suspicions.

Zara frowned. "What does that mean?"

"He means illusions," Ronan interjected. "As you know, archangels have abilities and powers like most creatures in Ribera—just more ethereal in nature. Erebus is able to make others see what he wants them to see. So long as he is able to touch them."

Zara's expression flashed with hurt. "I didn't know that. He never told me when we were together."

Something gnawed inside his chest at that. It soured him. Caused his jaw to tighten. Shit.

"I am not surprised," he said, smoothing out his expression. "Erebus never liked talking about or indulging in his powers. In the past he hardly ever used his ether, except for the occasional… interrogation."

Ezrah added, "If not handled properly, illusions can damage the mind of their victims. It is why many archangels who possess the ability don't wield it often."

Yes, both Ronan and his mentor were familiar with the white-winged archangel's methods. It was only after Erebus became a soldier that his powers were utilized to question prisoners. Many of them became insane: they'd yank their hair out, tear their nails out, or ram their heads against a wall.

Fiery light flared in Zara's eyes. "What did Erebus do to you, Axar?"

Axar looked pained. "He showed me Hakim and Eshe's deaths. I had to relive them over and over again. Erebus kept saying that the violence wouldn't stop there, not until you and Ronan were under the High Throne's control." He rubbed his temple. "The thing is, he manipulated the way I saw you both. In the illusions, he made you villains, ready to kill me, and told me you needed to be brought to him. That it was your fault Hakim and Eshe were killed."

Zara's breath hitched, and she brought a hand to her mouth. It took everything in Ronan not to go to her, hold her in his arms.

"You know that's not true, Santos," the shifter murmured to her, but it didn't look like she was listening.

Ezrah shifted in place, looking his way. "Erebus instilled a task in Axar's mind. By twisting how he views you and Zara, during the hallucinations Axar will believe you are his enemy, one that must be returned to the High Throne."

Ronan stilled. For Axar to have had his mind flayed open and violated in such a way… He curled his hands into fists. It was a miracle the shifter was still sane at all.

Erebus, what have you done?

Axar bunched the bedsheets. "I'm sorry, Zara. I promise that I will fix this. If I ever hurt you, I could never forgive myself—"

Zara cupped his cheek. "You don't need to apologize. I only wish I had saved you sooner." She turned to Ezrah. "How do we help him?"

The archangel seemed to be deep in thought. "Our healers have spent years specializing in ethereal-type wounds. Erebus touched Axar's mind, leaving his own fingerprints, you could say. His manipulation would have acted like a toxin, so it is simply a matter of removing it." Ezrah sat on a chair near the bed, leveling his gaze with the mercenaries. "We can treat him, but it is a delicate process. One that requires time and preparation."

"What kind of preparation?" Zara asked.

"Before we start the procedure, Axar will need to take a tonic for several months in order to lessen the frequency of these illusions." Ezrah's expression was serious, pinning the shifter with his gaze. "It's a gamble. The tonic does not guarantee that your mind will be ready for the treatment, and it may cause some… discomfort. And your abilities in battle may be weakened."

It was quiet for several minutes. Axar did not show fear, though a muscle flexed across his jaw as he said, "I will do it."

Ronan watched their interaction, his mind still on Erebus. An ache bloomed in his chest and he rubbed his hand over it. "It's settled then. Ezrah, I leave Axar's care in your hands."

The older archangel bowed his head. "Of course, Your Majesty."

Zara glanced at Ronan. "How can we repay you?"

Silly wolf. He should've been offended by that question. "You have done more than enough," he said softly.

Ronan could feel Ezrah's gaze on him. He ignored it.

Axar looked at Zara. He offered her a small, broken smile. "Stars made by the Suns?"

She nodded, smiling back. "We are stars made by the Suns."

Ronan didn't quite understand their little exchange but he didn't need to. Though Zara kept up a strong act, he could see the fear behind her eyes. She had lost two members of her guild, and now risked losing her brother. Perhaps the shifter saw past her bravado as well. Felt that fear just as much.

Seeing their sibling-like relationship, full of warmth and hope, left a gaping void in his heart. He thought of Hael—the little archangel would always follow him everywhere.

Right at that moment, Soraya walked in, a stack of towels in her hands. Their gazes clashed and she went taut with tension. They had been cordial whenever the situation called for it, but hadn't had another conversation alone.

Soraya looked away. She looked to be in pain.

Ezrah escorted Ronan and Zara out of the infirmary and into a breezeway.

"The situation is more dire than I thought," the archangel said. "May I suggest assigning some guards to watch over Axar whenever he visits the infirmary for treatment?"

In case the shifter acts out. Ezrah didn't have to say it out loud. Zara must've understood his meaning as well, and frowned.

Ronan nodded. "We need to be cautious."

Ezrah placed a hand on Zara's shoulder, giving it a comforting squeeze. "With the scouting party you encountered, and now Axar's hallucinations, I fear what else the High Throne and its Council may have in store."

Zara stared at the archangel's hand. As if in shock that someone from Damalis had seemed to accept her.

For a brief moment, Ronan looked out to where the ocean and sky met. "I've been making arrangements with the shadow dealers to help us reach Kairos safely. We will be able to leave soon."

"I actually have something to tell you, Ronan," she said. "I thought nothing of it at first, but with all that you have told me, I probably should've mentioned it sooner."

He held his breath as Zara continued, "Mikatán appeared in my dreams."

Ronan felt an icy chill run down his spine as she explained the brief interaction she'd had with the god. The Primordial of *Death* had visited her. He wasn't sure if he should be thrilled or worried.

One thing was certain though.

"Your *Izcali* has begun, and your ether will continue to mature. Powers you didn't think possible will begin to make themselves known to you." Ronan turned to Ezrah. "Our training must start now. We need to connect with the gods."

FIFTEEN

Under a sky of melted gold, Zara sat cross-legged in front of a lake. The jungle curled around the jade-colored water, the air smelling of paprika and soap. Somewhere in the distance she could hear the thunderous growl of a waterfall.

Ezrah had brought her and Ronan to a secluded area along the cliffs of the palace grounds. Ronan sat next to Zara, while the older archangel stood before them.

A knot had been twisting in her stomach ever since she'd told Ronan and Ezrah about her brief encounter with Mikatán. She wasn't sure what to expect next.

"Both of you are skilled warriors; for you, wielding steel is equivalent to drawing breath." Ezrah's sea-green wings stretched out behind him. "Primordial ether is just another weapon; it will strengthen and *heal* you at a much faster rate than those with regular ether. However, it requires a different approach: an indomitable strength of the mind."

At the word 'warriors', Zara had inwardly flinched. She had never associated herself with that term. It was a word of honor and glory, for those who fought and bled for a higher purpose. Not for mercenaries like her.

"Ronan, the last time you went through these teachings you were still very young. I imagine you don't recall much of it?" Ezrah asked.

The archangel gave a half-hearted chuckle. "No, I do not."

The light in Ronan's eyes seemed dull today. Duller than before. It pinched something in Zara's chest. They had been so consumed with preparing for Kairos and with other matters that she hadn't had the opportunity to speak more in private with him. She supposed the boundary they had drawn between them also played a part.

Ezrah continued, "I am going to provide you with the steps to get to a state of mind only those with Primordial ether can achieve. To reach into yourselves and know the shape of the ether inside you. While our mundane connection with the gods has been broken, everything that exists around us stems from the natural essence of ether. It is a tether, a way to connect with the gods."

Ezrah paced about, the lake glimmering behind him. "Mikatán appeared to you, Zara, so that formally makes the Primordial of Death your patron god. Your supporter as you face the trials that could ultimately lead to your godhood."

Zara gaped at him, her heart thudding against her ribs. "Are we sure about that?"

Ronan interjected. "No god would visit a mortal unless it was for good reason. Besides, it makes sense that he would come to you. The Horizons honor the Primordial of Death as their patron god, right?"

That was true. Throughout the Continent of Ribera, many Primordials were worshipped for different reasons.

Zara couldn't help but look at the blank space around Ronan's left bicep, where the ether-binding tattoo used to be.

"Who is your patron god?" She cocked her head. "I realized I never asked."

Ronan averted his gaze, pressing a hand to his chest. "I don't know. They have never made themselves known to me."

Zara gasped, a bit more dramatically than intended. She couldn't help it. "How can you not know? I assumed you would, since you attempted the Crossing before."

Ezrah let out a sound of disapproval and crossed his strong arms. "It may be due to the fact that Ronan was too young to attempt the Crossing in the first place. I told his parents the same thing back then."

Zara hadn't thought about that. She was curious to know what had really happened during that time. The details that drove Ronan to pursue the Crossing.

Ronan propped one leg up, resting his arm across his knee. The sunset light softened his features. Made him look younger.

"I think my parents went along with my request to go to Celestrea so that I could learn that truth myself," he said softly. "I still would have gone through with it, even if they'd said no."

Zara noticed how he dug his fingers into his fighting leathers, his knuckles whitening. There was more to the story. All she knew was that Erebus was at the center of it. More questions rushed through her, but she leashed them for now.

Ezrah watched Ronan carefully, as if he'd finally found an answer to a long-standing question. "Let us begin, then. To reach an ethereal state of mind, you will practice meditation. Meditation combined with ethereal power will sever you from your mortal shell and let you walk amongst the otherworldly. Through introspection and visualization, you will face the many broken mirrors that make you *you*. The ether in your blood will respond, thus creating a passage to the ethereal."

Zara didn't like the sound of that. "How will I know if I'm doing this right?"

"Your ether will let you know." The archangel's voice gentled. "It is about surrender, Horizon. Now, begin."

Zara might have grumbled to herself as she straightened her back and closed her eyes. Quieting the constant chaos in her mind was always a challenge. Fighting and wielding blades came easily, but it was finding peace within herself that never seemed obtainable.

The evening breeze curled around her neck. Crickets chirped and the grass brushed against her legs. The stresses and anxieties of yesterday, today, and tomorrow still plagued her. She practiced letting thoughts brush past her. Like silver clouds in the night sky.

Time trickled by. Ether pulsed. Soft at first, a distant heartbeat. And then it grew louder and louder.

Zara recognized it from her dream. She reached for that tether, wrapping her hand around the connection, and was propelled forward, launched into the void.

She careened through a sky of dusk and dawn and into a realm of darkness. And her eyes opened to a familiar chamber made of dark stone…

Mikatán sat on his throne. He tilted his head, the blades on his headdress clinking. "It's about time, young goddess."

That same cold breeze came with his voice. It was a deep and gentle sound, like the night and the moon.

Zara opened her mouth, but nothing came. The weight of the air grew heavy, pushing against her back. Her palms slammed on the ground as she bowed to the energy. Bowed to the god of Death.

"You won't be able to move or speak quite yet." Mikatán rose from the throne, *much* taller than she remembered. "In all of my existence, the natural ether still manages to surprise me. There must be a crack between the veils of our worlds, one that allows me to make contact with you. When your ether awakened, I felt its call. So full of resilience, so full of pain. I knew I had to answer it."

Sweat dripped down Zara's neck as the Primordial stared her down. The view before her flickered, and pain beamed through her head.

"I know you seek the Oasis of Dreams." Mikatán went to his haunches, the silver mists in his eyes swirling slowly. "Find me, Zara Santos. I can give you what you seek—power beyond measure. With my blessing, you will be a warrior with the ability to fight gods and monsters."

Hearing the god of Death say her name had her ether singing. A sensation that was all-consuming. It felt *good*. Zara could feel herself slipping from this reality. She dug her fingernails into the stone, desperate to cling to another moment with the Primordial.

She wanted to shout, but Mikatán was already taking a step back, returning to the darkness.

The black wolf appeared, rushing toward Zara, and for the first time she could hear it barking. Her heart squeezed tight to the point of pain. She thrust a hand out to the wolf, tears welling up in her eyes.

Before it could reach her, she was ripped away from that frayed fabric of existence.

Zara gasped, doubling over onto the grass. Her ether burned through her blood; it was bubbling within her, pressing against an unseen barrier.

It was darker now, the sun having sunk behind the cliffs. Ezrah was nowhere to be found, but she could sense Ronan near her.

"I saw him again," she said, pressing a palm to her head. "Mikatán wants us to go to the Oasis, too. Ronan—"

Zara twisted just in time to dodge the archangel as he rushed her. He stumbled on the grass, heaving for breath, his eyes filled with a deep blue light, the color of his ether. Whatever space Ronan had managed to reach through his meditation, it wasn't pleasant.

"Ronan, wake up!"

The archangel charged her again, his black wings sweeping out. Zara cursed out loud before slamming her body against his. Her ether was humming underneath her skin, a force able to withstand the male's weight.

She threw him into the jungle, stalking after him. "Come back to me, Menodora."

Ronan fisted his hair and screamed. Blue light shot out from him, lightning that smashed wood, torched grass, and flattened plants. Zara ducked before a bolt of ether could strike her.

If he lost any more control, the damage would be unfathomable. She leashed her red light and used it to speed through the chaos. She crashed into Ronan and slammed him against a tree as another explosion of his ether lit the world in electrifying blue.

He breathed heavily through his nostrils, whimpering, his eyes scrunched shut. "I'm sorry. I'm *sorry*."

The words weighed on her heart. This beautiful male before her, still lost to whatever trance he was in, sounded so broken.

Resorting to the first thing that came to mind, she pressed a dagger to his throat. "You better wake up *now*, archangel, or so help me gods—"

Ronan's eyes flew open. Sweat rolled down his face as he steadied his breath. "What—what—"

Zara shuddered with relief. "Fucking Suns, you scared me."

He scanned the destruction around them. "Did I do that? I didn't think I was moving." Ronan's throat bobbed against her blade. "Did I hurt you?"

She shook her head. "What did you see?"

"It was a memory of me and Erebus. We were in Celestrea; it was just before…" He let out a trembling exhale. "My patron god was there. I could sense their presence, though they didn't show."

Zara tried to focus on what he was saying, but her powers were now twisting her insides, as if wanting to burst out of her. It was so *hot* here. Sweat beaded her brow.

The archangel stopped and frowned at her. "What's wrong?"

She bowed her head, groaning. "It *hurts*."

Cursing under his breath, Ronan swept her up into his arms and flew through the jungle. Energy clapped around them, causing wood to snap and flocks of birds to scatter from the branches.

They crashed onto the ground, rolling down a slope until they came to a stop, Ronan landing on top of her. He held her wrists down as she squirmed. "We are reaching a new level of our ether, and it's going to be uncomfortable. I can feel it too, like it's clawing its way out of me. We are going to need to release our power—bottling it up will only hurt us more."

Zara clenched her teeth and kneed him in the torso and he grunted. Red smoke began to pour from her body.

"Yes." Ronan grinned under the growing night, though it was strained. "Fight me. Let it out."

"Shut up." She groaned as ether buzzed in her veins.

Tendrils of red curled around Ronan's arms and legs. His eyes widened a split-second before he was sent flying across the clearing.

Zara stood and swayed, wiping her mouth with the back of her hand. "To think the meditation was supposed to help us reach an ethereal state of mind—I think we are far from that at the moment."

"It means what we are doing is right. This is only the beginning."

Ronan crouched into a fighting position, his wings unfurling as an orange-blue mist wreathed his hands. "Come at me, mercenary!"

She raised a hand toward him, releasing a column of energy. Ronan veered to the side, his wings narrowly missing the fiery light as Zara's ether crashed into the stone behind him.

Power flared in his hands as he met her in close combat. She brought up her fists to parry against his attacks, every swipe and kick interspersed with bolts of ether. Their gazes met over the colliding energy, wicked grins stretched on both of their faces.

A rope of Ronan's light lashed out, cracking a tree trunk. "Shit."

Zara took advantage of his distraction to lunge at him; she wrapped her legs around his waist, her ether soaring around them.

"Are you trying to kill me?" Ronan shouted.

"No matter how much power I expel, the pain doesn't stop." Zara was panting now, sweat falling down her body.

Water thundered behind them, and she realized they'd reached the waterfall.

Ronan smiled. He wrapped his arms around her waist and flew toward the body of rushing water. They grazed the lake's surface, a ribbon of ether zipping behind them.

Zara screeched. "What are you doing?"

He tucked her head to his chest. "Hang on!"

His wings folded against his back just as he pierced through the waterfall. Heavy water pounded them for a breath before they crashed onto a stone platform on the other side, Ronan twisting them around so he could take the brunt of their landing.

The water was cold enough to cool their bodies down. Though only for a moment.

Zara was already on her feet, gasping for breath. She grabbed at her fighting leathers as if trying to rip them off. "I feel like I'm burning. What's happening to me?"

Ronan grabbed her face with his hands, forcing her to meet his eyes. "It's your ether evolving. You're all right, Santos. I promise. Take steady breaths—if we release it all at once, who knows the level of damage that could ensue."

She nodded her head, following his lead as they inhaled and exhaled slowly. Ronan pressed his forehead against hers and they allowed their ether to flow out of them. Mists of red, purple, blue, and orange swirled around their bodies.

Zara cried out at the pressure. She could feel her power building. Becoming stronger. Before she realized what she was doing, she'd bit into Ronan's neck. He groaned, holding her to him.

He pushed her back until Zara was pressed against the wall of the cave. She didn't let go, fingernails digging into his skin. They were in another type of battle, amid their spilling power. The energy was wild: claws that raked the stone, and wings that swept the air.

Ronan twisted her around so she was facing the wall. He slid his hand up her neck and wrapped it around her throat. Her breath hitched, only for a whimper to leak out of her lips. She arched against him—fucking Suns, what was she doing?

Her thoughts and desires were crashing into one another, every strand of emotion and ether becoming tangled. The lines blurring together.

The feel of his body behind hers. And something hard pressing against her. Zara rolled her hips against it. Ronan groaned, the archangel's grip tightening. His other hand lay flat on her lower abdomen as he moved with her. The feel of his length grinding on her from behind, together with their riling ether, was dizzying.

Zara turned back around to face him, her arms looping around his neck.

The pain lessened bit by bit as the tension left her. Slowly, their powers ebbed, till only embers floated around them. Ronan bowed his head and brought his brow to the slope of Zara's neck.

Silence hung between them, their heavy breaths echoing in the cavern.

She swallowed. While her ether had calmed, it had left behind a burning desire. One that she always carried, though it was more prominent and insistent now.

Zara shuddered out a breath. "Does the release of ether usually have an… aphrodisiac effect?"

"What?" Ronan jerked his head up. "Yes, sometimes. I'm sorry," he said, his voice ragged.

They were so close. Breaths apart. Their hair and clothes were soaking wet, though heat stirred between them, their bodies flushed together.

"Ether and emotion often cross over, but I should've shown more restraint." Ronan whispered. His gaze dropped to her lips. "I'm sorry, I won't do that again."

Zara tilted her chin up, staring at the scar on his mouth. "It's not your fault, we were both affected by our ether changing. My head has cleared now."

They leaned toward each other. His voice was rough. "Mine too."

Ronan brushed his lips against hers, and all she could see was… *blood.*

The ugly feeling returned with a violent vengeance, shattering any lust and desire and throwing Zara into a red-ridden temple where she lay on the ground, the deity Nadira pinning her down and—Her mercenary family was lined up before her, bound and on their knees, Raziel behind them. Behind Hakim.

Panic seized her as Nadira laughed and forced her to look. Her eyes went to the wicked dagger in Raziel's hand. "Stop, please—"

Hakim didn't move. Not even as Eshe and Axar fought against their own binds. His attention was on her, eyes glossed over with a sheen of admiration. "I am proud of you, Santos."

Tears burned behind Zara's eyes. "Don't."

The corners of his lips turned up, his own eyes glistening. A softness she hardly ever saw. "I love you, daughter."

Her mentor, a second pater.

"Close your eyes," he murmured.

But she couldn't.

And then, a slash of Raziel's dagger—

Zara's mouth opened into a scream… as blood fell from Hakim's throat. As the life dimmed in his eyes.

Raziel smiled wider and wider. He moved toward Eshe. Eshe. Zara clawed at the ground, her fingers breaking, blood bubbling.

My pup.

Another slash of Raziel's dagger—

Zara pushed Ronan away, gasping for breath. The images kept flashing through her mind, as if haunted her. She knew it wasn't his fault—so why was being in this enclosed space with him, with nothing but water and stone shielding them from the world, driving her to the edge of sanity?

"This can't happen again," she whispered.

He was staring at her, something like desperation in his gaze. "Zara, what's wrong? You can talk to me. This is *us*, we can work through whatever this is, together."

"There is no *us*," she snapped. Zara's eyes widened at how harsh the words sounded, shame crawling up her throat. She averted her gaze. "Not in that way."

The words tasted bitter in her mouth as her heart nearly cleaved in two. She hoped the archangel would grant her mercy and just leave.

Ronan must have heard her silent plea, and said nothing as he walked away with a sigh, hands clenched tight.

SIXTEEN

Ares held the vial to his mother's lips. "Drink every drop."

Morana swallowed the purple liquid. Her face soured as it always did when taking the medicine. "I should be used to it by now, but it is atrocious."

He crushed the glass receptacle in his hand, throwing the shards into the waste bin. Though it was not something Ares had to do, he tried to hide the expensive medicine as much as he could. King Matías knew of his mother's ailment, and it had still never stopped him from requesting her services on occasion. Ares couldn't be too careless: if the king found out how bad it was, he might throw Morana out on the streets.

He eyed the red rags that filled the waste bin, the blood his mother had coughed up; the Red Blight showed no sign of slowing. Ares had lost count of the number of healers he had hired to examine Morana. It had been a few months since Ronan had provided the last supply. Ares wondered when it would be possible to procure more vials.

"You look sad, son."

His mother's voice was soft and warm. Always filled with kindness. It broke his heart. She didn't deserve what the Fates had handed to her.

Ares lifted his gaze to meet her violet eyes. She lay in her lavish bed, sheets covering her legs as she rested her back against the head-board. More color seemed to have drained from her pale skin; her cheeks were sharper than before, lines creasing the corner of her eyes. Life was being sucked from her body. He steadied his breath against the rage that howled inside him.

"I am not," he said.

Morana didn't look convinced. "You may be able to fool others with that mean-looking demeanor, but you cannot trick me, boy. Is it Queen Daria?"

Ares shifted his large body on the seat beside her bed. "Why do you ask?"

The raid of Ikarria was public knowledge now. His mother didn't have to ask for details to know what happened.

"When you brought her to meet me, I saw how you—" Morana stopped herself, shaking her head. "I know you are not happy, Ares. There were times, when you were younger, that I wasn't sure how you felt about our new life, after the Lord of the Vampires took us in. I think I was too consumed with relief that you were finally being taken care of."

He didn't know where his mother was going with this. She gave him a smile that didn't reach her eyes. "Sometimes I wonder if I should have stopped you from accepting Matías's offer of becoming one of his soldiers. You were young and inexperienced, an easy prey to the king's pretty words."

Ares reached for her hand. "I was more than willing to do what was necessary to ensure our safety."

"In the *past*, yes. Now, it is different. I'd rather you be happy, my son—*that* is what matters to me. Do what you must for yourself. Not for me."

His heart stumbled in his chest. "I will not leave you behind."

Morana hesitated, but before she could speak, she started to cough, harsh, ragged sounds racking through her. Though she covered her mouth, red still seeped between her fingers.

Ares grabbed a rag and cleaned the blood from her face. Unease sunk low in his chest; he was running out of time.

"I'm sorry you had to see that." Morana shuddered. "Let's move onto brighter things. I meant to ask: how is Silas doing these days?"

Ares made a face. "Anything concerning Silas is the opposite of *bright*. The male is a thorn in my side."

"Don't be so harsh." She chuckled, covering her mouth with a clean rag. "Remember that, during your Academy years, I tended to his fighting wounds, too. Poor boy did not have anyone to go home to."

"Silas was frail and weak, but his sharp wit helped him survive the Academy. He proved to be a valuable soldier, otherwise I wouldn't have kept him by my side all this time. He has changed a lot."

"Well, I am glad he is your Second. He seems to serve you well."

"Hm." Ares held his tongue, not wanting to share more about Silas's violent side. He couldn't find it in himself to ruin whatever image his sickly mother had of the younger vampire.

Morana rolled her eyes good-naturedly. "Be sour if you want. Did you know that he still visits from time to time?"

Ares's eyes widened at that. How very uncharacteristic of the vampire he'd known for years.

He decided to change the subject. "Have you packed?"

For the first time that day, Morana's eyes brightened. That was more than enough for Ares to know it was the right decision.

She patted the sheets. "My bag is under the bed; I'm ready whenever you are."

Though Ares had been in Soleira a short time, he'd made quick work of setting up his plan. "We leave tonight."

At midnight, he led his mother out into the castle gardens. Water gurgled from the fountains, and crickets chirped to the moon. Marble statues were columns of silver light in the dark, guiding them to the gates of the palace. Ares's eyes darted to every corner and shadow. He could have gone for a bloodroot right about now.

"I have never seen you so nervous," Morana whispered, staying close to his side, though her breathing was growing more and more ragged with the effort. "I appreciate what you are doing, Ares, but I am happy to stay here. It would be safer if you go on without me."

He gritted his teeth. "You have sacrificed so much for me already. It is beyond time that you finally live the peaceful life you deserve."

"I am not the only one who has made sacrifices." Her eyes seemed to glisten as she reached for him.

She squeezed his arm and something in Ares's chest ached at the touch. He couldn't remember the last time he'd allowed himself to merely be a son...

They reached the stone ledge that faced the sea. In the distance, ships bobbed at the docks, the capital's torchlights twinkling like stars. This was the spot Daria used to frequent, where she would gaze at the capital spread out below, at the ocean, and the sky. The breeze would comb its delicate fingers through her hair, one strand sticking to the corner of her mouth—

He shook his head. The Queen of Ikarria should not be occupying his mind.

"Ares." His mother's grasp around him tightened, her wide eyes on something ahead of them.

Every bone in his body tensed as a coldness ran through his veins.

Someone was standing under an orange tree. An archangel with wings as white as snow.

The general inhaled a deep breath as he met the ice-blue stare of the newly crowned High King. *Erebus.*

"Good evening, General."

SEVENTEEN

Zara wasn't able to reach the Primordial of Death again for weeks. Nor did she have another sudden burst of strength, like she had in the jungle, near the waterfall. The only glimmer of hope was when an update from Daria arrived, courtesy of one of the shadow dealers' firebirds.

Her sister informed them that, as she was in good graces with Queen Kamari, she would request an audience with her and would help them get into the royal grounds of Nephtyr. Ronan thought it was a good idea: they would need to obtain permission to enter the Oasis.

The thought of seeing Daria had Zara's heart jumping in anticipation. Motivating her.

Under Ezrah's instruction, her mind was becoming stronger every day.

One night, she awoke in Mikatán's throne room. Dusk and dawn light illuminated the dark stone, causing the water channels around it to shimmer. The air felt cool and carried the scent of roses.

Zara groaned as she pulled herself up to her feet. She paused, her hand going to her throat. "Hello?"

"That's new." The god sat on his throne, half-shrouded by darkness and half-touched by the sky's light. "You are becoming more powerful, if you can now speak in this place."

Zara cleared her throat, her voice coming out raspy. "My body still feels heavy."

"Fortifying your mind is like building a stronger bridge for your spirit to connect with me," Mikatán said. "That's as far as you will get here. Speaking to me is all you need."

She tried to peek out the windows, only to see vast jungles and forests stretching out in the distance. "Is this place Celestrea?"

"It is my domain in Celestrea, yes. If you are wondering whether you can venture out there, it would be futile. These *dreams* are only meant for us, a patron god and their chosen mortal to speak with one another."

"May I ask… Why me?"

Zara met that ethereal gaze. The silver mists in his eyes swirled, fog above the sea.

"The ether may have selected you to have this power, but you have always been mine. As I have always been yours." Mikatán rose from his seat, sauntering down the dais and onto the slabs of stone that Zara stood on. The god paced around her. "You've been my reaper, mercenary. While you may not have wanted that life for yourself, know that I was always watching over you. In awe of your resilience."

Somehow those words softened the thorns in her heart; they were a gentle darkness that folded around her. Night woven with the stars.

"I wanted to ask you about the Oasis of Dreams," she said. "Can we use it to strengthen our powers without having to complete the Crossing?"

The Primordial of Death towered over her, his necklace of bones and teeth swaying with the breeze. "The Oasis can certainly amplify your ether, but that will be short-lived, as the Crossing is the only way to keep your abilities. Tell me, little goddess, is that what you want? To eventually lose your power? To have a shorter life-span?"

Zara's vision blurred, her connection to the god on the verge of dissolving. "Of course not. My power is a part of me, why would I want to be separated from it?"

The god chuckled, and the sound echoed throughout the dark chamber, causing the waters to ripple. "Because of your enemies? The very forces that threaten the existence of your kind? They want your ether. They'll kill to get it. Destroy the world as you know it."

"The world has never done anything for me, and yet I will still try to save it." She clenched her teeth. "*I choose what I can do with my abilities.*"

Mikatán leaned down toward her. "You sound like her."

The god's voice had softened. It piqued Zara's curiosity. "Like who?"

His gaze jerked up, looking somewhere in the distance above her head. "You need to wake up."

Her vision blurred again. "Why?"

"Zara Santos, find me in the Oasis. Now *wake up.*"

She staggered back a step. "No, I just found you again. I have so many questions—"

The god of Death pressed a skeletal finger against her brow. "*Someone is attacking you.*"

Zara opened her eyes to a heavy weight on her body and a thick hand clamped around her mouth. Silver armor, a pair of wings, and a dagger aimed for her chest. An Elios soldier—an assassin—was in her room.

The male glared at her under the moonlight. "Don't make a sound. I was ordered not to kill you, but if you make this difficult… *accidents* can always happen."

Hot fury and icy fear rushed through her. She bucked underneath the archangel, willing every tendril of ether to attack, but she had already expended her power speaking to Mikatán. Her limbs were sluggish, and her mind foggy.

The assassin squeezed her neck. Zara grabbed his wrist while punching his chest weakly with her other hand. Her legs slipped against the bed sheets as the male pinned her down. Stars scattered across her vision, darkness slipping in from the corners.

He was going to overpower her. The realization sunk low in her chest.

Zara tried to speak, but the archangel only tightened his grip, his dagger still pointed at her chest. She batted the weapon away and the tip of the blade sliced her skin.

A thin rope of blood splattered across the bed, her cry of pain muffled when the assassin slammed his hand over her mouth again.

As her world darkened, one image lingered. A single face adored by the night and the setting sun.

She thought his name. *Ronan.*

The doors to her room blasted open. A shadow, lined by ethereal blue light, yanked the male off her, hurling him across the room. The assassin crashed through furniture, an explosion of wood and stone.

Zara gasped for air, coughing and wheezing. Her vision swam, though she recognized the dark wings and silver eyes landing before her.

"My Zara, I'm sorry I'm late." Ronan's voice was low, kind, yet brimming with something more dangerous. He gently helped her sit upright. His hands hovered over her skin as he scanned her body. She noticed how he kept a modest distance from her. "Are you hurt? What did he do—"

Ronan froze, staring at where the assassin's blade had cut her chest. The blood no longer ran, but her nightwear was stained with red. The light in his eyes winked out, replaced by a darkness that caused Zara's senses to go taut. His gaze lifted to her neck and the air rumbled.

"Fingerprints," he said, quietly, as if speaking to himself. "There are fingerprints on your neck."

Zara's voice was ragged. "My ether is already starting to heal me." She touched her neck and winced.

Ronan bowed his head, his dark hair covering his eyes and hiding whatever expression was on his face. Zara thought she saw his body tremble before he straightened.

He was silent as he stalked toward the assassin who was still hunched over, struggling to get up. The bed chamber was bathed in night and starlight, but it was nothing against the blue ether that filled Ronan's eyes.

"How *dare* you." With a flare of his power, the archangel kicked the assassin in the gut, sending him flying against the wall. There was a loud crack and the Elios soldier shouted in pain. *"I will tear you apart."*

Ronan pinned the male to the ground and began punching him. He was relentless, slamming his knuckles against the assassin's face, the sounds of crunching bone and gurgled breaths reverberating in the room. The soldier tried to fight back, slapping his hands against Ronan's chest, his boots sliding along the ground. Blood splattered the floor, the walls.

Something about the scene before her had Zara moving toward them. "Ronan, I think that's enough." But the archangel didn't stop, as if he couldn't hear her. "Ronan, *stop.*"

Just then, Orion and Axar barreled into the room, the latter looking like he's just woken up.

"Are you okay?" the shifter breathed out, his eyes widening at the blood on her chest.

"Ronan, enough." The brawny archangel grasped Ronan's arm before he could land another hit and managed to pull him away. The assassin's face was broken beyond recognition. "Don't kill him yet. He's more useful to us alive."

Blue mist curled from the corners of Ronan's eyes. "No."

The archangel struggled out of Orion's grip and grabbed the assassin by the head and shoulder. Without another word, he snapped the male's neck.

Silence hung heavy in the room, except for Ronan's shallow breathing. The other two males stared at the blood-ridden scene in shock.

Ronan straightened. Red stained his clothes, droplets beading along the tattoos on his bare) chest. His ruined hands trembled.

Zara watched him. The male before her in that moment wasn't the King of Damalis but the leader of the Sombra Quarter. The one who had tamed the underworld. Or perhaps they were one and the same.

She slowly approached him. "Are you all right?"

Ronan looked at her, his eyes softening. But he didn't respond. Instead, he addressed Orion. "How in the fucking Suns did someone get past our defenses?"

Orion looked just as displeased. "They must have used the scouting party debacle in the jungle as a distraction, and snuck into the palace. I hate to say it, but for them to have remained undetected this entire time is impressive."

Ronan gritted his teeth. "Leave it to Erebus to send someone after us in the most underhanded way possible."

Zara's gaze lingered on the assassin's lifeless body. Red pooled across the floor, nearing her bare feet.

"Have staff clean up this mess and get the imperial soldiers to sweep through the palace as well as the city. Inform Riyad of what happened tonight." Ronan's expression was unreadable as he spoke to Orion. Those gray eyes met hers. "Apologies, Horizon, but it looks like I ruined your room. You're coming with me."

Zara frowned. "Wait, Ronan—"

He didn't answer as he swept her into his arms. The last thread of her strength was slowly fading, and Zara could only watch as Ronan carried her to his bedchamber.

Dark wooden furniture and indoor palm trees greeted them. Bookcases stretched high along the back wall, a massive desk before them. Scrolls, tomes, and canisters of tattoo ink were stacked atop its surface, heaps of swords and fighting leathers strewn about. Some weapons had been propped against the desk or on a dark blue rug on the floor, together with books and other objects. It was a mess. A beautiful mess. Just like Ronan.

And the room smelled like him, the scent of jasmine strong in the air.

On the far wall of the chamber, wooden doors were swung open onto a wide balcony, allowing the night breeze to brush against the ivory curtains.

Ronan took Zara into the bathing chamber, settling her on the counter before searching through cupboards for something. "Can you lower your shirt for me?"

She blinked at him. "Why?"

He placed ointments and bandages next to her as an answer. Of course. Zara gritted her teeth as she shrugged the nightwear down to reveal the cut across her chest.

The light was still dead in Ronan's eyes as he moved closer. "May I?"

Zara nodded. She was quiet while he cleaned her wound. As expected, her ether had already begun to seal the gash, though it left her flesh feeling tender. The energy around the archangel still rumbled, though it was much calmer compared to earlier.

He glanced at her neck, and something feathered along his jaw. "The bruises are starting to fade."

Zara thought of what she'd witnessed in her room. She grabbed his hand. "Do you want to talk about what happened?"

Ronan searched her gaze for a moment, the silence almost painful. His throat bobbed and his voice dropped to a whisper. "It's just… The thought of something happening to you *terrified* me. And I was lost."

He lowered his head, resting his brow against her knee. "Forgive me for crossing our boundary and touching you like this, but I—I'm sorry I didn't arrive sooner. I promised to be your blade, to protect you… and I *failed*."

Zara couldn't help the warmth running through her at the emotion in his voice. The sincerity there was undeniable. She didn't know what she'd done to deserve it.

She placed her hands on his head, in his hair. "Not once have you failed me, Ronan Menodora, and you didn't tonight."

They stayed like that for a while, the archangel on his knees before her. They lingered in the quiet together, silently tending to wounds that could not be seen by the naked eye. All while knowing this was only the beginning of their fears.

After Zara had washed and put on different nightwear, she sprawled out on Ronan's bed, the black silk sheets cool against the bare parts of her skin.

The archangel walked in from the bathing chamber. He was shirtless, wearing only loose-fitting trousers, the tattoos decorating his arms, chest, and neck on full display. His hair was damp, body now rid of the blood.

Ronan stilled when he saw her on his bed. His throat bobbed before he averted his gaze. "I'll keep watch tonight." He cut off her protests. "I won't be able to sleep, anyway."

Zara wasn't sure why he seemed so unsettled—he was the one who'd offered his bed to her in the first place.

"Thank you," she whispered.

Ronan nodded and sat on a cushioned seat beside the entrance to the terrace. The archangel looked so tired.

Nyota appeared through the open doors and settled beside him, leaning over the armrest to nuzzle his arm. Ronan sighed.

Zara stared at him for a while. She didn't think she'd be able to sleep knowing how distraught he was. Her gaze drifted to the needles and canisters of ink on his desk. It had been some time since Zara had seen him tattoo anyone, the last having been when he worked on Orion's back.

Ronan followed her gaze. "Looking to fill the fyrebrand's spot?"

"I hadn't thought of that." Zara glanced down at her wrist, at the empty space amid the myriad of tattooed skulls and vines all along her forearm. "Any ideas on what I should have?"

His expression was still tense. "Nothing will ever brand you again, so you are free to decide."

The fyrebrand had been forced onto her and the other mercenaries by Raziel. She was free to choose now, and the thought of Ronan tattooing her, when he'd had his own type of brand on him... felt fitting.

She smiled softly. "I'll think about what to have."

As the night deepened, the sound of chirping crickets rose louder. Eventually, the archangel seemed to relax.

Zara tried to sleep. The temptation to reach for him, to comfort him, that almost had her going to him, was invaded by that same *sickening* sensation. Hakim and Eshe's final words echoing in her mind...

Close your eyes.

My pup.

It bit through her insides, gnawing at her heart. The past could never be changed. Zara should remember her mistakes and be *satisfied* with what had been.

Whatever Zara wanted from the archangel could never go beyond this working relationship—this *friendship*. How dare she wish for more?

Those silver eyes lifted to hers, oblivious to the ache that howled inside her. "Sleep, Santos. I'll be right here."

EIGHTEEN

I t was deep into the night when Ronan decided to head to the royal training ground. He couldn't sit still any longer. Ever since his ether had acted out in the jungle, it hadn't quite calmed. The energy in his veins festered, constantly nipping at his skin.

Zara had been fast asleep when he left; he hadn't been able to stop himself from brushing the back of his hand against her cheek. She had been in danger—and so close to being taken from him. Seeing her there in his bed, knowing she was safe, was the only thing tethering him to sanity.

Ronan reached the palace gardens and trudged up the steps along the side of a limestone cliff, palm trees swaying below. Pink and blue plants tugged on his trousers. He stretched his wings, the tips of his black feathers blending in with the dark.

The back of Ronan's thighs burned, the pounding of his heart growing louder with every step. Dread grew the closer he got to the grounds. He stopped. *It's too soon*, he thought. He shouldn't be going there. What was he thinking?

He was about to turn back when something fluttered in Ronan's peripheral. In a blink of an eye, he had his dagger out—only for his blade to meet an explosion of silver light, like butterflies made of stars, dancing and twirling in the dark. For a breath it was too bright to see, but once his eyes adjusted, he saw a boy, an archangel, his back to Ronan.

The child wasn't corporeal; Ronan could see the trees and plants *through* the young male, his white wings shards of moonlight. So familiar. Now this was new. Ronan had come across many wondrous things that surpassed basic understanding, both within the mortal and ethereal world. However, never had he seen what looked to be… a ghost? Spirit? Some anomaly that was neither one of those things?

Before he could say anything, the boy turned around. Ronan's breath hitched. Water-blue eyes. Silver-white hair. He would never forget how Erebus looked as a young boy. He knew the male was alive, so it meant that this version of the archangel was neither a ghost nor a spirit. Something else entirely.

The child wore an older style of Damalisan fighting leathers, small and light to fit his body. His hair was shorter than it had been at the coliseum, barely reaching his shoulders.

The young archangel folded his arms. "*Hurry up.* You have already been late to training three times this past week! How many times do you expect the rest of us to wait for you?"

Yes, that was definitely Erebus. Something in Ronan's chest twisted. This was the work of ether, surely.

The archangel tried to take a step toward the boy, his knees nearly buckling. He opened his mouth to speak when another voice interjected—

"You can be such a busybody, Erebus. You're just as guilty as I am! Who helped me get those sweets from Ezrah's secret stash?"

Ronan felt the world slow as another child strode up the steps. He recognized his own face, big cheeks and a wide smile—he couldn't remember the last time he'd smiled like that. Young Ronan's hair was longer, tied back with a leather band that bore a silver sigil labeling him as the Crown Prince.

Erebus scowled, which only made Young Ronan laugh. The two archangels bumped their shoulders together as they continued walking up the steps.

Unseen hands clamped around Ronan's throat. There was a hum

in the air, and he knew it was the ether calling; his own power stirred within his veins, plumes of deep blue mist rising from his skin.

He reached out into the void and searched for Nyota's presence. His nahual was back in the palace, watching over Zara, but she still felt him.

Are you well? she asked. *I can sense your unease. What is happening?*

Ronan gritted his teeth against the strain of his ether. *Not sure, but it feels like my ether is reaching another level. Do not worry, I need to see this through by myself.*

Nyota growled through the veil though stayed put. It wasn't something she would be able to help him with. This was an obstacle designed only for him.

He blinked, and the world around him turned bright. The plants tugging at his pants were replaced by taller, thicker trees. Sunlight beamed from above, the sky filled with eagles and other winged beasts.

Ronan's skin paled when he realized he was staring at the Damalis from his youth. He forced his legs to walk, listened as the clang of swords and the chatter of people grew louder.

"That's it, my son. Keep your elbows tucked in."

"Well done, Erebus! You've been practicing your form."

The royal training ground sprawled out before Ronan. To the side was a building with a deep-red tiled rooftop, its sliding doors open to reveal a wide array of weaponry and cots. The training yard itself was paved with painted stone, etched with designs of jasmine flowers and suns.

Young Ronan and Erebus were there, fighting with wooden swords, their small forms bolts of lightning as they moved.

Ronan almost fell at the sight of the archangel observing the boys from the sideline. King Elijah looked younger than the last time Ronan had seen him, gray eyes sparkling with life. He paced back and forth, shouting command after command.

Ronan's father. And he was standing right *there.*

This was a memory. Through his ether, Ronan was somehow able to see the past.

Queen Miriam appeared. She looked beautiful… with her long

hair and dark eyes, little Hael in her arms. Ronan's mother cheered for the two boys while his younger brother watched with big eyes. The king turned and placed a kiss on each of their temples.

Ronan sucked in a breath. "Why am I seeing this? What is the purpose here?"

There would be no response, this he knew. The world shifted before him, the blue sky above peeling back into night. The trees around the grounds faded away as different plants reclaimed the dirt. The beautiful painted stone became faded and cracked; the red tiles deteriorated into broken shards.

And his family disappeared like sand within the wind. Ronan let out a pained breath.

It took every shred of willpower for him to move forward. His boots brushed against the dust. Weeds punctured through the cracks, reaching for the night sky.

The archangel stopped when he reached the blackened center of the courtyard. He couldn't tear his gaze away from the spot that had haunted him for so long. Cold sweat broke out across his skin.

Suns, why did he come here? Why did he think he was strong enough?

Ronan sank to his knees, the charred stone of the small crater mere paces away from him.

It was where he had killed them. His family.

He could see his mother and father, how they had tried to escape the ether he couldn't control. Their screams that followed him for years.

Ronan clutched at his chest and lowered his head until his brow touched stone. Tears spilled from the corners of his eyes, but he didn't wail. Not a single strangled cry tore from him as his heart continued to bash against his chest. It hurt to breathe.

His brother had been there as well, their parents trying to shield him from Ronan's untamed power.

"Hael," Ronan whispered. He gritted his teeth, sucking in air. "I'm so sorry."

The archangel couldn't shake the image of his little brother cowering on the ground as Ronan's ether washed over them all. It had blinded Ronan, his rage—his anguish.

Loose stones began to tremble. The air hummed and the surrounding trees rustled. Ronan didn't lift his head to watch his power pour out of him. How the energy of his ether caused pieces of rock to rise from the ground.

Ronan couldn't—couldn't do this. Suns, he shouldn't have returned home.

His body slackened, and he reigned in his power. The levitating stone thudded to the ground and the trees stilled. Ronan fought for breath, waiting until his heart rate slowed. He closed his eyes as he remembered the gentle touch of a particular mercenary, letting it ground him. His mind conjured green eyes and callused hands that touched his cheeks.

Ronan Menodora, you are safe.

Zara had said those words to him. But it was different now. These vivid memories hadn't come to him in a while, but it made sense for them to start again, now that he had returned to Damalis.

Ronan stayed like that for what felt like hours. Until a steady hand clasped his shoulder.

"I figured this is where I would find you." Orion Solterra's voice was warm and gentle.

Ronan's head felt heavy as he lifted his gaze to his brother, crouched beside him. "I think I have started the *Izcali.*"

"Didn't you go through the morphing of your power when you went to Celestrea all those years ago?"

"I did, but it wasn't like this. Back then, my ether did grow. Too much I suppose for my younger self to handle. My parents probably should not have agreed to my request to attempt the Crossing. Perhaps my father wanted me to learn on my own that I wasn't ready for it." He glanced at the empty space where his ether-binding tattoo used to be. "This time, the *Izcali* seems to include being able to see the past. Bits and pieces of it, at least."

For a few moments, neither of them said anything. Then his brother squeezed his shoulder. "I wanted to apologize to you, Ronan."

"Why?"

"You were struggling with so much more than a mere hatred toward your ether. A deep-rooted pain was connected to it, and all I did was push you to return to your powers. So that you could reunite with your *destiny*." Orion shook his head. "I was a selfish fool. I should have been a better brother to you."

Ronan swallowed the emotion that gathered in his throat. How could Orion believe he would ever think less of him? The male beside him had saved Ronan from the Iron Isles. Had helped him come to power in the Sombra Quarter.

"There is nothing to apologize for," Ronan said. "I was slipping toward an endless darkness, and you kept hold of me, even when you had your own pain. I should be thanking you."

Orion gave him a soft smile. "Let's go. The soldiers are doing their rounds; they found no other intruder in the palace. And I think Ezrah left some pastries in the kitchen."

Ronan slowly got to his feet, giving the blackened center of the courtyard one last look. All these years, he had run from his past, thinking the memories would disappear with time.

Everything was different now. There was more at stake—people he wanted to protect. Including a certain mercenary. Ronan was tired of hiding.

He would face the shadows.

Even if they killed him.

NINETEEN

"Your Majesty."

Ares bowed to the archangel, even as he took a subtle step in front of his mother. Fuck. This was not supposed to happen. Erebus had hardly made any public appearances since his ascension to the throne, keeping only to the necessary meetings with the court.

Ares hadn't seen him since the destruction of the coliseum. The damn Fates were playing a cruel joke for the High King to decide to come out tonight of all nights.

Dread churned inside him. He'd put his mother in danger. If Matías got wind of this—if the vampire king learned what they intended to *do*… Ares couldn't bear the thought.

Erebus's gaze went to Morana and then to the bag Ares held, his large wings flapping once before folding over his back in a graceful swoop. The archangel said nothing, his expression unreadable.

A breeze rustled the trees, carrying the scent of orange and salt, the low hum of distant music reaching them from the capital. Small clouds of glowing bugs fluttered by.

"Return to the suite," Ares said, offering his mother's bag to her. His voice was low and broken. "It really was a nice evening for a walk."

Morana took a step back toward the castle and murmured, "Are you sure?"

He kept his eyes on Erebus. "I will see you when I return to Soleira."

It wouldn't be until after his time in Ikarria, however long that would take. His mother knew this. She whispered another sad farewell that had his heart cracking before retreating back through the gardens.

It was only Ares and the High King now. The vampire took a moment to survey the archangel. His silver hair had grown longer since the last hunting season, almost reaching his waist. His blue eyes were ice and steel, sharp and unfeeling.

"A wise choice." Erebus's voice was low. Almost gentle.

Invisible hands squeezed Ares's lungs. He exhaled through his nostrils, willing the slight tremble in his fingers to still. Suns Above, he'd never experienced such visceral emotions before. It was unsettling.

"Will you tell Matías?" He knew it was foolish to ask such things, especially to the High King. But that didn't matter when the Lord of Vampires could harm his mother in retaliation.

Erebus brushed stray leaves from his sleeve. "There is no need to stir any unnecessary commotion, and I am not in the mood for Matías's erratic behavior." He walked toward the vampire, stopping mere inches from him. They were the same height, but somehow the archangel seemed to look down on Ares. "Your vampire business is none of my concern, and I need Matías focused. If I had let you continue your *evening walk* then your king would spend his time looking for you, and for his favourite courtesan. And unfortunately, I need him to complete his duties."

The High King cocked his head, the movement akin to a predator targeting its prey. Ares refrained from taking a step back, refusing to show any reaction.

Erebus's lips kicked up. "I do wonder where you planned to take your mother."

A bead of sweat trickled down the general's neck. Ares kept his expression smooth. "I suppose that doesn't really matter now, does it?"

He wasn't sure if he was being brave or outright stupid. Most likely the latter.

The archangel snorted. "I have been meaning to speak with you, Ares Valdemar. You have garnered my curiosity for some time now."

Ares should've definitely gone for a smoke. "How can I be of service?"

"You were once stationed at the Iron Isles, were you not?" Erebus hummed, as if he were speaking to himself. A whisper of a smile touched his lips. "Yes, I remember. You were assigned to Ronan Menodora. I know this because I was the one who advised Matías and Raziel to place you there."

Ares couldn't hide the shock from his face. Erebus's involvement with the High Throne truly ran deep. And the way the archangel had said Ronan's name... With such familiarity. Who was this male standing before him?

The general considered his next words. "I didn't realize it was you who chose me to watch the King of Damalis. May I ask why?"

Ares didn't want to say Ronan's name. He couldn't trust his own voice, worried that he would reveal the depth of his relationship with him.

Erebus looked to the stars, his profile bathed in moonlight. "When the War ended, everything was in disarray, the world ripe for the picking. Knowing I had the Damalisan king in my possession..." His words trailed off. "I wanted to ensure he had someone *capable* watching over him. Your rebellious spirit convinced me to have you assigned to him."

Ares was unsure what to make of that. Nor was he able to determine the emotion that stirred within the archangel's expression. "I see."

"I'll cut to the chase." Erebus met his gaze. "How did Ronan escape the Iron Isles?"

The world went mute, leaving only a thundering in Ares's ears. A darkness seemed to loom over him, with claws made of shadow, ready to push him over the edge.

Back then, Ares had tried to do his duty and ignore the archangel, alone and in pain. Had tried to tune out whenever the prisoner was tortured, beaten, whenever his shrieks echoed in the damp halls. Until he couldn't.

Something had cracked inside Ares one day. No. More than that. There had been a shuddering within his soul—and he couldn't stand by any longer.

He had started tending to the archangel's wounds after the other soldiers had had their way with him. Had cleaned the gashes across Ronan's body, spoon-fed him whenever the male had been beaten so badly he couldn't lift his arms.

And throughout it all, they would talk. The archangel would whisper stories of a faraway land filled with powerful people. Ares would share about his life with his mother in Adrastea. It shouldn't have happened, this odd, twisted bond between prisoner and guard. Perhaps it was simply the result of two lonely young men needing to confide in someone willing to listen.

Ares never believed it would go further than that. But when they tore Ronan's wings from his back, when Ares heard his screams… In that moment, he'd known needed to save—

After what felt like an eternity, Ares answered the High King.

"I saw him fling himself off the wall's edge into the sea." Prisoners had tried that method many times, though they always ended up dead. "His body was never found, but everyone thought that his broken wings may have gotten stuck somewhere below the surface, so they announced his death. Ronan had been showing signs of mania for a while—none of us questioned what he'd done. I never could have imagined he had survived." Ares bowed his head. "I failed my duty to you, Your Majesty."

The words he had made himself remember over the years spilled from his lips. There was no response at first. Erebus's eyes had gone distant, his gaze downcast. Almost as if he were far away. Alone.

"I truly thought he was dead." The archangel's voice was low, nearly a whisper.

Ares searched his face. Why did the High King look like he was in… pain?

Erebus blinked, the cracked expression gone. "When I found out that Ronan was still alive, it changed everything."

His wings unfurled, the feathers glowing like snow under the night, and he took to the dark sky, soaring over the capital lights. Ares was left with a thundering heart and sweat beading along his neck. He didn't know what to make of what just transpired. Only that Erebus, the High King, had some sort of connection to Ronan Menodora. He would need to ask that bastard for more details.

Ares rested his forearms across the wall's ledge, gaze lifting to the stars. Memories from the evening of Ronan's planned escape came to him so easily. He could still hear Ronan's manic laughter; it went on for several days, to the point that the soldiers had started to avoid him.

The archangel had fallen into that act, one that sold the idea that he was no longer a prisoner of worth. On that day, a prison fight broke out—initiated by the *insane* Ronan Menodora to distract the guards and prisoners.

Ares had been patrolling the outer walls, waiting, until the young archangel came sprinting down the stone bridge. His bare feet were bloodied, leaving red prints in his wake, a vampire guard chasing after him. The soldier yelled at Ares to grab the prisoner, but just as Ronan leaped, Ares ducked. He grabbed the oncoming soldier's sword, yanked it from its sheath and twisted around to pierce the vampire through his back.

The two young males gasped for breath, staring at each other with wide eyes, the gravity of what they had done settling heavily between them.

In the distance, a single boat bobbed, where Orion Solterra waited. It had been a pain for Ares to hunt down an archangel he'd never met, to convince him that the vampire soldier was indeed on their side. Somehow, however, they managed to pull it off.

Ares threw the dead vampire's body over the outer wall where nothing but rocks and saltwater waited below. Ronan stepped onto the edge of the stone wall and extended a hand to Ares. "Come with me!"

Ares had stared at that red-stained palm, at the cuts and blisters residing there. For the first time in his life, a feather-light sensation swelled in his chest. An excitement, a thrill, a sense of warmth overtaking him at the idea of leaving all he had known behind.

Yes, he wanted to say. *Take me with you.*

Ares reached for Ronan. No more having to kill and fight to show his worth. No more—He froze, his hand just inches from the archangel's fingertips. All Ares saw in his mind was his mother, the woman who had given so much, just so that he could live. The woman who had sacrificed her own dreams so that he could have a chance at creating his own. The woman waiting for him to return. How could he abandon her, after all she had done for him?

It was a moment that Ares would regret, as he took a step back from Ronan Menodora and the future they could've had.

"I'm sorry." Ares had said.

But Ronan had always been persistent. He gave Ares a firm smile, his eyes burning a silver fire. "Just you wait, Valdemar. I will come back for you."

Ares could only watch as the archangel flew into the dusk sky. The wings that should've been broken—healed by a mere soldier—carried Ronan over the sea into the awaiting arms of his home.

Ares closed his eyes, bringing himself back to the present. Suns Above, it had been... nice to relive that moment, despite all the disappointment that came afterward.

The cool ocean air kissed the sweat that had formed along his brow and neck, as he listened to the waters and the distant sounds of the city.

After all those years, Ronan *had* found him again. A long time after Ronan's escape, long enough that Ares had started to think he would never see the archangel again.

The day of their reunion had been a hot one. Ares had been promoted to the position of general and was patrolling one of the markets in the outer district. He stepped underneath a tarp of a shop to look at one of the trinkets in the stall.

"The deal for today is buy one, buy a second at half the price."

The voice, so familiar, had sent a wave of that familial warmth through Ares. Reminding him of that lightness he'd felt on the wall of the Iron Isles.

A small smile touched the vampire's lips as he glanced up toward the source of the voice. "I suppose today is my lucky day."

The archangel had one arm resting against the shop's threshold, and was grinning at Ares. The archangel had grown his hair out, and it had been pulled up with a leather band, a single braid entwined within. Ronan's body had healed from his time in the prison; he had more flesh to his bones, muscle that had filled out his arms and legs. Yet, on that particular day, his gray eyes were a gentle morning fog.

"I told you I'd come for you, Valdemar," Ronan said.

Ares sighed at the memory, a sense of sadness trickling through him. Now, everything was wrong.

The vampire pinched the bridge of his nose. "Why am I so sentimental these days?"

There was no point thinking about the past, what could've been. Ares pushed off the wall, heading to where his stallion waited.

TWENTY

The veil shimmered with a pearlescent sheen. Brighter than Erebus had ever seen it, though he knew it wouldn't last long. Soon it would begin to flicker and be cut off from this mortal world.

"Erebus, do you regret making a contract with me?"

On the other side, the goddess traced a slender finger across the ethereal fabric. The veil rippled like water, swirling across golden eyes. Though he couldn't see her or the world she stood in their entirety, Erebus would always recognize the Primordial who had paved the way for his dream. His Creator. His savior.

"Why would you ask such a thing?"

A smile. "You're right. If you'd had a change of heart, the contract would've killed you instantly. I only wondered if you would have wanted to return to Damalis—especially given the current circumstances."

Erebus could never forget the life he had in the guardian realm. The light that was shown to him, one crafted by the suns and stars. It had pierced through the darkness of his life. Only one person had managed to do that for him. No, two people.

That warmth would only exist in his memories now.

"Damalis couldn't offer the change this world needs," Erebus said.

Khaos was silent for a moment. "I was referring to the long-lost king being alive."

Erebus had known what the goddess meant. Every emotion and feeling connected to *him* were a nuisance. A detriment to his plans, but also what had breathed life into Erebus.

"My connection to Ronan changes nothing. We will capture him and the mercenary."

"I would hope so. Having two godlings against us puts our plans at risk; they would be uncontrollable. We only need *one* alive to satisfy our needs." Khaos's voice lowered. "And there's the matter of the Reborn seeking justice. You know what that means."

"I already agreed to it, did I not?"

There was an edge to his words but he didn't care. This plan had been brewing since the attack in the coliseum. Erebus would not get in the way of the Reborn's justice. He understood that feeling very well.

Khaos sighed. "If only we'd had the godlings on our side from the very beginning, everything would have gone much more smoothly. The Three Sun Gods would have been livid, though, the wretched things." She chuckled at that, the sound joyless, splaying her palm over the veil. "It has been a long time since you visited home. I may not be able to cross over but you can always come here."

Erebus gazed at the world that waited for him on the other side. A sense of familiarity tugged at his chest, though he did not feel the need to heed it. There was no place that was truly his home anymore.

As expected, the veil started to flicker. Ether shuddered, crumbling at the weight of the Primordial's presence.

His jaw tensed. "It lasted longer this time, but the gate is still far from complete."

"We need more ether-born. And we need one of *them*," Khaos hissed. "Continue your work with the portals, strengthen our forces. The others will have caught on to our intentions by now and will be making their next move. You must capture the elf and archangel."

Erebus bowed his head. "As you wish."

The veil moaned and started to disintegrate, a mist of crushed stars. Khaos spoke before the portal could close.

"As for the kingdom of Damalis, ensure that the guardian realm does not become too… bold. Remember my promise: I will make you into a Primordial."

Erebus had nothing to say about the last part—a lie—his expression unmoving.

She and the veil disappeared, a final sweep of energy blasting through his hair. He lingered in the quiet of the Elios catacombs. By now, Ronan and Zara would have realized what he had done to the wolf shifter's mind, and their ether would have started growing, morphing.

The look on Zara's face when he'd revealed his true intentions hadn't left him. The utter betrayal and despair. Erebus was surprised to have felt a slight sting from that—though he supposed that was only natural, given the time he'd spent with the mercenary.

And *Ronan*. It had been so long since Erebus had uttered his name aloud in such a casual manner. He still couldn't believe he was *alive*. A void opened its maws within him.

Two individuals entered the chamber, their aura crackling with energy. Only a certain kind of being could emanate this surreal strength.

Hadeon, a member of the Council, was as loud as ever. "How is our goddess faring?"

Erebus turned to face the deities. "Restless, as usual. She demands more progress."

"Then may I ask why we haven't sent armies to Damalis?" The second member of the Council was none other than Nadira Iryndel, one of the more violent of the group. Which made her more of a nuisance, in Erebus's opinion.

His lips twitched. "As I've mentioned before, the High Throne has been in a delicate position after Raziel's death. The civilians are uneasy and need to be reassured that I, their new ruler, am more than equipped to serve them. Things would be easier if the archangel were still alive, as now I have two roles to play." Erebus brushed a strand of silver hair over his shoulder. "Our battalion will be ready to attack much sooner than you think. I have sent forces to try and capture our marks. The shifter will already be going mad, and I suspect the assassin has made their move as well."

The ether in Hadeon's eyes waned. "You do realize that won't be enough to apprehend them?"

"The wolf might stand a chance. He is family to the mercenary after all—she won't want to hurt him." Nadira smirked. "I wish I could see that Zara Santos's face when the shifter attacks. The male is doomed."

Erebus stared at the deities with disinterest. "Did you think those were the only courses of action I resorted to? Even if they fail, what better way to capture two fugitives with growing godlike power than by wearing them down."

When he waved a hand, snarling creatures draped in dark fighting leathers and cloaks entered the chamber. They were strapped to the teeth with glistening blades, the mortal bodies they once possessed now replaced by their new form. Skin covered with scales. Jaws that no longer had lips or a mouth, only sharp metal-like teeth that stretched along what used to be cheeks. And sharp horns that protruded from their heads.

Surprise flickered across Hadeon's face; even the usually-unflappable Nadira took a step back.

"Specters," the male said. "Fully-transformed specters."

A female snapped her teeth at the deity. Erebus chuckled. "Careful, Hadeon, don't speak as if they are not here. They are one of the many ethereal races that have reached full maturity. Soon, the other specters possessing mortal flesh will reach their true forms, too."

Erebus met the female specter's gaze. She pressed a clawed hand to her chest, sinking to one knee. The others followed suit.

"Beloved Fallen, what is thy command?"

The language of the gods reverberated through the old stone. Words that Erebus had always understood, ever since his childhood in Celestrea, his birth place.

His eyes narrowed. "Send the archangel and mercenary a message: surrender. If they do not abide by my command, show them what you are truly capable of."

TWENTY-ONE

Despite the precarious situation Ikarria was in, business still continued in its capital. It was different, of course, with Adrastean soldiers patrolling the streets everywhere. They shoved and kicked any citizens carrying supplies or going about their day, whipping others as they saw fit. The sight caused Daria's blood to boil. She hid from a group of vampires, crouching between two buildings.

It had been several days since the shadow dealer visited her in the Primordial Sanctuary. The letter for Queen Kamari was tucked safely in Daria's cloak. She had heeded the shadow dealer's instruction to head to one of the businesses under the Sombra Quarter's influence. The woman in the Sanctuary had told her they would be able to deliver her message to Kairos fairly quickly.

Daria tucked her chin low, keeping to the outskirts of the capital. It had been some time since she'd ventured into the city, but she knew the roads well. Evening light bled across the sky, the air turning frigid; small clouds billowed with her every breath.

The streets widened the closer she got to the border. Citizens ambled about, their azure and crimson clothing bright against the dark stone buildings. More vampires monitored the area, their bronze armor grinning under the setting sun. They watched the

Ikarrian soldiers haul goods that were either entering or leaving the capital.

She pressed herself closer to the wall. The Sombra Quarter establishment Daria was looking for was a tavern near the main street that led out of the capital. And it was under the heavy eye of the vampires.

A male voice rose from behind her. "Ma'am, do you need help with something?"

Daria froze. Suns Above, she had been caught. One of the vampires had found her and if they searched her they would find the letter. Sweat broke across her skin. Any hope of finding the dragons and helping Zara would be lost.

"No, I'm fine." She hated how small her voice sounded at that moment. But still, she did not look the soldier's way.

There was the groaning of wood, as if something was being placed in a cart. "It's not safe to be out here, especially when it gets dark. Are you lost? Maybe I can be of help."

Would a vampire soldier be pushing a cart? But it was the gentle way in which the male spoke that had Daria turning around. She blinked in surprise when she saw an Ikarrian soldier. One of *her* soldiers.

The elven male wasn't wearing the usual Ikarrian silver armor, only simple garb. Muscles carved his dark skin, his long dark hair draped over his shoulders, many of the strands fashioned into braids.

His eyes widened. He looked around before ushering her into an alleyway. "Your Majesty, is that you?"

Of course he would know who she was. Daria had made it a goal to eventually learn all the names of her capital's soldiers, but couldn't place him, even though he looked familiar.

She nodded, offering an awkward smile. "I'm relieved to see one of our own."

"Why are you out here? It's not safe!" His words had dropped into a whisper-shout; as if remembering who he was talking to, he quickly bowed his head. "My apologies, Your Majesty. I meant no disrespect."

Daria waved her hand. "Please don't bow. I don't deserve that, not as things currently stand."

"I disagree, Your Majesty. Why are you here?"

She jerked her chin to the tavern. "I need to get into that building without the vampires seeing me. They don't know I have left the castle, and I need to hurry back before they find out."

The male glanced at the main road. "May I ask what business you have there?"

"It's probably safer that you don't know." Daria tightened the hood over head. "Though I will say that I am doing what I can to save Ikarria."

His eyes brightened at that. "Very well. I will help you." He went to the cart he had been hauling with him, and lifted the tarp to show the wooden crates of goods inside. "It just so happens I'm headed in that direction. You can hide in here."

A sense of relief swelled within Daria, and she extended a hand to the elf. "I apologize, I am still learning our soldiers' names. May I know yours?"

He smiled, taking her hand. "You hold the same grace as our King Calderón. My name is Vash, I was one of your father's generals."

That was why he seemed familiar. Daria must have seen the male about the castle in the past. She bowed her head before climbing into the cart.

Several minutes later, they were at the back of the tavern. Vash had managed to pass through the main street without garnering unwanted attention.

Vash helped her out of the cart. "I will wait for you and take you back to the castle, Your Majesty."

Daria tossed him a grateful look before sneaking through the back door. The tavern was practically empty, save for a couple of staff. Right. There would have hardly been any travelers making their way to Ikarria those days.

An attendant appeared from the hallway, throwing a towel over their shoulder. Recognition flashed in their face. "You work fast, Your Majesty. I was advised you would come here soon."

Daria eyed the individual, her low voice low for their ears only. "Are you a shadow dealer or a civilian?"

"Can't I be both?"

"I suppose." She handed them the letter. "Would you be able to have this sent off as soon as possible?"

In the blink of an eye, the attendant swiped the sealed envelope from her hand. They moved so quickly, Daria almost thought she'd imagined it.

"My Lord demands that we abide by any and all of your requests, Your Majesty. Most of our correspondence is handled by a hand-off system—and by our firebirds, the quickest mode of travel in the Continent."

As if on cue, there was a cawing sound from one of the rooms. Probably seeing Daria's uneasy expression, the attendant continued, "Rest assured, this will be dealt with immediately."

Daria nodded. Time was of the essence, they couldn't waste a single moment. After thanking the shadow dealer, she left through the back entrance of the tavern.

Vash was standing beside his cart, hands raised as he spoke to a group of… *vampires*. Daria's blood went cold. She had risked someone else's life over her own needs, and now one of her own would suffer because of her carelessness.

Fire sparked between her fingers; Daria may have still been a novice fighter but she wouldn't back down from defending her people.

She planted herself in front of Vash, fire hissing to life in her hands. The vampire soldiers backed up, drawing their weapons. The male in the front of the group bared his fangs.

His gaze went to Vash. "What's happening here?"

The elven soldier stepped around Daria. "Please don't attack, Your Majesty. These vampires mean us no harm."

Realizing who she was, the soldiers quickly lowered their weapons.

"Ridiculous," Daria hissed. "They are from *Adrastea*. Have you forgotten what they've done to us?"

Her words were blades, hitting them dead center. The head vampire flinched, and his expression dropped. "Queen Daria Calderón, I didn't realize it was you. I'm sorry if we frightened you."

Daria glared at the soldier but recognized him as one of the vampires who had been guarding the doors to the war room when Ares summoned her. The *kind* one.

The fire in her hands dissipated. She glanced at Vash. "Please enlighten me on what exactly is happening here."

He rubbed the back of his neck. "Nothing as grand as you might think, though it may be easier if I show you."

Night had fallen, the dark shielding them from sight. The elf led her to a nearby alleyway that opened up to one of the more secluded areas within the capital's outskirts.

Vash gestured to the clearing. "What do you see?"

Daria glanced back at the group of vampires they'd left at the beginning of the alley, before peeking out.

A group of Ikarrian soldiers were chatting and *laughing* with— with *Adrastean* soldiers. They surrounded a fire pit, lounging between crates and wagons.

She inhaled the scent of burning wood as she gaped.

Vash's gaze lingered on the scene before them. "Many vampires were misled about what the king intended to do in Ikarria. Not all of them participated in the initial fight, even though they were physically in the field."

"Even so, it doesn't excuse their behavior. Those vampires, regardless of their morals now, were still part of the raid."

"Yes, and that is something they will have to carry for the rest of their days," Vash said. He rested his back against the wall, his expression strained. "Is this world not painted in whorls of gray? The history of Ikarria is not so pure either; we had rulers of previous generations who ruled unjustly—against their own people as well."

"So you don't believe that we should free ourselves from Adrastea?" Daria asked.

"I didn't say that. None of this is good, Your Majesty. I am not excusing anyone, but I have come to realize that there are some who do not have much power in what they can or can't do. Some of the vampires you saw come from poor households and have to provide for their families back home. Others were led to believe they were fighting for a noble cause, only to find out that was false. All of them, however, regret what they've done here."

Daria's mind went to Zara. Her sister had committed atrocities on behalf of the High Throne as well, and even though she hadn't wanted that, it didn't remove the blood from her hands. Daria would not prevent anyone from pursuing the path of redemption—Suns Above, this was too much.

"Seeing this camaraderie brings me some hope," Daria said. "Although I am not sure what that means for us in the long term, I am grateful to have witnessed it. Thank you for showing me."

Vash bowed his head. "If anything, it's a reminder of what our world could be."

A comfortable silence fell over them. Until the male vampire approached. She narrowed her eyes at him and he held his hands up in surrender. "I apologize again for earlier, Your Majesty. You have every right to not trust us."

"If many of you have had a change of heart, why not leave Ikarria?"

"Guilt," the vampire said. "I think we all feel a sense of duty to stay and fix what we have done. We stay to support your soldiers, protect them from the abuse the other Adrasteans may want to inflict."

Vash clasped a hand around the male's shoulder. "What he says is true. They have aided us on many occasions." He turned to the vampire. "Would you and your lot be able to help me escort my queen back to the palace?"

The Adrastean soldier thumped a fist against his own chest. "Leave it to us. We will clear the way."

More laughter echoed from the clearing, and Daria's body slackened. She couldn't bring herself to fully trust the vampires yet, but her soldiers relied on them, and she trusted in her own people.

It was not as if Daria had anything more to offer the Ikarrians. She silently sent a prayer to the gods that this would not end in more ruin.

The vampires escorted them back to the castle and then disappeared into the night, blending in with the other soldiers patrolling the area. Torches flickered, amber light stretching toward the old trees that curled over the buildings as Vash walked her to the front courtyard.

Daria felt the same pang of loss when they passed the Seeker, the massive tree-turned-watchtower. Vampires could be seen walking up and down the stone steps curling around the trunk.

Long ago, the dragons had claimed that tree as their own, as part of their home. And now it was in the hands of the enemy. *Daria would make sure they reclaimed it.*

Vash bowed at her. "It seems my work here is done. I will take my leave, Your Majesty. If you ever need me in the future, I am at your disposal."

Daria had a feeling this wouldn't be the last time she'd see the soldier. "Thank you for all that you've done. Please know that this reality won't be for long, we *will* free Ikarria." She grabbed his hands and squeezed them.

His face softened. "I believe in you, Your Majesty."

The truth in his words wrapped around Daria like an embrace. With all the doubt her own court had in her, knowing that someone had faith in her capabilities was more than enough.

Vash's gaze lifted to something behind her and he stiffened, pulling his hands away. Daria felt a tingle along her skin and turned around.

Ares Valdemar stood in the courtyard, his black horse beside him.

The vampire's attire was worn and dirty, dark circles underneath his eyes. He must have just returned from Elios.

He stared, gaze drifting to Vash before returning to Daria. There was an odd look in his eyes, one that she had never seen before. She didn't know what to make of whatever emotion swam in his expression.

Ares cleared his throat. "Don't mind me, I didn't mean to interrupt."

He tugged on the reins and led his horse away. Daria cocked her head.

"Well…" Vash rumbled. "He is a scary fellow."

Daria arched her eyebrow. "Did you ever encounter him on the battlefield during the raid?"

"I did, briefly—but it was strange. The general of Adrastea is a vicious fighter; however, not once did he kill an Ikarrian citizen or soldier, even when they attacked him."

"That doesn't make sense."

"That is what I thought, but I know what I saw. While some of the other vampires killed and destroyed everything and anyone in sight, he did not. It seemed his only focus was reaching King Idris."

Daria frowned at that. "I suppose it could have been a battle tactic, have his armies hold our soldiers back while he accomplished the true mission."

Vash shrugged. She tried to imagine what Ares must have been thinking then. How he felt while betraying her. If there had been any remorse when he broke her heart.

TWENTY-TWO

The vampires were hosting a feast in honor of their general's return and it wasn't long before Daria was summoned to the dining hall. Dread pooled in her stomach as she pushed the main doors open. There was no reason for her to be here. None.

Glasses of blood and alcohol were arranged between the garlands lining the wooden tables, candles burning bright overhead from iron chandeliers. Humans sat amongst the soldiers, allowing them to drink from their necks or wrists. The scene made Daria think of those evening feasts in Soleira, where the salty air was touched with a citrusy scent.

It was during one of those parties that she'd seen Ares drink from a woman for the first time. Daria recalled how her cheeks had *heated*—from embarrassment and… something more.

Atop the back platform, the general sat at the head table. He was slouched in his chair and smoking a roll of bloodroot, one leg propped over the other. Even from this distance, she could see a tempest in his gaze. The vampire was lost in thought.

Silas stood from the seat next to him. He raised his cup. "The queen has arrived!"

All the vampires slammed their fists against the tables, jeering or whistling at her, some making crude gestures in her direction as others guffawed. Daria could feel her cheeks burning. Her fingers twitched at her sides.

"*Enough.*" Ares tapped the burnt end of his bloodroot on an ashtray on the table. "Don't make me kill one of you; I am not in the mood to dispose of your lifeless bodies."

Silas cackled. "Our general arrived grumpier than usual."

Soldiers laughed before returning to their business. Ares met Daria's gaze from across the hall. Somehow, even in the mayhem, a wave of deafening silence stretched between them.

The general beckoned to her with his finger. "Come. Sit with me."

Daria's lips thinned, but she started toward him. The small train of her dress glided across the floor, the silky fabric cool on her skin. Daria could still smell the lavender soap from her bath, her freshly washed hair now plaited in multiple strands.

A plate of cooked meat and steamy potatoes, as well as a tall glass of bubbly wine, were waiting for her. Daria frowned at the food. "Why am I here? I could've eaten in my room."

"It was easier for you to be here; we need to talk." Ares continued to smoke, his gaze straight ahead. "Eat, Your Majesty."

Daria wanted to protest but her stomach growled. *Fine.* She stole glances at Ares while she ate.

He had freshened up since their earlier encounter, his porcelain skin now clean of dirt, his long hair shiny. That familiar rose scent emanated from his long-sleeved shirt and trousers.

"General, are you not going to drink?" Silas asked, licking blood from his lips.

Daria realized she still hadn't seen Ares drink blood during his stay in Ikarria. He might have had his fill while in Soleira.

Ares took a long drag of the bloodroot. Red smoke unfurled from his lips as he turned to her. "I'm more hungry for your conversation."

Daria nearly choked on her food. She glared at him, wiping her mouth. "You must be bored or desperate for attention, if that is your desire. Considering I'd quite like to smash your head against the table."

Silas burst into a fit of laughter, but Ares didn't seem amused. Even though she was sure his lips twitched.

He reached a hand toward her, his fingertips brushing along her jaw. Daria didn't move, her gaze on his.

"I've missed your insolence." Ares tilted her chin up. "Have you been good at following your orders?"

Daria gnashed her teeth together. If only she could torch him from where he sat.

Ares's lips curled, the tip of a fang showing, as he still held her chin. "I've always suspected rebellion lurked underneath that royal exterior. So tell me, what have you learned about the dragons?"

A pause as Daria debated what to share. "I found out that the last dragon rider, King Arzhel of Ikarria, broke the bonds between dragon and rider. I am still researching the reasons behind it. History texts have been altered, so it is more of a challenge than I suspected."

"That is not good enough. You are risking Matías's wrath."

Anger boiled in her veins. Steam curled from her fingers. "It is not as though I have a plethora of information and resources at my disposal."

His expression turned smug. "Do you need Adrastea's help? If you ask nicely, I might grant it."

Hot. Everything was getting too hot. Out of pure emotion or her ether growing restless, she couldn't tell. A dagger of fire formed in Daria's hand and she smacked his fingers away, bringing the makeshift blade up to his neck. Her chair toppled to the ground, somehow hitting the table and spilling a goblet of blood across the surface.

Daria froze just as the tip of her ether-made weapon nicked Ares's neck.

Silence. Every gaze was on them; some of the soldiers had even stood up from their seats, their weapons drawn. Silas seemed more delighted than appalled.

Ares stared at Daria above her ether's flames. "Why the hesitation? You could've killed me and been done with it."

"You didn't try to stop me," she said in disbelief, her grip trembling around her dagger. "You could've done so easily."

"And I can assure you that had you not paused, you would've succeeded," he said, wrapping his hand around hers. The blade flickered out into embers. "Your skills have improved. You've surpassed my expectations."

Daria snatched her hand away. She didn't—didn't know what to think. But she couldn't deny how strong her body felt now, even if it was a mere shred more than what she was before. Perhaps her consistent training was beginning to pay off.

Tension feathered across Ares's jaw. "Looks like this one needs to remember her place."

The vampires began their ruckus again, cheering for their general. He stood from his seat, grabbed her wrist and started to walk out of the banquet hall. Daria struggled against his grip—though it was firm, it was more gentle than she expected.

"Follow me, or I will *carry* you out."

That was enough to get her moving. Anything—anything to get out of here.

They left the great hall and he let go of her wrist when they entered one of the spare offices. Ares was silent as he stared out the glass window, the dim candlelight illuminating his face.

"I finally have you alone." His deep voice cut through the quiet. "Your anger towards me made it easy for me to manipulate the situation in my favor."

Daria blinked in surprise. "You meant to get us away from the feast?"

"I came across something interesting as I entered Dae Asari." Ares turned away from the window, not answering her, a knowing look in his eyes. "Did you forget that I have connections with the shadow market?"

She paled.

"Imagine my surprise when I found out that a member of the Sombra Quarter had sent out a letter on your behalf."

Daria exhaled. "It seems I didn't truly have the confidence of the shadow dealers."

"They didn't say anything to me. I visited the tavern on Sombra business. One less firebird than usual and it wasn't difficult to determine who else would make use of their services in this realm." Ares tilted his head to this side. "Who did you send a letter to?"

Daria glared at him, but said nothing. The vampire chuckled. "Being rebellious again? You should be grateful that I am this merciful. I could discipline you for being disobedient."

Her breath hitched. Candlelight flickered between them, shadows stretching over the bookshelves inside the office. The warm air smelled like parchment and sandalwood.

Daria surveyed the vampire. She had expected this—so why did this distance between them hurt? "I sent a letter to Queen Kamari, asking for an audience."

Ares's brows lifted. "The look on your face tells me you have something up your sleeve. Consider me intrigued."

Daria supposed there was no harm in telling him. She grudgingly explained her findings about Arzhel and her theory that she wouldn't find anything more about the last dragon rider and the dragons' disappearance in Ikarria. How Kairos kept information on all things otherworldly and could even potentially shed some light on someone long-dead. Daria did not reveal about Zara and Ronan's plans to go to the Oasis of Dreams—that was not something Ares needed to know. If at all. The vampire listened in silence the entire time, his face betraying nothing.

"Asking Queen Kamari for an audience without asking Matías first is risky. She may very well turn you over to him," he said. "More work for me. I would have to clean up your mess and appease any tensions."

Daria scoffed. "This is the best way for me to have a chance at finding the dragons. Something *your king* wants."

"And how do you intend on leaving the city?"

The fires within her blood growled at his tone, though she didn't let it show on her face as something came to her. Daria slowly smirked. "Did you think I hadn't planned this far ahead? I need *you* to come with me."

The general folded his arms. "Now I am definitely surprised. I thought you would curse me out and avoid answering my questions. Instead, you want my help."

"Don't get confused on any of this. I merely need your status and influence to get me out of Ikarria and across the Continent safely." Daria stalked toward him, jabbing a finger at his chest. "And if the queen accepts my request, in Kairos, *my* title alone will help us. So if you even think about betraying me again before we get there, remember that I *know* you."

Before Ares could respond, Daria continued, "I imagine you wouldn't want your king and soldiers to know that you have links to the Sombra Quarter. That their beloved *general* has been in alliance with the leader of the shadow markets and long-lost King of Damalis for years."

"Blackmailing me, Your Majesty?" The vampire's fangs seemed brighter in the dim light. He lowered his head, his lips a mere breath from her ear. "Very well. Use me how you like, Queen Calderón."

Daria hated how deep his voice was, how it sent shivers along her spine. She stepped back. "If we are in agreement then we are done here. I will return to my chambers and wait to hear of any progress about our journey."

"I will make the proper arrangements to escort you out of Ikarria. Though that won't be easy."

"Figure it out, vampire." She turned on her heels and strode toward the doors.

Before Daria had made it halfway across the office, Ares said, "I saw your father… he is alive and managing well."

Her heart leaped. *Pater was alive.* As quickly as that relief came, the idea of Ares having been to see Idris in the prison had dread filling her veins.

"Why did you visit my pater? What reasons would you have to see him after the raid?"

Ares didn't respond. He prowled toward her, his broad shoulders lined by the amber light and shadows. "You've been busy while I was away."

A chill ran through her blood. "What do you mean?"

Ares stopped within inches from her. A sound rumbled in his chest. "With that male."

There was a bite to his words. Daria had to tilt her head up to look at him. "Are you referring to Vash?"

"He has a name."

For one absurd moment, fear stabbed through her chest, and she clutched onto the fabric of his shirt. "Don't hurt him, Ares. He was helping me with something. I beg you not to lay a finger on him."

Something swam in Ares's eyes. The violet there deepened… and maybe even cracked.

"The male is fortunate to have someone like you defending him." He gently picked her hand off his chest. "I don't bother with such frivolous matters. What you decide to do on your personal time has nothing to do with me."

How he sounded… No, it couldn't be. Ares couldn't possibly be *jealous?*

Ares gazed at her, as if peering into her soul. Trying to find an answer to an unsaid question.

Daria noticed then the black veins stretching out from the corners of his eyes—something she'd only seen once before.

He turned away and lit another roll of bloodroot, the air soon filling with its earthy, coppery scent.

"You smell good, Daria," was all Ares said as he left the room.

Daria could only stare after him, wondering what in the blazing Suns had just happened.

TWENTY-THREE

Another frustrating round of Junya's Hunt, and the érendira were quickly trouncing Zara. She let out a growl of frustration. Her throwing dagger ripped through the air, tearing the wide leaves apart before striking the center of a target.

Zara didn't have time to appreciate hitting her mark as Río leapt over some tree roots and she had to hold on for dear life. Sweat coated her lashes, nearly blinding her.

A month had passed, and they were still waiting for an update from Daria. There had been no other surprise attacks from the High Throne, so her usual meditation and training routine had resumed.

The next target emerged overhead, a jaguar already scaling the branches toward it. The warrior slid halfway down the animal's side, preparing to hit the mark.

If this were a real battle, what would Zara do? She jumped off her warhorse and landed precariously on the other side of the jaguar's saddle. The érendira didn't hesitate to lunge at her, a dagger in hand.

Zara relished the thrill. She knocked the warrior's arm to the side, swinging her own body onto the jaguar and kicking the érendira off.

The animal snarled at Zara and jumped onto an approaching branch, pushing off it to turn back toward its bonded érendira. The

Horizon used the momentum to launch off the saddle, leaning into her surging ether.

Wind hissed at her ears, tears flicking out of her eyes. She let out a cry as she slammed the dagger through the target.

Every breath burned through her lungs, the muscles in her limbs on fire. Zara hung there for a moment before letting herself drop onto a branch below her, heaving for breath as she lay on her back.

"Shit, that was harder than I thought."

Soraya pushed through the giant leaves, strutting onto the branch. "You're improving. Another soldier would most likely have tried to force their way through the jungle. Not you, though. You are understanding that every tree and vine can be used to your advantage."

"I have to admit, you are a great teacher." Zara threw an arm over her eyes. "I haven't had an exciting challenge like this in quite a while."

Soraya's training had been tearing her muscles and stitching them back, strengthening areas Zara hadn't realized needed the improvement.

The érendira sat beside her, dangling one leg over the edge. "That must be a compliment, coming from a Horizon."

They were alone, surrounded only by large trees shielding them from the sun. Feather-tailed monkeys could be heard chattering along with the songbirds.

Soraya stared out at the jungle. "May I ask you a question, mercenary?"

"Should I be worried? In the time we have spent training, you have never asked me anything."

The warrior clicked her tongue, but paused for a moment. "What—what was Ronan like, as the leader of the Sombra Quarter?"

Ah. Zara could sense genuine curiosity in the elf's tone. A younger sister wanting to know what her brother got up to during their time apart.

"Ronan was cutthroat. One time, I witnessed him cut a shadow dealer's ear off to reprimand them."

Soraya jerked her head to her. "Really?"

"It was disgusting. Many of the Sombra dealers were scared

shitless of him. Yet, the people at the Stone Orchard adored him. And he still held a sense of honor in what he did."

The elf smiled to herself at that. Zara felt her heart soften.

"My turn," she said. "Since we arrived in Damalis, you've been angry at Ronan. Why is that?"

That smile disappeared, replaced by a glare. "Straight to the point, aren't you?"

Zara shrugged. "You clearly care about him, but you have been distant and short with the archangel the whole time we've been here."

Perhaps she was overstepping, but the words had left her before she could take them back. Kenzo yawned loudly from somewhere within the branches, sending a group of birds flying.

Soraya hugged her knees to her chest. "It's not as if I am not happy to see him again—because I am. Truly, I am. But there *is* something that... hurt me, and is still hurting after all this time."

The warrior then told her, cutting her own wounds open and revealing the bruises on her heart. Zara's eyes widened as Soraya spoke, a sense of sorrow pooling in her stomach.

No. She couldn't judge Soraya for how she had behaved.

"I'm sorry." It was all Zara could say.

Tears pricked the warrior's eyes. "I know I should have handled this better, but whenever I see Ronan, I cannot help but feel this—"

"You don't have to push yourself if you're not ready," Zara said. "Though you will have to talk to him eventually."

Soraya didn't hesitate. "I know."

After a moment, Zara asked, "Other than that first day, you've been quite welcoming to us—to me. Aren't you upset anymore about having someone like me in your home? Training alongside you?"

"'Welcoming' is a strong word."

"Fine, you've been *cordial*."

The elf's face was unreadable. "I cannot deny the anger and sorrow I felt at the loss of my people's lives. It was *hard* having you here, but I cannot say the rest of us are innocent. None of our hands are stainless. We've all made decisions that weren't easy to make and done things that have hurt us deeply. So, I will... *tolerate* you."

Zara's lips tugged to the side. "I'd never thought you'd have a softer side, érendira."

Soraya rolled her eyes. "Don't ever repeat what's been said today."

They lingered on the tree branch for a while longer. The sun crested its peak, casting the sky in hues of orange and blue.

Suddenly, an imperial soldier stumbled out of the bushes. Blood coated his armor and he had a hand pressed to his side.

"Suns." Soraya was already scaling the tree down toward the soldier. "Don't move, we will bring you to a healer."

His gaze dragged up to them, his eyes glassy. "Monsters."

"What?"

Zara felt a cold chill run through her veins as the soldier said, "Monsters have crossed our borders."

Sounds of ringing steel and the clashing of ether reverberated throughout the érendira stronghold, the smell of iron and leather dancing above the greenery and glistening waters.

Zara pulled on Río's reins, slowing him to a halt. Soraya rode Kenzo, the imperial soldier clinging to her from behind.

Ronan was exercising on the central platform; Axar and Orion were with him as well—Zara's brother had finished a healing session earlier today.

Ronan was in a fighting stance, fists raised, wraps around his knuckles, sweat glistening along the tattoos of his naked chest. When Soraya shouted for him, he spun around, a wicked dagger of ether morphing in his hand as if he were ready to dive into battle.

When he saw the wounded imperial soldier, the blue ether flickered out from his grasp. "What happened?"

Soraya slid off Kenzo as other érendira came to help the male; Orion could be heard shouting for a healer.

The soldier breathed out, "We were stationed around the mountain region, just north of the border, when a group of—of those specters appeared. They don't look like anything we've ever seen."

Ronan's wings flared. "How so?"

"Their bodies didn't look like those of mortals. Creatures not of this world—" Blood spurted from his lips as he began to cough.

The archangel grasped the male's shoulders. "Keep your eyes open until the healer arrives."

"Our unit was separated," he rasped. "Most of them killed."

"I'm sorry. I will order a search for the others."

When the healers arrived, they placed the male onto a stretcher and carried him away.

Soraya frowned. "I will take a few of my warriors to search for the rest of the unit. But what about the specters? They must still be alive—"

"The specters are mine." Ronan ripped the wraps from his hands with his teeth. "Orion will go with me. Santos?"

Zara glanced at the archangel, just as he flashed her a wicked smile and said, "Like I would let you miss out on the entertainment."

Amusement touched her lips.

Axar puffed his chest. "I will help you, too."

"No offense, Tallon, but I am in a rush and I cannot risk you attacking us. You are already joining us to Kairos; don't push yourself."

It had been decided that Axar would travel with them on the condition that he kept taking the tonic Ezrah prepared for him. As the older archangel had mentioned, her brother had to wait before being able to start his treatment anyway, and Axar despised the idea of staying behind.

The shifter sighed. "Just keep *her* safe."

Not long after, the three of them stood at the edge of the limestone cliffs, the palace towering behind them. Golden sunlight spilled onto the capital below. The archangels were strapped to the teeth, their bodies clasped in dark fighting leathers.

Ronan dragged his gaze down her body and smiled. "Welcome back, Horizon."

Dark gray scales covered her shoulders and torso, a black cloak brushing against her legs. Her twin khopesh blades were strapped to her back. Zara was wearing her mercenary armor.

Putting on the leathers of the Ikarrian guild was like stitching a wound in her heart. Like she was finding herself again, bit by bit. Tears pricked her eyes.

He extended a hand to her. "Are you ready?"

A sense of familiarity and belonging settled in Zara's chest. She had missed the hunt.

"Lead the way, archangel."

TWENTY-FOUR

Days bled into weeks as Zara and the archangels ventured toward the southern region of Damalis. The specters had last been sighted near the mountains, and the landscape soon changed to rocky hills and plateaus.

They decided to spend a night in a gorge, on a stretch of land tucked between a stream and a steep rocky wall. Ronan and Orion started getting the campfire ready while Zara headed to the brook. She splashed water onto her face, the muscles in her legs whining as she stretched. Suddenly she stilled and looked up.

"Can you feel the energy in the air?" Zara asked. "How it silently screams. Agitated. The specters must be close."

Ronan was sitting on a smooth rock, his gaze on the rising flames. "I've been feeling it the past few days, too. It is an ugly sensation."

She sat near the fire, taking one of the meals Orion had unwrapped for her. "You mentioned that your *Izcali* has started. Have you experienced anything else?"

The archangel had told her about how he was able to see the memories of his past. Ronan, who had struggled to face his trauma, now had to walk through those shadows as part of his power's growth. A cruel irony.

"The memories haven't come in some time." He chewed on his food, glancing up at her. "How about yourself?"

"Nothing new yet."

Orion grunted. "There is no way for you to have a hint about the abilities you'll be manifesting, is there?"

Ronan shook his head. "No. It's said that as we get further into our metamorphoses—our *Izcalis*—the powers will provide an insight on the kind of Primordial we could become."

The kind of Primordial we could become. Like the gods of Death, Life, Nature, and all the others who represented different aspects of their world, she and Ronan could have a place in the pantheon.

Tell me, little goddess, is that what you want? To eventually lose your ether? Mikatán's question made her sick to her stomach. No, she didn't want to lose her power—it was what made her *her*.

Zara turned her attention to Orion. "What sort of ether do you possess? I have not seen it."

"It's nothing extraordinary. And you will find out soon enough when we fight the specters."

Ronan snorted. "Stop being humble." He flicked a piece of bark toward the brawny archangel. The male caught it in his large fist before it could hit his face.

Orion grinned. "This reminds me of our nights as soldiers. You would always wander off into trouble, and Erebus would have to drag you back into camp."

"Please, you joined me most times."

Zara listened to their stories while the two males reminisced. Her gaze was rapt on Ronan, his expression free of the shadows that so often plagued him, even while talking of Erebus.

"You'll be expected to attend the Festival of the Three Suns, Ronan," Orion said, tossing the bark into the fire. "The long-lost king has returned—the people will be very excited to celebrate this year. The Horizons are invited, of course. I already mentioned it to Axar."

Zara remembered them mentioning the holiday that honored Life, Death and Nature, but she hadn't planned on participating.

"Save it, I already received a lecture from Ezrah." Ronan sighed.

He glanced at Zara, a smirk dancing on his lips. "I recall a certain mercenary saying she liked dancing, though hasn't had the opportunity to try it. *Yet.*"

Zara ducked her head. "Don't tease me, archangel. I don't have a problem drowning you in this river."

He chuckled.

"It's settled, we'll all go to the Festival together." Orion smiled, before announcing he needed to go relieve himself.

Ribbons of stars shimmered above. Night creatures howled or chittered within the dark.

Zara felt something curl in her chest; it was the same sensation from before, like it was rushing *into* her from somewhere else. An odd warmth that made her think of the evening sky pouring into her soul, touching the dark crevices of her heart and filling the cracks there.

Zara met the archangel's gaze, his silvery eyes already on her.

Ronan looked at her like she had been touched by the light of the cosmos. Like Zara was so much *more* than what she believed.

That feeling still streamed into her. So powerful and pure.

"Ronan… have you ever been able to sense my emotions?"

He blinked at her like she had caught him doing something he shouldn't have. "What do you mean?"

"Just now, I felt this sensation. A strong wave of emotion *flowing* into me. I thought it was all in my head, but it's happened before."

Realization dawned on his face. "I've felt certain emotions push through me as well."

Zara's jaw slackened. "Are *we* doing this?"

"Empathetic projection," Ronan murmured. He grasped her hands. "It is the sharing of one's emotions. As if there is a door that connects us and our feelings. I think this might be a Primordial power of ours."

Projection of emotion. Suns, Zara's head was spinning. "So, that just now—it was you?"

She didn't want to describe the sensation out loud. It felt too raw, too real.

The archangel's expression flickered with something like pain. Devastation. "Yes."

Ronan was still holding her hands, and she withdrew from him. If it bothered him, he didn't show it.

"Santos." He waited until Zara met his gaze again. "You know how I feel, but I would never push you to do something you don't want, to be with me."

Suns, it *hurt*. Zara swallowed the heaviness in her throat. "I know."

"But know that I will wait for you. As long as it takes. And if you never want to be with me, that's all right too."

Zara clutched onto her chest, as if trying to rip out the agony there. The archangel watched her, the sound of rushing water the only sound between them for a few moments.

"Does being with me bring you pain?" Ronan asked, jaw tensing, something unreadable in his eyes.

Zara felt the back of her eyes burn. *No*, she wanted to shout. *It's not because of you. Never you.* Her lips parted—

A cacophony of screeches echoed from the mountainsides. Chills raced along Zara's skin. It had been some time since she'd last heard the cries, though these were different.

Orion came barrelling out of the shadows. "*Specters.*"

Zara and Ronan pulled away from each other, the absence of his large body near her leaving her feeling empty. She wanted to talk to him, explain that she was haunted by these ugly emotions that prevented her from moving forward. That she *wanted* to move forward.

The archangel glanced at her. "Let's go."

Zara nodded, unable to respond.

The sound of steel being unsheathed rang out, and she was eager to get lost in the sea of battle.

Specters were roaming the stone plateaus below the steep rock wall Zara and the others were on. Even from this distance, she could tell they looked *different*. Bigger.

"It's true, then: the specters are starting to reach their true forms," Ronan observed.

Orion growled. "They don't look like a mere scouting party. They've been sent with the intent to attack."

The hairs on the back of Zara's neck rose. In the distance, a dog barked. Was it a dog? It sounded deeper, throatier than the average animal.

"Do you hear that?" she asked.

"What?" Ronan cocked his head and listened. "I don't hear anything, Horizon."

She waited for the sound to come again, but nothing happened. She shook her head. "It's nothing, I must've imagined it."

They scaled down the rocky wall toward a vast area filled with plateaus, steep slopes and trenches. One misstep and they could slide off and fall into what looked like a gaping void.

They kept to the shadows, creeping closer to where they'd last seen the specters. But when they reached the plateau, it was empty.

Orion cursed under his breath. "Where did the creatures go?"

Her senses started to buzz. The barking started again, getting louder and louder, as if the animal were nearing her. Nyota lunged out of a slash of light, landing beside Ronan; the panther roared at Zara and whatever the nahual said had the archangel's eyes widening.

"Look out—"

Zara spun around, yanking out one of her swords, and clashed with a pair of claws. Black-blue nails wrapped around the steel of her obsidian blade as reptilian eyes met hers. The creature was female, with pointed horns and waist-long dark hair. She had no lips, but a jaw full of sharp teeth that looked made of metal. Patches of scales were scattered about her pale skin.

Blood rushed from Zara's face. So, this was a specter in its true form.

The creature seemed to grin. *"I caught your scent in the wind. Full of crackling light and power. You are who we are looking for, Daughter of the Dawn."*

That forsaken title, one the specters seemed to echo every time they saw Zara. Five other creatures burst from the darkness, charging at Ronan and Orion. Nyota dove into the fray with fangs bared.

Zara pushed her blade against the specter's grasp. Saliva dripped between those metal teeth as the creature grabbed onto Zara's sword and shoved her back.

The Horizon summoned her ether, using its strength to leap away. Zara sheathed her khopesh blade as red mist swirled around her body.

Like a comet, the specter rushed forward, the ground exploding underneath her. Her claws pierced through the small gaps in Zara's armor, puncturing skin.

Zara shouted in pain and struck the female, her fists wreathed in red light. It burned the specter's flesh, though the ethereal warrior didn't waver and crashed into Zara with a force that rippled the air and sent them sliding down a steep slope, darkness's open maws waiting below. The mercenary's stomach flipped—she couldn't grab hold of anything.

In her mind, it was as if a door blasted open, and an icy sensation washed over her. It was so tangible, a metallic taste formed on her tongue. Fear. Fear that was not her own.

Black wings unfurled above her a second before Ronan snatched Zara's hand and yanked her up. He pulled her close to his body as he shot a beam of blue ether toward the specter. Black blood exploded and the creature screamed, falling over the edge and into the trench. Ronan landed on the ground though didn't release Zara.

More specters charged at them from behind and Zara lashed out with arcs of red-purple light over Ronan's shoulder. The ether burned bright in the dark, slicing off one of the creature's arms.

The other specter dodged the attack, its wicked axe carving a path toward Ronan's wing.

He was still holding onto her—he wouldn't be quick enough to avoid the attack. Zara's mind raced. "Lower your wings!"

The archangel didn't question her and obeyed, angling his wings down as she clambered up his body and placed a foot on his shoulder. Ronan instinctively pushed her up and she leaped off. Ether gathered in her hands and she released a torrent of power against the specter.

The creature roared, pushing through the fiery light, its horns visible in the column of burning stars. Even though Zara's power was burning off its leathers and flesh, the specter still managed to press onward, its slitted eyes honed on her.

Zara's jaw slackened. They were so much stronger than before.

Orange-blue energy crackled along Ronan's wings. "Keep it going."

He lifted himself into the air, releasing a wave of power with a flap of his wings. The specter broke free from Zara's ether and, a mere moment before the archangel's attack collided with it, killing it, the creature swung its axe toward Ronan.

The blade tore through the air and struck his shoulder. He cried out, the sound sending her into a boiling fury. The axe clattered to the ground.

Red seeped through the corners of her vision as Ronan fell. Somewhere in the distance, Nyota roared. Before she could take another step, a burning sensation erupted along her own shoulder. Zara hissed.

Nothing had touched her, but the pain emanated from the same place where Ronan had been hit. Could it be possible…? Fucking Suns, this was becoming too much to handle.

That didn't matter. Not as Zara sprinted toward him. Blood pooled from where he lay. Her hands brushed over his face, neck, and chest. *Please, please, please.*

Ronan grabbed her hand, his silver eyes shining. "I can feel your worry, little wolf. I'm okay. See? I'm right here."

Zara couldn't help the shaky sigh of relief. "That was too close, Ronan."

"A mere flesh wound is not enough to stop me." He tried to smirk but it ended in a wince. "Though this one hurts."

Zara glanced at the axe. Its blade twinkled like starlight, made of an ore unknown to her.

"It's astral ore," Ronan said in explanation as she helped him sit upright. "You've seen it once before, remember?"

Ah. Zara had almost forgotten. Back when she had been poisoned,

Ronan had found an Elios emblem, one that only the deities of the High Throne wore. Made of astral ore.

"It can kill a god," Ronan continued. "Probably best to avoid getting hit by it in the future."

That had Zara gritting her teeth. "Are you sure you'll be all right?"

"I love it when you're worried about me." He groaned. "It will just take a bit longer than usual to heal and will most likely scar."

Zara frowned but turned toward another handful of specters running in their direction. Ether flared in her hands just as Orion slammed down in front of her, Nyota flanking him.

An invisible wall, threaded with silvery light, appeared before the archangel. A specter crashed into it, only to be thrown back across the plateau.

Zara's eyes widened. "Shieldwork?"

Orion looked at her, smirking. "Impressed?"

She nodded. "It's fascinating." Growing up as a mercenary, Zara had learned about a lot of fighting tactics and the many types of ethereal power known across the Continent, though she'd never seen a force field with her own eyes.

Ronan cursed under his breath as he struggled to his feet. "I hate to remind you both that we are in the middle of something quite pressing."

The specters came upon them. Ronan and Orion clashed with them, grappling horns and avoiding their metal teeth. Every time their attacks connected with the creatures, the sounds echoed between the cliffs.

Zara was about to dive into the fray when someone grabbed her from behind. She recognized the female specter from before; it had somehow survived the fall and climbed back up from the trench.

Zara could almost taste the dread—it filled her lungs and slowed her muscles. "I thought you were dead."

The specter wrapped her dark nails around Zara's throat. "*You underestimate us, Daughter of the Dawn.*"

Zara briefly met Ronan's gaze. The archangel was pale, trying to fight his way toward her, ordering Nyota to get to her. But there were too many creatures. Not even the panther could push through the horde.

Zara didn't realize how close to the edge of the plateau she was. She should've sensed the creature crawling back up from the ditch.

The specter tightened her grip and Zara scrambled to pull the hand off her neck, but there was no use. The female held Zara's gaze as she stepped off the edge—and they both tumbled into the abyss.

All she could hear was Ronan screaming her name.

TWENTY-FIVE

J agged rocks grazed Zara's side as she fell, spiraling through the darkness and hitting more stone jutting out of the cliff. A sense of helplessness overwhelmed her—she couldn't even scream. Air was punched from her lungs when she finally crashed onto a stretch of rock. She struggled to push herself up, her body protesting with every movement.

She was a long way down from where the others were still fighting. More plateaus and steep slopes stretched out before her, sharp stone peaks protruding from the abyss below.

The specter braced a hand on the wall, pulling herself up, and snarled at Zara.

Zara growled back. "How are you still alive?"

"Even if I were to die tonight, only more would come."

Blood dribbled down the side of the Horizon's face, blinding one eye. She bolted toward the specter.

The creature slashed with her claws, each swipe powerful enough to tear Zara apart, but she dodged the attack in time, the tips of those nails hissing above her skin.

"You will never be free! Do you hear me? There is nowhere you can flee. We will raze every corner of this land to the ground if we have to."

Zara let out a cry of frustration. Adrenaline pounded through her veins, heart roaring. How dare they? How *dare* they?

The specter grabbed Zara by the head and smashed her against the wall. Dark spots danced across her vision, already blurred by the blood as Zara threw up a shield of ether, trying to recreate what Orion had done, but the creature smashed through it. She was forced on the defensive, constantly summoning plates of ether to protect the parts of her body the specter aimed for. But the female was too quick, capable of withstanding the celestial heat of Zara's power longer than most. Other opponents would have fallen by now.

The specter slammed a fist against the arc of ether the Horizon created in front of her torso. Struck it again and again, obliterating the shield and striking Zara's ribs. She could've sworn she heard a crack.

She groaned a curse, sliding down to the ground. A heavy weight seemed to fall over her limbs as she lay slumped against the rocks— blinking through the red, watching the specter raise her claws.

A mirthless laugh escaped her lips. The specter cocked her head as Zara continued to laugh that cold, empty sound. How it wrenched such a visceral, familiar feeling from her.

A part of her had started to believe that she could defeat her enemies, protect her loved ones. But she was still weak. The monsters were stronger than her.

Zara lifted her shaky hands as wisps of ether coiled from her palms. Slowly. Weakly. The power inside her whined, unable to give her what she wanted.

No. Zara couldn't die yet. This was only the beginning. She was *more.*

Somewhere, a wolf howled. Her breath hitched. Was it the same animal she'd heard before?

Silver light exploded between her and the specter just as a black wolf darted out. The same one that had appeared when she needed it most. Back during the hunting season—back when she was on the run toward Damalis.

It dug its fangs into the specter's wrist, wrenching the bone in half. The female shrieked, stumbling back as the wolf grabbed her by the throat.

Zara pressed a hand to the wall, her heart racing. The ether in her tired body sang in the animal's presence. It had been some time since she'd last seen the wolf, except for in her dreams.

The specter screamed and screamed, her hands flailing and scratching at the stone as the wolf tore her apart. Blood pooled along the ground and the ethereal warrior's body went limp. Lifeless.

No nightbirds sang and no crickets chirped. The stars themselves seemed to still when the wolf swung its head to Zara, licking the blood from its muzzle. Waiting.

"You're here." She fought to catch her breath; the back of her eyes burned. "Where have you been?"

Zara didn't understand the surge of emotion that clogged her throat. This urge to reach for the animal whenever it appeared.

The wolf whined, pacing back and forth. It raised a paw toward her but didn't take another step. Or maybe it couldn't.

Zara tried to remember what Ronan had said when she confided in him back in the Kairos temple and told him about the mysterious wolf. What was it again? *Next time you see it, try summoning your ether.*

She extended a hand. Red wisps danced from her palm and floated toward the wolf. The animal touched her light with its snout and a gust of silver energy swept out from the contact, caressing Zara's hair.

It settled, leaving only orbs of silver light hovering in the air around them. Zara fell onto her hands and knees as a truth revealed itself to her. An understanding that went beyond the bounds of this world. One that touched the stars above.

Her throat thickened. "You are my nahual, aren't you?"

The wolf slowly pressed its snout against her arm. Its presence was like a blanket of gentle sunlight. *I've been waiting for you.*

The voice was that of a male, reverberating throughout the air, echoing in the empty spaces of her soul. A sound only she could hear.

Tears filled Zara's eyes. Her voice cracked. "Why didn't you tell me sooner?"

You weren't ready to hear me yet. I've been listening to your soul's cries all this time, but I couldn't reach you. He nuzzled her face as warmth poured along their connection. *Now your heart and mind are becoming stronger—even if you think otherwise. You are finding your place.*

Zara flung her arms around the wolf. The bond clicked into place, one that tethered her to her nahual. *Her nahual.* Her familiar.

She buried her face in its neck. "I'm sorry I took so long."

Zara understood what Ronan had meant. The feeling of finding a missing piece to the soul, one that she didn't even know was missing. The pure loyalty from the animal spirit. An unspoken vow that said the wolf would stand beside her until the stars turned to glimmering ash.

Zara tried to climb the steep stone to reach the archangels, the wolf whining below, but the wall was too steep, with barely any footholds. She didn't realize how long had passed until the two males came flying down to search for her, all of the specters now dealt with. Their leathers were drenched in black blood. They seemed fine except for the bandage wrapped around Ronan's shoulder, a thick red blotch there.

Her gaze turned heavy. "The astral ore truly does slow down your healing, doesn't it?"

"Orion had to treat it, but it is much better than earlier. Good thing it wasn't a critical injury, otherwise I might have been in trouble." Ronan paused when he saw the wolf beside her. "Are you all right?"

Zara nodded, the animal nudging her to her feet. She leaned against it, most of her own wounds already healing. "There's someone I want you to meet."

With the heap of shit they were in, no other moment that would have felt right. Suns, she was grateful for this mercy. This gift the Fates had handed her.

Zara could've sworn silver lined Ronan's eyes. He gazed at her, a warm smile growing on his face. "You have a nahual."

"Shit," Orion said in awe.

"He saved me from the specter." Zara placed her hand atop the wolf's head. "Meet Basim."

During her conversation with her familiar, she'd discovered the wolf had no name. Apparently, it was the bonded mortal's duty to name their nahual. Zara felt the strong-sounding name suited this beautiful creature.

Ronan bowed his head. "It is an honor. My name is Ronan Menodora."

Basim's ears flickered. *He's not bad, I suppose.*

Zara smirked. Hearing his voice still had her heart dancing. *The archangel is better than that, Basim. You know that.*

The wolf let Ronan pet his head and was soon wagging its tail. Orion joined in, murmuring warm welcomes to Basim. Even Nyota appeared, prowling around the wolf, either in challenge or curiosity. Apparently, the two nahuals could speak with one another.

As they started their journey back to Damalis, a firebird descended from the sky. It squawked, landing on Ronan's shoulder. Attached to its leg was a small capsule. One of his message carriers from the Sombra Quarter, Zara realized.

"Finally, an update." He took out a sealed envelope and handed it to her. "It's addressed to you."

When Zara saw the seal, she ripped the letter open, heart pounding.

"It's Daria," she said. Zara met Ronan's gaze. "Queen Kamari has accepted her request for an audience. We can now head to Kairos."

PART II

SILENT WARS WITHIN CRYING SOULS

TWENTY-SIX

Daria waited with bated breath to see whether Ares would follow through on his end of the deal and escort her out of Ikarria. It was a risk. She didn't know what to expect from the general.

Much to her relief, it didn't take long before he got the clearance to travel to Ikarria—much to Silas's annoyance. Perks of being the general of Adrastea. His Second made a fuss about the plan, claiming Daria was deceiving them. That she did not intend to find the dragons at all but beg the Queen of Kairos for help.

Ares had smirked. "Do you think I'll let the queen do as she pleases? Her pleas for aid would amount to nothing anyway—Queen Kamari is loyal to the High Throne. Besides, Daria Calderón is only wasting time here in Ikarria. Should she return empty-handed, she will face the consequences."

Before Daria knew it, she was on a horse—a red roan the general had prepared for her—in the middle of the ancient forest, the Ikarrian castle now several days behind her. She was surrounded by vampire soldiers, a travel party Ares had personally selected.

Her advisors had not been pleased with the plans either, though it was not like they had a choice in the matter. Daria could still hear their doubts ringing in the brisk air.

The Lord of Vampires must know this is pointless.

The dragons are lost! You will never find them.

Daria had resisted the urge to throw her hands up in the air. "How many times must I say that if I don't comply with their demands, our kingdom will be at risk. The vampire king won't listen to me, anyway. At least with the dragons we have a fighting chance against Adrastea."

One of the advisors had laughed. "It's a foolish dream, Your Majesty. You are wasting your time."

"I am doing *something* about our situation, unlike you. And last I checked, I did not need your permission. Remember your place."

She had been met with silence. It was Basira who said, "Can you trust you will be able to accomplish what you need, with the general around?"

"Ares and I have worked together in the past. I'll manage."

She remembered the vague sense of victory at the advisors' reactions, especially the look of genuine surprise on Basira's face. Her advisor had helped train her for weeks, and they had grown fairly close; perhaps Daria should have mentioned it earlier. It was too late now.

The swish of a tail caught her attention. Ares's horse was a beauty, with its shiny black coat and expensive saddle. It was obvious that the general took great care of the animal. He rode ahead of Daria, the night sky rolling out before them.

"Have you ever been to the sand cities, General?"

Daria stiffened as one of the soldiers spurred their horse to trot past her. The travel party rode on either side of her, wine-red cloaks flowing behind them.

The general stared ahead as he responded. "No."

"I heard they have oases filled with the spirits of the dead," said a second soldier.

"Must you always bring up depressing topics? How about we talk about their women? I heard their beauty and combat skill is otherworldly."

"Same with the men, actually. They're all so strong and they line their eyes with an ether-imbued kohl that helps them see through sandstorms."

"Incredible!"

The two soldiers continued chatting loudly and Daria was grateful for their distraction. She tucked her head low, her hood covering her face and sweat dappling the skin of her brow and neck.

They were approaching the border between Ikarria and the Estrella Territories; she would need to find a way to escape and meet with Zara soon. Ares would certainly be angry, but her threat to blackmail him would hopefully keep the general quiet. At least for the time being.

"I wonder if our queen has any exceptional skills…" Daria stiffened as the first soldier turned their attention to her. "King Matías insists on keeping her alive, but I don't get the appeal."

The second vampire chuckled. "Careful or you will upset our general. Word has it Ares has fed from her."

"That's right!" The male drew his horse closer to her. "Tell me, Your Majesty, did you enjoy it?"

Daria curled her lips. "Get away from me."

"I was wrong. I think I see the appeal after all." The soldier grinned. "The more feisty the prey, the sweeter they taste. I wonder if I can have a bite."

"Silence." Ares sounded bored as he finally stopped and turned around. "We'll make camp here. Make yourselves useful and unload our bags."

Daria's cheeks burned. Even though the general had cut the conversation short, it didn't stop the sting from the soldiers' unsavory comments.

Their entourage settled for the night in a small clearing within the forest. The vampires huddled around the fire, eating meat and drinking from blood bags. They laughed and conversed with little care in the world.

When Daria finished her meal, she crossed her legs and closed her eyes. As she had done every night since they left the castle. She sensed Ares watching her across the fire; she had caught him several times, though he never lowered his gaze.

"What are you doing?" he asked then.

Daria fought the urge to grimace at the sound of his voice and opened her eyes. "By the gods, whatever do you mean? I'm simply resting my eyes."

Ares surveyed her. "Don't be coy. You've been way too *cooperative* since we left the castle. It's suspicious."

"Why not simply be relieved that I am making things easier for you? It is only because of your efforts that I can move forward with King Matías's task." She cocked her head and smiled. "I should thank you, General."

Ares narrowed his eyes, but said nothing. The soldiers around them were loud, occasionally trying to engage the general in conversation. After a while, he left the campsite and strode into the forest, a fresh bloodroot tucked between his lips.

One of the vampires leaned forward, whispering to the others. "Our general has been smoking a lot more lately, hasn't he?"

"Rumor has it his thirst for blood has been unquenchable. The bloodroot helps tame it."

"I remember many years ago our king would send courtesans for Ares to feed from. I'm sure he had plenty to drink when he visited Soleira."

"What luck! I wish I was Matías's favorite."

Daria had closed her eyes again, hands back on her knees, though something about what the soldiers had said didn't sit well with her. She knew Ares hated being called Matías's favorite, and he'd never struck her as someone who would drown himself in drink and willing blood sources. He was always practical, never swayed by emotion. Then again, Daria could be wrong. She had been before about him.

An hour or so later, the camp turned in for the night. Except for Daria. When silence finally fell, she sat up from her bedroll. Ares still hadn't returned.

Legs crossed once more, Daria closed her eyes. She thought of the obsidian throne and the energy that emanated from it. The secrets resting beneath that black stone that she would expose. That thought was what helped her reach deeper into the unseen well of her mind until she could touch her ether. The flames shifted at her mental touch.

Every night since they'd left the castle, Daria had been suppressing her fire. Forcing it down, down, down. It boiled deep within her, pressing against the walls of her restraint—waiting for this moment. None of the soldiers had even bothered to question the strength of her ether.

Daria smiled. She opened her eyes and placed her palms against the grass. A plume of smoke seeped out of her lips as fire rushed beneath the ground. The power that had grown inside her funneled through roots and dirt, streaming out to every corner of the campsite.

It was a challenge to keep it under control. With every exhale, fire spiked up between the sleeping vampires and along the edges of the clearing before dropping back down again.

The soldiers didn't stir.

Daria sucked in a deep breath and drew back every tendril of ether. *Now.*

Flames exploded, the night turning a bright red. The fire caught on some of the soldiers' clothing or bedroll, waking them up and throwing the entire place into chaos.

She burned their supplies and food, went as far as singeing the ropes that tethered their horses to nearby trees, setting the animals free.

It happened so fast, though Daria couldn't help the swell of pride at how far her abilities had come. She sprinted to her horse.

"Put out the fire! Where's the prisoner?"

"The bitch ran off! Capture the queen!"

"Someone call for the general!"

The mayhem would give her a head start. Daria snapped the reins and her horse galloped into the forest. Cold air howled into the night, the moonlight occasionally peeking through the canopies of leaves above.

The vampires chased her. They were fast, some firing arrows her way; Daria veered the horse to the side and their weapons hit the trees. When she glanced over her shoulder, she saw the soldiers were dispersing, diving into the darkness.

Daria felt a stab of fear as she looked around, the brief moment of distraction enough for her to miss the low-hanging branches in front. Her roan leaped over a narrow ditch and Daria collided with the wood.

She hit the ground, the air being punched from her lungs. Adrenaline pounded through her veins as she got back up and forced herself into a run. She followed the direction of her horse, hoping it hadn't gone far.

A vampire darted out of the shadows. "Not so fast, Your Majesty!"

Daria twisted, flames curling from her palms, but the ether winked out when the soldier wrapped his arms around her. The momentum was too much and they tumbled down a slope, the vampire releasing her as they rolled. Branches and small rocks nipped at her skin before she slid to a stop. She didn't wait to see where the soldier was and scrambled back up, lunging over more wood and stone. Her breathing was harsh and her legs burned.

Darkness thickened around her as she slipped under an overhang of thick tree roots.

She pressed her body against the wall of dirt, clamping a hand over her mouth and nose. Above the overhang, soldiers ran past.

"Find her! She was right here!"

"I can't catch her scent!"

If she stayed here long enough, perhaps the vampires would venture farther and farther into the forest, and it would be safe for her to sneak away. Yes, she could do that—

Daria froze when a lone figure appeared in front of her. Their tall silhouette was shrouded in darkness, but she knew who it was. Knew it before they stepped into a thin pillar of moonlight.

Ares's jaw tensed as he surveyed her body. "What a mess you've made."

Soldiers appeared behind him but he held her gaze.

"General, you found the prisoner!"

No. Daria trembled. She'd already failed.

Ares gave her a sidelong glance, his expression unreadable. "Close your eyes."

The words were a command, laced with iron. Daria didn't

understand why—maybe it was the deep emotion tucked underneath the steel in his voice—but she obeyed.

All she heard was the sound of a sword being unsheathed.

"General?"

Silence.

"General, what are you doing?"

And then the soldiers began to scream. Daria flinched at the cries and sounds, and slowly opened her eyes. The blood drained from her face.

Ares had become the night breeze. A blade in the dark. His cloak unfurled behind him like wings.

Steel met steel, though the general always remained standing. His soldiers fell one by one, and soon, Ares's sword was dripping in red.

The last vampire, wounded and bleeding on the ground, tried to drag himself away, snarling. "You are no general of mine, Valdemar. Does Matías know his *favorite* is a traitor?"

Ares stalked forward. "How I've longed to kill every single one of you. I chose you all for a reason—I've seen the atrocities this party has committed, even before we came to Ikarria." Ares's sword seemed to shine brighter at his side. "Your souls were beyond saving. Though I'm glad I saved *you* for last."

He slashed his sword up the soldier's chest and the male rolled away, blood pouring from the wound. "I did nothing wrong. Nothing!"

The general bared his fangs. Even the violet of his eyes glowed. "You thought you could speak to *her* however you liked without consequences? You wanted to *feed* from her."

The soldier started to sob. "I didn't mean it, have mercy! I wouldn't have touched her!"

Ares said nothing at first, not as he drove his sword through him. The male let out one last gurgle as the general wrenched the blade deeper.

"You should be honored that King Matías's favorite ended your miserable life."

Daria stared wide-eyed, gasping for breath, as Ares straightened. What had she just witnessed?

"You planned to kill them all along," she breathed out after a moment. "Is that true?"

He wiped his blade clean and sheathed it at his side. "What is your true plan, princess?"

She blinked, ignoring the flutter in her chest at hearing him call her 'princess' again. "I don't know what you mean."

"I had a feeling you hadn't told me everything. My suspicions were aroused while I observed you in deep focus the past several nights; I knew you had a trick up your sleeve." Ares faced her, his long hair swaying with the movement. "You have become stronger at controlling your ether."

Daria couldn't hold back the frustration that boiled inside her. "No, don't avoid my question. Did you really plan to kill your soldiers all this time?"

Ares gave her a blank look. "It is a long journey from here to Kairos; it isn't unheard for a group of soldiers to be killed by a pack of demons these days. What a tragic loss."

The vampire glanced at the bodies littered around him.

Daria gave up, thinking he wouldn't answer her, when he added quietly, "I've wanted to get rid of them for a while, for my own personal satisfaction, yes—but also, to show you my loyalty."

His words wrapped around her lungs, making her unable to speak for a breath. "Your loyalty? To me?"

Ares's gaze lifted to hers. "I am on your side, Daria Calderón, whether you believe me or not."

Daria stared at him, something flickering in his violet eyes as the air between them heated, before he looked away.

"I can't say I'm upset that you got rid of them." She gestured at the lifeless soldiers. "However, you cannot expect me to fully trust you, just like that."

"No, I cannot. But I ask you to at least let me *help* you on this quest of yours." Ares reached a hand toward her, but stopped. His eyes went to the blood that stained his fingers. "Once you find the dragons, you can save Ikarria."

"How can you say that, after all you've done? How can I believe you?"

The vampire wiped his hands on his cloak. His voice was low. "Let's just say I have a bargain to fulfill."

Daria narrowed her eyes, ready to question him further, when Ares continued, "You already know my history of working both for the High Throne and with Ronan. I propose a truce. My life is quite literally in your hands now, just as yours is in mine. I have already removed any hindrances to your progress and safety, and I will continue to be a cooperative soldier at your side, till the end of your quest."

Daria considered his words. "And when all that is done? I doubt you would really let me try to save my kingdom."

He shrugged. "I've given you a fighting chance. Don't let all of my efforts go to waste."

"You are infuriating."

Once again, Daria found herself with limited options. This prospective alliance could help her right now. It was a temporary solution. Until she found the dragons and decided her next step in helping her people. It was a major gamble to trust the vampire with the rest of the plan, but she wouldn't make it on her own in the forest.

She sighed. "Fine. Though, let me make myself clear: I do not trust you. It is simply easier for me to survive if I have you with me. After this ordeal, you and I go our separate ways and return to being enemies."

Ares's expression shuttered. "I'm glad you're seeing reason."

Daria shoved away the unsettling feeling that rose within her; she couldn't afford to be distracted by her emotions.

Though she enjoyed the look of surprise on Ares's face when she said, "We are going to meet with Zara and your beloved Ronan. *Surprise.*"

TWENTY-SEVEN

Daria told Ares the extent of her plans. How Zara and Ronan needed to access the Oasis of Dreams to use as a catalyst for their powers' maturity and why she'd decided to visit Kairos as well. The moon dragged itself further across the dark sky as she spoke and they retrieved their horses, securing any food supplies that had survived the flames.

Ares furrowed his brows. "Do you know how Ronan and Zara are managing their ether's growth?"

"They didn't provide many details." She narrowed her eyes. "It sounds like you know more about what's happening than I do."

He shook his head. "No, not really. I have known about Ronan's… power for some time, and I assume your sister is going through something similar."

Daria realized there was a lot she didn't know. "I heard that Zara and Ronan are wanted by the High Throne because of it. Can you tell me about this ether of theirs?"

"It may be best if your sister has that conversation with you." Ares hesitated, his voice going soft. "You will speak with her soon."

A bitter feeling twisted in her stomach. This sense of helplessness at being in the dark, especially when it concerned her loved ones… Daria's knuckles tightened around the reins.

Ares asked, "Where are we meeting them?"

Daria recalled the directions Ronan had sent her through the shadow dealers. "In a city called Corduva; it sits at the border of the Estrella Territories and Kairos."

The vampire made a sound, like he was impressed and appalled all at once. "And you were planning on traveling that distance by yourself?"

"What else was I supposed to do?" she snapped. "And anyway, Ronan's shadow dealers provided me with a map of the businesses and taverns associated with the Sombra Quarter from Ikarria to Corduva."

Daria made a point to wave the letter from the archangel in front of the vampire. "I have places to stay and to get help from. You're not the only one with access to the Sombra Quarter's resources now."

"It is still dangerous for you to do that alone," he muttered. "You and your devious schemes…"

Daria barked out a mirthless laugh. "That's rich coming from you. You pretended to be my friend, all the while planning to betray me."

Ares halted his horse. She almost considered continuing, but something told her to look back.

The vampire was gazing at her, a silent plea there. "Our… *friendship* was never a lie. It was real. As real as anything like that can be for me."

Daria sucked in a painful breath, his words a stab in the chest. *Then why did you agree to raid my home? Why did you hurt me?* The questions burned through her.

She looked away. "It doesn't matter now. Nothing has changed."

Crickets chirped in the temporary silence, followed by the steady thumps of their horses' hooves as they moved off again. In the distance, four-winged owls soared into the air. Neither of them said anything else.

They soon crossed the border into the Estrella Territories, where rocky hills and valleys stretched out all around them.

For two weeks, they hardly spoke to one another unless they needed to, stopping in the towns and cities the shadow dealers had noted down for Daria. She appreciated the silence and solitude: it allowed her to wallow in her hurt and anger. What kept her spirits up was the fact she would be seeing Zara soon.

Since Ares also had access to the Sombra Quarter, he took charge of any arrangements with the local taverns and marketplaces, ensuring their needs were met.

Most days were sunny and bright, though a downpour had surprised them one afternoon, while they were in the middle of the woodland, and they had to find an alcove of trees to wait it out.

They huddled close, though not enough to touch—Ares always minded his distance with her. And yet, his presence in that moment was so cold it burned. She was always so painfully aware of it. Her damp clothes made her shiver, and she startled when Ares draped his cloak over her shoulders.

"How do you think the city of Nephtyr will help you learn more about Arzhel?"

Daria hugged her knees to her chest. His rosy scent still permeated the fabric of his cloak. "I am not sure yet." She considered telling him about the voices from the obsidian throne, but she wasn't quite sure what to make of that experience herself. And she still couldn't confide in him completely. "His story seems to have been removed from Ikarrian history and textbooks; Nephtyr may have other ways to find information about those who are no longer alive. And there's also the matter of the Primordial contract that I still don't quite understand."

After the incident with the other vampire soldiers, she had told Ares about King Arzhel telling her to find him. The general was quiet for a moment. "Someone went to great lengths to hide the truth behind the dragons' disappearance. I know you will find the answers you are seeking."

His words were touched with warmth, reminding her of their conversations and time together in Soleira. Back when she was the ambassador of her kingdom and he was her bodyguard. Her heart twisted, the back of her eyes burning. A small smile touched her lips. Then she remembered his behavior in the Ikarrian palace and her anger stirred once more.

Daria clenched her teeth. "Your demeanor right now is vastly different to how you treated me in my own home. Now that we are alone and away from the castle, you are almost like the male I used to know. Which one is the true Ares, I wonder."

He growled. "Listen to what you are saying. *Away* from the castle. It was for your safety that I acted that way. If I hadn't, the vampires would have continued to abuse their power. If they don't have me to fear, who knows what they would do to you."

She whipped around to face him, snarling. "And you think that is enough to justify your actions—for me to forgive you?"

Ares didn't wear his cold mask now. Not here. The light in his violet eyes flickered, the lines between his brows deepening.

"No, I don't," he said, softly. "You have every right to be angry with me. I am not asking for your understanding, nor for your forgiveness."

A torturous silence stretched between them. Then, Ares said, "This truce we have is only a means to an end."

Daria felt like she couldn't breathe. Even if he'd acted like the cold, merciless general of war against his will, to protect her somehow, it didn't change what happened. It didn't remove the pain. Her body quivered. Whether because of the chill or her need to cry, she couldn't tell.

That evening, when the rain lessened, they continued their journey and reached a tavern owned by the Sombra Quarter. It was in an isolated farming town, a popular rest stop for shadow dealers transporting rare goods in caravans.

Daria had just finished eating her dinner when Ares sat in the seat across from her. She arched an eyebrow at him. Normally, whenever they found a place to stay, they would part ways for the evening. They'd have their own rooms and eat meals on their own, providing each other the space they couldn't have while traveling through the woodland.

Though this town was much smaller than the others they'd visited, which made it harder for them to avoid each other. At least that's what she told herself.

Ares was making himself a roll of bloodroot, breaking their routine. She watched him sprinkle red powder onto the parchment and fold it.

"How is your mother?" Daria asked when she realized he had no intention of saying anything, or leaving.

It was a genuine question. She had been wanting to know how

Morana was faring. The vampire had been kind to her, and Daria had enjoyed their conversation.

Ares's expression seemed to soften under the dim candlelight. "My mother is doing as well as can be expected. Her illness is worsening, though I don't intend to give up."

"I recall you tried to find healers to treat her, correct?"

"Yes, but there is no cure for the Red Blight." Ares lit the bloodroot, exhaling red smoke. "The medicine Ronan sends helps my mother, but it only provides temporary relief."

Unease settled in Daria's chest. "Perhaps Kairos can serve you, too. Have you tried to see if the realm of the sands may be able to help?"

"I have, Your Majesty, to no avail." He gave her a sad look.

Daria considered if she should say more, though couldn't find the words, her chest squeezing. Perhaps it was something she could ask Queen Kamari.

She was about to head to her room when Ares spoke again.

"There's something you should know."

"Coming from you, I'm not sure I like the sound of that."

His lips thinned. "While I was in Soleira, I learned a few things about what Matías and Erebus are planning."

She listened as he relayed his findings about astral ore. Many civilians filled the tables surrounding them, chatting and clinking drinks, but all the noise seemed to drift away.

Barbed spears made to kill *dragons*… Weapons with the capacity to bring down *gods*. With all of these otherworldly blades, Daria wondered just how bloody the War of the Skies had been.

"Your king seems awfully confident that the dragons can be found," she murmured, meeting his gaze. "Why tell me this?"

Something blazed in Ares's eyes. "Because I want you to stay alive, and win."

Daria was left feeling like she was on uneven ground.

But knowing what Adrastea and the High Throne were up to only gave her the push she needed. So much was at stake. Daria was about to thank Ares for the information when he gave her a soft smile and stood up, striding toward the stairs where their rooms were located.

I want you to stay alive and win. His words lingered in her heart longer than she wanted to admit. Because all that came with them were questions and doubts.

A third week passed before they finally arrived in the city of Corduva, the largest settlement in the Estrella Territories, where the grasslands opened up to the vast sands. Golden dunes crouched along the horizon, waiting for brave souls to venture in their territory.

The city gleamed with ivory buildings and blue-colored domes, its borders delineated by a great white wall. The tall wooden entry gates were open, a constant throng of people filing in and out. Many were shifters and elves, holding baskets filled with food or linen. Others had vases propped atop their heads as they meandered through the crowd.

Large hyenas with patchy fur and thick hides carried sacks of flour and grain, their owners ambling alongside them. The air smelled of cumin and ginger, sprinkled with the fresh scent of mint.

Daria's heart pounded against her ribs as they grew closer to where they were supposed to meet Zara and Ronan. When evening came and the busy streets started to thin out, they stopped at what looked like a luxurious tavern, its tall front doors a glossy mahogany carved with images of flowers.

"I think this is the place," Ares said.

But Daria could barely hear him. Her body moved on its own as she practically ran inside the building. Tall blood-red tapestries hung along the walls, while other intricately-designed rugs rested underneath couches and settees. Diamond-shaped lanterns hung from the ceiling, some low enough to touch.

Guests wandered about the floor, either conversing or gambling. A pair of harp musicians and a singer performed in one corner. The Sombra Quarter was doing *quite* well.

Daria was acutely aware of Ares following her, though her eyes were scanning the place. And there she was. Zara had her arms crossed, her hip propped against the bar, a beautiful archangel standing in front of her. They were talking, whatever they were saying too low to catch, but something about it had Daria skidding to a halt. Their postures were slightly awkward and distant, the skin between her sister's brows pinched together, while the male's gaze was downcast.

Axar was there, too, sprawled in the sitting area, drinking and eating and flirting with a few other patrons. Oblivious to anything around him.

Daria felt the back of her eyes burn. *"Zara."*

The world seemed to slow as her sister turned at the sound. It looked as if Zara was witnessing a shower of shooting stars. As if light had finally broken through a stormy sky.

"Daria," she breathed, stumbling a step before sprinting toward her.

Daria bit back a cry of relief as she embraced her sister. Zara felt strong in her arms. Her scent made her think of wild freedom, vicious and full of power—in the best way.

"I'm so happy to see you." Zara squeezed her even tighter. "I was so worried."

Daria winced at the pressure. She was sure her ribs were about to break, but she would gladly take that pain if it meant never being separated from her sister again. A laugh escaped her. "We are together again."

Her heart was on the verge of exploding with joy. It overpowered the loneliness and pain she'd felt the past couple of months. The strength that flooded her entire being made her feel like she was capable of anything. *They were finally reunited.*

Zara looked over Daria's shoulder and slowly untangled herself from her arms, stepping around her. Daria stiffened at the energy wafting from her sister. It was the quiet before the storm, the subtle scent of embers and smoke before a fire. Her brows furrowed as she turned to see where Zara was heading.

Ares stood a few steps away from the bar area, his face impassive as always.

Daria raised her hand. "Zara, what are you doing—"

Her sister cocked a first and punched Ares.

TWENTY-EIGHT

aria's eyes widened. Ares's head snapped to the side, the force of Zara's punch sending him stumbling back.

He braced himself against the bar, cursing under his breath, and rubbed his lower jaw, where a red mark had already bloomed.

Zara slowly lowered her fist. "That was for raiding our home. As well as for hurting my sister."

Daria's heart raced.

The vampire glanced at her. Something flashed in his eyes before he shot a look at Ronan. The archangel folded his arms, an unreadable expression on his face, and then merely shrugged.

Ares sighed. "You are *much* stronger than you look, Horizon."

Zara glared at him, a promise of ruin written there. "I told you that if you harmed Daria in any way, I would rip out your spine."

The general had the decency to look ashamed. Daria tugged on her sister's arm. "Thank you, Zara. I think that's enough for now."

Her sister scoffed. "I hope you have a *very* good reason for bringing him here."

Daria stole a glance over Zara's shoulder. Ronan was leaning toward the general, an innocent gleam in his eyes and a faint smirk on his lips. He reached over, as if to inspect Ares's face, but the vampire slapped his hand away with gritted teeth. Ronan snickered.

Zara followed her gaze. "Ronan was actually hoping the vampire would make an appearance. Something about wanting to talk to him about… *something*. I don't know."

"*Calderón!*"

Daria's curiosity about that quickly disappeared when Axar noticed her in the tavern's chaos and rushed to embrace her. She grinned and squeezed him back. Being reunited with her family made her feel like she could finally breathe again.

Eventually, Ronan came over and bowed. "It is a pleasure to see you again, Your Majesty."

"I suppose I should address you properly as well, *Your Majesty*." Daria found herself smiling and bowing in return. "Thank you for arranging our path to Nephtyr. And for taking care of Zara and Axar."

He waved a hand in dismissal. "No need for that. Whether we like it or not, our paths are connected. And since we are all here, I'd like to introduce you to my interim leader of the Sombra Quarter, the one who has been helping me organize our journey to Nepthyr. Someone I think you mercenaries already know."

The archangel gestured to somewhere within the throng of guests just as a large male appeared. The elf's hair was shorn at the sides, save for the thick blond braid running down the center of his head.

Zara stiffened beside her, grabbing her arm, and Daria felt a flutter of worry. "Who is that?"

"That's Warrick, head of the Adrastean guild. He was a longtime friend of… Hakim. They used to fight together, before the guilds were separated to serve their designated kingdoms."

Daia didn't miss how Zara's voice strained at the mention of Hakim. She placed her hand over her sister's.

Warrick looked between Zara and Axar. "I am quite relieved to see you, young ones." His expression softened. "Allow me to extend my condolences."

"Likewise," her sister choked out. Zara's face seemed to crumple for a moment before she straightened, an impassive and emotionless

Horizon once more. "I imagine the rest of your guild is here as well." She glanced at Ronan. "Would you mind explaining why you have the Horizons of Adrastea working for you, archangel? And why have you never mentioned it before?"

The male almost looked smug. "I wanted it to be a surprise. When I went to the Elios mercenary temple to plead for the Horizons' help to fight with us at the coliseum, I offered them the Sombra Quarter's protection. I was asking the mercenaries to commit treason, so I wanted to make their sacrifice worth it. The Elios and Kairos guilds declined—but not Adrastea."

Warrick placed a hand over his chest. "Thanks to Ronan, my mercenaries and I are now able to call the Stone Orchard home. He gave us a new purpose, and we've been keeping the shadow dealers in check, ensuring they do not risk the safety of the secret city."

It seemed the archangel was always many steps ahead—perhaps Daria could learn a few things from a ruler like Ronan.

"I knew you had a hand in most things that happen in the Continent," she said, addressing him. "I just didn't anticipate it being a *helping* hand."

The archangel shrugged with a smirk. "That's me, hiring unemployed mercenaries here and there."

Zara rolled her eyes.

Whatever Daria had witnessed between her sister and Ronan earlier seemed to have dissipated. The tension now gone.

Ares, who had been silent throughout most of the conversation, took a step forward. "May I ask what made you turn your back on Adrastea?"

Warrick's eyes widened. "General? I didn't expect to see you here." He lowered his head. "One of our own was taken by those specters. I reported it to the Lord of the Vampires and requested aid to search for him. Well… nothing came of it. So, when Ronan approached us, the decision came easily to me."

Daria held her breath. She didn't know how Ares was going to react to this. What she didn't expect, though, was the vampire bowing his head to the mercenary.

"You're brave, Horizon," Ares said. When Warrick blinked in surprise, the general continued, "Do not worry, I won't report this to King Matías. My being here is already treasonous enough, so whatever happens here stays here."

Emotion stirred within Daria, though she suspected Ares had merely said those things to save his own skin. Only time would tell where his true intentions lay.

Ronan clapped his hands. "Now that the niceties and awkward small talk are out of the way, I think it's time for us to eat and get some well-deserved rest."

The archangel brushed past them, pausing to touch Zara's arm. "Catch up with your sister, Santos. Apparently there are some deities in town, but Warrick says they are scheduled to leave the city tomorrow night. So, we will rest here for another day before heading to Nephtyr."

That had her sister stiffening. "Which deities? Why are they here?"

"I am not sure, though it sounds like they've been meeting with the city's government officials. Either to review efforts in catching us or something else entirely. We need to lie low."

Zara sighed, nodding.

Ronan's gaze slid to Daria, shooting her a wink before grabbing Ares by the back of his collar. "As for *you*, you are coming with me."

Servers came by just then, offering her and Zara beverages. They watched as the vampire gave a half-hearted protest before allowing Ronan to drag him out of the tavern.

The skin on Ronan's knuckles was bright red. Ares had taken the punch gracefully, as if expecting it. He adjusted his cloak, wine-red fabric like blood in the dark.

"You've hit harder than that."

They stood behind the tavern, away from prying eyes. The establishment sat at the edge of the city, where the ground was more sand than dirt.

Ronan's lips twitched. "You're taunting me."

He moved before the vampire could blink, striking him square in the chest with his fist. Ares clenched his teeth—the look of pain so foreign on the male's usually-impassive face.

"This is what you want, right?" he said, silver eyes glowing in the moonlight. "To feel pain and to add to your self-loathing."

Ares snarled. He pivoted, swinging his leg toward Ronan's side. The archangel blocked it, but the force of the vampire's attack sent him sliding across the ground. They fell into close combat, a storm of punches and parries that only the sand bore witness to.

"If our situation were reversed, you would feel the same," Ares grunted, dodging Ronan's uppercut.

The archangel narrowed his gaze. "Why don't you tell me the reason you invaded Ikarria. I am not surprised by Matías's motives though, frankly, I can't believe you would have so easily agreed to it."

Ares swept his leg out again, but Ronan's wings lifted him up just before he could crash to the ground.

The vampire sneered. "You cheat."

"Don't avoid the question, Valdemar." The archangel lunged forward, meeting Ares in a series of blows.

Cuts and bruises ripped through skin with every attack. The vampire managed to graze his cheek. Ronan slammed a punch to Ares's jaw, right where Zara had hit him earlier.

The vampire stumbled back, but Ronan didn't relent. He grabbed Ares by the collar. "*Talk* to me. Why did you do it?"

Blood trickled from Ares's nose as he gazed at Ronan with that usual empty stare. "I am a general of Adrastea, and I serve my king."

The vampire's eyes slid down to where the emblem rested on his lapel. Ronan felt a rush of fury.

"Lies!" He yanked Ares closer. "If that were true then you would not have brought Daria here. You have been living a double life for as long as I remember. I *know* you—there must be a reason. And soon, you will need to own up to what you want or risk losing *everything* you care for."

Ares blinked, and that mask of his cracked. What Ronan saw there… it rendered him speechless.

Fuck, he recognized the pain that dwelled there. The self-loathing. The confusion. The fear, and everything terrible that came with that.

Ares's voice was low. Almost inaudible. "He was going to kill her."

"Who was going to kill who?"

The vampire clenched his jaw. "During the hunting season, Daria wasn't meant to leave Soleira alive. Matías planned to assassinate her and… My king was furious though I managed to convince him not to do anything rash. To save her, and my mother—I had to keep up appearances, and lead the raid on Ikarria. Keep the king appeased."

A cold sense of understanding rushed through Ronan. He slowly released him. "And you won't tell the queen."

It wasn't a question. Ares straightened, adjusting his collar and sleeves. "No, and neither will you. No matter the reason, I still hurt Daria. People died because of me. I don't deserve anything other than her hatred and mistrust."

Ronan despised what the outside forces of this world had done to those he cared about. And he understood. Because if he had been in Ares's position, he would've done the same.

"You are worthy of more, whether you realize it or not." Ronan sighed and dropped the topic, his wings slackening. Ares would have to find a way to forgive himself on his own time. Another thing Ronan could relate to.

He untied a leather pouch from his waist and handed it to Ares. "I brought you a gift. More bloodroot for my favorite vampire. And some more medicine for Morana. Give her my regards."

Ares eyed him for a moment before taking it. "You're being very nice to me—it's unsettling. Especially when I don't deserve it."

"Only for those who matter to me," Ronan said. "And it's not as if I haven't done terrible things myself."

The vampire popped open a small canister. A puff of red exploded into the air and the scent of copper followed. He exhaled, a faint smile forming on his lips before he looked up again.

"I saw Erebus while I was in Soleira. He asked about

you—specifically about the time you served in the Iron Isles. It was strange, the way he spoke of you... Almost with fondness."

Tension bracketed Ronan's body. The air in his lungs thinned as Ares met his gaze.

"What exactly happened between you and Erebus?"

The vampire knew most things about Ronan's past, except for this. No one was aware of what exactly had caused the fallout between him and Erebus.

Shit. Emotion clogged his throat. "Many years ago, I made a mistake. Erebus trusted me—and I failed him." Ronan stopped and looked away.

The vampire placed a hand on his shoulder. "I won't force you to tell me."

Ronan let out an awkward chuckle. "I'm sorry you have to see me so weak."

"If there is anything I know about you, it is that you are anything but weak."

Ronan cracked a smirk. "This is the first time I've heard you speak like that. You *do* care about me."

Ares rolled his eyes, lighting his bloodroot. "I don't know why I still stand by your side when you're this annoying. It astounds me."

The vampire turned his face away and took a drag of the burning bloodroot. Ronan didn't miss the blackened veins along the corner of Ares's eyes. He frowned, but before he could say anything, the vampire spoke again.

"Actually, there is something I wanted to discuss with you." Ares's skin was already a few shades brighter. "Remember how you gave me full access to the Sombra Quarter's services?"

Ronan arched an eyebrow. "Of course. It took several years, but you won that trust."

Ares's lips lifted slightly and he squared his shoulders. "There is something I need your help with."

Ronan grinned. "Now I like the sound of that. Tell me what you're thinking, vampire."

TWENTY-NINE

The following morning, Zara was leaning against the threshold of a local shop—one owned by a follower of the Sombra Quarter, of course. She blinked against the grains of sand that blew onto her eyelashes, feeling the warmth of the daylight against her skin.

Ronan draped a shawl over her head, the fabric thin and buttery soft. Elegant bronze shapes and patterns were woven into the dark green fabric. Zara ran her fingers along the hem of the shawl, tilting her head up to meet the archangel's eyes.

Dust sprinkled his cheeks, even stained the vines tattooed along his neck. His hair was messy, curling slightly at the ends; it gave him an almost wild look.

"Beautiful," Ronan murmured. He was staring at her, Zara realized. He took the fabric from her fingers and brought it up to cover the lower half of her face. "Keep your identity hidden as much as you can. Sneaking around in dark hoods would only bring us more attention here."

It had been some time since Zara had felt her cheeks heat. Surely, it was due to the sun. The audacity of the archangel to say such disarming things…

They hadn't properly spoken since that moment before fighting the specters. There was always something demanding their attention, and they were hardly ever alone, especially since leaving Damalis.

Zara cleared her throat, jerking her chin toward the bustling streets outside. "Did you know I've actually been to Corduva before? It was so long ago, though, that it feels like my first visit."

His eyebrows lifted. "How young were you?"

"It was during one of my first hunting seasons. We'd been assigned to kill several royal advisors—opponents of Raziel—and I remember scaling those white walls there. I may have fallen a few times, hardly an intimidating Horizon to our marks."

"I beg to differ," Axar interjected. He had been admiring the daggers splayed on the counter of the shop, their golden hilts embedded with gems. "I remember you dragging our marks from their beds and gutting them in alleys."

The shifter had changed from his mercenary clothes, now donning brown fighting leathers with a hooded shawl wrapped around his shoulders.

Even Daria wore a new silk stole that hugged her frame, her dark hair running freely down her back. She was sitting on a bench, Basim curled at her feet. Nyota was lying beside the wolf, licking her large paws. The nahuals were allowed to be out with them as long as they kept away from the public eye. *They would draw too much attention,* Ronan had put it.

Still, the sight warmed Zara's chest. The night before, she had told her sister everything that had happened, from training in Teotlan to finding out about the Primordial ether in her veins and the Crossing— and had introduced Daria to her nahual. Her sister had relayed all the terrible things that had occurred in Ikarria as well, including the details surrounding Matías's demand to find the dragons. Something Zara still seethed over.

Daria shuddered at Axar's words. "Suns Above."

Zara shot a glare at the shifter and he shrugged. Her sister was not used to this ugly side of her, the grim realities of life as a mercenary.

Daria glanced her way. "Your experience will definitely be of help when we save Pater."

Zara stared at her, dumbfounded. The sisters had vowed to save Idris, to get him out of that prison, and had shared the pain of not knowing what he was going through at that very moment.

Zara had to push back the thought, her stomach churning. Her last conversation with her pater hadn't left them on the best of terms, her feelings toward him twisted with love and disappointment. Disappointment that stemmed from his failure to spare her the fate of the hunting season and serving the High King.

Now Zara understood that her pater had done everything he could to give her a good life, even if it came with the heavy cost of her becoming the Rogue. Though it was too late to take her words back.

My storm… Her pater's words echoed through her chest. *I haven't stopped fighting for you, and I will continue to do so until my body joins the soil in the ground.*

Zara returned her attention to Daria, placing a hand on her shoulder. Her little sister, who had complimented her skills as a mercenary rather than being disgusted by it.

"We will get him back," Zara said. "I promise."

Daria's expression turned pained. Ares appeared from one of the dressing rooms, dark clouds seeming to loom over the male's shoulders as he stomped over to Ronan.

The vampire gestured to himself. "Does this suit your taste now?"

He wore a tan long-sleeved shirt made of cotton. The sleeves were rolled up to his elbows, billowing slightly around his arms. His dark brown trousers tapered down to his boots. A red sash was tied around his waist, matching pieces of cloth wrapped around his elbows. The vampire wore fingerless gloves to complete the ensemble, his long hair tied up with a leather band.

Ronan whistled. "I like this look on you, Valdemar. Very dashing."

Zara caught her sister staring at the vampire for a breath longer than necessary before she averted her gaze.

Ares rolled his eyes, tugging at his collar. "I am not used to this type of clothing."

"Removing anything connecting you to the Adrastean realm should make things easier for us. What made you think wearing your flashy armor and bright cloak around these parts was a good idea? No one likes your kingdom at the moment." The archangel folded his arms. "It is only when in Nephtyr that we'll need you to be the general."

Outside, packs of Elios soldiers patrolled the streets, their white armor bright under the blue sky. Zara stepped away from the threshold and farther into the shop, patting Basim's head. Her nahual licked her hand.

Ares grunted. "Your portrait on the wanted posters was terrible, by the way."

Ronan gasped. The archangel and vampire continued to bicker, while Axar stepped closer to where Zara and her sister were huddled. Daria sat up straighter, her amber-brown eyes honed on the shifter.

"Axar, what are you wearing around your neck?"

The shifter cocked his head before fishing out a familiar necklace that was tucked under his shirt. "This?"

It was a coin made of copper on a simple gold chain.

"Yes. What is it?"

His voice went low. "It's a talisman… Eshe got this for me."

Zara recalled when the vampire had bought the necklace for her brother, back in the Stone Orchard's markets. Grief squeezed her heart.

"It's lovely," Daria said softly. "Does it have some kind of power?"

"Depends on the talisman." Axar frowned. "Now that I think of it, I don't know what this one is supposed to do."

Daria smiled. "Whatever ability this piece has, I am sure Eshe knew it would help you. I know she loved you very much."

Axar averted his gaze as he reached down to pet Basim's head. "I—I appreciate it, Calderón."

Their group prepared to leave—now stocked with fresh travel clothes and shined weapons, plus other resources for their journey through the sands—and the nahuals returned to the other side of the veil. Zara was still deep in thought as she wandered outside.

She didn't notice how packed the streets had become. How civilians were pressed to the side of the main road.

Basim's voice rang through her head. *Careful.*

She jerked her head up and froze. Earlier there had only been Elios soldiers marching through the city, but now—now several *deities* stalked down the dirt path. They were surrounded by guards, the silver ether in their eyes making them look more beast than human-like.

They must have been diplomats, businessmen, or other influential figures here on behalf of the High Throne. Were they here as part of the search for her and Ronan?

The world around Zara fell into a hum the longer she stared at the deities. And then her blood turned cold.

Someone else was among them. Someone who had forced her to watch Raziel kill her mercenary family. Someone she had vowed to kill.

Nadira, a member of the Council, walked past her. Of all the places on the Continent, one of Zara's marks was now within killing distance. It was as if the Fates had handed her a gift.

"Make way for council member Nadira Iryndel!" A soldier announced. "All citizens and businesses must comply with the High Throne's organized search for the wanted fugitives, criminals Zara Santos and Ronan Menodora."

Ah. So they *were* here for them. Zara almost smiled under her shawl. The High Throne was trying to maintain the facade of being a peaceful ruling power ridding Ribera of threats, by apprehending and torturing any dissenting citizens. It was only a matter of time before it would crumble.

The civilians around her turned into colorful blurs. Zara took a heavy step forward, navigating through the crowd as she prowled closer to where the deities walked. Her daggers were tucked within the folds of her new clothes. One slid down her sleeve, ready to drop into her open palm.

This was foolish. So utterly insane. But it could be a quick kill. A single stab to the heart could kill a deity. She just needed the right opportunity.

"You! Halt!"

The voice snapped her back to reality. Zara blinked, finding herself on the main street. She pushed her dagger back up her sleeve before anyone could see it.

An Elios soldier stomped toward her. "What are you doing on the road?"

Zara kept her expression smooth, even though her heartbeat was pounding in her ears. Could she make a run for it? It was broad daylight, and there were too many people around. Fucking Suns, she'd allowed her rage to blind her.

Ares stepped in between her and the soldier. "Apologies, ma'am. My friend here got a bit too excited with everything going on. We will be more careful."

Zara stared wide-eyed at the vampire, shocked that he had come to her aid. The female soldier didn't seem to recognize Ares as the general of Adrastea.

"As long as you do." She stared at Zara longer than she would've liked before turning to him. "We have been asking civilians if they have seen anything strange that might reveal the traitors' whereabouts. Have you noticed anything amiss?"

Ares took a subtle step closer to Zara, blocking her face from the soldier. "We haven't, but if we do, we will report it. We apologize for interrupting your patrol."

Maybe it was how the vampire's tone seamlessly seeped into that of a war general, authoritative, firm, that had the soldier backing down.

"Carry on," the archangel said, before marching down the street.

Zara released a slow breath. "Thank you."

Ares looked at her, like he suspected why she was out here in the first place. He gestured for her to walk ahead of him and back to the others.

Zara looked over her shoulder, staring at where Nadira had disappeared. The Primordial ether in her veins growled. Begging to bare its fangs.

THIRTY

That night, Zara donned her mercenary armor and black cloak again. She waited in the shadows, listening to the night markets from the open windows. Blood and anger pumped through her veins, feeding her every minute that ticked by.

Her gaze scanned the main room of the penthouse she'd snuck into. It had high ceilings and was filled with statues of feathered beasts and celestial warriors. Above this floor were an office and various other suites. How extravagant.

After questioning several tradesmen—perhaps even threatening one or two—Zara discovered that this building was being rented by one of the deities. Whatever business the lesser gods were tending to in the city was not public knowledge, and anything concerning Nadira's whereabouts was closely guarded.

The door opened and the smell of expensive liquor spilled into the room. The deity walking into the penthouse was one of the many diplomats who had been at Nadira's side earlier today, someone Zara had seen before in Soleira working for the Council. They had been attending a dinner party in the lower levels of the building late into the night.

Zara silently scaled one of the statues. The still-drunk deity stumbled farther into the room, and didn't notice the mercenary stepping out of the wall of night. A steel-fanged beast made of heartache and turmoil.

She unsheathed her dagger and dove for him. The male spun around, snatching her wrist, the blade dangling above them.

"I'd almost missed your aura, but there it was. A flutter of shadow. The Rogue has skill indeed." The deity's ethereal eyes flared. "I never thought I'd have the honor of experiencing it firsthand."

Zara merely glowered at the male from beneath her hood. "Where is Nadira?"

The deity didn't seem surprised by the question. "She left the city. Which is unfortunate for you, as she is *quite* eager to see you again."

Disappointment sank through her, replaced by a thrumming in her veins. Zara should've attacked Nadira when she had the chance—damn the consequences.

"Looks like I will have to keep hunting," she said. The corners of her lips curled. "I can't very well let you walk away now though, can I?"

The deity grinned. With a powerful sweep of his silver ether, he leaped several yards away. However much alcohol the male had consumed, it didn't seem to slow him down. Zara chased after him, both of them sprinting between the statues. She threw daggers and slashes of light, the deity releasing his own ether at her.

Their attacks smashed into marble and stone. An arc of blinding silver raced toward Zara's face; she slid down to the ground, dodging the ether, heat caressing her face.

The deity's voice echoed in the penthouse.

"No one has killed a deity in years, mercenary! What makes you think you can?"

Zara climbed up another statue, ether flaring in her wake as she jumped from one to the next. There was a flicker of something across the deity's face, like genuine surprise that quickly morphed into worry. He started to run faster.

She threw another dagger. "You aren't a warrior, deity, just a mere official. You have no chance against me."

He snarled, lashing out with more arcs of ether. Silver light illuminated the statues before chunks of stone went flying across the room. Dust billowed in the air.

Zara took advantage of the mess, blending in with the shadows and smoke. The deity was huffing and puffing, ether flickering into a blade in his hand as he walked between the remaining statues.

"I heard the Council and the late Raziel killed your guild," he snarled. "If the Rogue had stayed an obedient mercenary, none of that would've happened. You could say it was all your fault your precious mercenary friends died."

Zara pressed her back against marble. Red flickered across her vision and her breathing turned shallow. She could see the temple now, its floor filling with Hakim and Eshe's blood.

The deity's voice echoed in the hall. "I suppose I should say 'good riddance,' they were only weapons meant to be discarded. One less useless guild to be concerned about. Now, we can finally move forward in creating our new world. Word is you're valuable, and our new High King needs that power of yours."

Her world was doused in a shade of crimson—it hurt to breathe, every inhale making her lungs burn. She turned toward the statue behind her. Every pain and heartache poured into the ether that gathered at her fist as she punched the stone.

The deity dodged chunks of marble hurtling toward him with giddy laughs, but when he looked up, he couldn't see Zara. Couldn't sense her aura. Didn't catch her sinking back into the darkness. She jumped.

Zara crashed into the deity, wrapping her legs around him, and plunged her dagger deep into his chest. Her ether sang at the spill of blood.

"Why does the High Throne want me? For what purpose does he need my power?" She snarled and drove the blade deeper.

An unseen energy blasted through the penthouse, crashing against stone and reaching for the high ceiling. It rolled from the deity's body in waves.

He rammed his elbow against Zara's ribs, but she still held on.

"You are a shit assassin," the male choked out. "To kill a deity, you have to pierce the heart. And you *missed*."

Zara lowered her mouth to his ear, ignoring his taunt. "Do they want to use my ether as a weapon?"

"Your power is a *tool*." The deity laughed. "An instrument that will open this world to new possibilities we never thought possible."

Her eyes widened. Zara was running out of time; she had to end this before anyone heard the mess they were creating. The deity struggled against her but she overpowered him—she was now stronger than a *deity*. His cry was cut short when she wrenched her dagger out and drove it straight into his heart.

Energy flowed out from the deity's body as he fell onto his back. Zara held onto him, her grip tightening around her blade. She didn't let go as the male squirmed against her. Not until the ethereal light in his eyes dimmed and he stilled.

Zara lay there for a moment, catching her breath. Blood shone across the steel of her dagger. *What had she done?*

A deity was dead. She had *killed* one of them. When was the last time a lesser god had died? Not since the War of the Skies, more than ten years ago. Zara had tipped the scales, and the world's gaze would soon sharpen on her. There was no going back.

There was no time to mull over what happened. Basim appeared, stepping out of the shadows.

You could've let me help.

The wolf grabbed the lifeless deity by the collar and dragged him toward the window. Zara followed.

Zara stumbled through alleyways. Moonlit dust spun about her boots as she dragged a hand along the pale walls. A quiet anger leaked from the cracks within her heart; it burned hotter with every step. And her ether *ached*.

It must have been the aftermath from the fight with the deity. Reality sank low in her abdomen the longer she walked.

Soon, soldiers would be alerted, perhaps even flood the streets. It might have been foolish, what she had done, but she couldn't bring herself to care.

Zara wanted to hunt down every follower of the High Throne, cut down all the members of the Council, one by one. None of these kills would rid her of her pain, this she knew. But that didn't matter.

Sparks flared into the starry sky, snapping her out of her thoughts. She halted in a narrow alleyway, staring at the night market still bustling with life. String music resounded in the chilled air as people lingered about the stalls.

An arm wrapped around her from behind, pulling her back before she could step out into the street. Zara threw a punch at the stranger, but a large hand caught her fist, and her gaze clashed with familiar stormy gray eyes.

"When I noticed that a certain mercenary had left the tavern, I couldn't contain my curiosity." Ronan's voice was dark liquid. "The little wolf has had an eventful evening, it seems."

Zara gritted her teeth against the pressure of her ether building inside her. "How did you find me?"

"I could feel your anger—my ether started to get agitated. It wasn't hard to follow your murderous aura through the city."

She tried to pull away from his grasp when the archangel suddenly pushed her against the wall. He bowed over her just as a patrol of soldiers marched past the alley.

"Are you trying to get caught?" he hissed under his breath.

"Like your massive wings aren't a giant beacon announcing where we are!"

Tendrils of blue light lapped across his tattooed neck and he shuddered. "Fuck, this ether is not letting up."

Zara's body trembled as her power pressed invisible hands against her mental walls. Ready to release.

She peered up at the archangel. "It's happening again, isn't it? Our ethers are becoming stronger."

Ronan stared at her with... *need*, and it made her knees weak. He cursed under his breath before wrapping his arms around her. "We can't let anyone see us."

The archangel soared into the air, flying over the rooftops. Firelight flickered in the streets below, sounds from the night markets rising toward them.

"I knew you had seen the deities. And Nadira." Ronan flapped his wings. "I had a feeling you would go after them."

"I killed one. A deity." The truth was a heavy weight between them. When he didn't say anything, she asked, "Are you disappointed?"

"No. I don't blame you for doing what you did."

She stared at him, speechless.

His grip tightened around her and a surge of energy swept through her bones. It was as if their ethers were communicating with each other, wanting to twist and dance together.

Ronan faltered in the air. "Shit."

He tried to land on a flat rooftop, but his restless power must have sent him off balance. The archangel crashed through a woven tarp that overlooked a lounge area and they landed on some cushions and a rolled out blanket.

Zara found herself on top of the archangel, her face pressed against his neck. His body was strong underneath her, his dark fighting leathers melded to the muscles of his chest. On any other day, she might have scampered away—but the ether was itching at her skin. The thrumming in her veins wouldn't stop.

Strong hands grabbed her waist. "We should probably put some distance between us."

Yes. She thought of the last time their ether had matured, of how close they had gotten, of Zara's reaction—the memories... But the need to release was stronger this time.

Her hands curled atop his chest. "No," she said, her voice strained.

"I don't want to do something that would hurt you." Ronan rasped, his body trembling.

Does being with me bring you pain? He'd never asked again after that night.

Hearing the words now cut through her, down to the core. Regret became the marrow of her bones, and her anger turned its fiery head toward herself.

"Being with you does *not* bring me pain." Zara's eyes watered as the truth barreled up her throat. She raked her nails down his chest, scraping nothing but leather. "The hurt comes whenever I feel *happy*."

Another wave of power rushed over her body. Ether leaked from her, ribbons of red energy dancing around her.

…her torn fingers slipped against the tiles as she crawled over to Hakim and Eshe's lifeless bodies. As she pulled herself to her mentor's side.

Zara's tears fell onto Ronan's cheeks as she stared down at him—fighting to breathe. "I think of Hakim and Eshe. All the time. How much they suffered while I was at peace—while I was with you—and then I get this terrible feeling inside and I can't—I can't get rid of it!"

The archangel pushed himself to sit up so that she rested between his thighs. He waited patiently as Zara waded through the battles within. Even as her power continued to howl and push against her restraints. Even as his own did the same.

"It's not your fault, this is my problem. Mine, alone."

Raziel pointed a finger at her. "You did this."

She cried out. Ether struck the tarp, ripping through fabric and shattering pottery. "Why am I like this? I must be broken. Anytime I think I made progress, that the pain has lessened, I find myself a thousand steps back."

Strong arms wrapped around her, a wave of warmth that threatened to break her. Ronan held her so firmly, his large hand pressed against the back of her head.

"You are not broken, you are grieving. There is not a single way to handle that kind of loss." His embrace tightened. "I knew it would take time for you to work through it, but I didn't realize how it was affecting you. Especially around me."

"I didn't want to tell you, because I didn't want to put another burden on you. You are already fighting your past." Zara pulled back to look at him. She brushed away her tears, even as more poured down her face. "I didn't want to add to your pain."

A groan was yanked out of her lips as the light brightened around her. The ether was more agitated; it snarled and snapped at the air.

Ronan grabbed her shoulders, silver light flashing in his eyes. "You're right, this is your fight to overcome, but you are not alone. Learn to separate your grief and love for them from the need to move forward."

He winced as he spoke, battling his own churning ether. "Not for my sake, but for your own. You are more than your past. You are allowed to be happy. It was *not* your fault, Santos—their deaths are not on you."

You are more. Zara clung to those words, to the comfort that Ronan offered her. The weight of her power was too much, needing to burst out of her.

Another cry peeled out of her as she gripped his shoulders, one filled with the anguish of her heart and raging power. Crimson light flared, spiraling around them.

"It's okay. Let it out, as much as you can." Ronan held her tightly. "You're safe with me. *Always.*"

Tears trickled down her cheeks. "As are you."

Zara shuddered, feeling the weight of her ether start to lessen. It sank back down into the depths, though she didn't release the archangel. His body still trembled.

"I know your ether is fighting you," she whispered. "Do what you need to."

The world spun. Ronan rolled her over onto her back and stared down at her, breathing heavily. Blue mist curled from his body.

Zara's heart betrayed her at this moment. She was at Ronan's utter mercy… and didn't *mind* it. At all.

The archangel slid his knee between her legs, stopping before actually touching her. More blue ether spun around them like a glittering river. Ronan leaned down, his lips inches from hers.

Zara's heart slammed against her chest. He was so close. Was he going to kiss her?

She might have parted her lips. Might have tilted her chin up. Could she have this?

A shudder racked through Ronan's body. He clenched his teeth against whatever his ether was doing to him and, instead, brushed his mouth against her throat.

Zara bit her lip, holding back the whimper that wanted to escape. Ronan sucked in a breath and his body tensed, as if he was leashing himself. He licked her neck.

That heat inside her turned hotter. Suns, this shouldn't be happening. They needed to stop.

Ronan nipped the column of her throat and she gasped. His ether suddenly brightened before exploding into clouds of shattered gems. His body slackened as he fought for his breath.

"What a frustrating experience." He gazed at her, like she was something precious. Someone who *mattered*, beyond steel and battle. "Thank you, Santos."

Whatever heat had curled inside her withered away, replaced by a warmth in her cheeks.

"Don't thank me, I should be apologizing to you," she said, averting her gaze.

Ronan brushed the corner of her eye with his thumb as they sat up. "You are strong enough to get through this. And I will do the same."

She gave him a grateful look. Time tended to be the answer to these things, didn't it? There was no telling when she would be able to overcome this grief, but she refused to let what the High Throne did break her.

Hakim and Eshe would be shaking their heads. Telling her to stop crying over them and to keep going. And she would. One day.

They sat there for a while, the broken tarp above them showing the gleaming night sky. Music and chatter still wafted from the streets.

Zara thought about the deity she'd killed—about the blood on her hands and the anger that boiled through her ether. She narrowed her eyes on the city stretched out before them.

"I can't let them win, Ronan," Zara said.

He knew who she was referring to. "Neither can I."

After a pause, he asked, "Where's the body?"

"I took care of it."

"Tell me. Warrick can have the shadow dealers get rid of any evidence."

Of course. It was only natural that the leader of the shadow markets knew how to remove any signs of murder.

Zara's tongue felt heavy. "I left him in an alleyway. I changed his clothes and cleaned his wounds so it would be less obvious he had died by a blade."

"Quick thinking. Sooner or later, the other deities will find out that one of them is dead. We need to stall them as long as possible."

Guilt curled in her stomach. "Will the city suffer for this?" The question took her by surprise. Since when was the wellbeing of others, of random strangers, a thought.

"No, the deities won't want this getting out, to keep the people's support. Over time, the Continent will realize who the real enemy is, but for now our priority is to get the power we need to defeat the High Throne."

Zara sighed. "I caused you more problems."

Ronan curled his fingers around her chin and gently turned her gaze to his. There was no judgment in those eyes, only a pool of stars.

"No, you didn't." The corner of his lips lifted. "But next time, invite me. I am your blade, remember?"

He was somehow easing the storm that constantly raged inside her. Zara was still gazing at the archangel, when the world before her changed. They were in Damalis—Ronan was standing in front of her. He looked upset, and was *shouting* at her. Something swam in his silver eyes, something that had her heart aching.

Before she could understand what was happening, Zara returned to the present. She shook her head.

The archangel cocked his head. "Where did you go? Just now? It looked like you were far away."

What was it that she had seen? Could it have been a vision? A weird phenomenon, like when she dreamed of Mikatán?

Zara had experienced this before though, back in Damalis, while exploring the capital's nightlife. She'd seen the city up in flames…

Zara shouldn't agonize over this. There was nothing to confirm that it had been a vision. Perhaps she was simply tired. "It was nothing."

"Cheers to a successful night!"

Zara couldn't help but chuckle as Ronan clinked his drink with hers. She gulped down the clear alcohol, hissing at the burn torching her throat.

"If by successful, you mean cleaning a crime scene without any issues, then yes it was a good evening," she said. "All thanks to you and Warrick."

Zara nodded her head to the massive elven mercenary, who raised his glass in return. "Being able to control the earth element has its advantages."

He lounged on an expensive couch with the other members of the Adrastean guild. Daria, Axar, and Ares had yet to join them; apparently the trio had gone into the city to make some final purchases for their journey to Nephtyr tomorrow.

The archangel lifted a finger and the human bartender scampered over. "Another serving for you and your guests, Lord Ronan?"

"Something stronger, please. I could barely get anything out of this one."

The human bowed before scurrying away.

Zara turned her attention to the head of the Adrastean guild. "How is the Stone Orchard faring?"

It shouldn't have come as a surprise, but she realized the secret city held a special place in her heart. Those caverns filled with stone trees had healed some part of her.

Warrick smiled. "The people are doing well, though the shadow dealers can be pricks. I don't know how Ronan managed to handle their attitudes without killing them."

The archangel snorted. "Oh, I have killed some."

Warrick seemed amused as he brought his cup to his lips. "They are worried about business in the rest of the Continent. Now that your identity has been revealed, word is spreading like wildfire. They're restless, wondering how the truth is going to affect them."

Shadows flickered across Ronan's face. "I will meet with them, eventually. To be honest, their comfort is low on my priorities. We have bigger threats to worry about."

"Right. The secrets you are unable to tell me about." Warrick glanced at Zara. At her hands. "Though I may have a hunch what it may be about, seeing the destruction both of you caused in the coliseum."

Zara fought the urge to shift in her seat. The elf was wise enough not to press further; it was safer for him and his mercenaries not to know the details.

The bartender returned with a tray filled with glasses of chilled alcohol. Zara took another swig of her drink as something came to mind.

"I wanted to ask about your mercenary, the one who was taken by the specters… I believe his name is Cyrus." She hesitated. "Did you know he was ether-born?"

The last time Zara had heard the missing Horizon's name was when Warrick had burst through the Elios mercenary temple, his body beaten, tears lining his eyes. The large male had seemed so fragile as he'd clutched onto Hakim, still in shock from what they'd escaped from.

Warrick's expression shuttered. "Ether-born." The word rolled over his tongue like a curse. Perhaps it was. "To be descended from a line of deities, no matter how thin the blood relation. No. I don't think Cyrus was aware of it himself. Not until the specters took him."

Ronan gulped down another glass. "Those born of pure ether, like the specters, can most likely sense it in others. They are gathering these people for a reason—it must be in connection with the Primordial Khaos." He looked up to meet the mercenary's eyes. "I will do everything in my power to bring Cyrus back."

Warrick gave a small smile. "In the short time I've known you, I've come to realize you are true to your word. Thank you."

He raised his glass, and the other mercenaries followed. Zara joined in, all of them toasting the archangel. Ronan almost seemed flustered, a streak of pink across his cheekbones.

The energy quickly changed as countless drinks were consumed. Some of the mercenaries began to play a game while others continued to converse, laughter and shouts filling the place.

Zara lifted her cup, realizing it was empty. She cocked her head. "This may sound insane, but I feel like the alcohol here isn't very strong. We've been drinking most of the night and I am just now starting to feel its effects."

Ronan looked offended. "I'll have you know that my establishments only offer top quality alcohol." He paused, glancing at the people around them. Everyone seemed to be *very* drunk. Everyone except for him and Zara. "Though, perhaps you're right. Our tolerance may have risen. Ironically enough."

Zara couldn't stop the smug expression appearing on her face. "You said I was right."

Ronan's lips twitched. "I did. Don't get used to it, Horizon."

Something about his low tone made her think back to their moment on the rooftop. Zara cleared her throat and swirled her empty glass. "Should we even be drinking like this? It feels irresponsible."

"I think it is too late for that. We *are* about to dive head first into the desert tomorrow, might as well enjoy this moment while it lasts."

He held her gaze as he raised a hand to the barkeep again for more alcohol. Zara found herself leaning closer and closer to the archangel throughout the night. His presence was becoming an addiction.

And the drinks continued to come.

THIRTY-ONE

Daria exchanged a pair of silver marks for some dried meat at one of the stalls. The brown paper crinkled as she shoved it into her bag, where bundles of vegetables already lay. She gulped down the air that smelled of chicken broth and coriander leaves. It was long past suppertime when Daria had awoken from a nap, her stomach rumbling. Axar had ventured out to the city with her, the shifter now chatting with a vendor several stalls away.

The night market was packed, bodies practically squished together. Corduva was full of many intriguing characters indeed. Some wore masks with antlers or the horns of a ram, while others had wide-brimmed hats with veils hiding their faces. Groups of people sauntered through the crowd with large, gleaming weapons strapped across their backs; demon fangs and claws adorning their clothes.

Daria turned to leave and let out an *oomph* as she knocked into a hard wall. No—it was a person's back.

"I'm so sorry." The words died on her tongue when piercing purple violet eyes landed on her.

Ares stared down at her, a roll of bloodroot between his lips. The crowd swerved around them, avoiding the scary vampire.

He raised an eyebrow, his gaze sliding to the bag hanging around her shoulder. "Did you go shopping?"

"Yes. Well, to be more accurate, Ronan did the buying. He refused to let me use my own funds as so many businesses here are part of the Sombra." Her finances were controlled by Adrastea anyway. Daria tightened her fingers around the leather strap. She glanced at the stall the vampire had been looking at, vials and canisters of crimson liquid laid out everywhere. It dawned on her that a blood bank was connected to the stall, the small building's entrance just behind the vendor. "It seems you did as well. Have you drunk your fill?"

Daria hated how her stomach dropped at the idea of him drinking from someone. It was his business, and it should not be *any* of her concern.

Ares grunted. "I suppose."

Suns Above.

"The blood's bland. None of it satisfies me." The vampire raised a bag filled with vials. "I am forcing myself to drink these for our journey. Otherwise I might die."

Oh. So, he hadn't drunk from someone else. That was a relief—*No, Daria. None of that.*

She huffed out a sigh. "Isn't that a little dramatic? I know vampires have their blood preference, but I'm sure you can manage not drinking from your source of choice for a few months."

Ares's gaze was heavy on her. "I have been… managing."

The way he said it. Daria felt her throat close up, her cheeks hot for some reason. She looked away, glancing around at the market. "We should probably get back. Zara and the others will begin to worry."

"Here, let me." Ares reached for her bag, gently sliding it off her and flinging it over his shoulder.

Daria didn't object to his help but froze when he took a step toward her and grasped her hand. Everything seemed to slow as his scent rushed over her. His broad shoulders blocked out the torchlights and colorful stalls, that long hair shifting with his movements.

Ares folded his palm over hers and leaned toward her ear. "Next time, allow me to pay for whatever you need."

Daria blinked in surprise, feeling a weight in her hand. She opened her palm to find several gold marks glittering there.

"Well, it's the least you could do," she said.

He caught the subtle touch of humor in her tone and his lips twitched. "I know my offer may seem foolish. You are a queen; you could probably buy *me* a thousand times over."

Daria tilted her head to the side. "Now there's an idea."

Ares held her gaze for a moment, and something fluttered in her chest, something she couldn't stop. He nudged her away from the stall and guided her through the crowd. Daria tried looking for Axar though couldn't find him.

"I will buy you dinner," the vampire said. "Your growling stomach is so loud, I can hear it from here."

Daria rolled her eyes. "Then I want the skewered meat they were selling across the street."

Not long after, while she was midway through her meal, Axar joined them, whining. "You ate without me?"

"*You* disappeared, not I."

Daria was acutely aware of Ares stepping away from their table and heading off somewhere. The shifter stared at the vampire a long minute before glancing back at her.

"Were you okay with him all by yourself?"

The worry in Axar's voice was so genuine, it brought a smile to Daria's lips. "Yes, don't worry about me. I can handle the male."

"Of course you can." The shifter chuckled. His expression turned serious as his gaze returned to where Ares walked off. "The vampire feels very guilty."

Daria stiffened. "What do you mean?"

"If I can see it, then I know you can too. He's trying to make amends—at least that's what it seems. I could be wrong, but I'm hardly ever wrong." The shifter shook his head. "Has he demanded anything of you in exchange for his help?"

"No," Daria said, catching on what he meant. "Ares keeps his distance from me, for the most part."

The shifter was silent for a moment. "I have some more respect for the male now."

Daria mulled over Axar's words. She could believe that the

vampire regretted his actions. But did that change anything? Did that change his loyalty to the vampire king?

Ares returned to the table then, and shoved a plate of skewered meat into Axar's hand. "Here."

The shifter made an exaggerated gasp. "You're *feeding* me? This is so kind of you, General. Now you're speaking my language. You're not so broody and cold after all."

The vampire sighed, though the corner of his lips lifted. Just slightly, but it was there. Daria chuckled, a feather-light sensation spreading in her chest. It felt good. Freeing.

Here, they were far away from their problems. For just a moment, she could push away thoughts of what awaited them, and simply *live* in this pocket of reality.

When they returned to the tavern, Daria faltered a step at the… utter *chaos*. It was the only way to describe the scene unfolding before her.

In the midst of a crowd of people Zara was arm-wrestling with Warrick. Ronan stood behind her, hands on his hips and a wide grin on his face, the other Adrastean mercenaries and tavern customers all hollering around them.

It was a surprising sight, maybe a little unsettling. Even Ares was frozen at her side. "What in the blazing Suns is happening here?"

Zara slammed Warrick's arm down, cracking the table. People cheered, some clinked drinks while others passed coins to one another.

Ronan clapped. "I told you that you couldn't beat Zara, but you didn't want to hear it!"

Was the archangel slurring his words? Warrick belted out a loud laugh. "I didn't doubt either one of you! I only wanted to experience this strength myself."

Zara propped one boot on the cracked table and flexed her arms in triumph. Her cheeks were tinted a rosy pink.

Ronan swept in, wrapping his arms around her legs to spin her around and Zara cackled.

Warrick noticed Daria and the others then, and his face brightened. He called out to Axar, gesturing toward the couple. "Tallon! Have you seen these two?" Ronan and Zara were *very* close, grinning in each other's arms, their faces inches apart.

"Fucking Suns," Axar muttered, though a smirk curled his lips. "Well, the only kind of male I would accept for my sister is one strong enough to beat me. And I think we all know just how strong the archangel is."

Warrick roared in laughter and he and Axar went to join some of the Adrastean mercenaries who were playing a drinking game. Daria didn't think Ronan or Zara had heard any of that. She wasn't sure they even comprehended what they were doing. Their bodies swayed as they laughed with abandon. The sound so pure it tugged on Daria's heart. How long had it been since she had seen her sister so carefree?

Ares groaned. "These two fools actually got themselves drunk."

She glanced at the vampire. "Is Ronan often like this? He never struck me as the drinking type."

"He isn't. Not really. This is a first for me." The longer he stared at the archangel, the more dismayed he seemed. Daria didn't think she had ever seen Ares genuinely surprised before.

The barkeep was now wiping the wooden bar down; the candles had been blown out, giving the impression he was closing for what remained of the night.

Ares stomped over to the human. "Did you try to stop those two from ordering more drinks?"

The male gaped at the vampire, cowering slightly. "Sir, I did! But Lord Ronan is my superior, I cannot say no to him. Those two are menaces! They kept complaining they weren't feeling anything from the drinks I served so they kept ordering until I ran out of stock!"

Daria noticed all the empty bottles along the shelves behind him. She glanced at Zara and Ronan who were now playing a game of darts. With daggers. Bystanders gasped as Ronan flipped a pair of the short blades, his grin a blend of mania and darkness, and sent the weapons sailing through the air. Each one struck the target at its center and the room boomed with applause.

The archangel was still precise with his aim, even while being so blatantly drunk. Daria had to admit it was terrifying.

She tugged on Ares's sleeve. "Their higher tolerance level has to be linked to their *Izcali.*"

The vampire glanced at her hand on his arm with a frown, and Daria quickly pulled back. His expression smoothed out in a blink of an eye. "Their bodies are maturing, getting closer to potential godhood; everything, including their alcohol tolerance, is at an otherworldly level."

Ares turned around to watch Zara and Ronan. The vampire folded his arms, his eyes stuck on the archangel. He looked like a guard dog on edge, ready to protect his friend at any given moment. Daria chuckled.

"You are enjoying this, aren't you?" He looked at her sidelong.

She waved a hand. "Oh, let them be. They hardly ever have the opportunity to relax and be free of their obligations. We can monitor them from here."

At that moment, Zara and Ronan noticed them watching, and the two drunkards came stumbling toward them. Her sister grabbed her arm.

"Daria, I missed you," Zara mumbled. "Where did you go? I couldn't find you… *anywhere!*"

Ronan flung his arms around Ares's shoulders, slurring his words. "*Valdemar,* can I tell everyone that you said you care about me?"

The vampire's face went white as a sheet. "I did *not* say that."

Daria couldn't stop herself from laughing. Ares shot her a glare; she beamed at him. "They aren't used to how fast their bodies are changing. They're like newborn deer learning how to walk."

Ares blinked at her. Before he could respond, Zara grumbled. "I'm not a deer."

Daria patted her sister's head. "I think that's enough for tonight." She jerked her chin to the archangel. "Help your friend, Ares. The one you care about *so much.*"

The vampire rolled his eyes as he slung Ronan's arm over his shoulders.

The archangel was still spouting nonsense in Ares's ear. "*I am the one who is blessed to have you in my life, Valdemar. Nyota and I cannot wait to show you Damalis one day. You'll love it.*"

For a moment, Ronan seemed younger. His demeanor more boyish and innocent. Daria wondered if it was because he was always taking care of others, and had hardly had the opportunity to just let go like this. She squeezed Zara at the thought.

Daria could've sworn she saw Ares smile. One filled with genuine affection, tinged with heartache.

"You're wrong, Menodora. It is I who is the fortunate one," the vampire murmured.

THIRTY-TWO

Zara raised a hand against the bright sun. She swayed to the gentle movement of one of the tusked-camels the Sombra Quarter had provided them when they left Corduva that morning, though she missed Río, who had stayed behind in Damalis. The sand mounds of the desert were almost gold beneath the blue sky.

She groaned. "It's too bright."

Daria chuckled from beside her, saddled atop her own camel. "You definitely *overindulged* last night."

Heat rushed Zara's cheeks at the vague memory of her drunken state. Never had she suspected that her tolerance to alcohol had strengthened to that unfathomable degree. Fucking Suns. She remembered being close to Ronan throughout the night, laughing so much it had hurt. Touching him *way* more than she normally would. Or should.

Her gaze darted up to where the archangel rode, Ares beside him. They hadn't spoken much since the night before; she could've sworn Ronan had even blushed when he saw her that morning.

Zara tugged her shawl farther over her head. "Don't remind me."

Axar snorted. "And you give me a hard time about indulging in my vices."

"You were flirting with most of the Adrastean mercenaries. *And* took some of them to your room!"

"Shut up."

At the sound of Daria laughing, Zara relaxed in the saddle.

Hours dragged by. Hot winds accompanied them until the sun started to descend, revealing the constellations above. They glimmered in a sky swathed in indigo and purple hues, the colors melting into deep orange and blue where the sun sat on the edges of the distant dunes.

Zara's head bobbed, a drowsiness ready to overtake her when the rustle of paper caught her attention. Ronan was chewing on a strip of dried meat, a map spread out on the camel's saddle. His brows furrowed the longer he stared at the inked lines.

"If I may have everyone's attention," the archangel said. "We need to make a decision."

Ares leaned forward to peek over Ronan's shoulder. "Will this explain why you have been glaring at the map?"

Ronan tapped the parchment. "See this? The main path to Nephtyr takes approximately three weeks. However, if we take this second path through the canyons, it will cut that to about half."

"The distances don't seem that different."

Ronan grimaced. "It is because we'd have to go through the Wraith's Den. Not all maps show it."

Zara perked up. "Wraiths?"

"Yes, Horizon. To answer Ares, this path shortens the travel time because the Den is imbued with an ancient form of ether. Somehow, time is manipulated there, and it'll *transport* us closer to Nephtyr."

Axar cursed under his breath. "The wraiths are tricksters. They are manipulative by nature, and love their riddles and puzzles. That Den will be dangerous."

"Great," Ares said dryly. "Shall we take the path through the sands or should we risk our lives with the wraiths?"

The sun finally sank behind the dunes, plunging the world into a glittering night, frigid air replacing any heat.

The group was quiet until Zara sighed. "It's obvious, is it not? We are to go through the Wraith's Den. More and more cities are getting destroyed by specters, more people are being taken or killed. We are running out of time. The faster we can get to the Oasis of Dreams, the sooner we can amplify our ether and formulate a plan of attack against the High Throne." She pointed a finger at her sister. "And, as much as I hate to say it, the sooner Daria can return to Ikarria."

"Would this place be able to offer some insight about matters of the afterlife—or anything in regards to the spiritual aspects of ether and the dead?" Daria asked. Zara looked at her.

"The wraiths are beings that are neither dead nor alive, so it is possible," Ronan mused. "What an interesting topic. Why do you need to know?"

"It would help me with the dragon search. I also say we should go there." Her sister shrugged.

Zara raised an eyebrow at that but said nothing. The aftereffects of her drunken state had waned—quicker than she expected.

The archangel stretched his wings, bunching the map in his hand. "To the Wraith's Den it is."

They reached the Wraith's Den a few days later. The entrance took up the face of a canyon, tall carved statues of cloaked figures guarding over its open doors. It was so massive that Zara had to tip her head back to admire the ancient place. Ronan and Ares unbridled the camels, slapping their rumps and sending the animals back to Corduva.

Zara's body tensed the longer she stared at the darkness of the entrance to the Den. It felt like the dark was staring back.

Daria stepped to her side, a ball of fire burning in her palm. "Are you ready?"

"As selfish as this sounds, I am *so* glad you are here."

Her sister snorted and nudged her shoulder. Their group entered the canyon, Daria at the head. The flames in her hand darted toward the unlit torches along the walls, igniting them.

Patches of dry grass stuck out of the cracked tiled ground. Dust covered stone and the occasional piles of bones and leathers—remnants of previous travelers who had not been so fortunate.

Axar's whisper echoed in the tunnel. "I feel like we are being watched."

Zara lifted her chin, her gaze coasting their dark surroundings. There was no sign of anyone or anything; they were completely alone. Yet, she could sense an energy here that caused the fine hairs on her neck to rise.

"You're right," she murmured. "The wraiths know we've entered their home."

Daria shivered. "That's a terrifying thought."

The hall widened slightly, the threshold into another chamber looming at its end. A *click* resounded in the silence, making Zara yelp, and the ground began to shake. Tiles beneath her boots cracked, some breaking apart and falling into darkness as the floor started to crumble and disappear beneath them.

Zara gasped. "Run!"

She pushed Daria on with all her might, Ares sweeping in to grab her sister by the waist, carrying her in his arms. The vampire was so fast, he was a rush of wind and dust, and they soon reached the threshold to the next chamber. Zara didn't have time to sigh in relief as she kept sprinting down the hall, tiles shattering in her wake.

Red light skittered around her legs, giving her more speed. Axar was just behind her while Ronan flew just above them.

The archangel shouted. "Watch out!"

Before her, a section of the floor fell into an abyss. Zara was going too fast, she wouldn't be able to stop herself. And neither would Axar.

She and the shifter lunged in opposite directions, running along the walls with enough strength and speed to not fall. They jumped and rolled onto solid ground, collapsing on their backs.

The shaking stopped, the floor no longer breaking apart. Pebbles tumbled down from the ceiling, the walls seeming to sigh.

Zara got to her feet, slapping the dirt from her trousers. "Well, that was unexpected."

She peered down into the massive hole. Below, where the floor had crumbled away, an array of protruding spears awaited. Bones and skulls already hung from the thick, sharp iron.

Ronan ran a hand through his hair. "An old fashioned trap; I suppose that's to be expected in a place like this."

"Fucking wraiths and their tricks," Axar said, breathing heavily.

Zara had never seen the creatures before, but from her brother's stories, she'd gathered that they were very clever and cunning creatures. She had a feeling this was only the beginning.

Her gaze shot to Daria, scanning her sister's body for any injuries. She seemed fine, though was now taking a few steps away from Ares, who had only just put her down. Her sister's face was half-cast in shadow, hiding her expression.

The vampire's jaw tightened. He grabbed a spare bone from the ground and sent it sliding across the stone into the next room.

Instead of the floor dropping, iron spears shot out from the walls, though remained attached to the stone. Zara's eyes widened. If they had kept walking, they would've been impaled.

"Fucking Suns," she muttered. "Is there a way for us to identify these traps before they're set off?"

Ares grunted. "Every contraption will have different parameters. We need to keep a sharp eye on everything around us."

They'd barely taken a step when Zara heard the sound of grating metal. Stone exploded from the wall where Ronan was walking, a spear aiming right for him. She opened her mouth to shout but the screech of iron *bending* drowned out the world.

Dust settled to reveal the spear bent in an awkward angle. Ronan stood there, holding the knotted iron in his hands.

He took a step back, blood covering his palms. "Seems like this one didn't set off in time. We should move quickly."

Zara sighed in relief. The thought of something happening to the archangel had the blood in her veins turning cold.

"How are your hands?"

Ronan opened them, the wounds already stitching back together. He cocked his head, a small smile on his lips. "Are you concerned for me, Horizon?"

She couldn't find it in herself to shrug him off like she normally would. Instead, Zara brushed her fingers over his palm.

"Yes. Always."

Ronan blinked in surprise, a soft light swimming across his silver eyes. She didn't give him a chance to say anything else and headed after the others.

They crossed the wide, arched doorway and entered the next chamber. It was large, with a very high ceiling. Daria let her ether light a few torches and the entire room was doused in amber.

The walls had murals painted on them, similar to those they had seen in the mercenary temples. Depictions of feathered beasts and skeletal warriors.

Her sister was muttering to herself. "I wonder if there'll be anything useful here."

Ares flanked her. "For your dragons? What are you looking for exactly?"

"Nothing." Daria grumbled under her breath as she observed the paintings. "Nope. Not what I need."

The vampire sighed, following her around the chamber, like one would do with a small child.

Zara leaned toward one mural of a creature with long hair and a jaw full of metal-like teeth. "This one looks like the specter I fought in Damalis. Why is it here?"

Daria sucked in a breath. "You fought that? Wait, is that what a fully transformed specter looks like?"

The sight was so unnerving that it even had Ares pausing. "Suns Above."

Zara reached to touch the painting when the colors shimmered, and the entire mural *shifted* into another image. An archangel with red hair and golden-brown wings had his arms spread as if in welcome, above him a red sky.

Ronan cursed. "Is that Raziel?"

More images shifted, following the first. There was an elf dressed in dark gray-scaled armor, holding dark, curved blades. An archangel with black wings, facing the elf head on. And then, cities swarming with people with glowing blue eyes.

"The wraiths know who we are," Ronan rumbled. His hand was outstretched, as if ready to reach for his sword.

Ares folded his strong arms, glaring at the walls. "Their ether is peculiar. I heard they can read your soul and the stories written there merely by looking into your eyes."

Zara took a step away from the image of Raziel. The painting changed again, now showing the archangel dying by Zara's bare hands. Her eyes glowed crimson red as ether swallowed them both, consuming Raziel.

Words emerged underneath the painting. *What will you do next?*

Zara snarled at the question. The mural shifted once more. This time, it was her, except…

She almost didn't recognize herself. The woman before her wore armor she had never seen before. It was crimson red and black, lined with an ethereal glow, as if power was spilling out of the gaps. She looked like a burning star. More scars riddled her body, a jagged line slashed across her face, her eyes radiating a crimson light.

Behind her was an army, though Zara couldn't make out any of the warriors' faces. The image of them was smeared, blurry, as if unfinished.

The question below misted away, replaced by another. *How far will you go?*

Zara staggered back a step. Her ether was hissing inside, its hackles raised. Everything inside her screamed to *run*. To turn away from this mural. What were the wraiths showing her? They were tricksters—nothing they did could be trusted.

She gritted her teeth. "I don't see how that is any of your concern, *Wraiths*."

The mural remained still. It was too silent in the chamber.

Daria tugged on her arm. "Zara, look."

She followed her sister's gaze to see Ronan taking a few steps away from another painting. His voice was ragged. "What is this?"

The world seemed to slow when Zara saw the mural the archangel had been looking at had changed as well. It was Ronan—yet it wasn't. It wasn't the male she knew. He wore similar armor as the Zara in the other mural, except his colors were dark blue and emerald green, his eyes swallowed by a deep ethereal blue. Burning ether spilled out of his armor as well, like molten lava and crackling light. Two angry gashes slit the sides of his neck and jaw.

What Zara hadn't realized at first was that the depictions of themselves were standing on… *bodies*. Piles of bones and torn limbs.

Her heartbeat was pounding in her ears. She couldn't breathe. "We need to leave."

No one objected. They backed away slowly as red paint started to pour from the top of the murals, trickling down the painting. Someone grabbed her arm.

"Look away," Ronan whispered, his voice soft yet firm as he urged her to head back into the hall.

Zara tried to ignore the new question on the mural. The final message.

The future rests in your veins.

THIRTY-THREE

"This cannot go unanswered." Hadeon slammed a fist against the stone table. "The fugitives were in Corduva, and we lost them!"

Erebus raised a hand. "Let us first excuse Lady Maira from the table." He addressed the female. "Thank you for the report."

The deity, who had the same olive skin, black hair, and blue eyes as Nadira, bowed her head. "Your Majesty."

She left the catacombs where the meeting was being held. Her footsteps echoed as she headed back up the stairs to King Matías's office.

News of the deity diplomat's death had been kept hidden from the public—not that the average citizen would even remember the official. One of the more draining tasks since Raziel's death; now Erebus had to tend to these exasperating things when he should be focusing his efforts on Khaos and the Spirits. That damned archangel should've stayed alive; Raziel had played the tyrant well, keeping some kind of order—until he was killed, that is. Useless male.

Zara Santos. This new kill also reeked of the mercenary's work. All those years working alongside the Rogue had taught him how to identify the way she hunted. One of the many benefits of acting as Hand of the High King had been seeing up close the birth of her potential.

Erebus dragged his gaze to the Council members gathered before him. Sunlight poured from the small opening above. The air was cool here, smelling of the sea.

When it was only him and the Council, Erebus leaned back in his seat. "It is obvious that Zara Santos was hunting *you*, Iryndel."

He turned to Nadira. The deity clenched her jaw.

"The bitch was so close, and I didn't even sense her."

Erebus's lips twitched. "That is useful information. Zara Santos and Ronan Menodora are stepping closer to their Crossing—their powers will soon be ready."

Hadeon drummed his fingers along the stone table. "The group of specters you sent to Damalis have not returned; we can assume they were all killed. With respect, your methods are not producing satisfying results."

"You doubt me."

Erebus didn't have to signal for more of the fully formed specters to step out from the shadows. They were always waiting for him. The power he had been craving for so long now in his palm. And yet, there was still so much he had to do.

The creatures prowled along the edges of the room, snarling at the deities.

Hadeon eyed them warily, his jaw clenching. "Don't forget it was *us* who put you on the High Throne. *We* brought you to Khaos in the first place."

Erebus could never forget that day, even if he wanted to, and the events that happened in the realm where the skies were a clash of dusk and dawn, when the pain had split his heart in two and pushed him to be the male he was today. When he'd abandoned all that he was.

"You all had grievances against the Primordials and the world they were leading—the ether they took for themselves. I'm giving you the vengeance each of you hungered for." Erebus stared at the broad-shouldered male. "Khaos chose me to lead this new age. Anyone who disagrees with her decision can speak to her directly."

There was no argument. Only a fool would do so. Erebus flicked his fingers and the specters around them slowly returned to the shadows.

Hadeon sighed. "So theatrical of you, Erebus, when you know I speak the truth. Can you not order the Spirits to go after the fugitives?"

"I cannot command them. They were created with the purpose of bringing about the end of the world. I can merely *request* their assistance. And we do not need them for this."

"Then what about the Reborn?"

Erebus narrowed his eyes. "The Reborn is none of your concern. I already suspected the forces I sent after the elf and archangel wouldn't be enough."

When Erebus met the deity's gaze again, Hadeon smiled. "You've been studying them. Tracking them."

"Finally, you're catching on. Zara and Ronan are heading to Kairos, that much is clear. The reason for it evades me…"

No, that wasn't true. He knew the archangel very well, understood that brilliant mind of his. If they were heading to the realm of the sands, it had to be worth risking their safety. Something that would give them an advantage against the High Throne.

Erebus thought back to when he'd served Ronan. They had stayed in Nephtyr once, so the archangel could continue his royal studies, and there had been mention of a place filled with ether, celestial power. Yes. A place that would certainly serve Zara and Ronan well. How could he have forgotten?

He placed a hand to his brow, chuckling. "It seems I spoke too soon. The fugitives are going to the Oasis of Dreams, in Nephtyr. If they succeed, they will magnify their ether."

Hadeon growled. "Is that something we should prevent?"

"You haven't been understanding our goals, Hadeon. We must continue as originally planned. Damalis is already weak from the War, so it will not be difficult to accomplish what we set out to do. As of right now, our attention shifts to Nephtyr." Erebus slid his gaze to another deity. "Are you ready to visit the capital of the sands?"

Arwan was an old-fashioned warrior who'd once fought alongside the very deities of Celestrea he betrayed. He wore dark fighting leathers, his body strapped to the teeth with blades. The male pushed up from his seat, placing a fist over his chest.

The ether in his eyes deepened. "The city is under my administration. I will go and oversee the *progress* we've been making there."

Out of all the deities at the table, Erebus preferred him. He was the quietest and most efficient of them. The corner of the High King's lips curled. "See if you can find our mercenary and archangel."

Arwan bowed. "Will do, Fallen."

"You'll need some help."

Erebus waved a hand. Mist gathered in the room, the air chilling as rain began to fall from the sky, pouring into the hole in the ceiling of the catacombs. A sky that had been clear and warm mere moments ago.

The being strode up to him, stopping at his side. A twisted satisfaction pooled in Erebus's chest at the deities' expressions. His thoughts went to Zara and Ronan. He would have to keep a closer eye on them than he originally thought.

THIRTY-FOUR

Ronan was seeing things. The sound of crunching bone filled the air as they walked through hallways, checking empty rooms for any more traps. Time was lost in this place—who knew how long it had been since they'd entered the Wraith's Den.

Meanwhile, the past whispered to Ronan.

It may have been another trick of the wraiths, but in the depths of his soul he knew it was his power at work. Another shift in his *Izcali*. Laughter rang out between the stone walls, the younger versions of himself, Orion and Erebus darting past him.

Ronan's chest ached at the sounds of pure innocence and joy. The world before him shifted, the hallways transforming into those of the Damalisan palace. His younger self sat on the steps beside a courtyard, his father next to him. The sight of King Elijah made Ronan's knees buckle.

Young Ronan was frowning. "Erebus is from Celestrea, right? Why doesn't he go home?"

"Do you want Erebus to leave?" His father looked amused.

"No! I just know he misses his family. Can't he at least visit?"

Elijah's expression smoothed out, though it didn't hide the warmth in his eyes. "It's not that he can't, it's just safer for him to stay here. I think Erebus understands this, too."

"But Father, you are the king! I'm sure if you say something to the Primordials and deities there, they will make it safe for him to go back."

"It's not that simple, my son." There was a hint of somberness in Elijah's voice. "One day, you will understand."

The older archangel stood up, ruffling Young Ronan's hair. "Erebus is working hard in order to become your Second. He will support you as you prepare to become king; why don't you show him the same encouragement?"

"I will! But once I come of age, I will *force* the gods to listen!"

Young Ronan raised a fist, not noticing the way his father watched him. With… pain. And maybe a little hope. However small it might have been.

Ronan watched as the memory shifted, silver light swirling around him. In the midst of the glimmering tendrils, he could see his father and mother speaking to Erebus. They were smiling and chatting, Elijah patting Erebus's head, like he would do with Ronan.

Something wet pricked the corners of his eyes.

The ether disappeared into the unknown, revealing Zara standing before him. She scanned him from head to toe.

"It hurts, doesn't it?" She rubbed her chest. "I could feel it."

For a moment, Ronan regretted the power of their emotional projection. Tension bracketed his jaw. "My power continues to revolve around my past. I know I must face it; there may be an answer to a question that is unknown to me."

"Perhaps the Oasis will provide some insight on that."

Ronan tapped her nose as he walked by. "We should probably learn to raise our mental shields. I'm sure it would provide you some relief."

They entered a massive chamber with a domed ceiling, torchlights and braziers erupting to life as they walked in. The walls were painted and a wide stone path ran through the chamber's center, leading to a statue on a raised dais.

"Look," Daria shouted.

Ronan stilled. It was the carving of a woman wearing a thin gown, strands of fabric twisted up and around her lean, athletic frame. Long, wavy hair spilled down her back as she extended a delicate hand, her face etched in a solemn expression. He recognized this woman.

"It's Khaos," Ronan and Daria said at the same time.

The Queen of Ikarria met his gaze, her eyes shining. "You recognize the Primordial?"

"I can only give credit to the education I received when I was Crown Prince."

Behind them, the iron door slammed closed, shutting them inside the chamber.

"Shit," Ares murmured.

Axar shifted into his wolf form, throwing himself against the stone. "*No! Let us out you bastards!*"

Ronan scanned the room. His wings flared. "Well, this is a predicament. There are no other exits."

The chamber rumbled and water burst from the ducts high up on the walls, pooling onto the stone pathway.

Zara took a step closer to Daria. "I don't see any drains for the water. Another trap?"

"Seems likely," Daria murmured. The Queen of Ikarria skirted around her sister, her eyes on the statue of the goddess.

Ronan followed her gaze. Behind Khaos were three tall, large alcoves, the Three Sun Gods sitting in each one. The sound of the rushing water pounded in his ears, questions filling his head.

He studied the painted walls around them.

There were five distinct panels depicting different scenes: a handsome male watching over a young, newly-created Continent of Ribera, filled with humans, elves, shifters, and vampires; the Three Sun Gods tearing the man away from a beautiful woman Ronan recognized as Khaos; the same male embracing the goddess; a Ribera overridden by corruption and despair, its people directing their hate towards the man; and finally, the male leading a charge of ethereal warriors against the Three Sun Gods.

At the base of each mural was an iron wheel.

Understanding dawned on Ronan. He placed a hand on Daria's

shoulder. "Do you see the paintings? They're of Deimos, the Primordial of Dread and Terror."

The queen's eyes widened. "How do you know? There aren't any portraits of him anywhere. After Khaos was banished by the gods, any depictions of them were removed."

"Based on the murals alone and the fact that Deimos is the only male who ever became that close to Khaos, it is the only logical answer."

Ronan didn't mention how he'd learned this during his time in Celestrea, as he prepared for his Crossing.

Zara's voice echoed from behind them. "May I remind you both that water is flooding this place? We need to find a way out of here!"

The sound of gushing water turned louder as it began to overflow off the stone pathway. It poured across the ground, quickly filling the chamber and rising over their ankles. Ronan gritted his teeth, while Daria gasped in *delight*. She looked from the statue, to the murals and the iron wheels below them.

"This place is a puzzle." Daria waded through the water. "Come, Ronan. You seem to know a lot about celestial history, I will need your help."

Ronan's jaw dropped. "Never thought being trapped in a rigged chamber with the risk of drowning would bring someone joy."

"I read about Khaos back in Soleira. She was favored by the Three Sun Gods; some would say they even considered her like a daughter. Yet all that changed when she fell in love with Deimos, an outsider— the pariah of the pantheon. Khaos was ousted, banished to the far corners of the universe." Daria pointed at the murals. "These depictions are telling Deimos's story."

Ronan trudged through the cold water. "It was said he was an enemy of the gods, so he was imprisoned in the depths of Celestrea. But these murals diverge from the common story."

It was true. The first mural showed Deimos as a refined, intelligent-looking man. He wore simple clothing and held a book in his hand, as if taking notes on the happiness that thrived in a young world.

Ronan and Daria walked up the dais to stand at the base of the statue, overlooking the puzzle the chamber laid out for them.

"We will leave the first mural be." The queen pointed at the second painting. "Can someone turn that iron wheel for me?"

Ares immediately leaped across the room, sailing through the air and landing beside the wheel. Daria startled, and Ronan smirked. The vampire started to turn the contraption and the mural above him moved. It changed from the image of the Three Sun Gods pulling Deimos and Khaos away from one another to the same painting as the first mural—of him admiring the young world.

The walls groaned and more water poured into the chamber. Slits opened along the stone, and daggers were released, flying toward Ares. The weapons hissed through the air, but he cut them down with a swipe of his sword.

The vampire straightened. "I suppose what I did was incorrect."

Zara scrambled onto Axar's back as water lapped up the wolf's legs. He pawed at his face, whining as if in pain. Unease twisted Ronan's stomach. They needed to act quickly.

Daria tapped her lips in thought. "The murals need to be arranged in the correct order of Deimos's history. This first painting must be the starting point—Deimos enters a young, innocent Ribera. What happens next?"

Ronan cursed under his breath. It wasn't like the deities of Celestrea had given him many details about history's most hated god. Why would they?

He sifted through the scenes, racking his brain. "After the god arrived in Ribera, it became tainted." Ronan looked at Ares. "Try turning the wheel to the painting of corruption."

"If it's wrong, I'll kill you," the vampire grumbled.

The water was higher now, wrapping around Ares's waist. He grunted as he pushed the iron wheel, the contraption more difficult to maneuver with the weight of the water, even for a vampire.

Above, the mural now portrayed a world lost to the evils of mortality. People were abusing one another, from murder and robbery, to other terrible acts. And Deimos looked… horrified.

Ares braced himself, ready to defend himself from any daggers. Nothing happened.

"It looks like we are starting to understand this puzzle." Ronan sighed in relief.

"Three more murals," Daria murmured. She pointed to Zara. "Rotate the third wheel to the scene of the people turning on Deimos."

While Ronan and Daria were standing at a higher elevation, the others had to traverse the flooded chamber. Axar was now paddling—Ares moving his arms and legs to keep himself afloat.

Zara gritted her teeth, pushing herself to her feet on top of the wolf. "Axar, you might as well head to the next wheel—"

The wolf snapped his teeth at her, causing Zara to fall into the water with a yelp. Axar dove in after her, and for a breath the chamber was silent.

Ronan could only stare, the blood stilling in his veins.

Daria's voice was a ragged whisper. "Did he just *attack* her?"

Columns of water burst toward the ceiling as Zara and Axar rose to the surface, grappling with each other. She was gripping onto his fangs, stopping him from biting her.

"You have impeccable timing, Tallon!" she shouted.

"*Erebus commanded me to bring you to him,*" Axar snarled. "*You are a danger to this world.*"

Cold fury roared through Ronan. "Nyota, go!"

The panther ran out of the veil just as Basim emerged too. The nahuales lunged at Axar, biting and puncturing his hide with their claws and teeth. Not enough to hurt him badly, but enough for him to jerk away from Zara.

Axar whimpered. "*Fuck! Why now? Everything was fine just moments ago!*"

"We don't have time for this," Ronan growled, even as adrenaline pumped through his body. He was about to dive in after them when Zara thrust a hand out.

"I can handle it!" she said, jerking her chin toward her sister. "Stay with Daria."

Ronan didn't object. He narrowed his eyes on Axar. "If you touch her, I'll fucking skin you alive!"

Zara spat out mouthfuls of water as she tried to coax her brother back to her. "Keep fighting the urge. I will come back to help you!"

She cut a path to the wheel that was now fully submerged. Axar struggled against the illusions and the nahuales, trying to fling them off him, but they didn't relent.

"No, no! The elf and the archangel need to be in chains! They need to suffer for all the pain they've caused!"

Daria pressed a hand to her mouth as she watched the shifter fall prey to the illness in his head. Ronan touched the queen's arm.

"Focus on this puzzle, otherwise none of us will survive this place."

Zara reached the third wheel, sucked in a breath and went underwater.

Several painful moments passed as they waited. Then the walls groaned and the mural turned to reveal Deimos in tears, surrounded by angry, hateful people. They were pointing their fingers at him, screaming, sneering, and throwing things at him—the mortals he once served had forsaken the god.

Time passed, and Zara still didn't rise. Ronan took a step toward the edge of the dais when a flare of red light exploded under the surface and the mercenary popped out, splashing the water and gasping for breath.

"I couldn't see what mural it was—if it's the right one," Zara spluttered.

Both Ronan and Daria sagged in relief, though that moment was disrupted when water suddenly rushed up the dais, toward the statue of Khaos and them. He quickly grabbed Daria, holding her against him as they were swallowed up.

The world turned cold and dark. Water plunged its icy fangs into his skin, threatening to tear into him. Ronan's wings moved sluggishly, the muscles under his feathers working hard as he swam to the surface, bringing the queen with him.

When they broke free, Daria shouted. "We need your help, Axar! Turn the fourth wheel!"

Axar tossed his head from side to side, his screams filling the chamber. Basim was still clinging onto the shifter, the nahual biting down on Axar's ear and pulling him towards the wheel.

The male reared his head back, ether flaring around his body as he shifted back into his human form. His face was pale, blood pooling from the wounds the nahuales had inflicted on him.

"Thank you for that, Basim." He patted the nahual's head, trying to calm his breathing.

Basim made a sound, almost sounding irritated. Axar looked defeated, exhausted, but he turned his attention to Daria. "What mural should I change it to?"

"The one where Deimos and Khaos were broken apart by the Three Sun Gods!"

The shifter dove underneath the water's surface. There was now more distance to swim to reach the wheel. Nyota and Basim waded through the water, staying close.

Ronan looked from Ares to Zara, both of them struggling to keep afloat in the rushing water.

The fourth mural started to turn ever so slowly, but then paused halfway between two paintings. A rumbling noise started behind the walls and Ronan paled at the sight of blood spreading in the water. The mural started to move again and the depiction of Deimos and Khaos being pulled apart by the Three Sun Gods appeared. The blood lessened in the churning pools.

Zara shouted Axar's name and the nahuales went after the shifter, dragging the male back up by his collar, spluttering and heaving for breath.

"Ronan, can you get the fifth wheel? We need it to be Deimos attacking the Three Sun Gods," Daria asked.

He nodded, tucking his wings as tight as he could and diving into the water. It was dark as he swam farther down, shadows curling around him, and he summoned a flare of ether to help him twist the wheel.

He heard the mural shifting and daggers shot out of the stone, aimed in his direction. Ronan ducked in time, one of the weapons grazing his leathers, and kicked his way back up to the surface.

"Are you sure that is the correct order? The chamber tried to attack me," he shouted up to the queen.

"This should be it." Daria gasped as she fought to keep herself afloat. "We played your game. Now let us go!" she called up toward the ceiling.

As if in response, more water rushed into the chamber. Desperation and perhaps even terror had Ronan's body going numb. "No, we must have it wrong."

Daria frowned. "That makes no sense. History says that Deimos was the Primordials' enemy. The mural shows him attacking the gods, but it must be the last event that occurred! After they separated him and Khaos."

Her gaze jumped between the last two murals as she started muttering to herself.

Zara's voice echoed from a distance. "Hurry! The water keeps rising!"

"It couldn't be. If it was true, then history was wrong; it would mean that Deimos didn't attack the Primordials; they attacked him. He was *defending* himself against them. Fighting for himself and Khaos," Daria whispered. She turned to Ronan and Axar. "Switch your murals so it's the Primordials attacking Deimos first before they separate them!"

Ronan's eyes widened. He knew that Celestrea was imperfect, but this was something that chipped at his understanding of the world. Deimos's betrayal was the foundation that started the War of the Skies. If that wasn't true, then what was the real truth?

He didn't question the Queen of Ikarria, and he and Axar both swam back down to switch the murals. Ronan quickly returned to Daria's side—there was no telling what the chamber would do next.

Suddenly, pebbles and dirt crumbled and fell into the water, something echoing from deep within the Wraith's Den. Behind the statue of Khaos, the carvings of the Three Sun Gods began to rotate in their alcoves.

As each Primordial turned, they were replaced by a Spirit of the Midnight Sun. In the center was the mummified woman they had encountered months ago, her milky white eyes covered by a veil. To the right was the skeletal warrior with curled horns and a spear latched to its back, while on the left was the cloaked spirit with the scythe who had tried to take Zara in the city of Adira, when it was overrun with specters.

Ronan squinted through the dark locks plastered to his face. "The Three Sun Gods turned their backs on Khaos, so she created the Spirits of the Midnight Sun."

Daria clung onto his arm. "The water is rising too high."

At the worry and vulnerability in her voice, for a moment Ronan thought of Soraya and all the moments she would run to him for help.

He tightened his hold around the Ikarrian queen. "Take a deep breath."

They both sucked in all the air they could just as the water rose above their heads. The chamber was now completely filled and they were suspended in pitch black. It didn't take long for Ronan's lungs to start burning. Shit shit shit. He frantically tried to look for Zara, but the water was too dark and cloudy.

The statues of the Spirits now stood behind Khaos, the Three Sun Gods no longer in sight, and the chamber shook. He could've sworn there was the sound of iron groaning.

Bubbles burst from Ronan's clenched teeth; Daria clambered for air, thrashing in his hold.

And then the water began to descend.

Ronan gasped for breath when he burst out, gobbling up every bit of oxygen. His gaze cut to every corner of the chamber just before the others broke the surface, the relief at the sight of Zara almost enough to sink him back down again.

The water drained away slowly and eventually they were back on ground level once more. Ronan sank to a knee, his hands trembling as he shoved wet hair from his face.

"You did it, Queen Calderón," he said. "Congratulations"

Daria was heaving for breath. "Same to you, Your Majesty. Job well done."

A door opened on one side of the chamber, a sharp breeze blowing from the darkness within the frame. Zara, Ares, and Axar made their way toward them and the nahuales disappeared. The shifter had a hand pressed to his side.

"Are you okay?" Zara gingerly placed a hand on his shoulder. "We saw the blood in the water."

"The wheel got stuck, and I don't think the chamber room liked that. Some daggers managed to graze me." The male waved a hand. "But thanks to the nahuales, I managed to escape. These are just flesh wounds, I will be fine."

Ares ran a hand through his long, wet hair. "Were the wraiths trying to tell us something with that ridiculous game of theirs?"

Daria stared at the vampire. Ronan could've sworn she was scanning his body—perhaps searching for injuries.

"The common story taught in the Continent is that Deimos was an enemy of Celestrea. That he embodied all that he represented—Dread and Terror—and wanted to rule over the ethereal realm." Daria frowned. "But here, his story seems the opposite of that. I didn't see a man wanting to destroy and conquer, I saw a man full of love and hope. And of sorrow."

Ronan had to agree with the queen. There was more to the story, he was sure of it.

"And now, Khaos is out there, in between the planes of existence, while Deimos is still imprisoned…" Ronan paused. "Where in Celestrea is the Primordial being kept exactly?"

A voice, made of broken bones, echoed in the chamber. "That is the question, isn't it?"

A presence, ancient and angry.

Ronan and the others moved at once. They unsheathed their weapons, turning to find a woman looming in the center of the chamber.

The female was more bone than flesh, had no eyelids and a skinless jaw. She wore a red skirt, decorated with skulls and crossbones. Strapped across her chest was a matching breastplate, arrowheads knitted along the hem, and on her head was a small headdress made of bone, its ends carved into stars. Blood painted her bare feet and knobbly hands.

"I must applaud your efforts and quick wit." She tilted her head, the movement quick and predatory, gazing at the elf standing beside Ronan. "Aren't you a bright one, Daria Calderón?"

THIRTY-FIVE

"Wraith," Axar hissed, his eyes flashing yellow.

The others held their blades steady. Daria didn't reach for her dagger. Maybe she was a little afraid, but she couldn't deny the pure curiosity that bubbled through her veins. The wraith was speaking to *her.*

She squared her shoulders. "We apologize for trespassing on your home. Your puzzle was entertaining. It was an honor to partake in it."

The creature before them was a living mystery. Not much was known about the wraiths across the Continent except for their crafty, proud nature.

"Flattery and apologies will get you nowhere, mortal. Though, I will acknowledge the strength of your will to live. Many others were not so fortunate." The wraith lifted a skeletal hand, stray flesh hanging from the bone. "Mortals hardly realize when they are dancing straight into our awaiting teeth. As we feast on their memories."

Dread tightened Daria's stomach. She watched the others slowly back up to where she stood, Ares angling himself in front of her.

"We bested your game, so are we not free to leave? Why go

through the trouble of these tricks if you planned to consume us all along?" Daria felt a surge of bravado. "It seems a bit a waste of time."

The sound of rattling shells echoed from the wraith's throat. "The game is not yet finished, mortal. You have merely received a precious shard of truth that may serve your party well in the battles to come—should you survive the Wraith's Den, that is."

Daria glanced at the murals. "I presume you are speaking about Deimos. How will his truth serve us?"

The wraith disappeared in a wisp of breaking stars, appearing inches before her. "*So you may know the kind of gods you are support-ing*," she hissed.

It happened so quickly. Daria lurched back just as Ares shoved himself between her and the wraith. The vampire raised his blade, snarling at the creature who vanished in tendrils of moonlight.

"What the Three Sun Gods did to Khaos and her lover was unjust. The same goes for the young world that turned its back on Deimos." The wraith reappeared in the center of the chamber. "The Primordial of Dread and Terror never forced those feelings into the mortals. No god or goddess can exert their will on a being of flesh and blood; every living creature in this world has free will."

Daria hadn't thought of that. That the Primordials didn't con-trol the values or emotions they represented.

The creature continued, "How unfair it is that mortals cannot acknowledge their faults. Instead, they always blame a third source. 'I was tempted,' they say. 'It wasn't me, it was the evil that possessed me. I'm innocent! A victim!' It is *disgusting*."

The wraith laughed, though there was no mirth in its tone. Daria felt her muscles tense, her body ready to flee at any given moment.

"I don't blame Deimos for what he did," the creature said.

Daria narrowed her eyes. "You mean when he sought to destroy and rule over Celestrea? That is what the common story says."

"I wish that were the case. No. Deimos decided to simply turn away from the world. He no longer had a desire to be associated with it. The Three Sun Gods didn't approve of this, of course, and their hatred only worsened when their beloved goddess crossed paths with him."

Daria's eyebrows lifted in surprise. The way the wraith spoke about Khaos… There was a tenderness there.

"What happened between Khaos and Deimos?"

Daria didn't know why she was entertaining this creature; she analyzed the wraith, a being that was not of death nor of life, but something in between.

The wraith ran her blood-painted fingers down her skeletal face, pulling stray hairs from her skull in the process. "My kind were not always called wraiths. Long ago, we were known as the *Tzitla*, and we served Khaos. We read the fabrics of the Fates, conjured possibilities of the future in order to support our goddess in her tasks as Primordial of Fate and Time," the wraith said. "When the Three Sun Gods banished Khaos, we became tethered to this mortal plane, losing our original name. Never able to return to the celestial glory we once had. Forced to feed off mortals to survive."

Ares took another subtle step closer to Daria. The others did the same, slowly herding themselves toward the exit.

"You haven't answered my question," Daria said, trying to keep the creature's attention on her. "What happened between Deimos and Khaos?"

"A story for another time. Your party has learned enough." The wraith's soulless gaze pierced through her. "The game is still playing, Daria Calderón. This time, you must survive for as long as possible. Or escape, if you can."

Shimmering smoke poured out from the walls as more wraiths appeared, charging toward them.

Axar cursed. "We need to go, now!"

Daria bolted, the group diving for the open doorway. Darkness surrounded them, something gooey sliding along the walls. She lit her flames to see that it was made of cobwebs and bones.

"Fucking Suns." Zara panted as she ran. "I hate this place."

A wraith materialized out of the wall, hands outstretched toward Daria. Ares swung his sword down, cutting the wraith's arm off. The creature did not stop moving; its arm regenerated, flesh and bone twisting back into place.

Ares leaped out of the way before the creature could slash his face. "How do we kill these things?"

More wraiths crawled out of the cracked walls. They clashed with Zara, Ronan, and Axar who were having difficulty harming the nimble creatures.

Daria's mind was spinning with theories. She released her flames onto the wraith that had attacked Ares. The creature screeched, shells scratching on stone, before it lunged for her.

The wraith snatched her wrist. Daria met her murderous eyes, her skinless jaw, teeth grinding on rot. She tried to yank her hand back when light flashed across her vision.

Not light. Images. *Memories.* From blurry depictions of her childhood to the sharp recollections of today.

"I hunger for what thrives within the mortal mind," the wraith hissed. "Which one shall I taste first?"

An image of her pater appeared. He was sitting at the dining table, a heap of books strewn about its surface. Idris lifted his gaze, the skin at the corner of his eyes crinkling.

"Firelight, where have you been?"

Daria gasped in pain, the memory fading as the wraith latched onto it.

"This one will satisfy me."

No. She gritted her teeth as she thrust a hand into the creature's face. Fire ignited at her palm and burned the wraith. Its screams rang through her bones and blood, ricocheting between her ribs and reaching the stone beneath her feet.

It exploded into a blast of stardust and Daria sank to the ground. Ares rushed to her side.

"Light! They thrive in the dark, so you need to douse them with light!" she cried out to the others. "Be wary though, they will eat your memories, and you'll forget them."

Daria wasn't completely sure if light would affect them, but given how the wraith reacted to her fire, she chose to take that gamble. They just needed enough light to overpower them.

The others heeded her direction. Ronan shot out bolts of his ether while Zara zig-zagged through the hall with her crimson light. Axar moved among the fray, sword in hand.

Ares helped Daria to her feet, and they continued to run, the others in tow. She continued to throw bolts of fire toward the creatures. They all scrambled into a massive foyer; it was too dark to see all the details, but Daria could make out tall, thick pillars lining their path as they sprinted past.

A wraith lunged from one column to the next, flanking Daria while she ran, its hands puncturing the stone. The sight chilled the blood in her veins.

Fire spilled from her hands. It crackled and twisted into a makeshift whip. She lashed it at the wraith, cracking a pillar as the creature leaped toward her.

Ares appeared behind it midair and decapitated the wraith, giving Daria enough time to throw out a blanket of bright flames. The creature dissipated, dusted galaxies sprinkling to the stone ground.

The vampire had barely landed when a swarm of wraiths rushed them.

A wraith ducked underneath him, reaching for her. Ares's face leached of color. "Daria!"

She created a short blade of fire and drove it up into the creature's face. The wraith crashed into her before withering away, and the force of it sent her rolling across the ground and slamming against a pillar.

Chaos howled as she tried to get to her feet. Ares came to kneel before her, and brought a hand to her face.

"Are you hurt? Did you hit your head?"

Daria tried to ignore the warmth in her cheeks at his touch.

"I'm fine." Suns Above, her throat felt rough.

Zara called out to them from the chaos. "There is no end to these things! We have to keep moving!"

Ronan and Axar were farther within the horde, the archangel's silver eyes seeming to glow in the dark. A shudder crawled down Daria's spine.

She looked over her shoulder to find a floor-to-ceiling door, their only exit, sealed shut. Daria nearly cursed.

She turned back to Zara. "Can we blast ourselves free with your and Ronan's ether?"

"We can certainly try, though I would like to leave that as a last resort. I'd rather not risk this entire place crumbling down on us."

Ronan and Axar managed to push their way to them, the archangel sending a powerful gust of his wings to draw the creatures back for a breath.

The wraiths drifted together, their carved crowns clanking against each other. Their unblinking eyes steady on them.

The first wraith they'd encountered in the other chamber appeared in front of the group. "We are beings that tread the line between life and death. However many of us you slay, more will be born. Our kind are endless."

A being that was neither of death nor of life, but something in between. Daria couldn't help the flicker of hope inside her.

"If your kind exists within the in-between, do you know if there is a way to speak to the dead?"

Zara hissed under her breath. "Is now really the time to be asking such questions?"

"I'm a bit desperate, sister, so *yes.*"

This was the reason she'd come to Kairos, was it not?

The other wraiths snarled in response while the head wraith moved closer. "An atrocity. You are asking about an atrocity! Necromancy is an act of barbarity, not something any mortals should tamper with."

Necromancy. *Necromancy?*

Daria couldn't ask any more questions as the wraiths began prowling toward them. Ares and the others raised their swords once more; tension bracketed their bodies as they fell into various fighting positions in a half-circle before her.

"Stay close to me," Ares whispered, his eyes never leaving the creatures. "Use everything you have been taught, and trust your ether. Release those flames; I will take care of the rest."

A part of her was angry—at the others, at herself. That she was still being protected while they put themselves at risk. Still a naive princess, with little to no experience of the real world. The feeling gnawed at her stomach, deeper and deeper.

The head wraith spread its arms, and the foyer was plunged into complete darkness.

Daria gasped. It was silent for a breath. A painstakingly long breath, and then steel began to ring out. Wraiths screamed and energy moaned.

Within the dark, she could see flickers of light. Shards of red and purple. Bolts of blue and orange. Zara and Ronan. Their ether followed the length of their limbs like smoke and mist as they tore through the creatures.

They dove in together, two living weapons that always seemed to fall in step with one another. Her sister charged forward, her twin blades angled at her sides, the archangel flying above, his midnight wings arched over them. Daria couldn't take her eyes off them.

Ares and Axar were fighting the wraiths near her, back to back. Their bodies were quickly gobbled up by the shadows that seemed to grow thicker with every breath.

"No." Panic seized Daria's senses, devouring all logic. "Don't hurt them."

Desperation to save her friends had her moving. Her body fell into position, her legs braced against the ground, hands raised. Every technique she'd read from the book in Soleira, all her training from Ares and Basira, every lesson she'd taught herself—it all came rushing back.

Ether bowed at her call. Daria twisted and turned in one of the many fighting sequences she had memorized, bringing her hands together in a controlled circular motion. Fire erupted, a fiery wheel that devoured all in its path. The flames became a river of fire flowing into the heart of battle, a burning torrent. She was the ruler, and the ether her subject. Wraiths screeched, many of them coming in direct contact with the brightness and flames bursting into smoke.

A shadow moved in her peripheral vision and Daria realized it was Ares. The vampire had reached her side again, cutting down any of the creatures who managed to slip past her ether.

He met her gaze and the world seemed to slow. "Look at you," he murmured. "A mortal queen, with the heart of a dragon."

Daria only gave him a soft smile. The fire burned brighter, thickening into a tall wall. She lunged forward and lifted her gaze toward the head wraith, still alive. It had drifted back to the opposite end of the stone chamber, safely tucked within the darkness.

Through the heat and fire, Daria gritted out, "Remember that it was I, Daria Calderón—a mere mortal—who bested you at your game."

She pushed her hands out to the side, and the flames fell over the remaining wraiths in a burning wave, reaching to the far ends of the chamber. Their screams echoed; clouds of stardust exploded. Devouring and devouring, until only silence remained.

Embers floated in the air, tendrils of shadows crawled along the floor. Daria's ether fizzled out, her legs wobbling, and she nearly collapsed before Ares caught her.

"You did so well," he whispered.

Sweat beaded her brow, her heart pounding in her ears. Daria let out a shaky exhale as she dragged her gaze to her sister.

Zara stood in the center of the battle's remains, her eyes gleaming with something Daria couldn't put her finger on. A surge of emotions she could certainly feel within her chest.

"Incredible." Zara smiled. "You are incredible."

Daria nearly cracked out a laugh. Her sister had always been the one sacrificing pieces of herself to protect Daria, most of their lives. It was long overdue for the same to be done for Zara.

They had survived the Wraith's Den. Now, they could find a way out of that place and—

Zara moved, but the sound of tearing flesh stopped her. She

stared at Daria for a breath, brows pinching together before she slowly looked down…

A clawed hand had pierced through her side. Daria's world came to a screeching halt at the sight of the blood dripping from long nails. The head wraith rose behind Zara, burns scattered about her skeletal body. Half of her crown singed off. It had somehow managed to survive Daria's ether.

"I wonder how your memories taste," the wraith said to Zara. "If all the blood that stains it has made it sweet."

Daria wasn't sure whether she screamed. Her throat burned as if she had.

But she heard nothing as the world began to shudder.

As Ronan roared in fury, his ether splitting the air, threatening to sever the fabrics of this existence.

THIRTY-SIX

Zara didn't feel the pain at first. Her vision blurred as more wraiths exploded from the ground. They were like a wave, rushing to hold everyone back. Away from her and the one that had stabbed her.

Zara didn't know how she hadn't noticed it until the very last second. There had been a subtle brush of air, a touch of shadow pressing against her senses. She had moved just in time, or the wraith would have pierced straight through her torso.

The world was rumbling. Rocks broke off from the ceiling as pillars shook. And light—blinding light seared through the darkness. *Ronan.* Zara couldn't quite see him through the mountain of wraiths holding him back, trying to pin him to the ground. The archangel managed to break free, ripping some of the creatures apart with his bare hands, blasting them with dazzling power, only for another horde to swarm him again.

Basim leaped out of the void, landing near Zara and snatching the wraith's skirt in his jaws. The creature ripped its hand out from the Horizon's side to smack her nahual across his snout, but the wolf held on. Zara staggered back a step, blood trickling down her clothes. Basim quickly returned to her side, snarling at the creature.

"Warriors fight in your name, godling," it said. "Everything that has come to pass is all because of you and the archangel."

What?

Zara unsheathed her blades, speaking to Basim. *Help the others.*

The wolf hesitated. *I don't want to leave you.*

You're not. Help them. Please.

Basim whined before charging toward the wraiths. Nyota appeared, and the two familiars began fighting side by side.

Zara faced the wraith in front of her. "My path doesn't end here."

The tip of her swords slashed through the fabric of its skirt as the creature dodged her. It twisted around to swipe at her chest, bony fingers ripping the leather there.

"So we've seen," the wraith said. "There are many paths you can take, and all lead to bloodshed and heartache."

It slashed its hands down again and again. Zara was forced to step back, too distracted fending off the quick attacks to summon her ether. Her blades went through the creature's torso but its flesh regenerated immediately.

"You have witnessed flashes of moments that have yet come to pass. And you still don't know what it means," it hissed, unfazed by her attack.

Zara's blood was pounding. It felt like her soul was laid bare for the creature to see. A being that once served Khaos somehow knew about her visions.

"Don't speak in riddles, beast. Tell me what you know."

The wraith caught her khopesh blades with its bare hands. "Daughter of the Dawn, you can *see* the future."

Zara nearly faltered a step. No, it couldn't be. That didn't make sense. How could she possess such an ability? The wraith was playing its usual tricks. Surely.

Her hesitation cost her.

The creature's grip tightened around the edges of her swords until they *shattered* between its fingers. Zara froze. There was a faint ringing in her ears as she stared at the obsidian shards falling to the ground.

The wraith laughed. "The opportunity to taste a godling has never presented itself before. Gluttony has overcome me."

Zara remembered when she first received her khopesh blades. It had been in the Ikarrian mercenary temple, after swearing her Oaths as a Horizon. Hakim had walked in, presenting her with freshly forged twin swords wrapped in ivory.

His smile was warm that day. She would never forget how he ruffled her hair as she clutched those weapons tightly to her chest.

And they were now broken at her feet.

Her khopesh blades. Hakim's gift to her. The only things she had left of him. *Gone.*

Zara could hear her sister crying out for her, but she couldn't tear her gaze from the broken obsidian steel. The sight tore through her heart, ripped it apart. Her arms were loose at her sides, fingers twitching. She moved her mouth, though no sound came from it at first.

Eventually, the words seeped from her red-stained lips.

"Why would you do that?" The wraith was silent, watching as red and purple ether wreathed her body. "What have you *done?*"

The creature drifted back, but Zara rushed forward with the speed of her ether. A trail of shattered crimson light followed her as she appeared before the wraith.

She clutched onto the collar of its breastplate. Zara froze, light flashing across her vision, memories racing through her mind. The wraith was sifting through them.

A whimper of fear escaped her. Zara tried to pull away, but the creature focused on an image of Hakim and her pater. One of the many times Zara found them speaking in the mercenary temple of Ikarria.

Idris had noticed her standing there, waving for her to join them. Hakim glanced over his shoulder and said… What did he say?

Why could she not remember?

The wraith hummed in delight. "I was wrong. Peaceful memories taste better."

Panic punched through Zara's ribs as the corners of the memory started to dim. No no no. The monster would not take this or any other memory away from her. *Never.*

"The lines of your mind taste like the sun rising upon an ended war." The wraith paused, head cocked. "Your eyes are glowing, like blood red rubies."

Zara wouldn't have seen it, how the others and the wraiths halted their fight, their gazes fixated on her. She wouldn't have seen how Ronan ripped free of the creatures, his lips parting at the sight of the ether dancing around her body.

A plume of Zara's power rose behind the wraith. She could feel a shift in her power.

A presence manifested within her ether. Created by *her*. Within the ethereal flaming light the shape of something humanoid was formed. Skeletal hands clasped in armor emerged from the shroud. They gripped the wraith's shoulders, keeping the creature still.

The wraith panicked. "M—mercy, god. Forgive me!"

Zara's lips curled in disgust. She conjured a thought, a fleeting image, and it turned into a command. One the manifested presence heeded. It grabbed the wraith's head and shoulder and ripped the creature apart. The wraith's blood-curdling screams reverberated in the chamber before Zara gave the killing blow with a flare of her light. The creature exploded into mist.

For a moment, Zara and the skeletal figure stared at one another; it was shaped like a tall warrior, though she could not see its features as it was hidden within the fiery light. Her ether withered and the mysterious being sank into nothing but embers.

The other wraiths were motionless, stunned.

Ronan suddenly swept toward her and gathered Zara into his arms. "Everyone to the door! Now!"

The nahuales disappeared as they all sprinted to the sealed exit. Ares tried to grab Daria in his arms, but gave up when she swatted him away. A wraith barked an order and the ground beneath their feet began to break apart.

"Fuck, they are still controlling the Den!" Axar shouted. "The doorway is closed—what's the plan archangel?"

Ronan spread his wings, blue mist rising with the motion. "Forgive me, friends. This may hurt."

Ares glanced over his shoulder. "I swear, Ronan, you better not—"

The archangel jumped into the air, still holding Zara. With a single flap of his wings, a wave of energy swept out. It shattered the sealed doors, an avalanche of dust rolling out.

Dirt blinded Zara's eyes and clogged her nostrils. She tucked herself into Ronan's embrace as he soared out of the doorway. The others stumbled out and landed in—in sand. *Sand.*

Clouds of dirt dissipated to reveal the night sky above and the entryway to the Wraith's Den blocked by broken stone behind them. Canyons stretched out from the Den, rolling toward the vast desert.

Zara rolled out of the archangel's arms when he landed, sucking in the desert air. The archangel reached for her. "Your wound."

His voice was tight, and she remembered his bright fury from moments ago. Zara let out a ragged breath, pressing the tender flesh at her side. "It hurts, but it'll heal."

Ronan didn't seem to like her answer. She slowly moved, her muscles screaming. Daria was holding something to her chest.

Her sister met her gaze, tears lining her eyes. "I didn't think you'd want to leave them behind."

Daria held out the broken pieces of Zara's twin swords, the obsidian steel darker than the night. Zara's heart twisted. She didn't know how her sister had managed to snatch them in the midst of the chaos, but she nearly cried out in relief.

Emotion gathered in her throat, making it hard to speak. "Thank you."

Ronan took out a thin blanket from their travel bags. "Here, I will wrap them."

A deep voice reverberated in the distance. "*We were convinced that you wouldn't survive!*"

Hooded figures stood atop the nearest cliffside. They were tall, taller than the average man. Zara unsheathed a dagger, keeping it at her side.

One of the figures jumped off the edge, landing in the darkness before her, and she thrust her blade forward. A claw wrapped around her wrist, stopping her. They were strong, and lifted the mercenary up, high enough that her toes hovered above the ground. Ronan snarled, but didn't move.

Zara's breath caught when a long snout and pointed ears emerged in the moonlight. When dark, glittering eyes met hers. A jackal-shifter.

A deep, guttural, voice echoed from the creature's unmoving mouth. The stars seemed to shudder. *"Look who we have here. The Rogue lives."*

THIRTY-SEVEN

The jackal shifter tugged Zara closer. *"A pleasure to see you again, Zara Santos of Ikarria."*

She narrowed her eyes. The jackal was tall, with a thick, dark hide and lean muscle. He wore brown fighting leathers with ivory sleeves, a crimson-colored pauldron clasping one shoulder, etched with designs unique to Kairos, and a pale scarf around his neck, the white tassels brushing the sheathed steel on his body. A cloak lined with red hung across his other shoulder, a quiver of arrows strapped to his back.

Zara had never met a jackal shifter before, yet there was something familiar about the male. Her eyes widened.

"You're a mercenary of Kairos," she said. "You brought me the glowing flower when I'd been poisoned. You are the Horizon who saved me."

The jackal tilted his head, a soft rumble in his throat. *"How did you recognize me?"*

Zara searched the dark glimmer in his gaze. She remembered that scalding pain from all those months ago. How her skin had peeled and her blood boiled. And it was during that awful night, when she'd hallucinated a sky of dusk and dawn, that the mercenaries of Kairos had come.

She would never forget the human warrior who had placed the

cure on the ground, winking at her before disappearing into the shadows.

"It's your eyes," Zara murmured.

Someone cleared their throat behind them. "If you do not mind, Horizon of Kairos, I'd be grateful if you released her. *Now.*"

Zara realized the shifter was still holding her up by the wrist, and that the blood flow in her arm was beginning to slow. She glanced over her shoulder to find Ronan glaring at the male. A shard of moonlight angled down across his face, making his eye shine like a freshly forged blade. Except there was a threat writhing there. A brewing storm within the dark sky.

"*What a scary face.*" The jackal let Zara go. She stumbled back, bumping against Ronan's chest. "*Though I shouldn't be surprised, King of Damalis.*"

Shit. Zara could feel every part of Ronan's body tense. The archangel lifted his dagger, angling it slightly in front of her.

"Who are you, exactly?"

The jackal snickered just as the other shadowy figures leaped down from the cliff. "*I can see why you would be wary. But there is no need for that, Your Majesty. I am not your enemy. We helped you, back in the Estrella Territories, in the city of Adira.*"

Three other jackals appeared then, followed by an elven woman.

Ether burst from the first jackal and he shifted into his human form, winking at Zara. Yes, it was definitely the same male from before.

He had brown skin and a short beard, trimmed neatly against a strong jawline. His dark hair was long, fashioned in intricate plaits that were gathered together into a single, thick braid. He was very handsome.

The male flashed a smile. "I am Tareq. My queen, Kamari, has sent us to escort you to the palace."

That was certainly not what Zara had expected him to say. Ronan was still taut like a bowstring.

"How long has she been aware of our presence?" the archangel asked.

Tareq shrugged. "Ever since you entered the Wraith's Den. Risky move—if I say so myself. Not even we dare venture in those tricksters' nests. "Still, the capital is a few nights away from here. You shouldn't have been able to reach us so quickly if you were not already tracking our movements."

Tareq tilted his head, his lips curling further. "You are sharp, Ronan Menodora. Yes, we have been watching you very closely—except when you disappeared into Damalis. We didn't cross into your region, and simply waited until you emerged from your hideout. But let me clarify something."

Zara stiffened when the mercenary pointed in her direction.

The male met her gaze and smirked. "The Horizons of Kairos have only been assigned to watch over *you*."

Realization dawned on her. "That explains why you knew I was poisoned in the attack in the abandoned city. You were also there when the city of Adira was overrun by specters. You saved us then too."

"Well done, Zara Santos." Tareq's smile sharpened, before his expression sobered. "To make a long story short, after the War of the Skies, Kairos was bullied into signing the treaty that created the Aligned Kingdoms. Our queen decided to focus on the few benefits the agreement brought—trade, business, and safety. Kairos could increase its political power while keeping the High Throne at arm's length." His eyes narrowed on Zara. "Though her curiosity was piqued when she learned that Raziel was interested in an elven girl who had been adopted by the Ikarrian king."

Tension feathered across Zara's jaw. Raziel had left a jagged mark on her life, and would always haunt her past. She wished she could kill him a second time.

"So, Queen Kamari wanted to keep an eye on the late High King's movements while having me tracked," Zara said. "To see what had caught Raziel's attention, if it was worth knowing about."

"For years, we watched over you. At first, nothing seemed special about you, other than the fact that you were gifted in the use of the blade. But we noticed you were becoming very skilled and powerful in a very short amount of time. That strength, that prowess...

To discover that it all stemmed from that unique ether of yours was quite surprising."

And useful. Tareq didn't have to say it for Zara to read between the lines. What was Kamari's angle?

Ronan turned to her. "And no one in your guild noticed that you were being watched all that time?"

"I hate to admit it but no." Zara clenched her jaw, then met Tareq's gaze. "Your guild is impressive."

The male shrugged. "What is more impressive is how you managed to travel alongside the Queen of Ikarria without being caught." He turned his attention to her sister and bowed. "Your Majesty, we received word that Kamari accepted your request for an audience, but we assumed you would be traveling with a proper entourage. Not with a band of wanted criminals."

Ronan snorted. "Charming."

Daria's amber-brown eyes had betrayed nothing as she'd listened to the conversation. "Queen Kamari was kind to me in Soleira. I am grateful for her willingness to meet with me."

"And she is quite curious about you." Tareq turned toward the desert, pulling up his hood.

Zara chewed on her lip, considering the question that brewed in her mind. She took a step forward before the shifter could set off. "Have you heard from the Elios guild?"

The jackal shifter was silent at first, glancing over his shoulder. "They're alive, if that's what you're wondering. We offered them protection; they stayed with us for a time, but eventually decided to return to Elios. The very realm that has forsaken them."

"Why would they go back?"

"It is their home. I guess Tamaya and her mercenaries can't turn their backs on it." He watched her. "That's who you are *truly* asking about isn't it? She actually asked me to relay a message to you. Tamaya said, and I quote: 'You better make this worth it, Santos.'"

Ah. Those were the same words the red-winged archangel had uttered when she'd saved Zara in the coliseum. The always-hostile mercenary had turned out to be somewhat of an… ally. Only time would tell if and when their paths would cross again. A small part of her hoped so.

Tareq waved a hand. "As much as I enjoy chatting in the middle of the desert, why don't we bring you to our camp? You may eat and sleep—perhaps a wash would do you all good. And maybe treat all those scrapes and wounds I see. Then tomorrow, we will escort you to the city of Nephtyr."

The temporary distraction of meeting the guild of Kairos had almost made her forget about the pain, all the adrenaline draining away now that she knew they were safe. The strength left her legs, but Ronan swept in to catch her.

"Lead the way, Horizon," the archangel grunted.

The moon guided them as they walked. Nothing could sway Zara's thoughts, the fight in the Wraith's Den burning through her mind. Her power—what she had *created* in that place… The phantom warrior had *obeyed* her, though she didn't know how she'd managed to do that.

All of her enemies, including Raziel, had said that her ether would lead to otherworldly possibilities. Opening doors she'd never thought possible.

In that moment, Zara might have started understanding what they meant.

The city of Nephtyr had been carved by the gods. It was the only conclusion Zara could draw at the sight of it: the buildings seemed made of warm sunlight and ivory, canopies atop their flat rooftops, arranged with colorful throws and decorated jars; tarps and banners hanging down walls while ropes and ladders connected one rooftop to another.

Zara touched her cloth mask, ensuring it covered her mouth. Many soldiers sauntered the streets and rooftops, either as or whatever other animal they could shift into. Their armor twinkled gold and jade, crescent-shaped breastplates strapped over dark green tunics.

While she had been assured that she and the others would not be arrested, the guild of Kairos couldn't guarantee that there wouldn't be any spies of Elios. Not to mention what the deities who lived here might do, their loyalty tied to the High Throne.

"Hakim and Eshe would've loved this place," Axar murmured as he walked beside her. "A shame our assignments never took us to Nephtyr—or any part of Kairos for that matter."

Her heart twisted.

"What would they think of us now?"

Axar didn't hesitate. "They'd be proud. Worried, of course, but they would rather us fighting to free the Continent than continue on in servitude to the High King. They'd want us to fight for something more."

You are more.

Zara stepped aside, evading a little girl pulling on her donkey's lead. People ambled up and down streets filled with vendors that made the air smell of saffron and honey. The sounds of citizens shouting their bargains and of ringing bells brought her a sense of comfort. A reminder that they had survived the desert and everything that had come before that—so far, at least.

"Axar, do you ever wonder about where you came from?" She glanced at him. Axar was found in the desert, so it was safe to presume he was from Kairos. "Do you ever wish to know more about your parents?"

A pair of soldiers passed by. The shifter tugged the hood and scarf over his head.

"Even after what we've gone through, the answer is still no." Axar's face softened as he met her gaze. "You are my family. You and Daria. Whatever happened to my parents is in the past. I can still honor them in my heart, but you are all I need."

Zara smiled, bumping his arm. "What about when you fall in love with someone?"

"Then they will join our family." He shrugged. "Though, I don't see that happening for me anytime soon."

Zara hummed. "You know… Soraya is smart and beautiful. An outstanding leader."

"Yes, she is." The words almost came out as a sigh before Axar clamped his mouth shut, shooting her a look. "Why are you mentioning her?"

She smirked. "No particular reason. I just thought if there was anyone who could be a good match for you, it would be someone like her."

"Don't even entertain the idea—Ronan would kill me."

Zara fought back a laugh. She couldn't deny the possibility of the archangel doing exactly that.

"And *you*?" Axar leaned toward her. "How do you feel about *him*?"

Zara glanced at Ronan who was walking ahead with Ares and Daria—Tareq and the rest of the Kairos guild leading the group. She checked that the walls around her mind were up, blocking the channel of emotions so that Ronan couldn't sense what she felt.

Her brother continued, as if her silence had said enough, "Are you still punishing yourself for what happened to Hakim and Eshe?"

Zara sighed. "One moment I think that time has helped me process that guilt. Then I have waves of remorse for *not* feeling it, if that makes sense."

Axar looked worried. He tugged her closer in a one-arm embrace. "Whatever you do from here, I will support you. As long as you're being honest with yourself."

She hugged him back, some of the weight lifting off her shoulders. Her brother had managed to keep a strong heart, despite the things that quietly ailed him. Throughout their journey, Zara had kept a watchful eye on his behavior, reminding him to take his medication, knowing he would never ask for help outright.

A flock of women passed by, many of them casting flirtatious glances toward Axar, who grinned in return.

Zara rolled her eyes and elbowed his side. Hard. "Forget what I said earlier—Soraya deserves better than you."

His grin fell.

Canals of water emerged as their group reached the belly of the capital. The man-made rivers ran through the city, many boats drifting along them.

However, not everyone was using a boat. Zara squinted at the groups of people atop odd-looking rafts…

Tareq halted at the edge of the dock where water lapped at the wood. "We will travel this way."

"Where's our boat?" Axar asked.

The Horizon seemed appalled by the question. "Who said anything about a boat?"

He whistled, while the elven woman—Sahar, Zara thought her name was—tossed a slice of meat into the canal. The other three mercenaries, twins Ayah and Faris, and a stoic male named Malik, had shifted back into their human forms, and were chatting animatedly with Ronan and the others.

Faris was beaming at the archangel. "Tell me, Your Majesty, is it true that you witnessed the fall of the Gates of Celestrea?"

Ronan nearly choked on air before giving an awkward smile. "No, I was in the heart of the battle. By the time the Gates fell, I had already been taken by Elios."

Malik swatted the younger mercenary's head. "Boy, be mindful of your questions. Don't pry into people's personal matters."

"I didn't mean anything by it! People tell stories about the archangel whose name was lost to history. Many say he was very brave, fighting against the rebelling deities, protecting his realm to the bitter end. I was only curious."

The young Horizon seemed absolutely starstruck. Ronan's mouth opened as if to say more, but didn't. Perhaps more shocked than anything at the news that people within the Continent *admired* him.

The meat Sahar had thrown into the water started to sink, when something *big* moved; it darted along the canal like a shadow, almost blending in with the murky green of the water.

Daria hid behind Ares—whether she was aware of doing that, Zara wasn't sure.

"What is that?" her sister asked.

A massive animal emerged, moving with such stealth the water barely rippled. The creature's skin was a dark green, ridges running down its wide back. Rows of jagged teeth clamped together, slitted pupils honed in on the dock.

Both Zara and Axar faltered back a step, the shifter grabbing onto her arm. "*Fucking* Suns."

She realized the *rafts* she'd thought people were sailing on were actually very, very large *crocodiles*. Zara could see the animals more clearly now, drifting up and down the canals, transporting all kinds of people.

Tareq laughed as he boarded the crocodile's back. "Isn't she the most stunning creature you've ever seen? These ancient animals have an agreement with the rulers of Kairos. To protect and serve one another." He gestured for them to follow. "Come, come. There is plenty of space—she's a strong one."

Axar's grip tightened on Zara. "I am not ready for this."

She chuckled uneasily. "The world is much larger than we thought, isn't it?"

Ronan stepped onto the animal's back and extended his palm to her. "Don't worry, my ferocious Horizons. I have you both."

Zara scowled but took his hand, feeling the rough calluses on his skin. "You seem quite comfortable. This isn't a first for you, is it?"

At that, Tareq looked over his shoulder to Ronan. "That's right! I recall seeing you here many years ago."

The archangel nodded as he helped Axar, the shifter gripping onto his hand like a lifeline. "My father would often send me here to learn and train from the people of Kairos."

"Not quite what I was referring to." Tareq smirked. "I mean *after* the War. You were a wild one, archangel. If my memory serves me well, you had a little tryst with our queen, too. Actually I think you had affairs with all sorts of people. Both of you held very interesting… parties."

Zara's heart flipped as Ronan's jaw slackened.

"How do you—Have we met before?"

It was natural for Ronan to have had past lovers, romantic or otherwise. Though something in Zara's chest squeezed as she wondered if he'd ever loved someone. If he'd held them in his arms and whispered sweet words and warm promises—*Fuck*. She couldn't think about that. It wasn't right for her to feel *jealous* when she'd pushed him away herself.

Tareq chuckled. "No, Your Majesty. I was still training to become a Horizon then. But over the years Kamari and I have become close friends—I know *everything* now."

Sahar arched an eyebrow at the archangel, a silent question and maybe even a challenge there. Zara chuckled at how flustered Ronan had become. It was endearing.

She clasped her hands behind her back and leaned toward him. "Ronan Menodora, a wild one? *And* a tryst with the queen?"

He gave her a pained look. "Stop it. That part of my life happened straight after my escape from the Iron Isles, before I decided to overthrow the shadow markets. I guess I was looking for some *distractions...*"

She cackled. "It's still part of your past. I must admit, I did not expect that of you."

Ares was shaking his head, too. "Honestly, Ronan."

"*You* are in no position to criticize, vampire."

Zara raised a finger. "Question: If Kamari knew you were alive after the War, then why did she never report you to the High Throne? Did she not want to betray her *lover?*"

Ronan pinched the bridge of his nose. "At the time, the Queen didn't know about Damalis's survival. She believed the Crown Prince was the only one left from the guardian realm, a royal heir without a throne or his people. A threat to no one. As for why she didn't report me..." He shrugged. "We kept each other company when we were both lonely. Kamari probably took pity on me, on what I'd been through. I'm grateful she kept my survival a secret."

"Blessed Suns, aren't you a dreary one." Tareq's voice echoed as they drifted under an arched bridge.

Ronan glared at the male. "What is the point of bringing up my past? What happened between me and your queen was a temporary, mutual arrangement."

The shifter laughed. "I apologize, Your Majesty. I only tease!"

The crocodile swam down the canal that ran straight through the center of the city. Canoes bobbed along the banks, stacked with baskets of fruit or grain. Colorful flower petals and lily pads floated on the water, filling the air with their sweet aroma.

Palm trees filled the streets, the buildings becoming taller and more pristine. The jade tiles were brilliant underneath the sun, their reflections on the water shimmering like gems.

Pillars of nephrite and ivory pierced the bright sky, surrounding the great domed-structures of the palace within walking distance of the canal. Jackal soldiers waited for them at the end of the docks.

The crocodile hissed a sound, swerving to the side to brush its flank against the dock. Zara's legs wobbled slightly as she stepped onto solid ground.

Sahar tossed another chunk of meat at the animal. Water rose in torrents of white foam as the crocodile dove to catch its meal, sprays of water hitting the group, a musky scent thickening the air. The creature sank beneath the surface and did not return.

Tareq pulled his hood back from his face. "Now then, time for our group to disperse. Queen Daria and the general of war will need to make their formal appearance in court, while I'll escort the *criminals* to the palace through a private passage."

Ronan rolled up his sleeves. "Did you have to put it that way?"

The twins shifted into their jackal forms, strutting over to Daria and Ares. They unsheathed their spears, slamming the ends against the ground. They would escort her sister and the vampire to the throne room to formally greet the Queen of Kairos.

Zara's stomach knotted with nerves, but she knew Daria would be fine. Though her sister might have looked like a guarded treasure, something lingering behind her eyes. Something dark and murky.

Daria started the trek toward the palace, her chin raised and expression smooth, and Zara realized then it was the Queen of Ikarria she was gazing at.

THIRTY-EIGHT

Daria avoided Ares's gaze.

They were alone in a narrow hallway near the throne room. Waiting. Apparently, a troupe of water-wielders were performing in front of the court, so the twin jackals had gone ahead to prepare their introduction, leaving Daria and Ares to simply wait their turn.

Except the air was too warm and Ares's presence was too strong. It tugged at her attention, making her unable to ignore how tense he was. How he fidgeted in place.

Daria huffed. *What was taking so long? Could she not have sat among the crowd and watched the performance too?*

She moved towards one of the intricately designed walls, pretending she didn't notice Ares's flinch when she passed him. Pretending she didn't feel the sting of it. "How long do you think they'll make us wait?"

When there was no answer, Daria turned around. He seemed to be looking anywhere but at her. She took a step toward him. "Ares?"

The vampire clenched his eyes shut, turning away.

Daria rolled her eyes. "Is there a problem, General?"

"You best not stand so close to me."

She gritted her teeth and took another step. "It's not like I have a choice, in such a small space. Why is this hallway so narrow, it's a *palace* for Suns' sake—"

In a flash, Ares pressed her against the wall. His long hair drifted forward, shielding her from the world. Daria gasped at the sudden movement, at the cool feel of stone against her back. There was an almost drunken expression on the vampire's face as he lowered it to the slope of her shoulders.

A languid warmth curled inside her and she arched against—

What was she doing? Daria wasn't moving away, even when she should have. And she found that she didn't *want* to.

Ares's breath brushed against her skin. "*Daria.*"

His voice was rough and deep, her name uttered with such reverence. She bit her lip, anticipation quivering throughout her body, his fingers coming to her hip and scorching her skin—when she noticed the veins around the corners of his eyes had darkened again.

Black lines stretched out, his face twisted in what looked like pain. Daria hitched a breath, reaching a hand toward him. "What's happening to you?"

Ares's eyes widened, and he staggered back, the dark veins disappearing. "I'm—I'm sorry."

Daria stared at him. "Do you need… blood? But I've seen you drink from blood bags."

"No, I'm fine." Ares covered his mouth with the back of his hand, his gaze downcast. "It may be best if you stay away from me, Princess."

His words stung. *Stung.* Daria blinked, before moving back to her side of the hallway. Her face was warm, more out of embarrassment than anything.

Silence dragged between them, though she couldn't stop herself from observing him. How Ares had been behaving lately…

"You're different," Daria said. The vampire stilled. "Ever since you left the Adrastean forces, you've seemed… *gentler.* There was always a sort of darkness looming over you, but the air about you feels lighter now."

Ares lifted his gaze. Those violet eyes were swimming with emotion, one she couldn't decipher. Or maybe she was afraid to acknowledge it. The vulnerability in his expression, like he had been caught doing something he shouldn't have been…

The vampire's voice was warm. "You have changed, too, Daria Calderón. You've become stronger."

Her heart thumped against her chest.

One of the jackals returned then, interrupting the tension between them. "We will introduce you to the court now."

Daria kept her gaze on the jade throne before her, its back carved in the shapes of lotus flowers. Pillars of gold mosaic tiles lined either side of the royal hall, and grand windows towered behind the throne, showcasing a bright sky over the sand dunes.

Queen Kamari was as beautiful as the day Daria saw her in Soleira. Her sleek, black hair was cut just below her ears, and her brown skin seemed to glimmer in the intricate ivory gown she wore. The fabric just covered her breasts, cutting inward at her stomach before spilling over her hips and legs. The sleeves, separate from the dress, stopped at her biceps, the fabric sheer and glittery.

Kamari wore a crown shaped in the face of a hawk, its golden beak protruding out and over her brow. The design was similar to that of her soldiers' helmets, also carved into the shape of crocodiles, hawks, cats, and jackals.

Seeing all the light and gold of the chamber, made Daria yearn for the obsidian of her throne room. The seemingly cold darkness was actually strength and safety to her. She preferred that.

The twins came to stand on either side of her, Ares just behind. Daria ignored how damp her palms were as she dipped into a bow. "It is a great honor, Your Majesty."

Queen Kamari's golden eyes were sharp on her. "Queen Daria, welcome. I trust that your journey was a pleasant one?"

Daria could have laughed. Her thoughts went back to the Adrastean soldiers, to Ares killing them, to the wraiths, and to Zara conjuring that warrior—*creature*—whatever it was.

"It was very… educational."

Delight seemed to shine through the Queen's expression. It lasted only a breath before she returned to that previously serene look. "Nephtyr hasn't had a guest from Ikarria in some time, though I understand the circumstances behind this visit are… *different.*"

Her gaze slid to Ares. He bowed. "Yes, Your Majesty, I am here as an escort for the Queen of Ikarria. She rules in the name of the Lord of Vampires, King Matías."

Daria clenched her jaw. It was another lash at her heart, though she knew it had to be said. With all the eyes and ears on them, they needed to keep up the image.

Kamari raised an eyebrow. "So it seems. In your letter, you mentioned you had some questions for me."

"When we met in Soleira, you left me with the impression that you might hold some of the answers I seek." It was not an entire lie. Daria bowed again. "It is all for the sake of Ikarria, that will in turn benefit Adrastea and the agreement between our kingdoms."

Agreement. She thought of the raid that had killed many of her soldiers and imprisoned her pater. Her chest tightened.

The Queen's smile turned feline. "I would like to hear every word of it. You will be guests in my palace for the duration of your visit. Come, let us speak privately."

Kamari walked down the steps, her gown whispering along the dark green marble floor. She gave Daria a sidelong look, a smile touching her lips before heading to the corridor behind the throne.

Daria sucked in a breath and followed, Ares flanking her. She could feel the curious stares from the court members.

The jackal mercenaries trailed after Kamari down a breezeway that opened into a small courtyard, behind which a grand villa sprawled out.

Pools of water surrounded it, ducks swimming in the makeshift ponds. String music echoed through the rose-scented air and palace staff ambled by.

"These are my private quarters—no one will disturb us here," Kamari said.

They passed through thin white curtains and entered a living space with an office to one side. The Queen of Kairos strode behind the grand desk and sat in a velvet seat.

"Let me start by saying that everyone here knows about the wanted fugitives my guild is currently escorting through the palace. You were traveling together, so by association you two are also guilty."

Daria stiffened.

Kamari glanced at Ares. "General Valdemar, I did not anticipate you to be among one of the traitors against the High Throne. Especially considering you are Matías's *favorite*. I am very surprised."

Ares didn't move, almost resembling a statue. He merely stared at the Queen, his deep voice practically vibrating through Daria's chest. "Well, Your Majesty, imagine how surprised *I* was when I heard that you knew the King of Damalis survived his prison escape and you never reported it."

Something sparked in Kamari's eyes. She looked at both of them. "What makes you think I won't run off to the High Throne now and reveal all that I know? I could throw Ronan Menodora and that Zara Santos into the waiting arms of the Council."

Daria lifted her chin. "I don't think you are that type of ruler. You have allowed us to come this far—and I think you wish to see how things will unfold. You are a spectator in this game because you wish to place your bet with another player who is *not* the High Throne."

When the Queen didn't respond, Daria continued, "Besides, I could easily use your betrayal as a bargaining chip to gain more power and influence for my realm." She cocked her head. "The safety of my people and those I care about are all that matter to me."

Queen Kamari stared at her. Nothing but the quacking ducks and occasional splashing of water could be heard.

"Then by all means, tell me why you are here." Kamari said. "I hardly believed it when I read that you were seeking a way to find the Ikarrian dragons. I am curious as to how I fit in with your grand quest."

Daria steeled herself, thinking back to what the wraiths had said. "I believe the journey to Nephtyr has provided me with the insight I needed. I hope to stay in your capital for a few days to conduct some research and, if you're willing, I would like to ask for your guidance."

She wanted to ask Kamari something else, but she couldn't bring herself to say it in front of Ares. Not yet, at least.

Kamari glanced at the vampire before meeting Daria's gaze once more. "In that case, I look forward to you sharing your findings with me soon."

Daria surveyed her. Everything seemed to be going smoothly. She didn't believe the Queen to be an enemy, since Kamari had sent the Kairos guild to watch over Zara. But she wasn't an ally either.

"There is something you want from us... from Zara and Ronan, isn't there? Does it have anything to do with the fact that one of the Council members, Arwan, is here?"

The Queen's golden eyes brightened. "You truly do have the makings of a fine ruler. Let us join the rest of your entourage, shall we?"

THIRTY-NINE

Pain came in the form of ghosts. Ronan's gaze was set on the pools of water in front of him. The Kairos guild had led him and the others to a luxurious villa to meet with Queen Kamari. He had come out for air to the pavilion, while Zara and the others mingled somewhere inside, waiting to be called. He hadn't thought much of the Nephtyr palace in the last few years, but this place was stirring up old memories.

Ducks swam by, wading between lily pads—

Ronan bowed over, clutching a hand to his chest. Ether shifted within, and the world around him changed. He looked past the thin curtains fluttering before him.

Young Erebus stood on the stone pathway between the pools, staring at the water with a calm, thoughtful expression. He was older here than in the last vision, a few years shy of turning eighteen, and was wearing the leathers of a Damalisan soldier, his long silver hair tied back with a band.

A pair of deities approached the archangel, both wearing pins that deemed them students of Nephtyr's academy. Diplomatic officials in the making.

One of the males placed his hands on his hips, the ether in his eyes glowing silver. "Archangel, what House do you serve?"

Erebus looked at the deity sidelong. "The Crown Prince of Damalis."

Ronan remembered this. His breathing quickened as a presence drew up beside him. It was his younger self, watching the scene unfold.

"No," the male drawled. "The *Deity* House you serve."

Erebus flinched. "How do you know I am from Celestrea?"

"You archangels are so easy to sniff out. The ones born in the Continent smell almost like freedom. As delusional as that might be. Untamed." The deity prowled closer, his lips curling. "Whereas the archangels born in Celestrea smell like *nothing*. They are the dirt underneath our boots. I am willing to bet you were only sent here as part of that program to bridge the ethereal realm with the mortal lands."

When Erebus said nothing, both of the deities laughed. "No matter what fine leathers you wear, or whatever position you hold in this Continent, it will never rid your soul of the grime you came out of."

Young Ronan burst out of the pavilion. "How fucking dare you speak to him like that?"

The deities stumbled back, immediately recognizing who he was. They couldn't say anything to the Crown Prince of Damalis, a formal guest of Nephtyr, without the risk of consequences.

The black-winged archangel didn't stop.

"I will report your disgusting behavior to your professors and supervisors," Young Ronan snarled. Ether thundered in his gray eyes like blue-tinted clouds. "Your reputation will be ruined."

Even after the deities scurried out of the courtyard, the Crown Prince still seethed. "I should've blasted them with my ether and sent them crashing into the water."

Erebus chuckled. "If this had happened a few months ago, you might have. I'm relieved you restrained yourself, though. A prince shouldn't conduct himself in such a juvenile manner." He clasped a hand on Young Ronan's shoulder. "Still… Thank you for coming to my rescue."

The Crown Prince didn't seem appeased—Ronan recalled very well that he did in fact ruin the reputations of those deities some time later, tarnishing their prospects of obtaining respectable occupations in politics. Last he heard, they'd been sent back to Celestrea.

"What they said to you—you mustn't believe any of it. You have worked so hard to be where you are now; you deserve it. And it is only the beginning."

Erebus gave him a soft smile. "I would never let myself be hurt by small people. You do not have to worry about me."

"I was wondering, though…" The Crown Prince cocked his head. "It's been years since you visited your family. Would you like to? I'm sure Father and I can make it happen now."

Something dimmed in Erebus's eyes. "It's actually been some time since I last heard from them. I've sent them many letters over the last few months, but I haven't received anything back."

The Crown Prince looked concerned, fiery determination blazing in his eyes. That was how Ronan wanted to remember his younger self.

"I will look into it. Maybe there's been an issue with the couriers, constantly having to cross the Jade Sea to get to the Gates. If not—" Young Ronan grinned. "We'll soon be off to Celestrea anyway. With my position as prince and the ether I've been selected to wield, we'll have a major advantage. They'll have to listen to me. And then you can see your family again."

A beam of sunlight shone on the two archangels. Back when the world seemed more alive, full of possibilities. Even Erebus's eyes glistened as he stared at the Crown Prince.

The memory began to fade and Ronan bowed over once more. He scratched at his throat, struggling to breathe. Why had he been made to see this? Why now, after so many years? Shit. Shit. Shit.

Ronan pushed through the ache, shoving it down into the void of his mind. He was alone on this side of the pavilion, no one was going to save him. Fuck—Ronan wasn't just a king, but the leader of the shadow markets, and he couldn't pull himself together.

Except he wasn't alone anymore. Axar was hunched over a table, his large hands sprawled across the wood. Tension lined the shifter's body. The medicine that Ezrah had given him tipped over on its side.

"Axar, are you all right? I didn't hear you come out here."

"My fucking head."

Ronan had only taken a few steps toward him when the shifter twisted around, grabbing the archangel by the collar and slamming him against the table.

Ronan was quick to summon a knife of ether in his hand, the blue-flamed blade flickering under Axar's jaw. He glared at the male, ready to scold him, maybe even harm him. But the words died on his tongue at the expression on the shifter's face.

Axar was breathing heavily, pain so clearly etched in his eyes. He gritted his teeth. "Ronan, the pain hasn't stopped since the Wraith's Den, and the assignment Erebus instilled inside me—it's echoing throughout my head. I can't stop hearing his command to hunt you down."

The shifter's grip on him trembled, though his voice was still firm. "If something happens, you have to promise me that you will kill me. Kill me before I hurt Zara."

Ronan thought of Erebus in the memory he just saw, how different he'd once been from the male who'd done this to Axar. It saddened him. It angered him.

The archangel's expression smoothened as he pressed the ether-made dagger against the shifter's neck. "I promise."

That seemed to satisfy the male. Axar pushed away, stepping back several steps. "I saw the shadow dealer in you just now. You are more terrifying than you let on."

The makeshift blade disappeared from Ronan's hand. "One must do what is necessary in order to survive this world."

Tareq walked through the curtains that separated the various rooms from the pavilion. "I apologize for interrupting, Queen Kamari will see you now."

"Never a dull moment where Ronan Menodora is concerned."

Kamari sat behind her desk, Tareq at her side. Daria, Ares, Axar and the twin jackals were in the lounge area of the room, all of their attention rapt on the conversation. Zara stood at Ronan's side.

The Queen of the Sands was no longer the carefree woman Ronan remembered. There was a harshness in her gaze now, a blade that had been sharpened over and over again.

Ronan gave her a smooth smile. "It's been a long time, Your Majesty."

"When you left Kairos all those years ago, you were so miserable; I thought you would have wasted away. Alas, I was wrong." Kamari crossed one leg over the other, the silky gown rippling down her golden brown skin. "There is something about your aura. Like lightning that could strike at any moment. I can understand why the deities have been so intrigued by you. By *both* of you."

Her eyes darted to Zara.

"I've been wanting to meet you for quite some time, Horizon. I suppose I wasn't wrong in having my guild watch over you, seeing as you've become more valuable to the High Throne than anticipated. Ether so powerful, it's equivalent to that of a *god*. Yours and Ronan's."

Zara watched the Queen. She was calculating, assessing, a wolf trying to determine what sort of beast was before her. Whether it was friend or foe.

"I'm not some mere commodity the Aligned Realms can pass around," Zara said. She glanced at Tareq. "But your guild did save my life, so I want to express my gratitude."

"Let's hope that helping you stay alive was worth the trouble." Kamari stood from her chair, and leaned against her desk. "Tell me what you need."

This was the moment they'd been waiting for. The future of their ether—whether it would morph into a greater power or they lost their abilities altogether—depended on this moment.

Ronan took a step forward. "You already know that the High Throne seeks our ether. What they intend to do with it is still unknown to us, but we need to harness it before the specters become stronger than they are now." He didn't know if Kamari was aware of the Crossing and its details; after the Gates were broken, knowledge about the ethereal realm had slowly started to disappear. "Our Primordial power will not last, while the Crossing remains unavailable to us. We seek access to the Oasis of Dreams."

Tareq narrowed his eyes. Even the other mercenaries began to murmur uneasily.

The Queen tapped her nails on the wood, considering his words. "So you wish to use it as a catalyst for your power, and to try and meet your Primordial patron. It brims with dangerous energy. Not just anyone can enter it."

"You are already giving us sanctuary. Imagine what it would mean for Kairos and the Continent if we are able to get rid of the High Throne and its forces."

"All the effort of keeping an eye on me would have been pointless if you were not to see it through to the end," Zara added.

The Queen observed them. Hot wind brushed through the curtains. Music from somewhere in the villa played in the incense-scented air.

Kamari's smile was sharp. "Fine, I will send a request to the acolytes of the Oasis—but there is something you must do for me in return."

The relief quickly twisted into nervous anticipation. Deep down, Ronan knew they wouldn't have been able to walk into the Oasis of Dreams without fulfilling some agreement first. That was the world he knew.

The other two Kairos mercenaries, Sahar and Malik, entered the villa. The shifter brought a fist over his chest as he bowed to the queen. "Nothing of concern to report, Your Majesty. The court was disbanded; many of the officials and advisors have gone off to carry out their duties."

Tension feathered around Kamari's jaw. "And the deities?"

"They weren't present."

Sahar brushed past Malik, walking toward the queen. The elven mercenary smiled at Kamari. "All is well."

Ronan didn't miss how the woman softly brushed Kamari's hand before turning to stand by her side, opposite Tareq. Nor did he miss Kamari's flushed cheeks.

A smile pulled at Ronan's lips. Good for her.

The Queen sighed. "A member of the Council lives among us. Arwan, a warrior of legend, has been assigned to oversee Kairos, and by extension *me*."

Zara stilled. "Do you not have control over your kingdom?"

"If you are asking whether I'm in the same predicament as Queen Daria, no, I am not a prisoner, but the High Throne has been testing its boundaries, stretching its authority beyond what the treaty originally entailed."

Ronan noted how Kamari's gaze flicked to Daria, softening for a moment before honing in on Zara once more.

The Queen's expression darkened. "My people have been disappearing. It started with the border towns, and is now getting closer to the capital. I have no inkling as to where they are being taken. The Kairos guild have been doing their part in tracking the specters, but our realm is vast and my resources are already stretched thin."

Kamari took a deep exhale. "Arwan and his officials mainly conduct their business in Nephtyr; however, my mercenaries have caught the council member leaving the capital in the dead of night. He will disappear for several days. Where the deity goes, we know not."

Ronan folded his arms, sensing where this was going. "So you'd like us to find out what Arwan is really doing in your realm."

"Work fit for a mercenary," Zara said. She cocked her head. "It's better to send us after the deity, rather than your own people. We are expendable."

Kamari grinned. "I'll grant you a visit to the Oasis, and in exchange, you find where the deity goes and his true motives. It's a rather good deal for you. It's not as though you were thinking of sneaking into the Oasis, a place we consider *sacred?*"

Ronan and Zara shared a look before they both said, "No, never."

Tareq snorted, though Kamari didn't look amused.

"Lighten up, Your Majesty," Ronan said. "Of course, we will help you."

"If I may add to this developing transaction…" Zara reached into her travel bag, taking out the thin blanket with the broken shards of her khopesh blades and extending them to the Queen. "Would you be able to have these repaired?"

"Suns Above, I am being asked many favors today."

Sahar gingerly touched the Queen's shoulder. "Look, my love, those weapons are of Kairos."

Kamari arched an eyebrow in surprise, observing the shattered obsidian. "How did you come across those weapons?"

No one else other than Ronan would've noticed the tremble in Zara's lips. "They were a gift."

The Queen stood and moved closer, brushing her fingers over the shards. "I will send them to my blacksmiths; their skills are unmatched." She took the blanket from Zara. "That being said, I make no promises."

Zara sucked in a sharp breath. "Thank you."

The little wolf always put on a brave face, even when she was hurting. Ronan placed a hand on Zara's arm, before addressing Kamari. "How would you like us to handle this assignment of yours?"

"I will be hosting a feast to celebrate the harvest season, and the deities will be in attendance. Daria and the general will come as my esteemed guests, while the three of you…" Kamari looked between him, Zara, and Axar, her lips dancing in amusement. "I've been meaning to hire more hosts."

FORTY

The following morning, the palace of Nephtyr was quiet, not a soul around. Statues of jackal warriors watched as Ares stormed down the hall.

Arched windows filled the wall on his right, one set of glass doors leading to a balcony. Ares nearly burst through them, gulping down the warm air. Palm trees towered over the stone railing, and the smell of frankincense and flowers wafted into his lungs. It wasn't enough to soften the burning ache inside.

He growled to himself and reached for the last blood bag tucked within the folds of his Kairos attire. He was grateful to have been able to wash his body and be rid of the mucky clothes, the Queen of the Sands having arranged for a new wardrobe for them during their stay. Red and white fabrics, long-sleeves with billowing trousers.

Ares's stomach dropped at the sight of the blood bag running low. He would have to go buy some more—though it wouldn't do much good. His fangs ached as he lapped up the rest of its contents.

An animalistic sound rumbled in his throat. The blood was of fine quality, but it was still bland to his tongue, failing to satisfy the fire that burned throughout his abdomen.

He was so, so hungry. It was already beginning to affect his body; it had been a fucking challenge to keep his grip on his sword while sparring. He'd left Ronan midway through their practice for some air, some space.

The bloodroot didn't get rid of the thirst, but he found it lessened the itch in his throat. Red smoke curled into the air as he lit a new roll. The drug sank deep into his lungs, spreading along his limbs.

The vampire glanced over his shoulder at the sound of Ronan yanking the balcony doors open, a furious glint in his eyes.

Ares turned away. "I already know what you're going to say."

"Your thirst is nothing to jest about, Valdemar. You are *suffering*." The archangel stomped over to his side. "Vampires are not meant to rely on blood bags this long."

He gritted his teeth. Fuck, his fangs hurt. "Don't you think I know that?"

Ronan sighed. "Then drink from me. I don't understand why you haven't sought a blood source yet, but at least allow me to help."

Suddenly Ares could hear Ronan's pulse: a delicate sound, like a boat bobbing on water. He could see the veins running under the archangel's sun-kissed skin.

"No, thanks," Ares said, tension bracketing the general's jaw. "Besides, I doubt archangel blood would taste good."

"I'm sure archangel blood tastes *amazing*." Ronan had the nerve to look offended. "Why won't you drink from someone at the blood bank?"

Ares growled. "Because I *can't*."

The archangel blinked at him several times. Then something dawned on him, eyes widening. "I heard it can happen sometimes to vampires. Where they are unable to drink from anyone, unless it is someone they—"

"*Don't say it*." The words ripped out from between Ares's teeth. His heart was pounding; it hurt more than his hunger. A different kind of pain. Though one he would gladly hold onto for the rest of his miserable existence—he deserved it.

Ronan's face fell. "You can't do this to yourself."

"I will do whatever I must."

Ares took another long drag of the bloodroot. He leaned across the stone of the balcony, looking over the edge. His gaze landed on a very familiar woman in the gardens. *Daria.* Just his luck.

Her presence was formidable. A calm strength. The princess—the *Queen*—wouldn't show her claws unless absolutely necessary, but when she did she was a force to be reckoned with. She was the light, a blazing sconce in the darkness, spearing through the cold.

Daria was training with her mercenary sister. Zara was sitting on a bench, meditating—she had been doing that a lot. So had Ronan. The Horizon opened her eyes to watch her sister, while Axar was curled up in front of a tall plant in his wolf form, asleep.

Daria swept across the ground, sending out a wave of flames from her feet. Fire rolled out and lapped at the air, before forming a small whirlwind. The mercenary clapped her hands, and the princess bowed, releasing her ether.

"Your control is impressive," Zara said. "I'm curious how you'll manage in a duel."

Light speared out of her palm into a makeshift blade, the sight of the rare ether never ceasing to amaze Ares. Daria, however, took a step back. "Are you insane?"

"Don't be scared. This will help you, I *promise.*"

Ronan chuckled beside Ares. The gray in his eyes shone like rippling water as he gazed at Zara.

"And you give *me* a hard time." Ares leaned toward the archangel as they both rested their arms on the balcony's ledge. "How do you feel about the mercenary?"

The smile on Ronan's face was gentle. Of a man who had been wandering dark, lonely nights and had finally found the sun. "Zara's everything to me."

Ares raised his eyebrows at the sincerity in Ronan's voice. In all the years he had known the archangel, the vampire wasn't sure if Ronan would ever be able to get past all the shit he'd gone through.

But now… Ares felt his chest tighten. What an odd sensation. "I'm proud of you. It took time and a lot of work, but you are starting to move on, allowing yourself to be happy."

"I meant what I said. Just being around her... It's more than enough." His expression fell slightly.

"I'm sure everything will work out for you both."

Ronan chuckled. "The vampire can be sentimental when he wants to."

"Enough." Ares pushed away from the ledge. Paused. "I wanted to ask about the status of my request?"

The archangel's expression turned serious.

"Of course. The package will have been received and taken to a safe house by now. I've told my shadow dealers to keep you informed. They are also to follow your orders."

Ares exhaled; he felt like he was finally able to breathe for the first time in a long while. "Thank you," he whispered, his voice ragged. "Thank you."

"Always, Valdemar." Ronan squeezed his shoulder. "How's Morana?"

"She's fine. Or as fine as she can be." The vampire smiled softly. "Eventually, I will need to tell her that you've been the one supplying her medicine."

"No need for that. It's safer for her not to know."

Ares thought about all the things he wanted to tell his mother. What he was trying to change, what he wanted out of life. He wanted to talk to her about the annoying, somewhat clingy archangel he'd stumbled upon—and about a certain queen, and what he felt for her...

Ronan nudged him. "Let us have some breakfast. You need to eat something."

The archangel walked back into the hall, and for a moment Ares wondered what he had done to deserve a friendship such as this one. He stopped himself. *Friendship.* The relationship he had with Ronan... He had never formally acknowledged it as that before.

Ares ground the bloodroot under his boot and followed his friend.

"Turn your face toward me. I'm almost done."

Zara gave Sahar a sidelong glance. "I never imagined a Horizon of Kairos would be dressing me and doing my make up for a party."

The elven mercenary hummed as she swept gold powder across Zara's cheekbones. "And I never thought I would be doing the Rogue's makeup for some light espionage."

"How the Fates weave and entangle our lives," one of the twin mercenaries, Ayah, chirped.

The younger jackal-shifter sat on the dresser, eating grapes and swinging her legs. She seemed to follow Sahar like a little shadow, her presence pure and just simply *good*.

Zara wished Daria could have joined them, but as her sister was a royal guest, she was already at the feast with Ares. Knowing that the vampire would watch over her gave Zara more comfort than she realized.

Outside the window of her bedchamber, torchlight flickered. Royal gazebos had been erected on the palace's rooftop, figures already meandering about the flower-kissed hedges. Music from string and wind instruments flowed from them.

"How long have you been a member of the Kairos guild, Ayah?" Zara asked. "You seem too young to be a mercenary."

Ayah's cheek popped out to the side as she stuffed more grapes into her mouth. "Weren't *you* quite young when you joined yours? I am twenty! Though I can't say for sure, I don't know when I was born."

"We thought Ayah and Faris were members of a circus… Turned out they were slaves bought from the shadow markets. Used and abused by the leaders of their troupe," Sahar explained, her jaw tense. "Tareq saved them. He bought them, while Malik and I snuck past their defenses. We destroyed that place from the inside out and freed the others."

At the mention of the shadow markets, Zara stiffened. "The Sombra Quarter *sells* people?"

Sahar blinked at her in confusion and then shook her head. "Oh, no. This was before Ronan Menodora controlled the shadow markets. When the archangel took the helm, one of his first commands was to disband the slave trade."

"I heard he killed a lot of the shadow dealers responsible then," Ayah said, mid-chew.

Zara sighed. A part of her wished she'd known Ronan at that time. She would've enjoyed the hunt at his side.

"You and the King of Damalis seem close." Sahar gave her a pointed look. "May I ask what your relationship is?"

"I was assigned to kill him," Zara said. She thought of midnight wings and silver-dusted eyes. As if summoned, memories of Hakim and Eshe appeared too. But for the first time in a long while… the ugly sensation was a bit more muted. It didn't attack her, twist the contents of her stomach. After what happened on the rooftop in Corduva with Ronan—the release of her power—the pain and guilt had morphed. They were still there, still present, but not as debilitating. "And now I find myself unwilling to leave his side."

Sahar's lips twitched. The elf dabbed a thin brush along the edge of Zara's eyelid. "Romantics would like the sound of that."

Zara thought of how Sahar had been with the Queen during the meeting. The obvious affection there. "How long have you been with Queen Kamari?"

"Four years now. I thank the Suns for the courage I mustered to finally confess my feelings to her."

"What is it like for a mercenary to be with the leader of a realm?" Zara was *definitely* not asking for herself. Definitely.

"There are challenges to being with someone who must carry the fate of thousands, but *she* has never been a challenge. Like any relationship, it depends on the quality of the effort of those involved. Kamari and I work together—even though it never *feels* like work."

Hearing the mercenary's words sent an ache through Zara's chest. Her heart squeezed.

"You must love Kamari very much."

"I do," Sahar murmured, eyeing her. The mercenary took a step back and clicked her tongue in approval. "You are ready."

Zara walked to the plated mirror perched in one corner of the room. The woman in her reflection was… not someone she recognized.

Her eyelids were painted with shades of green powder that blended into shimmering gold, lined with kohl. Her dark hair was styled with gems and stones to flow down her back. And her dress—Zara spread her arms and twisted her body side to side.

The two-piece gown was an olive green, silky fabric, threaded with beads of the same color in an expert design. It made her think of water droplets streaming down a glassy surface. Her strapless top criss-crossed over her abdomen, her midriff bare. Golden gems lined the fabric covering her breasts. Sheer sleeves fell from her biceps.

Her skirt, high-waisted and long and in the same beaded design, pooled around her heeled shoes, slits on both sides showing her muscular legs. Around her neck was a thick band of gold in the shape of wings. More jewelry was strapped around her wrists and fingers—even along her pierced pointed ears. It wasn't the first time she had worn earrings, but it had been so long the sight made her smile.

It was the most dressed-up Zara had ever been. Not even in Ikarria had she dared to adorn herself like this. This was more her sister's area of expertise. Not someone like *her*—a violent beast whose soul was stained with red.

"You look stunning," Ayah said with a grin.

Zara blushed. "Thank you."

Sahar snuck in between her and the mirror to fasten a veil that would hide her face, apart from her eyes. "Remember the plan, Zara: you are one of the entertainers for the feast. Charm and distract the deities and get as much information as you can"

The golden lining of the veil felt cool against Zara's skin. "I'm ready."

They headed out into the hall just as Tareq, Axar, and Ronan appeared from another door. Malik and Faris were with them as well, the latter almost skipping to keep up with the archangel, his eyes bright on Ronan.

"Did you fight any gods during the War? Who's your patron god? No wait, I want to know more about Damalis. What kind of food do your people eat? What's your favorite?"

Malik's voice sounded tired. "Boy, stop pestering him."

Ronan was chuckling. "I don't mind the questions. One of my

favorites… There is this sweet bread with a topping made of flour and sugar, designed to look like a seashell. It is *delicious*, you must try it."

"May I come visit then?"

"You are always welcome." The archangel ruffled Faris's hair.

Zara blinked once, twice.

Ronan was wearing a two-piece outfit: midnight blue fabric lined with gold, the long sleeves made of a sheer material while the rest was decorated with dark beads. It was cropped, revealing the strong muscles of his abdomen. His trousers were loose-fitting, and hung low across his waist. Like Zara, he too wore a thick band of gold around his neck. And his eyes were lined with kohl, causing the silver in them to burst like falling stars. There was a flutter in her chest. He was—

"Beautiful." Ronan's lips were slightly parted, his gaze searing into her. "You are beautiful, Zara Santos."

The compliment surprised her. She hadn't realized he had been staring at her too. Her cheeks heated. *Suns.*

Zara averted her gaze. "As are you… I suppose."

She could almost feel the heat of the archangel's smile on her face.

Before Ronan could reach for her, Tareq swept in to loop her arm with his own. "I must make all my enemies jealous, Horizon; please allow me to escort you to the feast."

Zara choked out a laugh. "You are speaking nonsense. I am to be an entertainer, not a formal guest, remember?"

The jackal-shifter shrugged and led her out of the hall, forcing the others to follow them. Zara didn't turn to look at Ronan but she could still feel his gaze on her. Hot as a brand. One that sent shivers down her skin.

Faris muttered to Ronan. "You were too slow."

Glasses of sparkling champagne and wine were like twinkling stars on the tray on Zara's palm. The firelight made the liquid gleam as she weaved through the crowd, avoiding the dancing plaza. Out of the corner of her eye she could see Daria at one end of the main seating area, on a wide sofa. Her sister was beside Kamari, Ares standing at her other side. The vampire caught Zara's gaze and gave her a slight nod before looking away.

Zara swung her serving tray in front of the male she had been approaching. "Have you truly run out of drinks?"

Axar snorted. His eyes narrowed above a silky, dark blue mask covering the lower half of his face. He set some of her glasses onto his tray. "What can I say? My charm makes me easy to talk to. The people of Kairos can really handle their drink. I'm impressed."

Zara surveyed him. "Have you been taking your medicine?"

"*Yes*," he drawled, flicking her arm. "You don't have to dote on me so much. My mind has been clear for a while now. I'm fine."

She grunted, eyeing him. "I take it you haven't heard anything noteworthy?"

"Not yet. The deities are always surrounded by other officials." Axar looked somewhere behind her and chuckled under his breath. "It seems your archangel is popular this evening, too."

"What?" Zara frowned, following her brother's gaze.

Various males and females were gathered around Ronan. Their eyes seemed to sparkle, some trying to get closer to him, brush their fingers along his arm, press themselves against his body. Zara's eye twitched.

The archangel wore the same dark mask as Axar's. He said something just then, making everyone laugh loudly. It couldn't have been *that* funny.

"The archangel is far too pretty for his own good." Zara made herself sound bored.

Axar choked on a laugh. "And how *pretty* exactly do you find him, Santos?"

"Shut up. Don't you have women to flirt with?"

Zara stomped away from her brother, the sound of his laughter fading behind her. She pushed her way through the crowd again, heading to where Ronan was. The archangel's presence was a glorious beacon amid the chaos. A beautiful, *irritating* beacon.

Zara trusted him—not that there was anything between them. So why had this absurd territorial feeling raised its ugly head?

A woman trailed a manicured nail down Ronan's chest while a man leaned on his shoulder. The archangel tried to move away from them but the woman stepped closer—

"Is there anything I can get you, milady?"

Abandoning her tray of glasses, Zara swayed her hips and strode toward them. She was supposed to be an entertainer, a performer for these guests. This was simply another challenge. As a mercenary, she had never been one to shy away from assignments.

The woman's eyes brightened on her. "My, how delectable."

Zara almost stumbled. What?

The female prowled around her. "Our Queen Kamari has a real eye for exquisiteness."

The woman moved her hips to the music, brushing against Zara's body as the man who had been beside Ronan, joined them.

Zara mentally shook her head. Now was not the time to be flustered. The female was quick off the mark, tipping Zara's chin up and giving her a sensual smile.

The Ikarrian mercenary had been with a woman before. More than once. Ah, and she couldn't forget when she'd slept with a woman *and* a man either… One of the many riveting escapades she'd experienced. Though she couldn't be enticed to be with someone else now, not when her feelings for a certain archangel were so visceral. And real. Even when she tried to push them away.

The man blocked her view from Ronan as Zara tried to wiggle her way out of the couple's embrace, but they mistook her movement as an invitation and closed in on her.

Zara managed to catch Ronan's gaze. His lips were parted in shock and he seemed frozen to the ground, an iron rod stuck to the stone. More patrons gravitated to him, swooning and fawning over the pretty archangel.

Ronan tilted his head, staring at her. The mental bridge between them blasted open and a hot, intense sensation rushed through Zara's mind.

A challenge rose within her. She held his gaze in an ironclad grip, and allowed the couple to dance against her. Zara might have moved her hips along with them, too. And for good measure, she slammed the mental door shut.

Silver sparked in the archangel's eyes, though the corner of his lips curled, and he kept his gaze on her, following the sway of her body.

There was a round of cheers and hoots. "What a lovely display!"

Zara glanced toward a booth of cushioned seats. Ah. She understood why Ronan had been lingering in this area. Deities were lounging there, their gazes now set on her and the couple.

Another deity chuckled. "I must say, Lord Arwan chose the right time to return to Nephtyr."

Zara forced herself not to react to the Council member's name. After several attempts, she finally managed to break away from the couple, retrieved her tray of drinks and presented them to the deities, batting her eyes.

"May I offer you some drinks, my lords and ladies?"

The deities looked at her approvingly, glancing up and down her body; it took everything in her not to sneer. Alcohol would not have the same effect on them as it would on the average mortal, but she had to try to loosen their lips somehow.

There was a hum in the air, and her ether raised its hackles. Zara didn't dare look toward the crowd, to the member of the Council who walked past them.

She had only seen Arwan a few times over the years, but his presence had a growl sitting at the edge of her teeth. He had taken part in her guild's execution.

The deities in the booth were watching him.

"Do you think the Queen knows?" one of them blurted out.

The others looked at the deity sharply, their gazes flicking to Zara. She pretended to be focused on clearing their table.

"Not here, idiot."

Without another word, the deities stood and left the seating area. After several seconds, Zara looked up to see they were heading to the gardens at the center of the rooftop.

She didn't glance at Ronan as she forwent her duties and followed Arwan's officials.

The mercenary dipped into the shadows, the smell of blossoms tickling her nose. A sigh leaked from her lips at the comfort of the dark, of the stars and moonlight. How they would bow over her all those blood-ridden nights as the Rogue…

Zara weaved between hedges and bushes, trying to find the deities. Small domed structures that acted as private seating areas were scattered throughout the garden. She stiffened when the officials suddenly turned the corner. A corner that led straight to *her*.

"Fuck." She ducked low and leapt into one of the alcoves.

The deities lingered in the clearing ahead, far enough for them not to be able to sense her presence, but close enough for her to still catch their voices. A small sofa and an arrangement of pillows were spread out around the structure. Zara peeked through the slits of the wooden shutters.

A familiar voice of dark liquid hummed from behind her, and goosebumps raised along her arms. "What do we have here?"

FORTY-ONE

R onan's scent was suddenly everywhere, jasmine layered with vanilla. He had removed his mask, his kohl-lined eyes brilliant underneath the night sky. Dazzling. *Distracting.*

"When I saw you skulking around the gardens, I knew you were on the hunt."

"I wasn't *skulking*." Zara scoffed, ripping off her own mask. She turned her gaze to the deities outside. "I'm surprised you had time to actually try and fulfill your task with all those patrons fawning over you."

The archangel was silent at first before he leaned forward, trying to catch her gaze. "Do I hear jealousy, mercenary?"

She folded her arms. "Hardly."

"Liar," Ronan purred. "I admit—I was jealous, too. Your ghastly behavior made me want to throw you over my shoulder and take you away from this place. And have you just to myself."

Fucking Suns, why did his words have her stomach tightening with anticipation?

"I—"

His body closed in, that scent of his wrapping around her. "I don't think you realized how *everyone* was gazing at you. Captivated by the beautiful woman with dark hair and colored eyes, who walked with confidence and power as sharp as a blade."

Zara's heart might have skipped a beat. Words couldn't find her.

"Now, focus," the archangel said. "We are here to work."

She scoffed again. "No, *you* should be working. *I* should go and enjoy the feast."

Ronan turned away, grabbing something from the table beside the settee. He returned with a tall glass of sparkling wine and a small plate of chocolates.

"We will need to eat a proper dinner, but I thought you might enjoy this in the meantime."

Zara gasped, snatching the glass and dessert from him. "Thank you," she grumbled as she stuffed her mouth.

Ronan smirked just as the deities' voices rose from the garden. Zara leaned toward the wooden door.

"Word from the High King is that our Creator wants faster progress," one of the deities said. "Arwan will be checking to see how many ethereal warriors have been summoned."

Summoned? Did they mean specters? Zara shared a look with the archangel, and Ronan's expression turned grim. She placed her plate and glass down, squeezing in front of him to look through the shutters.

Another deity grunted. "I heard a new caravan arrived. A good haul, too."

"The Kairosians have been a strong power source. More blood means more portals."

Ronan growled softly. "The ether-born—that must be what they're talking about. When Kamari mentioned her people going missing, I had a feeling this was why."

"More blood means more portals," Zara echoed in a whisper. Her stomach churned. "Who are the portals for? The specters? I thought they were possessing people in order to cross into our world."

One of the deities was still speaking. "Those beasts are unsettling to look at."

"At least you don't have to visit the mines. Arwan ordered that I go with him."

Zara perked up as the other lesser gods cackled.

"A mining city," she whispered. "Are you aware of such a place in Kairos?"

"We will need to inform Tareq. He will probably know what they're referring to."

They waited, listening. The officials were now complaining about the heat and how they wanted to return to Soleira.

After a while, Zara sighed. "I think we've obtained all the intel we can get from them."

She glanced sidelong at the archangel, realizing just how close they were, her lips mere inches away from his. Ronan's gaze was heavy and warm. His tattooed throat bobbed.

The boundary Zara had been desperately clinging onto was quickly slipping through her fingers. She sucked in a breath and faced the deities' direction once more. The archangel leaned forward, placing his hand on the wood above her head.

"You're right," he whispered. "I think our job is done here. We should probably go."

His breath tickled her ear and she shifted in place. That same burning desire coursed through her, one that had always been there but she had stubbornly been shoving away for so long.

Ronan's presence was all-consuming. Full of power and dominance, comfort and gentleness. She wanted to sink her teeth into it. Into *him*. Let him fill every part of her being.

Hakim and Eshe flashed across her mind again. Though this time they were speaking to her, laughing with her. Images of Ronan overlapped with them, the memories colliding and blurring together. Shifting. Tempting her to fall, to crumble again.

No. Zara pried the painful memories away, separating the archangel from her guild. From the guilt that seemed to be intertwined with the two. They fought against her before disappearing from her mental fingers. Leaving her heart racing.

The grief would always remain, would be an ongoing battle but…

We should probably go, Ronan had said.

"I don't want to," she murmured. The words slipped out, but she didn't regret them. "I don't want to go back. Not yet."

The archangel hesitated though didn't step away from her. His wings rustled within the shadows.

"Neither do I." Ronan's voice curled above her ear. "What would you like to do?"

Zara sucked in a breath. *To be with you.* Those were the words she wanted to say, but that gash in her heart wasn't fully healed. That inner wound still dripped down her bones.

"Can you… hold me?" Suns, she hated how small she sounded. Zara met his gaze once more. "Is that okay?"

Ronan looked at her with desire, though it was so much more than lust. He slowly wrapped his arms around her.

"Of course, it is. You never have to ask."

Emotion thickened in her throat. Slowly, Zara rested her back against his chest. Sank in the warmth of his body.

The shadows covered them in the domed alcove, save for the sparse moonlight through the shutters. The deities were *right there*— and yet, Ronan didn't protest.

"I've missed you," he whispered.

Zara was thankful that it was night. How it hid the small droplets of tears at the corner of her eyes.

"I've missed you, too," she said. "I'm sorry I've been taking so long when it comes to *us*. I… I want to get better."

The archangel held her tighter. "Don't apologize. If anything, I am glad you are taking the time you need. The last thing I want is for you to do something you're not ready for."

Hakim and Eshe were out there, in the depths of her mind. She could feel the pain of her love for them. Her love, and her guilt. Zara desperately pushed those emotions away, to another corner within her soul where she could allow Ronan to exist in a space that was free of those stains. Like he deserved.

Was she allowed this moment with him?

"Kiss me."

Ronan stilled. He said nothing for a painstakingly long breath. "Look me in the eyes and say that again."

Zara turned her head, her heart rushing through her chest.

"Kiss me, Ronan."

The archangel gently tilted her chin up. "Do you realize what you are asking—what you are doing? It's the equivalent of allowing a man who's been wandering endlessly in the dark to finally feel the sun on his face."

"Yes." Her voice was rough. Heavy with desire.

"What about our boundaries?"

The forsaken line she had drawn between them. One they both agreed to.

"I'm trying—" Zara's jaw clenched. "I want this… with you, Ronan. If you do, too."

Tension thickened in the air. The mental bridge between them strained, tightening to the point of snapping.

Ronan's gaze dropped to her mouth. "*Yes. I want this—you—so much.*"

They kissed. Their lips patient and gentle, as if it were the first time. His tongue brushed over hers and she responded in earnest. The archangel wasn't the only one who had been wandering in the dark. Right then, with him, she felt like she had the strength of the suns at her heels.

The archangel's scent rushed over her. She was slipping toward bliss. This sense of peace folded over her and—No, *stop*—

The same unseen wound, it bled through her. Death sat on her hands. It would never leave—

Stop. Stop. Stop.

A strong hand cupped her cheek. "I can feel the tremors through our connection, my Horizon. The pain that echoes behind it."

Zara pulled back slightly, their mouths just inches apart. She slammed the mental door shut. "Don't. That's not something you should have to feel."

Ronan smiled softly at her. There was a bit of sadness there. "I will take what you give me. If this moment is what you want, then let yourself lean on me, and we can figure out the rest later."

Was she allowed this?

A heavy feeling enveloped her heart. Zara wanted this. She wanted to keep pushing forward.

She kissed him again. Deeply. Though their Primordial connection was closed off, there was still a tether between them. Something that tugged at them, causing them to hold each other tighter and tighter. Hands gripping onto arms. Teeth gnashing against teeth.

The deities could be heard talking outside, but that meant nothing in that moment.

"I like having you all to myself, Horizon," Ronan moved down to nibble on her earlobe.

Whatever response was about to sneak onto the tip of her tongue was quickly cut off when his large hands began to roam her body, those rough calluses burning through the fabric of her gown. Zara sighed, as if finally breathing. Until he stopped.

"Is this okay?" he murmured.

"Yes. Yes, please don't stop."

Ronan slid his palms up her stomach. He was strong, confident—and it had her trembling in anticipation. His knuckles brushed the underside of her breasts, and she arched her back.

"When I first saw you in this dress, it made my heart ache," he whispered. "I thought how I was the luckiest male in the world to know someone as strong and beautiful as you. To just be near you."

Fucking Suns, this was unraveling Zara's resolve much more quickly than she expected. Languid heat pooled in her center, that undying thirst that had been building and building returning with such fury. Such wanton need.

The archangel's body tensed, as if it was taking every shred of willpower to control himself.

Zara wiggled against him. "Don't stop."

Ronan exhaled, and brushed his lips over the slope of her neck. His hand slid underneath the fabric of her gown and cupped her breast, while the other went to her lower abdomen, pressing her to him as he gently rubbed her nipple.

Zara let out a gasp and he placed a hand over her mouth.

"Hush," Ronan murmured. "Our unknowing neighbors are still outside."

Zara could hear them, chattering and laughing. The thought of anyone finding her and the archangel like this was… *thrilling.*

Ronan swept his fingers under the skirt's hem, pulling it up, his hand reaching her undergarments. She bucked against his chest as the archangel palmed her.

He let out a groan of satisfaction, pressing the pad of his thumb on her clit over the thin fabric. "You're already so wet."

Zara's whimper was muffled by his hand as Ronan worked her over. Moving his fingers in small circles, faster and faster. The heat inside her built, and she began rocking her hips.

"Tell me what you desire, Horizon." He dragged his hand from her mouth to tilt her chin to him again. "Do you long for release?"

Under the cover of the night, Ronan looked every bit the warrior he was known to be. The king the world had forgotten. The archangel his loved ones waited for.

Zara panted, desperate. The tether between them was becoming so taut that surely it was about to break. Her gaze dropped to his lips. "*Yes.*"

Ronan captured her mouth with his own. The taste of him threatened to consume her, destroy her, remake her.

Their kisses became more hurried as he tugged her underwear to the side and plunged a thick finger inside her. Zara moaned against his lips, gripping onto his strong arm. His other hand still held her jaw, and she liked how he'd caged her in. This feeling of being *claimed* was intoxicating.

Ronan slipped a second finger inside, driving his tongue into her mouth at the same time. Sighs leaked out of Zara's lips while he fucked her with expert touch. The archangel was breathing hard, his groans tumbling down the back of her throat.

Heat filled her veins, on the verge of obliterating her. Zara moved her hips, her ass sliding against his hard length. She needed to tear off the clothes separating between them. She needed to *feel* him, drown in his scent.

Just before release could find her, Ronan pulled away. Zara was about to cry out in protest when the archangel gently pressed a hand against her lower back, pushing her toward the window shutters.

"Bend forward," he ordered.

And then, he lowered himself to his knees. Ronan tugged on the hem of her skirt and paused, as if in question. Waiting for her to give him permission.

Zara bit her lip and nodded, glancing over her shoulder, and the archangel pulled her skirt down to her ankles. She still wore her underwear, her skin almost bare to the night air.

It was much darker now, the stone buildings of the garden alone in the heart of the shadows. Even the deities had gone. It was truly just her and Ronan now.

"Beautiful," he murmured as he pulled the small piece of fabric to the side once more. "So fucking beautiful, darling."

Zara moaned under his praise, but a hiss was ripped out of her when the archangel pressed his lips to her. And began *feasting*. Licking her, dragging his tongue up and down her center.

"Fuck," she groaned. She didn't care if any passersby heard her. "*Fuck*, Ronan."

He tightened his grip on the flesh of her thighs and thrust his tongue inside her. Plunging in and out the same way he had with his fingers. Zara's eyes rolled back. He was claiming her every coherent thought, every ragged breath.

As her legs began to shake, Ronan stood up. He wrapped an arm around her waist, turning to place her on the settee behind them.

A surge of boldness rushed over Zara. Before the archangel could climb on top of her, she twisted around and straddled him.

"What do you think you are doing?" Ronan challenged.

His hardened length pressed against her and her mouth watered at the memory of their first time together. How big his cock had felt inside her.

Zara slid her hands underneath his cropped shirt, but he grabbed her wrists, kissing her fingertips.

"My Horizon had so much to say earlier and now she's silent." Ronan's voice was rough with lust. "Where did that attitude go?"

Zara glared and ground herself against him, eliciting a hiss from his clenched teeth. She tried to give him a smug smirk but her lips parted, the friction of his hot length against her core more than she could handle, even through their clothing.

"Admit it." She panted. "You want this just as much as I do."

The silver in Ronan's eyes burned bright. He grabbed her waist and ground up against her. Zara gasped out a moan.

"I'm a selfish male, Santos." Ronan growled. "I want all parts of you, every moment of every day."

She could feel the sincerity behind his words, the strain in his voice. A spiral of emotions bubbled up inside her, ready to burst forth. There was so much she wanted to say to him.

Zara didn't know who reached for the other first, their lips crashing against each other in a desperate touch.

The archangel turned them over, Zara beneath him now, and she flung her legs around his waist.

Ronan continued to run the clothed length of his cock against her—so close to where she needed him most—and then slid down her body, settling his shoulders between her legs. He held her gaze and lowered his mouth to her core, Zara's moans filling the shadows as Ronan began to fuck her with his tongue.

She grabbed at his hair as she rode his face. Release was barreling toward her. "I… I can't. It's too much."

"Yes." Ronan tugged on her clit with his lips. Sucked on it. "You can."

Zara cried out.

"Please." She wasn't even sure what she was trying to say. "*Ronan.*"

Her climax found her, and she shuddered. Sweat dampened her skin as her body went slack.

Ronan licked up the remnants of her release. "So sweet and wet for me right in the middle of a party, my darling. How indecent."

Zara fought to catch her breath as she reached for him, yanking on the collar of his clothes. His eyeliner was smeared. Ah, fuck. She wanted to devour him—

She froze. The gashes in her heart tore open wider. Those buried feelings were rising, threatening to spill over. No no no. She had been fine. This peace, this happiness—she wanted to keep hold of it.

Ronan grabbed her hands, gently pulling her away from her madness. Somehow already calming her. He kissed her palms. "Are you okay?"

She fought for breath. "I am."

"Your eyes say otherwise." He searched her face. "Do you regret what just happened?"

Zara didn't hesitate. "Never. I just..." She clutched at her chest, unable to understand how to put the mess inside her into words. "I'm trying to push past this ugliness inside me. I... I'm *trying.*"

Ronan smoothed her hair, his voice kind. "I know you are, Santos. Take your time. You know I'm at your side for whatever you need."

Zara nodded. "Thank you."

Should she force that boundary between them again? Even when it was so painfully obvious that they desired more for each other?

Zara felt like she'd reached the end of a path, unable and unwilling to return to the road behind her, one filled with unease and self-loathing. She wanted to walk forward, cross that line she had dug. Even though the path before her was... terrifying. But she was starting to believe she could do it.

Ronan said nothing else as he gathered her skirt from the ground and helped her dress. The experience had left Zara dizzy, and she couldn't bring herself to speak.

"Perhaps we should go back."

"Really, I'm okay, Ronan."

"I don't want to push you. We have all the time in the world." He placed his lips on her forehead and gave her a soft smile before moving away. Zara eyed the archangel as he disappeared into the palace halls. As a plan formed in her mind.

She was a mercenary, and she wouldn't shy away from what she wanted.

Ronan went to his bedchamber as a fiery torrent of emotions warred inside him. This insatiable hunger rubbed against his skin and bones. No matter how hard he tried, his thoughts would always go back to *her*.

Zara Santos. The Horizon underestimated just how much power she held over him.

Her scent was fucking everywhere. Ronan could still taste her, hear her moans.

How long had he waited to hold her? To touch her? To make her feel so good so as to have her forget the painful world that surrounded her. For his Horizon to just *be*. Only with him.

The moment in the garden was something Ronan could never regret. But he'd had to get out of there, otherwise he would have been tempted to do *so* much more, and he didn't want Zara to cede to that pressure.

If they were ever to be with each other again, Ronan wanted no barriers to their relationship. He knew she was trying to overcome the pain inside her. It was not a simple feat. Ronan was… in awe of her efforts. A warrior who had stumbled but kept pushing onward.

He made his way to the bathing chamber, steam from the hot water soon rising in the air. His hair dampened as he began to shrug off his clothes.

Green eyes flashed in his mind. The sound of Zara's gasps. Her lips brushing his.

Ronan swallowed. Liquid heat curled deep within him and his cock hardened again. He sat on a stool and dunked buckets of water over his head and wings, Zara's drunken stare burning through his mind. His length swelled further, almost hurting.

"Fuck." Ronan fisted it, wings arched behind him.

He would have taken her in the middle of that garden. Kissed her so hard she'd have seen stars, their bodies getting slick with sweat as they made love over and over again.

There was a shift in the air, along with the faint smell of eucalyptus. His skin prickled with awareness. Ronan tipped his head back, still stroking himself.

"*Zara.*"

He opened his eyes slightly to glance at the Horizon, who was watching him from the bathing chamber's entrance. Zara might have been standing there longer than he thought. Sparkling light danced in her eyes, her lips parted.

"Keep going, I want to watch."

Ronan's throat bobbed as she moved closer, stopping behind him, her presence sending shockwaves of energy up his spine.

"The steam," he croaked. "You're going to get wet."

There was a smirk in her voice. "It's a little late for that."

Fuck. Zara took another bucket of warm water and gently poured it over his back, over his wings. He shuddered as he wrapped his hand around his hard length once more.

She touched *that* spot at the root of his wing, and a zap of pleasure struck him. He gritted his teeth. "I see your intentions now."

That silky laugh. Zara dragged her fingers along the space where skin met wing, eliciting a hiss from him.

"Touch yourself, Ronan."

He closed his eyes as he stroked his cock. The Horizon explored his body, trailing her hands down his wings, brushing the length of his feathers. Stars exploded across his vision.

Ronan panted and whimpered, entirely at the mercenary's mercy, as whips of hot desire spiraled across his lower abdomen.

"Right there, darling," he moaned. "Fuck."

Zara kissed the scars at the root of his wings. "I love hearing you like this."

Ronan tipped his head back, wet hair sticking to his face. She slid her other hand up his side. This wicked, beautiful woman. It wouldn't be much longer now.

"I want you so much it *hurts.*" He breathed out the words, not caring that this vulnerable truth had escaped him. "Please, Santos. I beg you."

Ronan didn't know what he was pleading for, except that the woman beside him was the only one who had the power to save him from this torment.

Zara sucked in a breath. Instead of responding, she went to stand in front of him. There was a knowing glint in her eyes, one twisted with hot desire, before she sank to her knees.

Ronan clenched his teeth as Zara gently pushed his hand away and began to stroke him. Her hand was soft yet firm, and had utter control over him. She held his gaze as she licked up his length.

The mercenary hummed, the sound thick with pleasure, and took him into her mouth.

He groaned. "Yes, darling, take me in deeper. Just like that. *Such a good girl.*"

Zara moaned at his words, the sound ricocheting throughout his body. Her head bobbed as she continued to suck him, wet, sloppy sounds echoing in the bath chamber, her nails digging into his thighs.

Ronan tenderly gathered her long hair with one hand. Zara gasped for breath, her eyes heavy with lust. Saliva dripped down her chin.

"Look at you. So beautiful taking my cock." Ronan gave her another moment before he started thrusting into her mouth. "I love what you're doing to me."

Zara took him again and again. Pleasure stroked through him, and his very existence narrowed in on the feel of her. Her gaze lifted to his and she pulled away for a moment.

"This is *my* cock. And mine alone." She swept her tongue along his tip. "Give it to me, Your Majesty."

Fuck. The mercenary was going to end him. Zara took Ronan once again in her mouth, and it didn't take long for the orgasm to spiral through him. He was sent flying over the edge, where nothing but stars and silver light existed. Ronan fisted her hair even tighter as she swallowed every drop of his release.

He brought his fingers to her face. "Did I hurt you?"

Her lips curled as she shook her head before pushing herself up. Ronan blinked up at her in surprise when she grabbed his chin.

"Do you want more, archangel?"

His mind nearly blanked.

"Yes," he begged.

Zara bent down, bringing her mouth to his. She brushed her tongue over his lips, lingering on the scar there.

He remembered how she'd looked back in the garden. How her eyes misted over with emotion. She had pushed through the barriers, had come to him. The mercenary pulled away from him, giving him a soft smile.

"Maybe later, I don't want to push you." Zara paused. "We have all the time in the world."

Ronan smirked at the echo of his earlier words.

Amusement danced over her lips, though there was still a hint of sadness in her eyes, which confirmed to the archangel that they shouldn't rush into anything, even if she was making progress. Zara stared at him a moment longer before leaving the room. And he was left alone with the feelings he wanted to share with her. The steam dwindled, and a mix of eucalyptus and jasmine remained. Droplets of water sounded within the chamber as Ronan ran a hand through his hair.

His ruthless beauty was fighting for herself. For them. And so was he.

FORTY-TWO

Daria stared Arwan approach their table. She had been conversing with Queen Kamari, observing the feast from a velvet sofa, a low table placed before them, when those ethereal eyes had emerged from the crowd.

The handsome deity didn't stop to speak with them, but paused long enough to bow to her and the Queen.

Kamari watched him with a smooth expression, dipping her head in response. The deity said nothing else before he disappeared.

"Where is he going? I thought he might be coming over to speak with us," Daria said.

"Arwan is very *reserved*. Though he is not to be underestimated." The Queen's gaze lingered on where the male had left, the tip of her nail tracing the rim of her glass. "As for where he's going, that is what the archangel and your mercenary sister are to find out."

Daria remained silent. The sound of tinkling glass and swaying jewelry hummed through her ears. People laughed and danced.

Ares, who had been standing by her side, bent low to whisper, "If you will excuse me, Your Majesty, I will be back in a moment."

She caught the strain in his voice. Daria twisted around in her seat, the vampire already pushing through the crowd. Her eyes narrowed.

"Well, perfect timing. Why don't we discuss business, Queen

Daria? I know there was something you wanted to ask me in private, without the vampire or anyone else present." Kamari's golden eyes seemed to glow under the torchlight.

Daria gestured to the party around them. "You consider this private?"

"The loudest of places can keep the best secrets."

She supposed it was true. Their lounge area was lined with jackal warriors. No one would interrupt them.

"All right, though I'm not trying to hide anything from the general or from the others; I will tell them, eventually." Daria stared after the general for a moment before turning to meet the Queen's gaze.

"But there is something I'd like to ask you first. Do your healers know of any cures for the Red Blight?"

Kamari blinked at her. "Are you asking on behalf of your vampire?"

Daria didn't say anything, though her expression must have given her away.

The Queen shook her head. "I'm sad to say, the answer is no. There is no cure for the Red Blight. There is much speculation and a lot of theories about the blood poisoning disease, but healers still do not have a true understanding of it."

Disappointment flooded Daria, her thoughts going to Ares's mother. "I had a feeling, but I thought to ask anyway." She sighed. "The other matter… As I understand it, the realm of Kairos is expert in all things ethereal in nature, correct?"

Kamari watched her for a moment. "One could argue the guardian realms were the ones more versed in celestial knowledge, but yes, Kairos would be next."

"In order for me to find the dragons, I must speak with someone who is… dead. I learned this might be possible in the Wraith's Den."

Color leached from the Queen's face. "What did those fiends tell you?"

"They spoke of *necromancy*." Daria sat up straighter. "What do you know about this spell?"

Those golden eyes burned. "It is a banned practice, Your Majesty. An abuse of ether."

"Please, I need to know."

"It is a risky gamble, Daria. It is work that tinkers with the afterlife, something only few would dare dabble in. Access to the dark practices of ether always requires a price."

Daria swallowed the emotion that gathered in her throat. "What kind of price?"

"It will punish you. You will be hexed. *Cursed.* The possibilities are endless, but you will suffer. I would advise against this path."

Daria thought of her sister, of her pater, her realm. All the people who were waiting to be saved, for someone to be their shield. Her heart squeezed.

"You've made terrible choices as well," she said, her gaze hardening. "To protect your kingdom, those you care for. When you signed that treaty and stood alongside the High Throne."

Kamari's expression turned grim and she was silent for a while. "I can teach you how to summon someone from the dead, if you so wish. Though I must ask, are you willing to take the risks? To endure whatever pain will undoubtedly find you?"

Daria didn't have the luxury of time to find another way. There were forces with fangs and wine-red cloaks back in Ikarria waiting to tighten the chain around her neck. She'd come all this way for an answer.

Whatever punishment her choices would bring about, she would take it. For everyone she loved and everyone under her charge, this was the least she could do.

"Yes. Teach me."

Daria didn't know long it had been since Ares left. The feast became more boisterous the later it got, and she used the excuse of wanting to look for the vampire to leave the party early. Daria told herself she wasn't actually concerned for the missing male, she just needed the escape, especially after Kamari taught her how to communicate with the dead. A spell composed of foreign words and devastating consequences. Daria tried to shake the looming sensation that crawled over her shoulders.

There was no reason for her to stay in Kairos. She would—she would have to tell Zara. Suns Above.

Daria entered a hallway of jackal statues and arched glass windows. It was dark, quiet, and peaceful. The fabric of her crimson-colored skirt was cool against her skin, a matching bodice clasped to her body. She welcomed the tinge of warmth as she dipped through the gentle columns of sunset light.

A familiar scent tickled Daria's nose. A strong, herbal-infused smell that sent her heart rate stumbling. She squinted, noticing a thin trail of red smoke billowing out of one of the glass doors, and followed it.

Ares was on the balcony. He didn't seem to have noticed her, his head bowed, long dark hair flowing in the desert breeze. The silver-dark sky caught the violet hues of those long tendrils.

His brows were bunched together, a tremble in his lips as he took another long drag of the bloodroot. The black veins around his clenched eyes were back. The vampire was in *pain*.

Daria pushed through the glass doors, shutting them behind her. "Do you mind telling me why you look like you're about to collapse?"

Ares froze. Eventually, he dropped the burnt out drug to the ground, twisting the heel of his boot over it. The male still wore the red sash Ronan had bought him, tied loosely around the sand-colored trousers and leathers strapped to his body. A brown cloak was pinned to his shoulders.

He averted his gaze, rubbing at the space where the black veins disappeared. "I'm fine."

"You're sickly pale, Ares."

"It is not worth your concern, Your Majesty." The vampire straightened, his expression serious. "Did you get the answers you were seeking from Queen Kamari?"

Uneasiness coiled between Daria's ribs. "I did."

"What did you speak about?"

It felt like Ares was prying her apart with his eyes.

"I wanted to get her insight on some ethereal matters," she said, in a poor attempt to be cryptic.

Ares prowled closer. "Can you give me more details? What ethereal matters?"

"The Wraith's Den piqued my curiosity about spirits and what lies *beyond*. I wanted to know more about necr—" Daria gasped. "Are you interrogating me like I'm one of your soldiers?"

"Answer the question, Daria."

The way he said her name. That authoritative tone... Suns Above, she should not have liked it as much as she did.

Daria crossed her arms. "No. It was nothing. She was telling me about the various spiritual practices of the realm."

Ares tilted his head to the side, observing her. "Am I making you uncomfortable?"

"Stop trying to analyze me! I came here because I thought you weren't feeling well, but you seem fine to me so I will take my leave."

Her fingers had barely brushed the door handles when Ares grabbed her other hand. Daria's heart might've jolted at the touch, sending her emotions into a total state of confusion.

"I know you're hiding something important, Calderón," he murmured. "Your voice pitches higher and you avert your gaze when you do."

An old anger raised its head. She met his gaze. "I don't have to tell you everything, General."

"No, you don't." He searched her eyes. "It doesn't change the fact that I want you safe."

"What makes you think I am not?"

He looked down at his hand on hers. "Truthfully, it started back in the Wraith's Den but I couldn't understand what it was—something that could put you in harm's way—until the wraiths mentioned *necromancy.*"

Daria felt her chest tighten. When she didn't say anything, Ares added, "Did you think I wouldn't bring that up? Those creatures spoke of it in front of everyone."

Of course, she'd expected this. Had felt Zara's confused stare.

She knew she didn't have to tell Ares everything. However, this entire endeavour was much bigger than her. It was dangerous territory, and she didn't want to risk those she cared about. Including him… She yanked her hand away.

"Listen, I am only sharing this information with you as a battle strategy. Not because of your poor attempt at interrogating me."

The vampire smirked. "Very well, Your Majesty."

Daria told him about necromancy, how summoning King Arzhel was the best option in understanding the mystery behind the Ikarrian throne and the dragons' whereabouts.

As she spoke, Ares's face paled even more. Daria thought the male would have stopped her mid-sentence in a fury, but he did not. Though something broke in his gaze.

"When you said Kairos could provide insight on someone long-dead, I didn't think it would lead to something like this." He closed his eyes. "You're not going to change your mind, are you?"

The vampire somehow understood her better than most people, and Daria was surprised to discover that she didn't mind it. "This is the closest I've come to finding the dragons."

"Then let me do it with you." Ares opened his eyes, the violet there deepening. "I will share the burden of the spell."

His words soothed something inside her. "I have to be the one to do it, since I am a descendant of Arzhel. Otherwise he may not respond… And I would not want you to risk yourself, either."

The balcony was bathed in the shadows of the nearby palm trees, the sounds of chirping crickets and the distant feast filling the warm air. It was only them in this corner of the palace.

Ares took another step closer. "I don't care. If you wish to do this, then let me be there with you. Let me stand by your side."

Daria suddenly did feel awkward, exposed, even as something within her chest cracked. Words that had been long suppressed began to rise, bubbling up her throat. This conversation was long overdue.

She gritted her teeth. "Why do you say this now?"

"Because I didn't feel like I had the right to before. I've been wanting to tell you for so long that—" The emotion in Ares's eyes swelled as he reached a hand toward her, but stopped himself before he could touch her cheek. "I'm *sorry*. I'm sorry that I hurt you, Daria."

Breath stilled in her lungs. Daria could do nothing but gaze at the vampire, at the turbulent cosmos in his violet eyes.

His voice was ragged. "I know you still don't fully trust me, yet, but there's something you should know—"

Ares suddenly grunted in pain. Black lines spread even further out from the corners of his eyes, like the rotted roots of a tree. Daria felt her stomach drop.

She lurched toward him, gently grabbing his face with both of her hands. "Ares, you're hungry."

He growled under his breath. "Leave me be, Princess. You weren't meant to see this."

"You haven't been feeding from anyone?"

Ares averted his gaze, half of his face cast in darkness. "I will drink later."

The black lines thickened, stretching down his sharp cheekbones. His expression twisted in pain as a cry peeled from his clenched teeth. The sound speared through Daria's chest.

As he swayed on his feet, it was obvious that the male would only weaken if he didn't feed soon. Daria didn't know how he had managed this long.

"Drink from me." The words left her lips as easily as spilled water.

Ares sucked in a breath, and tried to push away from her. "No, I could never ask such a thing of you."

"I am offering," Daria said, quietly, even though her heart was thundering.

"No. I didn't apologize just so you would feel some sort of obligation—"

Her fingers slid to his chin, guiding his face back to her. Under the moonlight, his skin was ghostly pale. The black veins thickened and he winced.

"Ares Valdemar, I am giving you permission to drink from me. You are weak, and knowing you, you've most likely been suffering in silence for a while. How can you protect me if you can't even hold a sword?"

Ares let out a small breath. His voice was quiet. "Very well."

Her racing heart now began hammering against her bones. Daria fumbled for words. "How—how would you like me?"

Through the pain, something dark flashed in his eyes, and it looked like he was desperately trying to hold himself back—from speaking, from grabbing her. "Just your wrist will do."

Ares gingerly took her hand, bringing it to his lips. He held her gaze as he grazed the tip of his fang along her skin. They both shuddered at the contact.

This sensation… It was beyond anything Daria had felt before. She had to clamp her mouth shut to avoid any other sounds escaping her.

Her cheeks flushed with embarrassment.. He'd barely touched her and she was already in shambles.

Ares brushed his fang over her wrist once more before the sharp tip pricked her skin. Daria winced as a bead of red rose from the small opening.

"I'm sorry," he whispered, and dragged his tongue over the bubble of blood. He groaned. "Fuck. Barely a drop and I'm ready to fall to my knees."

His voice roughened, and the sound caused heat to coil in her lower abdomen. Daria struggled to keep her own voice steady. "Just shows how… hungry you are."

Ares's eyes flicked up to hers. The violet there glowed under the night sky. "I'm *starving*—though not in the way you think."

Before Daria could comprehend what he meant, Ares wrapped his lips around the wound and began sucking her blood. Slowly, carefully.

Daria's breath hitched as the pain melted into something different. Warmth spread through her, unseen hands grazing her skin—a trail of embers that coursed within her bloodstream, setting her alight.

Ares muffled the groan tumbling through his throat. The sound was rough and deep, temptation and danger wrapped in one. Daria's toes curled.

Color seeped back into the vampire's face, the black veins already lessening. He took another long pull before running his tongue across the wound and moving away.

"That is enough." Ares met her gaze. "Thank you."

Daria still felt breathless. "You barely had anything."

"I'll survive. This was more than I could ask for."

Before she could fight back, Ares cupped her cheek. She froze at the soft smile on his lips. Daria wasn't sure if she trusted what she was seeing, feeling. The vampire was otherworldly—so *beautiful*.

"Go, Princess." He jerked his chin toward the glass doors. A part of her wanted to stay on that balcony with him.

Instead, the Queen of Ikarria cleared her throat and left without looking back.

Daria couldn't sleep. It had been hours since the moment with Ares on the balcony. The prick on her wrist had slowly started to heal, but there was still a faint throbbing where his fangs had pierced her skin. She tossed and turned, unable to push away the feelings conjured when Ares had drunk from her.

Just a mere sip from her wrist had sent her blood abuzz. What would have happened if he'd drunk from her throat? Would he have pressed himself closer while his lips were on her skin?

Daria gritted her teeth. Fine, she could acknowledge her attraction to Ares. And the fact that her body craved something more.

The thought of Ares holding her gaze while he sucked on her blood flashed in her mind. She imagined what it would have been like to remove his clothes, to have his naked body on top of hers, to have his hard length push inside her—*Suns Above*.

Daria rolled over to shove her face in the pillow, groaning in defeat. Her feelings toward the vampire had been carved of fire and anger, and even after all she had witnessed from the male… they were becoming *more*.

Ares had not only apologized to her, but had shown his remorse through his actions. What had he been about to say before his hunger overwhelmed him? *There's something you should know.*

Daria couldn't bear to sit with her thoughts and slipped out of bed. She padded down the hall to the next bedroom.

Zara was curled up in her bed, a single candle flickering on her bedside. She lifted her head.

"Can't sleep?"

Daria felt phantom hands squeezing her lungs. "I learned something during the feast."

"Is it about the dragons?"

She hated how her sister's face brightened. "Yes."

Zara must have caught the crack in her voice and sat upright, patting the space beside her. "Tell me."

She listened as Daria recounted the details of her conversation with Queen Kamari, about necromancy and what it meant.

When she finished, Zara's expression had darkened. "I had wondered how you were faring, ever since the Wraith's Den. And that spell… You can't do it, Daria. Ether works in mysterious ways—it can be beautiful, but it is also dangerous. Using it like this is prohibited for a reason."

"What other options do I have?" Daria's voice pitched higher. "Ikarria is under threat every day, and I can't wait for someone else to come save us. I have to do it."

Zara clenched her teeth. "This isn't fair. Why must it be you who has to be put in harm's way?"

Daria grabbed her sister's hands. "Like you haven't been putting yourself in danger for most of your life. This is my duty and I am choosing it."

"Then let me help you," Zara said.

"You know that is not possible. Not with armies and otherworldly creatures searching for you and Ronan. You need to focus on your ether reaching its full potential. I'll be going with Ares."

Zara looked down at their intertwined hands. "How do you feel about being alone with the vampire now?"

"He is already aware of everything I told you. I can rely on him."

Zara's lips twitched into a smile. "I knew it. Something happened." Her sister cocked her head. "Is that why you sounded so guilty when you first came into my room?"

"No, it's—" Daria shook her head, lips trembling slightly. "Now that I have what I came for… I have to leave."

Zara squeezed her hands. Silver lined her eyes. "My sister has a kingdom to save."

Daria didn't want to say the words out loud because then it would be true—reality would separate them once again. The truth was a dagger to the chest.

"After Ikarria is free, I intend to save pater."

"When that time comes, I will go with you. We will *both* get our pater back."

Daria didn't want to let this moment go.

"Can I spend the night with you?"

Zara laughed. "Don't ask silly questions when you know the answer."

When was the last time the two sisters had been able to spend time together like this? Even though their journeys had been a treacherous one, Daria would not have changed it for the world and cherished every moment spent with her sister.

As she did now.

FORYT-THREE

The next morning, Zara swallowed back the emotion that threatened to choke her as she left her sister. The dunes had seemed to bow to Daria as she rode out into the distance, Zara heading in the opposite direction. For one moment, Zara thought of turning back. Had considered tossing her quest for vengeance and power to the sands and letting the wind carry her home.

Mikatán had come to her mind instead. She only had the occasional visit from the god of Death during her meditations, where the Primordial had hardly said much, apart from demanding that she hurry to him. As he did in that moment.

Find me, Zara Santos. I can give you what you seek—power beyond measure. With my blessing, you will be a warrior with the ability to fight gods and monsters.

While she was pleased with the god's words, what she'd learned in the Wraith's Den about Khaos and her lover Deimos gave her pause.

I will be there soon.

Zara looked ahead. The twins were in their jackal forms, walking beside her and Ronan as they rode their tusked-camels. Axar had already left with Tareq and the other mercenaries to the mining city. Kamari had had an inkling about what city Arwan's officials had been referring to.

The Horizon touched the skin underneath her eye. "Remind me again why we're wearing kohl?"

In his jackal form, Faris was nearly the same height as the camel. He tugged on the ivory scarf at his nape with a claw. "Tareq suggested the two of you wear it as you're not used to the desert weather. If you haven't noticed, there is ether in the liquid."

Zara's jaw slackened. There had been a slight vibration when she first put on the eye-paint.

Ronan leaned forward on his saddle, black wings slack against his back. His silver eyes seemed icy blue with the kohl. And it was an irritatingly handsome look for him.

The archangel flashed his teeth. "It helps block out sand from our eyes, little wolf."

Her lips curled in disgust at his term of endearment. Disgust at *herself* that she didn't mind it one bit.

Hours rolled by, the sun scorching hot. At times, Zara would reach out to Basim, brushing against the nahual's presence in her mind. She even felt as though Basim pressed his snout against her temple. The wolf was never far, and she knew he would always come at her call.

Ronan chatted with Faris—or it was more like the young jackal throwing question after question to the archangel and Ronan attempting to answer all of them.

Zara chuckled, leaning down to speak with Ayah. "How come your brother is so obsessed with Ronan?"

The jackal shrugged. *"After we were rescued from the circus, Faris was having a hard time—I think the stories about the lost King of Damalis are what gave him hope. It's kind of annoying, though."*

"You say that but you don't mean it, do you?"

Ayah averted her gaze. *"Shut up."*

Zara fought back a smile. "What can we expect from the Oasis?"

"It's difficult to say; the experience is different for every visitor. It was created by Neheharu, the Primordial of Divinity and Prophecy. He is the patron god honored by many in Kairos."

Zara wasn't sure how fond she was of the idea of entering a domain that revolved around *divinity* and *prophecy*, whatever that meant.

Basim nudged her thoughts, the wolf still hidden within the veil. *Are you afraid?*

No... Yes.

Her nahual sounded amused. *Have no fear, I will be with you every step of the way.*

Basim, are you able to communicate with Mikatán?

All nahuales can speak with the gods, though I cannot reach out to him like you do. Not since I became your bonded animal spirit.

There seemed to be a lot of rules and regulations when it came to the nahuales. Basim had been waiting for Zara, wandering near the god of Death until she was able to receive him.

Wind picked up, howling at the sky. Zara scrunched her eyes shut, expecting the sand to pummel and scratch them. She felt nothing. Though the sand battered her clothes, her vision remained untouched. The ether-imbued kohl certainly had its benefits.

"Incredible," Zara whispered.

The camels' grunts grew louder as the winds suddenly silenced. The air changed. An energy tickled her skin, and the weight on her shoulders felt lighter. Zara opened her eyes.

Before her was a massive pool of crystalline water. Palm trees stood proud along its banks, towering over stones and tall grass. On the other side of the water, pillars lined a path leading to the open entrance of a pyramid-shaped building.

"Welcome to the Oasis of Dreams," Faris murmured.

Flecks of light floated by, the sky somehow looking different from the one Zara knew. It was a clash of purples, reds, and blues—it awfully reminded her of the place she had seen in her dreams with Mikatán.

The Primordial was nowhere in sight, but it felt like he was there, beyond the veil, beckoning her to keep going. *Find me.*

They approached the lone building's steps, a pair of guards waiting at its threshold. Energy shuddered through the air as Zara got closer to the two armored figures.

They weren't human, nor were they shifters. Whatever they were was not of this world, a truth that rang in Zara's blood.

One of the guards was a female, with a sharp jawline and long black hair, her reptilian eyes seeming to glow. Blood-red armor clasped her body, the pauldrons at her shoulders jutting out like the horns of an ancient beast, and a bronze headdress sat atop her head, covering her brow as red paint streaked her cheekbones and the bridge of her nose. Where her brown skin showed, patches of scales shimmered under the setting sun.

The other guard was dressed in a similar attire. Zara could not tell what kind of creature they were as a helmet in the shape of a cat's head covered their entire face. The only feature Zara could see were the eyes staring at her through the slits. Undeniably feline.

Zara stiffened and clenched her hands at her sides. The ether that surrounded these guards was otherworldly, nothing she had ever felt before. It was the smell of rain and warm air—an ocean storm brewing in the distance.

Ayah spoke under her breath. *"They are sentinels forged by the hand of Neheharu himself."*

Zara kept her eyes on the guards as their group walked up the limestone steps. "Forged?"

"They were given life, a consciousness, by him. Sentient beings charged to protect this sacred land."

Her mind was rushing in hundreds of directions. Sentinels. Creatures made by the gods themselves. What she'd done in the Wraith's Den—

The guards crossed their spears, blocking them from entering. It was the woman who spoke, her voice deep and rough. "Only the elf and archangel may proceed."

The twins turned to Zara and Ronan and bowed. Faris met their gazes. *"Do what you came to do. I hope the knowledge you seek is worth it."*

Zara's ether seemed to prowl in the back of her mind. A part of her wanted to run. A dark abyss waited for her, a silent beast with unseen talons ready to claw at her resolve.

Ronan brushed his knuckles against her hand. They shared a look before stepping forward as one, and entered the temple of the Oasis of Dreams.

Darkness thickened around them—but it was only the gray stone beneath her feet and the doors closing behind them. Zara exhaled.

Ronan's wing stretched out behind her back and she smirked. "Scared, archangel?"

"Don't act like you didn't take a step toward me just now."

Bastard. She'd hoped he hadn't noticed.

Soft red light bloomed from a wooden archway ahead that had no door. It sat in a pool of water, lily pads drifting across the surface and bulbs of blue light fluttering in the air.

They stepped into the water, which was shallow and warm, reaching up to their ankles. Only smooth stone and soft sand beneath their feet.

Zara narrowed her eyes on the bright doorway before a gasp ripped out of her chest. She clutched onto Ronan's arm. "Look, there's another—another *world* out there."

Through the threshold was a land full of sand and stars, the sky engulfed in twilight and ether. Monoliths of pale stone rose from the ground, riddled with an array of shimmering lights. *Cities.*

"A portal." The archangel angled his body in front of her as they moved closer. "I have to admit, Santos. I am a bit afraid."

Zara was too. Despite the awe, there was an underlying sensation, bitter to the tongue. It made her legs feel numb, and she almost questioned whether she was truly awake or not.

This was the moment they had been waiting for.

"Whatever happens inside, remember who you are and where you came from." She squeezed his arm as if to help the words sink in. "You can do this, Ronan. The archangel who survived when the world thought him gone. When *they* wanted to destroy him, he rose from the shadows. He never stopped fighting, and that speaks to his courage. The weight you carry inside does not have to hold you back from what you want to achieve."

Ronan's eyes shimmered. He tucked a strand of hair behind her ear, his fingers lingering on her jaw. "Same to you. You are brave, my Horizon. All that you've endured made you into a strong and capable warrior, one who is braving the unknown—who can face anything. It is admirable."

Zara's heart swelled with something that was both powerful and terrifying. She didn't know what to make of it. What she did understand was that no matter what happened within the Oasis of Dreams, she would be one step closer to destroying the High Throne. With Ronan at her side.

Together, they stepped through the archway and the world exploded into bright light.

PART III

SHATTERED TRUTHS IN THE SANDS

FORTY-FOUR

Sand and starlight twisted together, blinding Ronan. One moment Zara had been holding onto his arm, and the next she was ripped away from his grasp. The last thing he heard was her shouting his name.

"Santos!" His hands met light and ether.

It was too fucking bright—he couldn't see her. Couldn't see anything. Terror iced his blood. Ronan tried to claw his way through the light, but the power around him flared.

The brightness suddenly faded and he found himself standing on a paved road that held a crystalline sheen. Where in the fucking Suns was he?

A city rose around him, towers and buildings of fine stone shimmering under a dusk and dawn sky. Silver torchlights flickered here and there in the streets, evidence of life and civilization. A bridge connected it to another stretch of land where purple mountains loomed in the distance, jungles rolling across the expanse behind the rest of the metropolis.

Small, floating islands covered in rocks and wilderness hovered above, staircases and pathways connecting them to the mainland.

Ronan recognized this place. Had been here many years ago.

"Yes, this is Celestrea, the realm of the Primordials," said a deep voice. "But it is not the Celestrea you know. Strange that the Oasis chose this place to be your dreamscape."

Ronan twisted around to see a man standing at the peak of a sloped road between some buildings. They were both on a floating piece of the city, large birds with leathery wings and sharp beaks flying below.

The stranger wore ivory robes, the white fabric billowing out gently behind him. A hood was draped over his shorn head, his dark skin gleaming with tattoos. The inked etchings glowed the color of dusk, shaped like runes, some of the figures similar to the words Ronan had tattooed on Orion's back. The language of the gods and goddesses.

Thin strings of golden jewelry hung around the man's neck, along with a hooped ring that pierced one of his nostrils. He was an ethereal beauty, and his presence caused the air to hum.

Ronan's knees trembled. He gritted his teeth and forced himself to keep upright, the effort of it enough to make his body sweat.

The male scoffed. "The godling is stubborn. Welcome Ronan Menodora, son of Elijah and Miriam. I am Neheharu, the Primordial of Divinity and Prophecy."

The sweat on Ronan's body turned cold. He was standing before a *god*. In the fucking flesh. Back in Celestrea, he had only encountered higher-ranking deities. Not even he had been worthy of being in a Primordial's presence.

Ronan felt compelled to bow, though there was another part of him—a more primal part—that turned its head away at the idea. He fought the unnatural urge.

"Where is Zara Santos?"

There was a bite to his words, but he didn't care. Even if it was directed to a god.

The dusk light within Neheharu's tattoos flared. "She is fine. I am speaking to her now as well. You should be more concerned about yourself."

Ronan frowned. "This is the Celestrea that existed when I was a boy. Why am I here? I came to the Oasis to amplify my power."

A golden staff materialized in Neheharu's hands. "A half-truth.

You will never get what you seek when a part of you is still running away."

Ronan gritted his teeth. "I'm not lying. I am here so that I may strengthen my ether to save *my* world. The one *your* kind has forsaken."

Power pulsed from the Primordial, finally sending the archangel to his knees. Neheharu's voice was low, yet somehow it boomed through Ronan's bones. "Do not speak on matters you know nothing about. Our kind never forgot you mortals. Not *once*. The Oasis reads the jagged lines of your mind and soul, and chose this dreamscape for you to overcome."

A sense of dread unfurled inside Ronan.

The Primordial observed him for a moment. "You and the elf have been a popular topic among the gods, and I wish to see how the both of you will fare in this endeavour. Now, have your powers morphed even more since your *Izcali* began?"

"Yes, they have been growing."

"Not enough. The elven godling has made more progress than you. You are a mere mortal, stumbling about, trying to face forces you are not ready for."

Ronan gnashed his teeth together. "Your enemies have become my enemies, and they are only becoming stronger. I must hold my ether at its full strength before—"

"Before you lose it? The Crossing is inaccessible to you, so you are trying to find a loophole."

Of course, with all the options you fools left us. Ronan didn't say that part out loud. "Is it possible to keep my power without having to go through the Crossing?"

"No." The way the god said it—so plainly. Neheharu cocked his head. "Mortals can be so tenacious. I had forgotten."

Anger sparked through Ronan's veins. They had come all this way, only for a Primordial to shrug him off with a simple *no*.

Neheharu gestured to the world around them. "Though I will give credit where it's due. What you see is only possible *because* of your powers. The Oasis recognizes that, hence why we are standing in the past."

He released whatever energy that was weighing over Ronan, and the archangel pushed himself to his feet.

"Your potential is great, though there is a mental block. Remove it and you will get what you seek. Perhaps then your patron god will reveal themselves to you."

Ronan closed his eyes as his breathing quickened. Deep down, he'd known this was meant to happen—maybe not in this exact way, but he knew those scars that were etched into his soul would come back to face him. All the flashes of his past had proven that much.

"You can try your best at amplifying your ether, but that can only happen if you succeed in your trial here in the Oasis." The Primordial of Divinity and Prophecy pointed to something behind Ronan. "It is time you face those shadows."

A young archangel brushed past Ronan, seemingly unaware of his presence. The child's hair was a silver-white and reached his shoulders, a boy with water-blue eyes. Untouched by the blemishes of the world.

Ronan took a slow breath. *Erebus.*

Ronan watched as young Erebus scampered up the ivory path toward a luxurious estate. In his small arms was a basket stuffed with vegetables and fruit, many of which held an otherworldly glow. Silver-armored archangels and deities were stationed about the grounds, eyeing the little boy as he headed to the staff side entrance.

The supervisor posted by the oak doors gave Erebus a once-over and a cruel snort. "Once you've left the produce in the kitchen, report to His Lordship's office."

Ronan's lips twisted in disgust at the older male. "Neheharu, what am I looking at exactly?"

No one responded. He glanced over his shoulder to find the Primordial had disappeared. How convenient.

Nyota appeared in a flash of light, the panther a warm, welcome presence within this strange world. *I'm here, Ronan.*

He patted her head. *Thank you.*

Ronan returned his attention to this fragment of the past. Erebus stood in front of large gilded doors, smoothing out the fine fabric over his thin—*too* thin—chest before entering the room.

A deity stood behind the desk, frowning at a scroll in his hands. The male must have been the lord of this estate, the one who had owned Erebus and his family.

An archangel with white wings stood at the side, his long silver hair tied high on top of his head. While his eyes were not blue, it wasn't difficult to see the resemblance between him and Erebus. It was his father, Callum.

Ronan took a few eager steps deeper within the memory. Erebus had hardly ever spoken about his family, though Ronan knew enough.

Erebus's father beckoned his son closer with a jerk of his chin, the little archangel scampering to stand at his side.

The deity tossed the parchment on his desk. "The guardian realms are eager to strengthen the relationship between Celestrea and the mortal world—not that it's worth the effort. Damalis is proposing the leading Ethereal Houses select a promising youth to live in the guardian realm's capital and learn the ways of the mortal kingdom. They will be given the formal position of advisor on behalf of Celestrea, thus creating a bridge between the kingdom of mortals and the realm of gods."

He pointed at Erebus. "I want your son to go. If a member of my House is sent, it will raise my status tenfold. Maybe even in the eyes of the Primordials."

Callum stiffened. "My Lord, I am honored that you would consider a member of my family, but Erebus is much too young. There must be someone who is a better fit to serve this role in your name."

The archangel's voice remained liquid smooth, carrying an elegance that reflected his elevated station in the deity's household.

"Nonsense. This opportunity would also benefit your family." The deity waved a hand. "I could promote you and have you become an official of my House, removing the term 'servant' from your *cursed* lineage."

The lines around Callum's mouth deepened. There was a battle rising in that expression. A father who wanted to keep his child out of danger—who wanted to protect his whole family.

The deity's lips curled at the lack of response. "I will have what I desire. Be grateful I had the courtesy of telling you instead of ripping your son away from you while you slept."

Ronan glared at the male. "*Bastard.*"

Erebus was fighting to keep his expression neutral, pinning his lips with his teeth as his eyes began to glisten.

Ronan hated the Oasis for shoving this moment in front of him. He knew it had been difficult for Erebus to leave his family behind, but witnessing it unfold was tearing at his heart.

The deity sat in his seat. "We will discuss the logistics at a later date. I am hosting a feast tonight for the other officials and generals. There is a formal gathering with the Primordials next week and we wish to prepare our material."

Callum paled. He gently pushed Erebus toward the door. "Go to your mother, I will join you later."

Erebus obeyed, keeping his white wings tight across his back. Ronan followed after him, Nyota in tow. He could still hear Callum speaking.

"Sir, for your feast this evening, I implore you to seek other modes of entertain—"

"Don't forget your place, *archangel*," the deity snapped.

Erebus tucked his chin down and rushed out of the office. Ronan glanced over his shoulder and, just as the doors were closing, he saw the deity slap Callum across the face.

The memory shifted, leaving Ronan clenching his teeth, battling through a rush of emotion. Thank the Suns Erebus hadn't seen it.

They were transported to a banquet hall bathed in silver and amber torchlight. Deities lounged on expensive couches and cushions or were spread about conversing and drinking.

Dancers twisted and turned in white veils on the raised platforms about the hall, while musicians played their flutes and harps between the pillars. Most of the entertainers were archangels.

Ronan frowned. "This must be the feast the deity was talking about. Where is Erebus?"

He must be close. Nyota's tail swished from side to side. *I don't like this place—it reeks of evil.*

"What makes you say that?"

Doesn't that woman look familiar to you?

He followed his nahual's gaze to a female archangel with white wings singing atop a platform. Ronan saw the similarities.

Erebus's older sister, Nymeria. It had to be.

He gazed at the young woman, racking his brain for what Erebus had told him about her. *She loves to compose. She is a good singer. She is kind.*

Deities watched her sing, some of them with hungry gazes. Ronan's stomach churned.

"Erebus has an older brother too," he murmured, tearing his gaze away to scan the hall.

It didn't take long to find him. Kaiser was the most handsome male in the room. While Erebus had spoken little about his family, he'd mentioned his brother the most.

Kaiser was seated along the lower steps that led to the raised center of the banquet hall. He looked to be in his mid-twenties, with short, wavy silver hair that fell over his brow. His strong wings were gray instead of the family's usual white.

He sat at a male deity's feet. The lesser god, who looked a couple of years older than Kaiser, would occasionally pet the archangel's head, and it sent Ronan's blood roaring with fury. Even Nyota snarled at the sight.

"What in the fucking bleeding Suns?"

Ronan felt his body go numb when he noticed Kaiser's body blotched with bruises. The emptiness in his eyes—an unfathomable void.

The deity who owned Erebus's family appeared, addressing the lesser god beside Kaiser. "I trust that you are enjoying tonight's festivities?"

The male smiled. "Of course. You always provide me with the best entertainment—even if they sometimes fight back."

Ronan cursed under his breath. He *hated* this. He stood there, helpless to history and time, as the deity lord grabbed Erebus's brother by the jaw.

"Kaiser, behave with our guests. You will do whatever they desire of you, do you understand?"

The archangel looked defeated. "Yes, my lord."

The deity grunted in approval, though his grip tightened, causing Kaiser to flinch. "Behave. Obey. Entertain. You made an agreement with me, remember? To spare your sister from doing *more* than singing, as well as protecting your brother for when he comes of age."

No no no.

The contents of Ronan's stomach twisted and turned. *Erebus.* He still hadn't shown. Where was he?

Somehow, perhaps by the unknown forces of this ethereal plane, the energy pulled Ronan's gaze to one of the back pillars. Erebus was peeking around the blue stone, eyes wide on his older brother. His face was white as a sheet, tears streaming down his face. Ronan felt a stabbing pain in his chest and took a step toward the little archangel, as if he could somehow console this past version of his brother.

Still in the deity's grasp, Kaiser narrowed his eyes. "Yes, my lord—"

"Don't hurt him!"

Ronan sucked in a breath. "No. Don't come over here. *Please.*"

His words were useless. Erebus darted out of his hiding spot and threw himself into Kaiser's arms, forcing the deity to pull away.

The lesser god who had been sitting beside Kaiser arched an eyebrow. "This evening is becoming tedious."

Those words seemed to spark something in Kaiser. He clutched his brother close to his chest. "I'm sorry, my lord. He doesn't understand."

The deity's expression darkened. "Fortunately for your brother, he already has a duty for the household, so *you* will have to answer for this interruption."

Kaiser didn't hesitate to bow his head. "Of course."

Ronan knew that look. Understood it very well. The extent—the sacrifice—that Kaiser was willing to go for his brother.

A deity soldier ripped Erebus from Kaiser's arms, but the little archangel was relentless. "No, I'm sorry! Don't hurt him! I'm *sorry!*"

Kaiser only gave him a soft smile. "No more tears. Nymeria and I will see you at home later this evening."

Erebus was dragged away from the banquet hall, the young archangel forced to watch as the deity yanked Kaiser down the steps by his hair.

All the while their sister continued to sing. She sang as tears rolled down her cheeks like broken stars.

Ronan couldn't take any more of it. He bowed over and vomited.

Nyota nuzzled his leg. *I'm sorry you had to see this.*

"I think I know why I must bear witness to this part of Erebus's past." Ronan wiped his mouth. "He and I shared a dream—of a new world we wanted to create. Together."

Erebus's cries echoed in the distance. The sound of an innocent child desperate for safety and peace. Ronan pushed himself off the ground to run after him. To reach for his brother's hand.

Only to be met with mist.

FORTY-FIVE

Why? Zara stared at the blood filling the abandoned temple floor. *Why here?*

Ether cried from within her soul, its lament reaching the farthest corners of her being. The Oasis was playing a cruel joke, forcing her to stand in the same place where Hakim and Eshe were killed. Though their bodies were not here, that didn't stop them from appearing every time Zara closed her eyes.

"Stop." She slapped a hand to her brow. "Please, *stop.*"

Zara had barely taken a step when someone slammed into her. Pain exploded throughout her body as she was thrown on the ground. Blood pooled at the back of Zara's throat as her attacker yanked her by the collar. As she was forced to meet Raziel's gaze.

Her eyes widened. *No.*

Zara tried to scramble away but the archangel pinned her to the ground.

Golden-brown wings that glinted like freshly forged blades underneath a dawn sky. Wine-red hair against flawless, ivory skin. Golden eyes that burned with the hatred of unending wars.

Raziel's smile was cruel. "Surprise, my Rogue. It's been some time."

This couldn't be real. A cry stuck between fear and determination peeled from Zara's lips as she twisted to try and swipe the male's legs from underneath him. Raziel barely moved and threw her to the side. Zara rolled on the bloodied ground.

It's not real. This is not theirs.

She pushed herself to her feet. "Even in death, you come to haunt me. What a shit apparition."

"That's no way to speak to your maker." Raziel's wings unfurled to their full length. An ethereal warrior driven by malice. "I was summoned here by your deep-rooted anger."

She snarled. "I can kill you again."

They charged toward each other with no weapons other than their hands. Ether flared around Zara's fists as she struck the male, the archangel parrying every blow.

The world blurred. Raziel's wing knocked her off her feet before he slammed her onto the ground, pressing a boot on her chest.

"I am here in this dreamscape because you are still *weak.* All this pomp and flair doesn't hide the wounded girl beneath. You are alone, Rogue. Those who love you *die.* It will only be a matter of time before everyone still by your side leaves you too."

Desperation clawed up her throat. For some time, she'd believed that she could desire something more in life. Now that her fyrebrand had been destroyed, now that she wasn't forced to serve the High King through its bond. But Raziel was not too far away from the truth. All those she cared about were in constant danger.

As the archangel's boot pushed harder on her chest, Zara started to sink into darkness.

She could see it. The flicker of steel from Raziel's blade when he cut Hakim's throat. Then Eshe's. They had died because of her.

Basim's strained voice echoed through their bond. *Why are you allowing this male to tear at your soul?*

I don't know.

Your guild is no longer here, Zara, but you are. Though they'll always remain in your heart.

It was too quiet, but Zara could see them. They were standing at the end of a dirt road, the sun setting behind them. Hakim Salvador, his dreads tied back, whorls of tattoos along his throat. Eshe Abara, her dark hair tucked back with a headwrap. Her alabaster bow nowhere to be found. They were smiling at her. Was this a memory?

Is there something you want to say to them?

Hakim and Eshe pulled their hoods over their heads and turned away from her. Zara tried to reach for them, but she couldn't move. *I don't know!*

Yes, you do.

"It should've been me!" she screamed out loud, every tendril of guilt and pain leaking from the thorns within. "You needed me and I wasn't there! You were fighting for me—*and I wasn't there!*"

Raziel glared at her. "What nonsense are you spouting?"

Tears swelled in the back of Zara's eyes. She was not speaking to the archangel. Raziel dug his heel into her chest and darkness fell over her eyes.

She was suspended in nothingness, and that inner wound tore open again. *I wasn't there for you.*

The gash peeled apart, the blood of her guilt spilling over. *I'm sorry. I miss you so much it hurts.*

Silence. *Come back.*

Zara sank further into the abyss. Deeper and deeper. The emptiness filled the corners of her soul. Maybe she was meant to stay here…

"*Little warrior.*"

This voice—she knew this voice. Heard it so clearly in this expanse of night. Oh, how she wanted to cling to it.

"*On your feet, little warrior. Your journey does not stop here.*"

Strong hands pulled her up. Zara fell into what felt like a hard chest. This presence. She recognized it.

Zara grabbed onto him, nuzzled him, even as soundless sobs rocked through her. *I remember your words, but I haven't been following them. I'm sorry.*

Large arms embraced her. Warmth melted through the thorns within her as the tears fell. "*Daughter, how you have tortured yourself. It breaks my heart.*"

I'm sorry I wasn't there. Zara cried louder and louder, even if she couldn't hear herself. *I'm so sorry.*

"I wouldn't have had it any other way. To give you a chance at happiness was all I wanted." He held her tighter within the nothingness. *"We rise and fall like the sun, but we never die. Remember to desire more for yourself, little warrior. Promise me."*

Grief and guilt collided, rushing out of her soul. Zara clutched onto his chest, unable to breathe through the thick emotion.

Slender arms wrapped around her from behind. A feminine voice followed. *"It was never your fault. We love you, always will. Now, allow yourself to move on."*

No, Zara was never alone, was she? In the depths of her heart, she'd known this to be true. Their presence drifted away from her, but she kept standing. Pain still poured out but she did not fall.

Light bloomed in the distance. Zara gazed at it, heart racing. She didn't want to leave, and yet… She took a step forward. Paused.

Those strong hands mussed her hair. *"We never left your side. Now, go."*

Tears streaked down her cheeks as she reached for the light—

Zara snapped her eyes open, chest tight, and met the former High King's gaze. Her anger was ancient. She had been scarred by the tears and pain of those before her and her own, but now she would rise.

The mercenary spoke through bloodied teeth. "He made me promise."

Raziel hesitated.

The last of her tears slid down her temple as she said, "I can't break a promise."

The guild of Ikarria would live in her memory, in her heart, and her enemies would learn to fear her. Zara Santos was *more*.

"Go."

Zara reached out into the void. There was a slash of light behind the archangel as Basim lunged from the veil. The wolf wrapped his teeth around Raziel's wing, forcing the male to get off her.

Ether had been raking its claws against the invisible walls of the Oasis ever since she'd entered it. This place was burning with untapped energy—and she *wanted* it.

Power rose around Zara. This was the Oasis's doing, and it was testing her resolve. She had come with a purpose and she would see it through.

Zara released the ether. It surged forward, beasts made of fiery tongues. Power ate up bloodied ground, igniting the world in red and purple. Basim let Raziel go, and the ethereal flames devoured the archangel once more.

"I come to you as an omen!" Raziel seethed. "No matter what you do, no matter how strong you become, you will always be a pawn. Serving one master to another!"

Red light illuminated Zara's face. "And I will cut each and every one of them down."

The archangel howled in rage, pointing a finger at her as his form dissipated in fiery light. "I warned you, goddess."

The world around her started to tremble. The dawn sky was being peeled away as the energy around her screamed.

This plane is unraveling, Basim snarled. *We need to go.*

Light exploded in front of them. Zara trusted her instincts and started to run toward it. She had strayed from her path—but no longer. Zara barreled toward the unknown, leaving behind her blood-ridden past.

That deep voice echoed through her. *"Don't look back. Keep going."*

A war cry tore out of her as she lunged through the light. To where there was no beginning and no end.

"I love you."

Zara was standing in a vast wasteland. Nothing but wet dirt beneath her feet and a red sky above her.

"Intriguing," said a deep voice. "Your dreamscape was much different than the archangel's."

Zara jumped, and saw a man standing beside her. He had dusk-colored eyes and glowing tattoos. Her ether didn't seem agitated at his presence, but felt almost heightened.

Basim's ears twitched. *Primordial.*

"Neheharu," she whispered. Zara felt compelled to bow or fall to her knees—the energy was forcing itself on her body. She did neither. "Where is Ronan?"

The Primordial sighed. "The godlings are so protective of one another. He is fine, in a manner of speaking. What I am more interested in is how your ether has been maturing. I can already sense the kind of Primordial you could become."

Zara gritted her teeth. "I am not here for that."

"Yes, I know. You are here for *him*." Neheharu looked to the red sky. "He is very eager to meet with you."

She took a step forward. "Where is Mikatán? Can you take me to him?"

Neheharu's lips curled in disgust. "If it were so easy, Mikatán would have appeared by now. You have to find your way to him as you have before in your dreams."

Zara didn't question how the Primordial knew about those.

Smoke rolled from the beyond, clouding her view of the Primordial. Neheharu's white robes made him a gem among the ruins.

"Only you can reach the Primordial, once you understand the dreamscape you are in." The Primordial of Divinity and Prophecy then disappeared.

Zara cursed under her breath. "All these riddles and half-answers. Why can't these gods just be straightforward?"

Even the Primordials don't know what to expect. Basim paced around her, urging her to walk. *You and the archangel are anomalies.*

They waded through smoke, waves of embers flying past her and the air heating so much that Zara had to bring her arm up to cover her nose.

Her eyes stung, and she coughed at the stench of burned flesh and melted steel. Her boots crunched over ash and—and bone. Her eyes widened at the sight before her.

Broken armor and bodies. Puddles of blood and mud, the red sky thick with smoke. This was a battlefield.

"By the fuckings Suns," she murmured.

Torn banners fluttered in the wind, spears and swords discarded.

Zara neared one lifeless soldier, bending down to see the engraved emblem on their breastplate. The face of a dragon inside a crescent sun.

Zara's heart rate pounded through her blood, so hard it made her vision swim. These were Ikarrian soldiers. When had this happened?

An irrational thought bloomed in her head. *Daria.* What if her sister was here? What if her body was among the many in this graveyard?

Zara shook her head and ran her hand across her mouth, fighting the urge to retch. No. This wasn't real. It couldn't be. It must have been conjured by the Oasis.

Zara then noted the banners of Kairos, Elios—even Adrastea. Other realms she didn't recognize as well. It was difficult to determine who had fought whom.

The world was too silent; the fine hairs along her arms stood on end. Then, it was as if the red sky took a single inhale before starting a drum beat. And another. And another.

Something *big* was approaching, flying toward them. Zara crouched low, the smoke so thick she could see nothing at first, until the clouds of ash rippled like the surface of water, and a silhouette formed above.

It was massive, with a burly body and wings that threatened to reach the horizon.

Zara looked down to where a shadowy figure was walking through the mist. It stepped into view—and suddenly, Zara was staring at *herself.*

The woman before her was different. Terrifying. Her eyes were consumed with red light, face riddled with cuts and bruises. A gruesome scar stretched from her cheekbone to the bridge of her nose. She didn't seem to notice them.

Basim sidled closer to her, silent.

The creature dove from the clouds. Barely moving, the mercenary appeared a moment later in the air just above the flying beast. Her body was already coated in red, her blades dripping with blood, ribbons of liquid streaming out in her wake.

Blood spurted from several parts of the creature's body, the gashes widening before it exploded into red mist.

Zara fell to her knees. What had she just witnessed?

Her other self dropped to the ground, and stood under the rain of blood.

Fear stabbed Zara in the gut. Was this… No, it couldn't be. It was not possible.

Someone landed behind her. *"Santos."*

Her body stilled at that liquid dark voice, her senses crackling. It was thunder and pure power. She turned around as a pair of glowing blue eyes emerged from the smoke.

Her lips trembled. "Ronan?"

The archangel before her was also different. Gone was that usual glint of wicked humor and wit. Blue and orange mist followed his wings, his ether a force that pulsed out with each powerful step.

He stalked past Zara, unaware of her presence. Her breath hitched when she saw the scars on his body. New ones.

Ronan walked to the other Zara, his ether flaring at the sight of the blood on her. He brought a hand to the back of her neck, brushing his thumb along her jaw and smearing the red there.

They stood alone on the battlefield. Two forces of indescribable power.

Zara's vision blurred with tears. She knew what this was. Had known for some time, but didn't want to believe it.

She thought of the wraith's words. *The future rests in your veins.* The path they were on now would lead to this. Zara had seen glimpses of it already: flashes of Damalis burning, of Ronan being angry at her.

She nearly hurled.

The Zara and Ronan of the future looked toward her.

It was as if her realization had sent a signal to the Oasis. A jungle sprouted around her, tearing through the dreamscape, and Zara watched as the strangers before her were wiped away from this place.

Basim's ears twitched. *He's here.*

Chills crawled along her skin. The ether inside Zara sang.

Mikatán walked between the trees, his necklace of bones and teeth swaying with every heavy step. Starlight lined his headdress of daggers.

"You came here seeking power, but the Oasis had other plans. It forced you to discover what kind of Primordial you could become, should you take the Crossing." The god cocked his head. "So, what will you be, goddess-in-the-making?"

The realization that had flooded her returned as a quiet wave. One made of dawn skies and crimson hope.

Zara lifted her chin, meeting Death's gaze. "I am a god of the future."

FORTY-SIX

It was raining again. Daria stared at the downpour tearing through the Ikarrian trees and huddled closer to the stone wall providing a little cover.

"I wonder how Zara and Ronan are doing." Daria glanced at Ares.

The vampire observed the ancient woodland, his sheathed sword propped against his leg. "The Oasis of Dreams works in ways beyond our understanding—who knows how long they'll be in there. Ether is already something I am not familiar with, so I'd personally stay away from a land that acts as a conduit to the otherworldly." He met her gaze and smirked. "But Zara and Ronan are much more suited to that kind of thing. They'll be all right."

Their journey from Kairos had taken longer than Daria would've liked. They'd traveled back through the Sombra Quarter towns, arriving at Corduva to leave the camels and to retrieve Ares's horse.

However, anytime they stopped in one of the shadow dealers' businesses, Ares asked to speak privately with them, the vampire getting more restless after every conversation.

Daria hadn't asked about it. Yet.

"Things are going to be different now, aren't they?" She sighed.

There was a nervous flutter in her stomach. Dae Asari was a day's ride away. Life was going to shift once more. Her relationship with the general hung in the unknown.

Ares was silent for a moment. "We will need to return to the way things were before, yes."

The words caused her stomach to drop. "You mean, back to me being your prisoner as I serve Adrastea's needs."

"It's the best way to handle the vampires in your castle. At least, until you find the dragons—then you'll be able to do whatever you wish."

Anger flared within her, that old emotion from his betrayal crawling back up from the depths of her mind.

"Once I find the dragons, I will convince them to fight for *me*. I'm sure you will have assumed that much." Daria glared at him. "I know your king is preparing for that, given the astral weapons he has amassed. That does not matter—my pater also entrusted me to find them. So I have to do it, for him too."

"I understand." Ares held her gaze, and her heart started to pound.

"So I have to ask, will you be fighting against the dragons—fighting against *me*? Or will you stand by my side?"

When he didn't answer for a few moments, Daria scoffed and pushed herself to her feet. She stormed out into the rain, trudging through the large plants that tugged at her cloak. Anywhere but back there.

"Daria, please wait." Ares ran after her. "I may have the title of general, but not even I can trust my soldiers. And it would be easier if you kept on not trusting me too."

"That's what you keep telling me!" She spun around, her wet braids whipping her face. "I don't understand. Just what are you planning on doing next? Will you go right back to serving Matías?"

He searched her face, his lips parting. Daria pressed on, "Whose side are you on: Adrastea, mine—or your own? You go with me to Kairos, you help Ronan, you protect me, and yet you are *still* holding onto your loyalty to Adrastea."

"That's not true." Ares's voice was low. "Please, just trust me."

Daria's heart twisted. "I'll ask you again… Why did you agree to raid Ikarria?" She nearly sobbed. "*Why, Ares? Why—*"

"*Because I was afraid of losing you!*" Ares's expression was pained, as if it hurt to speak. "Back during the hunting season, just after the Summit, Matías had planned to have you assassinated."

Daria felt sick to her stomach. She opened her mouth to respond, but nothing came.

"He was going to kill you. And I—I *panicked*. I convinced him that you were more valuable to his cause alive. Matías agreed to spare you, only if I led the charge against Ikarria. He threatened you and my mother." His voice broke.

The world was ripped out from underneath her. Daria staggered back a step, nearly slipping on the damp ground.

Ares caught her, one arm wrapping around her waist.

The truth weighed heavily on her soul. If he hadn't advocated for her—if he hadn't protected her—Daria wouldn't be standing here at this very moment.

"Your father knows this," Ares said. "I told him during the raid. He almost killed me before I had a chance to, but the obsidian ring on my hand—the one you gave me—was enough to convince him to work with me."

Ares lifted his hand, the dark band swallowing the light. "King Idris surrendered to prevent more violence, and to keep you alive. Your father believes you can save Ikarria. That you're getting stronger."

It was becoming difficult to breathe. Her pater *knew*. Had known all along. "What about *him*? What about setting him free?"

"King Idris knew the cost. He willingly gave himself up so that you had a chance to rise." His jaw locked. "I won't let him stay in the Iron Isles any longer than he needs to."

Ares let her go, but instead of stepping away, he slid to his knees. In the pouring rain, the general of war bowed before the queen of the draconic realm.

"I'm sorry, Daria. I'm so sorry, for all I've done, for the hurt I caused. I hated what I had to do. Hated *myself*." The skin between his brows pinched as he stared at her. "Though I would have still done it all—to save you. You can despise me, but I would do it all over again if it means that you *live*."

Rain cried, leaves shuddered, and the trees watched them.

Daria could only gaze at the male before her, who had been her silent protector. For every wrong committed, Ares had tried to make amends tenfold. And she had been witness to his efforts without even realizing it. Daria was one step closer to finding the dragons also because of the role Ares had played—even if it was under the guise of serving Adrastea. He'd paved the way for her. Had helped the others fight for a better world.

None of her allies were innocent, not even her. They had all done atrocious things to survive. This dark world held no mercy for softness—Daria had learnt this the hard way.

The fires of her anger suddenly weren't as hot as before.

"I don't hate you, Ares. I don't think I ever could." Daria placed a palm on his cheek. "Why didn't you say anything?"

"Because I didn't deserve your forgiveness. Nor did I want it. Only Ronan knows. Since the raid, I have been working on making things right." Ares leaned into her touch, his eyes never leaving hers. "I've been a coward, always afraid of turning away from the life that I've known. It was you who inspired me to brave those storms. To fight for something worthwhile."

His words rang through her. Daria pulled him up, not knowing what to say for a few moments. He stood tall, staring at her as she let her fingers trail down the sleeve of his left arm.

"I never got to ask about the burns you sustained in the raid," she eventually murmured. "I assume they scarred your skin."

"Yes. A small price that hardly equates to what I've done."

Daria swallowed and reached for his hand, touching the obsidian ring she'd gifted him. "And you still wear this."

Rain filled the temporary silence, Ares's presence like a sharp cold breeze, but a comfort in this dreary world. "I could never take it off."

All this time spent at each other's side, the wounds within had slowly been stitching themselves back together. Daria knew there was a long road ahead of them, one filled with more danger and unknowns—but when it came to Ares, the broken pieces of their relationship were becoming one once more. Bit by bit. Day by day.

"You said you were trying to make things right." Daria met his gaze. Ares looked almost afraid for a moment, and she smiled. "Our esteemed general does not have to fight these battles alone. You can trust me too."

He searched her face, and the tension lining his body slowly lessened. Ares nodded. "Let me tell you what I've been planning with the Sombra Quarter."

When they reached the capital of Dae Asari, they went to the tavern managed by the Sombra Quarter. Inside, Warrick was pacing back and forth. Daria hadn't expected to find the large mercenary of Adrastea *here* in Ikarria. Unease coiled inside her.

Warrick looked up when the door closed behind them, his face pale. He stormed toward Ares, slapping a bunched letter to his chest. "I received this report a few days ago—I worried that our firebirds were being tracked so I wanted to deliver it myself. I came as fast as I could."

Her intuition had been right. Something was wrong.

Ares narrowed his eyes and opened the letter.

Warrick continued, "The shadow dealers' caravan that was scheduled to arrive at the Stone Orchard didn't show. It was destroyed on the outskirts of Elios—they never even made it out of the city."

The vampire didn't say anything for a moment, but Daria knew better. She could see the faint tremors rattling his chest. How he was restraining himself, fighting to keep his composure.

Her own heart was racing as she clutched onto his arm. "You need to go to Soleira."

Ares crunched the report in his hand, met her gaze. "I need to escort you back to the palace and help you plan—"

"I trust you, Ares. Do what you must, and return to Ikarria as soon as you can."

The look in his eyes was something between desperation and

panic. It wedged an unseen blade in her ribs. The matter in the report was bigger than all of them, and they both knew it.

Within moments, Ares was saddled atop his horse, red cloak waving in the breeze. Warrick had already taken off back toward the Stone Orchard to continue his duties leading the shadow markets. Though the mercenary had offered to join the vampire, Ares had declined.

He glanced down at her. "Wait for me, Daria," Ares whispered. "Don't attempt the Necromancy spell until I return. I won't let you go through the summoning alone."

Daria smiled softly. "I will wait as long as I can."

"I will return to you, Your Majesty."

She watched as the general of war left for Soleira. For the High Throne.

FORTY-SEVEN

Ronan stood in a breezeway that connected two towers and overlooked a vast jungle. He sucked in a breath as two young archangels walked his way, and pressed himself against the wall, watching his younger self and Erebus cross the mosaic floor.

"This was when we came to Celestrea for the Crossing," Ronan said.

I remember. Nyota tilted her head. *You were so excited when you left Damalis, but when you returned, you seemed… different.*

Ronan couldn't bring himself to respond.

Erebus's voice was soft. "I heard you tried speaking to the leading deities about the mistreatment of the servants in Celestrea."

There were dark smudges under Young Ronan's eyes. "Yes. The deities overseeing the Crossing have enough influence on the ethereal realm to make a change. I thought I could use my position to advocate for the working class, once I become one with my Primordial ether."

His expression darkened. "Instead of considering my words, they mocked me, claiming that, even if I succeed with the Crossing, I will never make a difference here. I am not a denizen of this realm, therefore I have no business interfering in their matters."

"That doesn't surprise me," Erebus said. "Their society has

functioned like this for decades. It will take more than speeches to sway these lesser gods."

They entered their shared suite, tall, square windows allowing starlight to spill into the main living room.

"Speaking of gods, I have not met any of the Primordials yet." Young Ronan plopped himself onto a cushion next to the window. "Do they not care about what's happening within their own realm? Our existence gives ether to the Primordials—they should be watching over us."

Erebus leaned against the windowsill, observing the Crown Prince's tired face. "A curious thing, is it not? It is as if they are hoarding power for themselves without regard for anything else."

"It doesn't make sense. They are supposed to be *better* than that—that's what the mortal world has been taught. The Primordials maintain balance." Ronan sighed before wincing. Blue tendrils flickered about his body.

Erebus tensed. "Your ether has become more agitated since we got here. Have you been training?"

"Only when I'm with the deities. It's odd, whenever I'm around them, my power scratches at my skin."

"That's because being in Celestrea is forcing it to grow at a faster—more dangerous—rate. You know you're supposed to be practicing everyday, otherwise you will become a hazard to yourself and others."

Young Ronan waved him off. "You're being a pestering mother hen again. Listen, this ether is my *destiny*, and it will give us everything we want. I don't have to do anything more than I already have—why else would I have been chosen? Don't worry about it, brother."

Erebus pinched the bridge of his nose. "Crown Prince, you can be really exhausting. You never listen to me."

The archangel gasped in mock outrage. "*What was that?*"

"Enough." Amusement trickled in Erebus's voice.

Young Ronan grunted in pain once more as another flare of blue flashed across his body. Erebus reached for him. The prince was breathing a bit harder than before, but waved his friend away and forced out a nonchalant yawn.

"I guess it hasn't been a complete waste of time yet. A deity told me the most guarded secret of Celestrea. Do you want to know what it is?"

"Someone of my status probably shouldn't."

"Don't talk like that," the Crown Prince scolded. "You know I don't care about that."

Erebus sighed. "Go on then. Though I'm going to pretend you didn't say anything."

"They told me the history of how the Gates of Celestrea were created—and what could *unmake* them. Apparently, it's something I must know before I fulfill The Crossing, especially since I will have to uphold Damalis's responsibility to protect them."

Erebus sounded uninterested as he picked at something on his shirt. "What is it?"

"The *blood* of a Primordial, spilled onto the gates, can destroy them. Isn't that ironic?" Young Ronan stretched his arms out. "Anyway, enough of this. Have you decided to visit your family?"

Erebus's expression softened as he went to sit across from the archangel. "Yes. Though, if I may, I'd like to see them alone first before I introduce you."

"You don't need permission from me. I look forward to meeting them, whenever you're ready." The Crown Prince poured tea into two cups and served the archangel. "I won't let these deities get in the way of our goals, I don't care how young or naive I seem to those ancient fools. Anything is possible."

Erebus smiled and took the drink, clinking it with Ronan's. "Anything is possible."

As the memory began to fade, Ronan stared at the two young archangels for as long as he could. To burn this sight into his memory forever.

"This was the last amicable conversation we had," he murmured, laying his hand on Nyota's head.

An orange sky appeared. Erebus was in front of a small house— his childhood home. Ronan recognized it from the first memory he'd been shown.

The door opened and an archangel, several years Erebus's senior, appeared. His long white hair lacked its previous shine, the braids slightly messy. The male looked older now, tired lines bracketing his eyes. At least ten years had passed since the last memory, but Ronan knew who this was.

Kaiser's eyes widened. "Erebus, is that you?"

Ronan's former friend suddenly looked so young. His lips parted as if he was trying to find his voice, his gaze dropping. "I'm—I'm sorry for not coming to you sooner—"

His older brother pulled Erebus into a tight embrace. "Suns Above, you're *here*. I am not dreaming."

Erebus stood frozen, arms raised at an awkward angle. Slowly, he brought a hand to Kaiser's back. It was a rare sight for the male to be physically affectionate. Ronan had lost count of how many times he'd teased Erebus about it.

The two brothers headed into the house. Ronan followed and found them sitting at the dining table.

Admiration shone in Kaiser's eyes. "Look at you, you've grown into a fine male." He leaned over to tap the Damalisan emblem stitched on his brother's lapel. "You've made something of yourself."

"I've been doing my best, I think. They treat me well in Damalis."

The older archangel let out a ragged breath. "Good. I'm relieved to hear that. In your letters you've always said things were going well, but I worried you were hiding the truth."

"Like how you are evading it right now?"

Kaiser stilled, his eyes searching his little brother's face. "What?"

Erebus jerked his chin to the rest of the home. "The only scent in this place is yours. There is no sign of anyone else. Not our father, mother, or sister." He released a shaky breath and looked away. "I had a feeling that something was wrong. The letters started out with Father's or Mother's handwriting, but within the past year it's only been you."

Kaiser bowed his head, a slight tremble to his body. "I wasn't trying to hide anything from you. I wanted to tell you, but after what happened, my lord began to screen my letters." He seemed unable to look his brother in the eyes. "Earlier this year, Mother passed away due to an illness no healer could cure. Father was so stricken with grief, he pleaded with the lord of the House to let you return home—at least to bury her. But the lord didn't want to. They fought, and it resulted in Father's death."

Kaiser lifted his gaze, face ashen. "As for our sister... She was sold off to another House. I don't even know where she is, or if she's safe. Somehow I am the only one left—to pay for the *strife* we caused our lord."

Ronan bent to his haunches to look at Erebus's face. Shadows loomed over him, his icy eyes distant. If the archangel felt any heartache, he was doing a fine job hiding it.

"You've never been one for tears," Ronan whispered. "You always thought you'd be a burden if you showed any emotion... even when I assured you otherwise."

He watched the two brothers silently grieve their reality. The memory must have sped through time, because the sun was even lower and stars now dotted the purple sky. Torchlights burned bright beyond the windows.

Erebus finally looked up at Kaiser, a new resolve in his gaze. "Come away with me. I know Ronan won't let this stand—he will fight for your freedom."

"Ronan?"

"The Crown Prince of Damalis."

Kaiser stared at his younger brother. "You speak his name with warmth, as if you're close."

Erebus didn't hesitate. "We are. We're friends."

"No person of royal standing cares that much, Erebus. Besides, he is only a prince, what can he really do?"

"Ronan isn't like that. He's different." Erebus's hands curled into fists atop the table. "I want you to meet him—you'll see what I mean."

Several beats of silence passed. Kaiser gazed at Erebus with a softness that squeezed Ronan's chest. It was the look of someone witnessing the fruition of all their sacrifice. The realization that all the pain he'd endured to save his sibling had meant something.

The older archangel's smile stretched wider. "As you wish, dear brother; only promise me you will avoid the lord of the House in the meantime. Why don't you return tomorrow evening with your friend?"

Erebus smiled then, grief and hope mixing together. "I will."

Ronan's expression fell as the pieces began to fall in place. He ran his hand through his hair, breathing heavily. What he had been running away from all these years, was now rushing toward him. All the bloodshed and tears.

"No, please, I can't see this." Ronan clutched onto his chest. "I don't want to. *Please.*"

Nyota pressed herself against his leg. *Dear one, you can't move forward until you face it.*

"*I know!*" Ronan shouted into the void as the world before him shifted another time. "I'm sorry, Nyota. But I feel like I am falling apart."

Then hold onto me. I won't let you break.

Erebus entered the suite, returning from his visit with his brother. "I have some news—"

His smile quickly died when he saw the Crown Prince. Young Ronan was glaring out at the celestial world, his hands braced on the threshold of the window.

"Let me guess." Erebus walked over to him. "The deities gave you a difficult time today."

Ronan's ether was aching, pressing against the barriers of his skin. Yanking on his heart and mind. He hissed at his younger self. "You selfish prick. Your foul mood ruined the only sliver of happiness and hope your friend had in the midst of his grief."

Young Ronan didn't look up. "The deities said I am not ready for the Crossing."

"What do you mean?"

"I suppose we shouldn't be surprised—I'm young and inexperienced. Eighteen years of age is nothing in the eyes of a deity." The

Crown Prince bowed his head. "They will not stop me from doing the ritual, but they do not believe I should."

Erebus stared at the archangel. "And what do you think?"

"Well, I am starting to doubt my capabilities as the Crown Prince. Maybe this was all for nothing, and it was stupid to think we could do it."

"The Crossing depends heavily on the willpower of the participant; if they care about what they're working toward—then their training will always be worth it." Erebus's expression fell. "Unless you never truly believed in our cause."

Ronan's eyes were stinging. Every emotion was mounting in his chest, on the verge of an explosion.

The Crown Prince snarled, turning to face Erebus. "Did you seriously say that?"

"You're afraid."

Erebus did not say it unkindly, but Young Ronan let out a mirthless laugh. "Of course, I am! My whole life, I believed this ether was my destiny, and now I'm at risk of losing my life. And if I avoid the Crossing, I lose my power. How is that fair? I am a *prince*, this is not what I wanted. I don't want to die for them. I don't want to die for *anyone!*"

Silence. Painful silence.

Erebus's voice went low, almost to a whisper. "By 'them' are you talking about me and my family? The archangels who are *beneath* you?"

"I didn't mean it like that." Young Ronan gritted his teeth. "But how can I help anyone if I am not alive? No, I won't do it."

"What about the promise we made?" Erebus raised his voice, white wings flaring. "I don't want you in danger, Ronan, believe me. But chances of someone of your immense power dying are very slim, and I know you don't want to lose your ether. You knew this going into it."

The veins of the Crown Prince's throat strained, blue light crackling along his skin. "The Primordials are supposed to help us. Maybe if I can force an audience with one of them, I can fix this."

"Fix what? The higher gods haven't bothered to show since we've been here. They don't care about what any of us are going through."

Emotion swam in Erebus's eyes. "Are you not even going to try to change things?"

Ronan was tempted to reach out to Nyota. Perhaps to run away from this nightmare—but he didn't. No, he needed to see this all the way through.

His younger self growled in frustration. The sparks of ether around him brightened. "I will find another way to help your family. We have time; I'll ask my father—"

"How many times has King Elijah tried to sway the deities of Celestrea in his favor to no avail? Even *he* couldn't do anything. That is why we believed in the Crossing—"

"And we were fools, Erebus! I can't take that risk."

"Can't or won't? *I* have made sacrifices all my life! What about you?" Erebus's lips curled in anger. "You can make a difference. 'Anything is possible'—you said so yourself."

"Now I am saying to *leave* this plan behind!" Energy thickened in the room, Young Ronan breathing heavily. "We will find another solution."

"How long will that take? How much time will have to pass for the *perfect* answer to arise? My family is already—"

"I know!" Ronan's ether lashed out. Beams of electrifying blue slammed Erebus against a wall, pinning him there. "*Your family. Your family.* Fucking Suns, maybe I'm not the one who should be responsible for your family's—for all of Celestrea's—liberation!"

The Crown Prince gritted his teeth, the white of his eyes swallowed with power. "I said leave it, Erebus. And that's an order."

Erebus struggled against the ether. He gasped for air, unable to speak. The blue light retreated with a snap, sending Young Ronan stumbling back. The archangel blinked, his eyes returning to normal as his body shook.

The Crown Prince stared down at his hands, his face pale. "What... What did I..."

"Your ether lacks control." Erebus coughed, sliding down the wall, staring up at Ronan as if he didn't recognize the male before him. His expression turned more distant—more *empty*—the longer he spoke. "You don't listen to me. You haven't been listening to me in months."

Young Ronan reached for his brother. "I didn't mean to hurt you. I didn't mean what I said—"

Erebus slapped his hand away, pushing himself to his feet. "Yes, you did." He took a step back, his expression smoothing out. "The ether selected you to have this indescribable power; it was your *destiny* to be filled with so much potential, as you said. And yet, you are choosing to shy away from it. The first *real* challenge you've ever faced in your life, and you are running away."

Young Ronan was still trembling, both from his aggravated power and his frustration. "You can't be serious. Just—just wait, Erebus! Until I am ready."

"What do you think I've been doing all this time?" His brother snapped, before turning away. "Don't worry, Your Highness, you are not responsible for saving my family. Nor for helping me anymore. You are released from this burden."

The archangel headed toward the door, and the Crown Prince sucked in a harsh breath. "Where are you going? Erebus, wait! I order you to stop and answer me."

Erebus didn't look back as he left the room.

When the door closed, the Crown Prince fell to his knees and pressed his brow on the ground. As crackles of blue ether continued to shudder down his body.

Ronan wanted to scream. He wanted to grab his younger self by the shoulders and shake him, but all he could do was gaze at the doors Erebus had left from. His brother would never return. They would never be the same after this night.

His scarred lips curled. "You idiot."

Erebus went back to his family home. He stood in front of the door, staring at it. His nostrils flared, as if he'd smelled something bad, eyes going wide, and he charged through the door.

"Kaiser?" he called out. "Kaiser, where are—"

Erebus's words died on his tongue. His brother was slumped against the wall, the dining table on its side. Blood smeared the floor, pooled beneath the archangel's body.

Ronan felt weak, his ether shuddering. "No."

Bruises mottled Kaiser's pale skin and led to a gaping hole in his chest. Dried red stained the corner of his lips.

Erebus dropped to his knees beside the archangel. He cupped the male's face, his voice cracking. "Brother?"

He gently pulled his brother into his arms and pressed his cheek to his head. Silence fell over the home, drowning the sound of chirping birds outside.

"I don't understand," Erebus whispered. "I just got you back."

No one would answer him. No one would comfort him. No one would save him.

Erebus began to tremble as he squeezed his brother's body, breathing heavily through his nostrils as he stared at the pool of blood.

Ronan almost fell to his knees. Sadness and regret burned into a fiery agony, a rage that quietly brewed in his bloodstream.

Did you know? Nyota asked.

He responded through their bond. *As the years went by, I suspected something terrible had happened to his family, but no, I didn't know.*

Someone walked into the room, the energy about them hissing and snapping unseen teeth. "I'd heard that a certain servant of mine had returned to Celestrea. Imagine my surprise when I didn't receive notice from the kingdom of Damalis, or when you never even came to visit the one who made your fortune possible."

The male's hands were stained red.

A growl ripped through Ronan's teeth. "*You.*"

When Erebus lifted his gaze, the lord of the House laughed. "Look at you, glaring at your lord and master. I almost thought you were Callum. That's how your father looked at me before I killed him."

"Why would you do this?" Erebus rasped out, still clutching onto his brother. "Kaiser always served you well. *Why?*"

The deity prowled closer, the ether in his eyes bright. "I no longer require your family's work when *you* are all I need."

Ronan snarled, placing himself between Erebus and the male. He knew there was no point but his body moved on its own. That understanding turned into a knife embedding itself in his chest as the deity walked through him.

"I've invested a lot to send you to Damalis." The male grabbed Erebus by the collar of his shirt, yanking him away from Kaiser. "Your position in both realms can grant me more power, more influence. I think it is time I received the rewards of my investment."

Erebus slapped the deity's hand away. "Get away from me. There is only one male I serve, and he is not you."

"It seems you still don't understand. No matter what fancy titles you bear, I still *own* you." The lesser god laughed, pointing at his own chest. "The Primordials themselves allowed me to be head of this House. Me! And I will do *whatever* I please with you!"

Erebus lunged at the male. He grabbed his face, fingers digging into skin so hard that blood seeped out. The deity struggled against him, but the archangel was strong.

Energy lifted around them, Erebus's clothes and hair billowing in the air. Silver light flared in his eyes and the deity started to scream.

"What are you doing to me? Where am I?"

Erebus's voice was lethally calm. "I am making you feel all the pain you put my family through."

Ronan watched in awe. This was Erebus's power as an archangel, his illusions at work. The god thrashed in his grasp; Erebus must have obliterated the deity's mind. But the male would not die yet, not until his heart was—

A sword pierced through the deity's chest, nearly stabbing Erebus. The young archangel released him as the blade pulled away, and the one who'd ruined Erebus's family crumpled to the floor. Dead.

Whoever had killed the deity was swathed in shadow, the memory beginning to fade.

No, wait.

Panic seized Ronan's lungs. He didn't want to leave this place, because then—then Erebus would never come back. His friend would never be the same.

Ronan reached for the archangel, the image twisting as he was plunged into another memory.

The memories began to race by.

In one, Erebus was bowing his head before a—a portal? Ethereal light shimmered across its surface, a shadowed figure standing on its other side, speaking to the archangel.

The corners of this memory were dark, as if Erebus was in some cavern. Ronan tried to walk closer but a weight pulled his legs down.

Erebus slashed his palm open with a knife, his blood splattering on runes and symbols carved on the ground.

A voice purred from the other side. "Our contract is now sealed. You serve me, and I will serve you. Make sure the empire that is Celestrea topples, and I will give you the power to create the world you always desired to live in. You will be remade into a Primordial."

Erebus's face was expressionless. "I will accomplish the task you bestowed upon me, so that you may be reunited with the one you love."

Ronan gritted his teeth. *'Reunited with the one you love'—Fucking Suns, that must be Khaos on the other side of the portal, and they are talking about Deimos. She is looking for him.*

"We will need to cut off Celestrea from its power source—the mortal world," Khaos said. "Without it, the realm will be too weak to defend itself."

"The Primordials never answered my pleas to save my loved ones, and now I will force them to acknowledge me. Celestrea will be destroyed, and the mortal world will be remade." Erebus lifted his gaze. "I know what to do."

Power flared from the other side of the archway, shattering the memory. The world spun as Ronan's ether rose from his body. Mists of deep blue unfurled, and energy crackled along his skin.

He closed his eyes. For he knew what he would see next—the day

Celestrea went up in flames, when the rebelling deities released themselves upon their fellow kin. Their forces had been gathering for some time before Erebus joined them. Many despised the celestial realm.

Ronan opened his eyes and witnessed once more the civil war between deities and Primordials, creatures of formidable power.

Erebus was on the docks of Celestrea, near the Gates, and facing Young Ronan.

Ronan clutched onto his chest. The old pain of his heart breaking at the sight of his brother leading the battle had never truly left him. The confusion he felt that day—the betrayal. It had scorched through his bones, torn his soul apart.

The Crown Prince stood at the end of the dock, a boat ready to leave back to the mortal world.

"Come home with me!" Young Ronan shouted, his face smeared with soot. "You can stop this violence from spreading further. Everything will be fine, just come back!"

Erebus did not move, destruction reigning behind him. Flames rose toward the sky, winged beasts tearing through buildings. Deities killed deities, while the archangel citizens were forced to fight or flee.

"You are a chosen one, Ronan. Such great power within your reach because the ether said so." The corner of Erebus's lips curled. "While you have abandoned your path, I have chosen mine."

"I don't want to leave you!"

Erebus turned away from him, and faced the chaos once more. "You left me the moment you gave up on our dream."

So, Young Ronan escaped Celestrea, and sailed the Jade Sea back to Damalis, to warn the guardian realms of the incoming attack.

Images rushed around Ronan. Ethereal beasts clawed through the Gates, the gods themselves storming through the mortal lands. Blood poured from above, smoke filled the air. The War of the Skies returned to haunt him.

Screams burned through his ears.

Ronan grabbed at his head. *"Enough!"*

Nyota curled around him, pressing herself against him. His vision blurred, but he forced himself to watch when the memories halted on the Gates of Celestrea. It had been so long since he'd last seen them.

Made of ancient stone, they arched high above the ground, the ethereal realm visible just beyond. Rippling like the water, eager to welcome anyone who desired to pass through.

One of the Council members, Hadeon, tackled a young Primordial—someone he didn't recognize—at the foot of the entryway. Astral chains were tied around the god's neck, the deity hauling them up like an animal. Hadeon forced the Primordial on their knees and pressed the edge of his astral blade against their skin. Ronan held his breath.

From Celestrea's side of the Gates, another Primordial was racing toward them. It was Junya, the Primordial of Harvest and Hunt. She screamed at Hadeon to stop, but the deity only smiled and slit the young god's throat.

The light shining within the rock of the Gates flickered as Primordial blood was spilled on its foundation. The runes darkened, cracks forming along the ancient threshold.

Across the Continent, any would have disappeared in flashes of angry light.

Ronan recalled those moments, how portals had seemed to rip the sky open and swallow up any gods or goddesses who'd tried to fight alongside the guardian realms.

The Gates of Celestrea crumbled, sealing any remaining Primordials within.

Ronan fell to his knees as this truth he hadn't been able to face was forced onto him.

It had been his fault—how the world broke. He'd failed in his duty as a citizen—as a prince—of a guardian realm. Erebus had used the information he'd so willingly given to him to destroy the Gates. And now, Ronan witnessed that destruction.

Ether exploded from Ronan's body. Torrents of fiery blue and orange light raged around him. He bent over, wrapping his arms around himself, screaming out into the void.

Tears ran down his face as he tore out every shred of pain from his heart. Beyond the swirls of ethereal light, he saw Erebus. It was still the younger version of him, flying across the Damalisan sands, while deities battled imperial soldiers and érendira alike. The day Erebus brought the rebelling forces to Teotlan.

Ronan clutched at his chest, breathing hard. That day had haunted him for so long.

Erebus stood on the royal training ground, King Elijah facing him from the other side. Miriam was there, Hael in her arms. The royal family gazed at the archangel who had betrayed them, the boy they'd considered as their own.

"All of you need to flee. Damalis and Valenzia should abandon their loyalty to Celestrea. Forget the Gates and *survive*. Your involvement will only drag the other mortal kingdoms into this war." Erebus pointed toward the war-ridden beaches. "Ronan's ether is too sensitive to the presence of all the ethereal beings in this realm—he won't be able to control it, and there is no telling what it will do."

There was no hatred or pity on Elijah's face. No, it was *compassion*. "I didn't do right by you, did I? Not me nor this world. But you've lost your way, my son."

Erebus clenched his teeth. "Don't call me that. You don't get to say those words to me. I am not your son."

"Even so, we can't leave Damalis." Elijah lifted his blade, the silver etched with suns. "And we will not leave Ronan to face this alone."

A single tear streamed down Erebus's face as he unsheathed his own sword. "Damn you! Damn all of you!"

The two males clashed on the training ground.

Ronan was still on his knees, watching. His heart was stabbing at his ribs. Waiting. Waiting. Waiting.

Until his younger self appeared from the cliff's steps. He remembered the Primordial ether writhing inside him, crackles of blue light flaring around his body. Testing his control and craving to lash out, disrupted by the presence of deities and Primordials in Damalis. The weight of so much ethereal energy in the mortal world resulted in an imbalance, one that Ronan's power could not handle. And the sight of Erebus fighting his father had thrown him over the edge.

Young Ronan cried out as his ether struck the training ground—struck his family—Erebus rolling out of the way in time. The light turned the world a brilliant blue, before twisting into something like flames. And they screamed.

Ronan watched in horror, his hands shaking over his face. "Gods, stop! Please, gods, stop this!"

He couldn't look away from how his ether devoured his mother, her figure disappearing in the fiery blue. Hael cried and cried, calling for her, before being swallowed too.

"It's my fault." Ronan sobbed. "I did this! I did this! I did this!"

His father was the last one standing, groaning in pain. But he was staring at his son as he cried in despair, and there was so much love in his expression as he mouthed something, words Ronan's younger self wouldn't have heard at the time.

"My boy, it's okay," Elijah whispered. "It's not your fault."

Those words cleaved through his heart. Pulled those red threads apart until Ronan was left broken. *Not my fault? Look what happened. You died because of me.* "I'm sorry."

Ethereal light still roared in the courtyard as Young Ronan charged at Erebus, but he was too weak—too distraught—to make a difference. The archangel who was once his brother had sheathed his sword and, with desperation in his eyes, brought up a dagger and slashed it across Ronan's face. The cut sliced his lip, a scar he would carry for the rest of his days.

The last memory started to dissolve as a lone Erebus turned away.

"I'm sorry." Ronan fell to his hands and knees, crawling toward where his family had last been. "Don't leave me."

Darkness surrounded him. The Oasis had nothing else to show him. Sobs cracked through his ribs as Ronan finally threw himself into the torrents of his ether. It roared, lashing out at the remnants of the dreamscape.

Nyota stayed huddled close to him, saying nothing as he allowed himself to feel every tendril of pain and heartache. To let go. To break. To be *remade*.

Ronan's soul was being submerged by the orange-blue light of his ether. Every truth had ripped him apart—though it was what he'd needed. To witness the secrets buried among ghosts. To suffer through the consequences. So that he could rise from this tomb, the death of his youth and innocence.

The full scope of his power, of who his Primordial-self could be, came to light.

"A god of the past." Ronan scoffed. "What irony."

Another world emerged then, one separate from these memories. He found himself sitting on the edge of a cliff, above him a twilight sky filled with burning stars.

Ronan tilted his head to the side. To the presence at his side, now the other. Until it appeared before him. Ronan's eyes widened.

"So… you're my patron god."

FORTY-EIGHT

Death had always followed Zara, walked beside her on the blood-stained path. It had crowned her with red, gilded thorns, where she was burdened to carry the weight of unseen darkness. Now, death had come to give her his blessing.

That earthy scent mixed with rosemary thickened as the Primordial bent low to meet her gaze.

"Goddess of the future," Mikatán mused. "It is similar to *fate*, though different."

Zara couldn't look away from those glowing eyes. They were pools of swirling ether, mists filled with mystery. He could probably see every jagged crevice of her soul and beyond.

Silver light flashed as the Primordial of Death morphed into mortal size, the god was still taller than her. He extended a skeletal hand, and a wooden sword lined with obsidian shards formed in his palm.

"Show me what you've taken from the Oasis. Show me your strength."

There was a tremble in her fingers, a coppery taste on her tongue. Fucking Suns—was she afraid?

Zara's ether took the shape of twin khopesh blades and she charged at the Primordial. Mikatán merely raised his weapon and blocked hers. It was like hitting an iron wall, sparks of ether crackling in the air.

"Yes," the god murmured. "I can feel the layers of strength underneath, ripe and ready for the blessing of a god."

Zara's muscles trembled. She had only attacked him once and was already winded. She twisted around, slamming her khopesh swords against Mikatán. The god walked on while he parried every slash.

"There is something I've been wanting to ask you, Primordial. Something I learned in the Wraith's Den." Zara swallowed, lunging forward.

"What's the truth behind Khaos and Deimos? What did the Primordial of Fate and Time mean to you and the rest of the Three Sun Gods?"

The sound of ether clashing clapped throughout the clearing, Mikatán said nothing, holding her in place with his blade.

Flecks of silver light danced between them. The orchards that floated above were filled with glowing fruit. Dark, hairless dogs could be seen darting through the giant trees.

The silver in Mikatán's eyes deepened. "Genesis, Aspidis, and I—Life, Nature, and Death—were tasked to create a pantheon of gods. Khaos was our first. Unlike you and the archangel, she was *born* of the natural ether, not a mortal who *becomes* a Primordial. Khaos is one of the original gods."

Original gods and gods that were once mortal. Zara wondered how many of the current Primordials had once been of flesh and blood, like her.

"Is Deimos also one of the original gods?"

Mikatán pulled his wooden sword back, abandoning their fight—whatever final test this was.

His voice sharpened. "Deimos was a threat to our vision of the world—he wanted to take Khaos away from us."

"That is not what I saw." Zara narrowed her eyes on the Primordial, shoving back her nerves. "The god of Dread and Terror seemed genuinely in love with Khaos. What need was there to separate them?"

"Whatever the wraiths showed you in the Den is a lie. Those creatures have always been loyal to Khaos, and will continue to cater to her narrative."

"Even if that were true, it doesn't change the fact that the fissure between the Three Sun Gods and their precious goddess has affected *every* living creature in the mortal world. You *must* fix it!"

"Why do you think I am here—with *you?*"

Zara stumbled back, her blades disappearing, as Mikatán prowled closer, his long steps swallowing up the distance. She fell onto her backside, and Basim quickly went to crouch protectively in front of her.

The god of Death paused. "I will give you my blessing, goddess. With it, that crimson light of yours will be amplified, and you will become strong enough to face an army. However, this power is not meant to fit within the bounds of flesh and blood. You will gain more Primordial abilities, but soon your body will not be able to take it anymore."

"You and the archangel now have one year. Unless you find a way to complete the Crossing, you will lose your powers and your lifespan will be cut short."

The world went mute. Zara searched the god's skeletal face. Looking for a sign that this wasn't true.

"There is truly no way for me to keep this part of myself without completing the Crossing?"

"I already told you this, and yet you insist on not believing me."

"One year," she murmured. Her gaze hardened. "I don't want to lose my power. Ronan and I will take down the High Throne's forces and will figure out how to save our ether before the time is up."

It sounded ridiculous. Even the god stepped back with a scoff. "Mortals think they can do anything and everything in their short lives. You think you can last long enough to annihilate *legions* of specters? Not to mention the Spirits of the Midnight Sun? How about all the mortal forces that will rise against you?"

Mikatán's eyes flared with power. "And what if Khaos decides to tear her way into your world? What then?"

Zara didn't want to consider that. She gritted her teeth and pushed to her feet. "We are the ones who must clean up your mess! I've been told that my options are limited, that I am capable of so much more, but I've been given such little time. *You* tell me: what else can be done?"

The Primordial of Death was silent for a moment. In the distance, ethereal dogs barked.

"What if there were a way to bring us back? To restore the Gates of Celestrea?"

There was a roaring in Zara's ears. "You never mentioned this before."

"Chances that this can succeed are slim. But it is worth trying."

Fucking Suns. "What is it?"

"There are some deities who have the ability to rip through the seams of this world. In other words, they can create portals from the mortal plane into ours." Mikatán walked past her, pacing about the jungle. "They are called Wardens. Before the War of the Skies, there were many of them. They were ferociously loyal to Celestrea—especially to us Primordials. That loyalty cost them greatly, and many died during the War."

Zara had a sense of where he was going with this. "You believe some Wardens may have survived?"

"We have witnessed many marvels, even without the Gates. Marvels such as yourself. If the powers of a Primordial can be born again from a mortal, then the ability of a Warden could be present, yet dormant, within some living deities." The god of Death gazed at the twilight sky, the shimmering light brushing against his skull face. "Only they can rebuild the Gates of Celestrea. Find one, Zara, and help us win this war."

Her heart slammed a fist against her chest. "Once the Gates are rebuilt and the realm is restored, the ether in this world can heal."

Mikatán's gaze landed on her. "Celestrea is already on the verge of death. With the recreation of the Gates, my realm will be able to rebuild. The Crossing would become an option for you and the archangel again."

Energy swept through the plane, and the trees shuddered. Even the skies seemed to groan.

Zara's mind was buzzing. She could actually complete the Crossing, keep her power. How long would her ether last otherwise? But the thought of immortality didn't seem quite real either. She would be forced to watch all her loved ones die before her.

"How will I know if a deity is a Warden?" she asked.

"There is no differentiator, aside from their power. You will have to trust the ether inside you to find them."

The Primordial of Death's presence all-consuming. He brought a hand to Zara's brow, and the ether that had been building inside her snapped free. Ribbons of it spiraled out, engulfing them both.

"Normally, there is a ceremony to honor the blessing between a patron god and their selected mortal—but this will have to do." Mikatán stared into her soul, her very being. "That archangel of yours is destroying the place. You must go now." he rumbled.

Zara frowned. "What?"

"Survive, Zara Santos. And return the Primordials to the world."

Zara held Death's gaze for as long as she could as the jungle disappeared in tendrils of ether, taking the god away too.

She now stood in a space made of a dusk and dawn sky. The world hadn't stopped shaking.

The Oasis is breaking, Basim said.

Ether called out to her, and she followed its song to Ronan. He was on his knees, tears trickling down his exhausted face as he stared out into the distance.

His gaze slid to hers and his eyes widened.

"My Horizon," Ronan whispered.

Zara choked back a sob and ran into his arms.

FORTY-NINE

The Oasis trembled again, breaking at the seams. None of that seemed to matter. Zara clutched onto the archangel as he lifted them in the air. She clasped his face, studying him.

Ronan seemed unharmed, despite the redness that lined his eyes. The shadows that normally hung around him had weakened, and there was a difference in the way he carried himself.

He was observing her too. The archangel brushed a tattooed hand down the back of her head.

"They were there." Zara's voice cracked. "Hakim and Eshe. I felt them. Told me that they'll always be with me."

Ronan looked at her, his smile gentle and full of warmth.

The archangel embraced her, and it was enough for more stray tears to leak out of her. "I hope it helped you in the way you needed, Santos."

They stayed like that for what felt like an eternity. She never wanted it to end. Eventually, Ronan pulled back enough to ask, "Were you able to achieve what we set out to do?"

Zara nodded. "The ether is different. More alive."

It was true. Her energy had always been restless, but now its presence was heavier. As if a pressure were building within her bones. She wondered the things she could do now with this *blessed* ether.

"But it comes at a cost," she said. "Mikatán gave me a task."

Ronan's brows furrowed as he listened to what happened in the dreamscape, including what the Primordial of Death said about deities that could open portals.

"Wardens," he murmured. "My patron god warned me of the limited time we have left with our heightened power too."

Zara cocked her head. "Your patron god?"

A softness fell on Ronan's expression as he told her. Her eyes widened.

"They came to me," the archangel said, "Let's keep it between us for now. I need to process it alone."

"Whenever you're ready." She brushed strands of black hair from his face. "You faced more than that in your dreamscape, didn't you?"

Ronan let out a ragged sigh. He slumped forward, pressing his brow against her shoulder. "I learned what led to Erebus defecting, the pain he endured before that, and... I witnessed the Gates falling. How I contributed to the start of the War of the Skies."

Zara kept her expression blank as the words spilled from his scarred lips, a crack forming within her heart.

"I saw their deaths. How I killed them. My father spoke to me then, said it wasn't my fault." He trembled against her. "But it was. All these years, I've been hating myself for it. Wondering what my family felt—thought—in those moments."

She wrapped her arms around him, holding the back of his head. "Your father was right, Ronan, it wasn't your fault. There were forces beyond your control, none of this was your doing. Your father loved you so much; he did till the very end." Zara paused. "And about Erebus..."

Ronan told her about the argument, how he'd lashed out. What had happened to Erebus's family...

He looked pained. "I hurt him. I pushed him away when he needed me. It led to his ruin."

"You were both so young, experiencing hardships you didn't quite understand." She continued to hold him. "Erebus made his choice, and you've been making amends for yours. You're not the same male you were back then."

Ronan started to cry and slowly embraced her. Tighter and tighter as he sobbed.

The past had put chains around them both, and while they had started to break free of those shackles, only now could they move forward. Zara held the archangel as he shed the last of his tears, until Ronan slowly relaxed in her arms.

"I had to reopen the wounds, let the pain spill out of me—so I could let them truly heal." Ronan stepped back to meet her gaze. His eyes were broken silver stars, though he still smiled.

Warmth seeped through her. "I understand how you feel."

They were standing so close to each other. Heat radiated from him, making her ether shiver.

Someone cleared their throat. "As endearing as this is—you both need to leave. The Oasis is falling apart."

Neheharu's presence was difficult to ignore, a pulsing beat of energy. One that seemed sharper now. He didn't seem too pleased.

The ground and sky shook, sending Zara and Ronan stumbling back from each other. Cracks split the air, light seeping through. The nahuales disappeared in a flash.

The archangel let out an awkward chuckle. "Apologies, Lord Neheharu. It seems we've done some damage to the Oasis."

"Yes, *quite*. I will have to go into a temporary slumber in order to return this plane to its original state." Neheharu waved a hand. "It would be best if you left now, before the Oasis seals you in here."

Ronan hesitated. "I saw something in my dreamscape, something that may benefit you and the other gods. Khaos is looking for Deimos. I think she is planning on returning to Celestrea to avenge him and take back her lover."

Zara sucked in a breath. Mikatán had said something similar, that Khaos might cross into their world too.

The Primordial stilled. "You have my thanks, godling. Now, go."

They bowed to the Primordial before scurrying toward the archway they'd entered through.

As soon as Ronan and Zara stepped through the portal, the realm on the other side of it winked out of sight.

They made their way out of the Oasis's temple. Zara blinked through the brightness to find the sentinels pointing their weapons at a group of people halfway up the steps—

"Axar?"

The shifter was in his wolf form, breathing heavily. Beside him was Tareq, the twins just behind him, all in their jackal forms.

"*We found the mining city—and it's much worse than we thought,*" Tareq said. "*You'll want to see it for yourself.*"

Zara listened as Tareq explained their findings, their entourage now deep within the desert.

"*There's an abandoned fortress that hasn't been in use for years, but the place is now teeming with specters and the captured civilians. Sahar and Malik are waiting for us there,*" Tareq said. "*It looks like Arwan was charged to oversee whatever madness they have going on there.*"

Cold air nipped at Zara's face as night approached. "Are the specters fully-transformed?"

"*No, many of them are still simply possessing mortal bodies, though they certainly feel different. Stronger and smarter.*"

Ronan grunted. "I suppose that's a relief. Specters in their true form are a challenge, even for myself and Zara."

Tareq glanced back at them, midnight eyes gleaming. "*Things may be different now. I can sense the energy around you has shifted.*"

"How so?" Zara asked.

"*It's quieter than before—it's a bit unnerving.*"

She wasn't quite sure what to make of that.

Midnight turned the sand into silver. The camels grew agitated the closer they got, most likely feeling the evil presence of the specters.

When they finally reached the fortress that hugged the side of a canyon, they found Sahar and Malik waiting for them along the border wall.

Zara took a moment to examine the place. The moonlight revealed a stretch of jade-colored domes and mosaic tiles. Behemoth mechanisms had been driven into the canyon's side, perhaps for acquiring the crimson ore Kairos was famous for.

The area was infested with specters. Armed Elios soldiers patrolled the rooftops and monitored the pathways where mortals walked in a line. Chains weeped to the sky, along with the cries of the people.

Still in his jackal form, Tareq growled. *"They will pay for this. Malik, what do you see?"*

"It reeks of terrible ether. The specters are herding our people like cattle. For what I cannot tell. Every exit point is blocked and watched, except for the city wall itself."

Faris squeezed himself between Tareq and Malik. The shifter pointed at the base of the wall below them. "We will need to create an escape route. This section is abandoned; we can create a path to lead the civilians out."

"There is much ground to cover and many people to rescue, so we must divide our forces. While the twins clear the area below and have the exit ready, the rest of us can scope out the buildings the people are disappearing into." Tareq looked between Zara and Ronan. *"I suggest splitting the two godlings up, spreading our advantage as much as we can. Ronan, Sahar, and Malik in one group, the other with Zara, Axar, and myself."*

The archangel folded his arms. "Why is it that *you* are paired with Zara? Why not be in my group?"

Tareq gave him a sly smile, which was more fangs than anything. *"I like spending time with her, what about it?"*

Zara could've sworn Ronan's eye twitched. She fought back a chuckle and squeezed his arm. "You know he's teasing you. I agree with the plan, we should split up."

He curled his lips in disgust but relented. "My group will search the western side of the city. Be as quiet as possible with your kills. It'd be best to avoid an all-out battle here."

Tareq snapped his teeth. *"Lead the people toward the twins and they will help them escape the city borders."*

Malik shifted into his jackal form, his lithe body flying off the edge of the wall and toward the buildings below. Sahar sprinted after him.

Faris paused beside Ronan, beaming. "After this, I expect a group trip to Damalis, Your Majesty."

The archangel grinned. "It's a promise."

He mussed the young mercenary's hair just before Faris shifted into his jackal form and dove off the edge. Zara jerked back as Ayah snuck up to her, a mischievous expression on her face.

"What's that look for?"

Ayah's eyes gleamed. "I know I teased my brother before but I'm no better."

"What do you mean?"

"I admire you, Santos. And the King of Damalis. You make a cute pair."

Zara was too stunned to speak. Ayah smirked, transforming into her jackal body and going after her twin.

A deep voice chuckled. "How sweet. And I agree with her."

Ronan swept in to give Zara a kiss on the cheek and followed the others. A scoff left her lips, even though her heart skipped a beat.

Axar snorted, shoving her shoulder as he passed. "I wish I hadn't seen that. Let's go."

Zara rolled her eyes. They jumped off the edge together, Axar shifting into his wolf form as she grabbed onto him midair.

They landed on a rooftop behind the others.

"*If any of you come across Arwan,*" Tareq said. "*Don't hesitate.*"

The groups separated, diving into the folds of darkness that stretched over the city. Zara slipped off Axar, the shifter transforming back into his human body. She scaled ropes tethered to the buildings, leaped over an alleyway and onto the tiled ledge of a building. The material cracked beneath her boots. Cries reverberated from within the structure.

Axar landed behind her. "Tareq is heading to the front, so we can surround the specters inside."

Zara nodded, unsheathing her dagger. Suns, she missed her khopesh blades.

"Don't fall behind, Tallon."

Axar rolled his shoulders. "It's been some time since I stretched my legs."

Her brother grabbed a wooden post that jutted out of the wall and swung through an open window and into the building.

Zara smirked. "Like old times."

She followed the shifter into what looked like the upper level of a warehouse. Woven baskets with old grains and spices sat forgotten along the floorboards. But it was the smell of dried blood and human waste that stifled the air.

Axar peered over the edge of the wooden railing, and pointed to a group of specters stationed on the first floor of the warehouse. The creatures were not fully transformed yet—which was somewhat of a relief—though it was still unfortunate for the mortals they'd possessed. Their human skin was peeling, showing scales and strange hides underneath, mortal teeth now replaced with fangs.

Zara silently communicated with her mercenary brother before diving over the railing. Air hissed in her ears for a breath and she landed on a specter's shoulders, slicing its throat.

Before the creature could fall to the ground, she lunged for the next creature in a blast of blood-red light. It grabbed Zara by the arm and threw her across the floor. She crashed into a large ceramic vase.

People screamed, and the specters charged toward her, too distracted to notice the mercenary emerging from the shadows.

Axar's sword was a flash of silver as he cut his way through them. More creatures in the warehouse turned their attention to him, raising their blades to clash with his.

Zara took advantage of the moment. "Let's see how the Oasis amplified this power."

Ether swelled within her bones, and she sped forward, appearing behind a specter. The world seemed to slow as she kicked the creature, the force of it enough to blast its head open. Blood and brain splattered the floor. She did the same to two others, before her legs started to wobble.

That was new. The sudden pull of her ether had been much stronger than she'd anticipated.

"Shit," Axar said. "I will not lie to you, Santos, but that was gross."

The shifter had already killed the remaining specters, their bodies scattered about.

"I thought to test my strength, though I didn't realize how taxing it would be on my body." Zara winced. "I'm not used to it."

"Don't exert yourself, then! Suns, you're like a child playing with their shiny new weapon." Axar was breathing much more heavily than normal.

She gestured between them. "Look at us defective mercenaries. The tonic affecting your skills?"

"My body feels sluggish, but I will push through it."

The main doors of the warehouse blasted open. A jackal stood in the entryway, holding a specter by its neck. He squeezed the creature until its flesh burst and then dropped the lifeless body, staring at the blood dripping from his claws.

"*These specters are so loud,*" Tareq said. "*How annoying.*"

"Good of you to finally join us, Horizon." Axar cleaned his sword and sheathed it.

The jackal's gaze slid to somewhere behind them. He snarled in disgust. "*I have never been fond of the High Throne, but they have gone too far.*"

Zara followed his gaze, and her blood turned cold. Cages filled the warehouse, people shackled within. From the looks of their thin bodies, covered with dirty rags, they must have been deprived of food and water. Now she understood where the smell of urine and waste was coming from.

In the center of the back wall was an entrance to a cavern, the threshold etched with foreign symbols. This warehouse must have been connected to the mines.

"Is this some sort of gate?"

A growl rumbled through the jackal's thick chest. "*Help the people first.*"

The civilians watched them now, their eyes wide with fear, shrinking back when the mercenaries approached them. An older woman grabbed the iron bars. "It's the guild of Kairos." Murmurs and sobs of relief echoed in the space.

Ether wreathed Zara's hands and she pried the locks open. The sound of chains breaking and iron snapping could be heard throughout the warehouse as the others began to free the prisoners.

The stench thickened the farther Zara went into the building. People murmured their thanks, others bursting into tears, their hands brushing her shoulders, her back, as they made their way out of their prisons.

It was odd at first to feel their gratitude toward her. In the past, citizens would always shy away from the Rogue.

Zara noticed wounds and marks dotting their skin on the mortals shuffling out—while some didn't move from their chains, their bodies already gone cold.

Fury burned hotter through her veins as she finished twisting off the iron wrapped around someone's ankles. "Don't worry, you're safe now."

The woman reached out to Zara, her arm shaking.

"Horizon, those creatures *spoke* to us. We could understand them, even though they spoke no language of this Continent."

Zara met the woman's eyes. Could see the pain and fear there. The specters were targeting 'ether-born', which meant these people shared some deity bloodline—even if just a drop—or descended from someone in Celestrea. It made sense that they could understand the specters.

"What did they say to you?" Zara asked, gently pulling her to her feet. "Anything you heard might be helpful to us."

"They were going on and on about bringing their Creator here, but that their brethren had to return first—and they needed *us* for it all."

Another man spoke. "They also said something about our blood being a power source to them."

Chills ran down Zara's arms. It was similar to what the deity officials had said at the party.

The woman touched her arm. "They take some of us away. Where, I do not know—but those who leave don't come back."

Zara's lips thinned. She needed to let the others know. Whatever the specters were doing here might have meant the Spirits were involved.

"I'm sorry you went through this," Zara said. "We'll help you get home."

"Thank you." The woman broke down. "You're a good person."

Zara blinked at her, unable to say anything, her chest tightening.

At the warehouse doors, Tareq was directing everyone to where the twins waited at the border of the city. Zara went to join Axar, who was staring at the entrance to the mine, his gaze on the intricate symbols along the threshold.

"Khaos and the High Throne want to remake this world without the Primordials' influence, right?" he said. "And we can assume the specters are taking people away for something terrible."

She grunted in agreement. Her thoughts went to what both Mikatán and Ronan had said in the Oasis. "The ether-born are a power source for them, and there's a strong possibility that Khaos is trying to tear her way into our world. There may be a connection between the two."

"I don't like the sound of that."

Axar was still breathing hard, sweat glistening across his body. Zara frowned, just as the mental door in her head exploded open.

It had her gasping for breath and clutching at her chest. She could feel Axar holding her up, hear him shouting her name, but an icy wave, an all-consuming fear, rushed over her, everything going muted—and it didn't come from her.

Her vision flickered. The warehouse before her shifted into another room swathed in ribbons of silver light. A human was strapped to a wooden table, veins on the verge of bursting from their skin as they screamed. Light trickled out of them, rushing toward a doorway filled with the same luminescence. The threshold was similar to the one she and Axar were standing in front of. What was she seeing?

The scene flickered once more and she looked down to a pair of tattooed hands, one reaching for a sword. Their breathing was hard and rushed, echoing in her ears.

Zara clutched onto Axar, fighting for air. *"Ronan?"*

FIFTY

Daria swallowed the cry that formed in her throat. The castle's obsidian marble was flecked with blood, furniture and banners broken and strewn about the floor, the corridors echoing with vampires' jeers. She followed the sounds to the main hall, where soldiers were gathered in a circle, tables shoved to the sides.

Her advisors were in the center, being forced to fight. Or it was more that they were being pushed around like rag dolls by their opponent. The vampire soldier sneered, throwing punches and sweeping kicks. Daria was sure there were even some bite marks along the elves' necks.

The vampires fell into silence when they took notice of the queen's presence. She slid her gaze to the table on the dais at the back, where Silas lounged like a king of his own world.

The Second had his legs propped up on the wood, swirling a glass of blood in his hand. His eyes brightened. "Queen Daria Calderón, welcome home! We've *missed* you."

Vampires guffawed, some spitting on the ground at her feet.

Her lips curled in disgust. "What is the meaning of this?"

Silas stood up and sauntered down the steps. "Where is our general? And the soldiers I sent to escort you both?"

Daria swallowed. "As we said in our report, we were attacked by a pack of demons—unfortunately your soldiers perished. As for General Valdemar, he was summoned to Soleira but will be returning soon."

"See, you're lying, Your Majesty. I've never seen any demons in your region." Silas chuckled, soldiers parting for him as he drew closer. "And there is only one individual I know who could kill an entire unit of soldiers and survive."

Unease sank low in the pit of Daria's stomach. She said nothing.

The Second flashed his fangs. "I knew the general was fond of you, but I merely thought he was toying with his food. Not that he killed his own kind, his own soldiers for you."

Daria swallowed bile. "I don't know what you are talking about. Your accusation is preposterous"

"Don't lie to me!" Silas snarled. "He has been helping you, hasn't he? Did you truly go to Nephtyr to find more about the dragons?"

"Yes!" Panic was riling up inside her. Her heart raced. "I have more information about where they could be. I've made progress, Silas. That's not a lie."

The vampire didn't seem to be listening. "I should have known the moment that traitor pleaded for your life. King Matías should've killed you before you left the Summit. Then, I wouldn't have had to report him."

Her knees nearly buckled. "What? You reported him?"

"Deep down, I always wondered where Ares's loyalty truly lay. When I received a tip, I sent word to my Lord of Vampires. There is no actual proof that Ares betrayed us, so it would require an investigation." Silas's glare turned smug. "I guess we have a certain advisor of yours to thank."

A faint ringing started in Daria's ears. The vampire waved a hand. "Basira, come forth. Don't be shy."

Soldiers snickered as the Ikarrian advisor stepped into view. Basira looked unharmed, well-fed even, and serene. While she still wore the ether-imbued bracelet, the woman seemed fine.

It was no wonder Daria hadn't seen Basira in the makeshift fighting ring. Her advisor had thrown them under the blade's edge to save herself.

"Basira?" Her voice cracked. "Is it true? Did you turn your back on Ikarria?"

"I did not betray my kingdom." Basira's face flushed with anger as she jabbed a finger in Daria's direction. "You're not equipped to be our queen. You're weak; it took you ages to master even the smallest of ether fighting sequences. Our Continent has a better chance at survival under the High Throne's rule."

The advisor who had stood by Daria's side, the only one who had supported her, even when the other officials didn't. It had all been a lie. Daria nearly heaved.

Silas laughed. "Put one of those bracelets on our beloved queen and throw her court into the dungeons. We will wait for our general together, Your Majesty."

Daria couldn't stop herself. Fire ignited from her palms, startling the vampires that moved toward her. The Second stared at the flames, disgust flitting over his expression.

"You still have a duty to uphold for my Lord of Vampires, Daria. Obey and your advisors won't die."

Her breathing turned ragged. She glanced at her court, at their bruised and mottled faces. They may not have believed in her as a ruler, but she would not let them perish.

Her flames dissipated, and Silas grinned.

An icy sensation strangled her heart when a soldier clamped an ether-imbued bracelet around her wrist. Daria gasped as the bind coursed through her veins, stifling the ether within.

Her fire sank further and further in the void until it disappeared. She tried to reach out to it, begging it to return. Nothing answered, and for the first time in her life, Daria felt a terrible kind of loneliness. As if a hole had been left inside her.

"I am sure our king will find a punishment suitable for Ares, once he's found guilty—it wouldn't be the first time. Our general was always rebellious, in his own quiet way." Silas tilted his head, watching her. "I can see the worry all over your face, Your Majesty. He's too valuable an asset to kill off, so you can rest easy."

It was the only thing that kept Daria afloat, though dread washed over her at what they might do to him.

The vampires began to disperse. Silas strolled toward the dining hall's doors. "King Matías will reward you for your cooperation, Basira."

The Ikarrian advisor bowed before following the vampire.

Daria let out a short, dry chuckle. "You're a fool, Basira. They will kill you once you are no longer of use to them."

The elf never looked back.

So be it. Daria knew what she had to do. A small crack formed in her heart, but she knew that Ares would understand.

The Sanctuary was empty at this time of night—Daria preferred it that way. As she passed the Primordial statues, she felt their eyes on her. Her hands curled into fists. They would judge her for this, but there was no other choice.

Daria entered the chamber room that held the *Mirari*. There was a chill in the air, and her skin prickled as she kneeled on the center platform.

She unrolled the parchment filled with Kamari's notes. *First, you must draw these runes...*

"Suns help me."

She may have been wearing an ether-imbued bracelet, but it would not prevent her from conducting the spell, as necromancy pulled ether from the outside world rather than within someone. A loophole that she would take advantage of.

Shadows from the candlelight danced along the walls. Daria wiped the sweat forming along her brow with the back of her hand as she followed the directions. Her fingers were tinted with black dust from the symbols she drew on the ground.

Despite everything, she was grateful Ares was not here and that she couldn't wait for him. She would be the only one at risk.

Daria slipped out her dagger. Its red jewel gleamed under the firelight, reminding her of the dragon's eye she'd seen when the obsidian throne communicated with her. The late King Arzhel had done a fine job taking his secrets to the grave.

Tears pricked the corners of her eyes as she slit her palm with the blade; she squeezed her bleeding hand over the runes and watched as the red droplets fell onto the stone. Steam curled into the air on impact, and an icy wind blew through the chamber.

The fire from the torches dimmed and darkness seeped from the corners. Daria took a deep breath.

"I request an audience with—"

"Firelight, are you sure you want to do this?"

She froze at the voice. Her hands began to shake but she forced them into fists atop her lap, biting down on her lip to fight back the swell of tears.

Suns Above. Kamari had warned her about this, that there would be a safeguard the dark ether would use against the summoner, a mechanism to try and protect the individual and coax them not to proceed with the practice.

Daria shut her eyes tight. Kamari told her that she was not to look directly at whatever form the ether would take. Those who laid eyes on these entities never returned to a sane state of mind.

But the voice it used now—

Tears managed to break through her closed eyes, Daria's voice echoing in the chamber, cracked and wounded.

"It's me, firelight… I've missed you."

So have I, but this isn't you.

How cruel that the ether would use *her mater* against Daria. Memories of her might not have been as clear as before, but she remembered the late queen's warm smile, her tight embraces. She had been a warrior, a sword always gleaming at her side. Though she still found time to take care of Daria, to play with her.

Her death had severed something deep inside Daria—though the same day she lost her mater, she gained a sister.

Daria sucked in a shaky breath, still keeping her head lowered and her eyes closed. "I miss you too. So much."

The thought that *something* was there, speaking with her mater's voice, sent Daria's skin crawling. She had to tread carefully.

"You have grown into a beautiful young woman. Why would you want to risk yourself for a future that may never come to be?"

"People are suffering, and are depending on me to help them."

"So, you must force your soul to bleed in order to try and save them? Simply to say that you did your part?"

The presence moved—Daria could feel it nearing her. It took everything in her to not shrink back. "No, it's not like that." She pushed the words through clenched teeth. "There isn't enough time to find another way. I must do what I can to help my people and those I care about."

"What you are doing is a grave sin in the eyes of our natural ether. If you proceed with this, a curse will befall you. It may not be today or tomorrow, it may be years from now, but your heart will suffer."

Daria could stop this now, wipe away the drawn runes on the ground and clean the blood from her hand. Her mind flashed with the broken images of her people. She thought of Ares—always walking in danger's shadow. And Zara, who had been forced by the treaty to kill her own innocence.

The being shifted closer. She froze when a hand rested on her head.

"Firelight, look at me. Look at your mater."

The ether was becoming more persistent. A force pushed against Daria's chin and her own eyes fluttered against her will, a morbid curiosity finding her.

Her mater was here. Standing right *here.* An old, familiar grief wrapped around her. If Daria could only see her one more time…

"I'm sorry, mater." She bit her lip so hard she tasted blood. "I choose to do this. I hope you know how much I love you."

Whatever was in the chamber withdrew its hand—it still used her mater's voice. *"May the Suns forgive you, Daria Calderón, Queen of Ikarria. Daughter of mine."*

The presence disappeared from the chamber, leaving a chasm in its wake. Daria crumpled forward and pressed her brow to the ground, a sob racking through her ribs.

"By my blood, I request an audience. I summon you, Arzhel Calderón, the Last Dragon Rider of Ikarria," she choked out the last command.

Daria opened her eyes to find her blood moving across the stone to line up with the runes. It bubbled and hissed, steam coiling into the air, thickening to the point that Daria had to squint. The smoke slammed into the ground and darkness flooded the room.

Daria gasped. It was too quiet—her own heartbeat the only sound. Until she heard the sound of boots on the ground echoing around her. Fear froze her.

Where the candles had once flickered, green flames rose—and a male stood before her.

Daria tightened a hand around her dagger. The man was an elf, tall, with broad shoulders. His black hair thick and long, some strands braided, his golden eyes bright against his dark skin. Angry scars ran down the side of his face.

Arzhel.

The male sneered. "You interrupted my rest, Daria Calderón."

His voice was strong, enough to rattle her bones. But Daria gritted her teeth and bowed her head. The Last Dragon Rider, and her ancestor.

"You know who I am?" she murmured.

"Yes." He was staring at her with a stern expression. "And I know why you summoned me through necromancy. The cost for it will be grave."

"I'm afraid circumstances had become too dire for me not to." She tried to stand but the muscles in her legs gave out. Daria winced. "Our kingdom is being threatened by forces that intend to stretch their poison to all corners of the Continent. Our people are suffering, and I seek the dragons' help."

Shadows still shifted along the edges of the chamber like rippling water. The darkness thickened as Arzhel paced around her.

"Secrets I carried to my death now want to see the light."

"I know about the god contract." Daria hesitated to say more.

Arzhel stopped in front of her, the scars on his face seeming harsher than before. "How? I tried very hard to ensure that records of myself were destroyed."

"When I visited the *Mirari* some time ago, it stopped working. It kept repeating the same words over and over again."

The bond between dragon and elf was a vow forged in fire and blood. A connection with the potential of achieving something grand, filled with purpose, only to be broken by one of the Ikarrian kings.

Daria summoned all her strength to push to her feet. "Then I heard your voice, telling me to find you."

Arzhel stared at her, the corner of his lips curling. "So, it is you who is meant to fulfill the contract."

"What do you mean?"

He glanced at the shadows that surrounded them. "I made an arrangement with a Primordial to put a seal on the Ikarrian throne. Genesis understood my reasons."

Suns Above. "Genesis, the Primordial of Life? The goddess—the First *Dragon Rider*—helped you get rid of the dragons?"

"The judgment in your voice is very telling of what you think of me." The male's expression darkened. "You don't know the half of it, young one. I did it to protect them and our world. The dragons had a mortal enemy: the *cipactli*. Hybrid crocodile beasts with wings of great eagles, created by a faction of Celestrea's spiritual warriors that have now returned to the mortal world as specters."

"Many battles were fought between the two beasts over land and water. The dragons were dying off, the Continent was being destroyed. The answer was to break the dragon bond and hide them."

"Where?"

Arzhel gave her a look. "The Dragon's Teeth."

Daria let out a sound of disbelief. "My pater has been doing his own research for years. I'm sure he's traveled to that region. And they were so close to home, all along."

"The contract I made with Genesis had a condition—the sealing power within the Ikarrian throne would speak only to the descendant with the purest of hearts. I could not allow the safety of the dragons to be in the hands of just anyone, just because they shared my blood."

Something pricked the corners of her eyes. "How can that be when I just violated the natural ether by practicing necromancy?"

"The contract still deemed you worthy. Curious, isn't it?" Arzhel walked about the stone chamber. "The dragons have been living in a safe haven I created. A place that can only be found through the energy inside the throne."

Daria's mind was racing. "It is the key to opening its doors."

"You will need to transfer the power to another item that can be its host, it cannot be sustained on by itself. The contract allows you to do so without needing an official agreement with a Primordial yourself. From there, the seal will guide you to where the dragons are being kept."

Arzhel's expression remained hard, and for the first time Daria noticed the scars that covered the rest of his body. Remnants of a seasoned warrior who had probably only experienced bloodshed and loss throughout his whole life.

Daria felt overwhelmed. The key to finding the dragons had been in front of her all along. Not only that, but she was *meant* to find the dragons. Somehow, in the eyes of forces beyond her, this was a path she had been destined to take.

"What happened to the *cipactli*?"

Arzhel's eyes shone. "With my allies—deities capable of opening gates and portals to other worlds—we were able to drive the remaining *cipactli* across the veil, banishing them to wherever the cosmos desired. And it was on that day that my dragon and I died."

"Sacrificing yourselves for the good of Ribera." Daria said what he didn't. "I was wrong about you."

Arzhel took a step toward her, a glowing heat emanating from him. Like the warmth of the morning sun. "Heed my words, descendant of mine. I will tell you the spell to release the sealing power, but you cannot force the dragons to recreate the bond. They have been living in peace for a hundred years, and may not wish to leave. You must swear to it."

For a moment, fear sliced through her. No, Daria would never pressure another into a world of violence and death. Still, the idea of not having a means to save Ikarria made her chest tighten.

Daria bowed her head. "I swear it, King Arzhel, with every part of my soul."

For the first time, Arzhel looked at her with approval. He proceeded to tell her the spell, how to pronounce the otherworldly words and control the power of the seal.

When they finished, the darkness behind Arzhel rose higher and higher. The male smiled. "Someone has come to pick me up."

Daria's brows furrowed until she noticed two red eyes within the smoke. Then black scales, along with teeth the size of a man, until the head of a dragon drifted out as if peering into the chamber. Shadows billowed and thickened, tethered to the beast.

She staggered back, jaw dropping. "H—how?"

Arzhel's smile didn't falter. "Seek the Guardian of the Dragon's Teeth, who goes by the name Aladaer, son of Kaigen."

Kaigen. The black beast looming behind Arzhel was his bonded— and Daria was now seeing a legend in the flesh.

She met Arzhel's gaze. "I can see how deeply you cared. It must have been difficult to have carried such a weight, to have been known unjustly throughout history as the one who caused the fall of the dragons."

The late King said nothing, though his eyes glowed. He stepped back toward his bonded. "Best of luck to you, Queen Daria of Ikarria. I hope you find a way to break the curse that will inevitably find you."

Darkness rushed out, swallowing Arzhel and Kaigen, taking them back to their place of rest. The darkness retreated and Daria fell to her knees.

The Last Dragon Rider and his dragon had sacrificed themselves for a future of new bonds. And now, it was his descendant that would bring back those fires to the world.

FIFTY-ONE

When Ares arrived at castle in Soleira, the air felt different. Wrong. Discomfort gnawed at his skin, burying deep between his ribs. Soldiers bowed to him, diplomats praised him. To Ares's ears, their voices seemed far away. Insignificant. They were all insignificant.

He avoided anywhere King Matías could be, the contents of the letter reverberating through his mind, urging him deeper into the halls. His pacing quickened, an ocean breeze catching the end of his cloak.

Ares entered the courtesan wing—and froze. An all-too familiar smell, tinged with copper, wafted through the indoor olive trees. Blood.

The general stared at the small crowd of palace staff and courtesans hovering by the last door of the hall. The world around him went dull, every sound muffled in his ears. Each step he took grew heavier and heavier. The people's eyes widened when they saw him, before fleeing down the hall. Except for the courtesans. Many of them were sniffling, their noses tinted red, tears streaming down their cheeks as they watched him.

One of them stopped him. "Ares, don't go in there."

The smell of blood was so strong now. No words found him as he brushed past the courtesan and entered the bedchamber.

Ares stilled at the threshold. His mother lay in red-stained bedsheets. She looked as if she were simply sleeping—but he knew the truth. He couldn't hear a heartbeat.

Numbness fell over him. Ares didn't even know if he was truly awake, his own voice sounding far away.

"I'm so sorry, Ares." The courtesan followed him. "A few weeks ago, Morana disappeared from the castle—we don't know why. King Matías found out. He was furious and sent soldiers to find her. Eventually, they brought her back here. We thought King Matías was going to punish her, but he did not. He ordered her to serve him more often, despite her health." Her expression turned grim. "We should've known better. When word arrived that you were returning to Soleira, he—"

She cut herself off, looking away. The general read between the lines. King Matías must have discovered Ares's betrayal.

His mother was supposed to have been safe in the Stone Orchard by then—he shoved all thoughts away. Buried them deep before he could break.

"Leave me," he whispered.

The courtesan let out a sob before ushering the others out. Ares waited another moment before closing the door.

Deathly silence burned a hole through his stomach as he slowly approached the bed.

Dried blood smeared Morana's lips and neck, which told him that her Blight must have worsened quickly. But that wasn't what killed her. Dark bruises covered her throat. His mother was dying of an illness, but she had been killed by the hands of another.

Ares slid a hand underneath his mother's head, gently nuzzling her brow. Her skin was cold.

"You weren't supposed to be here," he rasped. "Why are you here?"

His gaze snagged on the drawer beside the bed. The vials of medicine had been shattered, pieces of glass glimmering with the remnants of the purple liquid.

This was not supposed to have happened. In Corduva, Ares had asked for Ronan's help, and the archangel hadn't hesitated, making arrangements with his shadow dealers.

The brothel in Soleira, the *House of Roses*, had been informed that a woman, whose identity would remain anonymous, would arrive through the Sombra Quarter during an exclusive market hosted by local tradesmen, artists, and other craftsmen within the castle's courtyards, many of whom were allies to the shadow dealers.

It had taken some convincing but Morana had agreed to follow the plan, and had hid in one of their wagons, before being wheeled out of the castle grounds. She had made it to the House of Roses, and joined the shadow dealers' caravan. They must have been betrayed—King Matías found her before she could reach the Stone Orchard.

The details of what happened had been in the report Warrick gave him. It took everything in Ares not to fall apart at the thought of his mother under the mercy of the Lord of Vampires. That he hadn't been able to protect her.

This was his punishment. Matías wouldn't kill him outright. That would be too easy. It was clear from the mere fact that no guards had come to arrest Ares and drag him back to the vampire king.

He didn't speak. He didn't cry. Nothing moved within him, his soul a barren land. Ares didn't care anymore. Whatever came after this, he would welcome it with open arms.

The general of war scooped his mother into his arms and left the bedchamber. He walked down the halls of the castle, carrying her body for all to see. Bystanders, court members and royal staff, gasped, cried, while others averted their gazes.

Ares Valdemar walked toward the throne room where many diplomats and officials had gathered. *I will show them what he did to me. To us.*

People were chattering and drinking; like a wave, every one of them fell quiet when they noticed him. Even the musicians on the center dais stopped their performance.

Ares walked through the crowd, everyone giving him a wide berth. Whispers rose, some of horror or outrage. Some did not even blink twice at the sight.

He closed his eyes for a breath, and let the words slip through his lips. "This was done by King Matías. Morana Valdemar was a beloved courtesan from his private wing. If he can do this to a citizen of his own realm, how do you think he views you, mere political allies?"

The crowd's murmurs rose into an uproar. No one dared to approach him. It mattered not. The reason for all his sacrifice was lifeless in his arms. Ares Valdemar, the war general of Adrastea, was going to leave his mark on this place, and crack the pedestal King Matías had sculpted for himself.

FIFTY-TWO

Ronan heard his name. Somewhere out in the void, someone was calling for him. It tugged at his chest, though his gaze was pinned on the horror before him.

His group was in a grand warehouse. They had been in the midst of releasing dozens of civilians trapped in cages when he heard a bloodcurdling scream.

Ronan had followed the sound, Sahar and Malik at his side. They crossed a breezeway to a domed tower, the atmosphere feeling dark and ugly as they climbed. At the top floor they found a carved archway swelling with energy. A pair of fully-formed specters stood in front of a human male strapped to a table.

Silver light was being pulled from the mortal's body, feeding the pulsing archway, and he screamed, his eyes flashing a pure white. Ether flared from the entryway and another fully-formed specter walked through, *entering* their world. Saliva dripped from sharp, metal teeth, and it had massive horns and long dark hair.

The deities' conversation from the feast came barreling back to him as Ronan realized what was happening, his stomach dropping. The ether-born were being used to power the archways and allow specters to cross over.

The portal flickered out, leaving the human gasping and crying, steam rolling from his skin.

One of the specters grunted. *"We should have brought more than one mortal, this one is too weak."*

"The previous batch died almost instantly. Lord Arwan ordered us to be mindful of how many we use, otherwise there won't be any ether-blood left."

Sahar and Malik drew up beside him, the former cursing under her breath. "The male on the table is Cyrus, the missing Adrastean mercenary."

Ronan's grip on his sword tightened. He had promised Warrick he would do everything in his power to save his guild member.

"Try again, the human is still breathing."

One of the specters uttered something that sounded like a spell and silver light leaked out of Cyrus's body once more. The portal within the archway powered up again, and the mercenary arched his back, shouting in pain.

Ronan rushed forward. Ever since the Oasis, his ether had been brimming with power and a hunger to bite. A bolt of energy shot out from his hand, striking one of the specters. In that same breath, he swung his sword into an arc, ether crackling along the blade. The electrified steel cut through the second creature's flesh, burning a pathway along its body.

The smell of burnt skin was thick as Ronan landed on the third specter, sending it crashing to the ground, and grabbed its face. More inhuman screams tore out of Cyrus, the portal still tethered to him.

"How do you stop the gate from forming?" Ronan snarled.

The specter's metal teeth glinted as it smiled. *"It's too late for that, Son of the Dusk. The portals are powered for as long as the mortal can withstand it."*

Ronan yanked the specter's head up by one horn and slammed it down again. "Why create these portals when you were already crossing over by possessing mortals?"

"Possessing flesh and blood requires more time; our forces are rather eager to walk these lands."

"So it's a matter of how efficiently you can rally your warriors." Ronan growled, glancing up at Cyrus, his veins bulging as he shrieked. "Your time is up, specter. I hope you enjoyed it while it lasted."

The archangel grabbed the creature by its hair and swung it toward the portal. Before it could fall back into the void, the specter grabbed the threshold. Ronan rushed toward it, but the horned creature tried to shove him back. He remained firm, preventing it from crossing over again.

Ronan glanced over his shoulder. "Help Cyrus!"

The mercenaries were already beside the male, Malik holding a knife in his hand. "Apologies, fellow Horizon."

The jackal-shifter cut Cyrus's palm and the male jerked against his restraints. It was enough to distract the Adrastean mercenary and the light within the portal started to flicker.

Ronan grinned at the specter. "Farewell."

The creature slashed its claws at him, nails grazing his leathers. He kicked its torso just as the portal closed, cutting the creature in half.

Ronan gasped for breath, gazing at the empty entryway. Its border was made of bronze, etched with odd symbols. Without another thought, he let his power smash the threshold into pieces.

He turned back to Cyrus. Malik had unfastened the restraints but the human didn't move, other than the subtle rise and fall of his chest.

"Cyrus, I need you to hold on—Warrick sent me to save you. You remember your guild, right? They are waiting for you."

A raspy breath. "I knew they didn't forget me." The mercenary's voice was too soft. Too weak. "I'm glad they aren't here."

"Come on, we'll take you back to them." Ronan gently helped the male to sit up. "Can you tell me what's been happening here?"

Anything to keep the mercenary awake and talking. Cyrus's breath rattled. "The specters are not the only ones crossing over. They have beasts… monsters at their side. Some are already here."

Ronan shared a look with Sahar and Malik as they pulled him to his feet, the archangel and the elf taking each of his arms over their shoulders.

"Is this the only place they are bringing the ether-born?"

"No." The mercenary groaned in pain. "There is a prison, much grander than this one. More terrifying, more brutal. It is where they're holding the beasts and the other ether-born, the ones they consider *stronger* than the rest of us."

Cold sweat trickled down Ronan's tattooed throat. They started toward the stairs. "Have you been there?"

Cyrus gritted his teeth. "The specters… They said—"

The mercenary started convulsing, blood running from his mouth and his eyes. Ronan helped the male to the ground. "No no no. Cyrus, your guild is waiting for you. I need you to hang on so you can see them again."

He lay his palm over the male's chest, ready to do *something*—anything—to help him. Ronan couldn't let this life slip away from him too. Not when he'd sworn he'd bring the mercenary back. Cyrus's convulsions stopped, and he let out a slow, weak exhale.

Malik rested a hand on Ronan's shoulder and slowly shook his head. The archangel closed his eyes for a breath before meeting Cyrus's gaze.

The mercenary smiled faintly. "Tell my guild that my path of silver and red has ended… That I kept the Oath."

Ronan recognized those words, had heard them uttered between Zara and Axar. "I will."

He didn't look away as the light slowly left Cyrus's eyes. After what felt like an eternity, he cursed under his breath. Yet another promise he was unable to fulfill.

Sahar was silent as she pulled the Adrastean emblem from Cyrus's waistband and handed it to him. "For Warrick and the guild."

Ronan nodded, tucking it into the folds of his fighting leathers.

Something warm pooled in his mind, followed by a rough voice. *Ronan!*

He stilled. The mental door was open and a flood of emotions was traveling through it. He hadn't even noticed with everything he'd just witnessed.

But he recognized who this was. There was no place in this world where he wouldn't know the shape of this soul.

Zara?

She let out a gasp. *Shit, I can hear you.*

Ronan touched his temple. *How… Another development of our Primordial powers?*

It must be. The bridge between our minds, the sharing of our emotions—it is all one ability.

Ronan had never heard of any Primordials with a power like this. His vision suddenly flickered and he saw Axar tugging Zara forward.

"Where's Ronan?" the shifter asked.

The archangel shook his head and was back in the tower. *Did I just see through your eyes?*

Yes, Zara said. *I think this has happened before. Once. Back in the Damalisan jungle, when we were playing Junya's Hunt.*

Ronan recalled the moment where he'd felt a force slam into his head. He thought he was going mad—or was severely dehydrated—and thought nothing of it.

So I take it that you saw what happened here, then?

Yes. I didn't know Cyrus very well, but I know the Adrastean guild will be grateful for your efforts. They would appreciate having some closure.

There was an explosion of roars and steel; Ronan swerved around as possessed mortals started to spill into the room. They had been followed.

Malik ducked under a specter's swinging blade. "Our exit is blocked!"

"Soon the rest of their forces will know that we are here." Sahar lunged away from the horde, skidding along the ground as she fired her arrows. "We can't stay in this city for long."

More specters poured out of the stairway, clambering up the walls and crawling along the floor. Ronan let out a wave of blue light, enough to burn those in the front lines and stall the others. His vision wavered, shifting to what Zara was seeing. Her group was fighting another horde of specters through a maze of buildings. He could feel the cuts and bruises on her legs and arms, every wound healing as quickly as she received them.

We are heading to the main road, Zara said.

Ronan struck another line of specters as he rushed toward the other side of the chamber. He shouted to the mercenaries. "Follow me!"

A ball of fiery blue-orange ether formed at his fingertips, hissing in the air and making his skin tingle. He fired it toward the wall and the stone exploded, revealing the night sky.

With the mercenaries at his heels, Ronan leaped off the edge of the tower, wings flapping. He looked over his shoulder to see a few of the specters jumping after them. Those bastards didn't have wings, but they didn't seem to care.

Malik shifted into his jackal form and snatched one in his jaws. Ronan's ether boomed through the night sky, cracking like lightning before piercing another specter through the chest.

A horned creature was grappling with Sahar midair, the mercenary slamming her fist into its face as they fell. The specter loosened its grip and Sahar threw the specter toward Ronan with incredible strength. His vision flickered again and he grinned.

Ronan spread his wings, reached for the specter and swung it toward the elven mercenary rushing up from below in flares of crimson light.

Zara struck the specter in the gut with her dagger, taking it down with her to the ground. Exhilaration filled Ronan's veins.

They all landed—the mercenaries crashing and rolling safely onto stall tarps and rooftops. He hurried to Zara, the mercenary patting the dirt from her legs.

"What fine timing, crossing paths here," she said dryly.

Ronan patted her head. "Remember to raise those mental walls, especially in a fight. I wouldn't want it to hinder you."

She swatted his hand away. "I know. We'll need to practice with it."

Ronan smirked. "You agreed with me. This *must* be the end of the world."

Zara rolled her eyes, though couldn't stop her grin.

Axar emerged from an alleyway, his clothes stained red, Tareq appearing beside him, both in their human forms.

"We've searched the buildings on the eastern side; couldn't find anyone else," Tareq said.

"We've lost the element of surprise, and despite our strength, we are still outnumbered," Ronan muttered. "Looking for other survivors will put the people we saved at risk. Let's head to the border and help the twins."

Their group took the main road, running back to where they'd first entered the mining city. Moonlight beamed upon the dirt path, though most corners and alleyways were pitch-black.

Specters could still be heard screaming from the tower they'd left. Ronan expected more to come in flocks, but the streets were empty. The hairs on the back of his neck rose.

They turned a corner and stopped. In the distance, people were fleeing through massive cracks in the city wall. Many of them glanced over their shoulders frantically, tears in their eyes, screaming in fear.

Ronan understood why. Felt it twist his heart until it shattered.

In the clearing between them and the city wall, were the twins. A thick javelin was pinned to the ground, Ayah hanging over it, chest pierced through and her back arched. Her dark eyes open toward the sky, mouth slightly agape. The mercenary was already dead.

"No," Malik murmured.

Arwan stood in the center, holding Faris by his hair, a dagger already thrust in the mercenary's stomach.

The deity looked up. Tears lined his ethereal, glowing eyes. "I'm afraid the amount of civilians you let go is a problem I cannot ignore. I had to do this."

Tareq fell to his knees, his gaze on the twins, his breathing ragged. Sahar brought a shaky hand to her mouth.

"You took me by surprise. I knew something was amiss during the banquet but I didn't expect this," Arwan continued, a pained look on his beautiful, monstrous face.

Faris turned his head to look at Tareq and the rest of his guild, eyes glistening with unshed tears. "We gave the others time to escape... I'm sorry," he rasped.

"You did well, boy." Tareq's voice cracked. He looked to the deity. "Please, kill me instead. Spare him."

Arwan shook his head. "If only you had arrived sooner, I might have."

The deity yanked out the dagger, a river of blood flowing out. Faris's eyes widened before the light in them faded. His body slowly collapsed to the ground, while they all watched in horror.

Sahar and Malik grabbed Tareq as he screamed and thrashed. *"What did you do? What did you do?"*

It all happened so fast. Ronan and Zara rushed forward, their ether spiraling out in torrents. Surprise flashed across Arwan's face just as the world exploded in a clash of dusk and dawn.

Ronan's blood was burning with anger—with hatred—for these fucking monsters. Faris and Ayah had been so young, so full of life, even with their painful past. Smoke rolled toward the sky and the deity emerged, somehow untouched from their attack.

Rain started to fall. It was sudden—there had been no sign of the weather changing. Something was wrong.

The deity did not smile as he sighed and raised a hand toward them. An invitation to battle.

Zara let out a war cry before charging. Ronan followed, his wings sweeping through the smoke. Ether coiled around his hands, energy wrapping tightly as he snarled, ready to unleash it all on the deity.

Until a Spirit of the Midnight Sun shot out from the dark and snatched him from the ground.

FIFTY-THREE

Zara didn't sense the Spirit until it was too late. How it emerged from the darkness, as if materializing out of thin air. It was the Spirit with the gilded horns and the face of a human skull, a javelin strapped to its back. A crown of silver fire on top of its head.

There was a thunderous clap as it collided with Ronan, two forces of unnatural strength battling one another under the rain and stars. Zara wanted to go after them but Arwan was already at her throat.

"Distraction will cost you, Horizon."

Zara raised her dagger in time to block his short blade, energy exploding on impact. Her eyes widened, her vision already blurring from the sudden rain. Arwan was stronger than she anticipated, waves of power rippling from his grip and through the face of the blade. Nothing like the lesser god she had killed before. So, *this* was the true power of a deity warrior.

And Arwan was not the average deity, but a member of the Council. One of the first to rebel against the Primordials.

"Are you gauging your opponent?" he asked over the clashing steel, his expression still full of sorrow. "Never overestimate yourself, mercenary. It is one of the many downfalls of mortals."

Zara clenched her teeth. "Don't act like you regret what you did."

The twins had deserved better, and now the deity who had killed them was *crying* over them.

Arwan pushed against their blades and sent her flying back up the road and crashing into a domed rooftop. Zara cried out in agony. Rain was already seeping through her clothes.

She tried to get up when another wave of pain rippled up her body, and she gripped onto the cracked stone for support. It didn't come from her though—it was Ronan. Across the city the Spirit slammed his javelin various times into the archangel, before Ronan managed to move away, the two leaping from one building to the next.

The Spirit was stronger than all of them. If she and Ronan were together, then perhaps they would have had a chance… They were separating them on purpose.

Zara didn't have the opportunity to reach out to Ronan through their mental connection—not as Arwan burst through the stone.

In the streets, specters began to spill into the road, the Kairos mercenaries and Axar trying to fight them off. Her mercenary brother let out a yelp, the sound echoing toward the sky. Worry gnawed at her abdomen but she forced her attention on the deity.

Arwan sauntered toward her, blade in hand.

"You may not believe me, Horizon, but it did pain me to kill those young ones." Strips of moonlight fell across the deity's dark curly hair. "They forced my hand."

Zara breathed heavily through her clenched teeth, the pain in her side lessening. She thought back to that forsaken moment when the Council members had held Hakim and Eshe at blade-point. "Like how you killed *my* mercenaries? Did they force your hand too?"

"Unlike my counterparts, I do not take joy in the hunt. I despised that I had to execute formidable warriors." The deity pointed his weapon at her, a sympathetic expression on his face. "But in order for us to achieve our new vision of this world, we must push forward, leaving behind those who do not understand what we are trying to accomplish."

Zara shouted a curse, her voice filled with anguish. "The Council wanted to rid Celestrea of its rot and toxic influence. Don't you think the War of the Skies achieved just that?"

"No, there are Primordials who are still trying to make their way back to this world." Arwan gave her a look, like she was being naive. "The only reason they want access to the mortals is because they are dying."

He lunged. Steel rang out as their weapons clashed over and over again. They dove toward each other, colliding in brilliant bursts of ether and strength, before charging once again. Their battle continued across rooftops and buildings, chunks of stone erupting from the force of their ether-fueled collisions.

Arwan slid down the face of a tower as it began to fall. "We won't stop until every Primordial in Celestrea is dead. They deserve what's coming to them!"

He sent a slice of sparkling ether toward her. It hit Zara dead center in the chest and she crashed through a wall on the opposite side of the street. Smoke billowed out, making its way into her lungs. She coughed, blinking through droplets of red and rain.

Fucking Suns. Zara wasn't sure how she was still standing. If it hadn't been for the amplified Primordial power from the Oasis, she would have been knocked out. Or worse.

Zara stumbled back onto the main road. Ether hissed to life in her hands, recreating her khopesh blades.

"I don't care what happened between you and the gods." The red-purple light illuminated the snarl on her face, the blood trickling down her cheek. "You dragged us into your fight. It is *you* who forced our hand!"

Arwan landed in front of her. "You should care, Horizon. The way the Primordials treated us isn't different from how they will treat you, if they win."

Those words unsettled her. Zara rolled to the side before a wave of his ether could hit her. With her makeshift swords, she sent out arcs of fiery light.

Arwan cut through one, while evading the others. His movements were lethally quick. Even with her heightened ether, Zara could barely keep up with the deity. She dreaded what could've happened if she had attacked a member of the Council *before* the Oasis.

"I never cared for the gods, nor for this Continent, but the Primordials seem to be the only ones willing to give me power," she said. A smirk flitted across her lips. "I'd even say they owe it to me."

Crimson smoke rose around her as Zara sank into a fighting position, one that she'd seen Daria do before. The deity merely stared at her, unmoving.

She pushed off the ground and flew toward him, when a large gray wolf snatched her from the air. Fangs dug through the flesh of her arm. Before Zara could register the pain, the beast flung her to the ground.

Her face fell as she looked up. "Axar?"

Saliva dripped from her mercenary brother's jaws, his breathing hard and ragged. But that was not what tore at her heart.

It was the lack of recognition in his yellow eyes and the hatred in his voice as he said, *"You've caused me a lot of pain, mercenary. For that, I will pay it back tenfold."*

Ronan's body was screaming. Broken tiles bit into his palms as he struggled to stand, small pieces of stone tumbling from the gaping hole he'd made crashing through a building. Something glinted in the distance and Ronan scrambled to flee, his wings flapping hard.

A spear came soaring through the night, splitting the raindrops. Ronan swerved to dodge it but the blade grazed his side and ripped the leathers. He groaned, blood bubbling from the cut, as the spear flew back into the Spirit's hand.

The warrior did not need wings to fly—though he shouldn't have expected less from an ancient being created by Khaos herself. Its skull face held nothing but darkness beneath, a silent embodiment of wrath and ruin. It had been relentless, constantly eating up the distance the archangel tried to put between them. Something wet dripped over

Ronan's eyes, whether it was blood or sweat he couldn't tell. Maybe both.

He summoned bolts of ether, thrusting his hand toward the Spirit. The creature was quick but the archangel's power was faster. Its body jolted, smoke rising from its dark cloak.

"I can feel the youth in your ether." The Spirit's voice was low and raspy. *"It is strong and wild, far beyond your mortal understanding."*

Ronan grunted, pressing a hand to his side. "You will not have us, Spirit."

Rain seemed to fall harder, soaking through the fabric under his fighting leathers, as he swung his sword in time to meet the Spirit's spear, their storm of attacks coming in a show of silver and sparks.

The muscles in Ronan's shoulders burned but he met every blow, every slash. It was madness and chaos. Ether rose in torrents around his body, rushing out to connect with the Spirit. Ronan knew it hurt the creature. He could see it from the subtle twitches and tilts of the creature's head. The sight was enough for him to keep going. He could *kill* it.

They kept fighting in the air, surrounded by tall towers and domes. The Spirit slid his spear down the face of Ronan's sword before clutching onto the collar of his leathers.

"My Creator and the Fallen say to capture the two Primordials alive—though that doesn't mean you need the use of your limbs."

The Spirit twisted around to throw the archangel down toward the ground. Ronan let his ether strike the creature as he fell, his wings unable to hold him up from the speed, and he crashed through one building and into the next, fiery pain lighting him up inside. He rolled away in time to avoid a wall collapsing on him, pale dust spraying his face.

Ronan was on his hands and knees, shadows of the canyons now falling over him, grass and sand soft beneath him. The battle had managed to make its way to the outskirts of the mining city.

The Spirit slammed into the ground beside him and stalked toward the archangel, kicking him in the side. Ronan shouted and collapsed. The ethereal warrior turned him over to press a boot onto his back and grabbed one of his wings. The sound of silver being un-sheathed sent Ronan's heart racing.

"It might please my Creator to know her prized possession has its wings clipped. You can grow these back, can you not? Perhaps we can do something similar to the elf. Break her somehow so she cedes to our cause."

Ronan breathed heavily through his nostrils as he tried to crawl away.

"Don't fucking touch me."

The Spirit yanked his wing back and—

Suddenly Ronan was back in the Iron Isles, Elios soldiers beating him while cutting his wings off. The agony of it all. His senses were crumbling into pieces. Slipping past his fingers.

"No! Get off me!" he shouted weakly. "Don't touch me!"

There was the cold touch of steel at the root of his wing. He tried to shove the terror away and summon all his ether. Before he could do anything, the Spirit stopped.

Ronan couldn't see the warrior but its grip on his wing loosened, the weight on his back lifting. Despite still being in danger, he couldn't help a ragged sigh of relief and his wings slackened on either side of him. The adrenaline was already leaking out of him, his body trembling.

Ronan turned his face; the Spirit was looking somewhere ahead of them before sheathing the spear on its back.

"So be it," it said, facing him once more. *"I will see you again, archangel."*

The creature pushed off the ground, disappearing into the night. Soon after, the rain lessened until it stopped completely.

Ronan knew he wasn't alone as he slowly pushed to his feet. Standing before him, within the shadows of the canyons, was an archangel with white wings.

Ronan breathed through the pain. "Erebus?"

The brother he once knew gazed at him with cold, expressionless eyes.

"I'm glad I arrived in time."

FIFTY-FOUR

Ares cremated his mother. He stood along the edges of a sea cliff and watched as her ashes were swept away by the ocean wind.

She had sacrificed so much for him, and he'd fought to sustain their livelihood as long as he could. He only wished he could've given her more. She *deserved* more. A better life. A regret he would carry forever.

The olive trees rustled behind him, the breeze mourning with him. It echoed the sorrow he couldn't voice.

Something was wrong with him. A hollowness in his chest where his heart was supposed to sit. He felt… alone.

The last of the embers floated into the evening sky. Ares tipped his head back and closed his eyes. He wished Daria were here. He wanted to rush back to Ikarria, but there were matters he needed to tend to before leaving Soleira.

He headed to the Iron Isles. There was a short window of opportunity he needed to make the most of. Word would soon spread of the spectacle he'd made during the diplomats' feast, and Matías would come for him.

Some of the soldiers stationed on the island gave him puzzled looks, though none questioned him. Ares would miss that level of power.

He approached the hall of Idris Calderón's cell. "Have you made any friends since I last saw you?" he called out.

Ares faltered a step at the sight that met him.

Fuck. The draconic king was still chained, but his body was now mottled with cuts and bruises. And King Matías was there, *drinking* Idris's blood.

He had his fangs wedged in the space between the elf's neck and shoulder. Gods knew how long he had been feeding from him—Idris seemed on the verge of passing out. Ares cursed himself. He had been so engrossed in thoughts of what had happened, calculating the next steps of his plan, that he hadn't sensed the Lord of the Vampires.

Matías lifted his head. "Finally. If you had taken any longer, I would've killed our prisoner—and then High King Erebus would've had my head."

The vampire grinned with bloody teeth and pushed King Idris aside, the male so drained that he slumped to the ground. Though it did look like the elven king hadn't made it easy for Matías: there were blotches of purple along the vampire king's skin.

Ares clenched his jaw. All he saw now was his mother's killer. Not his years-long mentor, but his mother's end. The one who never provided her with the medicine she needed, the one who kept her a prisoner most of her life.

"How did you know I would be making my way here?"

"When I discovered that *my* courtesan was leaving in a caravan owned by the Sombra Quarter, it didn't take long to make the connection that you were involved. You once watched over Ronan Menodora, the ruler of the shadow markets—and the King of Damalis."

"*Your* courtesan? My mother wasn't your property." Ares unsheathed his sword, the sound ringing through the empty prison floor. "I should've taken your head a long time ago."

The vampire king wiped the blood from his lips with a cloth. "Had you tried, the outcome wouldn't have changed, boy—you will never be strong enough. I took you in from nothing; all that you are and have is because of *me*. I know you were never fond of me, but I never thought your arrogance and ingratitude would shift into full-out betrayal." Fury flashed across Matías's expression. "How wrong was I. It was you who freed the archangel from this very prison. Who else could it have been but my *loyal* general of war?"

Idris had been trying to sit upright. At Matías's words, his eyes widened, gaze lifting to Ares.

The general frantically went over his options to help Idris escape. Ares had done it once; he could do it again. And he had to save him, for the realm—for Daria.

"What do you want?" he asked Matías. "You've had every reason to arrest and execute me, but you haven't."

The vampire king grinned once more. "I can see the wheels turning in that head of yours. I suspected you would come here to take away our beloved prisoner—given the relationship you have with the princess."

Ares's lips curled into a snarl. "The *Queen* of Ikarria. I merely serve and protect her. You are not to harm her nor Idris, unless you want the wrath of the other realms unleashed on you."

"Along with the incident regarding your mother, your Second sent me a report with concerns about your behavior and loyalty." Matías raised an eyebrow. "You should probably hurry back to Ikarria."

Ares growled, something in his chest tightening, and he moved toward the door of the prison cell, but the vampire king was faster. He grabbed Idris, holding the male's chin up to expose his throat, and bared his fangs. "Take another step and I'll make sure Idris Calderón walks the edge of death without ever dying, until Erebus decides his worth has run out."

As if to prove a point, Matías bit down on Idris's neck. The elf cried out.

"*Stop.*" Desperation clawed at Ares. "Let him go, and take me instead."

The vampire king released Idris, licking his lips. "You have already received your punishment through Morana's death, and I would like to see what you do next. For my own amusement and curiosity. Your former soldiers will deal with you soon enough."

It was a game to him, Ares realized. Some twisted fascination the king still had for his beloved general. *Matías's favorite. Matías's toy.*

Ares couldn't leave this place, not without Idris. He had hoped to bring home two parents to safety. If he could bring home at least one—

"*Leave*, boy. The only way for your sacrifice to still have worth is for you to live," Idris rasped out. The Ikarrian king struggled to his feet, putting distance between him and Matías, those ether-imbued chains dangling between his wrists. He leaned against the wall, gaze hard on Ares. "Something has happened in Ikarria. Go to *her*, protect her, and continue to bring fire to what you started."

Matías tilted his head, watching them with a smirk.

War raged within Ares's chest, filled with heartache and anger, everything he had bottled up inside on the verge of breaking.

Idris gave him a small smile. A sad one. "*Run.*"

Ares clenched his teeth and took a step back from the cell. He didn't want to leave. He'd failed Daria once more. Shame and disgust curled inside him, even though he understood Idris's words. The battle wasn't over yet.

His gaze slid to Matías. "I will return to save King Idris and avenge my mother."

The vampire king snarled. "See if you can save Ikarria before your own soldiers kill you, boy. You are a traitor. You are nothing, never have been."

Ares turned his back on the vampire king and walked away, disappearing into the shadows as Matías continued to shout.

Ares needed to get rid of the astral ore weapons. A lantern swayed gently in his hand as he rushed down into the catacombs and the makeshift warehouse there, the stuffy air already threatening to suffocate him.

The barbed spears and their ballistas were hunched creatures in the dark. Waiting to see the light. Ares gritted his teeth.

He took out a bottle of oil that he had snagged from the soldiers' supplies and dunked the liquid over the space, the spears, the chains, the other weapons. The whole time, Ares imagined Matías's face full of rage.

"Let's see how you'll fare when your precious astral ore is of no use."

He tossed the lantern toward the far end of the chamber. Glass shattered and flames erupted, eating up the oil, growing larger, clawing their way up the walls and over the weapons.

Heat thickened the air, and Ares squinted against the harsh brightness. He slowly backed up toward the exit, scanning the destruction.

His gaze landed on the barbed spears, his face falling. Fire licked over the wicked weapons, dancing above the starlight steel, but it did nothing to damage it. The same happened with the chains, the javelins, the swords—everything made of astral ore was unharmed by the flames.

Ares let out a mirthless chuckle. "Of course. It would've been far too easy."

Perhaps the destruction would still stall the vampires enough to give them time.

Ares turned, ready to flee from this place, when he saw a hooded figure blocking the exit. He unsheathed his sword.

"It's been some time, General Valdemar." The figure pulled down their hood.

"Lady Maira?" Ares's eyes widened at the sight of the deity who had worked with Daria on the blood banks, twin sister to Council member Nadira. "What are you doing here?"

Maira glanced at the burning chamber behind him. "Mere flames are not enough to destroy ore designed to kill a god."

Ares took a few steps toward her, his grip tightening around his blade. He half-expected the deity to attack or stall him, but the female moved to the side, gesturing to the darkened halls of the catacombs. "If you take this path, you will reach the outskirts of Soleira."

He observed her, frowning. "Why are you helping me? Are you not going to try and stop me?"

"I will say the same thing I told Queen Daria when she was last here: not all of us deities agree with this *new world* the High Throne and Council are trying to create."

That made Ares stop, a memory flitting through his head. At the end of the hunting season, Silas had almost caught him and Daria sneaking around the royal offices for information on the High Throne's plans, but *Maira* had intervened, escorted the queen away…

"You helped Daria before," Ares said. "You've been hiding in the shadows all this time, Lady Maira."

In the distance, shouts of soldiers echoed in the catacombs, getting closer.

The deity pulled up her hood. "Go. I will take care of this mess you created."

Ares nodded. There was no time to dissect what was happening here or what the deity's true intentions were. He needed to leave. Ares sprinted down the darkened hall, fire and smoke roaring behind him.

He left this place, which had had such a hold on his soul. His mother would no longer be waiting for him to come back. His breath caught. He'd wanted… He'd wanted to save her. So badly.

In that moment, it was as if the crackling fire turned into a whisper in the air, one that tightened his chest. *Be happy, my son.*

Ares Valdemar broke into a run. He had set himself free.

FIFTY-FIVE

Ronan had to steady his breathing, fight the lump in his throat. He wanted to raise his fist and scream at the male before him. Wanted to throw his weapon down and embrace the brother he once knew.

But Erebus wasn't the same. With everything Ronan had learned, he now saw the archangel in a different light. All the different shades that made him.

Erebus stepped into the moonlight. The white armor of Elios adorned his body, pauldrons fastened over strong shoulders. His silver hair had grown long, now past his waist. The male did not look like a High King, but a warrior.

And it was the look in his blue eyes that Ronan tried to understand. Heartache. Anger. Desperation.

Erebus's expression pinched slightly, as if gazing at him was almost painful. It disappeared as quickly as it came. "I wasn't meant to come here. Though fortunately for you I did, otherwise the Spirit would have torn your wings off."

Ronan fought the shiver that trickled along the scars on his back. "Should I be *thanking* you then? You're here for the same reason the Spirit and Arwan attacked us—to capture me and Zara."

"Not exactly, Ronan. The truth is, I knew you were going to the

Oasis." The archangel stepped closer. "Arwan and the Spirit were ordered to observe the both of you, from a distance, but it seems they got carried away."

Dread sank low in Ronan's stomach. "What do you mean you knew about the Oasis?"

Erebus's gaze never wavered from him. "Did you forget all the years I served you? I suspected you would go there to strengthen your abilities—and from the sheer magnitude of the ether rippling off you, it seems my theory was correct." The archangel's lips curled. "The stronger your ether is, the more it benefits us."

Ronan paled as Erebus added, "I could've stopped you a long time ago; I *let* you attempt the Oasis."

Ronan sucked in a breath. And here he thought they had managed to thwart some of the High Throne's plans. But he was merely a pawn in the archangel's schemes.

Erebus looked at their surroundings. Nothing but broken buildings around them.

"It would've made things simpler if you'd simply joined me... It's too late for that though. I made the same offer to Zara Santos, so she wouldn't have to suffer what's yet to come. She didn't listen. Now you will both carry the Primordials' wrongs—the blood of the lost gods is on your hands."

Ronan recalled those burning moments in the coliseum. Erebus's final plea to Zara, and how she had denied him. Still, even under such terrible circumstances, the thought of the male wanting her by his side had Ronan seeing red.

"Do not touch her, Erebus," he snarled. "If you want to serve your goddess, so be it, but you will not have her. I will go with you, though I will not make it easy for you."

The archangel stared at him with that same, empty look, yet there was a flicker of something in his eyes. "You love her."

Ronan didn't hesitate. "I do."

Erebus averted his gaze, brows furrowing. Silence fell between them. The warm desert wind rolled sparse pebbles across the dirt around their boots. Stars shined above them, silver light lining their wings.

"I do not wish to hurt you any more than I already have, Ronan." Erebus sighed. "Though with the way things are, pain will continue to find its way to you and Zara."

Ronan felt at a loss. "Why are you acting like you care what happens to us?"

For a moment—for one weak moment he wondered if his brother was not completely gone. The memories he'd witnessed in the Oasis flashed through his mind.

"When we were young, you told me that you had been mistreated by the gods and deities in Celestrea," Ronan murmured. "The pain you endured was terrible and unjust. I didn't know about the abuse your family suffered. Your brother, Kaiser—"

Erebus rushed forward in a blast of silver light. Ronan didn't have enough time to react, not as the archangel slammed into him and they went crashing through the debris and against a stone wall. Erebus had a hand around Ronan's neck, his grip ironclad.

Blinding ether rose from the High King's body like steam, blue eyes bright with fury. "Peering into my past, are we? What exactly have you seen? And how?"

Ronan felt the air being sucked from him. He clawed at Erebus; ether flowed through him to add more power to each punch to the silver-haired archangel's chest. Erebus grunted with each blow, though he did not waver. His body was a wall of steel.

Ronan was already at a disadvantage, weakened from his fight with the Spirit. He thrashed against Erebus's grasp, nearly breaking free, but the archangel pushed him against the wall with more force. Ronan rasped out the words. "You killed the deity who owned your family, but how did you come to align yourself with the rebelling deities? Why didn't you come to me after your brother was killed?"

Erebus's lips curled into a snarl. "I suppose the Oasis played a part in this, letting you see parts of my past? I could consider Kamari's obvious involvement as treason."

"*Erebus, listen.* I am trying to talk to you! I know I failed you—I wasn't there for you when you needed me. I broke our promise to fix Celestrea." He shoved the archangel's arm again and freed himself. "But you also betrayed *me*! Was our friendship so weak that you couldn't ask for my help?"

"I tried telling you then, you didn't listen." Ether still wafted off Erebus. It was certainly not the power of the average archangel. Ronan was certain this was the High King's reward for serving the Primordial of Fate and Time.

"I know I was a stubborn, selfish ass, but it would've been different had I known. I tried to find you, I came for you after, to apologize—"

Tension feathered Erebus's jaw. "I no longer cared, Ronan! I saw Celestrea for what it was—a society filled with liars and powerful beings that did not care for lowly archangels such as myself and my family! No one was coming to save us, so *I* had to do what needed to be done!"

Ronan couldn't argue against the fallacies of the Primordial world, nor could he blame Erebus for his hatred. But—"There has to be another way..."

"There isn't." Erebus breathed hard. His voice softened a fraction as he said, "The only thing I regret is how you suffered for it."

Emotion thickened Ronan's throat, tears lining his eyes. The memories he had witnessed from his *Izcali* came to him again. Reminders of their youth and innocence.

"How can you say that?" He asked, anger rising. "You brought the deity armies to my shores. The forces you sided with destroyed our home. It was your home, too. My family—" His voice broke.

He swept Erebus off his feet and slammed him onto the ground. Ether exploded, and whatever walls still standing began to crack. The world shuddered beneath them as Ronan punched the archangel. Every crack of skin was followed with images of his father, mother and brother.

"They *loved* you!" Ronan roared through his tears. "Considered you as their own!"

Erebus clenched his teeth, breathing hard through every hit. "I loved them, too." He kicked Ronan in the gut, shoving him several feet away. The black-winged archangel leaped to his feet. "When the rebelling deities came to Damalis, I rushed to find them, to convince them to leave, because I knew your power would go berserk with all the new ethereal energy in the mortal lands. I didn't *want* to fight your father! Then you came and—"

Erebus closed his mouth. They both knew the ending of that story.

"And then I killed them," Ronan said. He looked down at his fingers, his vision flashing with that of his untamed ether. "It was me. No one else."

A dark truth that would forever stain his soul. Suddenly, it was as if all of his progress disappeared. He tried to hold onto the memory of Zara holding him while he grieved. He held onto her support, tighter and tighter. But it was hard. It hurt. So, so much—

"It wasn't your fault, Ronan." Erebus glared at him. "Do you hear me? It was not your doing that they died. It was *mine*."

Ronan stared at the archangel. Helpless. Utterly defeated.

"I killed your family the moment I brought the War to them." Erebus pointed a finger at him. "Their deaths are *mine* to claim."

It's not your fault. His father had said the same thing. It hurt to breathe.

Erebus watched him. "The High Throne's forces are preparing to march for Damalis."

No, not Damalis, too. Ronan's home was in danger, and here he was. So far away.

Anger laced his veins. "Fucking Suns, Erebus, you can't attack the guardian realm. It is I and the ethereal realm who failed you. Keep this fight between you and me!"

"Tempting, but I cannot. We only need one of you. Your power is great, though it is not ready." There was that unreadable expression again. "Train your ether. Prepare yourself for what's to come. Justice will be served."

Ronan didn't understand. The world shuddered again, but this time, it wasn't because of them. Something in the air cracked, distant ether screaming. He felt a tug, the need to run toward it overwhelming him—

Erebus looked toward the heart of the city. "Our conversation will need to end here. Zara Santos is causing trouble."

At hearing her name, panic seized Ronan's chest. He turned, preparing to go to her, but the archangel's ether lashed out and threw him back against the wall.

Pain burst at the back of his head and Ronan cried out, though his breath was cut short when Erebus wrapped his hands around his throat, choking him.

"I need you out of the way for now," Erebus said.

Somehow, tears started to fall. Ronan watched as the sight of his former friend blurred. He was losing his grip on his consciousness, but he tried to get the words out, otherwise he would regret it. "Please, brother. Come back to me... You can still stop this madness and fight with us."

The corners of Erebus's lips lifted only slightly. "I can't."

His grip tightened, Ronan struggled against him. He was so tired, his body battered. Ronan's eyelids grew heavy, though he could still hear Erebus murmur something.

"I want you to be the one to kill me one day."

Ronan strained to look at the white-winged archangel once more. Erebus held a soft smile, and for a moment Ronan saw the young man he once knew.

The world before him shifted. Erebus and the broken stone drifted away, replaced by familiar jungle and ocean. *Damalis.*

Ronan's family appeared. They were smiling at him—his father, mother, and younger brother. His mother reached out to him, grasping his face in her gentle hands. He couldn't feel the touch, but emotion clenched tightly around his heart.

Ronan cried out. This was Erebus's power, an illusion. Whether it was to soothe or pain him, he didn't know. Didn't care.

Darkness slowly swept in from the corners. His family continued to smile and wave, his little brother giggling, too, instead of sporting his usual frown. And it was his father's voice, in that familiar, rich timbre, that echoed. *"You are a guardian, my son. A true warrior and a true king."*

Ronan tried to embrace them, even though he knew he couldn't. *I miss you*, he wanted to say. *I love you.*

A heaviness fell over him and the soft blanket of night finally engulfed him.

Zara sprinted through the buildings, Axar at her heels. His claws nipped and scratched her skin whenever he caught up. She let out another slash of ether toward him.

"Tallon, you need to snap out of it!" Zara's throat was tender from how much she had been screaming at him.

Her power grazed Axar and he slowed to a stop. They faced each other on an empty road between abandoned structures.

Zara panted. "Please, I need you to hear my voice. You are being tricked!"

"*Silence, mercenary.*" Axar growled, clawing at the ground. "*Murderers such as yourself don't deserve mercy.*"

Those words stabbed at her.

"Words will not work anymore, mercenary," Arwan called from a rooftop. "The wolf's mind can no longer withstand our High King Erebus's illusions. He is lost."

Red light flared around her. "I refuse to believe that!"

"The only way for you to save him… is to kill him."

Zara screamed, and a wave of ether crashed into the building where Arwan stood. The deity evaded the attack but tumbled to the ground along with chunks of brick and stone.

Axar lunged for her. An ether-made dagger formed in her hand, but she paused. She couldn't hurt him, not her brother.

The hesitation cost her. Axar crashed into her, the weight of his body threatening to shatter her ribcage. Stars flashed across Zara's vision as they rolled across the ground.

Searing pain danced along her arm, followed by a splatter of blood. Shit, Axar was tearing at her skin. Zara let her makeshift dagger dissipate and bashed her fist against his head.

"Let go of me, bastard!"

The world spun as she was smacked against the ground again. Axar towered over her, growling.

"You will pay for what you've done. For the lives you took from me."

A different kind of pain latched onto her heart. "I—I don't want to hurt you, Tallon."

Arwan stood at the end of the road, watching the spectacle with a sad expression. "I understand that the bond within mercenary guilds is something profound. Tragic that it had to come to this."

Zara clenched her teeth, red light swirling around her hand. *Basim, hold him down.*

Her nahual appeared from a slit in the sky. He bit down on Axar's ear, yanking him away. Her brother bellowed, prepared to buck the wolf off.

"I'm sorry," she said, before slamming her light ether into Axar's side.

Her brother yelped. Zara rolled out from underneath him and pushed herself to her feet.

Zara, you will have to do a lot more than that. Basim growled through their bond as he evaded every slash of Axar's paws. *Mere flesh wounds won't be enough.*

We also have the deity to deal with, she said. Her gaze lifted to Arwan. *This is a ridiculous plan, but follow my lead.*

Zara summoned a whip of crimson light and waved her hand to Axar. "Over here, Tallon, you prick!"

Her brother howled at the air, standing on his hind legs and preparing to chase after her. Basim let go of him. Zara sucked in a sharp breath before sprinting around the wolf. She ran up the face of a wall, powered by her ether, just as Axar crashed into the stone, barely missing her.

She pushed off the stone, swinging the whip and wrapping it around Axar's neck as she landed on the ground again.

Now, Basim!

Arwan was caught off guard by the wolf appearing behind him. Basim bit down on the deity's shoulder, grappling with the male.

The silver ether in the lesser god's eyes flared. "It's been years since I've seen a nahual. What a nuisance your kind is."

Fear twisted Zara's stomach. The whip lengthened around Axar's neck and she twisted around to throw the wolf toward the deity, the effort tearing a cry from her throat.

Axar crashed into Arwan just as Basim vanished, the wolf and deity tumbling into a broken building.

Her nahual returned to Zara's side. *I would normally find such battle tactics childish, but I suppose it will do.*

Zara let out a dry chuckle. *Apologies, nahual. I will try something with more flare next time.*

I'd rather you not.

Before Zara could approach the ruins, her vision flickered. *Erebus* was stalking toward her. No, toward *Ronan*—she was seeing through his eyes. They were shouting at each other, and the pain that echoed in Ronan's chest… It was so strong, he didn't even notice her presence.

Zara was slammed back into her body. Why was the archangel here? No no no.

"Ronan needs us; we need to move."

They had to deal with the deity and her brother quickly. She waded through the broken parts of the building, dirt curling into the night, the air stuffy with dust. Axar was slumped over a chunk of stone, breathing heavily, still in his wolf form. Blood poured from the wound Zara had given him.

Axar won't be moving any time soon, Basim said. *I will watch over him. Take care of the deity.*

Zara didn't trust herself to respond as she stalked to where the lesser god must have landed. A figure flitted toward her and she summoned ether-made blades in time to meet Arwan's.

"Where are those tears you shed earlier, or was that sympathy a performance?" She hissed. "If you truly feel sorry for those you killed, why not drop your weapon and leave this *calling* of yours behind?"

"You think you know who I am, Horizon. That you understand me. I used to be a warrior for the gods," the male gritted out. "I fought countless celestial battles in their name, but none of those deaths were worth the reality that Celestrea was bringing forth. So am I wrong to try and right this injustice? To stave off the guilt that haunts my heart every day?"

Ether burned bright as Zara met the deity's gaze, energy sweeping through her hair. "Perhaps not, but your fight with the gods is a threat to *my* life. To the people *I* care about. I cannot let you continue"

Arwan smiled. "I understand. Until one of us remains standing then, Horizon."

Red-purple light engulfed her. Zara inhaled, feeling every tendril of it sink into her bones. Deeper. Down to the roots of her being.

A whisper of a smile touched her lips before she drove her ether forward, sending Arwan flying through the air.

She soared after the deity, not giving him a moment of reprieve, and slammed her ether into him.

Arwan parried the attack, though his eyes widened. For the first time, Zara could sense fear emanating from him.

"Your eyes," he rasped. "They are filled with crimson light."

A fiery spear, similar to the one that had been used to kill the twins, formed in Zara's hand, the blade angry and bright. Something moved in her peripheral, but she kept her gaze on Arwan.

"For all the lives you took," she said, her voice echoing around them.

She raised the spear over her head and threw it, striking the deity's chest. He cried out and the world trembled—everything seemed to still, as if the mortal plane were holding its breath.

Arwan wrapped his hand around the body of the blade. "You missed my heart, Horizon."

The corner of Zara's lips curled as she glanced sideways. "Did I?"

The guild of Kairos emerged from the folds of darkness.

Tareq didn't look her way, his gaze pinned solely on Arwan. Shadows bowed over his expression as he shifted into his jackal form and prowled toward the deity. Sahar and Malik flanked him, weapons in their hands.

Arwan tried to pull the burning spear from his chest until he realized the blade—Zara's ether—was pinning him to the ground.

The deity breathed hard. "I deserve a warrior's death."

Tareq snarled. "*You will not get that from me.*"

Zara watched as the mercenaries unleashed themselves on the lesser god. The Horizons pierced Arwan's heart, over and over again, darkness clinging to them.

The deity screamed and the world shuddered once more. In the distance, perhaps somewhere in the fabric between the mortal and godly worlds, the ether screamed, too.

Zara started toward the outskirts of the mining city, her pace quickening when she couldn't feel the archangel's consciousness through their mental bridge.

Ronan.

Zara followed the path of destruction that Ronan and the Spirit had made. The rain had stopped, the ethereal warrior nowhere to be found. Her heart stuttered at the sight of Erebus placing Ronan onto the ground—her archangel's eyes were closed. Her chest squeezed painfully.

"*What did you do?*" Zara shouted.

Erebus turned to face her. Something feathered across his expression. "He's not dead, only unconscious."

She forced herself to stay put, trying and failing to leash the anger, the grief, at being so close to the High King. Zara thought back to all the assignments she had taken as the Rogue; Erebus had been there as the Hand of the High King—as her friend. And all the things Raziel had made her do… Erebus had known—had let it happen. There were many things she wanted to say, though Zara simply summoned a dagger of ether.

"I sensed the deity's death," Erebus said. He did not draw any weapons. "One less Council member for you to deal with. Are you satisfied?"

The archangel seemed different from the last time she'd seen him.

Her grip on the blade tightened. "You already know the answer to that."

Erebus smiled softly. "I do. I know the both of you very well."

He walked toward her and Zara raised her blade higher, but the archangel brushed past her. She whirled toward him.

"Are you not going to finish what you started here?"

It was unsettling that Erebus was simply *walking away*.

"There is no need for me to do that, especially now that a member of the Council has been slain. The other deities will be angry, Zara, and they will come for you." The archangel unfurled his white wings, casting a wintery glow to the night. He met her gaze. "Armies of Elios soldiers and specters are preparing to march for Damalis. Take it as a formal declaration of battle and ready yourselves."

Zara could taste a bitterness on her tongue. Her voice came out soft. "Don't attack them, Erebus. There are thousands of innocent people there."

"Funny. You sound like you care." He raised his eyebrow. "I re-member you hating the world once, for what it made you do, for hat-ing *you*. They still all despise you for all the lives you took from them."

She clenched her teeth. "That we *both* took. You were there for every assignment, knowing full well what was happening."

"Oh, I have done a lot worse than you, Zara Santos." Erebus's gaze drifted to Ronan. It was slight, but Zara was sure his expression cracked. Perhaps with an echo of pain. "But for what it's worth, I'm sorry. Take care of him."

Zara cocked her head. Why was he saying these things? Were they true? She took a step forward just as the archangel prepared to take flight.

"I thought we were friends," she said, her jaw tightening. "I thought I knew you."

Erebus glanced at her sidelong. "No, you didn't know me, truly— though that was by design. You did nothing wrong. I should thank you, Santos, for being a small comfort when my life hadn't known any for years."

She remembered what Ronan had said a while ago. How he was glad that she and Erebus had had each other back then.

The archangel took to the stars, his wings blades of white. Zara understood then that it was Erebus's farewell. He would continue to tread this polluted path, and there was no going back.

She gathered all the hurt, temporarily shoving away the worry for what would come to Damalis, and ran to Ronan.

He still hadn't moved. Wounds slashed his body, along with a faint purpling across his neck. Something pricked Zara's eyes as she gathered the archangel in her arms. His breathing was slow and steady.

Zara ran a shaky hand through his hair and pressed her lips to his brow, holding him tight until the Kairos mercenaries found her.

FIFTY-SIX

Daria stood before the obsidian throne, the black stone singing with energy, with voices that she'd heard for so long—and only now she understood what they needed. What they were begging for. The ground beneath her feet trembled, though she did not cower in fear.

No one else would hear or feel this, especially not Silas, who was watching her from the base of the dais.

"Are you sure it's the key to finding the dragons? It seems like a normal throne to me."

Ever since Daria had conducted the necromancy spell, there had been more eyes on her, as if the vampires could sense a shift in the air. Silas had been pressing Daria for more information every day.

Her back was still to the vampire. "It's because the power here was not meant for you, Silas."

She hadn't told him about Arzhel or the Primordial contract her ancestor had made, designed to reach out to a member of the Calderón line—tt was not something he needed to know—though she had mentioned that the throne held the key to their where-abouts and that its energy needed to be transferred. Daria returned her attention to it. In her hands was the obsidian crown, its spires glimmering like midnight.

She lifted a hand, whispering the words Arzhel had taught her, beckoning the power within the throne to break free.

A weight fell over her palm as the sealing energy seeped from the obsidian, threads of silver light stretching toward her. It could not exist outside the bounds of the throne; it needed a new place to be held.

Daria urged the power to bind itself to the crown and the ether greedily accepted its new host. The pressure glided off her hand, the sealing complete, and Daria sagged, catching her breath.

Silas whistled. "I could see that at least. Impressive, Your Majesty. Now, we can move on to the next step and find the creatures."

Her satisfaction quickly disintegrated. Daria gnashed her teeth together but said nothing. There was no way the vampires could find out where the dragons were. Daria hadn't told Silas about them being in The Dragon's Teeth.

She needed to plan her escape from the castle, but she needed *him* to come back—

The doors to the throne room flung open. As if summoned by her thoughts, Ares walked in, his head bowed, the shadows and dim candlelight hiding most of his face. Her heart jumped.

Silas was already making his way toward him. It had been some time since the vampire general had left for Soleira. She hoped he'd been able to accomplish what he set out to do.

Daria froze at the sight of blood staining Ares's leathers. From how dark it looked, it must have been there for a while. He hadn't washed it off for some reason.

"General, you look terrible," Silas said. "Like you've seen a—"

The vampire cut himself off and Daria saw why…

Ares had always worn a cold and unfeeling mask, especially in front of his soldiers. The hard exterior hid the damaged soul beneath, so he could keep his tender heart safe. But the one he wore now was more of a shell. No light could be found in his violet eyes. He looked so *empty*.

"My mother." His voice was almost too quiet to hear. "My mother is dead."

No. Pieces of Daria's heart shattered, and her legs weakened. Not Morana. Not the woman who had sacrificed so much of herself to care for her only son. The same boy who had grown into a merciless man in order to keep a roof over her head and food on her table.

How could this be?

"That can't be true." Silas faltered back a step. He shook his head, his face leached of color. "You're lying, General. Morana can't be *dead*."

Daria had never heard the male like this. In shock and so… distraught?

Something in Ares's eyes flashed as he glared at Silas. "Has King Matías said anything?"

Silas stiffened. "Not yet. What happened to Morana—"

"Your *report* to Matías is what happened," Ares snarled. "Because of your accusations, he decided to punish me."

Before leaving for Soleira, Ares had told Daria everything. How he had been working with the Sombra Quarter to have his mother escorted from the castle to the secret city of the Stone Orchard. King Matías must have discovered Ares's plans.

Daria's stomach twisted.

"I was doing my duty, Ares." Silas's breathing quickened as the corners of his eyes glistened, the emotion thick in his voice. "I would never have put Morana in danger—she was the only person who considered me as someone of *worth*."

Ares blinked. Suns Above, even she was taken aback.

The general stared at his Second for a long time, something churning in his eyes. Slowly, his expression returned blank. "It doesn't matter anymore. I hope you'll no longer question my authority, Second."

There was a quiver along Silas's shoulders. He gritted his teeth and shoved past Ares, disappearing into the castle halls. The other vampire soldiers gave the general one look and scurried away.

It was only them in the throne room now. Ares did not move, his downcast gaze stuck on the black marble floor. Something clenched in Daria's chest as she slowly approached and took his hand. "Come with me."

Cool night air swept through the windows as Daria led the vampire to her bedchamber. He didn't say a word the entire time.

Once she'd locked the door behind them, Ares's voice cut through the silence. "I'm sorry, I haven't changed into clean clothes."

"That doesn't matter," Daria murmured. She moved to stand in front of him. "Is there anything I can get you? Some tea or water?"

"I saw your pater," he said quietly. "I wanted to get him out."

Unease wrapped around her. Her voice was steady. "What happened?"

"Idris is alive. They have no intention of executing him." The vampire's gaze remained distant. "I wanted to bring your pater back. Make at least one family whole—but I couldn't. Matías has him."

Daria closed her eyes for a moment, pushing away the tears forming at her eyes. "You did what you could."

"It wasn't enough."

She cupped his cheek. "All that means is that *we* will get him back together."

Ares frowned, looking down at her wrist. "Why do you have the bracelets? Did Silas do this?"

She clamped a hand over the ether-imbued shackle. "Things happened while you were away, but we can discuss them later."

"I'm sorry," he murmured. "I will get the key to remove them."

"Don't—at least, not yet. Adrastea seems to be at odds with you already; I don't want to make it worse."

Ares nodded but said nothing else. Daria didn't push him to talk, and simply brought her other hand to his face, brushing her thumb over his cheek.

Eventually, Ares slowly lifted his gaze to hers. "This whole time,

I have been trying to save my mother from Soleira. To help free her from Matías."

Her heart cracked. "I know."

The way he opened and closed his mouth, as if it hurt to speak. "I thought—" His voice broke and he closed his eyes. "When we reached Nephtyr, I thought she was safely en route to the Stone Orchard—but he found her. He found her and took her back to Soleira—"

Daria's eyes began to water. She took his hands in hers and noticed how cold they were. How they shook.

Ares pressed his brow against hers. "Matías killed my mother with his bare hands."

Tears streamed down Daria's face as her breath caught. She wanted to rage, but she did not fall, not with Ares breaking before her.

He grinded his teeth, a grunt laden with sorrow escaping him. "She's *gone*. My mother is gone."

"I'm so sorry, Ares." Daria gently guided him toward the seating area beneath the window. She sat on the edge of the cushions and he sank to his knees before her.

"I'm so sorry," Daria whispered, running a hand over his hair. "I'm so sorry."

Ares's body trembled. For a while, he did not say or do anything else. Instead, he remained like that, head in her lap as she wrapped her arms around him.

"I'm here, Ares. I'm not letting you go."

And it was in Daria's embrace that he finally broke. Droplets spilled onto her dress and sobs racked through the vampire general's body.

Daria stayed there, holding the vampire in her arms.

From the moment he saw his mother's body, Ares had felt like he couldn't breathe. Pain and anguish had been welling up inside him.

His heart had been falling apart for so long; he may have been breaking from the moment Matías picked him out of the slums of Adrastea.

What a long, treacherous battle it was to hide one's emotions.

But here, in this room, in a castle within the ancient Ikarrian trees—*with Daria*—years' worth of bottled emotions began to seep through those defenses Ares had worked so hard to keep up.

The death of his mother had snapped the last thread that kept him together.

Being with Daria now—it was all he needed. He couldn't bring himself to shout or scream, nothing like that. Nor would he want to in front of his queen.

Ares's chest twisted and pulled in every direction, and he let himself feel every stab of emotion. Allowed himself to cry in the arms of the woman he cared for so much.

The woman he yearned for.

FIFTY-SEVEN

The following evening, Daria sat with Ares during the evening's banquet. Well, *sat on his lap* was a more accurate description. She kept her expression dejected, which wasn't too difficult to do since she was still a prisoner. The ether-imbued bracelet still gleamed around her wrist.

Daria lifted a cup of wine to Ares's lips. The vampire was regality and beauty all wrapped in one, with fine leathers and trousers clasping his muscular body. His long violet-tinted hair shone in the dim light, the skin of his face pale and ethereal. One would have never known that he'd cried in her arms the night before.

Vampires relished their blood sources and other foods. The soldiers were more *tame* than during previous feasts, most likely sensing the tension between their general and Second.

"Why did you demand we hold this banquet?" Silas stared at Ares, a faint curl of disgust on his lips. "Is now really the time for it?"

Ares drank from the cup Daria held, not even looking at her. "I'm in a shit mood, Silas. So *yes.*"

The Second was grieving too, but unlike the general's quiet sorrow, Silas was like a vulnerable, wounded animal. Bristling and lashing out. His expression was dark, no sign of the prideful, arrogant male she knew him as.

Daria didn't realize how close the Second had been to the general's mother—not even Ares had known. The night before, after they'd mourned the loss of Morana, they had to force themselves to concoct a plan.

She told him what happened with Arzhel, though Ares hadn't been pleased that he wasn't there with her. They didn't speak about the consequence of using the necromancy spell. There was already too much to worry about.

Ares told her of how he'd tried to burn the astral ore weapons intended for the dragons. While he was unable to damage them, for the vampire to commit such a thing... It was truly a severing of his role as general. It wouldn't be long before the vampire forces in Ikarria received news of it.

And *Maira* had helped Ares flee the catacombs. Assisted him like she had with Daria before. The Ikarrian Queen hadn't realized just how opposed the female was to the High Throne's ideals. The deity could make a powerful ally.

Ares had done so much. Daria almost didn't recognize him from the male who had led the armies of Adrastea to her home. Had this been the *real* Ares all along? The side he hadn't let others see.

Ares beckoned to the castle staff. "Bring more alcohol to my soldiers! Tonight we drink our sorrows and grievances away."

The vampires slammed their cups against the tables and cheered. Even Silas chugged a drink down to its dregs. Basira sat beside him, stuffing her face. The advisor hadn't looked Daria's way once; the elven queen tried to ignore the sting of it.

She was very aware of the eyes on them as the general brushed strands of her hair back. "Beautiful," he murmured. Daria wasn't sure what was part of the act anymore.

She purposely shifted on his lap, and he groaned under his breath. "General, as *honored* as I am that you forced me to attend this banquet of yours, what is it that you want from me?"

Their conversation was loud enough for the soldiers to hear, especially Silas.

"Such attitude." Ares wrapped his fist around her hair. He

clenched his jaw, as if leashing himself. "My Second informed me that you managed to unbind the key from the Ikarrian throne. We will need to arrange a travel party to escort you."

Daria glared at him, even as a prick of desire stirred inside her at the feel of him slightly pulling on her hair. "No, that's not what we agreed on. You told me it would only be you and me looking for the dragons."

"As if I would allow that to happen." He scoffed. "You've been played, Your Majesty. If you haven't noticed, there are consequences to crossing King Matías."

She went to slap him but he caught her wrist. The surrounding vampires braced themselves, hands hovering over their weapons, though they did not move.

"Let me go, *vampire*," Daria gritted out.

"That's enough from you." Ares wrapped an arm around her waist and stood up.

Daria yelped, feeling her cheeks go hot as he carried her out of the banquet hall like a sack of potatoes. This time, Basira watched them leave.

Ares waved a hand to Silas. "I'll handle it from here. Please try to find some reprieve tonight."

For once his Second had no snide remarks. He seemed defeated and merely nodded, while the other vampires whistled and shouted crude words after their general. Suns Above.

Daria smacked her fists against his back—she wouldn't go down that easily. "How dare you! Put me down at once!"

The vampire only chuckled. "I know you can do better than that, Your Majesty. Don't hold back now."

When they arrived in the hallway, there were no guards or patrols, not with the banquet happening.

Ares lowered her to the ground. He fumbled with a pair of keys from his pocket and unlocked the ether-imbued bracelets on her. "That went as well as it could."

Daria's ether returned in a rush of heat, quickly filling her veins. She never wanted to part with it again. She sighed and rubbed her wrist. "It was a bit theatrical, but your vampires seem to enjoy that sort of thing."

"They will be too drunk in the morning to notice your absence. We have to make the best of the opportunity."

They made their way to her bedchamber, darkness and silence trickling between them. It had been part of their plan to have the vampires gathered in one place, drinking their fill and being as distracted as possible. Anything—*anything* to give her and Ares as much advantage as they could get.

Daria would leave to find the dragons while he stayed behind...

Her stomach twisted. "Word about your betrayal will come soon. You will be in danger."

"I am a general. You don't need to worry about me—there are greater things at stake."

She didn't doubt his resolve. Ares had made his decision to betray his kingdom a long time ago, ever since he'd made that agreement with her pater. No, it went even further than that. His rebellion had started when he befriended the long lost King of Damalis. Ares had been trying to fight back all this time, in any way he could.

Daria had been so lost in her thoughts she hadn't noticed they'd arrived in front of her bedchamber. Her stomach dropped. This was where they were meant to say goodnight. Daria would spend the night alone, and then they would part ways in the morning.

"Your Majesty?"

Daria looked up to see Ares staring at her, standing close—*very* close.

Her cheeks grew hot. "I suppose I will see you in the morning."

Moonlight streamed from the windows, touching Ares's pale skin. The tip of his fangs peeked over his lips as he took ragged breaths, like he was holding himself back from something. Black veins appeared along the corners of his eyes.

Daria clutched his arm. "You're hungry."

The small amount of blood he'd taken from her back in Nephtyr had only satiated him for a short while.

Ares averted his gaze. "I just need to sleep; I will get more blood bags tomorrow."

"That isn't going to help, though, is it? We know that already." Daria gripped his sleeve tighter. "Tell me, why does other blood not work for you?"

His throat bobbed and he shook his head. "It can happen to some vampires. I'm sure it will fade over time."

"Well, what I do know is that you must have strength. Once I leave, you will need it more than ever." She brought her hand to his jaw and gently turned his face to her. His eyes widened at her touch. "Drink, Ares."

He searched her gaze, his fingers brushing her wrist. "I... I don't deserve it, Daria."

How he said her name. As if he were a worshipper kneeling before his god. Begging for forgiveness, writhing in self-hatred.

Suns Above, she hated seeing him like this.

A fire lit inside her. Daria tightened her grip around his jaw and spoke through clenched teeth. "Take my blood, Ares. I am giving it to you. I want to."

Ares's gaze lowered to her lips, his eyelashes casting shadows across his skin, before meeting her gaze once more. He surely must've seen the desire in her eyes. He bent to brush the bridge of his nose along the slope of her neck, his hand cradling the back of her head, the other going to her waist.

Daria melted under his touch. They had been through so much, had navigated pain and grief. She didn't know why but this moment felt different. He wasn't just about to drink from her—this was something more.

Her breath caught when Ares licked her neck.

"You smell exquisite, Your Majesty." His voice was rough. "Thank you."

Ares bit her then. His fangs struck deep, yanking a gasp from her lips. He drank, his tongue grazing her skin with every swallow. Daria's body buzzed with warmth—it was so much better than she remembered. Each drag of blood sent a rush of pleasure through her. Her breasts grew sensitive, nipples hardening under her dress. A deep groan shuddered through Ares's body, and the sound went straight to her core.

They lingered in strips of shadow and candlelight. Daria tilted her head back, allowing him more space. Suns, she had been avoiding her desires for so long—always agonizing over matters of right and wrong, always carrying the weight of obligation and leadership. This felt almost liberating.

Ares's fingers curled into her hair. "You taste so good."

For some reason, a lump formed in her throat, though it soon morphed into something languid and hot as he continued to drink. A thrill went through her, the feel of his mouth moving against her absolutely sinful. Ares pressed a hand on the door behind her, still cradling her head with the other, and slowly lined his body with hers.

She felt something hard against her lower abdomen, and heat coiled within her. Daria wanted *more*, and she knew it went beyond the ecstasy of Ares drinking from her. Pushing aside her shyness and obvious inexperience, she let instinct and desire take control and rolled her hips.

Sparks lit across her body, a fire unlike anything she had known coursing through her veins. This feeling was all-consuming—and it wasn't enough.

Ares cursed against her skin. His mouth moved with desperation, as if the hunger was too much to bear. He drank from her like he wanted to devour her. Like he wanted to make love to her.

Daria's eyes rolled back as she continued to move her hips against his. Her hands went to his chest, tracing her fingers along his collarbone and down his body.

Having Ares like this, in such an intimate way, tightened her heart, squeezed it so much it nearly brought tears to her eyes.

Even though they'd been working together for months now, it felt like they were reuniting only now. Truly returning to one another.

"I've missed you," Daria whispered.

Ares's fangs tugged at her skin as he pulled away, resting his brow against her shoulder, his arms sliding around her waist. The general of war held her, his heavy breaths warm on her skin.

"I've missed you, too, sweetheart. So much," Ares murmured. He planted a soft kiss to the bite wound. "You have changed my world, Daria. Helped me see that it is not as cruel as I once believed."

Daria wrapped her arms around him, burying her face into the crook of his neck. That ocean scent wasn't as strong anymore, now being replaced by the fresh smell of the forest, touched with his usual rose fragrance. It was intoxicating.

"If you will have me," Ares added. "I vow to be at your side, and help you reclaim what is yours."

A shiver went through her and she nodded. Daria couldn't help it; her lips brushed against his skin and Ares's fingers dug into her back.

They both moved as one. Their heads tilted toward each other as they slowly pressed their lips to each other's. His mouth was soft, yet commanding—and Daria surrendered to him. Allowed him to guide her as he tugged on her bottom lip before slanting his mouth over hers once more. Their tongues brushed, and a tightness coiled within her.

Ares's kisses gave an icy bite to her resolve. He was so tender, almost reverent, his hands roving over Daria's body as if he couldn't comprehend that this moment was real.

Daria fumbled with the door handle behind her, gasping against his lips when he grazed her breast. "Come inside."

"Fuck, Daria." He groaned. "We should stop here."

"We should." She nodded before their lips crashed against each other again, Ares pulling her tighter to him for a moment. He moved away slightly, though kept her pressed against the door. It felt like he was struggling to create distance between them. Color had already seeped back into his cheeks and light had returned to his eyes.

Daria went to hold his face in her hands. "Kiss me."

He shuddered out a breath. His expression turned almost pained, tilting his head and placing a hand over hers. "You are not yourself right now. It's the blood drinking."

Daria's brows furrowed. "You know that's not true. At least—it's not *just* that. I want this, I want *you*."

"Trust me, I have longed for this, from the moment I first saw you. The pleasure I want to give you—the things I want to *do* to you…" Ares tucked a strand of hair behind her ear, his gaze holding hers. "When I fuck you, it will be when we are truly alone, and I can make you scream as loudly as you want."

Her heart raced, as something fluttered low in her core, her frown slowly melting away. She fought against the urge to squeeze her thighs together as she nodded. Daria still didn't want to let him go.

"Stay with me tonight anyway," she whispered. "I don't want to be alone."

Ares kissed her firmly on the lips. "I'm not going anywhere."

He reached behind her and pushed the handle down. Daria yelped when Ares scooped her up with one arm and entered the room, a shocked laugh leaving her. "What are you doing?"

Ares kicked the door closed behind them. The room was dark, save for the starlight that poured through the window and splashed the bedsheets where he placed Daria.

She brushed a hand through the long hair spilling down his shoulder. There was a sheen in the vampire's eyes, a warmth that shattered the usual iciness there as he bowed over her. And it was only for her.

Ares said nothing, gathering her face in his hands and kissing her. His tongue swept between her lips and their movements became more hurried. Daria grasped at his leathers, but the vampire stopped her.

"Though I still think we should wait, I want to touch you. Make you feel good, as a thank you for allowing me to drink." He held her gaze. "If that is what you would like."

Daria's breath hitched and she nodded.

"Yes." Daria breathed out the word and he lowered his mouth to hers briefly before dragging his lips away and kissing a path down her throat.

His hand went to the collar of her dress and he tugged at it in question. "May I?"

Daria's heart thundered. "Yes."

Ares slipped the gown off her body, brushing his lips between her breasts and down stomach as he did so until Daria was left wearing only her lacy undergarments.

The vampire hissed as he stared at her. "You are so beautiful, Your Majesty."

Daria looked away, placing the back of her hand over her mouth. "It's been a while since I've done this."

"The only thing you need to do is enjoy yourself." He leaned forward to kiss her hand still covering her mouth. "Feel my touch—feel how much I missed you."

Ares traced his fingers along the hem of her already-wet underwear and lowered himself so he was level with her core. Daria felt a hot flare of embarrassment and involuntarily closed her legs.

"Are you all right?" Ares gently ran his hands along her thighs, waited for her, kissing the skin around her knee. Such an intimate gesture, Daria felt like she was about to cry again. "Yes… I guess I'm a little nervous."

"Take the time you need," Ares murmured. He pressed his lips against her thigh again. "You are doing so well, my Queen"

Daria whimpered. She knew she wanted this—with him. More than anything. He was patient, running his palms down her legs, breathing sweet words to her, helping her feel at ease. Slowly, she spread her legs.

"Good girl," he whispered.

His breath coasted over her skin, right where she ached for him. Daria shivered. Ares pulled the fabric of her underwear to the side and kissed the area just above her clit, making her moan with frustrated need. He bided his time, nibbling and licking the skin along her hips. Then he lowered his mouth, lingering on a sensitive spot that caused her legs to jerk.

He chuckled, the sound rough. "Do you like that?"

The words caught in her throat when Ares grazed his fangs along her inner thighs. His eyes lifted to hers, the corners of his lips curling, as he bent down again and dragged his tongue up her center. She arched under his touch, sparks shooting up her spine.

"Oh," she moaned.

A groan rumbled in Ares's throat and the sound traveled through her. His tongue was thorough, stroking her soft and hard. He spread her thighs further apart, grip tightening as he worked her over.

Daria bowed at every touch. Ares focused on her most sensitive spot, swirling his tongue there before sucking. When she felt the slight prick of his fang, Daria could swear she saw stars.

Ares was still fully dressed in formal attire, while Daria was practically naked before him. His to devour. His to feast on. She liked that.

"Ares."

"Your Majesty, the way you say my name will undo me." His eyes flicked up to hers, gaze burning bright. "Say it again."

He pushed a finger inside her and her mouth dropped open, spilling his name in a strangled whine. Ares growled as he kept stroking her, licking at her core at the same time.

Daria was breathing hard, her moans filling the darkness. She touched her breasts, her thumbs sweeping over her nipples.

"There you go, sweetheart. Just like that."

The pleasure was too much, it would've surely burned her alive. She was pulled away from the edge of bliss when Ares stopped, his finger leaving her. Daria lifted her head with a frustrated groan, the sight of this stunning male between her legs enough to make her heart skip beats.

"You didn't want me to slow down?" The vampire gave her a wicked grin. "I'm sorry."

She fought for breath. "You sound anything but sorry."

Ares's fangs seemed brighter in the dark as he lifted his finger, glistening with her wetness, and slipped it into his mouth. He licked it clean. Licked *her.* "I merely want to savor this moment with you."

Daria bunched the sheets at her sides. "Please."

He grinned at her before leaning forward to press his mouth to hers, letting her taste herself. His touch melted through her and she slowly sank back down onto her back.

Ares gave her another peck on the lips. "Don't worry, I'm not done yet."

He splayed a hand on her stomach, pinning her to the bed as he returned to feasting on her sex. Daria rolled her eyes back, writhing under him. A rush of courage found her and she pulled on his hair, bringing him closer to her, while he swirled his tongue around her entrance.

"I love the little sounds you make, princess."

Ecstasy filled Daria to the brim. She went back to gripping the bedsheets as Ares dipped his finger inside her. He was fucking her so well. That steady rhythm picked up, pulling more gasps from her mouth.

"Ares." Daria arched against the bed. "*Ares.*"

He groaned in response, slipping another finger inside as he kept licking her clit. She cried out—and came undone. Her legs trembled as her orgasm spiraled through her, groans and cries escaping her.

The vampire moaned her name, giving her center a few more licks until she was wholly spent. He kissed her inner thighs again before crawling back up to lean over her.

"Next time we do this," he whispered. "The kingdom of Ikarria will be free."

Daria shuddered as he pressed his mouth over hers. She grabbed his sleeve. "Don't you think about leaving."

"I won't." Ares tilted her chin up. "I'll be right beside you. As long as you'll have me."

Those words echoed through her heart and mind. Daria watched Ares remove his shirt, the burn scars on his skin more apparent under the moonlight. Her chest squeezed at the sight.

"What's that look on your face?" he asked with a smirk, slipping under the sheets next to her.

She watched him for a moment, partly still disbelieving that the vampire general was in *her* bed. This strong male feared by so many. The male who had protected her over and over again. The words she truly wanted to say wouldn't come. Not yet. "Nothing."

Daria snuggled against him. Ares tensed before immediately relaxing to her touch. He wrapped his strong arms around her. They lay together in silence, darkness and night folding over them.

He ran his fingers along her arm. "I hope you know that I care about you, Daria. More than you imagine."

"What's this now?" she teased, even as a fuzzy warmth clenched her heart. Even as she pressed her cheek against his chest. "I care about you too, Valdemar."

Ares chuckled, his voice softening. "Sleep. You have an early morning."

Daria inhaled his rosy scent. She wanted to savor this moment too, remain tethered to his warmth forever. To this sense of safety, with his strong body curled around hers, his gentle breathing soothing her worries, even if for just a moment. Daria sank into his embrace and fell asleep.

At the break of dawn, Ares escorted Daria to the border of the Ikarrian forest, the Dragon's Teeth looming in the distance. Sunlight peered through the morning clouds and there was a chill in the air.

Daria patted her horse's rump, the animal already saddled and holding her bags. Ares took this moment to take her in. She was wearing royal riding wear, black as night, a dark cloak over her shoulders.

Out of all the choices he'd made, being at Daria's side was the one he would never regret. It was why he would cherish the moments shared with her the night before. Of having been able to kiss her, touch her, *taste* her. A night woven from dreams and bliss.

Daria deserved the best this mortal life could offer. For as long as she wanted him beside her, he would be there for her, and strive to be worthy of that privilege.

"I think that's everything. The crown is safe." Daria secured her saddlebag before gesturing to the dagger strapped to her waist. "I'm ready."

His chest tightened. "Please, be safe. Return to me."

It was bold of him to say such things. Nothing between them had been defined yet, but he couldn't run away anymore. From her, from what he felt.

Daria smiled, and it was the light pouring from cloudy skies. "I will."

A chilly breeze rushed by, scattering the leaves, and Ares wrapped his arms around her.

"I will be waiting," he said before kissing her. Deeply.

Something like fear flickered over her face when they pulled back. "What will you do in the meantime?"

Ares cupped her cheek. "I will right my wrongs."

"Haven't you already done that?"

He smirked. "Not quite."

Daria wanted to say more—he could see the curiosity brimming in her amber-brown eyes. Ares jerked his chin to the forest. "Go, Queen Daria Calderón, and return with the dragons of Ikarria."

She got onto her horse, the length of her cloak flying in the crisp air. Daria would come back with a force that could set the skies on fire, he was sure of it.

Ares stayed there, watching as the woman he was falling for disappeared within the ancient forest, hope and promise following her.

He didn't care for the gods, though in that moment, he couldn't help but whisper a plea to whoever would listen. A plea—and a threat.

Protect her, or I will ensure that you won't be able to hear any prayers for the rest of your miserable existence.

The sun rose higher, sweeping away the morning mist. His wine-red cloak brushed against his legs as he kept his gaze ahead. Even as he felt the presence of Adrastean soldiers approaching from behind.

"Are you ready?" Ares asked.

"We have gathered all the soldiers from our realm who believe in our cause."

Ares almost smiled. The general turned to face his small army. There were many he recognized. The group was even larger than he'd hoped for.

The male who'd spoken bowed. "There are more of our vampires coming, and we're coordinating with an Ikarrian soldier and his forces."

"Vash, correct?"

"Yes, General."

Ares recognized the name. One of the elven soldiers who'd supported Daria while he was away.

This had been in the works for so long. Before Ares had left for Elios.

"That's not all. Reinforcements provided by the Sombra Quarter will also be joining us," Ares said. There was a soft smile on his lips. "I thank you. You did well."

"You honor me, General."

Ares clasped his hands behind his back, eyes scanning the vampires of Adrastea watching him. "If you do this with me, there is no going back. You will be considered traitors. Many of you have loved ones at home, and I will not hold it against you if you change your mind. This is your final chance to step away."

None of them moved. Instead, they slammed their fists against their breastplates or weapons. For the first time when it came to his forces, Ares felt pride flood through his chest.

He'd led violence for so long, and had only known brutality. This was different. There was purpose, something to fight for. Ares wondered if his mother would've been proud of him. He wished he could show her how he'd changed, so that she'd know her son was not all lost. The ache thickened his throat.

Ares bowed to his soldiers. Many of them shifted in place, glancing at each other. No leader had ever shown them this level of respect.

"I am honored to have been able to lead you. Thank you for allowing me to continue." He straightened. "Now, you may all still be loyal to your realm—that is well within your right."

"As for me—" Ares Valdemar whipped out his dagger and cut the emblem of Adrastea from his leathers. He lifted his gaze, his lips curling. "I fight for my Queen."

FIFTY-EIGHT

Sorrow loomed over the city of Nephtyr. Zara had never seen a capital mourn like this, grieving the citizens who hadn't survived the mining city, and the mercenaries who gave their lives trying to protect them.

Preparations for the funerals had started. Flags were being lowered, the crowds in the streets and on the canals thinning as people headed toward the palace. Even the air seemed to have a permanent scent of frankincense. Zara observed the people as they dropped white flowers at the gates.

Her gaze drifted to the other Kairos mercenaries who had come to see her group off. She wished they could stay longer, but with the High Throne waging war on Damalis, they had to leave now.

Tareq was wearing his usual mercenary garb, except for a black sash wrapped around his shoulders—as were Sahar and Malik.

The shifter's face was pale as he stared out at the procession. "Ayah and Faris were so young, with their whole lives ahead of them. I wished I'd handled things differently—given another command. Maybe they would still be here."

It was always painful to linger in the past. To suffer for things that *could* have been. But it never helped to dwell or cast blame. Zara was also learning this.

"We are Horizons. We rise and fall like the sun, but we never die." She grasped Tareq's shoulder. "Hakim would always say those words to me. I didn't quite get the meaning of them at first, but I think I do now. Even when our souls leave this world, we are never truly gone, as long as our memories live on through our loved ones."

"You understand this pain very well. Thank you for your words, Horizon." There was a glimmer of admiration in his eyes. "We will make our way to you… after the funerals. I imagine the Damalisan forces would like some extra warriors alongside them. Perhaps we can track down the Elios guild, too."

The Elios mercenaries were still missing, though 'had gone into hiding' was probably the more correct way to put it. They were adamant on not being found.

"And you think they'll fight with us?" Zara asked.

"Chances are quite high, I'd say," Sahar said. The jackal-shifter winked. "Tamaya was the first of the mercenaries to turn against the High Throne. There is more to her than we think."

If Zara were to ever run into the red-winged Horizon again… well, she would like to thank the archangel for saving her, back in the coliseum.

She smiled softly. "Thank you. We will need the support."

Her chest swelled with something warm and fuzzy. A rare sensation. Zara looked at Sahar and Malik, the two mercenaries bowing their heads to her.

"What of Axar?" Tareq asked, gesturing to the wagon beside Zara. "How is he faring?"

A tarp was pitched overhead, providing shade to a sleeping Axar. Baskets and chests of medicine, herbs, food, and drink filled the wagon. All thanks to the Kairos guild.

After the battle in the mining city, the Kairos armies had cut down the remaining specters with their crimson-colored blades, freeing any other survivors they could find.

Axar had shifted back into his human body, but still hadn't woken up. Zara had barely left his side, checking his pulse and temperature regularly. They were all recovering from the battle. Bandages were wrapped around Zara's arm and torso. Her body was tender to the touch, though the ether in her blood had already made quick work healing most of the wounds.

"The tonic he was given was to prepare him for his treatment," Zara said. After Axar went berserk in the mining city, she had to explain to the mercenaries what had happened to her brother. "Ronan says that the medicine must have reached its limit and can no longer help him. He will need to start treatment as soon as we reach Damalis. I can only hope it's not too late."

Tareq sighed, lifting the flap to peer into the wagon. "I know that Tallon will be able to fight this."

She nodded, her jaw locked, and lowered the tarp when a soft voice called out to her.

"Zara Santos."

Her gaze snapped to Queen Kamari; she was walking down the steps of the palace, Ronan beside her. He had gone to talk battle strategies with her and her royal generals, in the event the High Throne decided to attack her realm. Kairos was under high-alert now that Erebus was aware of their involvement with Zara and Ronan.

The Queen bowed to Zara. "Thank you for finding my people. My guild and I couldn't have done it with you. For that, allow me to give you a parting gift."

A jackal soldier stepped around Kamari and presented Zara with two sheathed weapons. Her chest tightened when the soldier revealed her khopesh blades.

They were whole again; strips and pieces of red ore webbed throughout the obsidian steel—the crimson metal was a speciality of Kairos, strong and almost indestructible.

"They're beautiful," Zara murmured, hands hovering over the swords. "Your blacksmiths were able to save them."

"As I said, their skills are unmatched." Kamari's kohl-lined golden eyes burned bright.

Zara took the sheathed blades from the jackal and bowed.

"You and the Queen of Ikarria have my full support," Kamari said. "I will be working to ensure my people's immediate safety—no doubt there will be political complications ahead—but you can expect the forces of Kairos to stand alongside you."

A chill ran over her skin. Mikatán was right. The power at their fingertips was not going to be enough. Their foes were becoming too strong. They needed as many allies as they could.

Zara and Ronan bid their farewells and rode their camels out of Nephtyr, Axar's wagon being pulled by a large hyena behind them.

She looked at the archangel—he had been silent for a while.

"What are you thinking?"

Ronan stretched his black wings out and sighed. Bandages decorated his arms and neck, a faint line of bruises resting along his cheekbone. "Our patron gods told us to find a Warden, or a deity who can become one. I don't even know where to begin."

Zara eyed him. "That's not really what's on your mind."

He kept his gaze ahead and let out a sigh. Sand whistled across the desert and the sun beamed above them.

"I've failed so many people: Erebus, my family, my people… Guilt has followed me for so long, and I can't stop thinking about how my mistakes played a hand in the War of the Skies. Erebus could've taken us both in the mining city—but he didn't. Said we 'weren't ready'. Now he's waging war against the guardian realm."

The archangel met her gaze, his silver eyes dull. "I'm worried, Santos. I'm worried for Orion and Soraya back home. For my realm. The Festival of the Three Suns will be starting soon. Erebus knows that—it can't be a coincidence."

Zara didn't hesitate. "We will defend your kingdom, and everything you fought so hard to keep. I promise you, Ronan: Damalis will not fall."

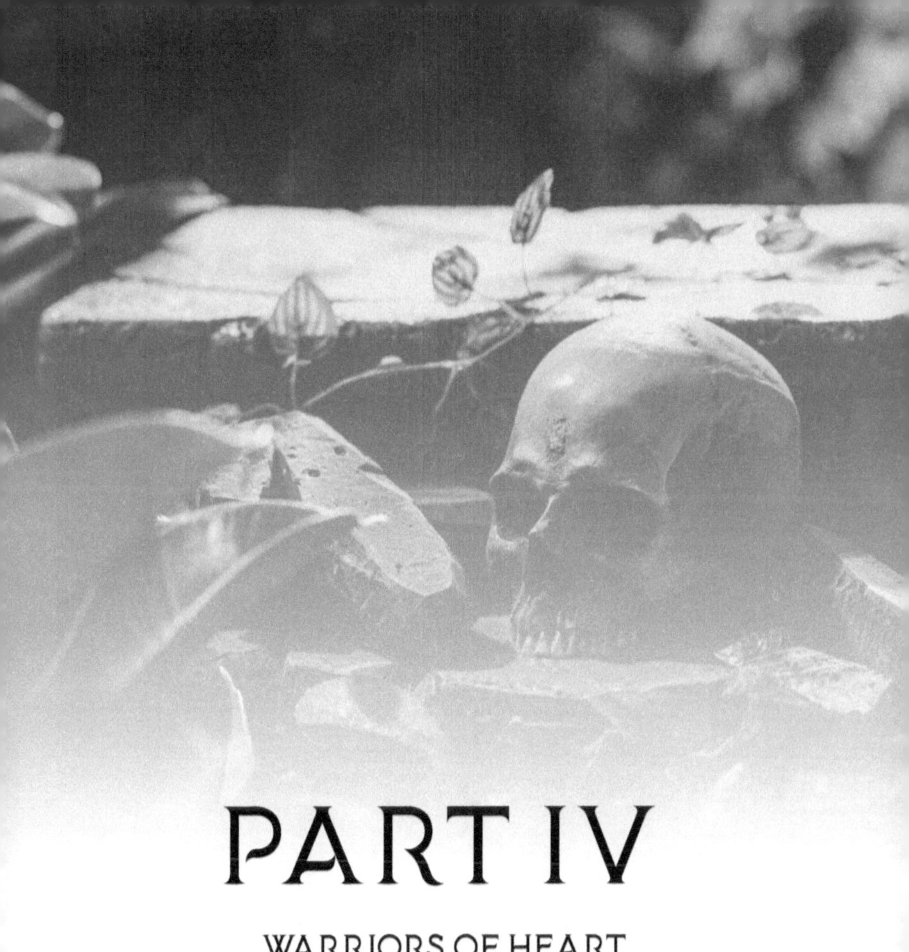

PART IV

WARRIORS OF HEART

FIFTY-NINE

By the grace of the Suns, Daria had been able to reach The Dragon's Teeth within a week. Terrain had shifted from dense forest to rocky hills with each passing day, making the trek slower, and the insides of her thighs ached from riding with little to no rest, but she'd managed. If there was anything Daria had learned from this past year, it was how to survive in the wilderness.

She stared up at the paths weaving through the steep slopes. The mountain ranges could've passed for sleeping beasts, their ridges and peaks piercing the sky.

Daria shoved the wrinkled map into her saddlebag, her red roan nudging her arm.

"I'm sorry I don't have any more apples," she said. "You ate them all."

The horse snorted. The food Ares had packed for her had been enough to sustain her throughout the entire journey, though Daria might have indulged the horse a bit more than she should've.

She took out her crown and placed it on her head. "The map brought me this far. Now, it is up to you to help me find them."

Arzhel's spell came much easier this time, spilling like water on a barren land. Daria pulled herself onto the saddle and clicked her tongue, urging the horse forward.

She tapped a nail against the obsidian. Energy pulsated from the crown, sending her deeper down the paths between the mountains. She groaned, her stiff muscles protesting.

"Let's get on with it." Not like she had a choice.

Days passed as they trudged up and down the slopes. Nights were spent either under arching rocks or tree alcoves. Thankfully, the fire in Daria's blood kept her warm through the elevation and chill. She kept to the streams, refilling her waterskins whenever she could before diving deeper into the mountains.

Animals watched them—four-winged owls, horned deer, and other critters. Daria could sense them hunkering in the rocks above or skittering along the branches around them. At night, she cast a large fire as a barrier from the outside world.

One day, as they were traveling along a river in a gorge, the energy in Daria's crown began to vibrate again. The voices that had been whispering to her all this time, now grew louder. They clawed at the air, yanking on the unseen tether between her and the spell.

Daria hissed at the sensation, observing her surroundings. "Where do you want me to go?"

The waters were a sky blue, rippling along the stone, and greenery and trees clung to the walls of the cliffs. Daria's clothes were dirty and torn—it was already the third set she had brought. Her stomach rumbled, even though she had just been nibbling on some dried meat.

The crown was urging her to go *deeper* into the mountain. She wanted to scream. Maybe even cry. The energy nudged her again, as if impatient.

"I hear you. You want me to go *up* this cliff," Daria called out, raising her hands in the air, whining. "And now I am talking to a crown, for Suns' sake. I'm going crazy."

Her horse trotted up an incline, the sound of clopping hooves calming the anticipation in her chest. *Go, go, go,* the voices seemed to say. *Hurry, hurry, hurry.*

A ribbon of silver energy appeared before her eyes. Winding through the air, guiding her deeper into the wilderness toward a slit in the rock at the base of a mountain.

Daria slipped down from the saddle, observing the path that dipped down to a small clearing in front of a smooth wall, tall and wide.

She cocked her head, watching the silver light from the tall gap she was standing in press against the face of the stone. Her heart thundered.

Daria turned to her horse. "I think this may be the end of the road for us. You will be able to return home much more quickly without me." She unsaddled and patted the gentle animal, her heart twisting at the sweat that gathered along its coat. "Off you go, my friend."

When the horse turned away, Daria slid down the slope. There was no indication that this space held any significance, but the whispers were growing frantic.

"I understand that Arzhel wanted to keep the dragons safe—" Daria muttered, running her fingers along the wall. "But couldn't he have left behind a statue or a sign of some sort?"

Still, a thrill ran through her veins. Daria wasn't quite sure what to expect, but if she could solve puzzles in decrepit dens hosted by ethereal creatures in the middle of the desert, then she could surely figure this mystery out.

The sealing power within the crown was the *key* to the dragons' safe haven. Daria held it in her hand, the obsidian glimmering under the weak shards of sunlight. The smell of wood and pine was thick, the air cool on her skin. She sucked in a deep breath.

The spell echoed in the cave. Voices hummed around her excitedly, and she could almost feel invisible hands brushing against her. As if in gratitude for releasing them.

Out of pure instinct, Daria guided the sealing energy toward the wall. It rushed through the stone, rippling along it as if the rock were water. The humming in her crown suddenly stopped.

Daria's fingers tightened around it before shoving it in her bag. She couldn't tear her eyes away from the wall, a layer of ether now shimmering over it—no, over the entire mountain. "What in the bleeding Suns..."

She reached for the stone, her hand slipping through it as if the wall wasn't actually a wall but a doorway. Daria squared her shoulders and walked through.

Light. Her vision was suddenly filled with brilliant golden light—until it slowly peeled away to reveal another *world*. She stood on the edge of a cliff, an expanse of land stretching out before her. A land full of beauty and life.

Grand trees, similar to the ancient forests of Ikarria, and more mountains stretched out toward the horizon, rivers curving around them like silver blades. The sounds of birds and animals echoed through the air. Massive colorful plants and flowers hugged the cliffsides. It was humid and a musky aroma of damp dirt reached her.

Daria raised her hand against the bright sun, more red-hued than the one in her world. Her knees buckled and she crashed to the ground. This was another *dimension*, tucked within the mortal world. How was such a thing possible?

The fires in her blood sang. This was the haven that Arzhel had designed for the dragons.

"Pater, I think I did it," she whispered. A breeze rushed through her braids and cloak, warmth kissing her cheeks. "I found them."

The fine hairs on the back of her neck rose. There was something behind her. She scrambled up, kicking her leg out as she turned and releasing a wave of flames.

A bone-chilling shriek responded. Daria almost wished she hadn't looked. The creature was unlike anything she'd seen before. It had a sleek, black coat that gleamed almost like liquid, eyes shaped like crescent moons, and a feline-like body. The creature was definitely some breed of demon.

Daria gulped. She had never seen this type of creature before, but she'd heard the stories from Zara's adventures. There were many kinds of demons living in different parts of the Continent—but why were they *here*?

She dug her heels into the dirt, flames gathering at her hands. If other living things were here with the dragons, then Arzhel couldn't have created this safe haven out of thin air; it must have existed before and he'd merely cleaved a gate into it.

The demon launched itself at her, its roar more of a shrill. Daria's flames burst in a thick, messy blast, turning the air hot. Energy swept her hair back and she gritted her teeth against the force of her ether.

She dodged to the side as the demon landed right where she had been standing, and she formed a thin rope of fire, whipping it out against the creature. It caught her flames in between its teeth.

Daria might've cursed for the first time in her life as the demon threw its head back, sending her flying through the air and crashing onto the ground, snuffing out her ether.

Her stomach flipped and she nearly hurled. Run. Run. Run. Alarms were blaring throughout her muscles, her senses. Daria clawed at the ground, stumbling to get away from the demon.

She sprinted down a narrow slope of a cliffside, climbing down rock as quickly as she could. Sweat dripped down her face, every breath burning her lungs.

The demon lunged toward her, following her down and slamming into the cliffside. Rocks broke free, nearly taking her down in the process. Daria shrieked, swallowing and inhaling dirt.

The path widened as she finally reached the foothills and the edge of a forest. Anywhere was better than that cliff. The demon was still pursuing her, eating up the distance between them, with curved claws that could shred her skin as if it were parchment.

Trees towered above her, proving enough of an obstacle for the demon as it struggled to maneuver between them.

"Dammit," she hissed to herself over and over again. "*Dammit!*"

If only Ares could hear her now; the vampire would have been amused—and maybe a little concerned. Suns Above, she couldn't think about the male right now. Gods knew what was happening in Ikarria right now.

All the more reason for her to survive *now*.

Daria's boots kicked up leaves and dirt as she tore through bushes, twigs and branches scratching her face and arms, a stray root almost sending her flying, before she stumbled into a wide clearing. The demon leaped out from the trees a few moments later, a rattling sound coming from its throat.

Flames materialized in thick rings around her, tongues of fiery red lapping at the air. The demon flicked out a forked tongue, its horned tail slamming on the ground. It tried to claw at her but Daria thrust out a column of fire from one of the rings.

She fought to keep standing—her muscles were crying, her breath laboured, her ether quickly eating up her energy—as her fire spiraled upward before charging the demon. The flames singed most of its sleek hide, though the creature didn't seem fazed by her attack.

It burst through her ether, its maw of teeth and saliva ready to swallow her whole. Daria stumbled back, raising her hands up—nothing came, her flames guttering out. She couldn't move.

A massive shadow fell over her and the world shuddered.

Daria didn't understand what was happening until it was too late.

SIXTY

"When will the Queen return?" Silas asked.

Ares placed the pen down on his desk, allowing silence to fill the office. "Soon."

His Second glared at him from where he leaned against the wall. "Remind me again why we didn't send our soldiers along with her? We should be monitoring all her movements."

Silas had only just noticed Daria's absence that morning, days after she'd left, and Ares had spouted out some lies and pulled rank to prevent him or any soldiers from going after her. Rank he technically didn't have anymore, though they didn't know that—*yet*. Silas hadn't seemed to care about what was happening in the castle the last few days, the male keeping to himself, probably mourning Morana. Until today, when he'd come to the general's office in a foul mood.

Word of Ares's betrayal still hadn't arrived from Soleira so Silas couldn't act on his suspicions. The destruction Ares had caused in the castle's catacombs must have delayed Matías's plans, the temporary setback giving Daria more time to reach the Dragon's Teeth. Still, Ares could not let his guard down.

His hand drifted under the desk to the dagger sheathed at his side. Waiting. "As I mentioned before, a group of armored vampires appearing before the dragons may not give them a good first impression. The goal is to have them under our control and on our side, no?"

"You are a fucking liar, Ares." Silas curled his lips. "The audacity to sit in that chair and pretend you are still our general, when Matías dismissed you from the position."

A pause. Ares smirked—he had been waiting for this moment. "When did you find out?"

"A letter arrived this morning, detailing what you did in the catacombs of the Soleira castle, how you attempted to free the King of Ikarria. I still can't believe you were so stupid as to throw away everything you've worked for."

"You never knew me, Silas. I never enjoyed the work that Matías assigned us, but you did. You've always been a cunning snake, eager to serve others worse than you."

Silas flashed his fangs before charging at him. Ares kicked the desk toward him, unsheathing the dagger as his Second tore through the wood with his bare hands. The general barely managed to nick the vampire's side before Silas swerved and unsheathed his own knife.

They clashed, but Ares was bigger and stronger, and their blades locked together. Silas was persistent, though—Ares could give him that.

"What are you going to do next? Fight the vampires you once led? Your own people?" he shouted. "I have soldiers who will follow my command much more quickly than yours and I will drag your beaten body back to Matías."

Ares grinned. "Try me, Second. I will withstand anything you bring at me, every fucking day, until Daria returns."

Silas trembled with rage; the circles under his eyes seemed darker than before. "Fuck you, you arrogant bastard." His voice wavered. "Morana died because of *you.*"

The words pierced through Ares, shoving past the hard walls he'd erected again with his mother's death. Straight to the core of his soul.

He snarled as he slammed Silas against the wall, cracks exploding along the stone. No soldiers barreled in yet. It hurt even more because Silas was right.

His Second grimaced, his expression crumpling. "It should've been me. *I* should've been her son. At least with me, she would still be alive."

Ares's breath caught. He searched the male's face. How had he missed this, in all this time? Silas had always been like a shadow, benefitting from Ares's ruthlessness. How had the general not realized that the male before him had *cared* for Morana. Loved her like a mother.

He remembered how warmly his mother had spoken of Silas. His Second had shown her a side Ares hadn't known existed.

"She asked about you," Ares said, his voice dropping to a near-whisper, even as he kept Silas pinned to the wall, his dagger pressed to the younger vampire's side. "You never told me that you visited her. And often too."

Silas snarled, shoving him off. Ares let him. "You didn't need to know. Morana was *kind* to me. One of the few who was." The male brought a hand to his chest. "And I will never forgive you for this."

Ares wondered for a brief moment how different things would have been if he had opened up to Silas. If they could have been brothers in a cruel life. A part of Ares was glad that someone else mourned his mother, maybe just as much as he did.

Ares straightened. "You know what happens next."

"Yes. You're probably rallying soldiers and Ikarrians to fight for your cause." Silas fixed the sleeves of his fighting leathers. "This is now a civil war amongst the Adrastean soldiers—try to survive for as long as you can."

Silas walked toward the door, but paused. "There's something I forgot to mention. When the letter from Matías arrived, some *shipments* came with it." He glanced over his shoulder with a smirk. "Would you like to take a guess on what they were?"

Ares clenched his jaw, dread twisting his stomach.

"Ballistas, equipped with barbed astral ore spears," Silas continued. "Ready for when your precious queen returns home."

Matías had taken his time informing the other vampires about his betrayal. The Adrastean king had wanted to send a parting gift.

A soldier barged in. She was out of breath, gripping the threshold.

"Silas, the elven soldiers—somehow their chains have been removed. They've revolted."

Silas jerked his head toward her. "What? Their elemental ether is free?"

"Yes sir. Battles have started in the streets; citizens have already gone into hiding. It's like they knew about this already."

Silas turned his glare on Ares. "What did you do?"

The former Adrastean general merely stared at him, a shadow of a smile on his lips.

Silas stormed out of the room.

His loyal vampire soldiers were out there at this moment. They would have quietly unlocked every ether-imbued bracelet on every elven soldier during their day-to-day duties, making the most of changes in shifts and guards.

Every Ikarrian soldier would have been waiting to break free from the unlocked chains and was now cleaving the capital with the elements.

Their rebellion had begun.

Ares strode into the castle's prisons. Each step echoed along the stone walls, followed by the clink of amor, his hand resting on the pommel of his sword. The cells were primarily empty, save for the few where the Ikarrian advisors were being kept.

They cowered at the sight of him.

"What do you want from us?" one of them said.

Ares didn't particularly want to help the people who had doubted Daria's potential as their queen, though he needed them to witness what was happening outside.

"A battalion of my soldiers has freed your warriors. As we speak, they are battling against the vampires who are still loyal to Adrastea and the High Throne." He tilted his head. "Your queen will arrive soon with forces more than capable of saving your kingdom. You will bear witness to the fight, so that you know how worthy she is in being your ruler."

One of the advisors scoffed. "Like we would believe a mongrel like you."

"I understand," Ares said. "It is why I brought someone along to act as proof of my allegiance to Ikarria."

The Ikarrian soldier called Vash emerged beside him. The male had been one of the first to be freed and came running when Ares asked for his help. *For Queen Daria,* he had said.

The advisors balked at the sight of one of their own next to an Adrastean soldier. "General Vash!"

"What the vampire says is true."

Ares was surprised to find the Ikarrian soldier watching the advisors with a hint of disdain. "My soldiers are outside risking their lives to save this kingdom. I suggest you listen to Ares Valdemar if you want Ikarria freed."

Vash glanced at the general. His eyes drifted down the vampire's body and he smiled. "I like your outfit."

Ares's lips curled. "So do I."

Gone was the bronze and wine-red cloak, replaced by silver and dark gray. The colors of Ikarria.

SIXTY-ONE

By the time the Festival of the Three Suns began, there was still no sign of the High Throne's forces. Ronan and the Elders had initially considered canceling the celebration altogether. Everyone knew the peace that existed within the jungles and beaches was temporary, but it didn't seem right to sap the people's joy of life. Their determination to thrive.

While the Damalisan imperial soldiers patrolled the region, the capital of Teotlan exploded in color and festive spirit. Garlands of orange and red blossoms hung across nearly every railing and around homes and businesses. White banners flapped above the streets, dancing from one building to another. The air carried the scent of sweet bread—which Zara never failed to demand from Ronan.

She entered the infirmary wing, holding a basket full of seashell-shaped sweet bread. Axar had been bedridden since they'd arrived in Damalis; he had awoken during their journey back, only to try attacking her and Ronan again. The archangel had had to shackle the shifter to the caravan until they reached the healers.

"How is he?" Zara asked.

Ezrah was placing damp cloth on Axar's brow. The shifter was in such deep sleep, he didn't even stir. Perhaps that was for the better.

"We have to be patient so as not to disturb his mental state too much. I will say, the tonic did its part but Axar is still fighting the poison in his mind."

Progress. Even if very small, that was still progress. Zara kept repeating those words over and over again in her head as she placed the basket of sweet bread on the counter.

"These are for—for you and the other healers," she said, not looking directly at Ezrah. "I'm… I'm grateful for your kindness."

Her cheeks reddened. Fucking Suns. It wasn't often that people decided to *help* her and that she had to show her gratitude. She was usually the one to take care of herself and her loved ones.

Ezrah chuckled. "A mercenary feared across the Continent, but really, you are just a young woman fighting battles that were never your responsibility to begin with."

Zara met his gaze. The older archangel's eyes held warmth, and she was tempted to look away again.

"You know, I practically raised Ronan when his parents couldn't, and I can tell he is quite attached to you—he is *happier* than he was years ago, even with his past. A lot of that must be due to you," Ezrah said. He smiled.

She felt too exposed, like the softer shades of her soul were more brilliant than the dark, murky parts. Like her blackened heart still had worth.

Ezrah saved her from having to respond as he turned to Axar.

Zara went to stand at her brother's bedside. His cheeks were sallow, the skin under his eyes bruised with exhaustion. Yes, it was definitely better that he hadn't woken or seen her. Her presence would only hurt him.

"Keep your heart alight, little warrior," Ezrah said. "I know life has presented its challenges, but you are much stronger than you think."

Little warrior. A pang went through her chest at the familiar term of endearment. *I'm no warrior,* she wanted to respond, but a part of her was tired. Tired of fighting against the stubbornness that made her. The self-loathing, the doubt.

You are more.

Ezrah continued with a soft smile, "You look beautiful, by the way. Are you excited for this evening?"

Zara winced. She'd forgotten how she looked. Her face was painted like a skeleton, with gems and lines of black and white paint dotting her cheekbones, and her eyelids had been dabbed with red-orange powders, like the wings of a firebird. Zara's hair fell in dark curls down her back while a crown of orange blossoms sat on her head.

Her crimson two-piece gown was made of a buttery soft fabric and clung to her hips, with slits revealing her thighs as well as a sliver of midriff. Thin pieces of lace were woven into the outfit as it flowed down her arms and legs.

Apparently it was tradition to wear this for the Festival of the Three Suns.

"Soraya helped me with all this," Zara muttered, gesturing toward herself.

"Soraya saved the day, is what you meant to say." The érendira sauntered into the suite. "Be grateful I was merciful enough to help you prepare for the Festival and not kick you out."

"*Delgado,*" Ezrah chided.

"I tease!" She was dressed similarly to Zara, though in green-blue colors. The warrior looked Zara over, nodding her head in approval. "You are ready. Let's go, the parades have started."

Parades? It had been some time since Zara had been to or enjoyed any sort of holiday like this.

A warm presence knocked on her mental walls. Her lips twitched into a smile and she lowered those barriers.

Little wolf, where are you? I finished reviewing the security measures and I came to the palace to bring you some candies I thought you might like. Ronan released a dramatic sigh. *Oh well, I suppose I will eat them by myself.*

She couldn't fight the warmth that pooled in her chest. It was still odd to hear the archangel speak to her through their connection.

Soraya is about to take me into the city now. If you finish any of the sweets, I will throw you off the cliff.

A deep chuckle echoed through her mind. *I will see you at the Festival.*

Zara suddenly felt this fiery urge to defend and protect the new *home* she'd managed to find. She looked at her brother, fighting for his life, as thoughts swirled in her mind of the archangel with midnight wings who would cross the edges of this world for her. There were so many people relying on them, and the *Rogue* would do her best to save them.

The streets were teeming with citizens, many of whom were either wearing skeletal masks or had painted their faces as such. Some wore floral gowns and skirts that rippled with red and green ribbons, while others donned black suits with white collared shirts underneath.

Music swelled, the sound of violins, guitars, and trumpets echoing in the air. Various groups of fire and water ether dancers moved down the main street, musicians walking beside them while playing their instruments. Zara couldn't take her eyes away from the beauty of the world before her.

Soraya gripped her hand as they—and a group of the érendira—brushed through the edges of the crowd. The people were so pleasantly distracted by the parades, they paid no attention to her. And probably couldn't recognize her under all the makeup and colorful garb.

Soraya shouted over her shoulder. "We have to hurry or we'll miss it!"

Zara frowned. "Miss what? Where are we going?"

"It's a surprise!"

Zara wasn't sure if she liked the sound of that. They reached the central plaza, bordered by a spectating crowd.

The warrior tugged her arm and pointed ahead. "*Now* do you see?"

A group of males in dark suits stood among the crowd, designs of serpents and jaguars etched on their backs. There were archangels, shifters, elves, and humans—and even the occasional vampire. But only one among them called to her attention.

The one who always seemed to have her ether singing.

Ronan Menodora was dressed in the same black suit as the others, the pale etching of a feathered serpent across his back. Several plumes of his powerful wings were coated in an array of green, blue, and red dye. His face was elaborately painted as a skeleton's, silver swirls and whorls dancing along the edges of his temples and brow. Beside him, Orion was also dressed in similar attire, laughing boisterously at something an elven male said.

Soraya grasped Zara's shoulder. Suns, the érendira was strong, her grip almost making the mercenary wince. "There's an all-male dance popular within the guardian realms; Valenzia had it too—back when it was around. They express gratitude to their mothers and fathers, guardians, friends and loved ones."

Zara felt a pang of longing for the destroyed realm, her first home, even though she barely remembered anything of it.

"The male also makes a promise to love and protect the one they intend to spend their life with," Soraya added.

That should not have caused Zara's heart to skip the way it did. She tried to shrug it off. "Ronan never mentioned he would be performing."

"He wanted it to be a surprise." The érendira sounded amused.

As if he'd heard his name, Ronan looked their way, his grin faltering when his gaze landed on Zara.

The world surrounding them blurred. Colors twisted and morphed, nothing but the strands of music between them. Echoing the songs that rang in their hearts.

Ronan's eyes dropped, drinking in the sight of her. A spark ignited brighter and brighter in that gaze.

Zara Santos. His voice purred in her head, and she nearly sighed at the sound. *My ruthless beauty, the Suns and stars are nothing compared to you.*

She cocked her head as warmth spread through her chest. *His* emotion pouring into her. *Don't say words that could offend the gods.*

I am your blade, and I would cut through the veil for you. Ask me whether I care if I insult the Primordials.

Amusement danced on her lips. Even as this sensation that coiled and burned in her chest grew stronger.

Zara whispered through their connection. *You're beautiful, Ronan.*

The archangel nearly tripped and Orion caught him before he could fall. Soraya was looking between her and Ronan.

The érendira smirked. "Both of you need to give it up already and confess."

Zara jabbed a finger at the warrior's chest. "And *you* need to talk to Ronan about what you've been harboring all these years. He will understand."

Soraya blinked at her before averting her gaze. "I will."

A group of musicians began to play a new tune. Ronan—eyes still on Zara—bowed his head and moved in line with the other dancers.

Trumpets and violins resounded in the air, and the males clasped their hands behind their backs, beginning to move in tandem with one another. Their dark-slicked boots stomped the ground as they pivoted, tapping the tips of their shoes and then slamming their heels into the stone. Rows of dancers would veer to the right while another line moved to the left.

Everyone clapped to the rhythm of the music, cheering the males in the center. And Ronan—Ronan was *beaming*. His eyes were bright as he shared smiles with Orion and the others, as they swayed their hips and spun around. Zara couldn't help but move to the beat as well, a grin plastered to her face.

You look happy.

Ronan's silver eyes darted to her. *With you here, how can I not be?*

People cheered, throwing their hats in the air when the song ended with a blast of strings and brass. The noise pounded through her ribs all the way to her toes. Soraya and many of the érendira were clapping and whistling.

Ronan and Orion laughed, slinging their arms over each other's shoulders, and made their way toward them.

The music melted into something slower, swelling with a sense of longing and passion. Zara's heart nearly stopped when she realized what dance was next. She looked at Soraya with wide eyes and the érendira nearly burst into laughter.

"Is the mercenary nervous?"

"Yes," Zara hissed. "And I'm not ashamed to admit it."

Soraya patted her back. "Don't be. We've practiced the movements many times. I wasn't lying when I said you are quite a natural."

People started to couple up, heading to the dance floor. Before Zara could wipe the sweat gathering in her palms, Ronan extended a hand to her.

"Dance with me."

Her cheeks reddened but Zara let the archangel guide her out into the center of the plaza, and saw Orion taking a grinning Soraya's hand, too. Many eyes burned Zara's back. The atmosphere shifted, brimming with hostility and frustration. Ah. They had recognized her.

Ronan squeezed her hand. *Pay no attention to them. You deserve this joy just as much as them.*

He tugged her to his chest, his right hand resting on her waist. When Zara sank into the first stance, he raised an eyebrow.

"Are you familiar with this dance?"

A surge of confidence took hold—this was just another type of battle. Zara grinned, leaning forward. "It has become one of my favorites."

Ronan gave her a curious look as the song began with the rhythmic clap of the bongos. Guitars strummed a melody that made her think of sparrows flying, of colorful banners fluttering in the wind, and the smell of flowers and sweet fruit.

As one, Zara and Ronan dove into the dance. She fell into that three-step count, giving a gentle sway of her hips at the third step before repeating the movement in the opposite direction. The archangel mirrored her, his midnight wings swishing in the air.

Every breath was controlled as her body recalled Soraya's training. A thrill gathered in her limbs and her heart jumped in time with the music.

Ronan's breath hitched. "You've been *practicing*. Now I know where you've been running off to these past days."

Zara couldn't help but laugh. "Soraya taught me. How am I doing so far?"

His hand drifted to her lower back, pressing her even closer to him. The comfort and power of his presence fell over her like a blanket, softening the tension that had been bracketing up her spine. Hakim and Eshe's deaths didn't hit her now. Didn't send her crashing to her knees. The ache had shifted to a quiet throb. She could tend to it, face it. Zara wanted to rest her head against his chest—but stopped herself, aware of the eyes on them.

Ronan's low voice felt like an unseen finger trailing down her skin. "Anything you do is perfect to me, though I will say you are doing *very* well. Now allow me to take control."

His painted wings unfurled to their full length and Zara followed the call of the music, letting Ronan twist them around and guide her into a spin. She had done this a few times with the érendira, but with him it yanked another type of emotion from her. A visceral sensation that had her heart squeezing.

Orange flower petals floated in the air, drifting over their clothes and kissing the sweat on their skin. Ronan spun her out before having her twirl back into his arms. As the music deepened, they clung to one another. Tighter and tighter. Zara melted further into the archangel's touch, even as her feet began to burn. Ronan dipped his head, pressing his temple against hers.

They didn't speak. They didn't need to. Not when their movements spoke for them. Not as each brush of their fingers echoed every desire, every promise that ached day by day.

"I'm proud of you," Ronan said suddenly. He pulled back enough for her to see the dusted starlight in his eyes.

"For what?"

The archangel picked the flowers off her head, his fingertips trailing down her jaw. Their movements had slowed. "A while ago, you told me you liked to dance but never had the opportunity to do it. Now here you are, dancing in front of everyone, and looking breathtaking."

The back of Zara's eyes burned. Her past had been ridden with steel and blood, never allowing her to believe she could have anything else. But here she was, having moved from dancing on the blades to swaying in the breeze of the forgotten jungles.

The music had ended but the melody was still soaring between their hearts. Ronan placed a hand over his chest and bowed to her.

If you will, my Horizon, he said through their connection. *There's something I'd like to show you.*

Trails paved through the jungle, leading them to grand statues of the Three Sun Gods. The Primordial of Life, Genesis, had her hands extended as if to receive prayer, while Aspidis and Mikatán had their gazes fixated on the golden sunset.

Orange blossoms filled the base of the statues, people dropping their own flowers to join the rest. Many lowered their heads, either whispering to themselves or kissing the petals.

Ronan stood behind Zara, bending to speak to her. "This is one of many sites of remembrance. It is not so much to honor the gods, but to pay respects to those who have passed on."

More paths weaved through the trees, lined with lit braziers. Jaguars prowled through the bushes, people murmuring to each other and praying, though no one paid attention to them.

Zara understood then why the archangel had brought her, Orion and Soraya here. She eyed the bouquet of flowers in his tattooed hand.

Ronan plucked a blossom and gave it to her. "Honor your family. You need not say anything, if you wish—this moment is only for you and them."

Golden light gilded the male's wings and dark hair. Zara may have stared at him longer than appropriate in public. But she didn't care. No, she didn't care at all. Ronan was giving her the opportunity to properly mourn Hakim and Eshe. She hadn't had the chance to do that before.

Orion swiped the bundle of flowers and Soraya gave one of them to Ronan.

"Same goes for you, Your Majesty," she said. "It's the first time you've celebrated the Festival in years. You can honor your family's memory too."

It was the first time Zara saw the érendira giving Ronan a soft smile. A sad one.

The archangel stared at the elf in shock. Zara shot Soraya a grateful look, before tugging on Ronan's sleeve.

"Let's go."

They approached the base of the statues. Zara lifted her gaze to Mikatán. Since the Oasis, she hadn't visited the god in her dreams, nor had he reached out to her. Maybe he was giving her time to consider their last conversation.

To find a deity who could be a Warden, capable of opening portals to other worlds. To decide whether or not she would pursue the Crossing or *lose* her ether forev—

No. None of that now. This moment was for her. For her family.

A salted wind kissed her face and she closed her eyes.

"Thank you," she whispered. "For the strength you gave me. I love you. And I miss you—*so* much."

Zara kissed one of the petals, letting the blossom float to the statues' feet. She wished Axar were here to do this with her. Next time, maybe. Something tightened in her chest.

Hakim and Eshe would continue to live through them. Through every teardrop, every roar of laughter. They would never leave, even now that they'd walked across the veil. Her family's love stretched beyond the sun and stars. Beyond time. And their sacrifice wouldn't be in vain, not as long as she kept fighting the shadows that plagued this world.

Zara would be the steel of these lands, even if they didn't want her. She'd be vengeance made flesh.

Ronan gazed at the sky, beads of silver forming at the corner of his eyes. A soft smile touched his lips as he held the flower to his chest and let it go.

Grief took many forms; sometimes it became claws or fangs. Yet it was also the gentle rain on a spring day, or the warm fires on a winter's night. But it always came from something real, worthwhile. Love.

After Soraya and Orion had made their own offerings, they all started to make their way back to the capital, when a screech shredded through the sky.

A golden eagle tumbled through the tree branches above. Blood spilled from its torso in vicious slashes as the creature swayed and banked... toward *Ronan*. Bystanders fled in time before the animal crashed to the ground, near the archangel's feet.

Gashes lined the eagle's hide, wounds too large to have come from any mortal. Zara's blood chilled.

The creature heaved, each breath a rattle of bones. Its eyes honed in on Ronan, even as the light within dimmed.

Ronan touched its beak. "The eagle knew it wouldn't survive—it came to me as a warning."

"A warning?" Orion tensed. "Our soldiers are stationed throughout the region, there's been no sign—"

Screams broke out as people began running and stumbling back to the city. Zara twisted around, her hand flying to her back to—nothing. Fuck. None of them had their weapons.

There was little time to think, especially when hordes of specters began to spill out of the jungle.

SIXTY-TWO

A shadow fell over Daria. She shut her eyes, expecting to feel jaws clamp around her body. Wind knocked her onto her backside, and when she looked up, a giant, dark figure was snatching the demon from the air before it could reach her.

Every limb in Daria's body froze at the sight of a four-legged beast with the head of a crocodile and feathered wings, twice the size of the demon. Arzhel had told her of this creature, the dragons' natural enemy. A *cipactli*.

The demon's squeals raked the air, but its cries were cut short as the cipactli chomped down on it. Daria flinched at the wrenching of flesh, the shattering of bone. Gore spilled down onto the ground as the crocodile-eagle-hybrid flew over the clearing, tossing the lifeless demon up and into its throat. She clambered away to avoid the splash.

What was a cipactli doing here? This safe haven had been created due to the constant battles between these very creatures and the dragons.

The cipactli suddenly turned and angled lower, diving straight for her.

"*Suns Above.*"

Daria tore into the trees behind her, sprinting farther away from the mountain she had emerged from, her bag rattling against her back.

She wished she had the time to mark her whereabouts—so she would at least know how to get home.

The cipactli bellowed. It soared above the trees, its shadow blocking out the light. The beast was hunting her. If she could somehow shake it off her trail…

There was no time to plan or even think as the creature crashed into the trees, swiping its claws through the branches, trying to reach her. Daria bit her lips to hold back her cries.

The beast shoved its long snout down through the canopies. Rows and rows of teeth aimed right at her. Daria flung out a beam of flames toward its jaws, and the cipactli reared back, roaring in pain.

The momentum—and the sheer fear running through her body—had Daria flailing out of the treeline and crashing onto smooth ground. She pushed herself to her feet but stopped at the edge of a cliff.

Suns Above. Suns Above. Suns Above.

Daria breathed heavily. It was so hard to fight the terrible, terrible thought that this might be the end.

The cipactli landed on the ground, its rumbles vibrating through the dirt and her ribcage. Unable to back up any farther, she was forced to watch as the creature prowled toward her, its thick tail sweeping across the grass, knocking some trees over.

"I realize I am quite at a disadvantage," Daria breathed out, fire forming between her hands. "But you are a fool if you think I'd just give up."

The beast snapped its jaws and charged for her.

Her flames billowed out like wings as she let them surge forward, releasing all the ether left in her veins. The cipactli screeched and clawed at the fire. The beast pushed through it, its teeth close enough to get her.

The smell of burnt hide filled her nostrils, causing her stomach to churn. Daria couldn't falter now. She couldn't give up.

Something flew up over the edge of the cliff behind her. Wings unfurled, swallowing the sky. Daria kept her hands steady, willing the ether to keep going, and too scared to look up. If this was some other animal ready to make her its next meal, then maybe she'd take her chances off the cliff—

A dragon with crimson scales hovered in the air, its sun-colored eyes on the cipactli. The creature opened its maws as ruby light swelled within its scaled chest.

Daria felt the heat before it happened and ducked her head as a torrent of fire blasted out from the dragon's jaws. Flames that were larger, hungrier than hers, folded over her ether. Devoured her power, washing over the cipactli.

The feathered reptile pushed off the ground, screeching from the burns and ramming itself against its opponent. The dragon dug its ebony claws into the creature's hide, whipping at the cipactli's underbelly with its dagger-tail.

Daria's flames withered out as the strength was sucked out of her body, and she fell to her knees. The cliff trembled as the dragon pinned the creature to the ground, prying its mouth open to blow another beam of fire into it.

The cipactli was burned from the inside out, its body convulsing several times before going slack. Dead.

Daria shuddered, but stilled when the dragon turned to face her. Horns reached out from its diamond-shaped head, a smaller pair extending out just beneath. Scales rippled in various shades of crimson down to a deep red-black, and light spilled through the velvety skin of its wings, revealing ruby veins along them. Sharp frills carved a line down its long neck, before shifting into spikes all the way down to its dagger-shaped tail.

Daria's heart thrummed. It was as if the voices from the obsidian throne came back, reminding her that she had seen these scales before. That this dragon had appeared before Daria already. Maybe the sealing power within the throne had been trying to tell her all along who would come to her.

"Thank—thank you." Her lips were dry as she rasped the words out.

The dragon said nothing. Its golden eyes roved over her, as if she were a foreign, unknown creature. In a manner of speaking, Daria could say she was.

Smoke curled from its nostrils before the dragon slunk off the edge of the cliff, taking flight. *Leaving* her.

"*Wait!* Please, I beg you!" Daria reached a hand out. "I need to speak with you—"

There was a loud crack and she looked down. The weight of the two giant beasts fighting had fractured the stone of the cliff. A big chunk of rock broke off, taking Daria and the lifeless cipactli along with it.

Her screams burned her throat, the forest below rushing up toward her.

This was the end. Not the cipactli. Not the demon. Daria was going to die falling off a *rock*.

She was swept up mid-air, the air punching out of her lungs. Her hands met a smooth and rough texture. Daria didn't realize she had closed her eyes until she tried to peel them open.

A claw. She was sitting in a large, very sharp claw. The crimson dragon had returned, saving her from falling to her death.

Its grip was surprisingly gentle.

A voice rumbled. "*You are far away from home, elven queen.*"

His voice. A deep timbre that was undeniably male echoed from the dragon's unmoving mouth, similar to how shifters spoke. It was neither old nor young.

Daria glanced down and shrieked, seeing just how high they were. She wrapped her arms tighter around the dragon's talon. "*You left me!* You left me and you were going to let me die!"

"*I came back, did I not?*" The dragon almost sounded *annoyed*. "*I couldn't leave you, anyway. I think… I think I've been waiting for you.*"

Daria breathed through her nostrils. His words tugged on her heart. "You called me *elven queen*. Do you know who I am?

"*I can smell the obsidian crown in your bag. Unless you are a thief— though I cannot imagine you'd have been able to pass through the seal if you were.*"

"You knew I had entered this place."

The dragon flapped its great wings. "*I am the Guardian of the Dragon's Teeth. I was charged to sense whenever anyone passes through the seal.*"

Arzhel's words rang out in her head. This was the dragon she had been searching for. The one who had protected this safe haven throughout the years. Of course, he would be the first she came across.

"Aladaer," Daria murmured. The dragon tensed. Her heart thundered. "Son of Kaigen, the Last Dragon. I've been looking for you. My name is Daria Calderón."

Aladaer was silent for a moment. "*I will take you to our den, Daria Calderón. It seems we have much to discuss.*"

He took a sharp turn, angling down. She swallowed the bile that threatened to lurch up her throat, gripping onto the dragon, but the terror quickly fled when she saw the sprawling canyons and forest below.

Sparks of green, blue, and yellow sailed past and below them. Roars that were deep and fierce, like twisted thunderstorms, pounded through her bones.

Dragons. So many of them, flying and winding around the canyons. Gleaming gems with large powerful wings. They were *here*.

Daria couldn't stop the tears from flowing.

SIXTY-THREE

Specters tore through Teotlan. Their half-morphed bodies—mortals with horns and claws, some even with tails—ravaged buildings, uprooting statues and fountains in the public square. Zara noticed the creatures that had been sent here were not fully-fledged specters. She wasn't sure if that was a good thing.

Citizens sprinted through the streets, making their way to the far-end of the city or into nearby buildings. They avoided the imperial soldiers' path as the warriors rushed to meet the specters. The Damalisans had been preparing for this moment.

Zara sailed through the air. The sky above her darkened with gray clouds, and the smell of smoke reached her nostrils as flames erupted from the destruction. She leaped from rooftop to rooftop, cutting down specters with her ether. Slit bone and burnt flesh ricocheted from the arc of her light.

Ronan and Orion charged toward the jungle. If the specters had managed to get this far into the guardian realm, then there must have been greater forces throughout the territory, where many of the imperial soldiers were stationed.

Soraya whistled for Kenzo, swinging herself onto the jaguar before diving toward the other side of the capital.

Ether surged out in a flood of red and purple. Zara blasted her power along the plaza, incinerating any specters clambering up the walls. The fabric of her skirt had already ripped, the floral crown upon her head having long disintegrated, blossoms stuck to the strands of her hair.

A young family was racing out of the plaza, the children crying and holding onto their parents, specters nipping at their heels. Zara summoned a blade, the red-purple light heating the air beside her face, and landed on the stone between the people and the creatures.

Zara maneuvered the blade through the horde, slashing a specter's abdomen. She leaped away to evade another's attack while thrusting her weapon through the gut of a third. Her heartbeat was a drum in her ears, and every breath burned.

She let go of her makeshift sword, sweeping out her light, letting it grow, grow, grow. The ether plunged forward, swallowing the specters in its path, as the Damalisan soldiers picked through the remaining creatures.

Basim emerged beside Zara, covering her blind spots. The wolf's voice was a welcome warmth in the chaos.

More are coming from the jungle.

Zara nodded, breaking the control of her ether to duck from an incoming sword. She swept out her leg and knocked the ethereal warrior off its feet before jamming a light dagger into its throat. Basim pounced on a charging specter before its metal teeth could reach her, tearing it apart, and his fangs dripped with black blood and saliva.

What Zara didn't know was how she must have looked to the people of Damalis in those moments. The mercenary who had slain so many of their own was now *defending* them, going against the High Throne, no longer its weapon. A blazing shard of crimson, flecked with purple—like the dawn. A warrior and her wolf, her nahual.

They slayed the last of the horde, and Zara's ether-made weapons dissipated. She gasped for breath, legs shaking slightly, her amplified power still taking its toll on her. *This may sound odd, but this battalion of specters wasn't that strong.*

Basim licked his chops. *Not only that but their numbers weren't anywhere near enough to overwhelm the Damalisan soldiers.*

More battles were still being fought throughout the capital. Imperial soldiers and érendira alike facing their own bands of specters. Massive jaguars charged through the streets, pinning many of the ethereal beasts to the ground with their fangs and killing them.

Archangels could be seen diving from the sky to join in the various fights.

This was a strategic decision, Zara said. *More is coming.*

Basim growled. *You need to find the archangel. The two of you cannot be separated.*

Rain suddenly started to fall. Muddied water and blood already pooling near her shoes. She brought a hand to her face as the droplets smeared the paint on her face, dark and red streaks running down her cheeks.

The sky was shifting at an unnatural pace. One of the Spirits was here.

Someone screamed. Zara ran toward the sound, her body moving before she could even think.

Specters were attacking a blacksmith's shop that faced the mouth of the jungle. People were screaming from inside—citizens who had tried to find a safe place to hide.

Zara narrowed her eyes, allowing the red light to crackle over her body again. Smoke curled from her skin, and she was sent flying across the distance, appearing in front of the specters.

The creatures startled, before snarling and lunging at her.

She summoned a double-edged spear, sweeping them off the ground. Light flared as she twisted to jab a specter, wrenching through its scales to meet flesh and bone. One of the creatures smacked the weapon from her grasp, the blade disappearing in broken shards of ether.

It punched Zara's torso, yanking all the air from her lungs. She sucked in a sharp breath before surging forward to grab the specter by its horns and jamming her knee into its face.

They are less strong than their fully-transformed counterparts, she said to Basim. *But they are still very irritating.*

Her nahual grappled with another, chomping through its neck until black gushed out onto the grass. *And they taste horrible.*

A dry chuckle escaped her. Zara killed the last of the specters, relishing in her temporary victory. She tipped her head back as the rain pelted her hair and face even harder. Clouds of red energy billowed out from her lips, power still thrumming through her veins.

The people in the blacksmiths' shop slowly emerged, their gazes on her. Zara stilled. They were watching her with an odd *light* in their eyes that she couldn't name. A small boy bowed his head to her, thanking her softly, which prompted the others to do the same.

Fear and hatred had always followed her throughout her life. This was different.

Zara slid her gaze to a figure emerging from the jungle. The general of the Damalisan Imperial soldiers, Elder Riyad. The elven male wore midnight blue armor with shards of emerald green; cuts sliced through the steel along his shoulders, while various bloodstains had blossomed along his body. But the elf held himself tall, seemingly unbothered by the wounds.

Riyad watched her with an unreadable expression as he approached, glancing over at the people. Zara braced herself for some kind of admonishment or threat.

"Thank you, Horizon," he said, instead, meeting her eyes.

Zara let out a rough exhale. She definitely hadn't expected that.

She stared at him for a moment. "Riyad… The elven male you mentioned back when we first met—the one I killed. He had a human girl alongside him—" Her brows furrowed, "He was my uncle. Raziel told me so."

The Elder's eyes widened. "He was my cousin—had no children of his own. If he was your uncle… then you must be his *sister's* child. Are you… Thalia's daughter?"

Zara sucked in a sharp breath. The name stirred something within her memories; it yanked and pulled, but was unable to reveal what rested beneath.

"I recognize that name," she murmured.

"That makes you my niece." Riyad took another step before hesitating. "Do you know where Thalia is?"

Emotions flashed across the male's face. Zara could make out grief, disbelief and… hope.

Her hands twitched at her sides. "She's dead."

Riyad slowly shook his head. "Are you sure? We—we never found a body."

"*Yes*, I'm sure. I would know what happened to my—" The words caught in Zara's throat.

She stared at the elf, her vision blurring. Her memories of the War were broken fragments. Chunks of darkness and red skies. Roars that shook the ground and mountains.

Zara remembered hiding between the statues of the Primordials, clinging to the God of Death's feet. That was when her pater, Idris Calderón, had found her. Had there not been someone else with her before that? Someone with dark hair and a gentle voice…

More cries from Damalisan soldiers echoed into the sky and they both jumped. The sounds stopped. Nothing but the pounding rain answered. Until one of the Spirits emerged from the jungle. Zara's fists tightened.

It moved as quietly as a shadow. It was different from the one that had attacked them in the mining city. A hood was draped over its bronze skeletal face, a scythe strapped to its back. A crown of silver fire burning bright on its head.

Twin fiery blades formed in Zara's hands. She angled herself in front of the elf and the other Damalisans. "I trust that you can escort these people to safety, Elder Riyad?"

He nodded warily, his eyes on the Spirit. "We will finish our conversation later, mercenary."

Her answer was a grunt, and Riyad slipped into his role as general, beckoning the people to follow his lead.

Zara prowled from side to side as she kept her gaze on the ethereal warrior. "I assume you are here for me?"

The Spirit unsheathed its scythe, the steel whipping soundlessly through the rain. It ran a gloved finger along the edge of the blade. *"Daughter of the Dawn. On behalf of the Fallen, I come to warn you."*

A voice as powerful and deep as the sea. It made her think of the cosmos, and the darkness between the stars and moon. Zara felt her knees tremble, though she did not fall.

"Save your warnings for someone who cares."

"The Daughter of the Dawn has grown cocky." The warrior sank into a fighting stance. *"But she is a mortal like the rest, nothing else."*

The Spirits were more than the creatures who wrought the end of the world. More than simple creations of Khaos.

The world exploded in red light and rain as they collided. Zara's blades hissed at every contact with the warriors's scythe. It was a force greater than any man's, stronger than any ether she had encountered.

The Spirit slid the face of the scythe down her weapons before striking her in the gut with its boot. Zara sailed through the air and slammed into a tree, chunks of bark flying off, and pain exploding along her whole body, her swords having winked out.

She fell into mud, surrounded by the thick jungle. The sound of birds and wildlife stopped. It was darker now, the rain splattering loudly on the canopies above. The smell of damp wood and sweet flowers was strong, though it was unable to distract from the heavy energy that came charging her way.

The Spirit raised the scythe over its head. Zara thrust out slashes of ether but the warrior cut through them, devouring the distance between them.

She scrambled out of the way and began scaling a tree. The mossy wood was slippery beneath her feet, though the adrenaline pulsating through her veins pushed her to keep moving.

Zara threw her power against the ethereal warrior as she jumped between the massive branches. It was Junya's Hunt, she realized, her body falling into muscle memory, as the Spirit chased her through the tree branches.

It was relentless, toying with her. Not taking this duel with her seriously. It caught up and grabbed her arm.

"*The Fallen is merciful, for he is giving you the opportunity to make a decision.*"

Zara cried out when the Spirit threw her down onto the jungle floor. The muscles in her body screamed as she landed on her stomach, and her ether flickered. She crawled away from the creature as it landed near her, clawing at the dirt before pressing her back against the trunk of a tree.

"What decision?" She spat out a wad of blood.

The Spirit stalked toward her and forced her to her feet, gripping onto her arm. Those endless eyes staring right through her.

"*The destruction you witnessed today is nothing but a shred of what the High Throne intends to do with the realm if you do not abide by their demands. We only need one of you.*" It tilted its head, the hood still draped over the bronze of his face. "*And I would be very curious to see what would happen if it were you.*"

Zara clenched her teeth, ether forming around her. "You only need *one* of us? For what?" She hadn't sensed or seen Ronan. Where was he? Had they taken him?

Blue light crashed in between them, and she was ripped away from the Spirit's hold and tucked against a solid chest. This ether was not hers; it crackled and popped, humming through the air.

Black wings unfurled and she met Ronan's gaze through the pounding rain and blazing light. He sent a glare toward the Spirit, a wicked blade of blue ether in his hand.

"Your forces here have been killed off," the archangel said through gritted teeth. "Consider your terms received."

The Spirit took a step back. "*Heed my warning, godlings. The Fallen has amassed the High Throne's armies in the bordering lands of Damalis as we speak. We will raze the guardian realm to the ground. Surrender, or throw your own forces into the fray to die. It does not matter to us.*"

The rain began to lessen. The ethereal warrior sheathed its scythe, sweeping a gloved hand down in a low arc. Fire hissed to life at its command.

"*The first phase of the end is done. Rain is now silenced,*" it said, "*Now the fires will begin.*"

The Spirit disappeared in a flash of light, leaving a ring of singed grass and dirt. Zara's heart pounded. Water had been the first stage of the end. Next was fire. So anytime the Spirits of the Midnight Sun appeared now, they would bring *flames*.

Strength seeped from her limbs and she nearly went slack in Ronan's arms. He tightened his hold on her.

Zara met his gaze. His face paint had been smeared by rain and blood. The archangel brushed her cheek with his thumb as he landed with a squelch on the muddy ground.

"Are you hurt?" Ronan's voice was ragged.

Zara shook her head. "I was worried about you."

He cupped the back of her head and pressed his brow against hers. His lips inches away. As they stood in the growing darkness, beneath the shield of trees where lingering droplets fell, she still felt warm. Safe.

"The thought of them taking you away from me," Ronan whispered. The light in his eyes cracked. "It terrifies me, Zara."

She sank into his touch, pressing her lips to his. He let out a sound of surprise before deepening the kiss, his hands cradling her face, groaning in a mix of relief and need. Feeling him here, right now, this beautiful warrior who always found his way to her side—it anchored her. And Zara would blaze the ends of this Continent to be at his.

Later, after washing and tending to her wounds, Zara went to the war room. The Elders argued for hours about what to do now that the High Throne's armies had been confirmed to be approaching the heart of Damalis. Apparently, while the attack in the capital was happening, Elios soldiers and specters had fought several of the imperial forces stationed along the borders.

Elios had sent some of its specters to weaken and scare Damalis, and distract it from the main army marching through the valley of the guardian realm.

The capital of Teotlan had taken significant damage, but only in a certain quadrant of the city—which could only be credited to the imperial soldiers and the érendiras' fighting skills. Healers were tending to the injured as they spoke.

Taraji, the head of the Elders, discussed reconstruction and rehabilitation efforts with Ezrah, while Orion and Soraya debated battle tactics.

Riyad was uncharacteristically silent, his gaze drifting to Zara from time to time. She didn't have time for that, her mind racing with what had occurred during the battle, especially the Spirit's warning.

The memories of the city up in flames flashed through her mind again. She had witnessed this before. Her Primordial power had shown what would happen, and it came to pass. And she hadn't done anything to change it.

The mental door must have been slightly open because Ronan's gaze jerked up to hers.

"I will go," Zara said. The others around the war table fell silent, their gazes on her. "They want one of us for our powers, and it can't be the King of Damalis. Send me to create a diversion; I am sure you can concoct a plan to drive the Elios forces back."

"Absolutely *not*! They want to *separate* us, and gods know what they'll do to the one they take." Blue mist swept out from Ronan's wings. He glared—a look he had never directed at *her* before.

No, that wasn't right. She *had* seen it before. In a vision.

"Better it be me, than you."

The archangel kept his gaze on her as he commanded the rest of the room. "Leave us. *Now.*"

SIXTY-FOUR

Daria had stood before assemblies of diplomats and politicians, before elves and archangels and vampires, before allies and enemies who wanted her dead—and now she stood before *dragons*. The den was a big gash within a canyonside, a small waterfall beside its entrance pouring into a large pool. Nests were spread out on various plateaus and ledges inside the cave.

Dragons watched her from wherever they were perched, large eyes with slitted pupils focused on her. The deep flap of their wings or the trills from beneath their scales were enough to rattle Daria's bones.

Aladaer stood in front of the others, his hide a wave of flames under the golden light. *"Much has changed in the Continent of Ribera. Rebelling deities, a corrupted High Throne, and the rise of specters and Spirits led by Primordial Khaos. Now Ikarria is under siege and you wish for us to fight for you."*

She had informed the majestic beasts of what had been happening, every word like a weight on her tongue. Daria looked about their haven. Water rushed outside, birds chirped in the distance, the smell of wood and sweet fruits thick in the air. Suns, there were even eggs in some of the nests.

"I know I am being selfish with this request, and I don't blame you for your hesitation to join me." Daria's expression softened. "This place has been your home for a hundred years—I wouldn't want to leave it either."

Arzhel had made that final request of her, had he not? To not force the dragons to leave their haven. And she wouldn't, but circumstances had become too dire for her to do nothing.

The crimson dragon was analyzing her. Had been for some time now. *"You want us to return, but you did not mention the bonds. The late King Arzhel abolished those connections in order to spare us the urge to find a rider while here. Do you wish to rekindle them?"*

"I would leave that choice to all of you," Daria said. "I understand it is a significant binding, and not to be taken lightly."

Aladaer snorted. *"It is more than a binding, elven queen. It would make us yearn to align ourselves with an Ikarrian whose soul echoes with our own. To bond with a rider means to tie our lives—and deaths—together."*

Daria nodded; she had read many passages about the ancient phenomenon. A question probed her mind.

"So the lifespan of the rider is connected to that of their dragon, correct? For as long as the dragon lives, so does their rider. If either one of them dies, then the other would perish, too."

"You are aware of it. Good. Then you understand what this new age could bring to your kingdom."

Daria sucked in a breath. "Are you considering my proposal then?"

Aladaer looked over to the other dragons in question. Their booming voices suddenly filled the cavern, questions and concerns ricocheting up the stone walls.

A purple dragon swept down from somewhere above, landing beside Aladaer. *"While I favor the thought of finding my rider, we must consider how this will affect us in the long-term. Our way of life has changed this past century, and so has life in Ribera."*

Aladaer grunted. *"I was told long ago that our kind would return to the mortal world, and I would understand when the time came. The shift in the veil and the arrival of our elven queen here are no mere coincidences."*

"The cipactli have been appearing more often recently."

The red dragon grunted. "*Yes. I was hunting one earlier today, and that is how I found Daria. She was fighting the creature.*"

Daria wasn't quite sure what the dragons were talking about, but the last part was received with curious rumbles and—and maybe approval. That she had been fighting the demon? She felt a flare of embarrassment. It was more Daria flailing and running away from the crocodile-eagle-hybrid in a screeching panic than an actual fight.

She stepped forward. "'Shift in the veil'—does that have anything to do with how the cipactli managed to enter this place?"

The red dragon paced before her, every heavy step causing her stomach to flip. "*We felt a rift in the ether sometime ago—as if it were agitated. Then those beasts started to show. I suspect that something, or someone, made it possible for them to cross into this world.*"

It was similar to how the specters had started entering the Continent. Maybe there was a relation between the two. Dread pooled in Daria's stomach at the thought.

The dragons hadn't given her an answer. It was understandable, given the potential danger involved, and she wouldn't press. Daria had been allowed to spend the night in their den on an empty ledge in the corner of the massive cave, had washed herself in the pool and eaten what was left in her travel bag. Daria's body quivered with exhaustion, but sleep still evaded her. Even well into the night.

Stars shined brightly here, brighter than in the world she knew. The sky was also different. Constantly rippling, like gentle waves.

Daria pushed herself up from the bedroll. Many of the scaled beasts watched her leave, and she stifled a shiver at the sight of their large teeth.

She exited the cave and climbed to the top of the canyon, her body warm and sweaty from exertion. Sleep was definitely out of the question now.

"How's the night watch?"

Aladaer was curled along the stone, his red tail swaying gently over the edge. *"Quiet, for now."*

She went to sit near his front claws, looking out over the expanse of trees and mountains. "It's incredible how King Arzhel managed such a feat: a pathway to a foreign world where your kind could heal and repopulate."

"Aye, and it is no ordinary feat to be able to reach this place. You must have made some sacrifices for you to find the seal and use it."

The dragon's gaze was heavy on her. Daria swallowed. "I take it you are aware of the Primordial contract Arzhel made?"

Aladaer gave a slow nod of his large head. *"The obsidian throne would eventually speak to the rightful heir who is meant to find us."*

"My ancestor did a fine job hiding his secrets. For me to even find out what the voices in the throne were, I had to… I had to make a difficult decision."

The dragon was silent as she told him about the necromancy spell. How she would be cursed for defying the natural order.

"You went through all of that to find us?" Aladaer's voice was soft. Curious. Like he was trying to understand her in a deeper, meaningful way.

Daria looked up just as the dragon lowered his head enough so she could meet him at eye level.

She smiled, even though there was a heaviness behind it. Even though her heart couldn't rise as high as it had in the past. "I had to. My home and my people need me."

A slitted pupil lingered on her. *"Tell me more about you, Queen of Ikarria."*

"Where would you like me to begin?"

"How about your father? You mentioned he was taken by the High Throne—do you know how he is faring?"

Daria pulled her knees up to her chest. "As far as we know, he is still alive, but with all that's happened, I don't know how long—" Her lips thinned. No, she couldn't think about that. "I intend to save him, after we've freed Ikarria."

Aladaer made a rumbling sound. *"Your father must have treated you well for you to love him so."*

"Yes, he did his best raising me and my sister alone, all while leading a realm."

"You have a sister. What's her name?"

"Zara," Daria said warmly. "We aren't blood-related—she originally came from Valenzia—but, we are sisters in every way that matters."

"Valenzia, the lost guardian realm… I feel like there is much more to the story."

"Well, we have all night."

They spoke for what felt like ages. Daria told him more about her life, about the ongoing conflicts with the High Throne. Aladaer did not share much about himself; the dragon seemed more interested in learning about her, for whatever reason. But she was fine with that.

Then an explosion sounded in the air. Flocks of large birds with spear-pointed beaks fluttered out from the trees. And deep roars answered.

Aladaer lifted his head as Daria scrambled to her feet. Her gaze fixated ahead. "What is that?"

Silver light flared in the distance, ether sparkling on the horizon and crawling up the sky like the electrified roots of a tree. Shadows moved in the forest below it.

The crimson dragon got to his feet. *"I will scope the area."*

"Wait! Take me with you." Daria waved her hands at him before he could leave her. *Again.* "I need to know what's happening here too."

Aladaer snorted, sliding his front leg forward and lowering himself to the ground. *"I will take you… if you can make it onto my back."*

Her heart lurched. Daria gulped and started climbing up the tough hide of scales. She slipped, his leg offering no purchase for her to hold onto, and she nearly fell off.

"I'll pretend I didn't notice that poor attempt."

Daria gritted her teeth and pulled herself back up. She slid down once more.

"You want to be a dragon rider, do you not?

"If you could keep your thoughts to yourself, that'd be lovely," she growled.

The muscles in her legs burned and the skin of her palms were torn by the time she reached the space between the tall frills and spikes on his back. There was a smooth patch, as if designed to be a seat.

Aladaer sounded amused. *"It's about time you arrived."*

"You need a ladder or a rope!"

"I think not." He shifted his body weight and slowly rose to his full height. Daria yelped, her stomach flipping over. Suns Above. *"The dragon riders of Old never needed such trivial items."*

She reached for the stem of a frill, large and strong enough for her to hold on to.

"What if I fall off?"

"Then you would die."

Great.

"No need to worry, though."

As Aladaer spoke, a ripple of energy swept down the valley of his back. Daria could feel a weight fasten her to him. She could still move freely but an invisible shield secured her to him so she wouldn't fall off.

"You could still fall if you don't hold on. It is only once a Rider becomes bonded to a dragon that our ether provides a layer of protection to the mortal. While they may still feel the wind, nothing will get into their eyes and they won't be immediately thrown off when their dragon takes to the air. You and I are not bonded, though I can still lend you some of my ether."

"Right." Daria drew in a deep breath, steadying her nerves. "Makes sense."

With a powerful beat of his wings, Aladaer pushed off the cliff. The world dropped below them and Daria clung onto him, surprised to feel the gentle weight of his power holding her close. Wind whistled in her ears, though nothing went into her eyes or altered her vision.

Aladaer climbed and the sudden incline and the awe of the moment caused her grip to loosen. Daria gasped and was thrown off her seat. She cried out, palms sliding against the scales on his back as she tried to grab onto him again. Somehow she mercifully missed the horns that protruded from his spine and spiraled toward the forest below.

"Help me!"

The dragon swerved around, diving low to catch her, and Daria landed on his back with a loud grunt.

"Honestly, I just said that you need to hold on or you could still fall."

She pressed a palm to her chest in an attempt to calm her racing heart, this time gripping the ridges. "Well, pardon me. It is not like I *fly regularly.*"

Aladaer's ether wrapped tighter around her, keeping her firmly on his back. *"Be careful."*

Daria could sense his concern and fought back a smile. The dragon flew into the night, surrounded by trees and darkness. She felt like she could reach the stars, run a finger in the ink above.

Aladaer soared toward the silvery light that still flared up into the sky.

Her grip on him tightened. It wasn't the sky the ether was climbing up, but a *veil*, extending out in both directions, with the same strange ripple she'd noticed earlier on the entrance wall.

"Is the safe haven bordered all around by this?"

Aladaer grunted. *"Yes, this world is connected to another, and the veil prevents us from wandering any farther. And it keeps whatever lives beyond it out. Though, as you know, some creatures have still managed to get through."* He flapped his wings, veering closer to the border. *"I had never seen that flare of light before. "*

Daria's eyes widened. "There's something moving on the other side." Shadows with glowing, cerulean eyes. She couldn't see them properly but their bodies were twisted and distorted in an array of forms. Horns, wings, tails, pointed ears.

"Aladaer." Her voice wavered. "Those are specters. Fully-transformed specters. There are so many of them. What are they doing?"

A rumble echoed from the dragon's throat. *"They're marching. Those are armies, Queen Calderón."*

"I thought the specters were from Celestrea. Is the world on the other side—"

"No, that is not Celestrea. It is another plane that exists within the fabric of this universe; the specters must be walking between worlds."

How was such a thing possible? Daria's mind was buzzing. It would have explained the explosion and the flares of light: maybe the armies had tried to force their way into this plane.

Flying above the specters were feathered beasts with long snouts—

"Cipactli," Aladaer rumbled. *"They are fighting alongside the specters."*

Suns Above. "Khaos has been strengthening her forces to a degree we didn't anticipate. She is preparing for an all-out war—a complete purge of the mortal world as we know it."

Before the dragon could respond, a massive shadow smashed against the veil in front of them, causing another explosion of light. Aladaer reared back, and Daria hunched down, gripping onto his horn.

A cipactli had spotted them. It clawed at the veil, bellowing from the other side. More of the crocodile-eagle-hybrids crashed into it, their roars enough to rattle the sky.

Daria was sweating. "Aladaer, we need to leave."

The armies of specters marching on the other side did not stop; they didn't seem interested in entering the dragons' haven. But many of their gazes slid to them, thousands of cerulean eyes watching from the shadows. Watching *her.*

Her skin chilled as one of the cipactli managed to tear through the veil. Bit by bit, its claw ripped a slit in the border.

"I see now, the explosion was due to the armies of specters crossing different worlds. Their large numbers and presence are disrupting the ether and weakening our borders, thus allowing cipactli to sneak into our haven." The red dragon growled. *"This place is no longer our home."*

The cipactli peeled the veil farther back. Not enough for its body to squeeze through but enough for Daria to hear its hungry snarls.

"There are too many of them for you to fight," she said. "We need to leave!"

Aladaer snapped his teeth in frustration, swerving around to return to the cavern. The cipactlis' roars echoed behind them.

When they reached the top of the canyon, Daria slid down the dragon's front leg, stumbling onto solid ground. Aladaer had been silent on their flight back, but when he spoke, his voice was calm.

"A new age of dragons and dragon riders."

Daria stilled. "What did you say?"

Aladaer towered above her. *"For a while now, I have felt this longing, as if a piece of myself has been missing. I only realize now why that was: The time to return to Ikarria has come."*

Daria felt a confusing mix of emotions. "The cipactli—this haven—I'm sorry your home is no longer what it was. That you're being made to leave…"

"None of it is coincidence. You were meant to find us." Aladaer exhaled a wisp of smoke from his nostrils. *"I choose you, Daria Calderón. I choose you to be my rider."*

Tears swelled in her eyes. An unseen energy flickered to life between them. "Are you sure? You barely know me, and you know what I did to get here. The curse that will befall me… I don't think the dragon bond is impervious to its effects."

"I know your heart, Queen of Ikarria, I can sense your intentions. There is no other mortal I would rather tie myself to. I will be cursed alongside you."

Daria's tears fell. She smiled. "I accept, Aladaer, son of Kaigen. Be my dragon, and I will be your rider."

There was no spell to create the bond. It was the work of vows, the sincerity of the hearts making them. A power that had existed for hundreds of years, forgotten and left to the void of time.

The connection snapped into place as if the natural ether that made their world, that created every living thing, had heard their promise. A thread tethered them to each other, a burst of heat that spread throughout her soul, her blood. Flames that overlapped with the fires of her ether—the entwining of two forces.

Aladaer bowed his head, his large horns reflecting the starlight. *"Let's alert the others, Your Majesty. We must save our* true *home."*

Dawn broke as the dragons finally gathered. They stood on top of the canyon of their den, claws puncturing stone, wings spread. Sunlight broke through the horizon, turning their scales into shimmering oceans.

Daria sat atop Aladaer, the bond they'd forged burning beautifully within the depths of her being. It was still a foreign concept to her, something she was eager and honored to explore.

While the other dragons had been preparing to leave, Daria and Aladaer had taken the time to practice flying and releasing her ether while doing so, especially for the battle they were heading toward. The energy from the bond fastening her to Aladaer much more strongly than before. Daria had still fallen a handful of times—much to Aladaer's amusement—but was getting better.

Her dragon unfurled his wings, a brilliant red that reflected the dawn like sconces of fire. A loose piece of rock fell down the cliff as his claws curled around the edge and he glanced back at the beasts behind them. *"We have long rested in this corner of the universe. It is time we reclaim our realm!"*

Aladaer lifted his head high and let out a roar, and the others followed. Daria's heart was so full. It beat with warmth and hope, stretching out over her body.

She placed the obsidian crown on her head, the weight of it now felt light and *good.*

Aladaer pushed off the cliff, flapping his wings as he took to the sky. All the colors rushed by in brilliant streaks as he soared toward the mountains from where she'd come. The Dragon's Teeth.

Daria's eyes widened, the dragons flying faster, straight toward the stone. She had no idea how they were going to exit this realm—the throne's spell had already been cast and had dissipated.

"Brace yourself!" Aladaer shouted.

She cried out in shock, ducking her head as the dragon shot toward the mountain—and dove *through* it. He ripped through the veil, and entered the Continent of Ribera.

Daria gasped for breath, turning around to see every dragon emerging from the Dragon's Teeth and into Ikarria. The releasing of the spell must have also released their binds, allowing them to leave the haven.

A laugh suddenly broke out of her, the staggering realization hitting her. She was a *dragon rider*.

Daria lifted her gaze and spread her arms as her army of dragons soared to Dae Asari.

SIXTY-FIVE

Zara and the archangel were alone in the war chamber. Unable to bear the expression on Ronan's face any longer, she pushed off the table and strode to the stone archway. The jungle canopies rustled in the breeze, dragging cold fingers through her hair.

"Why are you so willing to sacrifice yourself?" Ronan's deep voice was not loud, though strong enough to reverberate through her bones.

She glared at him. "What do you mean?"

"The Zara I know wouldn't resort to such *theatrical* measures, not on a scale like this. It isn't the Horizons' way." He stalked toward her, wings flaring. "Do you think you offering yourself up will truly stop them?"

"Of course not," Zara hissed. "I know it's a foolish idea, a *desperate* one, but you have seen what they can do. You have witnessed their atrocities. If giving myself over to them can give you a chance at defeating them, then we should consider it."

The archangel narrowed his eyes. "Then *I* should be the one to surrender. They had me before, they can have me again."

"No!" Zara stomped closer to him. They stood inches away from each other, the light of the setting sun bending over their bodies. "Anyone but *you.*"

He stared at her. "I can feel your emotions fluctuating. What's truly on your mind?"

Fuck. She thought she had shut that mental door tight.

"Offering myself, it's what I should do…" she said, her voice wavering. "This is how I can repay the people of Damalis and Valenzia for all the blood I shed."

"Who said you need to repay them?"

"I *saw* this, Ronan! My ether showed me Teotlan in flames, and I—I didn't know what to think of it. I was confused by what my Primordial powers were trying to show me. If only I had done something different, had taken the vision more seriously, then *maybe* the future could have been changed."

"Santos, how could you have known?" Ronan's expression cracked. "We barely understood our Primordial powers, especially before the Oasis. We knew it was a possibility that they'd attack during the Festival, and we prepared as much as we could."

"It doesn't matter. In the eyes of your people, I am just a mercenary—I am the Rogue. *You* are the one who needs to survive this. You are their *King* and you just returned to them—"

He grabbed her shoulders, forcing her to meet his gaze. To see the tears that lined his gray eyes.

"I don't *care* that I am the King. Do you hear me? I don't *fucking* care." Ronan gritted his teeth. "I will gladly let my name be removed from history once more if it were to keep you safe. If it were to keep you with me."

Zara's heart twisted in pain. Heartache and something else— something that was so much more. It threatened to consume her.

"You are *everything* to me."

Ronan went to cradle her face in his hands. Those strong, warm hands. Always protecting her. Always fighting for her.

She couldn't trust her voice as her lips trembled. "I don't want you to have to make any more sacrifices. You've already done so much. I want to be the one to save *you*."

"Zara Santos, you saved me a long time ago. I am your blade, but you have my heart. It's always been yours." He brought her hand to his chest, holding it there. "Tell me the truth. What do you really want?"

This beautiful male. Her warrior. He was the silver of the moonlight, the shimmer of the stardust, ever igniting the dark of the sky.

Her restraint broke, and the swell of emotions punctured through the walls over her heart.

"I want to live," Zara whispered. She breathed out the truth that had resided within her for so long. "I want *you*."

Ronan let out a soft, ragged breath. Like he'd finally received a long-awaited answer to a prayer.

"I've been waiting for you, my Horizon," he murmured. His gaze dropped to her mouth. "I've been waiting to hear those words from your lips."

Their breaths mingled as they leaned in. And Zara showed him how she felt through their kiss. In the way she swept her tongue with his, her hands going from his jaw down to his shoulders, her nails digging into his leathers.

Zara could feel his need—his desperation—as he pressed her against the pillar, the vines and leaves scratching at her sides, and she melted into his hold.

Their kisses became hurried, frantic, every thread of emotion weaving between clashes of teeth and lips. He broke away to kiss a hot line down her throat, his tongue finding the sensitive spot along the slope of her neck.

"You want me." Ronan's breath was warm against her skin. It sounded more like a question and it gently tugged her from the haze.

Zara sensed what he was asking. That languid heat spread throughout her lower abdomen, her hips rolling forward to feel that hard length.

"I'm yours, Ronan," she breathed out. "And you are mine."

His grip on her tightened and he lifted his gaze.

"Forever yours, my ruthless beauty," he replied. "Always."

His words were a promise, one that brought tears to her eyes. Ronan guided Zara deeper into the chamber as they started to unfasten each others' leathers. She let her fingers dance across the hot skin of his chest and the tattoos there.

Ronan twisted her around and bent her over the war table, pushing her now untied clothes out of the way, her skin bare to the cool air. Anticipation rippled throughout Zara's body as the archangel dragged a hand down her spine.

"My beautiful Horizon, I want to show you how much you mean to me."

Zara panted as she heard him unzip his trousers. She was already wet for him, the evidence clear when he stroked two fingers down her throbbing core. Her nails bit down into the wood.

Ronan lined up his cock with her center and pushed into her. Slowly. They both groaned as his length sank deeper and deeper. Zara clenched her teeth, breathing through it.

While working side by side these past months, there had always been this crevice between them. A terrifying wedge that, if crossed, could change everything. Now she wanted to leap over that line more than anything.

Him. It was always going to be him.

Ronan grabbed her waist, a groan rumbling from his chest. "You are so tight, darling."

He pulled back only to thrust back into her. Zara jolted at the sensation, how it struck her where she needed him most. "*Fuck.*"

Ronan thrust into her over the war table; the sound of skin slapping on skin echoed in the chamber, followed by Zara's moans. His hot length fit her so perfectly, making her squirm and claw at the wood. The stone ornaments used for battle tactics that were strewn across the surface tumbled off to the ground.

Ronan gently grabbed her hair, guiding her to him so that her back was against his chest.

"So beautiful," he whispered as he licked her throat. "You're making a monster of me—and I'm on the verge of losing all control."

She gave him a drunken smile. "Don't hold back, I want it all."

He turned her around to lay her down on her back. Zara's hair was splayed out on the war table as she spread her legs for him. Ronan held her thighs and plunged back into her, making her gasp.

"Do you like that, Horizon?"

She whimpered, nodding her head. The archangel's wings flared as he plunged his cock in and out of her, every movement becoming harder and fiercer.

"This is for coming up with that stupid plan of yours," Ronan said through clenched teeth.

Zara's moans grew louder. More desperate. She clutched onto her breasts, kneading the flesh. "I'm sorry."

Ronan leaned down to give her a hot kiss. His teeth grazed her lips as he drank in her whines. He bent down to lick and suck on her nipples.

"Together," he rasped. "We do this together."

Zara knew what Ronan meant. They would take on the world as one. Together, they were so much more.

She grasped his face with her hands and ran her tongue along the scar on his lips. "Yes. I'm with you, Ronan."

Zara wrapped her legs around his waist all while he plunged into her, harder—faster. So deep—and she was so full. Over and over until her orgasm crested, rippling through her.

Her core clenched around Ronan, driving him over the edge, too, his wings stiffening as he came inside her.

Devotion, power, and something much stronger were tied together in this blazing moment. A thread of passion that connected their souls, their hearts.

Unsaid promises lingered between their panting breaths, their lips inches apart. Ronan ran a hand through her hair. "I'm not done with you yet."

Ronan led Zara to his bedchamber. Thank the Suns it was late enough for most of the staff to have gone back to their own homes, leaving the palace empty. His heart was full to the brim with this brightness. Light poured throughout his soul, ready to ignite him from the inside.

He wasn't sure what he'd done to deserve this. To deserve *her*. What he'd found was something no crown or scrape of power could have ever offered him. What he felt for her was all-consuming, as wild as the flames of the sun and as calm as the morning waves that lapped at the shore.

The way they'd unleashed themselves upon each other had been a desperation to reunite. They'd proclaimed their devotion to one another through wild, untamed desire. He would never stop wanting her.

Ronan took Zara on all the surfaces of his room, losing count of how many times they came. It was as if they were making up for lost time. His body was riddled with love marks and he repaid the favor.

He made love to her, the silk sheets beneath them already slick with sweat.

Zara was on her back, the muscles of her body flexing as she moaned. Ronan lifted one of her legs to drive himself deeper inside her. Every steady thrust had a fire burning inside him.

Fuck, she felt exquisite. The sounds she made were music to his ears, a melody he never wanted to stop listening to. Her nails bit into the flesh of his thighs and he welcomed every fiery nip of pain.

"I can't get enough of you, my darling." Ronan groaned. "You feel so good."

He lowered her leg, sliding out of her and moving down her body, kissing every inch. Zara whined at the loss of him inside her but stilled when Ronan nipped at the tender flesh of her inner thigh. He smiled against her skin before moving to her wet core.

Fucking Suns, he loved tasting her—it sent his blood pounding. Ronan loved how Zara grabbed his hair, his shoulders, needing something to hold onto while she rocked against his mouth.

Ronan swirled his tongue over her clit in tight circles that had her legs quivering—and then stopped, just as she reached the edge. He grinned at the loud groan she let out in protest, and crawled back up her body, his wings rising on either side of him.

"Ronan," Zara whimpered. She grabbed his length, stroking it. *"Please."*

He hissed with pleasure before lowering himself to kiss her on the lips as he pushed his cock back in. Her mouth fell open and he swept his tongue in to taste her moan. She grabbed at his backside, squeezing tight.

Ronan rolled his hips, driving his length into her in deep, merciless strokes. Again and again.

"Come, my beautiful Horizon," he whispered. "Come for me. I want to feel it."

Sweat gathered between their flushed bodies, the bed's headboard hitting the wall. Zara's fingers dug into his skin and she shouted his name as she came. He drove into her a few more times before pressing his lips to her neck as he found his own release.

They sank into the sheets, catching their breath. Night had deepened, and there was no telling how late it was. It might have been close to dawn.

Perhaps it had been foolish to let go like this, given the battle that was waiting for them. But he didn't care. No. The truth resonated throughout his soul as he stared at the beautiful woman beneath him, at her parted lips as she caught her breath, at the sweat beading along her breasts. How she gazed at him with that powerful light. No, Ronan didn't care what awaited them.

He carried Zara to the bathing chamber. Ronan drew her a bath and washed her hair, admiring the marks he'd left on her skin. Some part of him deep inside growled in satisfaction at the sight.

He kissed her as he washed and dried her body. As he took her back to the bed.

Zara yelped when he dragged her close to his chest. The mercenary stiffened for a moment before slowly resting her cheek on his chest.

"You saved me, too," Zara said suddenly, her voice soft. "I hope you know that."

Ronan kissed the top of her head. A fierce need to protect her overwhelmed him. He would claw through the ends of this mortal world for her. To protect this life they'd created together and would continue to forge.

For her, he would do anything.

Shortly after dawn, Ronan returned to the royal training ground.

He stared at the place where his family had died, the place that had haunted him for so long. Even though it still hurt to be here, no memories came to haunt him now.

That pain might never truly go away but he would no longer be crippled by it. He'd faced and come to accept the part he'd played in his family's death, accepted the things he'd done wrong, the things he could've done differently, though he also knew that, in that awful moment, nothing could have stopped his ether from lashing out. Not him, nor anyone else. His father, mother—his little brother… Ronan's soul cried when he thought about Hael. He wished he could hold him again like he had when they were young. Maybe he could've been a better brother, let Hael join Ronan and his friends on their mischievous adventures.

Fuck, those regrets would never leave, would they? It was something he would have to learn to carry. He tipped his head back and inhaled the ocean air.

The scars would stay with him, and he would never want to part with them—but he wouldn't suffer as he had before.

Leaves danced across the training ground, skipping over the charred stone. The sounds of waves crashing against the cliffs and of the morning songbirds in the trees echoed through his heart.

Ronan sighed and looked over his shoulder. "It's been some time since you and I spoke."

Soraya stood at the top of the steps, her hair more golden under the morning light. Those green eyes blazed with emotion as she pulled awkwardly on the sleeves of her long, loose blouse.

"Orion told me you would be here."

Ronan arched an eyebrow. "I thought you were keeping your distance from me."

Soraya winced, her gaze going downcast. "I—I've been angry."

She slowly approached him. Ronan had never pressed her to explain, giving them both time to heal their wounds.

"I know," he said, his expression falling. "You're upset that I didn't reach out to you while I was living in the Stone Orchard. And I understand your anger."

Soraya shook her head, her brows bunching together. Ronan stared at her—he hadn't seen her like this in a long time.

"No, that's not it." Her voice broke, eyes misting. "I've been angry at *myself*."

That made him go still. Soraya continued, "When the rebelling deities first raided our home and we took part in the battle... *You* saved me from a group of deities. You saved me and that was when they—when they took you." She looked up at the sky as tears began to flow. "I'd told you and Orion that I was with another battalion of érendira and that I would be fine—but that was a lie. I'd gone to confront the deities alone, and..."

Understanding fell over him like a warm ripple of water. The memory resurfaced in a gentle wave.

Soraya had been much younger and shouldn't have been in the battlefield to begin with, but they had rallied every able-bodied warrior they could. He saw his younger self plowing through the armies. His family had just been killed and he didn't want to lose anyone else.

He had found the young érendira fighting a group of lesser gods, alone and wounded. He'd assumed the other warriors had already been killed. Ronan had killed the deities, had thrown himself on top of her when more came. The way those soldiers had peeled him away from her, yanking him by the wings, wrapping a chain around his throat as if he were a wild animal.

Soraya had screamed for him but he'd forced her to stay back. She had been the last sight of home before the soldiers beat Ronan unconscious.

Now, Soraya gazed at him, tears silently streaming down her

face. "It was because of *me* that you were taken as a war prisoner. It was *my* fault you had to endure all that pain. The *torture*. All because you protected me when I couldn't defend myself. When I didn't listen, too arrogant and naive." She sobbed. "I'm sorry for taking my anger at myself out on you, and for what happened then. I'm sorry, Ronan—I'm so sorry."

Ronan's heart broke. How long had his little sister suffered through these thoughts? He knew exactly how it felt, the guilt consuming you from the inside for years.

He embraced her, one of his wings extending behind her protectively. "Soraya, it is not your fault that I was taken. Do you hear me? It was *not* your fault."

It was as if a dam had fallen. Soraya wept into his chest, clinging to him. More apologies spilled from her lips, and all he could do was hold her tight.

Ronan pressed his cheek to her head. "They were going to take me one way or another. And I'm glad it was me rather than you."

"It shouldn't have been that way!" she cried. "It isn't fair. What happened to you—what's *been* happening—it isn't fair."

He smiled. "Thank you for telling me how you feel."

Soraya's body shook as she shed the last of her tears. She sniffed, lightly pushing him away. "You should be more disappointed in me."

"Why would I be?" Ronan smirked as he ruffled her hair. "You've always been stubborn, and were always more sensitive than you let on, constantly crying about something. Usually Orion was the cause. Do you remember when he—"

Soraya playfully punched him in the gut even as she fought a smile. "Please don't bring any of *that* up." She looked up at him, green eyes shimmering. "It's long overdue, but I wanted to say that you have always been my hero."

His breath caught. Hearing those words from Soraya, the warrior he considered his little sister, was something he would carry close to his heart.

"My hands are not that clean," he said as they started to make their way back toward the steps.

"Whose are?" Soraya glanced up at him. "Zara was the one to encourage me to talk about this with you… I should go thank her, too."

He hadn't expected that. It seemed the little wolf and Soraya had been getting along far better than he thought.

"I didn't realize the two of you were close."

Soraya's expression turned sly. "Of course you wouldn't have noticed—you are always gawking at her when she's around."

A loud laugh left him. "I can't help it."

She snorted, jabbing an elbow into his side. "I'm happy for you, brother."

Ronan smiled as he wrapped an arm around her shoulders. "And I'm so proud of you." Together they ambled down toward the palace.

All the pain he had endured… It was worth it, if it meant having moments like *this*.

SIXTY-SIX

Erebus sheathed his sword at his hip. Armies from Elios were already marching through Damalis and he would soon join them. He never thought he would return to that place. Part of him had hoped not to.

The Primordial contract he had made with Khaos hissed within his veins. Blackened chains that wrapped around his heart, ready to puncture him from the inside out should he ever turn against their agreement. Not that he would. Not while this world he *despised* still existed.

The Primordials and deities had wronged him. The first phase of his retribution had been completed, and it would only be a matter of time before he could give that final blow.

Erebus crushed vials of preserved ether-born blood across the threshold, spreading the red liquid all over it. The power within it caused the carved runes on the makeshift doorway to glow.

This would have been easier if he'd had a Warden at his behest. Yet another forsaken task he needed to tend to. A deity capable of creating portals would allow more of Khaos's specters and other monsters to cross into this plane. If they couldn't find one, then they would have to garner enough energy from the ether-born to force those portals to open.

The veil sparked to life, a liquid-like curtain shimmering within the frames of the threshold. An incredible feat. Its opalescence reflected the white of his armor, nearly blinding him.

And yet, Erebus couldn't stop thinking about what had transpired in Kairos. Images slashed across his mind like blades. Tattooed hands reaching out to him. Silver tears lining storm-gray eyes. Midnight wings trembling with exhaustion and pain.

Erebus had been furious with Ronan, but more so with himself. With the world. Now, anytime he thought of the archangel, it struck the blackened shackles around his heart. Piercing through him.

How Ronan had discovered the ugly details about his childhood—about his family—he didn't know. He'd never wanted the archangel to know that side of him. He and the Crown Prince came from different worlds, Erebus's past full of stains. He would always be the archangel that came from nothing. The Ronan he'd known was still there, always helping those he cared about. Erebus needed to squash that. There was no going back now.

And Zara Santos. The energy around the mercenary had changed, shifted into an invisible beast with claws that curled around her shoulders, snarling at anyone who dared approach her. Erebus had been impressed.

He hadn't lied to the mercenary. She had been a light in his life—still was, in a way. It had been a long time since he'd allowed himself to be close to someone, especially after all he had done to the guardian realms. Maybe it had been Zara's unseen scars, the blisters that riddled her soul, that had him opening up to her over the years—as much as he could, at least. Erebus had underestimated his loneliness, and had found comfort in that fiery, battle-worn presence of hers.

Those connections now had been frayed. The next time Ronan and Zara saw him, they would surely hate him. As it should be.

The veil crackled and popped, reminding him of what he was doing in the first place. Erebus lifted his gaze as a figure approached from the other side, along with the clinking sound of armor and steel.

"My armies are ready to charge at my command," Erebus said. He placed a hand on the pommel of his sword. "You asked for this. Are you ready?"

SIXTY-SEVEN

The Damalisan forces gathered in front of what would become the fighting ground. Across a stretch of grassland and rocky hills surrounded by jungle, was the Elios army. Even from this distance, Zara could see the fully-formed specters amongst the archangel soldiers.

Healer tents had been erected within the trees. The smell of smoke and burnt metal scratched the back of Zara's throat, but she kept her gaze on the sea of midnight blue around her.

Sunlight shattered on the Damalisan soldiers' armor, their blue steel beacons against the greenery. Their helmets, shaped like the jaws of jaguars, made them look as if they were prowling through the clearing. Riyad was at the front, riding his war horse, while armored archangels flew above.

Something nudged Zara, and she looked down to find Kenzo billowing hot air against her skin.

"Fucking Suns, you scared me," she whispered to the jaguar, petting his large head. "When we first met I thought you were going to eat me. Glad that hasn't happened."

"*Yet*," Soraya added, saddled atop him. "It hasn't happened yet."

Zara rolled her eyes just as other érendira and their jaguars brushed past them, heading toward the main forces. "Shouldn't you be joining them?"

"I will in a moment." Soraya flicked her skeletal mask over the lower half of her face and tapped the bronze. "Put yours on, mercenary."

Zara faltered, her fingers mindlessly going to the mask hanging around her neck. Ah. It wasn't her usual mercenary attire. She wasn't back in the hunting season. Zara tried to calm her breathing.

After much debate, Soraya had convinced her it was better to wear Damalis's armor. Midnight blue fighting leathers clasped her body like a second skin, colorful gems decorating her chest, while a threaded design lined the rest.

"I told you already, I'm not an érendira," Zara grumbled, yanking up the skeletal mask over her face.

"Well, it suits you." Soraya looked at her and chuckled. More maniacally than she should've. "Did you not bring Río along?"

"No, he deserves to rest. I wouldn't force him into another battle again."

Her old warhorse was safe in the palace grounds. The thought alone was more than enough to comfort her.

My ruthless beauty, look at you.

Ronan's voice sank through her mind and into her bones. Her gaze drifted to the archangel approaching them. He too was wearing the attire of a Damalisan soldier, the jaguar helmet tucked in the crook of his arm.

Zara's eyes lingered on the scar across his lips, remembering how she'd licked it just that morning. She would never forget those moments together, entangled in the sheets or pressed against a random flat surface in his bedchamber. How his kisses had scorched her skin, how his whimpers had echoed through her blood, how the space between her legs still ached.

Wicked woman, Ronan said. *I can practically see what you're thinking.*

I'd like to take you right now.

Desire flared in his silver eyes.

"—There is no sign of Erebus or any of the Spirits."

That snapped her gaze away. Orion was talking to Soraya. When did the brawny male arrive?

"If the two of you can stop ogling each other, we are in the middle of a *very* important discussion!" Soraya shouted at them.

Orion gave Ronan a dry look. "Aren't you the king? Shouldn't you be paying attention?"

"I heard you loud and clear, Solterra," the archangel said, a smirk curling his lips before he turned to them, his expression sobering.

"Erebus will show. He personally called for this battle—he will not shy away from it."

"We continue with the original plan: We will deal with the main forces, while the two of you handle the Spirits and Erebus." Orion's face turned grim. "Fighting against him like this… I hate it."

Ronan clasped a hand around his shoulder. "I know. I do too."

A temporary silence cut through them as the cold reality reminded them of what they were up against. *Who* they were up against. Zara clenched her hands into fists, the last image of Erebus waving in her mind. *I should thank you, Santos, for being a small light in the dark when my life knew nothing else.*

Horns blared, the blunt ends of spears pounding against the ground. It was time.

Soraya grunted, urging Kenzo forward. "We move at your signal."

Orion took to the sky to join the other archangels while Ronan put on his helmet. He met Zara's gaze. "Ready?"

Red ether whispered around her body in response. Together, they stalked out to the front line.

The High Throne's forces didn't hesitate to charge. The clattering of armor and shields mixed with war cries hollowed out her ears. Her heart thumped painfully against her ribs as the specters sprinted toward them. Many of them had long, dark hair, with skinless jaws and metal teeth.

Zara exhaled a plume of crimson. Ether flowed from her body and Ronan's, their powers yawning out to the grass and sky, as if clawing for something. Her red-purple light danced with the blue-orange of the archangel's, an entwining of two celestial forces.

Together, eyes glowing, they unleashed their powers. It was a swelling of energy, pulling every thread of strength from within and manifesting out in the form of light. A blast of red and blue exploded from their palms and shot across the field.

The initial force of it was silent, as if the world had sucked in a breath. Then a massive battalion of Elios soldiers burst on impact, incinerated.

Zara gasped for air. It was as if something heavy had been yanked from her chest, leaving her trembling. Ronan looked just as winded as she.

He stared at his shaking hand. "Incredible. All that meditation and training has paid off."

Zara swallowed, her throat dry at the immensity of her power.

It was their signal to Damalis. Their forces charged, tearing over the grass as they cried out for their realm. For their king. Ronan raised his fist, spreading his wings, just as the elven forces spilled out on either side of them.

Wind blasted through Zara's hair as a line of elves leaped into the air. They slammed their fists into the dirt, twisting their hands in motions that had the ground *rolling* forward. The earth cracked and dropped several feet, causing another large chunk of the Elios soldier to fall into it.

Some of the High Throne's archangels took to the air, firing hundreds of arrows that turned the sky dark. Orion and his soldiers summoned their shields, an array of sparkling silver that blocked most of the projectiles. The arrows that managed to sneak through were swept away by elves bending the air.

The two armies met and the world exploded in clashing steel and crackling ether. Fire and water snaked between enemy forces, while specters poured through gaps, metal teeth puncturing armor and flesh.

Zara punched a specter with a lion-like face and pointed ears with her ether, its claws grazing her leathers as it fell. She spun around to jab her light through another creature, black gore spilling onto her skin.

Behind her, the first specter rose from the ground. It lunged at Zara just as Ronan slammed down on it, piercing it with his sword.

The archangel wrenched the blade deeper into the specter before yanking it out. He pulled his helmet off and smirked at her.

Zara heard the shrill cry of an oncoming arrow and slashed her weapon down in an arc, cutting the projectile before it could hit the archangel.

"Pay attention," she grunted.

In the chaos, Ronan yanked Zara by the waist, tugging her mask down to crash his lips against hers. A kiss that burned through her heart.

"Together?" he asked.

She kissed him back. "Together."

Ronan shoved his helmet back on and flew into the sky as she shot ahead with her ether, dragging her mask back up. The red light sent her sailing over the soldiers; she unsheathed her newly forged khopesh blades and dove into the battle.

Her swords were slashes of obsidian within the mass of white Elios armor, cutting through steel and leather to pierce skin and bone. Ether sprang out in fiery beams, burning the specters who launched themselves at her.

Blood and gore quickly soaked through her fighting leathers, Zara's hair getting plastered to her skin. She spun out in sharp angles, hacking and slashing.

The érendira tore through the wave of soldiers, jaguars snatching many from the ground and crunching them in their jaws. Soraya bolted toward her and Zara grinned, reaching a hand out. The warrior grabbed her, yanking her onto Kenzo's saddle and sent out a wave of water, drowning the soldiers that flanked them. "Needing a ride?"

Zara laughed. "I just wanted to catch my breath."

In the corner of her eye, she saw Ronan clashing with the Elios archangels in the air. His ether cracked through the sky, rendering the world in blinding flashes of blue.

"I must get to the other side," Zara shouted. "To find Erebus and the Spirits."

More waves of Elios forces rained down on them. Pools of red began to form on the grass, trickling over the rocky hills as soldiers from either side fell.

"We are going to be overpowered," Soraya said, her voice grave.

Zara shot out more beams of ether, and a row of specters exploded. Her energy was lasting longer now; she could feel it thrumming through her.

The érendira was right, though. Specters kept coming in waves, tackling entire lines of Damalisan soldiers. The warriors screamed, and many of them retreated to find higher ground.

Elios soldiers filled the skies with their arrows. Many of the Damalisan warriors fell, while jaguars and their érendira tried to flee out of their range, though Zara couldn't ignore the sharp animalistic cries that reached her.

She thought back to the Spirit's warning. It had been right, the first attack on Teotlan was nothing compared to what the High Throne could really do. There were no deities in sight either. Gods knew the destruction that would happen if they were to show now. The sweat on her body turned cold.

Someone shouted from above. Orion's eyes were wide on Ronan, who had a big gash on his arm and was battling another archangel. The soldier threw a dagger toward him and Ronan's head snapped back, his helmet flying off.

A wrangled cry tore from Zara, pain shooting across the same spot where the archangel was wounded. Ronan lurched forward then, the dagger caught between his teeth. He grinned as he took the weapon in his hand and hurled it back.

The blade hit the archangel in the shoulder, but before he could react, an eagle shot down and ripped the male away, puncturing his wings and throwing him to the ground.

"Fucking Suns," Zara breathed out. She might've clung onto Soraya a bit tighter. "The eagle saved Ronan."

More eagles emerged from the sky then, their shadows running over the battlefield. They plowed through the Elios soldiers, spearing them with their powerful beaks or plucking them from the grass.

Roars echoed from the jungle and the air nearly trembled.

Rhinoceros burst from the trees, their iridescent hides gleaming as they rammed their way through the fray, cutting down any specters and Elios soldiers.

"Not just them," Soraya murmured in awe. "The animals have come to protect their home."

Zara glanced up to see an eagle share a look with Ronan before diving into the battle. The mercenary let out a ragged laugh.

"Thank you for the ride, Soraya."

The érendira let out a warrior's cry, one that echoed after Zara as she sailed through the air once more.

She landed on a rhinoceros, cutting down any who tried to claw their way up the animal's hide, half-expecting the beast to throw her off. It didn't—it must've known she was an ally.

"Thank you, fellow warrior." Zara patted the animal before leaping onto the back of another.

Again and again, she jumped from one rhinoceros to the next, slashing down their opponents. Her blades were soaked with the black and red blood of both specter and mortal. Her body was hot with adrenaline, though the ether inside was still brimming with life.

A line of the rhinoceros were running toward a blockade of specters, the creatures snarling through their metal teeth, ready to attack. Zara sheathed her weapons and slammed into the ground between them.

Red ether surged up from the dirt, geysers of fiery light, and the specters screamed, scrambling away from her power. Zara tampered it down in time for the rhinoceros to plow through the creatures— followed by the érendira.

Jaguars poured into the melee, the warriors doing the same as Zara had, leaping between the animals, taking down their enemies.

Hands up, Horizon. Ronan suddenly commanded through her mind.

She raised her arms in time for the archangel to sweep her off the ground.

That was incredible, he said. His heart was laughing with manic joy—the male might have been more insane than her when it came to the hunt.

Keep going. She grinned. *We are over halfway across the field.*

Ronan gave a powerful flap of his wings. He swung her forward onto an eagle waiting for her. Zara's stomach flipped but she didn't hesitate as an archangel of Elios charged toward them and she took him down with a shot of ether.

Wind screamed at her ears and Zara could see the world rushing beneath her. She cursed aloud. The eagle banked lower, diving toward the heart of Elios's forces—way too fast. Zara cursed even louder.

She pulled her arms back and red-purple flaming light hissed to life beneath her fingertips into a makeshift bow and arrow. Bigger, larger than the average weapon.

The world tilted for a brief moment, the eagle's wings shifting to the side. There was a bright flare of flames below them. Flames that erupted from *nowhere*. Zara's chest tightened as she redirected the arrow toward Ronan—and released it.

It whistled through the air, the celestial flames around them growing larger and larger. Zara counted the seconds and watched the arrow collide with the Spirit that had been veering toward the archangel.

Zara had seen something shooting toward Ronan out of the corner of her eye.

As the Spirit barreled down to the ground in a fiery cloud of smoke, Ronan flew toward Zara. He wrapped a strong arm around her waist and carried her off the eagle.

"Thank you." His voice was soft against her ear.

"The Spirit came out of nowhere," Zara said, shuddering. "I was afraid I might miss him."

Ronan squeezed her tighter. "It seems our honored guests finally decided to show themselves."

He soared down to the narrow valley where the Spirit had crashed, away from the battleground. Trees rustled and smoke billowed from heaps of broken wood as Ronan landed, letting Zara go.

The Spirit sauntered out of the destruction, looking unharmed, scythe in its hand. Zara gritted her teeth, unsheathing her twin blades once more, while the ether inside her bristled.

Fire rippled out, surrounding the clearing they stood in, closing them in—the flames caused by the Spirit's presence. The second phase. They weren't alone in the ring. Erebus appeared, his white wings bright against the burning jungle behind him.

Ronan growled. "Where is your precious Council?"

The blood drained from Zara's face. The archangel was right. The Council wasn't here, and there was only *one* Spirit. Where were the other two?

Erebus stared at the archangel. "The deities don't need to be present for what we need to accomplish."

Zara didn't have time to process that as the Spirit and Erebus rushed them, forcing her and Ronan to move in tandem. The four of them fell into battle. No order, no sense of reason existed within the gnashing of their blades.

The Spirit was tall and broad-shouldered, and towered a few feet over her and the archangels. Its scythe struck Zara's weapons, the weight of his attack threatening to snap her bones. Erebus was an angry slash of winter and ice, agile and lethal. He moved around the Spirit, battling Ronan and Zara, blocking the archangel's sword before jabbing at her.

She met Erebus's gaze over their clashing weapons. "Is there a way to break a contract with a god?"

The agreement Erebus had made with Khaos. Zara didn't know why she asked. Maybe some weak, pathetic part of her hoped to still find the male she had considered a friend in him.

Erebus's lips twitched. "Only through death."

Ronan collided with the archangel, blue energy crackling along his body. "The binding cannot be reversed?"

Erebus shoved him away. "As I said, even if I ever wanted to betray Khaos, the contract would kill me."

Suns, it was almost like an even more twisted version of the Reckoning. The dreadful consequence that used to loom over the Horizons when they were bound by the fyrebrands.

Air was punched out of Zara's lungs as the Spirit rammed the blunt end of his scythe into her gut, before slicing her side with the blade. It *burned*. The steel was strong, piercing through the érendira armor and raking her skin.

Zara cried out, pressing a hand to the bloody wound.

Ronan roared. Lightning struck the Spirit and the warrior fell to one knee as the archangel dove in front of Zara, crouching in a protective stance.

His voice was rough. *How badly did it get you?*

It fucking hurts, but it's fine. Zara forced herself to stand. *I can manage.*

Relief shuddered through their connection, cooling the tension that had bracketed her mind. As the Spirit regained its bearings, Erebus lunged toward Ronan.

The archangels crashed in the center of their small battlefield. Fighting with weapons and fists. Slashes of ice and shadow.

To see Ronan and Erebus like this, it shifted something in Zara's chest. A bond that had been born out of love and companionship, now torn and bent by wrath and hurt.

Silver energy spiraled out from Erebus, a strong wind that yanked at Zara's hair and even dragged her a few feet across the ground.

Tears lined Ronan's eyes as he struggled against Erebus, pushing forward against the male's sword, their blades locked. "I haven't forgotten our dream. I still believe in it."

For a breath, Erebus looked pained. It was quick, a temporary flare of emotion before he bent forward and murmured something. The King of Damalis frowned.

Then Erebus twisted his blade free, the steel winking under the ashen sunlight, and drove the weapon through Ronan's side.

His scream tore at Zara's heart. Ripped it to shreds.

Fighting for breath, the High King looked up to the sky. As if in plea. As if searching for something.

Rage consumed Zara, burned through every vein in her body. She felt Ronan's pain through their connection, scorching her side. Tears burned the backs of her eyes.

Mikatán appeared in her mind—whether it was real or not, she couldn't tell. The god of death touched her brow like he had in the Oasis of Dreams, and an unknown sensation echoed through her soul, brilliant light flashing before her eyes.

Zara thrust a hand out into the void, commanding whatever ethereal power was left in her mortal body. She latched onto the tether of burning stars and bent it to her will.

Red smoke rose before her, curling up from the grass. Rising higher and higher. Zara allowed her imagination to take hold. In her mind, she saw the figures painted on the murals of the mercenary temples.

Feathers were the first to appear, crowning a skeletal face. Its body was broad, clasped in dark fighting leathers, the gaps filled with crimson light. A thick wooden sword embedded with obsidian blades formed in its hand.

Zara Santos—a mortal who stood on the threshold of immortality, who bore the powers of a Primordial in her hands—had made a soldier. A *sentinel*.

The skeletal warrior roared and rushed toward Erebus.

SIXTY-EIGHT

A res wiped the grime from his face, his lungs burning. He stepped over the lifeless body of an Adrastean vampire, their blood splattered across his gray armor. Smoke and ash filled the air, from the many battles that had erupted from their rebellion. Battles that had stretched on for days and nights. He wasn't sure how they had survived this long. Bodies had piled up with every sunrise and sunset.

Elven soldiers rushed past him, leaping over their dead comrades. They spilled onto the saltillo roads, commanding the elements as they met the vampires head-on. Wind howled, fire roared, water hissed, and the earth rumbled. The dark stone of buildings shuddered, but remained standing. The Ikarrian capital had been built to withstand the elemental elves.

Vash strode beside Ares, panting hard. "As successful as we've been so far, we are spread thin. If the Adrasteans don't kill us, exhaustion will."

"I know. The weapons provided by the Sombra Quarter have sustained us for now. But we'll need reinforcements soon."

"I am still baffled by that, by the way. How did you manage to secure their support?"

Ares averted his gaze. "I have my means."

He couldn't have done it without Ronan's help. The archangel had given him authority to command the shadow dealers in Ikarria, who were surprisingly willing to fight. The Sombra Quarter had shipped extra weapons and aid to Dae Asari before the battles started, and now many of its members were disguised as Ikarrian soldiers, hiding their identities from the public, but still taking arms against Adrastea.

A pair of vampires appeared before them. "How dare you betray us, General! You fucking traitor!" one of them bellowed at him.

Ares swept low, swinging his sword in a swift, upward strike, catching the soldier in a gap on their armor. Ares drove forward and pinned the vampire against a nearby wall, wedging his blade deeper until he heard the gush of blood and flesh. The soldier tried to grab him, gurgling more insults until they slumped.

Vash used the wind to coil around the other soldier's head, yanking all the air out of their lungs until they suffocated.

Ares tore his sword free, the vampire's body sliding down the wall. Exhaustion quaked through him. "Queen Daria will be here soon—we must keep this city standing for her."

There was no other alternative he would accept. Out of all the battles he had led, this was one that could not fail. Even if it left him battered and bleeding.

A vampire ally burst from an alleyway. "General, we have located the astral spears. There are giant ballistas stationed on the outskirts of the city."

"Any news is better than nothing," Ares said, sheathing his weapon. "Has Silas been found?"

The vampire shook his head. Ares had spotted his Second in some of the battles, but anytime they crossed paths, the male would disappear, ordering other soldiers to fight their former general instead. Silas was avoiding him.

"He will be where the spears are." Ares glanced at the blood-filled street. "I know Silas: he stands where he has the most advantage."

"One of those launchers was taken to the top of a tower, General."

Vash cursed aloud. "He's preparing for when the Queen returns."

Ares marched into the alleyway. He didn't look back as he said, "We need to destroy all of them."

Vash, the vampire, and other soldiers followed after him. They walked into a clad of smoke, leaving one battle to enter another.

Howls of pain scratched at Ares's ears as he carved his way through wine-red cloaks and bronze armor, moving closer to the outskirts. To the tower.

Fangs emerged before him, an Adrastean soldier aiming for his throat. Ares took a silent step back, grabbing their neck before they could make contact.

He tilted his head to the side, his long hair falling over his face. "How bold of you. Or how *foolish* of you."

Ares bared his fangs and the soldier blanched. Their cry was cut short when he punctured their jugular, tearing the flesh apart with his teeth. Someone laughed from somewhere above as Ares dropped the lifeless body and glanced up.

Silas stood at the edge of a building's rooftop, the structure sitting beside a tower. His own mouth was stained with blood. "I would've said the same thing to the bastard. He was practically walking into the lion's jaws."

Ares's brows furrowed. "Get down and fight me, Silas."

"Why? I came here to tell you that I want to join your side!" The vampire snickered, lifting a spear and aiming it at Ares. "King Matías has been generous enough to send me two specialty weapons to test out. Shall we?"

Silas grinned and fired one of the weapons down toward the vampire soldier standing next to Ares. The astral ore pierced through the male's chest, and his body exploded on impact.

Ares paled as guts and gore sprayed him and the street. So this was how the celestial ore could affect the average mortal.

His former Second laughed. "The realm of Celestrea has been hiding fineries, indeed!" He picked up a second spear. "And no one else is more deserving of this than you."

Ares snarled. Vash and the other soldiers were attacked by Adrastean vampires. It was only him against Silas now.

His Second pulled the weapon back. "See you in the Otherworld, bastard."

Sunlight glinted off the spear, almost blinding Ares. He ducked, preparing for the whistle of flying steel or for the agonizing pain of dying by astral ore.

Nothing happened. Ares exhaled a slow breath.

Silas wasn't looking at him anymore. No, he was staring at the sky. Eyes wide, face white as a sheet.

The dirt beneath Ares's feet rumbled. Loose tiles tumbled off rooftops. Broken window shutters and doors rocked on their hinges.

Ares sucked in a sharp breath, rushing to scale the building opposite the one Silas stood on. Once he reached the rooftop, he lifted his gaze to the sky.

An army of creatures was cutting through the air toward them. Their giant wings and wicked horns visible even from this distance.

Dragons. Beasts of radiance and terror. Suns, they were here. The dragons had returned to Ikarria.

"She did it," Ares murmured.

His eyes landed on the crimson dragon that led the charge. On the woman who rode it. The obsidian crown lay on her head, holding her braided hair back, her royal riding clothes somehow looking more like the fighting leathers of a warrior under the harsh light.

Queen Daria Calderón showed no fear as the dragons dove low over the capital.

Like a wave, the Ikarrian soldiers' voices rose. They raised their gloved fists, pounding them against their armored chests.

"*The Queen of Ikarria!*" they shouted. "*The Queen of Ikarria has returned!*"

A glorious sight. One Ares had dreamed of witnessing. A royal leader and her people.

Daria was nearing the heart of the city, where many Adrastean soldiers were huddled. Her war cry cleaved the air, as powerful as the sun. Her dragon drifted even lower, its dagger tail brushing the rooftops.

Ares's eyes widened when he realized what she was about to do. A yell reached his ears.

"Take cover!"

Daria's dragon opened its maw and released a brutal torrent of fire. Flames obliterated flesh. The screams raked across Ares's skin—he had never heard sounds like that before.

The dragon burned a path through the city, nothing but ash and charred rock in its wake. The other creatures followed suit. Their roars filled the sky, piercing through the clouds as they filled the streets with fire.

A dragon landed on a rooftop, smashing its snout into the neighboring building and yanking out mouthfuls of Adrastean soldiers. The vampires could do nothing as the beast chomped on their bodies, limbs flying.

Daria's dragon continued to fly across the capital, getting closer to where Ares was. And to the tower.

He turned around to find Silas running toward the tower. The vampire glanced over his shoulder. "Don't worry. I will kill you next, *General.*"

Ares pushed off the ground, leaping onto the building Silas had been on, before sprinting after the male. The tower's roof had a wide deck that overlooked the city, and a ballista gleamed at its edge. Another vampire was already there, the astral spear locked and at the ready. Aimed right at the crimson dragon.

No. Something clenched his stomach in a tight fist. Dread.

Silas's laughter turned distant. "Shoot, you fool!"

Ares could only watch in horror as the vampire launched the astral spear and as the barbed weapon of starlight sailed through the ashen air toward Daria's dragon.

Daria saw a flare of silver charging toward them. Fear tightened her throat. It moved too quickly for her to think, but Aladaer was faster.

His tail swatted at a nearby building, sending chunks of stone into the spear's path. The onslaught slowed its original trajectory, but the astral weapon still managed to pierce through the rock. Aladaer's wings gave a mighty beat and he lurched up into the air, causing her stomach to flip.

The dragon was too big to avoid the spear. Aladaer swerved to the side just as the weapon grazed his side. He let out a roar of pain, blood splattering out.

"Are you all right?" Daria gasped. Her grip on him tightened. "How bad is it?"

"Nothing to fret about. Better that it hits the tougher parts of my hide."

Relief washed over Daria. Her gaze followed the path the spear had taken, landing on a tower, and the ballista at the top. Vampire soldiers skittered about the structure like ants. More launchers were stationed on other towers farther back.

Fire snarled through her veins. "Warn the others. Tell them to keep an eye out for any projectiles."

Aladaer released a roar that threatened to make her ears bleed. The dragons had been tearing through roads and gobbling up any Adrastean soldiers they could find. Gliding over buildings and shooting fire.

At her dragon's warning, they pushed off the ground or dove in between buildings for cover. More astral spears were fired, looking like shooting stars, slamming into structures or puncturing the streets across the capital.

"We need to destroy those machines," Daria said.

"Very well." Aladaer flapped his wings, his scales a bleeding red. *"Hang on tight, dragon rider."*

Despite the danger of the falling spears, the Adrastean vampires still attacked. Relentless, even if against huge, scaled beasts.

Aladaer veered toward the tower, keeping low. Soldiers sprinted along the rooftops, firing arrows and throwing javelins—but those meager weapons simply bounced off her dragon's scales.

Daria swept out her ether, flames crashing over the Adrasteans. The vampires were quick, many of them able to leap away. A few were not so fortunate.

The smell of burnt armor and flesh clogged her nostrils. With the binding power from the dragon bond holding her steady, she stood on Aladaer's back and shot more flames.

A vampire slid under a column of fire, leaping off the ground toward them. Daria braced herself. She may not have been well-versed in combat, but she would rely on sheer willpower.

Before the soldier could land, someone slammed into him. It was as if the world slowed. Another vampire had come to her rescue, and Daria recognized him as the one she'd dubbed 'the *nice* vampire', Vash's ally. He wasn't wearing the bronze and wine-red of Adrastea now.

No, he was wearing Ikarrian colors, his dark cloak waving like a flag.

The vampire saluted her mid-air. He fell back onto the rooftops and grappled with the enemy soldier, just as Vash appeared. The elf was hacking his way through vampires before he and the 'nice' vampire began to run alongside Aladaer.

Daria realized what was happening in her capital. Tears swelled in her eyes.

"That's twice you've helped me now, soldier! What is your name?"

The male smirked. "I am Kenji, Queen Daria—and consider it overdue amends. The general made all this happen."

Vash called out to her. "It's true, Your Majesty. Ares has been planning this from the beginning."

Ares had mentioned that he was rallying people to fight for her when he'd told her of his plans. But she'd expected a small group of supporters, not a full-on *rebellion*.

I will right my wrongs. And to see how his actions had united two peoples, how he was fighting in *her* name…

"Where is he?" she shouted through the rushing wind.

The two males pointed toward the tower. Of course, that's where Ares would be. Daria pushed aside the unease that wanted to curl around her.

"Incoming."

Another astral spear whistled through the air. Aladaer angled himself to the side again to dodge it, one of his wings knocking tiles off buildings. Vash and Kenji leaped off the rooftop in time.

Another spear followed straight after, angled at Aladaer's head. Fire swam in Daria's blood. She brought two fingers to her lips and an orb of fire manifested above the dragon's snout. With a mental command, the flames rushed out into a shield, the mass of ether enough to block the spear.

Her muscles strained as she kept the weapon from penetrating her fire. Daria gritted her teeth. She pushed her ether, tilting the spear upward and it shot into the sky.

Aladaer dove, flying along the street, breathing flames on any Adrasteans who tried to rush him. More spears hissed by as they were fired across the city.

A flash of astral ore had Daria looking up. A brown dragon was flying high above the city, and dodged the barbed weapon. Her relief was quickly snuffed out when another spear was fired immediately after. It snarled through the air and pierced the dragon's chest.

Its scales burst, thick streams of blood rippling down as the beast fell from the sky. Its wrangled roar shook the clouds, shattering Daria's heart. The dragon crashed behind some buildings, and a massive plume of dust rose. Adrastean soldiers could be heard cheering.

Aladaer trembled. She tightened her hold on him as he lifted his head and let out a bellow of sorrow, the other dragons crying out with him for their fallen companion.

Tears swelled in Daria's eyes. Guilt knotted through her ribs. "I'm sorry, Aladaer. I'm so sorry. If I hadn't brought you here—"

"*None of that.*" He snapped. "*We knew the risk when we agreed to return.*"

She closed her eyes for a painful moment. His rage was so heavy through their bond. "I understand."

Aladaer roared. "*We end this now.*"

They reached the tower, and her dragon banked, pushing off the wall and snapping his wings wide as he soared to the top. Daria heard the clashing steel before she saw the battle taking place.

Ares was fighting Silas. Other Adrastean vampires lay lifeless around them, one slumped next to the launcher. The general must have killed the soldier that had been firing the astral spears.

The two males paused when Aladaer's shadow fell over them. The dragon's nails pierced the stone, his tail wrapping around the tower, and he knocked the roof clean off with his snout.

The vampires ducked in time, falling through the crumbling rocks to the next level, now exposed to the blaring sunlight and the crimson dragon. The ballista fell with them, now lying on its side, though still undamaged.

Silas glared up at Daria. "Feeling mighty, Your Majesty? Hiding behind huge, fire-breathing beasts?"

"*Mortals like you have always existed, since the dawn of this world,*" Aladaer rumbled. "*You are but pests that need to be eradicated.*"

Silas slunk back a step at his deep, roaring voice, seething. Light flashed from somewhere in the city before an array of spears tore free from their towers.

Daria shouted, even though it was pointless. The dragons roared, diving down or angling themselves upward to avoid the astral ore weapons. Except one. A spear was hurtling through the air toward a younger, smaller beast, when the purple dragon knocked it out of the way, taking the blade in its shoulder.

Aladaer bellowed in outrage, but the purple dragon didn't stop. It folded its wings across its back, shooting down to the launchers, the spear still lodged in its scales. It flung its wings out, unleashing a plume of flames and destroying a line of ballistas.

Vampires screamed as they were burnt alive, while others fled toward the city's border as the dragons turned on them once more.

"It looks like your soldiers are retreating." Daria breathed through the ache in her chest. "And I'm taking back what's rightfully mine."

She glanced at Ares at that, her lips curling slightly. The general had been watching her. Soot smeared his pale cheeks, though it did not hide the sheen of emotion in his violet eyes.

Silas looked at his soldiers, before letting out a laugh, the sound twisting in a snarl. "You may have the advantage now, Calderón, but it will be short-lived. Until next time, Your Majesty."

Ares grabbed the vampire before he could leave. Daria turned to the launcher, but hesitated. The damage would be too great and Ares was so close—

"Do it!" the general shouted. "Do it now!"

She sucked in a sharp breath and spoke through the dragon bond. *"Destroy it."*

Aladaer reared back, amber light rising up his throat. Ares struggled against Silas, both of the vampires now within range of the dragon fire. Daria shouted as the torrent blasted the projectile, the wood exploding, astral ore melting.

Stone loosened beneath the dragon's weight and the tower began to crumble. The building sank down a few levels—huge chunks of rock crashing onto the streets below—before stopping halfway. Plumes of dust curled around them, stretching gray fingers toward the sky.

Aladaer straightened and shook off some debris as Daria looked at their surroundings. Adrastean vampires were running away. All ballistas had been demolished by the other dragons. They had done it.

Her heart lurched as she turned back to the destruction of the tower before her. There was no sign of Silas nor of Ares.

SIXTY-NINE

Ronan lurched back in time for Zara's warrior to crash into Erebus. Power rippled through the world, surging between the blades of grass and echoing up the feathers of Ronan's wings. It was unlike anything he had ever seen. Not even in the War of the Skies.

Whatever ability Zara possessed, it belonged to her arsenal as a Primordial-in-the-making.

Her warrior rammed its bladed club against Erebus's raised sword. Ripples of crimson ether spun out at the collision. The warrior roared in the archangel's face, the sound like a roll of thunder.

It swung its heavy weapon down once more, driving Erebus back with so much force that the archangel's eyes widened in shock. In fear.

Ronan groaned, staggering back a step. Blood spilled from the wound at his side. No time to falter now. He needed to take advantage of the opportunity Zara had given him.

He didn't want to kill Erebus. Despite everything that had happened, something in his heart rejected the possibility. But now—there was no time to reconsider.

He flapped his wings, digging his heels into the dirt, yanking on the last dregs of his power. The warrior smacked Erebus's sword out of the way, raising its weapon high above its head. Erebus summoned silvery ether. They were about to collide—

Zara's warrior disappeared, exploding in sparks of red. As quickly as it had come, it was cut off from its mortal bounds.

"No," Ronan whispered, pain shooting across his throat.

A chilling dread, one he wasn't sure he could ever overcome, sank into his bones as Zara's scream cleaved his heart in two.

The Spirit had moved so quickly. In its hands were chains, now wrapped around the mercenary's neck.

Astral ore. An otherworldly source that could kill a god, and also cut off the power of its bearer, without having to be imbued with ether.

To destroy the warrior Zara had created, the Spirit had gone straight to the source of its existence.

The Horizon paled. She must have had the same realization as Ronan. Her panic tunneled through their connection—something that surpassed the effect of the astral ore—tightening his lungs.

I can't feel my ether. I can't feel it!

The Spirit kicked her feet out from under her and slammed her into the grass. He brought out more astral bindings, tightening them around Zara's wrists. There was a crack of bone and she screamed.

Ronan's blood boiled, agony running through his body, and blue mist rose from where he stood.

"I'll kill you," he seethed.

Zara cried out. "Basim!"

The wolf appeared in a blazing light. He snarled and attacked the Spirit, forcing it to step away from the mercenary. The nahual had been waiting and clawing anxiously at their connection.

Ronan and Zara had agreed to keep their nahuales away from the heart of the battle unless it was absolutely necessary. They couldn't risk their safety.

Basim snapped his teeth around the Spirit's forearm, thrashing from side to side. The tall warrior grunted.

"*What a troublesome creature,*" it said.

The Spirit flung the nahual across the clearing with such speed and force, the wolf slammed against a tree, barely missing the flames. Basim yelped in pain.

"No." Zara's eyes were wide on her familiar. Basim couldn't fight a Spirit of the Midnight Sun. Not yet. The animal snarled in protest when she told him to leave. Basim rose to his feet, limping toward her.

She shook her head. "I need you to listen to me."

Basim whined.

"*Now!*"

Her nahual howled before disappearing in clouds of ether. The Spirit stomped over to Zara, yanking on her chains. Ronan was shaking in fury.

"I'll kill you," he murmured again. "I will hunt down every one of you Spirits and destroy you."

Erebus was staring at him, something swimming in his gaze. He closed his eyes before looking up to the sky.

"Well? You've been asking for the right moment," Erebus murmured. "Here it is."

Gray clouds gathered, a clap sounding from within. A shuddering of the skies.

Power, in the form of inky plumes, shot down from above. Ronan barely made out the silhouette of wings before a figure rushed him.

Ronan didn't move fast enough and the sharp coldness of a blade ripped a path up his body. He cried out, blood spilling with his every staggering footstep, and pressed a gloved hand against the torn skin on his neck, staring at who had attacked him. He vaguely heard Zara's scream of pain.

Shadows rippled around an archangel, tendrils that greedily clung to his body. The male shook the blade that now dripped with Ronan's blood.

A blade of astral ore. *Shit.*

The archangel lifted his gaze, and Ronan stilled. *No.* It wasn't possible.

He recognized the angular jawline, the straight nose. Eyes that were so dark they almost seemed black. The male was taller now, stronger too. His athletic frame was lean yet muscular, evidence of years of rigorous training. The archangel's black hair had grown slightly past his ears, half of it tied back into a knot while wavy strands brushed sun-kissed olive skin.

Midnight blue wings unfurled from the darkness around him.

Ronan's knees nearly buckled. The male had been but a boy the last time he'd seen him.

"*Hael?*"

The archangel—his *brother*—narrowed his gaze, shadows flaring around him. His power. Before Ronan's imprisonment—before… *everything*—Hael had been too young for his ether to manifest. And now it seemed he could control the darkness.

Ronan struggled to keep himself on his feet, his mind reeling, his wound burning. His brother was here, standing in front of him. *Alive.*

"What—*how?*" Ronan's breathing turned shallow, his voice breaking. "I thought I'd *lost* you."

He was acutely aware of the Spirit still holding Zara—he needed to get to her.

Hael said nothing, but Ronan saw the recognition in his eyes. His brother knew who he was, and yet…

Ronan snapped his attention to Erebus, snarling. "What have you done to him?"

The High King's expression was unreadable. "You thought Hael burned along with your parents, but he didn't. He is a survivor." His gaze went to the younger archangel, lingering. "I saved him."

All these years… Hael had been *alive.* The crack in Ronan's heart wedged deeper, gnawing down at the core.

Suddenly, his brother's wings snapped out and he sailed toward Ronan, sword in hand. Shadows flanked him, temporarily blinding Ronan, but he managed to raise his weapon in time to block the attack.

A strangled groan was yanked out of Ronan's teeth. Blood still poured from the wound on his neck, his body unable to heal as quickly as before. *Fucking astral ore.*

"I don't want to hurt you, Hael." Ronan gritted his teeth. "*Brother.*"

The archangel's jaw clenched. He twisted his sword free and attacked again. Shadows coiled around his wings and legs.

Ronan parried every swing and jab. Silver rang out; sparks flew. Exhaustion racked his body, aggravating his flayed skin. Hael threw out a column of darkness toward him, but Ronan was able to evade the mass of angry power..

They moved at the same time. The younger archangel was so much faster than him—and Ronan didn't see the flash of silver. That bright astral blade in his brother's hand tore up the other side of his neck and dug into the skin over the edge of his jaw.

Zara screamed. Cried out his name. He wanted to reach out to her, to take her away from this place.

Hael kicked him square in the chest, knocking him flat on the ground. Pools of red welled up along his chest and spilled down his sides.

A silent command echoed through Ronan's nahual bond. *Nyota.*

His panther shot out from the veil, attacking the younger archangel.

Hael hadn't expected it. Nyota slashed at his leathers, red flinging out. The male roared in outrage, his shadows pinning the panther to the ground. The nahual wriggled herself free and lunged at the archangel once more, only for him to slam the pommel of his sword against her torso.

The two tussled for a breath, dark wings and sharp fangs in a terrible collision. Blood sprayed, armor punctured through. Shadows wrapped around the panther's body, tightening around her so tightly that the animal started to choke.

Ronan's heart lurched in fear. *Go back, Nyota! It's not worth it, return to safety!*

You're worth it, bonded.

Don't you fucking dare! I order you to leave!

You are pushing me away again. Like last time. I won't do it.

His chest tightened. *Please, Nyota. I beg you to go. I won't be able to survive if something happens to you.*

Ronan's nahual closed her eyes in pain before disappearing in a flare of light. The temporary relief was a weight that pinned him to the ground, unable to move.

Hael loomed above him, red trickling down the side of his face.

The tip of his sword pointed at Ronan. And yet, Ronan reached out a trembling hand. "Hael, please."

His brother's eyes were bright with fury. "Stop saying my name."

Ronan froze at the sound. The young archangel's voice was so much deeper.

The archangel pressed down with his boot. Ronan cried out when some ribs cracked, and breathed through the burning pain, holding Hael's gaze.

"Why are you doing this? What *happened* to you?"

His brother leaned forward, lips peeling back into a snarl. Tears pricked the corners of his dark eyes. "I am not obligated to answer to a *murderer*."

The world dulled in Ronan's ears. "What?"

His voice sounded far away, as if he were slipping out of consciousness. Perhaps he was. There was so much red staining his chest and hands. Hael sharpened into view.

"You killed my parents," he seethed. "You brought the deities to Damalis's shores. It was *your* ignorance and pride that brought the gods' war to its lands."

"I'm sorry for—what happened to our parents." Ronan's face crumpled. "I never meant to hurt them, I swear, brother." The air thinned in his lungs—so much so that it hurt to breathe. "But the gods' war had been ongoing for years before it came to us. I—I didn't cause it."

"Lies," Hael snarled.

Zara was still struggling against the Spirit. Ronan needed to help her. Save her. He tried to get up only to feel Hael's sword nick his skin.

"I'm not lying. Has Erebus tampered with your mind?"

"Erebus doesn't shy away from the *truth*. I know everything, and I will *never* forgive you. You ruined my family." Hael glared at him, his dark hair falling forward, his shadows thickening. "I hate you."

Ronan's eyes widened. The past swam before him, his Primordial power at work.

He saw little Hael falling from the cliff, the image of Ronan burning their parents with his ether the last thing he saw.

Little Hael waking up in a foreign land, not part of the world he knew.

Little Hael holding Erebus's hand as he was led to a house. A house he came to call home.

Glimpses. Shards of memory. What Erebus had said was true: He had saved his brother. Raised him.

The past faded, leaving Ronan at his younger brother's mercy.

Hael lifted his sword, both hands wrapped around its pommel. Ronan squirmed in place, trying to move out of the way. His body was failing him, his limbs weakened from all the damage he had absorbed.

The astral blade winked in the ashen light, grinning in madness. Ronan's long-lost brother roared to the sky, and drove the sword down in a perfect arc and through the center of his chest.

Hael yanked the sword out, only to drive it back down. Again. Again. Again.

Blood spewed out of Ronan's lips. It hurt. It hurt so much.

Hael cried out, the sound wrought with despair and anger. Ronan tried to speak, to at least tell him he was glad to see his little brother alive.

Darkness seeped over the corners of his vision. A coldness was enfolding Ronan's body.

Ah, no. He wasn't done yet. He couldn't leave.

Zara hadn't stopped screaming for him. Every stab of silver was followed by the feel of her heart breaking. Was she feeling his pain? He wished he had the strength to close that mental door.

Ronan clung to the cries of the woman he loved. The woman he'd failed. Blood covered him, his flesh torn, his ragged breathing growing softer as he slowly turned his head to look at his Horizon.

His mind reached out a red-stained hand toward her. *Zara.*

"*Ronan!*"

Zara's throat burned from shouting his name, over and over. There was no rational thought, not as she flailed and struggled against the

Spirit. The chains had sapped her ether to the dregs, rendering her useless. Pain flared throughout her broken bones.

Still, she didn't stop fighting. Anything—*anything* to get to Ronan.

Zara couldn't remove her gaze from her archangel, couldn't tear her eyes away from the blood coming out of his body. There was so much of it, it would have been impossible to staunch it. She trembled at the sight of the fucking sword protruding from his chest.

Ronan turned his head to look at her, his gray eyes dull.

Zara.

She shook her head and bit back a sob. She didn't want to accept the resignation in his voice.

Ronan's brother yanked the astral sword out of his body with a squelching noise. Ronan made no reaction. No sound.

So, so still, lying in a pool of his own blood. Only his eyes twitched.

Hael sheathed the stained weapon, retreating to Erebus's side. The white-winged archangel had been staring at Ronan, a blank expression on his face.

"I will see you at home," Hael said before pushing off the ground with a powerful flap of his wings. He flew high, disappearing into the sky. Erebus didn't react to that, and merely returned his gaze to Ronan.

"The Reborn has received his justice; one of the godlings has been eliminated—just as Khaos demanded. I will call the Elios forces back," Erebus said, quietly. "We can leave."

The Reborn? Hael?

The High Throne had meant to kill one of them all along. They never intended to take them *both* of them alive. *We only need one.*

Ether howled inside Zara, ramming its head against the shackles around her wrists and neck. Weak sparks of red light skittered across her body and she managed to swing her leg at the Spirit.

The male grabbed her ankle before Zara could hit him. The Spirit gazed at her from underneath that bronze skull and tightened his grip, fracturing the bone there. She shouted, bucking in his grasp.

Ronan made a wheezing sound, his bloodied fingers lifting from the grass as if he was trying to reach her. His chest moved weakly and he coughed out more blood.

Little wolf… Listen to me.

Zara grunted through the pain. *Whatever you're going to say, don't.*

The Spirit's grip loosened and she slumped to the ground. Zara crawled to her archangel, moving through his blood.

Hot tears ran down her dirty cheeks. Muscles throbbed in pain. Bones burned in agony. She pulled herself to Ronan's side, cradling him in her arms. The archangel was so heavy, and she was so, so weak.

Ronan still gazed at her, like she had crafted the silver stars and hung the moon. Even as streams of red ran from his lips. He moved his mouth but couldn't speak. Instead, his voice seeped through her mind.

I'm sorry—this is something you need to hear. Before I go.

Zara sobbed. *Stop talking like that. You're scaring me, Ronan.*

It was as if a pair of midnight wings wrapped around her, the phantom touch giving her little comfort. As if his large hand, rough and callused, swept along the curve of her jaw.

My ruthless beauty, I will tread the stars, travel the veils of the celestial world to return to you.

More sobs racked through her. She brought his bloodied hand to her face, pressing his palm against her cheek. *You are my warrior, Ronan. I need you to fight.*

His eyes glistened, the sound of his voice growing weaker and further away even in her mind. *Zara… My Horizon…*

Ronan Menodora, leader of the Sombra Quarter and King of Damalis, spoke three words to her. Three words that turned the world around her into fiery, shattering light.

It terrified her. It meant he didn't believe he would have another chance to say them.

"Take them back," she said out loud. "Take them back, Ronan!"

Erebus had been watching them in silence all this time. He narrowed his eyes at her outburst. "What are you saying?"

The Spirit's voice echoed from behind her. *"The elf has gone mad."*

"You can't say that to me. Not yet. Do you hear me?" Zara ignored them, placing Ronan's hand on his wounded chest, squeezing it tight.

The archangel kept his eyes on her until they slowly closed, a sigh leaving his scarred lips. She felt his body slacken in her arms.

"No. No. No." Zara crushed him to her chest.

Ronan? Can you hear me? She reached out to him through their connection, only to be met with nothing but mist. *Answer me, Ronan!*

The future flashed before her eyes, her Primordial power surging back at this shift in the mortal world. As the Fates weaved a different thread, creating another path. The same vision from the Oasis rushed back to her, of Zara and Ronan of the future standing in a battlefield under a red sky.

Only this time, Ronan started to disappear. He drifted away in dusted starlight, leaving future Zara alone. That version of herself sobbed, falling to her knees. And the world around her burst in crimson light.

The future was changing. Panic seized every fibre of Zara's being as she was slammed back into the present.

Please Ronan! She shouted into the void. There was nothing for her to grasp, no tether. *No, you can't leave me!*

Zara screamed out loud, holding her archangel's body. "Please gods, please! Don't take him away from me!"

Hysteria clawed at her. Her ether rammed against the bindings. Sparks of red flickered around her shackles, brighter and brighter. No one would answer her. No gods or goddesses would hear her. Not even Mikatán, the God of Death still nowhere to be found.

"Take her." Erebus's voice was low. "Our forces are retreating."

Her heart jolted when the Spirit pulled her away, leaving her archangel slumped in the grass. Nyota returned to Ronan's side then, crying beside her bonded. Even Basim howled from within the veil.

"No! Let me go! *Ronan!*"

Zara screamed, and while her ether had been bound by astral ore, its power was still felt throughout the land. Every gaze lifted to the gray sky at the ripple of unseen energy.

The world shuddered at her pain. At the heart-wrenching truth that cleaved her soul in two.

Ronan was dead.

SEVENTY

"Daria."

Aladaer's voice gently tugged her attention to the scene around her. To *her* soldiers, gazing up at her from the rubble, from buildings, rooftops. And to the Adrastean vampires who'd fought on their side. Everyone cowered back as the dragons gathered around them, some hovering in the air.

Daria climbed down Aladaer and walked to the tower's edge. Silence stretched in the remnants of the battle. Dae Asari was no longer the same city she had known, but they would rebuild. Her relief was shadowed by dread as she looked about the debris, her heart racing. Searching and searching.

Her breath caught when a figure stepped through a cloud of smoke in the street below, the Ikarrian armor shining brilliantly on him. Brighter than any she had seen. Like he was *meant* to wear it.

Ares. He was safe. He was alive.

The vampire held her gaze as he approached the broken tower she stood on. The war general dropped to one knee, placed a gloved hand on his chest and bowed.

The other soldiers followed suit. A wave of armor and steel flashed as they all sank to their knees. Vash smiled at her before lowering his head with the others.

To *her*. They were bowing to her.

Behind Daria, her dragon unfurled his wings and lifted his head to the sky, roaring in triumph. Every dragon joined in, and the soldiers cheered.

"Long live the Queen! Long live Queen Calderón!"

Tears fell down her face. The draconic realm had once been dragon-less for a hundred years. No longer. The dragons had returned to Ikarria and her kingdom was free. Her heart was so full it was about to burst.

Daria looked at Ares again. A breath of a moment passed before they moved. She slid down the tower and stumbled onto the street, as Ares tore through broken stone and discarded steel.

She let out a cry of relief as she leaped into his arms. The vampire crushed her to his chest, sweeping her off her feet.

"Daria," Ares breathed. "You're home."

Yes. Yes, she was. And it meant more, with him at her side.

Her sob was muffled against his chest. "You—You failed to mention an actual rebellion in all your plan-making. Why didn't you say?"

Ares placed her on the ground but did not let go. "You had many other things to worry about, my Queen. Besides, I had to do something, since I started all this mess."

He grinned, and Daria smiled at him through her tears, cupping his face. "Thank you, Ares. Thank you for everything."

Pain and heartache had followed them for so long, but they'd kept pushing forward. Even as life nicked their skin, even when they were tempted to fall to their knees, they'd blazed their own path and come out victors.

"It was you, Daria Calderón, who saved your home. Who saved *me*." Emotion swam in the vampire's eyes. "I will stand beside you, defend you, and fight in your name until the sun and stars fall."

A vow. One forged by their renewed bond and something even more powerful.

Daria swept her thumb along his cheek. "Stay with me, Ares. Stay with me, always."

They leaned in at the same time. Ares cradled the back of her head, guiding her lips to his. His scent of rose and forest filled her lungs as Daria kissed him back.

The Queen of Ikarria and the war general had waded through battles on their own and had emerged together. And they would stand side by side, baring their fangs and wings to the forces that threatened to pull them apart.

Ikarria was healing. The people who had fled the city before the battle slowly began to return, and the soldiers—Ikarrian and Adrastean—started the rebuilding efforts. It would take a long time for Daria's kingdom to go back to its former glory.

The dragons mourned the death of their own, while healers tended to those who were gravely wounded. Aladaer was with them now, the male often checking in on her through their bond.

Daria was informed that the Sombra Quarter had been a great support in the rebellion. She would have to thank the shadow dealers somehow.

Daria was in the palace's library, shelving the books about dragons her pater had procured. Her heart felt heavy, and she curled her fingers against the spine of the tome in her hand.

"I will save you, Pater," she whispered. "Zara and I will come to you soon. Hold on just a little longer."

She hadn't heard from her sister yet, but there was much to do in the meantime, such as ensuring the other cities and towns within her region were free of the vampires and strengthening their defences. Aladaer had sent some of the dragons to help protect the rest of Ikarria.

There had been no sign of Silas, and it was concluded that he had managed to escape. The traitor Basira was found *trying* to flee, but Vash had apprehended her, the advisor now locked away in the prisons. Daria never saw the advisor during the battle, but it wouldn't have surprised her if the coward had hid throughout it all.

Her court was broken, though the other advisors had finally been showing their support and had accepted Daria as queen. Having a dragon companion probably helped.

Suddenly, a patch of skin just under her left ear started to burn. Daria hissed in pain, stumbling over to the oval-shaped plated mirror in the corner of the room.

"What in the bleeding Suns—"

A tattoo of a lotus flower had appeared below her ear, and Daria's stomach sank at the sight. It was no regular tattoo. *Suns Above.*

The necromancy spell's warning rang through her head. Somehow, in some way, her heart would suffer.

Vash knocked on the door, already ajar. "Your Majesty, a moment?"

Daria turned away from the mirror with a strained smile. "What is it?"

"We have a visitor." She didn't like the grim expression on the elf's face. "Under normal circumstances, I wouldn't have brought them to you like this." Vash hesitated before walking into her office. "However, I think the situation calls for it."

Before Daria could question him, a brawny archangel appeared at the threshold. He had long dark hair and dove-gray wings, and was wearing midnight blue armor. What gave her pause though was the redness that lined his eyes. Like the male had been crying.

"My name is Orion Solterra." His voice was rough. "I am from Damalis and I… I come bearing news."

Daria recalled the name. Ronan had mentioned it multiple times throughout their journey to Kairos. Dread thickened in her bones.

"What happened?"

Ares strolled down a castle hallway, his mind still on the meeting he'd had with his soldiers—Adrastean and Ikarrian alike—about the rebuilding efforts. And on Daria. On his Queen. The next dragon rider of the new age. He hadn't thought he could be more in awe of her, but Daria kept surprising him. He was on his way to see her, anticipation rushing through him at being able to hold her in his arms again—after a mere hour of being apart.

Ares suddenly stopped as a cough racked through his chest.

He clamped a gloved hand over his mouth, blood spilling between his fingers. The sudden swell of it in his throat had him bowing over until the coughing stopped.

Ares stared down at the red liquid that coated his hands. Confusion warred inside him, an image of his mother's frail body flashing through his mind, of her shaking from a bout of coughing. The Red Blight.

A burning sensation curled beneath his left ear, yanking out a hiss from his teeth. Ares stumbled over to the nearest armored statue in the hallway to see his reflection. There was a tattoo of a lotus flower, his skin tender to the touch.

It was obviously the work of ether. Ares straightened, his gaze dropping to the blood on his hand once more. Realization shifted into place, and he let out a soft, broken laugh.

"So, my own reckoning has begun," he said, wiping his mouth.

Ares was grateful the curse had chosen him and not her. It was better that way.

He heard the sound of Daria *crying* out and he sprinted the rest of the way, skidding to a halt when he saw the archangel standing at her library's threshold. It had been some time since he had seen the male.

"Solterra?" he asked. "What are you doing here?"

Orion glanced over his shoulder, his eyes puffy and red. "Valdemar…"

Ares's gaze drifted to Daria. She had a hand over her mouth, tears streaming down her face as she slowly slid to the ground. As Orion told him what had happened.

No, it couldn't be true. Ares sank to his knees, staring down at his trembling hands.

No.

EPILOGUE

The Pit was louder today. Prisoners gathered in the pool of light at the center, their bodies huddled close as they tried to absorb as much sun as they could. Hands outstretched toward the gap in the ceiling, their groans filling the space. How irksome.

The young man wanted silence. Craved it. He shuffled forward, following the specter who held onto the chains tied around his wrists. His throat was still tender from his screams, the wounds on his body fresh.

It had been the same agony of the night before. And the night before that. And the one before that. The specters had tried to probe into his past, his upbringing. Who his mentors were. What region he came from. They believed he was hiding something of value.

Like he would ever reveal the truth about himself. He would rather die.

The young man wanted to laugh, but the cuts on his lips had him wincing in pain. He hadn't experienced the worst of the Pit though. There was worse punishment than this.

The deities hadn't visited him. Nor had those Spirits. They hadn't even put him against the *monsters* that lurked within the darkest corners of this place yet. Creatures that were not born in this world.

Pain throbbed in the young man's temples. He squinted as they moved closer to where shadow and light met in the center of the large chamber. The crowd thickened, sweaty bodies pressing against him. It was too fucking *loud*.

He gritted his teeth. "What's going on? It's even more hectic than usual."

The specter jerked its chin toward the sunlight, the tuft of spotted fur on the tips of its pointed ears flicking with the movement. *"We have a new resident."*

Strange. It had been a while since their last newcomer.

"They're here." The specter stopped, facing the excitement.

The young man's lips thinned. He didn't want to see them. The fresh state of terror that would suck the color from their skin, or how they would beg for mercy. It always ended with them either shitting or pissing themselves. There was nothing entertaining about it.

It might have been a long time since a new prisoner had been thrown into this place but he still remembered each of those first dreadful moments.

Specters stormed through the crowd, shoving people. *"Make way! Make way!"*

An archangel lowered himself into the Pit. The one with white wings and blue eyes. The young man would've preferred to never see the archangel again, but he was not in a position for such wishful thinking.

His blood went cold when he saw the Spirit. The hooded warrior with the wicked scythe strapped to its back floated down the Pit's opening, landing on the ground beside the archangel.

In the Spirit's arms was a woman. An elf. A thick cloth had been wrapped around her eyes—to keep her from identifying the prison's location, no doubt. Even her ears were stuffed with pieces of cloth.

It must have meant that this person had the skillset to figure out their surroundings at a more heightened level than the average mortal. It also meant their captors were wary of her. Who was she?

The female was badly wounded, blood and dirt coating her muscular body. The elf thrashed in the Spirit's arms, its fiery crown flickering as he held her against him.

Her screams were like a knife gliding through the young man's chest. Though he couldn't make out her words over the noise and chaos, there was a deep, deep pain in her voice. Agony, and an undeniable anger.

The white-winged archangel didn't look her way and strode down the pathway the specters made within the crowd.

Somehow, by the grace of the Suns, the woman kicked herself free from the Spirit's grasp. She slammed the heel of her boot against the skeletal warrior's chest and toppled to the ground. Many of the prisoners cheered. Jeered. There were no allies in this place.

The elf struggled to her feet, the chains at her wrists jingling. An iron band was wrapped around her throat—and the young man could've sworn he heard the steel *groan*. She threw her head side to side, causing the cloth to slip down her face.

Crimson light swallowed the irises and whites of her eyes. Some of the prisoners—and specters—took a step back.

"I will kill you," the woman snarled. "I will kill all of you!"

The archangel finally turned around, his eyes widening slightly. "Get ahold of her, and fetch more astral ore!"

The Spirit moved in a flash of black. It slammed its gloved hand on the back of her neck and kicked her legs out from under her. She gasped for air and crashed back onto the ground.

The young man winced. It was difficult to watch.

The Spirit picked the limp woman up and carried her through the crowd. She was still conscious, though the red light dimmed from her eyes.

Something was different here. There was an energy that followed her—one that felt like an old memory.

The young man watched as the Spirit of the Midnight Sun carried this mysterious, powerful woman into the arms of darkness.

Hours—or days, he couldn't tell—later, there was the sound of jingling keys. The young man cracked his eyes open to see the Spirit dragging the elven woman inside the cell beside his.

Her body looked like it had been cleaned, and she now donned the simple tanned garb of the Pit. More bindings of astral ore were being strapped to her wrists and ankles, tied to long chains and pinned to the walls, just long enough for her to walk about the small enclosure.

The Spirit locked the door and began to walk away. He paused before the young man's cell, slowly turning his head to look at him.

The young man cowered back, cold fear striking his limbs numb. He could see no eyes, only pits of darkness within that skeletal face. The Spirit said nothing and kept walking, leaving them alone.

There were no other prisoners within that section of the Pit. It was a curious thing that they'd decided to place her here, next to him. Should he say something? Some bleak words of encouragement?

"How are you?" His voice cracked, unused to much else other than screams.

It was a stupid thing to ask. Her eyes were closed, but tears ran down her cheeks.

"You killed him," she whispered. "He's *gone*."

It was clear that the woman wasn't speaking to him. She might've gone mad. Wouldn't be the first time here.

The young man said nothing. Some time passed before the woman rolled to her side, groaning in pain. She looked up and scanned her surroundings. Nothing to see but darkness, stone, and dim torchlight.

There was an almost animalistic way to how she moved. No, this woman was definitely not the average prisoner.

Her gaze finally landed on him, and her breath hitched. "You are—Who are you?"

"My name is Micah." The words felt heavy on his tongue. "You?"

"Zara."

She pushed herself up, resting her back against the wall. The redness around her eyes showed that she must have been crying for a long time. Long before today.

Zara slowly cocked her head to the side, staring at him. Studying him, as if he too were her enemy. "So, Micah, why's a deity like you imprisoned here?"

ACKNOWLEDGMENTS

Hi there, my lovely reader, you made it to the end. Do you hate me? Please don't, I loveee you! We are halfway through the series and the thought is wild to me. Zara Santos and the gang have lifted me up, carried me through hardship and moments of heartbreak. I could never thank them enough for the support they have given me. This is just the beginning for the Dusk and Dawn series, for this incredible cast of characters, and I am so honored to be able to write their story.

I'd like to start off by thanking my parents, my mama and papa, as well as my brother, Ronnie. I love you so much and I am so grateful for all that you do. Thank you for encouraging me to pursue the things I love. Los quiero mucho. Forever and always.

Thank you to my little sister, Emily. You have heard about my goals from the start and have been supporting them since then. I am incredibly lucky to have you in my life, and I cannot wait to see where your successes take you. Always cheering you on.

To Reme, I can't thank you enough for your friendship and your love. For being there during the rough times as well as the beautiful moments. Look at us now: it's crazy to think how much has changed—in the best way. I am so lucky to have you as my best friend. Thank you for always encouraging me. I love you so much and I admire all that you do and all that you are.

A thousand thank-yous to my dear friend and editor, Jen. Where would I (and this series) be without you? It's been a helluva journey, and I am so grateful for all the time and effort you put in this work, as well as the support and guidance you provided me. I feel like I come out of this better than before and so much of that is thanks to you. Thank you, thank you, thank you. Love you!

Thank you, my Dani phantom, for your love and support. You are my ROCK. I am so lucky to have you in my life. Thank you for all the laughs. I am cheering you on and I cannot wait to squeeze you in real life.

A big shoutout to my all author colleagues. Seeing you pursue your goals and achieve so much throughout your journey is so inspiring. Much love to you all!

Thank you to Good Girls PR for being part of the publishing journey and for managing the ARC process. It was a massive help and I am so glad to have been able to work with you!

To the ARC team, THANK YOU! For taking a chance on my books and for supporting me. It means so much.

And a final thanks to all my readers, from the bottom of my heart. Your comments and messages lift me up—and make me laugh so much. (I have the best readers, don't I? You guys are too funny.) Thank you for the constant support.

Until next time. Love you!

MEET THE AUTHOR

 Jessica is a graduate of the University of California, Irvine and received her Master's Degree in Business Administration in 2022. Jessica has always been passionate about writing and has often found herself creating stories ever since childhood. When not writing, she can be found weightlifting, watching anime, playing video games, or wandering around a bookstore. She currently resides in Southern California, and is most likely listening to Epic music in search of creative inspiration.

www.jessicajayala.com
Instagram: @authorjessicajayala
TikTok: @authorjessicajayala

www.ingramcontent.com/pod-product-compliance
Lightning Source LLC
Chambersburg PA
CBHW030326010826
48973CB00004B/879